UNDER HEAVEN

ALSO BY GUY GAVRIEL KAY

The Fionavar Tapestry:
The Summer Tree
The Wandering Fire
The Darkest Road

Tigana

A Song for Arbonne

The Lions of Al-Rassan

The Sarantine Mosaic:
Sailing to Sarantium
Lord of Emperors

The Last Light of the Sun

Ysabel

Beyond This Dark House
(poetry)

UNDER HEAVEN

GUY GAVRIEL KAY

A ROC BOOK

ROC
Published by New American Library, a division of
Penguin Group (USA) Inc., 375 Hudson Street,
New York, New York 10014, USA
Penguin Group (Canada), 90 Eglinton Avenue East, Suite 700, Toronto,
Ontario M4P 2Y3, Canada (a division of Pearson Penguin Canada Inc.)
Penguin Books Ltd., 80 Strand, London WC2R 0RL, England
Penguin Ireland, 25 St. Stephen's Green, Dublin 2,
Ireland (a division of Penguin Books Ltd.)
Penguin Group (Australia), 250 Camberwell Road, Camberwell, Victoria 3124,
Australia (a division of Pearson Australia Group Pty. Ltd.)
Penguin Books India Pvt. Ltd., 11 Community Centre, Panchsheel Park,
New Delhi - 110 017, India
Penguin Group (NZ), 67 Apollo Drive, Rosedale, North Shore 0632,
New Zealand (a division of Pearson New Zealand Ltd.)
Penguin Books (South Africa) (Pty.) Ltd., 24 Sturdee Avenue,
Rosebank, Johannesburg 2196, South Africa
Penguin Books Ltd., Registered Offices:
80 Strand, London WC2R 0RL, England

Published by Roc, an imprint of New American Library,
a division of Penguin Group (USA) Inc.
Previously published in a Viking Canada edition.

First ROC Printing, May 2010
10 9 8 7 6 5 4 3 2

 REGISTERED TRADEMARK—MARCA REGISTRADA

Library of Congress Cataloging-in-Publication Data is available upon request.

Printed in the United States of America

to Sybil,
with love

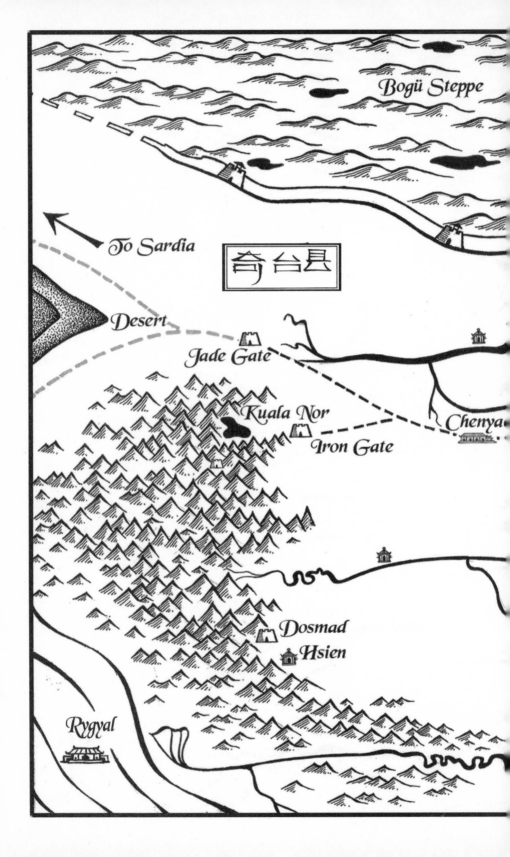

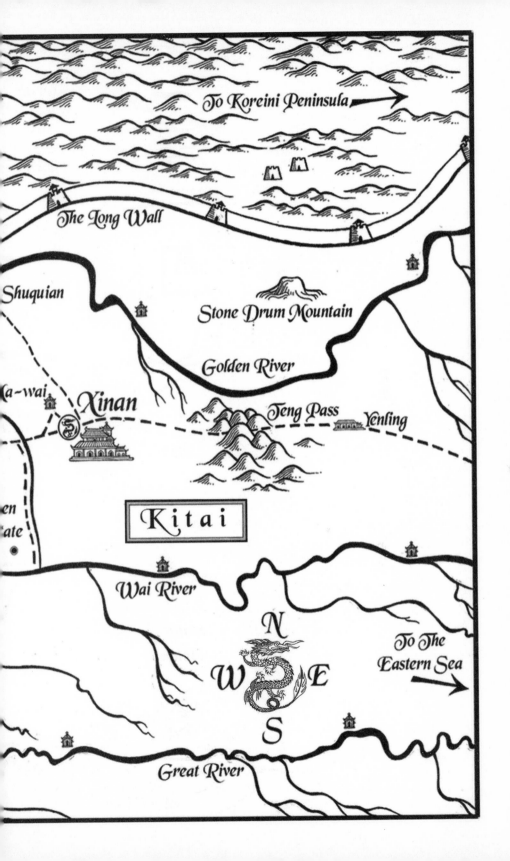

PRINCIPAL CHARACTERS

The Imperial Family, and Ta-Ming Palace mandarins
Taizu, the Son of Heaven, emperor of Kitai
Shinzu, his third son, and heir
Xue, his thirty-first daughter

Wen Jian, the Precious Consort, also called the Beloved Companion

Chin Hai, formerly first minister, now deceased
Wen Zhou, first minister of Kitai, cousin to Wen Jian

The Shen Family
General Shen Gao, deceased, once Left Side Commander of the
  Pacified West

Shen Liu, his oldest son, principal adviser to the first minister
Shen Tai, his second son
Shen Chao, his third son
Shen Li-Mei, his daughter

The Army

An Li ("Roshan"), military governor of the Seventh, Eighth, and Ninth Districts

An Rong, his oldest son

An Tsao, a younger son

Xu Bihai, military governor of the Second and Third Districts, in Chenyao

Xu Liang, his older daughter

Lin Fong, commander of Iron Gate Fortress

Wujen Ning, a soldier at Iron Gate

Tazek Karad, an officer on the Long Wall

Kanlin Warriors

Wan-si

Wei Song

Lu Chen

Ssu Tan

Zhong Ma

Artists

Sima Zian, a poet, the Banished Immortal

Chan Du, a poet

In Xinan, the capital

Spring Rain, a courtesan in the North District, later named Lin Chang

Chou Yan
Xin Lun } students, friends of Shen Tai

Feng, a guard in the employ of Wen Zhou
Hwan, a servant of Wen Zhou
Pei Qin, a beggar in the street
Ye Lao, a steward

Beyond the borders of Kitai

West

Sangrama the Lion, ruling the Empire of Tagur
Cheng-wan, the White Jade Princess, one of his wives, seventeenth
    daughter of Emperor Taizu

Bytsan sri Nespo, a Taguran army officer
Nespo sri Mgar, his father, a senior officer
Gnam
Adar } Taguran soldiers

North

Dulan, kaghan of the Bogü people of the steppe
Hurok, his sister's husband, later kaghan
Meshag, Hurok's older son
Tarduk, Hurok's second son

With bronze as a mirror one can correct one's appearance; with history as a mirror, one can understand the rise and fall of a state; with good men as a mirror, one can distinguish right from wrong.

—LI SHIMIN, TANG EMPEROR TAIZONG

PART ONE

CHAPTER I

Amid the ten thousand noises and the jade-and-gold and the whirling dust of Xinan, he had often stayed awake all night among friends, drinking spiced wine in the North District with the courtesans.

They would listen to flute or *pipa* music and declaim poetry, test each other with jibes and quotes, sometimes find a private room with a scented, silken woman, before weaving unsteadily home after the dawn drums sounded curfew's end, to sleep away the day instead of studying.

Here in the mountains, alone in hard, clear air by the waters of Kuala Nor, far to the west of the imperial city, beyond the borders of the empire, even, Tai was in a narrow bed by darkfall, under the first brilliant stars, and awake at sunrise.

In spring and summer the birds woke him. This was a place where thousands upon thousands nested noisily: fishhawks and cormorants, wild geese and cranes. The geese made him think of friends far away. Wild geese were a symbol of absence: in poetry, in life. Cranes were fidelity, another matter.

In winter the cold was savage, it could take the breath away. The north wind when it blew was an assault, outdoors, and even through the cabin walls. He slept under layers of fur and sheepskin, and no birds woke him at dawn from the icebound nesting grounds on the far side of the lake.

The ghosts were outside in all seasons, moonlit nights and dark, as soon as the sun went down.

Tai knew some of their voices now, the angry ones and the lost ones, and those in whose thin, stretched crying there was only pain.

They didn't frighten him, not any more. He'd thought he might die of terror in the beginning, alone in those first nights here with the dead.

He would look out through an unshuttered window on a spring or summer or autumn night, but he never went outside. Under moon or stars the world by the lake belonged to the ghosts, or so he had come to understand.

He had set himself a routine from the start, to deal with solitude and fear, and the enormity of where he was. Some holy men and hermits in their mountains and forests might deliberately act otherwise, going through days like leaves blown, defined by the absence of will or desire, but his was a different nature, and he wasn't holy.

He did begin each morning with the prayers for his father. He was still in the formal mourning period and his self-imposed task by this distant lake had everything to do with respect for his father's memory.

After the invocations, which he assumed his brothers were also performing in the home where they'd all been born, Tai would go out into the mountain meadow (shades of green dotted with wildflowers, or crunching underfoot with ice and snow) and—unless there was a storm—he would do his Kanlin exercises. No sword, then one sword, then both.

He would look at the cold waters of the lake, with the small isle in the middle of it, then up at the surrounding, snow-draped, stupefying mountains piled upon each other. Beyond the northern peaks the land sloped downwards for hundreds of *li* towards the long dunes of the killing deserts, with the Silk Roads running around either side of them, bringing so much wealth to the court, to the empire of Kitai. To his people.

In winter he fed and watered his small, shaggy horse in the shed built against his cabin. When the weather turned and the grass returned, he'd let the horse graze during the day. It was placid, wasn't about to run away. There was nowhere to run.

After his exercises, he would try to let stillness enter into him, a shedding of the chaos of life, ambition and aspiration: to make himself worthy of this chosen labour.

And then he would set to work burying the dead.

He'd never, from first arrival here, made any effort to separate Kitan from Taguran soldiers. They were tangled together, strewn or piled, skulls and white bones. Flesh gone to earth or to animals and carrion birds long since, or—for those of the most recent campaign—not so very long ago.

It had been a triumph, that last conflict, though bitterly hard-won. Forty thousand dead in one battle, almost as many Kitan as Taguran.

His father had been in that war, a general, honoured afterwards with a proud title, Left Side Commander of the Pacified West. Rewarded handsomely by the Son of Heaven for victory: a personal audience in the Hall of Brilliance in the Ta-Ming Palace when he returned back east, the purple sash presented, words of commendation spoken directly, a jade gift extended from the emperor's hand, only one intermediary.

His family were undeniably beneficiaries of what had happened by this lake. Tai's mother and Second Mother had burnt incense together, lit candles of thanksgiving to ancestors and gods.

But for General Shen Gao, the memory of the fighting here had been, until he'd died two years ago, a source of pride and sorrow intermingled, marking him forever after.

Too many men had lost their lives for a lake on the border of nowhere, one that would not, in the event, be held by either empire.

The treaty that had followed—affirmed with elaborate exchanges and rituals and, for the first time, a Kitan princess for the Taguran king—had established as much.

Hearing the number from that battle—*forty thousand dead*—Tai, when young, had been unable to even picture what it must have been like. That wasn't the case any more.

The lake and meadow lay between lonely forts, watched by both empires from days away—to the south for Tagur, east for Kitai. It was always silent here now, save for the sound of wind, the crying of birds in season, and the ghosts.

General Shen had spoken of sorrow and guilt only to his younger sons (never to the oldest). Such feelings in a commander could be seen as shameful, even treasonous, a denial of the emperor's wisdom, ruling with the mandate of heaven, unfailing, unable to fail or his throne and the empire would be at risk.

But the thoughts *had* been spoken, more than once, after Shen Gao's retirement to the family property on their south-flowing stream near the Wai River, usually after wine on a quiet day, with leaves or lotus blossoms falling in the water to drift downstream. And the memory of those words was the principal reason his second son was here for the mourning period, instead of at home.

You could argue that the general's quiet sadness had been wrong, misplaced. That the battle here had been in necessary defence of the empire. It was important to remember that it hadn't always been the armies of Kitai triumphing over the Tagurans. The kings of Tagur, on their distant, completely defended plateau, were hugely ambitious. Victory and savagery had gone both ways through a hundred and fifty years of fighting by Kuala Nor beyond Iron Gate Pass, which was, in itself, as isolated a fortress as the empire knew.

"A thousand miles of moonlight falling, east of Iron," Sima Zian, the Banished Immortal, had written. It wasn't literally true, but anyone who had ever been at Iron Gate Fortress knew what the poet meant.

And Tai was several days' ride west of the fort, beyond that last outpost of empire, with the dead: with the lost crying at night and the bones of over a hundred thousand soldiers, lying white in falling moonlight or under the sun. Sometimes, in bed in the mountain dark, he would belatedly realize that a voice whose cadences he knew had fallen silent, and he would understand that he'd laid those bones to rest.

There were too many. It was beyond hope to ever finish this: it was a task for gods descending from the nine heavens, not for one man. But if you couldn't do everything, did that mean you did nothing?

For two years now, Shen Tai had offered what passed for his own answer to that, in memory of his father's voice asking quietly for another cup of wine, watching large, slow goldfish and drifting flowers in the pond.

The dead were everywhere here, even on the isle. There had been a fort there, a small one, rubble now. He'd tried to imagine the fighting sweeping that way. Boats swiftly built on the pebbled shore with wood from the slopes, the desperate, trapped defenders of one army or the other, depending on the year, firing last arrows at implacable enemies bringing death across the lake to them.

He had chosen to begin there two years ago, rowing the small craft he'd found and repaired; a spring day when the lake mirrored blue heaven and the mountains. The isle was a defined ground, limited, less overwhelming. In the mainland meadow and far into the pine woods the dead lay strewn as far as he could walk in a long day.

For a little more than half the year under this high, fierce sky he was able to dig, bury broken, rusted weapons with the bones. It was brutally hard work. He grew leathery, muscled, callused, ached at night, fell wearily into bed after washing in water warmed at his fire.

From late fall, through the winter, into early spring, the ground was frozen, impossible. You could break your heart trying to dig a grave.

In his first year the lake froze, he could walk across to the isle for a few weeks. The second winter was milder and it did not freeze over. Muffled in furs then, hooded and gloved in a white, hollow stillness, seeing the puffs of his mortal breath, feeling small against the towering, hostile vastness all around, Tai took the boat out on days when waves and weather allowed. He offered the dead to the dark waters with a prayer, that they might not lie lost any longer, unconsecrated, on wind-scoured ground here by Kuala Nor's cold shore, among the wild animals and far from any home.

WAR HAD NOT BEEN CONTINUOUS. It never was, anywhere, and particularly not in a mountain bowl so remote, so difficult for sustained supply lines from either country, however belligerent or ambitious kings and emperors might be.

As a consequence, there had been cabins built by fishermen or by the herders who grazed sheep and goats in these high meadows, in the intervals when soldiers weren't dying here. Most of the cabins had been destroyed, a few had not. Tai lived in one of them, set north against a pine-treed slope—shelter from the worst winds. The cabin was almost a hundred years old. He had set about repairing it as best he could when he'd first come: roof, door and window frames, shutters, the stone chimney for the fire.

Then he'd had help, unexpected, unsolicited. The world could bring you poison in a jewelled cup, or surprising gifts. Sometimes you didn't know which of them it was. Someone he knew had written a poem around that thought.

He was lying awake now, middle of a spring night. There was a full moon shining, which meant that the Tagurans would be with him by late morning, a half dozen of them bringing supplies in a bullock cart down a slope from the south and around the lake's level shore to his cabin. The morning after the new moon was when his own people came from the east, through the ravine from Iron Gate.

It had taken a little time in the period after he'd arrived, but a routine had been arranged that let them each come to him without having to see the other. It was not part of his purpose to have men die because he was here. There was a peace now, signed, with gifts exchanged, and a princess, but such truths didn't always prevail when young, aggressive soldiers met in far-away places—and young men could start wars.

The two forts treated Tai like a holy hermit or a fool, choosing to live among the ghosts. They conducted a tacit, almost an amusing warfare with each other through him, vying to offer more generosity every month, to be of greater aid.

Tai's own people had laid flooring in his cabin in the first summer, bringing cut and sanded planks in a cart. The Tagurans had taken over the chimney repair. Ink and pens and paper (requested) came from Iron Gate; wine had first come from the south. Both fortresses had men chop wood whenever they were here. Winter fur and sheepskin had been brought for his bedding, for clothes. He'd been given a goat for milk, and then a second one from the other side, and an eccentric-looking but very warm Taguran hat with flaps for the ears and a tie for knotting under his chin, the first autumn. The Iron Gate soldiers had built a small shed for his small horse.

He'd tried to stop this, but hadn't come close to persuading anyone, and eventually he'd understood: it wasn't about kindness to the madman, or even entirely about besting each other. The less time he spent on food, firewood, maintaining the cabin, the more he could devote to his task, which no one had ever done before, and which seemed—once they'd accepted why he was here—to matter to the Tagurans as much as to his own people.

You could find irony in this, Tai often thought. They might goad and kill each other, even now, if they chanced to arrive at the same time, and only a genuine fool would think the battles in the west were over for good, but the two empires would honour his laying the dead to rest—until there were newer ones.

In bed on a mild night he listened to the wind and the ghosts, awakened not by either of them (not any more) but by the brilliant white of the moon shining. He couldn't see the star of the Weaver Maid now, exiled from her mortal lover on the far side of the Sky River. It had been bright enough to show clearly in the window before, even with a full moon. He remembered a poem he'd liked when he was younger, built around an image of the moon carrying messages between the lovers across the River.

If he considered it now it seemed contrived, a showy conceit. Many celebrated verses from early in this Ninth Dynasty were like that if you looked closely at their elaborate verbal brocades. There was some sadness in how that could happen, Tai thought: falling out of love with something that had shaped you. Or even people who had? But if you didn't change at least a little, where were the passages of a life? Didn't learning, changing, sometimes mean letting go of what had once been seen as true?

It was very bright in the room. Almost enough to pull him from bed to window to look out on the tall grass, at what silver did to green, but he was tired. He was always tired at the end of a day, and he never went out from the cabin at night. He didn't fear the ghosts any more—they saw him as an emissary by now, he'd decided, not an intruder from the living—but he left them the world after the sun went down.

In winter he had to swing the rebuilt shutters closed, block chinks in the walls as best he could with cloth and sheepskin against the winds and snow. The cabin would become smoky, lit by the fire and candles, or one of his two lamps if he was struggling to write poetry. He warmed wine on a brazier (this, also, from the Tagurans).

When spring came he opened the shutters, let in the sun, or starlight and the moon, and then the sound of birds at dawn.

On first awakening tonight he had been disoriented, confused, tangled in a last dream. He'd thought it was still winter, that the brilliant silver he saw was ice or frost gleaming. He had smiled after a moment, returning to awareness, wry and amused. He had a friend in Xinan who would have cherished this moment. It wasn't often that you lived the imagery of well-known lines.

Before my bed the light is so bright
it looks like a layer of frost.
Lifting my head I gaze at the moon,
lying back down I think of home.

But maybe he was wrong. Maybe if a poem was true enough then sooner or later some of those who read it *would* live the image just as he was living it now. Or maybe some readers had the image before they even came to the poem and found it waiting for them there, an affirmation? The poet offering words for thoughts they'd held already.

And sometimes poetry gave you new, dangerous ideas. Sometimes men were exiled, or killed, for what they wrote. You could mask a dangerous comment by setting a poem in the First or Third Dynasty, hundreds of years ago. Sometimes that convention worked, but not always. The senior mandarins of the civil service were not fools.

Lying back down I think of home. Home was the property near the Wai, where his father was buried in their orchard with both his parents and the three children who had not survived to adulthood. Where Tai's mother and Shen Gao's concubine, the woman they called Second Mother, still lived, where his two brothers were also nearing the end of mourning—the older one would be returning to the capital soon.

He wasn't sure where his sister was. Women had only ninety days of mourning. Li-Mei was probably back with the empress, wherever she was. The empress might not be at court. Her time in the Ta-Ming had been rumoured to be ending, even two years ago. Someone else was in the palace now with Emperor Taizu. Someone shining like a gem.

There were many who disapproved. There was no one, as far as Tai knew, who had said as much, openly, before Tai had left to go home and then come here.

He found his thoughts drifting back to Xinan, from memories of the family compound by the stream, where the paulownia leaves fell along the path from the front gate all at once, in one autumn night each year. Where peaches and plums and apricots grew in the orchard (flowers red in spring), and you could smell the charcoal burning at the forest's edge, see smoke from village hearths beyond the chestnut and mulberry trees.

No, now he was remembering the capital instead: all glitter and colour and noise, where violent life, in all its world-dust and world-fury, was happening, unfolding, would be *erupting*, even now, in the middle of night, assaulting the senses moment by moment. Two million people. The centre of the world, under heaven.

It wouldn't be dark there. Not in Xinan. The lights of men could almost hide moonlight. There would be torches and lanterns, fixed, or carried in bamboo frames, or suspended from the litters borne through the streets, carrying the high-born and the powerful. There'd be red candles in upper windows, and lamps hanging from flower-decked balconies in the North District. White lights in the palace and wide, shallow oil lamps on pillars twice the height of a man in courtyards there, burning all night long.

There would be music and glory, heartbreak and heart's ease, and knives or swords drawn sometimes in the lanes and alleys. And come morning, power and passion and death all over again, jostling each other in the two great, deafening markets, in wine shops and study halls, twisted streets (shaped for furtive love, or murder) and stunningly wide ones. In bedrooms and courtyards, elaborate private gardens and flower-filled public parks where willows drooped over streams and the deep-dredged artificial lakes.

He remembered Long Lake Park, south of the rammed-earth city walls, remembered with whom he'd been there last, in peach-blossom time, before his father died, on one of the three days each month she was allowed out of the North District. Eighth, eighteenth, twenty-eighth. She was a long way off.

Wild geese were the emblems of separation.

He thought of the Ta-Ming, the whole palace complex north of the city walls, of the Son of Heaven, no longer young, and of those with him and around him there: eunuchs, and nine ranks of mandarins, Tai's older brother one of them, princes and alchemists and army leaders, and the one almost surely lying with him tonight under this moon, who *was* young, and almost unbearably beautiful, and had changed the empire.

Tai had aspired to be one of those civil servants with access to palace and court, swimming "within the current," as the phrase went. He had studied a full year in the capital (between encounters with courtesans and wine-cup friends), had been on the brink of writing the three-day exams for the imperial service, the test that determined your future.

Then his father had died by their quiet stream, and two and a half years of official mourning came, and went from you like a rainwind down a river.

A man was lashed—twenty with the heavy rod—for failing to perform the withdrawal and rituals due to parents when they died.

You could say (some would say) he *had* failed in the rites by being here in the mountains and not at home, but he'd spoken with the sub-prefect before riding this long way west, and had received permission. He was also—overwhelmingly—still withdrawn from society, from anything that could be called ambition or worldliness.

There was some risk in what he'd done. There was always danger when it came to what might be whispered at the Ministry of Rites, which supervised the examinations. Eliminating a rival, one way or another, was as basic a tactic as there was, but Tai thought he had protected himself.

You could never truly know, of course. Not in Xinan. Ministers were appointed and exiled, generals and military governors promoted, then demoted or ordered to kill themselves, and the court had been changing swiftly in the time before he'd left. But Tai hadn't *had* a position yet. It wasn't as if he'd risked anything in the way of office or rank. And he thought he could survive the whipping rod, if it came to that.

He tried to decide now, in a moonlit cabin, wrapped in solitude like a silkworm during its fourth sleep, how much he really missed the capital. If he was ready to go back, resume all as before. Or if it was time for yet another change.

He knew what people would say if he did make a change, what was already said about General Shen's second son. First Son Liu was known and understood, his ambition and achievement fitting a pattern. The third son was still young, little more than a child. It was Tai, the second, who raised more questions than anything else.

Mourning would be formally over at the seventh month's full moon. He would have completed the rites, in his own fashion. He could resume his studies, prepare for the next set of examinations. That was what men did. Scholars wrote the civil service tests five times, ten, more. Some died without ever passing them. Forty to sixty men succeeded each year, of the thousands who began the process with the preliminary tests in their own prefectures. The final examination was begun in the presence of the emperor himself, in his white robe and black hat and the yellow belt of highest ceremony: an elaborate passage of initiation—with bribery and corruption in the process, as always in Xinan. How could it be otherwise?

The capital seemed to have entered his silvered cabin now, driving sleep farther away with memories of a brawling, buffeting tumult that never wholly stopped at any hour. Vendors and buyers shouting in the markets, beggars and tumblers and fortune tellers, hired mourners following a funeral with their hair unbound, horses and carts rumbling through dark and day, the muscled bearers of sedan chairs screaming at pedestrians to make way, whipping them aside with bamboo rods. The Gold Bird Guards with their own whipping rods at every major intersection, clearing the streets when darkfall came.

Small shops in each ward, open all night long. The Night Soil Gatherers passing with their plaintive warning cry. Logs bumping and rolling through Xinan's outer walls into the huge pond by the East Market where they were bought and sold at sunrise. Morning beatings and executions in the two market squares. More street performers after the decapitations, while good crowds were still gathered. Bells tolling the watch-hours by day and through the night, and the long roll of drums that locked the walls and all the ward gates at sundown and opened them at dawn. Spring flowers in the parks, summer fruit, autumn leaves, the yellow dust that was everywhere, blowing down from the steppes. The dust of the world. Jade-and-gold. Xinan.

He heard and saw and almost caught the smells of it, as a remembered chaos and cacophony of the soul, then he pushed it back and away in the moonlight, listening again to the ghosts outside, the crying he'd had to learn to live with here, or go mad.

In silver light he looked over at his low writing table, the ink-block and paper, the woven mat in front of it. His swords were against the wall beside it. The scent of the pine trees came through the open windows with the night wind. Cicadas whirring, a duet with the dead.

He had come to Kuala Nor on impulse, to honour his father's sorrow. He had stayed for himself just as much, working every day to offer what release he could to however small a number of those unburied here. One man's labour, not an immortal, not holy.

Two years had passed, seasons wheeling, and the stars. He didn't know how he would feel when he returned to the crash and tumble of the capital. That was the honest thought.

He did know which people he had missed. He saw one of them in the eye of his mind, could almost hear her voice, too vividly to allow sleep to return, remembering the last time he'd lain with her.

"And if someone should take me from here when you are gone? If someone should ask me … should propose to make me his personal courtesan, or even a concubine?"

He'd known who *someone* was, of course.

He had taken her hand, with its long, gold-painted fingernails and jewelled rings, and placed it on his bare chest, so she could feel his heart.

She'd laughed, a little bitterly. "No! You always do this, Tai. Your heart never changes its beating. It tells me nothing."

In the North District where they were—an upstairs room in the Pavilion of Moonlight Pleasure House—she was called Spring Rain. He didn't know her real name. You never asked the real names. It was considered ill-bred.

Speaking slowly, because this was difficult, he'd said, "Two years is a long time, Rain. I know it. Much happens in the life of a man, or a woman. It is—"

She had moved her hand to cover his mouth, not gently. She wasn't always gentle with him. "No, again. Listen to me. If you begin to speak of the Path, or the balanced wisdom of life's long flowing, Tai, I will take a fruit knife to your manhood. I thought you might wish to know this before you went on."

He remembered the silk of her voice, the devastating sweetness with which she could say such things. He had kissed the palm held against his mouth, then said, softly, as she moved it a little away, "You must do what seems best to you, for your life. I do not want you to be one of those women waiting at a window above jade stairs in the night. Let someone else live those poems. My intention is to go back to my family's estate, observe the rites for my father, then return. I can tell you that."

He had not lied. It had been his intention.

Things had fallen out otherwise. What man would dare believe that all he planned might come to pass? Not even the emperor, with the mandate of heaven, could make that so.

He had no idea what had happened to her, if *someone* had indeed taken her from the courtesans' quarter, claimed her for his own behind the stone walls of an aristocrat's city mansion in what was almost certainly a better life. No letters came west of Iron Gate Pass, because he had not written any.

It didn't have to be a case of one extreme or the other, he finally thought: not Xinan set against this beyond-all-borders solitude. The Path's long tale of wisdom taught balancing, did it not? The two halves of a man's soul, of his inward life. You balanced couplets in a formal verse, elements in a painting—river, cliff, heron, fishing boat—thick and thin brush strokes in calligraphy, stones and trees and water in a garden, shifting patterns in your own days.

He could go back home to their stream, for example, instead of to the capital, when he left here. Could live there and write, marry someone his mother and Second Mother chose for him, cultivate their garden, the orchard—spring flowers, summer fruit—receive visitors and pay visits, grow old and white-bearded in calm but not solitude. Watch the paulownia leaves when they fell, the goldfish in the pond. Remember his father doing so. He might even, one day, be thought a sage. The idea made him smile, in moonlight.

He could travel, east down the Wai, or on the Great River itself through the gorges to the sea and then back: the boatmen poling against the current, or towing the boats west with thick ropes along slippery paths cut into the cliffs when they came to the wild gorges again.

He might go even farther south, where the empire became different and strange: lands where rice was grown in water and there were elephants and gibbons, mandrills, rosewood forests, camphor trees, pearls in the sea for those who could dive for them, and where tigers with yellow eyes killed men in the jungles of the dark.

He had an honoured lineage. His father's name offered a doorway through which Tai could walk and find a welcome among prefects and taxation officers and even military governors throughout Kitai. In truth, First Brother's name might be even more useful by now, though that had its own complexities.

But all of this was possible. He could travel and think, visit temples and pavilions, pagodas in misty hills, mountain shrines, write as he travelled. He could do it just as the master poet whose lines he had awakened with had done, was probably still doing somewhere. Though honesty (and irony) compelled the additional thought that Sima Zian seemed to have done as much drinking as anything else through his years on the boats and roads, in the mountains and temples and bamboo groves.

There was that, too, wasn't there? Good wine, late-night fellowship. Music. Not to be dismissed or despised.

Tai fell asleep on that thought, and with the sudden, fervent hope that the Tagurans had remembered to bring wine. He had almost finished what his own people had delivered two weeks ago. The long summer twilight gave a man more time to drink before going to bed with the sun.

He slept, and dreamed of the woman with her hand on his heart that last night, then over his mouth, her shaped and painted moth-eyebrows, green eyes, red mouth, candlelight, jade pins pulled slowly one by one from golden hair, and the scent she wore.

THE BIRDS WOKE HIM from the far end of the lake.

He had attempted a formal six-line poem several nights ago, their strident morning noise compared to opening hour at the two markets in Xinan, but hadn't been able to make the parallel construction hold in the final couplet. His technical skills as a poet were probably above average, good enough for the verse component of the examinations, but not likely, in his own judgment, to produce something enduring.

One of the results of two years alone had been his coming to think this, most of the time.

He dressed and built a fire, washed himself and tied back his hair while boiling water for tea. He glanced in the bronze mirror he'd been given and thought about taking a blade to his cheeks and chin, but decided against such self-abuse this morning. The Tagurans could deal with him unshaven. There was no real reason to even tie his hair but he felt like a steppes barbarian when he left it on his shoulders. He had memories of that, of them.

Before drinking or eating, while the tea leaves were steeping, he stood at the eastern window and spoke the prayer to his father's spirit in the direction of sunrise.

Whenever he did this, he summoned and held a memory of Shen Gao feeding bread to the wild ducks in their stream. He didn't know why that was his remembrance-image, but it was. Perhaps the tranquility of it, in a life that had not been tranquil.

He prepared and drank his tea, ate some salt-dried meat and milled grain in hot water sweetened with clover honey, then he claimed his peasant-farmer straw hat from a nail by the door and pulled on his boots. The summer boots were almost new, a gift from Iron Gate, replacing the worn-out pair he'd had.

They had noticed that. They observed him closely whenever they came, Tai had come to understand. He had also realized, during the first hard winter, that he'd almost certainly have died here without the help of the two forts. You could live entirely alone in some mountains in some seasons—it was a legend-dream of the hermit-poet—but not at Kuala Nor in winter, not this high up and remote when the snows come and the north wind blew.

The supplies, at new and full moon without fail, had kept him alive—and had arrived only through extreme effort several times, when wild storms had bowled down to blast the frozen meadow and lake.

He milked the two goats, took the pail inside and covered it for later. He claimed his two swords and went back out and did his Kanlin routines.

He put the swords away and then, outside again, stood a moment in almost-summer sunshine listening to the shrieking racket of birds, watching them wheel and cry above the lake, which was blue and beautiful in morning light and gave no least hint at all of winter ice, or of how many dead men were here around its shores.

Until you looked away from birds and water to the tall grass of the meadow, and then you saw the bones in the clear light, everywhere. Tai could see his mounds, where he was burying them, west of the cabin, north against the pines. Three long rows of deep graves now.

He turned to claim his shovel and go to work. It was why he was here.

His eye was caught by a glint to the south: sunlight catching armour halfway along the last turning of the last slope down. Looking more narrowly he saw that the Tagurans were early today, or—he checked the sun again—that he was moving slowly himself, after a moon-white, waking night.

He watched them descend with the bullock and the heavy-wheeled cart. He wondered if Bytsan was leading the supply party himself this morning. He found himself hoping so.

Was it wrong to anticipate the arrival of a man whose soldiers would rape his sister and both mothers and joyfully sack and burn the family compound during any incursion into Kitai?

Men changed during wars or conflict, sometimes beyond recognition. Tai had seen it in himself, on the steppes beyond the Long

Wall among the nomads. Men changed, not always in ways you liked to recall, though courage seen was worth remembering.

He didn't think Bytsan would grow savage, but he didn't know. And he could easily imagine the opposite about some of the Tagurans who had come here through two years, arriving armoured and armed, as if to the stern drums of a battlefield, not bringing supplies to a solitary fool.

They were not simple, easily sorted encounters, the ones he had with the warriors of the Empire of the Plateau when they came down to him.

It *was* Bytsan he saw, as the Tagurans reached the meadow and began circling the lake. The captain trotted his bay-coloured Sardian horse forward. The animal was magnificent, breathtaking. They all were, those far-western horses. The captain had the only one in his company. Heavenly Horses they called them in Tai's own land. Legends said that they sweated blood.

The Tagurans traded for them with Sardia, beyond where the divided Silk Roads became one again in the west, after the deserts. There, through yet more harsh mountain passes, lay the deep, lush breeding grounds of these horses, and Tai's people longed for them with a passion that had influenced imperial policy, warfare, and poetry for centuries.

Horses mattered, a great deal. They were why the emperor, Serene Lord of the Five Directions and the Five Holy Mountains, was steadily engaged with the Bogü nomads, supporting chosen leaders among the *kumiss*-drinking yurt-dwellers north of the Wall, in exchange for a supply of their horses, however inferior they might be to the ones from Sardia. Neither the loess-laden soil in northern Kitai nor the jungles and rice-lands of the south would permit the grazing and breeding of horses of any real quality.

It was a Kitan tragedy, had been for a thousand years.

Many things came to Xinan along the guarded Silk Roads in this Ninth Dynasty, making it wealthy beyond description, but horses from Sardia were not among them. They could not endure that long desert journey. Women came east, musicians and dancers. Jade and alabaster and gems came, amber, aromatics, powdered rhinoceros horn for the alchemists. Talking birds, spices and food, swords and ivory and so much else, but not the Heavenly Horses.

So Kitai had had to find other ways to get the best mounts they could—because you could win a war with cavalry, all else being equal, and when the Tagurans had too many of these horses (being at peace with the Sardians now, trading with them) all else was not equal.

Tai bowed twice in greeting as Bytsan reined up—right fist in left palm. He had acquaintances—and an older brother—who would have judged it a humiliation had they seen him bow so formally to a Taguran. On the other hand, they hadn't had their lives guarded and preserved by this man and the steady arrival of supplies every full moon for almost two years.

Bytsan's blue tattoos showed in the sunlight, on both cheeks and the left side of his neck above the collar of his tunic. He dismounted, bowed, also twice, closed fist in palm, adopting the Kitan gesture.

He smiled briefly. "Before you ask, yes, I brought wine."

He spoke Kitan, most Tagurans did. It was the language of trade in all directions now, when men were not killing each other. It was believed, in Kitai, that the gods spoke Kitan in the nine heavens, had taught it to the original Father of Emperors as he stood, head bowed on Dragon Mountain in the past-that-lay-behind.

"You knew I would ask?" Tai felt rueful, a little exposed.

"Longer twilights. What else can a man do? The cup is a companion, we sing. It goes well?"

"It goes well. The moonlight kept me awake, I am slow to begin this morning."

They knew his routine, the query had not been idle.

"Just the moon?"

Tai's own people asked variants of that question every time they came. Curiosity—and fear. Very brave men, including this one, had told him directly they could not have done what he was doing here, with the dead unburied, and angry.

Tai nodded. "The moon. And some memories."

He glanced past the captain and saw a young, fully armoured soldier ride up. Not one of the ones he knew. This man did not dismount, stared down at Tai. He had only one tattoo, wore an unnecessary helmet, did not smile.

"Gnam, take an axe from by the cabin, help Adar chop firewood."

"Why?"

Tai blinked. He looked at the Taguran captain.

Bytsan's expression did not change, nor did he glance back at the soldier on the horse behind him. "Because that is what we do here. And because if you do not I will take your horse and weapons, remove your boots, and let you walk back through all the passes alone among the mountain cats."

It was said quietly. There was a silence. Tai realized, with a kind of dismay, how unaccustomed he'd become to such exchanges, a sudden tension rising. *This is the way the world is*, he told himself. *Learn it again. Start now. This is what you will find when you return.*

Casually, so as not to shame the captain or the young soldier, he turned and looked across the lake towards the birds. Grey herons, terns, a golden eagle very high.

The young man—he was big, well-made—was still on his horse. He said, "This one cannot chop wood?"

"I believe he can, since he has been digging graves for our dead for two years now."

"Ours, or his own? While he despoils our soldiers' bones?"

Bytsan laughed.

Tai turned quickly back, he couldn't help himself. He felt something returning after a long time. He knew it for what it was: anger had been a part of him, too readily, as far back as he could remember. A second brother's portion? Some might say that was it.

He said, as levelly as he could, "I should be grateful if you'd look around and tell me which of the bones here is one of yours, if I should feel inclined to despoil it."

A different silence. There were many kinds of stillness, Tai thought, inconsequentially.

"Gnam, you are a great fool. Get the axe and chop wood. Do it now."

This time Bytsan did look at his soldier, and this time the other man swung himself down—not hurrying, but not disobeying, either. The bullock had pulled the cart up. There were four other men. Tai knew three of them, exchanged nods with those.

The one called Adar, wearing a belted, dark-red tunic over loose brown trousers, no armour, walked with Gnam towards the cabin, leading their horses. The others, knowing their routine here, guided the cart forward and began unloading supplies into the cabin. They moved briskly, they always did. Unload, stack, do whatever else, including cleaning out the small stable, get back up the slope and away.

The fear of being here after dark.

"Careful with his wine!" Bytsan called. "I don't want to hear a Kitan weeping. The sound's too unpleasant."

Tai smiled crookedly, the soldiers laughed.

The *chunk* of axes came from the side of the cabin, carrying in mountain air. Bytsan gestured. Tai walked off with him. They stepped through tall grass, over bones and around them. Tai avoided a skull, instinct by now.

Butterflies were everywhere, all colours, and grasshoppers startled at their feet, springing high and away in all directions. They heard the drone of bees among the meadow flowers. Here and there the metal of a rusted blade could be seen, even on the grey sand at the water's edge. You needed to be careful where you stepped. There were pink stones in the sand. The birds were raucous, wheeling and swooping, breaking the surface of the lake for fish.

"Water's still cold?" Bytsan asked after a moment.

They stood by the lake. The air was very clear, they could see crags on the mountains, cranes on the isle, in the ruined fortress there.

"Always."

"A storm in the pass five nights ago. You get it down here?"

Tai shook his head. "Some rain. Must have blown off east."

Bytsan bent and picked up a handful of stones. He began throwing them at birds.

"Sun's hot," he said eventually. "I can see why you wear that thing on your head, though it makes you look like an old man and a peasant."

"Both?"

The Taguran grinned. "Both." He threw another stone. He said, "You'll be leaving?"

"Soon. Midsummer moon ends our mourning period."

Bytsan nodded. "That's what I wrote them."

"Wrote them?"

"Court. In Rygyal."

Tai stared at him. "They know about me?"

Bytsan nodded again. "They know from me. Of course they do."

Tai thought about it. "I don't think Iron Gate's sending messages back that someone's burying the dead at Kuala Nor, but I may be wrong."

The other man shrugged. "You probably are. Everything's tracked and weighed these days. Peacetime's for the calculating ones at any court. There were some at Rygyal who saw your coming here as Kitan arrogance. They wanted you killed."

That, Tai hadn't known either. "Like that fellow back there?"

The two axes were chopping steadily, each one a thin, clean sound in the distance. "Gnam? He's just young. Wants to make a name."

"Kill an enemy right away?"

"Get it over with. Like your first woman."

The two of them exchanged a brief smile. Both were relatively young men, still. Neither felt that way.

Bytsan said, after a moment, "I was instructed that you were not to be killed."

Tai snorted. "I am grateful to hear it."

Bytsan cleared his throat. He seemed awkward suddenly. "There is a gift, instead, a recognition."

Tai stared again. "A gift? From the Taguran court?"

"No, from the rabbit in the moon." Bytsan grimaced. "Yes, of course, from the court. Well, from one person there, with permission."

"Permission?"

The grimace became a grin. The Taguran was sunburned, square-jawed, had one missing lower tooth. "You are slow this morning."

Tai said, "This is unexpected, that's all. What person?"

"See for yourself. I have a letter."

Bytsan reached into a pocket in his tunic and retrieved a pale-yellow scroll. Tai saw the Taguran royal seal: a lion's head, in red.

He broke the wax, unrolled the letter, read the contents, which were not lengthy, and so learned what they were giving to him and doing to him, for his time here among the dead.

It became something of an exercise to breathe.

Thoughts began arriving too swiftly, uncontrolled, disconnected, a swirling like a sandstorm. This could define his life—or have him killed before he ever got home to the family estate, let alone to Xinan.

He swallowed hard. Looked away at the mountains ranged and piled around them, rising up and farther up, the blue lake ringed in majesty. In the teachings of the Path, mountains meant compassion, water was wisdom. The peaks didn't alter, Tai thought.

What men did beneath their gaze could change more swiftly than one could ever hope to understand.

He said it. "I don't understand."

Bytsan made no reply. Tai looked down at the letter and read the name at the bottom again.

One person there, with permission.

One person. The White Jade Princess Cheng-wan: seventeenth daughter of the revered and exalted Emperor Taizu. Sent west to a foreign land twenty years ago from her own bright, glittering world. Sent with her *pipa* and flute, a handful of attendants and escorts, and a Taguran honour guard, to become the first imperial bride ever granted by Kitai to Tagur, to be one of the wives of Sangrama the Lion, in his high, holy city of Rygyal.

She had been part of the treaty that followed the last campaign here at Kuala Nor. An emblem in her young person (she'd been fourteen that year) of how savage—and inconclusive—the fighting had been, and how important it was that it end. A slender, graceful token of peace enduring between two empires. As if it would endure, as if it ever had, as if one girl's body and life could ensure such a thing.

There had been a fall of poems like flower petals in Kitai that autumn, pitying her in parallel lines and rhyme: married to a distant horizon, fallen from heaven, lost to the civilized world (of parallel lines and rhyme) beyond snowbound mountain barriers, among barbarians on their harsh plateau.

It had been the literary fashion for that time, an easy theme, until one poet was arrested and beaten with the heavy rod in the square before the palace—and nearly died of it—for a verse suggesting this was not only lamentable, but a wrong done to her.

You didn't say *that*.

Sorrow was one thing—polite, cultured regret for a young life changing as she left the glory of the world—but you never offered the view that anything the Ta-Ming Palace did, ever, might be mistaken. That was a denial of the rightly fulfilled, fully compassed mandate of heaven. Princesses were coinage in the world, what else could they be? How else serve the empire, justify their birth?

Tai was still staring at the words on the pale-yellow paper, struggling to bring spiralling thoughts to what one might call order. Bytsan was quiet, allowing him to deal with this, or try.

You gave a man one of the Sardian horses to reward him greatly. You gave him four or five of those glories to exalt him above his fellows, propel him towards rank—and earn him the jealousy, possibly mortal, of those who rode the smaller horses of the steppes.

The Princess Cheng-wan, a royal consort of Tagur now through twenty years of peace, had just bestowed upon him, *with permission*, two hundred and fifty of the dragon horses.

That was the number. Tai read it one more time.

It was in the scroll he held, recorded in Kitan, in a Taguran scribe's thin but careful calligraphy. Two hundred and fifty Heavenly

Horses. Given him in his own right, and to no one else. Not a gift for the Ta-Ming Palace, the emperor. Not that. Presented to Shen Tai, second son of the General Shen Gao, once Left Side Commander of the Pacified West.

His own, to use or dispose of as he judged best, the letter read, in royal recognition from Rygyal of courage and piety, and honour done the dead of Kuala Nor.

"You know what this says?" His own voice sounded odd to Tai.

The captain nodded.

"They will kill me for these," Tai said. "They will tear me apart to claim those horses before I get near the court."

"I know," said Bytsan calmly.

Tai looked at him. The other man's dark-brown eyes were impossible to read. "You *know*?"

"Well, it seems likely enough. It is a large gift."

A large gift.

Tai laughed, a little breathlessly. He shook his head in disbelief. "In the name of all nine heavens, I can't just ride through Iron Gate Pass with two hundred and fifty—"

"I know," the Taguran interrupted. "I know you can't. I made some suggestions when they told me what they wished to do."

"You did?"

Bytsan nodded. "Hardly a gift if you're ... accidentally killed on the way east and the horses are dispersed, or claimed by someone else."

"No, it isn't, is it? Hardly a gift!" Tai heard his voice rising. Such a simple life he'd been living, until moments ago. "And the Ta-Ming was a brawl of factions when I left. I am sure it is worse now!"

"I am sure you are right."

"Oh? Really? What do you know about it?" The other man, he decided, seemed irritatingly at ease.

Bytsan gave him a glance. "Little enough, in the small fort I am honoured to command for my king. I was only agreeing with you." He paused. "Do you want to hear what I suggested, or not?"

Tai looked down. He felt embarrassed. He nodded his head. For no reason he knew, he took off his straw hat, standing in the high, bright sun. The axes continued in the distance.

Bytsan told him what he'd written to his own court, and what had been decreed in response to that. It seemed to have cost the other man his position at the fortress in the pass above, in order to implement his own proposal. Tai didn't know if that meant a promotion or not.

It might, Tai understood, keep *him* alive. For a time, at least. He cleared his throat, trying to think what to say.

"You realize," Bytsan spoke with a pride he could not conceal, "that this is Sangrama's gift. The king's generosity. Our Kitan princess might have asked him for it, it is her name on that letter, but it is the Lion who sends you this."

Tai looked at him. He said, quietly, "I understand. It is an honour that the Lion of Rygyal even knows my name."

Bytsan flushed. After the briefest hesitation, he bowed.

Two hundred and fifty Sardian horses, Tai was thinking, from within the sandstorm of his forever-altered life. Being brought by him to a court, an empire, that gloried in every single dragon steed that had ever reached them from the west. That dreamed of those horses with so fierce a longing, shaping porcelain and jade and ivory in their image, linking poets' words to the thunder of mythic hooves.

The world could bring you poison in a jewelled cup, or surprising gifts. Sometimes you didn't know which of them it was.

CHAPTER II

Bytsan sri Nespo was furious with himself, to the point of humiliation. He knew what his father would have said, and in what tone, had he witnessed this shame.

He had just bowed—far too deferentially—when the Kitan, having removed his stupid hat for some reason, said he was honoured that the Lion knew his name in Rygyal, so far away in glory.

But it was a gracious thing to say, and Bytsan had found himself bowing, hand wrapped around fist in their fashion (not that of his own people), before he was able to stop himself. Perhaps it had been the hat, after all, the deliberate self-exposure of that gesture.

The Kitan could do such things to you, or this one could.

Just when you'd decided, one more time, that they were all about their centre-of-the-world arrogance, they could say and do something like this from within the breeding and courtesy they donned like a cloak—while clutching a completely ridiculous straw hat.

What did you *do* when that happened? Ignore it? Treat it as decadence, softness, a false courtesy, unworthy of note on ground where Taguran soldiers had fought and died?

Bytsan wasn't able to do that. A softness of his own, perhaps. It might even affect his career. Although what defined military promotion these days—with warfare limited to occasional skirmishes—was more about whom you knew in higher ranks, had gotten drunk with once or twice, or had allowed to seduce you when you were too young to know better, or could pretend as much.

In order to be judged on courage, on how you fought, there had to be fighting, didn't there?

Peacetime was good for Tagur, for borders and trade and roads and raising new temples, for harvests and full granaries and seeing sons grow up instead of learning they were lying in mounds of corpses, as here by Kuala Nor.

But that same peace played havoc with an ambitious soldier's hopes of using courage and initiative as his methods of advancement.

Not that he was going to talk about that with a Kitan. There were limits: inward borders in addition to the ones with fortresses defending them.

But if he was going to be honest about it, the court in Rygyal knew his name now, as well, because of this Shen Tai, this unprepossessing figure with the courteous voice and the deep-set eyes.

Bytsan stole an appraising glance. The Kitan couldn't be called a soft city-scholar any more: two years of punishing labour in a mountain meadow had dealt with that. He was lean and hard, his skin weathered, hands scratched and callused. And Bytsan knew the man *had* been a soldier for a time. It had occurred to him—more than a year ago—that this one might even know how to fight. There were two swords in his cabin.

It didn't matter. The Kitan would be leaving soon, his life entirely changed by the letter he was holding.

Bytsan's life as well. He was to be given leave from his post when this Kitan left for home. He was reassigned to Dosmad Fortress, south and east, on the border, with the sole and specific responsibility—in the name of the Princess Cheng-wan—of implementing his own suggestion regarding her gift.

Initiative, he had decided, could involve more than leading a flanking attack in a cavalry fight. There were other sorts of flanking manoeuvres: the kind that might even get you out of a backwater fort in a mountain pass above a hundred thousand ghosts.

That last was another thing he didn't like, and this he'd even admitted to the Kitan once: the ghosts terrified him as much as they did every soldier who came with him bringing the wagon and supplies.

Shen Tai had been quick to say that his own people from Iron Gate Pass were exactly the same: stopping for the night safely east of here when they came up the valley, timing their arrival for late morning just as Bytsan did, working hastily to unload his supplies and do whatever tasks they'd assigned themselves—and then gone. Gone from the lake and the white bones before darkfall, even in winter when night came swiftly. Even in a snowstorm once, Shen Tai had said. Refusing shelter in his cabin.

Bytsan had done that, too. Better ice and snow in a mountain pass than the howling presence of the bitter, unburied dead who could poison your soul, blight the life of any child you fathered, drive you mad.

The Kitan beside him didn't appear to be a madman, but that was the prevailing explanation among Bytsan's soldiers at the fort. Probably at Iron Gate, too. Something two outpost armies could agree upon? Or was that just an easy way of dealing with someone being more courageous than you were?

You could fight him to test that, of course. Gnam wanted to, had been spoiling for it even before they'd come down from the pass. Bytsan had briefly harboured the unworthy thought that he'd like to see that challenge. Only briefly: if the Kitan died, there went his own flanking move away from here.

Shen Tai put his absurd hat back on as Bytsan told him what they were going to do in an effort to keep him alive long enough to get to Xinan and decide how to deal with his horses.

Because the man was right—of course he was right—he'd be killed ten times over for that many Sardian horses if he simply tried to herd them back east openly.

It was an absurd, wildly extravagant gift, but being absurd and extravagant was the privilege of royalty, wasn't it?

He thought about saying that to the other man, but refrained. He wasn't sure why, but it might have been that Shen Tai really did look shaken, rereading the scroll again, visibly unsettled for the first time since Bytsan had been coming here.

They walked back to the cabin. Bytsan supervised the unpacking and storing of supplies—metal chests and tight wooden boxes for the food, to defeat the rats. He made another joke about wine and the long evenings. Gnam and Adar had begun stacking firewood, against the cabin wall. Gnam worked fiercely, sweating in his unnecessary armour, channelling fury—which was perfectly all right with his captain. Anger in a soldier could be used.

It was soon enough done, the sun still high, just starting west. Summer's approach made the run down to the lake easier in obvious ways. Bytsan lingered long enough for a cup of wine (warmed in the Kitan fashion) with Shen Tai, then bade him a brisk farewell. The soldiers were already restless. The other man was still distracted, uneasy. It showed, behind the eternal mask of courtesy.

Bytsan could hardly blame him.

Two hundred and fifty horses, the White Jade Princess had decreed. The sort of overwrought conceit only someone living in a palace all her life could devise. The king had approved it, however.

It was never wise, Bytsan had decided on his way here from the fort, to underestimate the influence of women at a court.

He'd considered saying that, too, over the cup of wine, but had elected not to.

There would be one last supply trip in a month's time, then life would change for both of them. They might never see each other again. Probably would not. Better not to do anything so foolish as confide in the other man, or acknowledge more than curiosity and a rationed measure of respect.

The cart was lighter on the way back, of course, the bullock quicker heading home. So were the soldiers, putting the lake and the dead behind them.

Three of his men started a song as they left the meadow and began to wind their way up. Bytsan paused in the afternoon light at the switchback where he always did, and looked down. You might call Kuala Nor beautiful in late spring—if you knew nothing about it.

His gaze swept across the blue water to the nesting birds—an absurd number of them. You could fire an arrow in the air over that way and kill three with one shot. If the arrow had room to fall. He allowed himself a smile. He was glad to be leaving, too, no denying it.

He looked across the meadow bowl, north towards the far, framing mountains, range beyond range. The tale of his people was that blue-faced demons, gigantic and malevolent, had dwelled in those distant peaks from the beginning of the world and had only been barred from the Tagur plateau by the gods, who had thrown up other mountains against them, wrapped in magic. The range they were re-entering now, where their small fortress sat, was one of these.

The gods themselves, dazzling and violent, lived much farther south, beyond Rygyal, above the transcendent peaks that touched the foothills of heaven, and no man had ever climbed them.

Bytsan's gaze fell upon the burial mounds across the lake, on the far side of the meadow. They lay against the pine woods, west of the Kitan's cabin, three long rows of them now, two years' worth of bone-graves in hard ground.

Shen Tai was digging already, he saw, working beyond the last of them in the third row. He hadn't waited for the Tagurans to leave the meadow. Bytsan watched him, small in the distance: bend and shovel, bend and shovel.

He looked at the cabin set against that same northern slope, saw the pen they'd built for the two goats, the freshly stacked firewood against one wall. He finished his sweep by turning east, to the valley through which this strange, solitary Kitan had come to Kuala Nor, and along which he would return.

"Something's moving there," Gnam said beside him, looking the same way. He pointed. Bytsan stared, narrowing his eyes, and then he saw it, too.

∽

He'd gone back to digging the pit he'd started two days ago, end of the third row in from the trees, because that was what he did here. And because he felt that if he didn't keep himself moving, working to exhaustion today, the chaos of his thoughts—almost feverish, after so long a quiet time—would overwhelm him.

There was always the wine Bytsan had brought, another access, like a crooked, lamplit laneway in the North District of Xinan, to the blurred borders of oblivion. The wine would be there at day's end, waiting. No one else was coming to drink it.

Or so he'd thought, carrying his shovel to work, but the world today was simply not fitting itself to a steady two-year routine.

Standing up, stretching his back, and removing the maligned hat to mop at his forehead, Tai saw figures coming from the east over the tall green grass.

They were already out of the canyon, in the open on the meadow. That meant they had to have been visible for some time, he just hadn't noticed. Why should he notice? Why even look? No one came here but the two sets of troops from the forts, full moon, new moon.

There were two of them, he saw, on small horses, a third horse carrying their gear behind. They moved slowly, not hurrying. Perhaps tired. The sun was starting west, its light fell upon them, making them vivid in the late-day's glowing.

It wasn't time for supplies from Iron Gate. He'd just said farewell to Bytsan and the Taguran soldiers. And when men did arrive, it wasn't just a pair of them with no cart. And—most certainly—they did *not* reach the lake in the later part of the day, when they'd have to stay with him overnight or be outside among the dead after dark.

This, clearly, was a day marked for change in his stars.

They were still some distance away, the travellers. Tai stared for another moment, then shouldered his shovel, picked up his quiver and bow—carried against wolves and for shots at a bird for dinner—and started towards his cabin, to be waiting for them there.

A matter of simple courtesy, respect shown visitors to one's home, wherever it might be in the world, even here beyond borders. He felt his pulse quickening as he walked, beating to meet the world's pulse, coming back to him.

ख़

Chou Yan had expected his friend to be changed, in both appearance and manner, if he was even alive after two years out here. He'd been preparing for terrible tidings, had talked about it with his travelling companion, not that she ever replied.

Then at Iron Gate Pass—that wretched fortress here at the world's end—they'd told him Tai was still among the living, or had been a little while ago when they'd taken supplies to him by the lake. Yan had immediately drunk several cups of Salmon River wine (he had been carrying it for Tai, more or less) to celebrate.

He hadn't known, until then.

No one had known. He'd assumed when he left Xinan that he would be journeying ten days or so along the imperial road and then down through civilized country to his friend's family home with what he had to tell him. It wasn't so. At the estate near the Wai River, where he'd managed to remain uncharacteristically discreet about his tidings, the third brother, young Shen Chao—the only child still at home—had told him where Tai had gone, two full years ago.

Yan couldn't believe it at first, and then, thinking about his friend, he did believe it.

Tai had always had something different about him, too many strands in one nature: an uneasy mingling of soldier and scholar, ascetic and drinking companion among the singing girls. Along with a temper. It was no wonder, their friend Xin Lun had once said, that Tai was always going on about the need for *balance* after too many cups of wine. Lun had joked about how hard keeping one's balance could be on muddy laneways, weaving home after that many cups.

It was a very long way, where Tai had journeyed. His family had not heard from him since he'd gone. He could be dead. No one could reasonably expect Chou Yan to follow him, beyond the borders of the empire.

Yan had spent two nights among the Shen women and youngest boy, sharing their ancestor rites and meals (very good food, no wine in the house during mourning, alas). He'd slept in a comfortable mosquito-netted bed. He'd poured his own libation over General Shen Gao's grave, admired his monument and inscription, strolled with young Chao in the orchard and along the stream. He was unhappily trying to decide what to do.

How far did friendship carry one? Literally, how far?

In the event, he did what he'd been afraid he'd do from the time they'd told him of Tai's departure. He bade farewell to the family and continued west towards the border, with only the single guard he'd been advised to take with him, back in Xinan.

She had told him it was an easy enough journey, when he mentioned where his friend had gone. Yan didn't believe her, but the indifferent manner was oddly reassuring.

As long as he paid her, Yan thought, she wouldn't care. You hired a Kanlin Warrior and they stayed with you until you paid them off. Or didn't pay them: though that was, invariably, an extremely bad idea.

Wan-si was hopeless as a companion, truth be told, especially for a sociable man who liked to talk, laugh, argue, who enjoyed the sound of his voice declaiming poetry—his own verses or anyone else's. Yan kept reminding himself that she was simply protection for the road, and skilled hands to assemble their camp at night when they slept outdoors—rather more necessary now than he'd expected at the outset. She was not a friend or an intimate of any kind.

Most certainly not someone to think about bedding at night. He had little doubt what she'd say if he raised that matter, and less doubt she'd break a bone or two if he tried to give effect to the desire that had begun to assail him, aware of her lithe body lying near him under stars, or curving and stretching in her exercise rituals—those elegant, slow movements at sunrise. The Kanlin were fabled for discipline, and for how efficiently they killed when need arose.

Need hadn't arisen as they'd journeyed down the river road to Shen Tai's family home. One twilight encounter in light rain with three rough-looking men who might have had theft in mind had they not seen a black-clad Kanlin with two swords and a bow. They'd absented themselves quickly down a path into dripping undergrowth.

Once they started west, however, everything began to feel different for Yan. He was at pains to light candles or burn incense and leave donations at any and all temples to any and all gods from the morning they left the Shen estate and began following a dusty track northwest, and then farther west, towards emptiness.

North of them, parallel to their route, lay the imperial road through the prefecture city of Chenyao, and beyond that was the easternmost section of the Silk Roads, leading from Xinan to Jade Gate and the garrisons in the Kanshu Corridor.

The imperial highway had lively villages and comfortable inns at postal stations all the way along. There would have been good wine, and pretty women. Maybe even some of the yellow-haired dancing girls from Sardia, working in pleasure houses, perhaps on their way to the capital. The ones who could arch their bodies backwards and touch the ground with feet and hands at once—and so elicit arresting images in the mind of an imaginative man.

But Shen Tai wasn't up there, was he? Nothing so sensible. And it didn't make sense to go five or six days north to meet the highway, when their own path was to Iron Gate by Kuala Nor, not Jade Gate Pass.

That left his friend Yan, his *loyal* friend, feeling every hard-boned movement of his small, shaggy horse towards the end of a day's silent ride through late-spring countryside. He wasn't going to drink that wine or hear music in those inns, or teach fragrant women how he very much liked to be touched.

It was Wan-si who decided how far they'd ride each day, whether they'd reach a village and negotiate a roof under which to sleep, or camp outside. Yan ached like a grandfather each morning when he woke on dew-damp ground, and the village beds were hardly better.

For anything less than the tidings he was bearing he wouldn't have done this, he told himself. He simply wouldn't have, however dear his friend might be to him, whatever parting verses and last embraces they'd exchanged at the Willow Inn by the western gate of Xinan, when Tai had left for home to mourn his father. Yan and Lun and the others had given him broken willow twigs in farewell and to ensure a safe return.

The others? There had been half a dozen of them at the Willow Inn, fabled for the partings it had witnessed. None of the *others* were with Yan on the road, were they? They'd been happy enough to get drunk when Tai left, and then praise Yan and improvise poems and give out more willow twigs at that same inn yard when he set out two years later, but no one had volunteered to go with him, had they? Not even when the expected journey was only ten days or so, to Tai's family home.

Hah, thought Chou Yan, many hard days west of that estate. At this point, he decided, he himself could fairly be called heroic, a testament to the depth and virtue of friendship in the glorious Ninth Dynasty. They would have to admit it when he returned, all of them: no more wine-cup jests about softness and indolence. It was too pleasing a thought to keep to himself. He offered it to Wan-si as they rode.

As idle an expenditure of mortal breath and words as there had ever been. Black clothing, black eyes, a stillness like no one he'd ever known, this warrior-woman. It was irritating. A tongue was wasted on her. So was beauty, come to think of it. He couldn't remember if he'd ever seen her smile.

That night she killed a tiger.

He didn't even know it until morning when he saw the animal's body, two arrows in it, at the green edge of a bamboo grove, twenty paces from where they'd slept.

He gaped. Stammered, "Why didn't ...? I didn't even ..."

He was in a sweat, hands shaking. He kept looking at the slain beast and quickly away. The dreadful size of it. Fear made him dizzy. He sat down, on the ground. He saw her walk over and reclaim her arrows. A booted foot on the tiger's flank, twisting the shafts free.

She'd already packed their bedding and gear on the third horse. Now she mounted up and waited impatiently for him, holding his horse's reins out for him. He managed to stand, to get up on the horse.

"You never even told me last night!" he said, unable to take his eyes off the tiger now.

"You complain less when you've slept a night," she said, which counted as a long sentence. She started off, the sun rising behind them.

They reached the fort at Iron Gate Pass two evenings later.

The commander fed them for two nights (mutton stew and mutton stew), let Chou Yan entertain with gossip from the capital, and sent them west, with advice as to where to spend three nights on the way to Kuala Nor, so as to arrive at the lake in the morning.

Yan was entirely content with this counsel, having no interest at all in encountering ghosts of any kind, let alone angry ones and in the numbers (improbably) reported by the soldiers at the fort. But Wan-si disdained belief in such matters and did not want to spend an unnecessary night in the canyon among mountain cats, she said bluntly. If his friend was alive by the lake, and had been there for two years ...

They pushed on through two long, light-headed days (Yan was finding it difficult to deal with the air this high), past the commander's suggested stopping places. On the third afternoon, with the sun ahead of them, they ascended a last defile between cliffs and came suddenly out of shadows to the edge of a meadow bowl, of a beauty that could break the heart.

And moving forward through tall grass, Chou Yan had finally seen his dear friend standing at the doorway of a small cabin, waiting to greet him, and his soul had been glad beyond any poet's words, and the long journey came to seem as nothing, in the way of such trials when they are over.

Weary but content, he brought his small horse to a halt in front of the cabin. Shen Tai was in a white tunic for mourning, but his loose trousers and the tunic were sweat- and dirt-stained. He was unshaven, darkened, rough-skinned like a peasant, but he was staring at Yan in flattering disbelief.

Yan felt like a hero. He *was* a hero. He'd had a nosebleed earlier, from the altitude, but you didn't have to talk about that. He only wished his tidings weren't so grave. But then he wouldn't be here, would he, if they weren't?

Tai bowed twice, formally, hand in fist. His courtesy was as remembered: impeccable, almost exaggeratedly so, when he wasn't in a fury about something.

Yan, still on horseback, smiled happily down at him. He said what he'd planned to say for a long time, words he'd fallen asleep each night thinking about. *"West of Iron Gate, west of Jade Gate Pass / There'll be no old friends."*

Tai smiled back. "I see. You have come this long distance to tell me poets can be wrong? This is meant to dazzle and confound me?"

Hearing the wry, remembered voice, Yan's heart was suddenly full. "Ah, well. I suppose not. Greetings, old friend."

He swung down stiffly. His eyes filled with tears as he embraced the other man.

Tai's expression when they stepped back and looked at each other was strange, as if Yan were a ghost of some kind himself.

"I would not ever, ever have thought ..." he began.

"That I would be one to come to you? I am sure you didn't. Everyone underestimates me. That is supposed to confound you."

Tai did not smile. "It does, my friend. How did you even know where ...?"

Yan made a face. "I didn't think I was coming this far. I thought you were at home. We all did. They told me there where you had gone."

"And you carried on? All the way here?"

"It looks as though I did, doesn't it?" Yan said happily. "I even carried two small casks of Salmon River wine for you, given me by Chong himself there, but I drank one with your brother and the other at Iron Gate, I'm afraid. We did drink to your name and honour."

The ironical smile. "I thank you for that, then. I do have wine," Tai said. "You will be very tired, and your companion. Will you both honour me and come inside?"

Yan looked at him, wanting to be happy, but his heart sank. He was here for a reason, after all.

"I have something to tell you," he said.

"I thought that must be so," his friend said gravely. "But let me offer water to wash yourselves, and a cup of wine first. You have come a long way."

"*Beyond the last margins of the empire,*" Yan quoted.

He loved the sound of that. No one was going to be allowed to forget this journey of his, he decided. Soft? A plump, would-be mandarin? Not Chou Yan, not any more. The others, studying for the examinations, or in the North District laughing with dancing girls as a spring day waned, listening to *pipa* music, drinking from lacquered cups ... they were the soft ones now.

"Beyond the last margins," Tai agreed. All around them, mountains were piled upon each other, snow-clad. Yan saw a ruined fort on an isle in the middle of the lake.

He followed his friend into the cabin. The shutters were open to the air and the clear light. The one room was small, trimly kept. He remembered that about Tai. He saw a fireplace and a narrow bed, the low writing table, wooden ink-block, ink, paper, brushes, the mat in front of them. He smiled.

He heard Wan-si enter behind him. "This is my guard," he said. "My Kanlin Warrior. She killed a tiger."

He turned to gesture by way of proper introduction, and saw that she had her swords drawn, and levelled at the two of them.

His instincts had been dulled by solitude, two years away from anything remotely like blades pointed towards him. Keeping an eye out for wolves or mountain cats, making sure the goats were penned at night, did nothing to make you ready for an assassin.

But he'd felt something wrong about the guard even as Yan had ridden up with her. He couldn't have said what that feeling was; it was normal, prudent, for a traveller to arrange protection, and Yan was sufficiently unused to journeying (and had enough family wealth) to have gone all the way to hiring a Kanlin, even if he'd only intended to go west a little and then down towards the Wai.

That wasn't it. It had been something in her eyes and posture, Tai decided, staring at the swords. Both were towards him, in fact, not at Yan: she would know which of them was a danger.

Riding up, reining her horse before the cabin door, she ought not to have seemed quite so alert, staring at him. She had been hired to get a man somewhere, and they'd come to that place. A task done, or the outbound stage of it. Payment partly earned. But her glance at Tai had been appraising, as much as anything else.

The sort of look you gave a man you expected to fight.

Or simply kill, since Tai's own swords were where they always were, against the wall, and there was no hope of notching arrow to bowstring before she cut him in two.

Everyone knew what Kanlin blades in Kanlin hands could do.

Yan's face had gone pale with horror. His mouth gaped, fish-like. Poor man. The drawn sword of betrayal was not a part of the world he knew. He'd done something immensely courageous coming here, had reached beyond himself in the name of friendship ... and found only this for reward. Tai wondered what his tidings were, what had caused him to do this. He might never know, he realized.

That angered and disturbed him, equally. He said, setting the world in motion again, "I must assume I am your named target. That my friend knows nothing of why you really came here. There is no need for him to die."

"But there is," she said softly. Her eyes stayed on him, weighing every movement he made, or might make.

"What? Because he'll name you? You think it will not be known who killed me when they come here from Iron Gate? You will have been recorded when you arrived at the fortress. What can he add to that?"

The swords did not waver. She smiled thinly. A beautiful, cold face. Like the lake, Tai thought, death within it.

"Not that," she said. "He insulted me with his eyes. On the journey."

"He saw you as a woman? *That* would have taken some effort," Tai said deliberately.

"Have a care," she said.

"Why? Or you'll kill me?" Anger within him more than anything now. He was a man helped by rage, though, steered towards thought, decisiveness. He was trying to see what it did to her. "The Kanlin are taught proportion and restraint. In movement, in deeds. You would kill a man because he admired your face and body? A disgrace to your mentors on the mountain, if so."

"You will tell me what Kanlin teachings are?"

"If I must," Tai said coolly. "Are you going to do this with honour, and allow me my swords?"

She shook her head. His heart sank. "I would prefer that, but my instructions were precise. I was not to allow you to fight me when we came here. This is not to be a combat." A hint of regret, some explanation for the appraising look: *Who is this one? What sort of man, that she was told to fear him?*

Tai registered something else, however. "When you came here? You knew I was at Kuala Nor? Not at home? How?"

She said nothing. Had made an error, he realized. Not that it was likely to matter. He needed to keep talking. Silence would be death, he was certain of it. "They thought I would kill you, if we fought. Who decided this? Who is protecting you from me?"

"You are very sure of yourself," the assassin murmured.

He had a thought. A poor one, almost hopeless, but nothing better seemed to be arriving in the swirling of these moments.

"I am sure only of the uncertainty of life," he said. "If I am to end here by Kuala Nor and you will not fight me, will you kill me outside? I would offer my last prayer to the water and sky and lie among those I have been burying. It is not a great request."

"No," she said, and he didn't know what she meant, until she added, "It is not." She paused. It would be wrong to call it a hesitation. "I would have fought you, had my orders not been precise."

Orders. *Precise* orders. Who would do that? He needed to shape time, create it, find some way to his swords. The earlier thought really was a useless one, he decided.

He had to make her move, shift her footing, look away from him.

"Yan, who suggested you hire a Kanlin?"

"Silence!" the woman snapped, before Chou Yan could speak.

"Does it matter?" Tai said. "You are about to kill us without a fight, like a frightened child who fears her lack of skill." It was possible—just—that goaded enough she might make another mistake.

His sheathed blades were behind the assassin, by his writing table. The room was small, the distance trivial—unless you wanted to be alive when you reached them.

"No. Like a Warrior accepting orders given," the woman amended calmly.

She seemed serene again, as if his taunting had, instead of provoking, imposed a remembrance of discipline. Tai knew how that could happen. It didn't help him.

"It was Xin Lun who suggested it to me," Yan said bravely.

Tai heard the words, saw the woman's hard eyes, knew what was coming. He cried a warning.

Yan took her right-hand sword, a backhanded stroke, in his side, angled upwards to cut between ribs.

The slash-and-withdraw was precise, elegant, her wrist flexed, the blade swiftly returned—to be levelled towards where Tai had been. No time seeming to have passed: time held and controlled. The Kanlin were taught that way.

As it happened, he knew this, and time *had* passed, time that could be used. Timelessness was an illusion, and he wasn't where he'd been before.

His heart crying, knowing there was nothing he could have done to stop that stroke, he had leaped towards the doorway even as she'd turned to Yan—to kill him for speaking a name.

Tai shouted again, fury more than fear, though he expected to die now, himself.

A hundred thousand dead here, and two more.

He ignored his sheathed swords, they were too far. He whipped out the open door and to his right, towards the firewood by the goat pen. He had leaned his shovel on that wall. A gravedigger's shovel against two Kanlin swords. He got there. Claimed it, wheeled to face her.

The woman was running behind him. And then she wasn't.

Because the faint, foolish, desperate idea he'd had before entered into the sunlit world, became real.

The wind that rose in that moment conjured itself out of nothing at all, without warning. From within a spring afternoon's placidity, a terrifying force erupted.

There came a screaming sound: high, fierce, unnatural.

Not his voice, not the woman's, not anyone actually alive.

The wind didn't ruffle the meadow grass at all, or stir the pine trees. It didn't move the waters of the lake. It didn't touch Tai, though he heard what howled within it.

The wind poured *around* him, curving to either side like a pair of bows, as he faced the woman. It took the assassin bodily, lifted her up, and hurled her through the air as if she were a twig, a child's kite, an uprooted flower stalk in a gale. She was slammed against the wall of his cabin, pinned, unable to move.

It was as if she were nailed to the wood. Her eyes were wide with horror. She was trying to scream, her mouth was open, but whatever was blasting her, claiming her, didn't allow that either.

One sword was still in her hand, flattened against the cabin. The other had been ripped from her grasp. She had been lifted clean off the ground, he saw, her feet were dangling in air. She was suspended, hair and clothing splayed against the dark wood of the wall.

The illusion, again, of a moment outside of time. Then Tai saw two arrows hit her, one and then the other.

They struck from the side, fired from the far end of the cabin, beyond the door. And the wild ghost-wind did nothing to mar their flight, only held her pinned to be killed like a victim for sacrifice. The first arrow took her in the throat, a flowering of crimson, the second went in as deep, below her left breast.

In the instant of her dying the wind, too, died.

The screaming left the meadow.

In the bruised stillness that followed, the woman slid slowly down the wall, crumpled to one side, and lay upon the trampled grass beside his cabin door.

Tai drew a ragged, harrowed breath. His hands were shaking. He looked towards the far side of the cabin.

Bytsan and the young soldier called Gnam were standing there, fear in their eyes. Both arrows had been fired by the younger man.

And though the wild wind-sound was gone, Tai was still hearing it in his mind, that screaming, still seeing the woman pinned flat like some black-robed butterfly, by what it had been.

The dead of Kuala Nor had come to him. For him. To his aid.

But so had two men, mortal and desperately frightened, riding back down from their safe path away, even though the sun was over west now, with twilight soon to fall, and in the darkness here the world did not belong to living men.

Tai understood something else then, looking down at the woman where she lay: that even by daylight—morning and afternoon, summer and winter, doing his work—he had been living at sufferance, all this time.

He looked the other way, towards the blue of the lake and the low sun, and he knelt on the dark green grass. He touched his forehead to the earth in full obeisance, three times.

It had been written by one teacher in the time of the First Dynasty, more than nine hundred years ago, that when a man was brought back alive from the tall doors of death, from the brink of crossing over to the dark, he had a burden laid upon him ever after: to conduct his granted life in such a manner as to be worthy of that return.

Others had taught otherwise over the centuries: that survival in such a fashion meant that you had not yet learned what you had been sent to discover in a single, given life. Though that, really, could be seen as another kind of burden, Tai thought, on his knees in meadow grass. He had a sudden image of his father feeding ducks in their stream. He looked out over the lake, a darker blue in the mountain air.

He stood up. He turned to the Tagurans. Gnam had gone to the dead woman, he saw. He dragged her away from the wall, ripped his arrows out of her body, tossing them carelessly behind himself. Her hair had come free of its binding in that wind, spilling loose, pins scattered. Gnam bent down, spread her legs, arranging them.

He began removing his armour.

Tai blinked in disbelief.

"What are you doing?" The sound of his own voice frightened him. "She's still warm," the soldier said. "Do me as a prize."

Tai stared at Bytsan. The other man turned away. "Do not claim your own soldiers never do this," the Taguran captain said, but he was staring at the mountains, not meeting Tai's gaze.

"None of mine ever did," said Tai. "And no one else will while I stand by."

He took three strides, and picked up the nearest Kanlin sword.

It had been a long time since he'd held one of these. The balance was flawless, a weight without weight. He pointed it at the young soldier.

Gnam's hands stopped working his armour straps. He actually looked surprised. "She came here to kill you. I just saved your life."

It wasn't wholly true, but close enough.

"You have my gratitude. And a hope I can repay you one day. But that will be prevented if I kill you now, and I will do that if you touch her. Unless you want to fight me."

Gnam shrugged. "I can do that." He began tightening his straps again.

"You'll die," said Tai quietly. "You need to know it."

The young Taguran was brave, had to be, to have come back down.

Tai struggled to find words to lead them out, a way to save face for the younger man. "Think about it," he said. "The wind that came. That was the dead. They are ... with me here."

He looked at Bytsan again, who seemed strangely passive suddenly. Tai went on, urgently, "I have spent two years here trying to honour the dead. Dishonouring this one makes a mockery of that."

"She came to kill you," Gnam repeated, as if Tai were slow-witted.

"Every dead man in this meadow came to kill someone!" Tai shouted.

His words drifted away in the thin air. It was cooler now, the sun low.

"Gnam," said Bytsan, finally, "there is no time for a fight if we want to be away before dark, and, trust me, after what just happened, I do. Mount up. We're going."

He walked around the side of the cabin. He came back a moment later, on his magnificent Sardian, leading the soldier's horse. Gnam was still staring at Tai. He hadn't moved, the desire to fight written in his face.

"You've just won your second tattoo," Tai said quietly.

He looked briefly at Bytsan, then back to the soldier in front of him. "Enjoy the moment. Don't hurry to the afterworld. Accept my admiration, and my thanks."

Gnam stared at him another moment, then turned deliberately and spat thickly into the grass, very near the body of the dead woman. He stalked over and seized his horse's reins and mounted. He wheeled to ride away.

"Soldier!" Tai spoke before he was aware he'd intended to.

The other man turned again.

Tai took a breath. Some things were hard to do. "Take her swords," he said. "Kanlin-forged. I doubt any soldier in Tagur carries their equal."

Gnam did not move.

Bytsan laughed shortly. "I'll take them if he does not."

Tai smiled wearily at the captain. "I've no doubt."

"It is a generous gift."

"It carries my gratitude."

He waited, didn't move. There were limits to how far one would go to assuage a young man's pride.

And behind him, through that open cabin door, a friend was lying dead.

After a long moment, Gnam moved his horse and extended a hand. Tai turned, bent, unslung the shoulder scabbards from the dead woman's body, and sheathed the two blades. Her blood was on one sheath. He handed them up to the Taguran. Bent again and retrieved the two arrows, gave them to the young man, as well.

"Don't hurry to the afterworld," he repeated.

Gnam's face was expressionless. Then, "My thanks," he said.

He did say it. There was that much. Even here, beyond borders and boundaries, you could live a certain way, Tai thought, remembering his father. You could try, at least. He looked west, past the wheeling birds, at the red sun in low clouds, then back to Bytsan.

"You'll need to ride fast."

"I know it. The man inside ...?"

"Is dead."

"You killed him?"

"She did."

"But he was with her."

"He was my friend. It is a grief."

Bytsan shook his head. "Is it possible to understand the Kitan?"

"Perhaps not."

He was tired, suddenly. And it occurred to him that he'd have two bodies to bury quickly now—because he'd be leaving in the morning.

"He led an assassin to you."

"He was a friend," Tai repeated. "He was deceived. He came to bring me tidings. She, or whoever paid her, didn't want me to hear them or live to do anything about it."

"A friend," Bytsan sri Nespo repeated. His tone betrayed nothing. He turned to go.

"Captain!"

Bytsan looked back, didn't turn his horse.

"So are you, I believe. My thanks." Tai closed fist in hand.

The other man stared at him for a long time, then nodded.

He was about to spur his horse away, Tai saw. But he did something else, instead. You could see a thought striking him, could read it in the square-chinned features.

"Did he tell you? Whatever it was he came to say?"

Tai shook his head.

Gnam had danced his horse farther south. He was ready to leave now. Had the two swords across his back.

Bytsan's face clouded over. "You will leave now? To find out what it was?"

He was clever, this Taguran. Tai nodded again. "In the morning. Someone died to bring me tidings. Someone died to stop me from learning them."

Bytsan nodded. He looked west himself this time, the sinking sun, darkness coming. Birds in the air, restless on the far side of the lake. Hardly any wind. Now.

The Taguran drew a deep breath. "Gnam, go on ahead. I'll stay the night with the Kitan. If he's leaving in the morning there are matters he and I must talk about. I'll test my fate inside with him. It seems that whatever spirits are here mean him no harm. Tell the others I'll catch you up tomorrow. You can wait for me in the middle pass."

Gnam's turn to stare. "You are staying here?"

"I just said that."

"Captain! That is—"

"I know it is. Go."

The younger man hesitated still. His mouth opened and closed. Bytsan's tattooed face was hard, nothing vaguely close to a yielding there.

Gnam shrugged. He spurred his horse and rode away. They stood there, the two of them, and watched him go in the waning of the light, saw him gallop very fast around the near side of the lake as if spirits were pursuing him, tracking his breath and blood.

CHAPTER III

The armies of the empire had changed over the past fifty years, and changes were continuing. The old *fupei* system of a peasant militia summoned for part of the year then returning to their farms for the harvest had grown more and more inadequate to the needs of an expanding empire.

The borders had been pushed west and north and northeast and even south past the Great River through the disease-ridden tropics to the pearl-diver seas. Collisions with Tagurans to the west and the various Bogü tribal factions north had increased, as did the need to protect the flow of luxuries that came on the Silk Roads. The emergence of border forts and garrisons farther and farther out had ended the militia system with its back-and-forth of farmer-soldiers.

Soldiers were professionals now, or they were supposed to be. More and more often they and their officers were drawn from nomads beyond the Long Wall, subdued and co-opted by the Kitan. Even the military governors were often foreigners now. Certainly the most powerful one was.

It marked a change. A large one.

The soldiers served year-round and, for years now, were paid from the imperial treasury and supported by a virtual army of peasants and labourers building forts and walls, supplying food and weapons and clothing and entertainment of any and all kinds.

It made for better-trained fighters familiar with their terrain, but a standing army of this size did not come without costs—and increased taxes were only the most obvious consequence.

In years and regions of relative peace, without drought or flood, with wealth now flowing at an almost unimaginable rate into Xinan and Yenling and the other great cities, the cost of the new armies was bearable. In hard years it became a problem. And other issues, less readily seen, were growing. At the lowest ebb, of a person or a nation, the first seeds of later glory may sometimes be seen, looking back with a careful eye. At the absolute summit of accomplishment the insects chewing from within at the most extravagant sandalwood may be heard, if the nights are quiet enough.

A QUIET-ENOUGH NIGHT. Wolves had been howling in the canyon earlier, but had stopped. The darkness was giving way, for those on watch on the ramparts of Iron Gate Fort, to a nearly-summer sunrise. Pale light pulling a curtain of shadows back—as in a puppet show at a town market—from the narrow space between ravine walls.

Though that, thought Wujen Ning, from his post on the ramparts, was not quite right. Street theatre curtains were pulled to the side—he'd seen them in Chenyao.

Ning was one of the native-born Kitan here, having followed his father and older brothers into the army. There was no family farm for him to rely upon for an income, or return to visit. He wasn't married.

He spent his half-year leave time in the town between Iron Gate and Chenyao. There were wine shops and food sellers and women to take his strings of cash. Once, given two weeks' leave, he'd gone to Chenyao itself, five days away. Home was too far.

Chenyao had been, by a great deal, the biggest city he'd ever seen. It had frightened him, and he'd never gone back. He didn't believe the others when they said it wasn't that large, as cities went.

Here in the pass, in the quiet of it, the dawn light was filtering downwards. It struck the tops of the cliffs first, pulling them from shadow, and worked its way towards the still-dark valley floor as the sun rose over the mighty empire behind them.

Wujen Ning had never seen the sea, but it pleased him to imagine the vast lands of Kitai stretching east to the ocean and the islands in it where immortals dwelled.

He glanced down at the dark, dusty courtyard. He adjusted his helmet. They had a commander now who was obsessed with helmets and properly worn uniforms, as if a screaming horde of Tagurans might come storming down the valley at any moment and sweep over the fortress walls if someone's tunic or sword belt was awry.

As if, Ning thought. He spat over the wall through his missing front tooth. As if the might of the Kitan Empire in this resplendent Ninth Dynasty, and the three hundred soldiers in this fort that commanded the pass, were a nuisance like mosquitoes.

He slapped at one of those on his neck. They were worse to the south, but this pre-dawn hour brought out enough of the bloodsuckers to make for annoyance. He looked up. Scattered clouds, a west wind in his face. The last stars nearly gone. He'd be off duty at the next drum, could go down to breakfast and sleep.

He scanned the empty ravine, and realized it wasn't empty.

What he saw, in the mist slowly dispersing, made him shout for a runner to go to the commander.

A lone man approaching before sunrise wasn't a threat, but it was unusual enough to get an officer up on the wall.

Then, as he came nearer, the rider lifted a hand, gesturing for the gates to be opened for him. At first Ning was astonished at the arrogance of that, and then he saw the horse the man was riding.

He watched them come on, horse and rider taking clearer form, like spirits entering the real world through fog. That was a strange thought. Ning spat again, between his fingers this time for protection.

He wanted the horse the moment he saw it. Every man in Iron Gate would want that horse. By the bones of his honoured ancestors, Wujen Ning thought, every man in the empire would.

"Why you so sure that one didn't bring her to you?" Bytsan had asked.

"He did bring her. Or she brought him."

"Stop being clever, Kitan. You know what I mean."

Some irritation, understandable. They'd been on their eighth or ninth cup of wine, at least—it had been considered ill-bred among the students in Xinan to keep count.

Night outside by then, but moonlit, so silver in the cabin.

Tai had also lit candles, thinking light would help the other man. The ghosts were out there, as always. You could hear their voices, as always. Tai was used to it, but felt unsettled to realize this was his last night. He wondered if they might know it, somehow.

Bytsan wouldn't be—couldn't be—accustomed to any of this.

The voices of the dead offered anger and sorrow, sometimes dark, hard pain, as if trapped forever in the moment of their dying. The sounds swirled from outside the cabin windows, gliding along the rooftop. Some came from farther off, towards the lake or the trees.

Tai tried to remember the dry-mouthed terror he'd lived with on his first nights two years ago. It was hard to reclaim those feelings after so long, but he remembered sweating and shivering, clutching a sword hilt in bed.

If cups of warmed rice wine were going to help the Taguran deal with a hundred thousand ghosts, less the ones buried by Shen Tai in two years ... that was the way it was. That was all right.

They'd buried Yan and the assassin in the pit Tai had begun that afternoon. It wasn't nearly deep enough yet for the bones he'd planned, which made it good for two Kitan just slain, one by sword, one by arrows, sent over to the night.

They'd wrapped them in winter sheepskin he wasn't using (and would never use again) and carried them down the row of mounds in the last of the day's light.

Tai had jumped into the pit and the Taguran had handed down Yan's body and he'd laid his friend in the ground and climbed out of the grave.

Then they'd dropped the assassin in beside Yan and shovelled the earth from next to the open pit back in and pounded it hard on top and all around with the flat sides of the shovels, against the animals that might come, and Tai had spoken a prayer from the teachings of the Path, and poured a libation over the grave, while the Taguran stood by, facing south towards his gods.

It had been nearly dark by then and they'd made their way hastily back to the cabin as the evening star, the one the Kitan people called Great White, appeared in the west, following the sun down. Poets' star at evening, soldiers' in the morning.

There hadn't been anything in the way of fresh food. On a normal day, Tai would have caught a fish, gathered eggs, shot a bird and plucked it for cooking at day's end, but there had been no time for that today.

They'd boiled dried, salted pork and eaten it with kale and hazel-nuts in bowls of rice. The Tagurans had brought early peaches, which were good. And they'd had the new rice wine. They drank as they ate, and continued when the meal was done.

The ghosts had begun with the starlight.

"You know what I mean," Bytsan repeated, a little too loudly. "Why're you so sure of him? Chou Yan? You trust everyone who names himself a friend?"

Tai shook his head. "Isn't in my nature to be trusting. But Yan was too proud of himself when he saw me, and too astonished when she drew her swords."

"A Kitan can't deceive?"

Tai shook his head again. "I knew him." He sipped his wine. "But someone knew me, if they told her not to fight. She said she'd have preferred to kill me in a combat. And she knew I was here. Yan didn't know. She let him go first to my father's house. Didn't give away where I was—he'd have suspected something. Maybe. He wasn't a suspicious man."

Bytsan looked at Tai narrowly, considering all this. "Why would a Kanlin Warrior fear you?"

He wasn't so drunk, after all. Tai couldn't see how it would hurt to answer.

"I trained with them. At Stone Drum Mountain, nearly two years." He watched the other man react. "It would take me time to get my skills back, but someone may not have wanted to chance it."

The Taguran was staring. Tai poured more wine for him from the flask on the brazier. He drank from his own cup, then filled it. A friend had died here today. There was blood on the bedding. There was a new hole in the world where sorrow could enter.

"Everyone knew this about you? The time with the Kanlins?"

Tai shook his head. "No."

"You trained to be an assassin?"

The usual, irritating mistake. "I trained to learn how they think, their disciplines, and how they handle weapons. They are usually guards, or guarantors of a truce, not assassins. I left, fairly abruptly. Some of my teachers may still feel kindly towards me. Others might not. It was years ago. We leave things behind us."

"Well, that's true enough."

Tai drank his wine.

"They think you used them? Tricked them?"

Tai was beginning to regret mentioning it. "I just understand them a little now."

"And they don't like that?"

"No. I'm not a Kanlin."

"What are you?"

"Right now? I'm between worlds, serving the dead."

"Oh, good. Be Kitan-clever again. Are you a soldier or a court mandarin, fuck it all?"

Tai managed a grin. "Neither. Fuck it all."

Bytsan looked away quickly, but Tai saw him suppress a smile. It was hard not to like this man.

He added, more quietly, "It is only truth, captain. I left the army years ago, have not taken the civil service exams. I'm not being clever."

Bytsan held out his again-empty cup before answering. Tai filled it, topped up his own. This was beginning to remind him of nights in the North District. Soldiers or poets—who could drink more? A question for the ages, or sages.

After a moment, the Taguran said, also softly, "You didn't need us to save you."

Outside, something screamed.

It wasn't a sound you could pretend was an animal, or wind. Tai knew that particular voice. Heard it every night. He found himself wishing he'd been able to find and bury that one before leaving. But there was no way to know where any given bones might lie. That much he'd learned in two years. Two years that were ending tonight. He had to leave. Someone had been sent to kill him, this far away. He needed to learn why. He drained his cup again.

He said, "I didn't know they would attack her. Neither did you, coming back."

"Well, of course, or we wouldn't have come."

Tai shook his head. "No, that means your courage deserves honour."

Something occurred to him. Sometimes wine sent your thoughts along channels you'd not otherwise have found, as when river reeds hide and then reveal a tributary stream in marshland.

"Is that why you let the young one shoot both arrows?"

Bytsan's gaze in mingled light was unsettlingly direct. Tai was beginning to feel his wine. The Taguran said, "She was flat against the cabin. They were going to crush the life from her. Why waste an arrow?"

Half an answer at best. Tai said wryly, "Why waste a chance to give a soldier a tattoo, and a boast?"

The other man shrugged. "That, too. He did come back with me."

Tai nodded.

Bytsan said, "You ran outside knowing they'd help you?" An edge to his voice. And why not? They were listening to the cries outside right now. And screams.

Tai cast his mind back to the desperate moments after Yan died. "I was running for the shovel."

Bytsan sri Nespo laughed, a quick, startling sound. "Against Kanlin swords?"

Tai found himself laughing too. The wine was part of it. And the aftermath of fear remembered. He'd expected to die.

He'd have become one of the ghosts of Kuala Nor.

They drank again. The screaming voice had stopped. Another bad one was beginning, one of those that seemed to still be dying, unbearably, somewhere in the night. It hurt your heart, listening, frayed the edges of your mind.

Tai said, "Do you think about death?"

The other man looked at him. "Every soldier does."

It was an unfair question. This was a stranger, of an enemy people not so long ago, and likely again in years to come. A blue-tattooed barbarian living beyond the civilized world.

Tai drank. Taguran wine was not going to replace the spiced or scented grape wine of the best houses in the North District, but it was good enough for tonight.

Bytsan murmured suddenly, "I said we had to talk. Told Gnam that, remember?"

"We aren't talking enough? A shame ... a shame Yan's buried out there. He'd have talked you to sleep, if only to find a respite from his voice."

Buried out there.

Such a wrong place for a gentle, garrulous man to lie. And Yan had come so far. Carrying what tidings? Tai didn't know. He didn't even know, he realized, if his friend had passed the exams.

Bytsan looked away. Gazing out a window at moonlight, he said, "If someone sent an assassin they can send another—when you get back or while you are on the way. You know that."

He knew that.

Bytsan said, "Iron Gate saw them come through. They will ask where the two of them are."

"I'll tell them."

"And they will send word to Xinan."

Tai nodded. Of course they would. A Kanlin Warrior coming this far west as an assassin? That had significance. Not empire-shaking, Tai wasn't important enough, but certainly worth a dispatch from a sleepy border fort. It would go with the military post, which was very fast.

Bytsan said, "Your mourning's over, then?"

"It will almost be, time I get to Xinan."

"That where you'll go?"

"Have to."

"Because you do know who sent her?"

He hadn't expected that.

It was Xin Lun who suggested it to me. Yan's last words on earth, in life, under nine heavens.

"I might know how to start finding out."

He might know more than that, but he wasn't ready to think about it tonight.

"I have another suggestion, then," said the Taguran. "Two of them. Trying to keep you alive." He laughed briefly, drained another cup. "My future seems to be bound up with yours, Shen Tai, and the gift you've been given. You need to stay alive long enough to send for your horses."

Tai considered that. It made sense, from Bytsan's point of view— you didn't have to think hard to see the truth of it.

Both of the Taguran's suggestions had been good ones.

Tai would not have thought of either. He would need to get his subtlety back before he reached Xinan, where you could be exiled for bowing one time too many or too few or to the wrong person first. He accepted both of the other man's ideas, with one addition that seemed proper.

They'd finished the last of the flask, put out the lights, and had gone to bed.

Towards what would soon enough be morning, the moon over west, the Taguran had said softly from where he lay on the floor, "If I'd spent two years here, I would think about death."

"Yes," said Tai.

Starlight. The voices outside, rising and falling. The star of the Weaver Maid had been visible earlier, shining in a window. Far side of the Sky River from her love.

"They are mostly about sorrow out there, aren't they?"

"Yes."

"They would have killed her, though."

"Yes."

ৎ৶৾

Tai recognized the guard above the gate; he'd come to the lake at least twice with the supplies they sent. He didn't remember his name. The commander was named Lin Fong, he knew that. A small, crisp man with a round face and a manner that suggested that the fort at Iron Gate Pass was only a way station, an interlude in his career.

On the other hand, the commander had come to Kuala Nor a few weeks after arriving at the fort last autumn, in order to see for himself the strange man burying the dead there.

He had bowed twice to Tai when he'd left with the soldiers and cart, and the supplies being sent had remained completely reliable. An ambitious man, Lin Fong, and obviously aware, during that visit to the lake, of who Tai's father had been. Traces of arrogance, but there was honour in him, Tai judged, and a sense that the commander was aware of the history of this battleground among mountains.

Not someone you'd likely choose as a friend, but that wasn't what he was here to be at Iron Gate.

He was standing, impeccable in his uniform, just inside the gate as it swung open. It was just after dawn. Tai had slept through the first night travelling but had been awakened by wolves on the second. Not dangerously near, or hungry, as best he could judge, but he had chosen to offer his prayers for his father in the darkness and ride on under stars instead of lying on high, hard ground awake. None of the Kitan were easy with wolves, in legend, in life, and Tai was no exception. He felt safer on horseback, and he was already in love with Bytsan sri Nespo's bay-coloured Sardian.

They didn't sweat blood, the Heavenly Horses—that was legend, a poet's image—but if anyone had wanted to recite some of the elaborate verses about them, Tai would have been entirely happy to listen and approve. He'd ridden recklessly fast in the night, the moon behind him, borne by an illusion that the big horse could not put a hoof wrong, that there was only joy in speed, no danger in the canyon's dark.

You could get yourself killed thinking that way, of course. He hadn't cared, the pace was too purely intoxicating. He was riding a Sardian horse towards home in the night and his heart had been soaring, if only for that time. He had kept the Taguran name—Dynlal meant "spirit" in their tongue—which suited, in many ways.

Exchanging horses had been Bytsan's first proposal. Tai was going to need some mark of favour, he'd pointed out, something that identified him, alerted people to the truth of what he'd been given. One horse, as a symbol of two hundred and fifty to come.

Dynlal would also get him where he was going faster.

The promise of Sardian horses, to be claimed *only* by him, was what might keep him alive, induce others to join in tracking down those who obviously did not wish him to remain alive—and help Tai determine why this was so.

It had made sense. So also, for Tai, did his modification of the suggestion.

He'd written it out before they parted in the morning: a document conveying to Bytsan sri Nespo, captain in the Taguran army, his free choice of any three horses among the two hundred and fifty, in exchange for his own mount surrendered at need and at request, and in grateful recognition of courage shown against treachery at Kuala Nor, arriving from Kitai.

That last phrase would help the captain with his own commanders; they both knew it. Nor had the Taguran argued. He was clearly relinquishing something that mattered a great deal to him with the big bay horse. Moments after starting into the sunrise, running with the wind, Tai had begun to understand why this was so.

Bytsan's second suggestion had involved making explicit what might otherwise be dangerously unclear. The Taguran had taken his own turn with ink and paper at Tai's desk, writing in Kitan, his calligraphy slow and emphatic.

"The below-named captain in the army of Tagur has been entrusted with ensuring that the gift of Sardian horses from the honoured and beloved Princess Cheng-wan, offered by her own grace and with the lordly blessing of the Lion, Sangrama, in Rygyal, be transferred to the Kitan, Shen Tai, son of General Shen Gao, to him and to no one else. The horses, which presently number two hundred fifty, will be pastured and maintained ..."

There had been more, stipulating location—in Taguran lands near the border, close to the town of Hsien in Kitai, some distance south of where they were—and detailing the precise circumstances under which the horses would be handed over.

These conditions were designed to ensure that no one could compel Tai to sign instructions against his will. There were, in Xinan, men trained and often gifted in methods of inducing such signatures. There were others equally skilled in fabricating them.

This letter would go with Tai, be handed to the commander at Iron Gate to be copied, and the copy would proceed ahead of him by military post to the court.

It might make a difference. Might not, of course, but losing the empire those horses would very possibly cause any new assassin (and those who paid him, or her) to be hunted down, tortured for information, and creatively disembowelled before being permitted to die.

Tai had been aware, even as he rode east, and certainly now as he cantered Dynlal through the open gate of the fort and reined up before Lin Fong in the main courtyard, that a second assassin might be sent when word came back that the first one had failed.

What he had not expected was to see one waiting here at Iron Gate Pass, walking up behind the commander, clad in black and bearing crossed Kanlin swords in scabbards on her back.

She was smaller than the first woman had been, but with the same lithe movements. That walk almost marked someone as Kanlin. You learned those movements, even a way of standing, at Stone Drum Mountain. They made you dance there balanced on a ball.

Tai stared at the woman. Her black hair was unbound, falling to her waist. She had just risen from sleep, he realized.

Didn't make her less dangerous. He pulled his bow from the saddle sheath and nocked an arrow. You kept arrows and bow ready in the mountains, for wolves or the cats. He didn't dismount. He knew how to shoot from the saddle. Had been in the northern cavalry beyond the Long Wall, and had trained at Stone Drum after. You could find irony in that last, if you were in a certain state of mind. Kanlins were being sent after him. By someone.

The commander said, "What are you doing?"

The woman stopped, fifteen paces away. She had wide-set eyes and a full mouth. Given what she was, fifteen paces might be too close if she had a dagger. Tai danced his horse backwards.

"She's here to kill me," he said, calmly enough. "Another Kanlin tried, by the lake."

"We know about that," Commander Lin said.

Tai blinked, but never took his eyes from the woman. Moving slowly, she shrugged her leather straps off one shoulder and then the other, keeping her hands visible all the time. The swords dropped behind her into the dust. She smiled. He didn't trust that smile.

A crowd of soldiers had gathered in the courtyard. A morning adventure. There weren't many of those here at the edge of the world.

"How do you know about it?" Tai asked.

The commander glanced briefly at the woman behind him. He shrugged. "This one told us last night. She came pursuing the other. Arrived at sunset. Would have ridden on by night towards you. I told her to wait until this morning, that if something unpleasant had happened at Kuala Nor it would have done so already, since the others were days ahead of her." He paused. "Did something happen?"

"Yes."

The commander was expressionless. "They are dead? The fat scholar and the woman?"

"Yes."

"Both of them?" The woman spoke for the first time. Her voice was low but clear in the dawn courtyard. "I regret to hear it."

"You grieve for your companion?" Tai was holding in anger.

She shook her head. The smile had gone. She had a clever, alert face, high cheekbones; the unbound hair remained a distraction. "I was sent to kill her. I grieve for the other one."

"The fat scholar," Lin Fong repeated.

"The scholar was my friend," said Tai. "Chou Yan came a long way from the world he knew to tell me something that mattered."

"Did he?" The woman again. "Did he tell you?"

She stepped closer. Tai lifted a quick hand as he held the bow with the other. She stopped. Smiled again with that wide mouth. A smile from a Kanlin Warrior could be unsettling in and of itself, Tai thought.

She shook her head. "If I were here to kill you, you'd be dead by now. I wouldn't have walked up like this. You must know that."

"You might want questions answered first," he said coldly. "And you know that."

Her turn to hesitate. It pleased him. She'd been too sure of herself. At Stone Drum you were taught how to disarm a person with words, confuse or placate them. It wasn't all blades and bows and spinning leaps that ended with a kick to the chest or head and, often as not, a death.

His friend was dead, killed by one of these Warriors. He held that within himself, a hard fury.

Her gaze was appraising now, but not in the way the other woman's had been. She wasn't sizing him up for a fight. Either she was biding her time, at a momentary disadvantage, or she was telling the truth about why she was here. He needed to decide. He could just shoot her, he thought.

"Why would you be sent to kill another Kanlin?"

"Because she isn't Kanlin."

The fortress commander turned and looked at her.

The woman said, "She went rogue half a year ago. Left her assigned sanctuary near Xinan, disappeared into the city. Started killing for a fee, then was hired by someone, we learned, to travel here to do the same."

"Who hired her?"

The girl shook her head. "I wasn't told."

He said, "She was a Kanlin. She wanted to fight me, said the only reason she didn't was strict orders."

"And you think those orders could have been given to someone still serving the Mountain, Master Shen Tai? Really? You were at Stone Drum. You know better."

He looked from her to Lin Fong. The commander's expression was alert. This was all news to him, of course, and news was bright coinage this far west.

Tai really didn't want his life discussed in an open courtyard. She probably knew that, he thought. She had ignored his question about why she'd been sent here. That could be discretion, or a way to get him into a smaller space.

His life had been very simple, just a few days ago.

"The commander can have someone search me," she said in that low, crisp voice. It was as if she'd read his thoughts.

She added, "I have a dagger in my right boot. Nothing else. They can also tie my wrists so we can talk in a private place, with the commander present or not, as you wish."

"No," said Lin Fong, glaring. He wouldn't like a woman being so decisive. No military officer would. "I will be present. You do not set conditions here. You are both under my jurisdiction, and it seems people have been killed. I have questions of my own, there are reports to be filed."

There were always reports to be filed. The empire could drown in the reports that were filed, Tai thought.

The woman shrugged. Tai had the feeling she'd anticipated or even intended this. He needed to make a decision.

He sheathed his arrow and bow. Looked up to his right. The gap-toothed, balding guard was still on the wall, looking down. Tai gestured. "That one to look to my horse. Walk, water, feed him. I remember that he knows horses."

The man's expression of joy would have been gratifying, at any easier time.

HE HAD A FEW MOMENTS ALONE to wash and change his clothes. He switched from riding boots to brocaded slippers they provided. A servant—one of the border people serving the soldiers—took his clothing and boots to clean them.

It had occurred to Tai many years ago that one usually expected important decisions in life to emerge after long and complex thought. Sometimes this was so. But on other occasions one might wake in the morning (or finish drying one's hands and face in a dusty border fort) with the abrupt, intense realization that a choice had already been made. All that was left was putting it into effect.

Tai could see no clear pattern in his own life as to this. Nor was he able to say, that morning, why he was suddenly so sure of something.

A waiting soldier escorted him through two courtyards to the commander's reception pavilion at the eastern end of the compound. He announced Tai's presence and drew back a canvas flap that covered the doorway, blocking the wind. Tai walked in.

Lin Fong and the Kanlin woman were already there. Tai bowed, then sat with them on a raised platform in the centre of the room. He settled himself on a mat, crossing his legs. There was tea, unexpectedly, at his elbow, on a blue, lacquered tray decorated with a painting of willow branches and two lines from a poem by Chan Du about willow trees. The pavilion was sparely decorated.

It was also more beautiful than any space Tai had entered in two years. There was a pale-green vase on a low side table behind the commander. Tai stared at it for a long time. Too long, probably. His expression, he thought wryly, was probably something like the soldier's on the wall had been, looking down at the horse.

"That is a very fine piece of work," he said.

Lin Fong smiled, pleased and unable to hide it.

Tai cleared his throat and bowed at the waist without rising. "Untie her, please. Or don't bind her on my account."

Folly, on the face of it. He was alarmingly certain it wasn't.

He looked at the woman, who had been carefully trussed at both ankles and wrists. She was sitting placidly on the other side of the platform.

"Why?" Commander Lin, however happy with a compliment to his taste, evidently didn't like making adjustments.

"She isn't about to attack me with you here." He'd realized this while washing his face. "The Kanlins exist because they can be trusted, by both court and army. They have lasted six hundred years because of that. But that trust is badly damaged if one of them kills the commander of a military fort, or someone under his protection. Their sanctuaries, their immunity, could be destroyed. And besides, I think she's telling the truth."

The woman smiled again, large eyes downcast, as if the amusement was private.

"The commander could be part of my plot," she said, looking down.

In the intimacy of the room, out of the courtyard wind, her low voice was unsettling. It had been two years since he'd heard this sort of voice, Tai thought.

"But he isn't," he said, before Commander Lin could express outrage. "I'm not important enough. Or I wasn't, before."

"Before what?" the other man said, distracted from whatever he'd been about to say.

Tai waited. Lin Fong looked at him a moment, then nodded brusquely at a soldier. The man stepped forward and began untying the woman. He was careful not to step on the platform; discipline was good here.

Tai watched until the man was done, and then continued to wait politely. After a moment, the commander took the hint and dismissed the two soldiers.

The woman crossed her legs neatly and rested her hands upon her knees. She wore a hooded black tunic and black leggings for riding, both of common hemp. She had used the interval to pin up her hair. She didn't rub her wrists, though the ropes had been tight, would have chafed. Her hands were small, he noted; you wouldn't have thought she could be a Warrior. He knew better.

"Your name is?" he asked.

"Wei Song," she said, bowing slightly.

"You are at Stone Drum Mountain?"

She shook her head impatiently. "Hardly, or I could not have been here so soon. I am from the sanctuary near Ma-wai. The same as the rogue was, before she left."

A short ride from Xinan, near a posting station inn and a celebrated hot springs retreat with its pavilions and pools and gardens, for the emperor and his favourites.

Tai had said something stupid. Stone Drum, one of the Five Holy Mountains, was far to the northeast.

"Before what, please, Master Shen?" the commander repeated. "You have not answered me."

He made some effort to keep irritation out of his voice, but it was there. A brisk, fussy man. An important person for Tai just now. Tai turned to him.

It was time, evidently.

He had a vivid sense of roads forking, rivers branching, one of those moments where the life that follows cannot be as it might otherwise have been.

"I have been given a gift by the Tagurans," he said. "From their court, our own princess."

"Princess Cheng-wan has given you a personal gift?" Astonishment, barely controlled.

"Yes, commander."

Lin Fong was clearly thinking hard. "Because you were burying their dead?"

The man might be in a dismal posting, but he wasn't a fool.

Tai nodded. "They have done me too much honour in Rygyal."

"Too much honour? They are barbarians," Commander Lin said bluntly. He lifted his porcelain bowl and sipped the hot, spiced tea. "They have no understanding of honour."

"Perhaps," said Tai, his voice carefully neutral.

Then he told them about the horses and watched them both react.

CHAPTER IV

"*Where are they?* These horses."

It was the right question, of course. The commander had gone pale, was clearly thinking hard, fighting agitation. Experience could only take you so far in dealing with some kinds of information. Two deep, horizontal lines etched his forehead now. Lin Fong looked afraid. Tai didn't entirely understand that, but it was there to be seen. The Kanlin woman, by contrast, seemed to have withdrawn into repose, attentive but unperturbed.

Tai had been on Stone Drum Mountain, however. He recognized this as a posture, a way of trying to make herself tranquil in the act of seeming so. Which meant she wasn't. She was very young, Wei Song, he realized suddenly. Younger than the assassin had been, probably the same age as his sister.

"I don't have them," he said simply.

Lin Fong's eyes flashed. "I did see you come in. I know that much."

Irritation for some men was their response to strain.

"You'll never get to court alive with Sardian horses, unless you have an army escort," the woman said. "And then you'll be indebted to the army."

Young, but a quick brain working.

The commander glared. "You are all indebted to the army. You would do well to remember it, Kanlin."

It begins, Tai thought.

The old, old tale of the Kitan people and their rivalries. Petty kingdoms warring with each other, once; ambitious men and women at the imperial court, now. Military governors, prefects, mandarins rising through their nine ranks, religious orders, palace eunuchs, legal advisers, empresses and concubines, and on, and on ... all of them striving for eminence around the emperor, who was the sun.

He had been back in the empire for part of a morning, no more.

Tai said, "The horses will be held at a fort across the border, near Hsien. I have letters to be sent to court with the military post, explaining this."

"Held by whom?" The commander, working it through.

"By the Taguran captain from the pass above Kuala Nor. He's the one who brought me word of the gift."

"But then they can take them back! Keep them!"

Tai shook his head. "Only if I die."

He reached into his tunic pocket and drew out the original letter from Rygyal. He had a sudden memory of reading it by the lake, hearing the squabble of birds. He could almost feel the wind. "Princess Cheng-wan signed this herself, commander. We must be careful not to insult her, by suggesting they'd take them back."

Lin Fong cleared his throat nervously. He almost reached for the letter but did not; it would have been demeaning to Tai if he'd checked. He was an irritable, rigid man, but not unaware of due courtesy, even out here in the wilderness.

Tai glanced across at the woman. She was smiling a little at Lin Fong's discomfiture, not bothering to hide it.

He added, "They will keep them, unless I come myself." It was what he'd worked out with Bytsan sri Nespo at the end of a long night in the cabin.

"Ah," said Wei Song, looking up. "That is how you stay alive?"

"How I try."

Her gaze was thoughtful. "A difficult gift, that puts your life at risk."

The commander's turn to shake his head. His mood seemed to have changed. "Difficult? It is more than that! This is … this is a tail-star burning across the sky. A good omen or a bad one, depending on what it traverses."

"And depending on who reads the signs," Tai said quietly. He didn't like alchemists or astrologers, as it happened.

Commander Lin nodded. "These horses should be glorious—for you, for all of us. But these are challenging times to which you are returning. Xinan is a dangerous place."

"It always has been," Tai said.

"More so now," said the commander. "Everyone will want your horses. They might tear you apart for them." He sipped his tea. "I do have a thought."

He was clearly thinking very hard. Tai almost felt sorry for the man: you were posted to a quiet border fort, sought to do well there, maintain order, efficiency, move onwards in due course.

Then two hundred and fifty Heavenly Horses arrived, more or less.

A tail-star, indeed. A comet streaking from the west.

"I will be grateful to learn any thoughts you have," he said. He felt formality reasserting within himself, a way of dealing with unease. It had been so long since he'd been part of this intricate world. Of any world beyond lake and meadow and graves. He did think he knew what was coming. Some moves in a game could be anticipated.

"Your father was a great leader, mourned by all of us, in the west, especially. You have the army in your blood, son of General Shen. Accept these dragon steeds in the name of the Second Military District! The one nearest Kuala Nor itself! Our military governor is at Chenyao. I will give you an escort, an honour guard. Present yourself to Governor Xu, offer the Heavenly Horses. Can you imagine the rank you will be given? The honour and glory!"

As expected.

And it did explain the man's fear. Lin Fong was obviously aware that if he didn't at least try to keep the horses for the army here it would be a mark against his own record, fairly or not. Tai looked at him. In some ways the idea was tempting, an immediate resolution. In others …

He shook his head. "And I do this, Commander Lin, before appearing at court? Before relating to our serene and glorious emperor or his advisers how the princess, his daughter, has so honoured me? Before also telling the first minister? I do imagine Prime Minister Chin Hai will have views on this."

"And before letting any *other* military governors know of these horses?" The Kanlin woman spoke softly, but very clearly. "The army is not undivided, commander. Do you not think, for example, that Roshan in the northeast will have thoughts as to where they belong? He commands the Imperial Stables now, does he not? Do you think his views could matter? Is it possible that Master Shen, coming from two years of isolation, needs to learn a little more before surrendering such a gift to the first man who asks for it?"

The look the commander shot her was venomous.

"You," he snapped, "have no status in this room! You are here only to be questioned about the assassin, and that will come."

"It will, I hope," Tai agreed. He took a breath. "But I would like to give her status, if she will accept. I wish to hire her as my guard, going forward from here."

"I accept," the woman said quickly.

Her gaze met his. She didn't smile.

"But you thought she was here to kill you!" the commander protested.

"I did. Now I believe otherwise."

"Why?"

Tai looked across at the woman again. She sat gracefully, eyes lowered again, seemingly composed. He didn't think she was.

He considered his answer. Then he allowed himself a smile. Chou Yan would have enjoyed this moment, he thought, would have absolutely savoured it, then told the tale endlessly, embellishing it differently each time. Thinking of his friend, Tai's smile faded. He said, "Because she bound up her hair before coming here."

The commander's expression was diverting.

"She … because …?"

Tai kept his voice grave. This remained an important man for him for the next little while. Lin Fong's dignity had to be protected.

"Her hands and feet are free, and she has at least two weapons in her hair. The Kanlin are trained to kill with those. If she wanted me dead I would be, already. So would you. If she were another rogue, she wouldn't care about the consequences to Stone Mountain of killing you. She might even manage to escape."

"Three weapons," Wei Song said. She pulled one of her hairpins out and laid it down. It rested, gleaming, on the platform. "And escape is considered preferable, but is not expected with certain assignments."

"I know that," said Tai.

He was watching the commander, and he saw a change.

It was as if the man settled into himself, accepted that he had done what he could, would be able to absorb and deflect whatever criticism came from superiors. This was beyond him, larger by far than a border fortress. The court had been invoked.

Lin Fong sipped his tea, calmly poured more from the dark-green ceramic pot on the lacquered tray at his side. Tai did the same thing from his own. He looked at the woman. The hairpin rested in front of her, long as a knife. The head of it was silver, in the shape of a phoenix.

"You will, at least, attend upon Xu Bihai, the governor, in Chenyao?"

Lin Fong's expression was earnest. This was a request, no more. On the other hand, the commander did not suggest he visit the prefect in Chenyao. Army against civil service, endlessly. Some things never changed, year over year, season after season.

There was no need to comment. And if he also went to see the prefect, that was his own affair. Tai said simply, "Of course I will, if

Governor Xu is gracious enough to receive me. I know that he knew my father. I will hope to receive counsel from him."

The commander nodded. "I will send my own letter. As to counsel ... you have been much removed, have you not?"

"Very much," said Tai.

Moons above a mountain bowl, waxing and waning, silver light upon a cold lake. Snow and ice, wildflowers, thunderstorms. The voices of the dead on the wind.

Lin Fong looked unhappy again. Tai found himself beginning to like the man, unexpectedly. "We live in difficult days, Shen Tai. The borders are peaceful, the empire is expanding, Xinan is the glory of the world. But sometimes such glory ..."

The woman remained very still, listening.

"My father used to say that times are always difficult," Tai murmured, "for those living through them."

The commander considered this. "There are degrees, polarities. The stars find alignments, or they do not." This was rote, from a Third Dynasty text. Tai had studied it for the examinations. Lin Fong hesitated. "For one thing, the first thing, the honoured empress is no longer in the Ta-Ming Palace. She has withdrawn to a temple west of Xinan."

Tai drew a breath. It was important news, though not unexpected.

"And the lady Wen Jian?" he asked softly.

"She has been proclaimed as Precious Consort, and installed in the empress's wing of the palace."

"I see," said Tai. And then, because it was important to him, "And the ladies attending upon the empress? What of them?"

The commander shrugged. "I wouldn't know. I'd assume they went with her, at least some of them."

Tai's sister had gone to Xinan three years before, to serve the empress as a lady-in-attendance. A privilege granted to Shen Gao's daughter. He needed to find out what had happened to Li-Mei. His older brother would know.

His older brother was an issue.

"That is indeed a change, as you said. What else must I know?"

Lin Fong reached for his tea cup, put it down. He said, gravely, "You named the prime minister. That was an error. Alas, First Minister Chin Hai died last autumn."

Tai blinked, shaken. He hadn't been ready for this, at all. It felt for a moment as if the world rocked, as if some tree of colossal size had fallen and the fort was shaking with the reverberation.

Wei Song spoke up. "It is generally believed, though we have heard it suggested otherwise, that he died of an illness contracted with an autumn chill."

The commander looked narrowly at her.

We have heard it suggested otherwise.

These could be called words of treason.

Commander Lin said nothing, however. It could never have been said that the army held any love for Emperor Taizu's brilliant, all-controlling first minister.

Chin Hai, tall, thin-bearded, thin-shouldered, famously suspicious, had governed under the emperor through a quarter-century of growing Kitan wealth and fabulous expansion. Autocratic, ferociously loyal to Taizu and the Celestial Throne, he'd had spies everywhere, could exile—or execute—a man for saying something too loudly in a wine shop, overheard by the wrong person.

A man hated and terribly feared, and possibly indispensable.

Tai waited, looking at the commander. Another name was coming now. Had to be coming.

Commander Lin sipped from his tea. He said, "The new first minister, appointed by the emperor in his wisdom, is Wen Zhou, of … of distinguished lineage." The pause was deliberate, of course. "Is his a name you might know?"

It was. Of course it was. Wen Zhou was the Precious Consort's cousin.

But that wasn't the thing. Tai closed his eyes. He was remembering a scent, green eyes, yellow hair, a voice.

"And if someone should ask me … should propose to make me his personal courtesan, or even a concubine?"

He opened his eyes. They were both looking at him curiously. "I know the man," he said.

ℭℱ

Commander Lin Fong of Iron Gate Fortress would not have named himself a philosopher. He was a career soldier, and had made that choice early in life, following older brothers into the army.

Still, over the years, he had come to realize (with proper humility) that he was more inclined to certain ways of thinking, and perhaps to an appreciation of beauty that went deeper in him than in most of his fellow soldiers—and then fellow officers—as he rose (somewhat) through the ranks from humble beginnings.

He enjoyed, among other things, civilized conversation so much. Sipping wine alone in his chamber late at night, Lin Fong acknowledged that a disturbing measure of what had to be called excitement was keeping him awake.

Shen Tai, the son of the late General Shen, was the sort of person Lin Fong would have wished to keep at Iron Gate for days or even weeks, such was the spark of the man's thinking and the unusual pattern of his life.

Their conversation over dinner had forced him to acknowledge, ruefully, how impoverished his daily routines and company were here.

He'd asked the man an obvious (to him) question. "You have now gone twice beyond the borders for extended periods. The ancient masters teach that danger to the soul lies in doing that." He had offered a smile, to take any sting or offence from the words.

"Some teach that. Not all."

"That is so," Lin Fong had murmured, gesturing to a servant to pour more wine. He was a little out of his depth when it came to variant teachings of the ancient masters. A soldier did not have *time* to learn these things.

Shen Tai had looked thoughtful, however, the oddly deep-set eyes revealing a mind working on the question. Courteously, he'd said,

"The first time, commander, I was a very young officer. I went north among the Bogü because I was ordered there, that's all. I doubt, respectfully, you would have chosen to come to Iron Gate, had your wishes been considered."

So he had noticed! Fong had laughed a little self-consciously. "It is an honourable posting," he'd protested.

"Of course it is."

After a short silence, Fong had said, "I take your point, of course. Still, having been beyond the empire once without any choice of your own, the second time ...?"

Unhurried, unruffled, a man of obvious breeding: "The second time I was honouring my father. That is why I went to Kuala Nor."

"There were no other ways to honour him?"

"I'm sure there were," was all Shen Tai said.

Fong had cleared his throat, embarrassed. He was too hungry for such exchanges, he'd realized, too starved for intelligent talk. It could make you cross social boundaries. He'd bowed.

This Shen Tai was a complex man, but he was leaving in the morning to pursue a life that was unlikely ever to bring the two of them into contact again. With reluctance, but an awareness of what was proper, the commander had turned the conversation to the matter of the Tagurans and their fortress north of the lake, what Shen Tai could tell him of that.

The Tagurans, after all, were within his present sphere of responsibility, and would be until he was posted elsewhere.

Some men seemed able to slide in and out of society. This man appeared to be one of them. Lin Fong knew that he himself was not, and never would be; he had too great a need for security, routines, for such uncertainty. But Shen Tai did make him aware that there were, or might be, alternative ways to live. It probably did help, he thought, to have had a Left Side Commander for a father.

Alone in his chamber later that night, he sipped his wine. He wondered if the other man had even noticed that they'd been drinking tea earlier, how unusual that was out here. It was a new luxury, just beginning to be taken up in Xinan, imported from the far southwest: yet another consequence of peace and trade under Emperor Taizu.

He had heard about the drink from correspondents and asked for some to be sent. He very much doubted the new custom had been adopted by many other commanders in their fortresses. He'd even ordered special cups and trays, paid for them himself.

He wasn't sure he liked the taste of the drink, even sweetened with mountain honey, but he did enjoy the idea of himself as a man in tune with court and city culture, even here on a desolate border where it was almost impossible to find a man worth talking to.

What did you do when faced with this as your life? You reminded yourself, over and again, that you were a civilized man in the most civilized empire the world had ever known.

Times were changing. The prime minister's death, the new first minister, even the nature and composition of the army—all these foreign troops now, so different from when Lin Fong had first enlisted. There were great and growing tensions among military governors. And the emperor himself, aging, withdrawing, with who knew what to follow? Commander Lin did not like change. It was a flaw in his nature, perhaps, but a man could cling to basic certainties to survive such a flaw, couldn't he? Didn't you *have* to do that?

ॐ

There was only one private chamber for guests at Iron Gate.

The fort wasn't a place where distinguished visitors came. The trade routes were to the north. Jade Gate Pass, aptly named, guarded those and the wealth that passed through. That was the glamour posting in this part of the world.

The guest room was small, an interior chamber on the second level of the main building, no windows, no courtyard below. Tai regretted not having chosen to share a communal room where there might at least be air. On reflection, however, it hadn't been an option: you needed to make choices that reflected your status or you confused those dealing with you.

He'd had to take the private chamber. He was an important man.

He had blown out his candle some time ago. The chamber was hot, airless, black. He was having trouble falling asleep. His thoughts were of Chou Yan, who was dead.

There were no ghost-voices in the darkness here, only the night watch on the walls, faintly calling. There hadn't been ghosts in the canyon, either, the two nights he'd spent coming this way. He hadn't been used to that: stillness after sunset. He wasn't used to not seeing the moon or stars.

Or, if it came to that, to having a young woman just the other side of his door, on guard—at her absolute insistence—in the corridor.

He didn't need a guard here, Tai had told her. She hadn't even bothered to reply. Her expression suggested that she was of the view she'd been retained by a fool.

They hadn't talked about her fee. Tai knew the usual Kanlin rates, but had a feeling he also knew what she would say when that came up: something to do with her failure to be at Kuala Nor in time to save him, being required by honour to serve him now. He needed to learn more about that first woman at the lake: most importantly, who had sent her, and why.

He had a name—Yan had named their scholar friend Xin Lun—and Tai also had a growing apprehension about another.

The fee for Wei Song hardly mattered, in any case. He could afford a guard now. Or twenty. He could hire a private *dui* of fifty cavalry and dress them in chosen colours. He could borrow any sum he needed against the Sardian horses.

He was—no other way to shape the thought, no avoiding it—a wealthy man now. If he survived to deal with the horses in Xinan. If he sorted out *how* to deal with the horses.

His family had always been comfortable, but Shen Gao had been a fighting officer commanding in the field, not an ambitious one at court straining towards recognition and the prizes that came with it. Tai's older brother was different, but he wasn't ready to start thinking about Liu tonight.

His mind drifted back to the woman outside his door. That didn't lead him towards sleep, either. They'd put a pallet in the corridor for her. They'd be used to doing that. Guests of any stature would have servants outside or even inside this chamber. It just wasn't how he thought of himself. A guest of stature.

The other Kanlin—the rogue, according to Wei Song—had likely slept out there when Yan was in this same bed a few nights earlier.

You could look at that as symmetry, two well-balanced lines in a verse, or as something darker. This was life, not a poem, and Yan, loyal, gentle, almost always laughing, lay in a grave three days' ride back through the ravine.

West of Iron Gate, west of Jade Gate Pass,
There'll be no old friends.

For Tai, there would be one there forever now.

He listened, but heard nothing from the corridor. He couldn't remember if he'd barred the door. It hadn't been a habit for some time.

It had also been more than two years since he'd been close to a woman, let alone in the stillness after dark.

Against his will, he found himself picturing her: oval face, wide mouth, alert eyes, amusement in them under arching eyebrows. The eyebrows her own, not painted in the Xinan fashion. Or what had been the fashion two years ago. It had likely changed. It always changed. Wei Song was slender, with quick movements, long black hair. It had been unbound when first seen this morning.

Too much, that last recollection, for a man who'd been alone as long as he had.

His mind seemed to be sailing down moonlit river channels, pulled towards memory as to the sea. Unsurprisingly, he found himself thinking of Spring Rain's golden hair, also unbound, and then—unexpectedly—there was an image of a different woman entirely.

It was because of what he'd been told this afternoon, he suspected, that he found himself with a clear memory of the Precious Consort, the emperor's own dearly beloved concubine.

Wen Jian, the one time he'd seen her close: a jade-and-gold enchantment on a springtime afternoon in Long Lake Park. Laughing on horseback (a ripple in air, like birdsong), a shimmer about her, an aura. Appallingly desirable. Unattainable. Not even safe for dreaming about or reveries.

And her handsome, silken-smooth cousin, he had learned today, was now first minister of the empire. Had been since autumn.

Not a good man to have as a rival for a woman.

If Tai was even halfway intelligent, in possession of the most basic self-preservation instincts, he told himself, he would stop thinking about Spring Rain and her scent and skin and voice right now, long before he came anywhere near to Xinan.

Not easily done.

She was from Sardia, as the horses were. Objects of desire, coming as so many precious things seemed to do, from the west.

It was another existence entirely, this world of men and women and desire, Tai thought, lying in darkness at the empire's edge. That truth was beginning to come back, along with so much else. One more aspect of what he was returning to.

It was unsettling, pushed away sleep, twisting with all the other disturbances in his mind like silkworm threads inattentively spooled. And he was still on the border, in a back-of-beyond fortress. What was going to happen as he rode east on his bay-coloured Sardian to the brilliant, deadly world of the court?

He turned restlessly, hearing the mattress and bedposts creak. He wished there were a window. He could stand there, draw breaths of clear air, look up at summer stars, seek order and answers in the sky. *As above, so below, we are a mirror in our lives of the nine heavens.*

He felt confined in here, fought an apprehension of permanent enclosure, restraint, death. Someone had tried to kill him, *before* they'd known about the horses. Why? Why would he have been important enough to kill?

Abruptly he sat up, swung his legs over the side of the bed. Sleep was vanishingly far away.

"I can bring you water, or wine."

Her hearing had to be extremely good, and she couldn't have been asleep.

"You are a guard, not a servant," he said, through the closed door.

He heard her laughter. "I have been retained by people who saw little distinction."

"I am not one of those."

"Ah. I shall light an ancestor candle in gratitude."

Gods above! He wasn't ready for this.

"Go to sleep," Tai said. "We start early."

Laughter again. "I'll be awake," she said. "But if you can't sleep because of fears tonight, you'll slow us down tomorrow."

He *really* wasn't ready for this.

There was a silence. Tai was acutely aware of her presence out there. After a moment he heard her say, "Forgive me, that was presumptuous. Accept that I am bowing to you. Respectfully, however, might you have declined the princess's gift?"

He had been thinking the same thing for three days. That didn't make it easier to hear someone else ask it.

"I couldn't," he said.

It was odd, talking through door and wall. Someone could be listening, easily enough. He doubted it, however. Not here. "They were offered to me by royalty. You can't refuse."

"I wouldn't know. Her gift will probably kill you."

"I am aware of that," Tai said.

"It is a *terrible* thing to do to someone."

Youth in the voice now, in that aggrieved sense of injustice, but her words were true, after a fashion. The princess would not have meant for that to happen. It would not even have occurred to her that it might.

"They know nothing of balance," Wei Song said from the corridor. She was Kanlin: balance was the essence of their teaching.

"The Tagurans, you mean?"

"No. Royalty. Everywhere."

He thought about it. "I think being royal *means* you need not think that way."

Another silence. He had a sense of her working it through. She said, "We are taught that the emperor in Xinan echoes heaven, rules with its mandate. Balance above echoed below, or the empire falls. No?"

His own thought, from moments before.

There were women in the North District—not many, but a few—who could talk this way over wine or after lovemaking. He hadn't expected it here, in a Kanlin guard.

He said, "I mean it differently. About how they think. Why should our princess in Rygyal, or any prince, have an idea what might happen to a common man if he is given a gift this extravagant? What in their lives allows them to imagine that?"

"Oh. Yes."

He found himself waiting. She said, "Well, for one thing, that means the gift is about them, not you."

He nodded, then remembered she couldn't see him.

"Go to sleep," he said again, a bit abruptly.

He heard her laugh, a richness in the dark.

He pictured her as he'd first seen her, hair down her back in the morning courtyard, just risen from her bed. Pushed that image away. There would be women and music in Chenyao, he thought. Five days from now.

Perhaps four? If they went quickly?

He lay down again on the hard pillow.

The door opened.

Tai sat up, much more abruptly than the first time. He gathered the bed linens to cover his nakedness, though it was dark in the room. No light came in with her from the corridor. He sensed rather than saw her bowing. That was proper, nothing else about this was.

"You should bar your door," she said quietly.

Her voice seemed to have altered, or was that his imagination?

"I'm out of the habit." He cleared his throat. "What is this? A guard's sweep of the chamber? Am I to expect it every night?"

She didn't laugh. "No. I ... have something to tell you."

"We were talking."

"This is private."

"You think someone is listening? Here? In the middle of the night?"

"I don't know. The army does use spies. You need not fear for your virtue, Master Shen." A hint of asperity, tartness returning.

"You don't fear for yours?"

"I'm the one with a blade."

He knew what bawdy jokes would have been made in the North District as an immediate response to that. He could almost *hear* Yan's voice. He kept silent, waiting. He was aroused, distracted by that.

She said, softly, "You haven't asked who paid me to follow the assassin."

Suddenly he wasn't distracted any more.

"Kanlins don't tell who pays them."

"We will if instructed when hired. You know that."

He didn't, actually. He hadn't reached that level in twenty months with them. He cleared his throat again. He heard her move nearer the bed, a shape against darkness, the sound of her breathing and a scent in the room now that she was closer. He wondered if her hair was down. He wished there were a candle, then decided it was better that there wasn't.

She said, "I was to catch up to the two of them and kill her, then bring your friend to you. I followed their path to your home. We didn't know where you were, or I'd have come directly on the imperial road and waited for them here."

"You went to my father's house?"

"Yes, but I was too many days behind."

Tai heard the words falling in the black, like drops of water from broad leaves after rain. He felt a very odd tingling at his fingertips, imagined he heard a different sound: a far-off temple bell among pines.

He said slowly, "No one in Xinan knew where I was. Who told you?"

"Your mother, and your younger brother."

"Not Liu?"

"He wasn't there," she said.

The bell seemed to have become a clear sound in his head; he wondered if she could hear it. A childish thought.

"I'm sorry," the woman said.

He thought of his older brother. It was time to begin doing that.

"It can't be Liu," he said, a little desperately. "If he was behind this, he knew where I'd gone. He could have had the assassin and Yan go straight to Kuala Nor."

"Not if he didn't want it known he was behind this." She'd had more time to sort this through, he realized. "And in any case ..." She hesitated.

"Yes?" His voice really did sound strange now.

"I am to tell you that it isn't certain your brother hired the assassin. He may have only given information, others acting upon it."

I am to tell you.

"Very well. Who hired you, then? I am asking. Who told you all of this?"

And so, speaking formally now, almost invisible in the room, a voice in blackness, she said, "I was instructed to convey to you the respect and the humble greetings of the newest concubine in the household of the illustrious Wen Zhou, first minister of Kitai."

He closed his eyes. Spring Rain.

It had happened. She had thought it might. She had talked to him about it. If Zhou offered the demanded price to her owner, whatever it was, Rain would have had essentially no choice. A courtesan could refuse to be bought by someone privately, but her life in the North District would be ruined if she cost an owner that much money, and this *was* the first minister.

The sum offered, Tai was quite certain, would have been more than Rain could have earned from years of nights spent playing music for or slipping upstairs with candidates for the examinations.

Or slipping towards loving them.

He was breathing carefully. It still didn't make sense. Neither his brother nor the first minister had had any reason to want—let alone need—Tai dead. He didn't *matter* enough. You could dislike a man, a brother, see him as a rival—in various ways—but murder was extreme, and a risk.

There had to be something more.

"There is more," she said.

He waited. He saw only an outline, the shape of her as she bowed again.

"Your brother is in Xinan. Has been since autumn."

Tai shook his head, as if to clear it.

"He can't be. Our mourning isn't over yet."

Liu was a civil servant at court, high-ranking, but he would still be whipped with the heavy rod and exiled from the capital if anyone reported him for breaching ancestor worship, and his rivals *would* do that.

"For army officers mourning is only ninety days. You know it."

"My brother isn't ..."

Tai stopped. He drew a breath.

Was all of this his own fault? Going away for two years, sending no word back, receiving no tidings. Concentrating on mourning and solitude and private action shaped to his father's long grief.

Or perhaps he'd really been concentrating on avoiding a too-complex world in Xinan, of court, and of men and women, dust and noise, where he hadn't been ready to decide what he was or would be.

Autumn? She'd said autumn. What had happened in the fall? He had just been told today that ...

There it was. It fit. Slid into place like the rhyme in a couplet.

"He's advising Wen Zhou," he said flatly. "He's with the first minister."

He could see her only as a form in the dark. "Yes. Your brother is his principal adviser. First Minister Wen appointed Shen Liu as a commander of one thousand in the Flying Dragon Army in Xinan."

Symbolic rank, symbolic soldiers. An honorary palace guard, sons of aristocrats or senior mandarins, or their cousins. On display, gorgeously dressed, at parades and polo matches, ceremonies and festivals, famously inept in real combat. But as a way to shorten mourning with military rank, to bring a man you wanted to the capital ...

"I'm sorry," she said again.

Tai realized he'd been silent a long time.

He shook his head. He said, "It is a great honour for our family. I am still not worth killing. Wen Zhou has power, and Spring Rain is his now. My brother has his position with him, and his rank, whatever it is. There's nothing I could do—or would do—about any of this. There is another piece here. There has to be. Do you ... did Rain know anything more?"

Carefully, she said, "Lady Lin Chang said you would ask me that. I was to tell you that she agrees, but did not know what this might be when she learned of the plot to have you killed, and sent for a Kanlin."

Lin Chang?

She wouldn't have a North District name any more. Not as a concubine in the city mansion of the first minister of the empire. You weren't called Spring Rain there. He wondered how many women there were. What her life was like.

She'd taken a tremendous risk for him. Hiring her own Kanlin: he had no idea how she'd done it. It wouldn't be difficult for them to figure out who might have sent this woman after the other if ...

"Perhaps it is best you didn't reach me in time," he said. "There's no easy way to trace you back to her now. I found and hired you on the road. The assassin was killed by Taguran soldiers."

"I thought that, as well," she said. "Although it is a mark against my name that I failed."

"You didn't fail," he said impatiently.

"I could have somehow found out, come straight here."

"And given her away? You just said that. Kanlin honour is one thing, foolishness is another."

He heard her shift her feet. "I see. And you will decide which is which? Your friend might be alive if I'd been quicker."

It was true. It was unhappily true. But then Rain's life would be at risk.

"I don't think you are meant to talk to me that way."

"My most humble apologies," she said, in a tone that belied them.

"Accepted," Tai murmured, ignoring the voice. It was suddenly enough. "I have much to think about. You may go."

She didn't move for a moment. He could almost *feel* her looking towards him.

"We will be in Chenyao in four or five days. You will be able to have a woman there. That will help, I'm sure."

The tone was too knowing for words, a Kanlin trait he remembered. Wei Song bowed—he saw that much—and went out, a creaking of the floorboards.

He heard the door shut behind her. He was still holding the bed linens to cover his nakedness. He realized that his mouth was open. He closed it.

The ghosts, he thought, a little desperately, had been simpler.

CHAPTER V

Some decisions, for an officer accustomed to making them, were not difficult, especially with a night to consider the situation.

The commander of Iron Gate Fort made clear to his guest from Kuala Nor that the five guards being assigned to him were not to be seen as discretionary. His premature death, should it occur, would be blamed—without any doubt—on the incompetent fortress commander who permitted him to ride east with only a single (small, female) Kanlin guard.

In the courtyard, immediately after the morning meal, the commander indicated, courteous but unsmiling, that he was not yet ready to commit an ordered suicide and destroy the prospects of his children, should a tragic event overtake Shen Tai on the road. Master Shen would be properly escorted, military staging posts would be made available to him so that he might spend his nights there on the way to the prefecture city of Chenyao, and word of the horses—as discussed—would precede him to Xinan.

It was possible that the military governor would wish to assign further soldiers as escorts when Shen Tai reached Chenyao. He was, naturally, free to make his own decision about sending the five horsemen back to Iron Gate at that time, but Commander Lin presumed to express the hope he would retain them, having come to see their loyalty and competence.

The unspoken thought was that their presence, entering into the capital, might be some reminder of the priority of Iron Gate in the matter of the horses and their eventual safe arrival, one day in the future.

It was obvious that their guest was unhappy with all of this. He showed signs of a temper.

It might have to do, Commander Lin thought, with his having been solitary for so long, but if that was it, the man was going to have to get out of that state of mind, and the quicker the better. This morning was a good time to start.

And when the Kanlin guard also made clear that she could not be held accountable for guarding Shen Tai alone, especially since the Sardian horse he himself was riding was so obvious an incitement to theft and murder, the late general's son acceded. He did so with—it had to be admitted—grace and courtesy.

He remained an odd, difficult fellow to pin down.

Lin Fong could see why the man had left the army years ago. The military preferred—invariably—those who could be readily defined, assigned roles, understood, and controlled.

This one, intense and observant, more arresting than conventionally attractive in appearance, had had a brief military service, with a cavalry posting beyond the Long Wall. And then there had been a period among the Kanlin on Stone Drum Mountain (there had to be a story to that). He had been studying for the civil service examinations in Xinan when his father died. More than a sufficiency of careers, already, for a still-young man, Lin Fong would have thought. It spoke to something erratic in him, perhaps.

Shen Tai also—and this signified—had evidently had dealings with the new first minister, not necessarily cordial. That was problematic, or it might be. *I know the man* did not offer much, but the tone in which it had been spoken did, for someone inclined to listen for nuance.

Considering all of this, Commander Lin had, sometime in the night, made his decisions.

These included offering a considerable sum from his own funds to the other man. He named it a loan—a face-saving gesture—making clear that he expected reimbursement at some point, but stressing that a man travelling with the tidings Shen Tai carried could hardly undertake such a journey, or arrive at court, without access to money.

It would be undignified, and perplexing to others. A discord would emerge between his present circumstance and the future's promise that would unsettle those he met. In challenging times it was important to avoid such imbalances.

The solution was obvious. Shen Tai needed funds for the moment and Lin Fong was honoured to be in a position to assist. What was left to discuss between civilized men? Whatever the future would bring, it would bring, the commander said.

Men made wagers with their judgment, their allegiances, their resources. Commander Lin was making one this morning. If Shen Tai died on the road or in Xinan (distinctly possible), there was still a distinguished family to approach for the return of his money.

That didn't need to be said, of course. One of the pleasures of dealing with intelligent men, Lin Fong decided, watching seven people ride out the eastern gate in early-morning sunlight, was how much did not have to be spoken.

The five soldiers represented protection for Shen Tai and for the Second District's interests. The strings of cash were Fong's own investment. It was frustrating, had been from the beginning, to be tied down in this impossibly isolated place, but when that was the case and there was nothing to be done about it, a man cast his lines like a fisherman in a stream, and waited to see if anything chanced to bite.

He had done one other thing, was quietly pleased with himself for thinking of it. Shen Tai now carried documents, and so did the couriers who had already ridden out, establishing that the commander of Iron Gate Fort had made him an officer of cavalry in the Second Military District, currently on leave to attend to personal affairs.

If he was an officer, Shen Tai's mourning period was now over. He was free to return to Xinan. This was, Commander Lin had pointed out, not trivial. If there had been people willing to kill him even before the horses, they would hardly hesitate to invoke failure to honour ancestral rites to discredit him. Or even smooth the way towards confiscating his possessions, which might include ...

You could say a great deal, Lin Fong had always believed, with properly chosen silences.

Shen Tai had hesitated. He had prominent cheekbones, those unusually deep-set eyes (a suggestion of foreign blood?), a way of pressing his lips together when in thought. Eventually, he had bowed, and expressed his thanks.

An intelligent man, no doubting it.

The commander stood in the easternmost courtyard to see them leave. The gates swung closed, were barred with the heavy wooden beam. They didn't need to do that, no one came this way, no dangers loomed, but it was the proper thing to do and Lin Fong believed in acting properly. Rituals and regulations were what kept life from spinning towards chaos.

As he walked back to deal with paperwork (there was always paperwork) he heard a soldier on the wall begin to sing, and then others joined him:

> For years on guard in Iron Gate Pass
> We have watched the green grass change to snow.
> The wind that has come a thousand li
> Beats at the fortress battlements ...

The air felt unnervingly still all the rest of that day. Towards evening a thunderstorm finally came, surging from the south, sheets of lightning shattering the sky. A heavy, percussive rain fell, filling the cisterns and wells, making muddy lakes in the courtyards, while thunder rolled and boomed. It passed, as storms always passed.

This one continued north, boiling away as quickly as it had come. A low, late-day sun returned, shining red down the wet ravine that led to Kuala Nor. The storm explained his day-long feeling of brittle tension, Commander Lin decided. He felt better for the realization. He preferred when there were explanations for what occurred—in the sky, on earth, within the loneliness of the self.

ᘒᘓ

Their path trended downwards out of the mountain foothills, to grain fields and hamlets, and eventually through a low-lying marshland south of the river. This was tiger country. They posted guards the one night they chose to camp between posting stations, heard the creatures roaring, but never saw one.

There was some tension between the soldiers and the woman, but no more than might be expected. Wei Song kept mostly to herself, riding at the front. That was part of the problem—her taking the lead—but once Tai realized that, he turned it into an order he gave her, and the men from the fort accepted it that way.

She kept her hair tightly coiled, her posture alert. Her head was always moving as she scanned the road ahead and the land to either side. She said almost nothing at night, at campfire or the inns. There were enough of them—seven, well armed—that they hadn't feared to light a fire when they camped, though there would be bandits in this countryside, too.

As they descended, riding east, the air felt heavier to Tai. He had been in the mountains for so long. One morning he caught up to the woman, rode beside her. She gave him a glance, then looked ahead again.

"Be patient," she murmured. "Chenyao tonight, or early tomorrow at the latest. The soldiers can surely tell you the best house for girls."

He saw—couldn't miss—the amusement in her face.

This did need to be dealt with. At least it felt that way to him.

"But how would it satisfy *you*," he asked earnestly, "if I slake my passion with a courtesan, leaving you to weep, unassuaged, on some marble stair?"

She did flush. It made him feel pleased, then slightly contrite, but only slightly. She had started this, in his room back at the fort. He knew who had to be behind what this one had said then, about women. Was it normal for Rain to have confided in a hired bodyguard the intimate nature of the person she'd be protecting?

He didn't think so.

"I will manage to control my longing," the woman said, looking straight ahead.

"I'm sure you will. You seem well-enough trained. We *could* have the others wait, take a short ride together past those trees …"

She didn't flush again. "You'll do better in Chenyao," she said.

They had entered more densely populated country. Tai saw mulberry trees and a path leading south towards a silk farm—the buildings were hidden behind the trees but a banner was visible.

He had spent three weeks on one of those, years ago, obscurely curious. Or without direction, more accurately. There had been a period in his life when he was like that. After his time in the north, beyond the Long Wall. Some things had happened to him there.

He remembered the sound in the room where the silkworms were kept on stacked trays and fed, day and night, hour by hour, on white mulberry leaves: a noise like rain on a roof, endlessly.

While that happened, in that time of needful, important perfection, the temperature was controlled, all smells were prevented from entering the room, all drafts of wind. Even lovemaking in chambers nearby was done without sound, lest the silkworms be frightened or disturbed.

He wondered if this Kanlin woman knew this. He wondered why he cared.

Shortly after that, a fox appeared at the edge of the trees, alongside the road to their right.

Wei Song stopped, throwing up a quick hand. She turned in the saddle, eyed the animal. One of the men laughed, but another made a gesture averting danger.

Tai looked at the woman.

"Surely not!" he exclaimed. "You think it a *daiji*?"

"Hush! It is beyond foolish to name them," she said. "And which of us do you think a fox-woman would be here for?"

"I don't think she'd be here at all," Tai said. "I don't think every animal seen by the woods is a spirit-world creature."

"Not every animal," she said.

"What next, the Fifth Dragon appears in a red sky and the Ninth Heaven falls?"

"No," she said, looking away.

It was unexpected, that this crisp, composed Kanlin Warrior would so obviously believe in fox-woman legends. She was still watching the fox, a stab of colour by the woods. It was looking back at them, Tai saw, but that was normal. Riders were a possible threat, needed to be observed.

"You should not be so careless, speaking of spirits, naming their names," Wei Song said softly, so that only Tai heard. "We cannot understand everything about the world."

And that last phrase took him hard, sent him spinning back a long way.

The fox withdrew into the woods. They rode on.

಄

The only other time he'd been in command of cavalry had been north of the Wall, on campaign among the nomads. He'd led fifty soldiers, not just five riders, as now.

Command of a *dui* had been more than he deserved, but Tai had been young enough to feel that his father's fame and rank had simply opened a doorway for him to show what he could do, what he honestly merited. He'd welcomed the chance to prove himself.

He didn't want to dwell on it now, all these years after, but being among soldiers again, riding in open country towards a changed life seemed to make it inevitable that his thoughts would drift.

That time among the Bogü had begun the changes in his life. Before that, he'd thought he knew what his course would be. After, he was shaken, unsure. Adrift for a long time.

He'd told what had happened, how it had ended, as best he could. First to his superior officers, and then to his father when they were both home. (Not his brothers: one was too young, the other not a confidant.)

He'd been permitted to honourably resign rank and post, leave the army. It was unusual. Going to Stone Drum Mountain some time later had been a useful, perhaps even an appropriate next stage, though he doubted the Kanlin masters on the mountain saw it that way, since he'd left them, too.

But after what had happened on the northern steppes that autumn, it had not been considered unexpected that a young man would want to spend time searching for spiritual guidance, discipline, austerity.

Tai remembered being surprised that his military superiors had believed his northern tale, and even more at the hint of understanding among them. Understanding was not seen as a strength, let alone a virtue, in the higher ranks of the Kitan army.

Only later did he realize that he and his men might not have been the first or the only ones to encounter some terrifying strangeness among the Bogü. He'd wondered over the years about other stories; no one ever told him names, or what had happened.

He was not blamed for what had happened.

That had also surprised him. It still did. Military rank carried responsibilities, consequences. But it seemed the official view was that some encounters between civilized men and savagery in barbarian lands were not to be anticipated or controlled by any officer. Ordinary soldiers' conduct could break down in such places.

The Kitan felt a defining superiority and contempt for those beyond their borders, but also fear whenever they left home, even if that was denied. It made for a dangerous intermingling.

For a long time their armies had been going among the nomads to ensure the succession of the chieftain—the kaghan—they favoured. Once you went north of the Wall and its watchtowers you were living in the open or in isolated garrison forts among the Bogü or the Shuoki, fighting beside or against the barely human. It was unreasonable to expect men to conduct themselves as if they were doing domestic duty on the Great Canal or among summer rice fields, guarding peasants against bandits or tigers.

Manipulating the Bogü succession was important. The Ta-Ming Palace had a considerable interest in who ruled the nomads and how willing they were to offer docility along the border and their thick-maned horses in exchange for empty, honorary titles, lengths of lesser silk, and the promise of support against the next usurper.

Unless, of course, the next usurper made more attractive overtures.

The nomads' grazing lands, fractured among rival tribes, stretched from the Wall all the way to the bone-cold north among birch and pine forests, beyond which the sun was said to disappear all winter and never go down in summer.

Those farthest ice-lands didn't matter, except as a source of fur and amber. What mattered was that on their nearer margins the nomads' lands bordered Kitai itself—and ran alongside the Silk Roads—all the way from the deserts to the eastern sea. The Long Wall kept the nomads out, most of the time.

But the northern fork of the great trade routes curved up through the steppes, and so the lucrative flow of luxuries into the glorious Kitan empire depended to a great degree on camel-trains being safe from harassment.

The Taguran empire in the west was another threat, of course, and required different solutions, but for some time the Tagurans had been quiet, trading for themselves with those taking the southern branch of the route, exacting tolls and duties in far-off fortresses they controlled. Acquiring Sardian horses.

Xinan wasn't happy about this, but could live with it, or so it had been decided. Tagur and its king had been bought off from worse with, among other things, a slender Kitan princess, in the aftermath of wars that had drained both empires.

Peace on his various borders might reduce an emperor's chances of glory, but Emperor Taizu had reigned for a long time and had won battles enough. Wealth and comfort, the building of his own magnificent tomb-to-be north of Xinan (colossal beyond words, overshadowing his father's), languid days and nights with his Precious Consort and the music she made ... for an aging emperor these appeared to be adequate compensation.

Let Wen Jian's sleek, clever cousin Zhou be first minister if he wished (and if *she* wished it). Let him be the one to sort through, after a forty-year reign, the complexities of court and army and barbarians. One could grow weary of these.

The emperor had a woman for the ages making music for him, dancing for him. He had rituals to follow and carefully measured powders to consume—with her—in pursuit of longed-for immortality. He might never even need his tomb if the three stars of the Hunter's Belt, the asterism of this Ninth Dynasty, could be aligned by alchemists with the emperor's merit and his desire.

As for ambitious younger men in the empire? Well, there *had* been steady fighting among the Bogü against their eastern rivals, the Shuoki, and in their own internal tribal wars, and these continued.

Military officers and youthful aristocrats (and brave men of no particular birth) had always been able to assuage a hunger for blood and sword-glory somewhere. For this time it was in the north, where the emptiness of the grasslands could dwarf a man, or change his soul.

For Shen Tai, second son of General Shen Gao, that last had been what had happened, years ago, during an autumn among the nomads.

IT WAS EXPLAINED to them that evil spirits, sent by tribal enemies, had afflicted the soul of Meshag, the son of Hurok.

Hurok had been the Ta-Ming's chosen kaghan, the man they were in the steppe lands to support.

His eldest son, a man in the prime of health, had fallen suddenly, gravely ill—unresponsive, barely breathing—in the midst of a campaign. It was determined that shamans of the enemy had invoked dark spirits against him: so the nomads told the Kitan soldiers among them.

The imperial officers did not know how that understanding had been arrived at, or why the alleged magic was directed at the son and not the father (though some of them had views, by then, as to which was the better man). This business of Bogü magic—shamans, animal totems, spirit journeys from the body—was simply too alien, too barbaric, for words.

It was only reported to them as a courtesy, along with what apparently was going to be done in a desperate effort to make the sick man well. This last information had compelled some hard thinking among the army leaders sent north from Kitai.

Hurok was important and, therefore, so was his son. The father had sent private earnests of allegiance and offerings to the Long Wall in the spring—good horses and wolf pelts and two young women—his own daughters, apparently—to join the emperor's ten thousand concubines in their palace wing.

Hurok, it emerged, was willing to contemplate a revolt against the ruling kaghan, his brother-in-law, Dulan.

Dulan had not sent as many horses or furs.

Instead, his envoys had brought weak, small-boned horses, some with colic, to the wide northern loop of the Golden River where the exchange was done each spring.

The kaghan's emissaries had shrugged and grimaced, spat and gestured, when the Kitan pointed out these deficiencies. They claimed the grasses had been poor that year, too many gazelles and rabbits, sickness among the herds.

Their own mounts had looked sturdy and healthy.

It seemed to the senior mandarins charged with evaluating such information for the celestial emperor that Dulan Kaghan might have grown a little too secure, perhaps even resentful of his annual commitment to far-off Xinan.

It had been decided that a reminder of the power of Kitai was past due. Patience had been abused. The emperor had, once again, been too generous, too indulgent of lesser peoples and their insolence.

Hurok had been quietly invited to contemplate a more lofty future. He had done so, happily.

Fifteen thousand Kitan soldiers had gone north late that summer beyond the loop of the river, beyond the Wall.

Dulan Kaghan, with his own forces and followers, had been in strategic retreat ever since, maddeningly hard to pin down in the vast grasslands, waiting for allies from north and west, and for winter.

There were no cities to pillage and burn on the steppe, no enemy fortresses to besiege and starve into submission, no crops to ravage or seize, and they were acting for the man who needed to claim the trust of the nomads afterwards. It was a different sort of warfare.

The key was, clearly, to find and engage Dulan's forces. Or just kill the man, one way or another. Hurok, however, in the growing opinion of the Kitan expeditionary army's officers, was emerging as a feeble figure: a weak piece of pottery containing nothing but ambition.

He drank *kumiss* from first light, was drunk most of the day, sloppily hunting wolves, or lolling in his yurt. There was nothing wrong with a man drinking, but not on campaign. His eldest son, Meshag, was a better-fired vessel, so they reported back.

In the event, Meshag, in turn privately approached, did not appear to have any great aversion to the suggestion that he might aspire to more than merely being the strongest son of a propped-up kaghan.

They were not an especially subtle people, these nomads of the steppe, and the empire of the Kitan, amongst everything else, had had close to a thousand years and nine dynasties to perfect the arts of political manipulation.

There were books about this, any competent civil servant had them memorized. They were a part of the examinations.

"Consider and evaluate the competing doctrines emerging from Third Dynasty writings as to the proper conduct of succession issues among tribute-bearing states. It is expected that you will cite passages from the texts. Apply your preferred doctrine to resolving current issues pertaining to the southwest and the peoples along the margins of the Pearl Sea. Conclude with a six-line regulated-verse poem summarizing your proposals. Include a reference to the five sacred birds in this poem."

Of course, the appraisal of this work also included judging the quality of the candidate's calligraphy. Formal hand, not running hand.

With whom did these ignorant, fat-smeared barbarians, bare-chested as often as not, hair greasy and to their waists, smelling of sour, fermented milk, sheep dung, and their horses, think they were dealing?

But before this newer plan for the Bogü succession could be implemented, young Meshag had fallen ill, precisely at sundown, in his camp one windy autumn day.

He had been standing by an open fire, a cup of *kumiss* in one hand, laughing at a jest, a graceful man—then his cup had fallen into trampled grass, his knees had buckled, and he'd toppled to one side, barely missing the fire.

His eyes had closed and had not opened again.

His women and followers, extravagantly distressed, made it clear that this had to have been done by sinister powers—there were unmistakable signs. Their own shaman, small and quavering, said as much but admitted, in the morning, after a night spent chanting and drumming at Meshag's side, that he was unequal to shaping a response capable of driving malign spirits from the unconscious man.

Only someone he named as the white shaman of the lake could overmaster the darkness sent to claim Meshag's soul and bear it away.

This lake was, it appeared, many weeks' journey north. They would set out the next morning, the Bogü said, bearing Meshag in a covered litter. They did not know if they could keep his soul near his body for so long but there was no alternative course. The little shaman would travel with them, do all he could.

Whatever the Kitan expeditionary force thought about this, there wasn't much they could do. Two army physicians, summoned to take the man's pulses and measure auras, were at a loss. He breathed, his heart beat, he never opened his eyes. When the eyelids were lifted, the eyes were black, disturbingly so.

Meshag was, for good or ill, a component of imperial strategy now. If he died, adjustments would have to be made. Again. It was decided that a number of their own cavalry would go north with his party, to maintain a Kitan presence and report back immediately if the man died.

His death was what they expected. Advance word would go to Xinan immediately. The assigned cavalry officer riding north with the Bogü was to exercise his best judgment in all matters that arose. He and his men would be desperately far away, cut off from all others.

Shen Tai, son of Shen Gao, was selected to lead this contingent.

If that decision carried an element of unspoken punishment for the young man having a rank he hadn't earned, no one could possibly be faulted later for giving him the assignment.

It was an honour, wasn't it? To be sent into danger? What else could a young officer want? This was a chance to claim glory. Why else were they here? You didn't join the army to pursue a meditative life. Go be a hermit of the Path, eat acorns and berries in a cave on some mountainside, if that was what you wanted.

THEY WORSHIPPED the Horse God and the Lord of the Sky.

The Son of the Sky was the God of Death. His mother dwelled in the Bottomless Lake, far to the north. It froze in winter.

No, this was not the lake of their journey now, it was much farther north, guarded by demons.

In the afterworld, everything was reversed. Rivers ran from the sea, the sun rose west, winter was green. The dead were laid to rest on open grass, unburied, to be consumed by wolves and so returned to the Sky. Dishes and pottery were laid upside down or shattered by the body, food was spilled, weapons broken—so the dead could recognize and lay claim to these things in the backwards world.

The skulls of sacrificed horses (horned reindeer in the north) were split with an axe or sword. The animals would be reconstituted, whole and running, in the other place, though the white ones would be black and the dark ones light.

A woman and a man were cut to pieces at midsummer in rites only the shamans were allowed to share, though thousands and thousands of the nomads gathered for them from all across the steppe under the high sky.

Shamans engaged in their tasks wore metal mirrors about their bodies, and bells, so demons would be frightened by the sounds or by their own hideous reflection. Each shaman had a drum he or she had made after fasting alone upon the grass. The drums were also used to frighten demons away. They were made from bearskin, horsehide, reindeer. Tiger skin, though that was rare and spoke to a mighty power. Never wolf pelts. The relationship with wolves was complex.

Some would-be shamans died during that fast. Some were slain in their out-of-body journeys among the spirits. The demons could triumph, take any man's soul, carry it off as a prize to their own red kingdom. That was what the shamans were all about: to defend ordinary men and women, intervene when spirits from the other side came malevolently near, whether of their own dark desire, or summoned.

Yes, they could be summoned. Yes, the riders believed that was what had happened here.

Moving slowly north with thirty of his own *dui* and fifteen of the nomads, accompanying the carried, curtained litter of Meshag, Tai couldn't have explained why he asked so many questions, or hungered so deeply for the answers.

He told himself it was the length of the journey through an expanse of emptiness. Day after day they rode, and the grasslands hardly changed. But it was more than tedium and Tai knew it. The thrill he derived from the crystals of information the riders vouch-safed went beyond easing boredom.

They saw gazelles, great herds of them, almost unimaginably vast. They watched cranes and geese flying south, wave after wave as autumn came, bringing red and amber colours to the leaves. There were more trees now and more rolling hills as they moved out of the grasslands. One evening they saw swans alight on a small lake. One of Tai's archers pointed, grinned, drew his bow. The Bogü stopped him with shouts of menace and alarm.

They never killed swans.

Swans carried the souls of the dead to the other world, and the carried soul, denied his destination, could haunt the killer—and his companions—to the end of their own days.

How could Tai explain how hearing this quickened his heartbeat, set his mind spinning with the strangeness of it all?

It was almost undignified: the Kitan were famously dismissive, never allowing themselves to be more than languidly amused by the primitive beliefs of the barbarians on their borders. Beliefs that confirmed their barely human nature, the appropriateness, in a world rightly ordered, of Kitan pre-eminence. Really: a people that left their dead to be devoured by wolves?

He told himself he was gathering information for his report, that it would be useful to have a fuller understanding of the Bogü, make it easier to guide and control them. It might even be true, but it didn't explain how he felt when they told him, riding past crimson-and golden-leaved birch woods, of three-eyed demons in the north among sheets of ice, of how the men there grew autumn pelts like bears and slept the snowbound winter away. Or—again—of midsummer's Red Sun Festival, when all wars stopped on the grass-land for the rites of the Death God, performed by shamans of all tribes with bells and pounding drums.

The shamans. The *bogï* lay behind or at the heart of so many of the tales. They were taking Meshag to one of them. If he lived so long. This one was a mighty shaman, Tai was told. She dwelled on the shore of a lake, remote and mysterious. If sufficiently rewarded, and ardently beseeched, she might intervene.

She. That was interesting, as well.

The journey was taking them into territory controlled by the current kaghan, Dulan, their enemy. That was another reason why Tai and thirty of his cavalry were with this party, riding through an increasingly up-and-down russet-coloured autumn land, past jewel-bright stands of larch and birch, into a growing cold. They had an interest in what happened to Meshag, in his survival, however less likely that seemed every day.

He was still breathing. Tai looked in on his litter to confirm it each morning, at midday, and at sunset, enduring tired, hostile glares from the little shaman who never left Meshag's side. The patient lay on his back under a horsehair blanket, breathing shallowly, never moving. If he died the Bogü would leave him under this sky and turn back.

Tai could see his own breath puffs when they mounted up at first light now. The day warmed as the sun climbed, but mornings and the nights were cold. They were so far from the empire, from any civilized place, in unnervingly strange lands. He had grown used to the howling of wolves by now, though all Kitan—a farming people—hated them with an ancient intensity.

Some of the big cats that roared at night were tigers, which they knew about, but some were not. These had a different sound, louder. Tai watched his men grow more uneasy with every *li* they rode away from all they knew.

They were not travellers, the Kitan. The occasional exception, a far-farer who returned, was celebrated as a hero, his written record of the journey widely copied and read, pondered with fascination and disbelief. He was often regarded, privately, as more than slightly mad. Why would a sane man choose to leave the civilized world?

The Silk Roads were for merchants and wealth to come to *them*, not so that they could go—or ever wished to go—to the far west themselves.

Or the far north, for that matter.

Heavier forests now, brilliant and alarming with autumn colour under the sun. A scatter of lakes strung like necklace ornaments. The sky itself too far away. As if, Tai thought, heaven was not as close to mankind here.

One of the Bogü told him, around a night fire under stars, that as winter approached, so did darker spirits. That, the nomad added, was why the magic that had assaulted Meshag this season had been harder for him to resist and required a powerful shaman to redress.

The shamans were divided into white and black. The division turned on whether they cajoled demons in the spirit world they left their bodies to enter, or tried to battle and coerce them. Yes, some were women. Yes, the one they were approaching was. No, none of the riders here had ever seen her, or been so far north themselves. (This did not reassure.)

She was known by reputation, had never allied herself with any kaghan or tribe. She was one hundred and thirty years old. Yes, they were afraid. No living creature or man frightened a Bogü rider, the thought was laughable, but spirits did. Only a fool said otherwise. A man did not let fear stop him, or he was not a man. Was this not also so among the Kitan?

The creature roaring the night before? That was a lion. They were the size of tigers, but they hunted with others of their kind, not alone. There were different bears in these woods, too, twice the height of a man when they reared up, and the northern wolves were the largest—but men of other tribes were still the greatest threat this far from home.

They saw riders the next morning, for the first time.

Ahead of them on a rise against the horizon, about fifteen or so. Not enough to fear. The horsemen fled their own approach, galloping west and out of sight. Tai considered pursuit, but there was no real point. The riders had come from the north. Tai didn't know what that meant, he didn't really know what anything meant. The leaves of the trees were crimson and amber and gold and beginning to fall.

They saw arrows of geese overhead all the time now, countless multitudes, as if they were fleeing something that lay where the riders were headed, the way animals fled a forest fire. They saw two more swans on another lake at dusk, floating strange and white on darkening water as the moon rose. None of Tai's men threatened these.

A fear of ongoing transgression had grown in the Kitan riders, as if they had crossed some inward border. Tai heard his men snapping and quarrelling with each other as they broke camp in the morning, as they rode through the day. He did what he could to control it, was unsure how successful he was.

It was difficult to feel superior here, he thought. That, in itself, was disturbing for the Kitan, altering the way they dealt with the world, intersected it. He wanted to call the forest colours and the autumn landscape beautiful, but the word, the idea, didn't rise easily through the apprehension within him.

He'd finally admitted that fear, acknowledged it, the night before they came to the shaman's lake.

There was a cottage, he saw, as they halted on the slope above and looked down in afternoon light: unexpectedly large timbers, well fitted, with an outbuilding and a fenced yard and firewood stacked against winter. This was not a yurt. Houses changed with the climate and they had left behind the grazing lands for something else.

Meshag was still alive.

He had not moved all the way north. It was unnatural. They had shifted his body at intervals, to prevent sores, but he'd done nothing but breathe, shallowly.

Someone came out from the cabin, stood by the door staring up at them.

"Her servant," the little shaman said. "Come!"

He started quickly down, with the litter-bearers carrying Meshag, four of the Bogü riders flanking them.

A gesture was made, rather too emphatically: the Kitan escort were being told to remain on the ridge. Tai hesitated (he remembered that moment), then shook his head.

He spoke to his next-in-command, a quiet order to stay for now and watch, then flicked his reins and moved down the slope alone, following the unconscious man and his escort. The nomads glared at him, but said nothing.

He was here to observe. His people had an interest in this man, in the Bogü succession. It was *not* the place of barbaric herdsmen to deny them the right to go anywhere they wanted. Not when fifteen thousand Kitan were assisting Hurok in his rising. That many soldiers gave you rights.

One way of looking at this. Considered another way, they had no proper place here among nomads' spell-battles, no business being this far away from home at all: alien sky, bright, green-blue lake, leaf-dazzle forest behind and beyond in sunlight, and the first hint in a far blue distance of mountains to the north.

He wondered if any of his people had ever seen those mountains. Or the cold jewel of this lake. That possibility should have excited him. At the moment, easing his horse down the slope, it didn't. It made him feel terribly far away.

The riders reined up before the doorway. Those carrying the litter also stopped. There was no fence in front of the cottage, only around the back where the outbuilding was. Tai assumed it was a barn or animal shed. Or maybe this servant slept there? Were there others? There was no sign of the shaman herself, or any life within. The door had been carefully closed when the one man came out.

The nomads' leader dismounted, he and the shaman approached the servant, spoke quietly, with unwonted deference. Tai couldn't make out the words, too quick and soft for his limited grasp of their tongue. The servant said something brisk in reply.

The Bogü leader turned and gestured to the slope. Two more riders detached from the company. They started down, leading two horses, these carrying the gifts they'd brought all this way.

Magic and healing did not come without cost.

It was the same back home, Tai thought wryly, and that realization somehow calmed him. You paid for healing, whether or not it worked. It was a transaction, an exchange.

This one would be appallingly strange, but elements of what was to come would be exactly the same as going to an alchemist in Xinan or Yenling to cure a morning-after head, or summoning the plump, white-haired physician from the village to their home by the stream when Second Mother couldn't sleep at night, or Third Son had a dry cough.

A memory of home, with that. Very sharp. Scent of autumn fires, smoke drifting. The ripple of the stream like the sound of time passing. The paulownia leaves would have fallen by now, Tai thought. He could see them on the path from their gate, almost hear the noise they made underfoot.

The shaman's servant spoke again as the horses approached with their gifts. It wasn't a suitable tone, even Tai could tell that, but he did know that shamans carried enormous honour among the Bogü, and that the one here was of particular significance—and power. They'd come a long way to her, after all.

The riders unloaded the gifts. The servant went inside with some of them, came out, carried another armful back in. It took him four trips. Each time, he closed the door behind him. He didn't hurry.

After he went in for the last time, they waited in the sunlight. The horses shuffled and snorted. The men were silent, tense and apprehensive. Their anxiety reached into Tai, a disturbance. Was it possible they could come all this way and be rejected, sent back? He wondered what his own role should be if that looked to be happening. Would it be his task to try to coerce the shaman into seeing Meshag? Would he be sparing the Bogü riders from doing that, if the Kitan took it on themselves? Or would he be performing a gross impiety that endangered all future relationships?

It occurred to him—belatedly—that he might have a serious decision to make in a few moments and he hadn't given it any thought at all. He had considered that Meshag might die before they came here, or that whatever the shaman tried to do would fail. He had never contemplated being refused treatment.

He looked around. There was smoke rising from the cabin chimney. Little wind today, the smoke went straight up before drifting and thinning towards the lake. From where he was, a little to one side, he saw two she-goats in the yard behind, huddled against the back fence, bleating softly. They hadn't been milked yet. It didn't make him any more impressed with this servant. Perhaps there *were* others, it was not his task?

The man came out again, finally, left the door open behind him for the first time. He nodded, gestured at the litter. Tai drew a breath. One decision he wouldn't have to make. He was angry with himself; he ought to have anticipated possibilities, worked them out ahead of time.

Their own shaman looked desperately relieved, on the edge of tears. His face working, he quickly drew the litter curtain back. Two of the men reached in and eased Meshag out. One cradled him like a sleeping child and carried him into the cabin.

Their shaman made to follow. The servant shook his head decisively, making a peremptory, stiff-armed gesture. The little shaman opened his mouth to protest, then closed it. He stayed where he was, head down, looking at no one. Humiliated, Tai thought.

The servant went into the cabin, reappeared an instant later escorting the man who'd carried Meshag. The servant went back in. Closed the door. They still hadn't seen the old woman, the shaman of the lake. They were left outside, in front of the cabin, in the bright, clear stillness of an autumn afternoon.

Someone coughed nervously. Someone glared at him, as if the sound might undermine whatever was happening inside. Their shaman was still staring at the ground before the door, as if unwilling to meet anyone's gaze. Tai wanted to be inside, then realized that, no, he actually didn't. He did *not* want to see whatever was taking place in there.

The nomads clustered before the cabin, looking more uncertain than Tai had ever seen them. The rest of the riders, including Tai's own men, remained above on the slope. The lake glittered. Birds were overhead, as always now, streaming south. Some were on the water. No swans that he could see.

Restless, edgy, he dismounted, left his horse to graze the sparse grass and walked around to the back where the outbuilding was and the yard with the two goats. He had a thought of milking them if he could find a pail. Something to do. A task. He slipped the gate latch and went in, closing it behind him.

The fenced yard was good-sized. Two fruit trees, a tall birch for shade. An herb garden at the far, eastern end. He could see the lake beyond it, across the fence. The goats huddled against the shed at the back, clearly unhappy.

No pail to be seen. Probably inside, but he wasn't about to knock on the rear door of the cabin and ask for one.

He crossed the yard towards the garden and the birch. He stood under the tree, gazing across the fence at the small lake, the brightness of it in sunshine. It was very quiet except for the soft, distressed bleating of the two animals. He could milk them without a pail, he thought. Let the servant suffer for his laziness if the shaman had no milk today.

He was actually turning to do that, irritated, when he noticed the freshly dug mound of earth at the back of the garden.

A single thump of the heart.

He could still remember, years after.

He stared, unmoving, for a long moment. Then he stepped carefully to the edge of the neatly ordered garden space, the order undermined—he saw it now—by boot marks and that narrow, sinister mound at the back, right against the fence. The goats had fallen silent for the moment. Tai felt a stir of wind, and fear. It was not a shape, that mound, you could confuse for something else.

He stepped into the garden, fatuously careful not to tread on anything growing there. He approached the mound. He saw, just the other side of the fence, an object that had been thrown over, discarded.

Saw it was a drum.

He swallowed hard, his mouth suddenly dry. Too much silence now. Trembling, he knelt and, drawing a steadying breath, began digging at the earth of the mound with his hands.

But he already knew by then. One of the goats bleated suddenly, making Tai's heart jump in fear. He looked quickly over his shoulder at the rear door of the cabin. It remained closed. He kept digging, scooping, his fingers shifting the black, freshly turned soil.

He felt something hard. A low cry escaped him, he couldn't help it. He looked at his fingers. Saw blood. Looked at the earth he'd moved.

A head in the soil, emerging as from some desperate nightmare into hard sunlight, or from the other world, where the dead went.

There was a single deep, downward gash in it, almost splitting the face in half—and the blood from that blow lay thick in the soil of the garden, and on his own hands now.

Tai swallowed again. Made himself move more earth, wishing so much he had a tool, didn't have to do this with shaking fingers.

He did, however, he did do it. And in a few moments he'd exposed the blade-ruined face of a woman. A very old woman, her eyes still open, staring upon nothingness or into the sun.

He closed his own eyes. Then opened them again and, pushing and digging more quickly now, uncovered her body farther down. She was clothed, wearing tangled bone necklaces and a strange, glinting collection of metal polished to be ... to be mirrors on her body, he realized.

Mirrors to frighten demons away. His fingers, clawing at the soil, shifted her a little, inadvertently. He heard muted bells in the blood-wet earth.

Tai stood up. A very old woman. Drum, mirrors, bells.

He looked at the heavy cabin door that opened on the yard.

He ran, sunlight overhead, darkness behind him and before.

CHAPTER VI

In Xinan, some years later, after he had found Spring Rain among the singing girls in the North District (or, more accurately, once she had noticed and chosen him among the student-scholars) and they had begun to talk frankly when alone, before or after music, before or after love, she asked him one night why he never spoke about his time north of the Wall.

"It didn't last very long," he said.

"I know that. Everyone knows that. That's what makes it talked about."

"It is talked about?"

She shook her golden hair and gave him a look he knew well by then. *I am enamoured of an idiot who will never amount to anything* was, more or less, the import of the glance.

Tai found it amusing, sometimes said so. She found his saying so a cause of more extreme irritation. This, too, amused him, and she knew it.

She was a glory and a wonder, and he worked hard at not thinking about how many men he shared her with in the North District— one, in particular.

"You were permitted to withdraw from the cavalry. With honour and distinction—during a campaign. That doesn't happen, no matter who your father is. Then you go to Stone Drum Mountain, but leave there *not* a Kanlin ... and then you show up in Xinan, having decided to study for the examinations. It is all ... mysterious, Tai."

"I need to clear up the mystery?"

"No!" She put down her *pipa* and, leaning forward, tugged hard at his hair, which he'd left unbound. He pretended to be in pain, she ignored that.

"Don't you see ... being mysterious is *good*. It is a way of being noticed. That is what you want!"

"I do? It is?"

She made to seize his hair again and he lifted his hands to forestall her. She settled back on the couch and poured more rice wine from the flask upon the brazier at her elbow—pouring for him first. Her training and manners were flawless, except when she was attacking him, or when they were making love.

"If you pass the examinations this spring, and you hope for a position that means something—that doesn't leave you sending little begging poems to senior mandarins for their help—yes, it is what you want. You are trying for rank in the palace, Tai. To swim within the current. At this court, you need to know how the game plays or you will be lost."

He had taught her to use his given name. He insisted on it when they were alone.

"If I am lost, will you come find me?"

She glared at him.

He grinned, at ease. "I've been lucky, if you're correct. I've managed to become noticed without even trying. Rain, I just prefer not to discuss that time above the Wall. It isn't a good memory. I never thought about any of the things you are saying."

"You need to think about these things."

"I could let you keep doing it for me?"

She stiffened, shifted. He regretted his words as soon as he'd spoken them.

"I am," Spring Rain said, "a humble singing girl of the North District, hired by the hour or the night, owned by the proprietor of this house. It is inappropriate that one such as I be offered such a role. It is cruel to say so, even in jest. You will need to master these subtleties for yourself. It is your life we are talking about."

"Is it? Just my life?" he asked. Which *was* a little cruel, but her self-description had wounded him—and he knew at least one man who could afford to buy her from the Pavilion of Moonlight, for the impossible sum she'd command, if he chose to do so.

She flushed, a curse of the fair-skinned from the northwest, which was what she was.

She said levelly, after a moment, "If you pass the examinations you will enter among the most ambitious men on earth. You can decide to leave Xinan—leave yet another life—but if you stay here, at court, those are the people you will be among. They will eat you for breakfast, throw your bones to the dogs, and not know they dined."

Her green eyes—her celebrated jade-green eyes—were hard and cold.

He laughed, a little nervously, he remembered. "That's not poetic language."

"No," she said. "But I'm not a poet. Would you prefer a girl who is, Master Shen? There are some downstairs, and in other houses. I can make suggestions, sir."

A revenge, of sorts, for his own remark a moment before. But this *was* about her life, too. Of course it was …

A woman smooth as jade
Waiting all night above marble stairs
At a rice paper window wet with autumn rain.

Tai shook his head. He remembered looking at her beside him on the low couch, wanting simply to enjoy beauty and intelligence and nearness, but wrestling with what she'd said.

He murmured, "Women have usually been better at this than men, haven't they? Pursuing these subtleties?"

"Women have no choice but to be this way if we want any kind of influence, or simply a little control of our own lives."

"That's what I meant," Tai said. He tried a smile. "Do I get credit for subtlety?"

She didn't respond to the smile. "A child can know that much. You will be, if you ever decide to study enough to pass the examinations, among grown men who use words like blades and are in mortal combat with each other for position every day and night."

And to that he remembered saying, quietly, "Men like my brother, you mean?"

She'd just looked at him.

☯

Sprinting across the autumn grass from the shaman's grave, Tai thought about screaming a warning, then about running around the front to summon the others. He didn't do either. He couldn't have said, after, that he'd been thinking with clarity. This was an utterly remote, terrifying place. He'd unearthed a murder, and he was very young.

Those truths didn't entirely address why he broke into the cabin alone.

When pressed—and he was, by his officers later—he'd say that if they were going to save Meshag, which was their reason for being where they were, it was unlikely to happen if he alerted those inside by shouting, and he didn't think he had enough time to go around the front.

It sounded true. It *was* true, if you considered it. He didn't remember considering anything at the time, however. You could say his instincts had been at work. Tai didn't have any idea if that was so.

His sword was on his saddle, so was his bow. There was a shovel leaning against the back cabin wall. He had a fair guess by then how that had been used.

Without pausing to think, plan, to do anything coherent at all, he seized it, grabbed the door latch, and pushed, with no idea what he'd find, what he would actually do in there.

Or what they were doing, whoever these people were who had killed the shaman, buried her in earth to deny her soul access to the sky, and deceived them out in front.

It wasn't locked, the back door. He stepped inside.

It was dark in the cabin. It had been very bright outdoors, he was nearly blind. He stopped. And just made out the shape of someone turning towards him from within the room.

Tai stepped forward and swung the shovel as hard as he could.

He felt it bite—the sharp spade edge—into flesh, and sink. The figure, still only half seen, threw up an empty hand as if in entreaty or placation, and slumped to the earthen floor.

Soundlessly. Which was good.

Tai had never killed anyone at that point in his life. He didn't have time to consider what had just happened, what it meant, if it meant anything. He blinked rapidly, willing his eyes to adjust to shadow and dark.

Heart pounding, he made out an interior archway, a curtain over it, no actual door. A two-room cabin. He stepped over the fallen man, then—tardily—turned back and exchanged the shovel for the man's sword.

He did kneel and check, cautiously, he was aware enough to do that. The man was dead. Another brief disturbance: how swiftly, smoothly, silently life could be present, pulsing, and then be gone.

That thought pushed him forward, treading lightly, towards the fabric curtain. He shifted a corner of it.

There were candles burning in the other room, for which Tai gave thanks. Three men. Two near the front door, whispering fiercely to each other. Tai saw that the door was barred. They wouldn't have been able to crash in that way. Not without giving a great deal of warning.

Meshag lay on a pallet near the hearth. Tai saw that his tunic had been cut open, exposing his chest. His eyes were still closed. He looked terribly vulnerable. The third figure, tall and bulky, with animal horns attached to his head, was standing over him.

This one wore mirrors and bells and was softly beating a drum and chanting, rocking from side to side, occasionally spinning completely around. A kind of dance. There was a sickly-sweet smell in the room, something burning on a brazier. Tai had no idea what it was.

But he did not believe for a moment that this third man—it was a man, the woman was dead in the garden—was doing anything benevolent for the unconscious figure. They had killed the shaman who dwelled here. They weren't trying to help Meshag.

They hadn't killed him yet. Tai didn't know why. Why should he understand any of this? But, watching through the slightly lifted curtain, breathing carefully, Tai had a disturbing sense that what was happening here was intended to be worse than killing.

He was a long way from home.

That was his last clear thought before he screamed at the top of his voice and exploded through the curtain into the front room.

He went straight for the shaman, not necessarily what an experienced soldier would have done (take out the guards!) but he *wasn't* experienced, and surely his task was to try to stop whatever was being done with drum and chant and gathered powers to the man on the pallet.

He had not yet been on Stone Drum Mountain—his time among the Kanlin was a result of what happened that autumn day in the north—but he was the son of a soldier. He had been trained from earliest memory in ways and means of fighting, the more so since his older brother, soft and slightly plump even as a child, had made clear that his own inclinations and path in life did not involve swords or spinning, twisting manoeuvres against other armed men.

The dead nomad's sword was slightly curved, shorter than Tai's own, heavier as well, meant for downward blows from horseback. No matter. You used what you had. He had time to see the shaman turn, see fevered eyes open wide, blazing surprise and rage, before he struck a slashing blow above the metal mirrors draping the shaman's body, protecting it.

A part of Tai, his bearings lost so far away from everything he'd ever thought he knew, enmeshed in sorcery, was surprised when the sword bit the way it should.

He felt it grind on bone, saw blood, heard the shaman cry out and fall (a sound of bells), dropping drum and mallet on the hard-packed floor. He shouldn't have been startled: they'd killed a shaman woman, hadn't they? These mirror-and-drum people, they were holy and feared, but they weren't immortal.

Of course it was also possible that killing one put a curse on you for life. Not a matter Tai was in a position to address just then.

He wheeled and dropped, fear giving him urgency. He saw the nearer of the guards—the one who'd pretended to be a servant outside—rushing to where a bow lay against a wall. Tai sprang after him, twisting to dodge a knife thrown by the other man. He heard shouts outside.

He screamed again, words this time: *"Treachery! Get in here!"*

The false servant scrabbled for his bow, for an arrow, turned, dodging to avoid Tai's thrust sword—or trying to avoid it.

Tai caught him in the shoulder instead of the chest, heard the man shriek in pain. Tai jerked free his blade and—instinctively—dropped and rolled again, careful of the sword he held. He banged against objects scattered on the floor (their offered gifts) but the second enemy's sword sweep whistled over his head.

First time in his life for that sound: the sound of death averted, passing close. He heard thudding outside, and wild cries as his companions tried to get in, pounding against the barred front door.

"Around the back!" he screamed. "It's open!"

But in the same moment he took another chance, hurtling to the door. He flung the heavy wooden bar back. Just in time he dodged again, avoiding a downward slash that bit past him into wood.

He was sent staggering as the door flew open, hitting him in the back, but something—pride and anger and fear interwoven like threads in silk—made him step towards the man left standing. Tai slashed at him, parried a hard return as the others spilled into the room behind him.

"They killed the shaman!" he cried over his shoulder. "She's dead out back! Meshag's over there! Watch the one on the ground! I only wounded him!"

The one on the ground was seized by three men and dragged upright, off the ground, held like a child's doll. He received a bone-splintering blow to the side of his head. They didn't kill him, however. Tai noticed that. And in the same moment he heard one of the Bogü say, "Leave the last one, too. We will use him."

At those words, the man facing Tai abruptly changed his expression. Tai would remember that look, as well. He could sometimes see it when he closed his eyes in years of nights to come.

The man moved back towards the curtain. He reversed his sword, fumbling for the grip with both hands. He was trying to stab himself, Tai realized. But before that could happen, two carefully placed arrows took him one in each shoulder. The sword fell to the ground.

The man screamed then. A terrible sound, beyond any possible pain of his wounds, Tai thought.

A little later he would begin to understand.

HE'D HAVE SCREAMED like that, he found himself thinking on the ride back south (they had left that same evening, unwilling to remain by the lake, needing as much distance from it as possible).

He'd have tried to kill himself, too, if he'd had any idea what was to come before he was allowed to die. And the man had clearly known. In some ways, that was the most horrific thing.

The Kitan cavalry—Tai's own men—had come rushing down the slope when the shouts and screaming had begun, but it was all over within the cabin before they were near enough to do anything.

Tai had walked across the grass to join them when he came out. It had been disorienting, to be back in mild sunshine with so little time having passed. The world could change too swiftly.

The thirty Kitan riders had remained apart, together, to see what the nomads would do. Watching in impassive silence at first, then with increasingly intense, shattering revulsion.

The Bogü began by claiming the body of the old shaman from out back and burning it on a pyre they built between cabin and lake. They did this respectfully, with chants and prayer. She had been defiled by murder and burial under ground, it seemed. She had to be returned to the sky—left in the open to be devoured by wolves and other animals—or she could be consumed by flame and rise with the smoke.

They chose fire, because they were beginning a greater burning. They set the outbuildings alight, and then the cabin itself, but not before they brought out Meshag upon his pallet and laid him down in the yard. They dragged out the two men Tai had killed, the guard and the shaman, and finally they brought forth the two who were still alive. They were drinking by then, the Bogü: there had been *kumiss* in the cabin.

The shaman's bells chimed as they pulled his body across the trampled grass. His mirrors glinted, splintering sunlight. Tai had wondered if he'd transgressed in killing this man. It was not so, he understood now. He had done something, in the nomads' eyes, that marked him as a hero. He was to be honoured, it seemed.

They invited him to join in what was now to follow, with the two dead men and the two left deliberately alive. He declined. Stayed with his men, his own people, from a civilized place.

He was physically sick, wrackingly so, when he saw what came next. What he had been invited to share. Many of the Kitan cavalry became violently ill, stumbling or riding away, retching into the grass.

The empire of Kitai had not been shaped through nine dynasties by a placid, pacifist people. Theirs was a violent, conquering grandeur, built upon slaughter through nearly a thousand years, in their own civil wars, or carrying warfare beyond shifting borders, or defending those borders. Such was their history: fires such as these, or greater burnings by far, blood and blades.

There were texts and teachings as far back as the First Dynasty about the tactical utility of massacre, killing children, mutilation, rape. The useful fear all these could spread in foes, the overcrowding of besieged cities as terrified refugees fled before advancing armies. These things were a part of what men did in warfare, and warfare was a part of what men did in life.

But the Kitan did not roast dead enemies over fires and eat their flesh with invocations to the sky. Or cut off slices from men still living, staked out naked upon the ground, and let them watch, screaming, as their own body parts were consumed, cooked or raw.

There was a great deal of smoke, spilling thickly upwards, hiding the sun. A stench of burning in a once-serene space beside a northern lake. The crackling of several fires, howls (humans, not wolves), ritual chants, and someone's desperate, slowly fading plea for death replaced the sound of birds and wind in leaves. The ugliness of men erasing solitude and autumnal beauty.

It went on for some time.

One of the nomads eventually approached the Kitan where they waited, gentling their nervous horses a distance apart. He was bare-chested, grinning widely, and he was waving the severed forearm of a man. Blood dripped from it, and from his chin.

Unsteady on his feet, he extended the human flesh towards Tai, as to a hero worthy to partake of this great bounty. Giving the Kitan, the stranger, one more chance.

He took an arrow in the chest as he stood before them. He died instantly.

Tai could not, for a moment, believe what had happened. It was *entirely* wrong, shockingly so. He stood in numbed disbelief. Which was, however brief, too long an interval for a commander of men in a place such as this one had become.

His soldiers, as if released by that single arrow to their own demons, their frenzied response to the horror they were being made to witness, mounted up suddenly, all of them, with smooth, trained efficiency, as if an order had been given.

Seizing bows and swords from saddles, they swept forward—avenging spirits, in and of themselves—into the fires and smoke, infused with a clawing fury, with the sense that this hideous savagery could only be expunged, erased, with savagery of their own.

This understanding of events came to Tai only afterwards. He wasn't thinking clearly at the time.

His cavalry knifed into and among the outnumbered, on-foot, drunk-on-*kumiss* nomads, the stumbling, blood-soaked men they'd come north to aid—and they slaughtered them between the fires.

And when it was done, when none of the Bogü were left alive amid the black smoke and the red burning, the blurred sun setting west now, the lake a dark, cold blue, the next thing happened.

Meshag, son of Hurok, stood up.

He looked around the unholy scene created by men in that place. He had been a graceful man. He wasn't any more. He had changed, had *been* changed. He moved awkwardly now, as if oddly jointed, had to shift his whole body to turn his gaze, moving stiffly through a full circle. Black smoke drifted between him and where Tai stood rooted to the ground with a gaping horror. He was seeing this, and refusing to believe what he saw.

Meshag stared towards the Kitan riders for a long moment. The last men alive here. Then, shifting his shoulders as if trying to throw back his head, he laughed. A low, distorted sound.

He had not moved or opened his eyes since falling unconscious by another fire to the south weeks before.

It was not his remembered laughter. The way he stood and moved was appallingly different, this shambling, slack-limbed, unnatural posture. The Kitan soldiers, in an alien place among burning and the dead, stopped wheeling their horses about, stopped shouting. They clustered together, close to Tai again as if for protection, keeping their distance from Meshag.

Looking at this man—if he was still a man—Tai understood that the evils of this day had not ended.

He heard sounds beside him, arrows clicking from sheaths, nocked to strings. He stirred, he rasped an order—and was not sure if what he did was right. He might die not knowing, he would decide on the ride back south.

"Hold!" he cried. *"No man shoots an arrow!"*

What was left of Meshag, or what had become of him, turned, cumbersome and slow, to look at Tai, tracking the sound of his voice.

Their gazes locked through smoke. Tai shivered. He saw a blankness in those eyes, something unfathomable. Cold as the end of all life. It occurred to him, in that same moment, that his task, his *duty* to what had once been a man, might be to grant him the arrows' release.

He did not. He knew—he could not deny knowing—that something evil had been happening in that cabin (still burning, a red, roaring chaos) before he burst in and killed the shaman. It might have been interrupted, incomplete, but what that meant, what it implied for the figure standing stiffly before him, holding his gaze, as if committing Tai to memory, he couldn't hope to grasp.

"Like the swans," he said loudly to his cavalry. "Killing it might curse us all. This is not our affair. Let it ... let him go. He will find his fate without us."

He said that last as clearly as he could, staring at the soul-wracking figure of Meshag. If the creature moved towards them the soldiers would panic, Tai knew. He'd have to allow the arrows to fly, and live with that.

He didn't believe his own swan comparison. He hadn't even believed killing a swan would curse them ... that was Bogü fear. The Kitan had their own animal legends and fears. But the words might offer something to his men, a reason to listen to him. They didn't normally need reasons: soldiers followed orders, as simple as that. But this northward journey and today's ending to it were so remote

in all ways from their normal lives and world that it seemed necessary to offer one.

As for why, in his own mind, it felt proper to give this dead-eyed,
impossibly reawakened figure the chance to leave this place and
live—if living was what it was—Tai could only call it pity, then and
after.

He wondered if that came through in his voice, in the look they
exchanged. He wouldn't have said it was an entirely human gaze,
Meshag's, but neither would he have said it wasn't, that there was
some demon in there. Meshag was altered, and it seemed to Tai he
might well be lost, but he didn't know.

Killing him might have been the truest answer to what had been
done to him, offering the kindness of release, but Tai didn't do it, and
didn't allow his soldiers to do it. He wasn't even sure this figure could
be killed, and he really didn't want to test that.

After a long stillness, barely breathing, he saw Meshag—or what
had been Meshag—move one hand, in a gesture he could not interpret. The figure turned away from him, from all of them, living and
dead and burning. Meshag didn't laugh again, and he never did
speak. He loped away, around the burning cabin and then along the
shore of the lake, towards the fire-coloured autumn trees and the
distant, almost-hidden mountains.

Tai and his men stayed together, watching him through the
smoke until he passed from sight, and then they started the other
way, towards home.

☙❧

They had left the silk farm and the orange flare of the fox far behind.

The sun was going down, also orange now. Tai realized he'd been
wrapped in reverie for a long time, tracing memory, the paths that
had led him here.

Or, one particular path, that journey north: past Wall, past river's
loop, beyond the steppes to the edge of winter's land.

In the eye of his mind, riding now with six companions on a glorious Sardian horse, he still saw Meshag, son of Hurok—or whatever he had become—shambling away alone. It occurred to him that, having seen this, having been a part of that day, he ought not to be so quickly dismissive of someone else's belief in fox-women.

Or, perhaps, because of his own history, that was *why* he needed to be dismissive? There were only two people in the world with whom he could even have imagined talking about this feeling. One of them was in Xian and it was very likely he would never be able to speak with her again. The other was Chou Yan, who was dead.

No man can number his friends
And say he has enough of them.
I broke willow twigs when you left,
My tears fell with the leaves.

Wei Song was still up front. The stream they were following was on their left, a wide valley stretching from it, fertile lands, both banks. The forest that had flanked them to the south had receded. This was farming land. They could see peasant huts clustering into hamlets and villages, men and women in the fields, charcoal burners' fires against the darkening trees.

Tai had come this way heading west, approaching Kuala Nor two years ago, but he'd been in a strange state of mind then—grieving, withdrawn—and he hadn't paid attention to the land through which he rode. Looking back, he couldn't say he'd begun to think clearly about what he was doing, what he intended to do, until he'd ridden beyond Iron Gate Fort up the long ravine and come out and seen the lake.

He needed to become a different man now.

Spring Rain had warned him so many times about the dangers of the Ta-Ming Palace, the world of court and mandarin—and now he had the army, the military governors to consider as well.

Someone wanted him dead, had wanted that *before* he'd received the horses. He couldn't keep them, he knew he couldn't keep them.

Not in the world as it was. The issue was what he did with them, and—before that—how he could live long enough to claim them back at the Taguran border.

He twitched Dynlal's reins and the big horse moved effortlessly forward to catch up to the Kanlin woman. The sun was behind them, shining along the plain. It was almost time to stop for the night. They could camp out again, or approach one of these villages. He wasn't sure where the next posting station was.

She didn't turn her head as he pulled up beside her. She said, "I'd be happier inside walls, unless you object."

It was the fox, he guessed. This time he didn't make a jest. He still carried the long day's dark remembering, a smell of burning in his mind from a northern lake.

"Whatever you say."

This time she did look over, he saw anger in her eyes. "You are indulging me!"

Tai shook his head. "I am listening to you. I retained you to protect me. Why hire a guard dog and bark yourself?"

Not calculated to appease her, but he didn't exactly feel like doing that. It did occur to him to mildly regret hiring her. The soldiers from the fort would surely have been enough protection. But he hadn't known that he'd be given a military escort.

There was more ... *person* in her than he'd expected. She'd been chosen by Spring Rain, he needed to think about that. He had many things to think about, it seemed.

He said, "You never did tell me that night if Rain knows anything, or told you, about why someone sent a Kanlin to kill me."

A weak question ... he'd have been informed by now, if she knew. He expected a remark to that effect, didn't get one. "A false Kanlin," she reminded him, reflexively. Then added, "If the Lady Lin Chang knew, I do not. I don't believe she did know. Your friend was bringing you tidings, and it seemed you weren't to know them."

"No." Tai shook his head. "It is more than that. Or they'd have killed Yan before he reached me. It would have been easy to have him die along the way. They were alone."

She looked at him. "I never thought of that."

"They didn't want me alive to act on whatever he was coming to tell me, if I found it out some other way."

She was still staring. Tai grinned suddenly. "What? You are astonished I can think of something you didn't?"

She shook her head, looked away. Watching her, Tai felt his mood darken. The joking felt shallow. He said, not sure why he was confiding, "He was a dear friend. Never harmed a soul in life that I know of. I am going to want to know why he died, and do something about it."

She turned again to look at him. "You may not be able to do anything, depending on what you discover."

Tai cleared his throat. "We had better choose a village soon, if you want to negotiate for shelter."

Her turn to smile, as if to herself. "Look ahead."

Tai did so. "Oh," he said.

The land rose slightly before them. He saw that the road widened, three lanes now, the middle one reserved for imperial riders. In the distance, caught by the setting sun, he could just make out the walls of a fair-sized city, with banners flying.

Chenyao. They had arrived. And closer to them, beside the road, obviously waiting, Tai noticed a small group of men. They had horses but had dismounted, respectfully. One of them, formally dressed, lifted a hand in salute.

"You are being met outside the walls," Wei Song murmured. "It is an honour. Iron Gate sent word of your coming, with the courier."

"The horses," Tai said.

"Well, of course," Song replied. "You will probably have to meet with the military governor and the prefect, both, before you can go find a woman. So very sorry."

He couldn't think of a rejoinder.

He lifted a hand in a return salute to those waiting. They immediately bowed, all of them, as if pulled downwards by his gesture, like puppets in a street theatre.

Tai drew a breath and let it out. It was beginning.

CHAPTER VII

It might have been thought that the most beautiful and talented of the singing girls, the courtesans who could break a man's heart or bring him to a climax in ways he had never imagined, would all be in Xinan, with its world-dazzling wealth and the palace by the northern walls.

That would have been a fair assumption, but not an accurate one. Market and canal-side towns could emerge as celebrated or notorious for a variety of reasons, and the grace and skill of their women was one. The south had its own traditions in the matter of lovemaking, as far back as the Fourth Dynasty, some of these sufficiently subversive to be discussed only in whispers or after too much wine.

The northeast was a wasteland in this regard, of course: soldiers and camp followers in the wind-scoured fortresses by the Long Wall, repressive cities (also wind-scoured) dominated by an ascetic aristocracy that saw the last *three* imperial dynasties as new arrivals, barely worth acknowledging.

Chenyao, however, was at the other end of the empire, and the Silk Road passed through it, becoming the imperial highway, bringing traders and trade goods into the market square and pleasure district of a prosperous, lively city.

Lying so far west, Chenyao also had a reputation for Sardian girls—the fair-haired, blue- or green-eyed goddesses from beyond the deserts, so very appealing in Ninth Dynasty Kitai.

One such woman was called Spring Rain, who *was* in Xinan, and whose name now appeared to be Lin Chang, and who belonged as a personal concubine to the new first minister of the empire.

There were a number of reasons, Tai decided, that it was past time for him to become extremely drunk.

One was a friend's death. He kept reclaiming images of Yan: laughing until he spluttered and choked in a wine-cup game in the North District, or studying on a bench next to Tai, in ferocious concentration, chanting under his breath to memorize a passage, or the two of them climbing a tower outside the walls during the Festival of Chrysanthemums, which was *about* friendship. And now this friend was lying in a lakeside grave beside the assassin who had killed him. The second reason for needing wine (*good* wine, one might hope) was that someone had tried to kill him and he didn't know who, or why.

The third was Rain.

She had foreseen her departure from the North District more than two years ago, had warned Tai about it. He hadn't believed it could happen—or had denied it to himself. Not the same thing.

Against his will, he found himself remembering a night in the Pavilion of Moonlight, Rain and three other girls entertaining the students, laughter and music in the largest room.

A silence had fallen. Tai's back had been to the doors.

He'd seen Rain glance over, and then—without the slightest hesitation—stand up and, carrying her *pipa*, walk away from them towards the man Tai saw in the doorway as he turned to watch her go.

Wen Zhou had not been first minister then. But he was wealthy, well-born ... and a favourite cousin of the emperor's favoured concubine, which mattered most of all. He was a big man, handsome and knowing it, elegantly dressed.

He could have had any woman in Xinan sent to him. He'd wanted Rain. It amused him to come to her in the city, and there was no question of scholars claiming any kind of priority once such a man arrived—the idea was laughable.

Tai remembered that night, though it wasn't the only time. Zhou's gaze had flicked over the party of students before turning to Rain, accepting her graceful homage. She'd led him out, towards a private room.

Tai tried to sort out why that memory was the one that had returned, and decided it was because Zhou's gaze had actually held his a moment, a too-long moment, before looking away.

There was a poem by Chan Du about powerful men and women of the court enjoying a feast in Long Lake Park, suggesting that with certain men it was better if they never noticed you.

He'd been noticed that night.

He didn't want a yellow-haired girl in Chenyao.

He did need a woman, after so much time alone. And, he decided, assorted ghosts and malign spirits could choose amongst themselves which would torment the smug Kanlin Warrior he'd mistakenly hired at Iron Gate.

He'd arranged with the escort waiting outside the walls that he would call upon the prefect and the military governor—in that order—in the morning. They both wanted him tonight. He declined, politely.

Tonight was his own.

They were inside a city patrolled by soldiers, safe from roaming bandits—or spirit-world fox-women. He'd had Wei Song book the best available inn for the seven of them.

He'd also decided to keep the cavalrymen from Iron Gate. It was a small enough gesture of acknowledgement to Commander Lin, who had given him cash for the road, including the inn here, and what turned out to be a handsome room with a good-sized bed and sliding doors leading out to a garden.

Five guards from a border fortress were not going to link him too closely to the Second Military District when he got to the capital, but

their presence with Tai might be of use to the commander who had
assigned them.

There had been competing invitations from the welcoming party
on the way into the city, to be the honoured house guest of both the
men in power here: a competition that made it easier for Tai to take
his own lodging. The governor was more powerful (they always were,
these days) but the prefect had the title that signified in protocol, and
Tai had studied in Xinan long enough to know how this matter
needed to be dealt with, come morning.

THERE WERE GIRLS at his inn, of course, in a pavilion behind the first
building, red lanterns hanging from the eaves there. One of the
women, he noticed, when he strolled across the courtyard and
looked in, was charming—or could that be due to his not having
been close to a silk-clad woman in two years?

There was a *pipa* being played, and another girl with wide red
sleeves was dancing. He stayed a few moments to watch in the
doorway. But this was a comfortable inn, not the entertainment
district, and Tai had been cheerfully advised by the escort sent out to
meet him which of the courtesan houses was most likely to please a
man of taste with some reserves of cash.

He left the inn to make his way there.

The night streets of Chenyao were crowded, lit by hanging
lanterns on walls and carried by torches. That was something else he
hadn't experienced for a long time: men pushing the darkness back,
so the nights might hold more than fear. He wouldn't have denied
feeling a measure of aroused anticipation.

In Xinan, nightfall marked the curfew, the city gates and those of
each ward locked until the dawn drums, but this was a market town
on the merchants' road and rules were slack here, of necessity. Men,
many of them foreigners, emerging from the hardship of the long
passage around the deserts, would not readily submit to limits on
their movements when they finally arrived at a civilized place,
knowing their journey was over.

They'd pay their duties and taxes, submit to inspection of goods, bribe clerks—and the prefect—as required, but they wouldn't stay in one place after dark.

There were enough soldiers in Chenyao, this close to the Taguran border, to ensure relative good order even if travellers were abroad at night. Tai saw clusters of soldiers here and there, but they looked relaxed, not oppressive. Moonlit carousing was encouraged here: men feasting and drinking spent money, left it in the city.

Tai was prepared to be one of those.

Music, graceful women dancing, good food and wine, and then a chosen girl, eyes dark with promise, the nearly forgotten scent of a woman, legs that could wrap themselves around him, a mouth and fingers skilled in provoking, in exploring ... and a candlelit private room where he could begin to feel his way back into the world he'd left behind at Kuala Nor.

He was distracted, he would later decide, his thoughts running too far ahead through the noisy streets, or else he'd not have been so easily trapped.

He ought to have been alerted when the short laneway he turned down, following directions given, was suddenly *not* noisy, or thronged. He was alone, he realized.

Figures appeared at the head of the lane, blocking it.

There was no lantern at that end, it was hard to be sure of their number. Tai stopped, swearing under his breath. He looked quickly behind him. Was unsurprised to see more men at the lower end now, where he'd entered. Eight of them in all, he guessed. He was in the middle of an empty street. The doors of shops and houses on either side were, naturally, barred.

He had only one of his own swords. It was considered bad manners to carry double blades into a courtesan house, but it was also regarded as foolish to go unarmed through night streets in any city.

He might have been foolish just now. He drew his sword.

There were tactics prescribed on Stone Drum Mountain, early levels of teaching, for dealing with a challenge such as this. It was set as a formal lesson. One was unlikely to defeat or break free of eight men. Four was possible.

Tai drew two quick breaths and then sprinted forward, shouting at the top of his voice for the city guards. He heard a yell behind him, but he'd have a few moments with half of these men, whomever they were.

And he did, as it happened, know how to fight.

He hadn't had much use for those skills in years, but the second son of General Shen Gao, trained by the Kanlin on their holy mountain, ran towards this new set of assassins with a rising, useful anger—he recognized it, let it surge, channelled it.

Sword extended, he whipped through a full, running circle as he neared them, to confuse, cause hesitation. He leaped at the last house wall on his right, driving himself with three or four short steps, running *up* the wall, and then he sprang back from it, flying above the heads of the men—three only, not four, which was good—and he stabbed one and slashed another with his first two airborne passes, the good blade cutting deep, both times.

He landed behind the one who remained. That man whipped around, lifting his sword to parry.

It was at that point Tai saw that the man wore a uniform—the colours of the army of the Second District. The same as his own five cavalrymen. These *were* the military guards he'd been shouting for. Tai froze, blade levelled.

"What is this?" he cried. "I am one of your officers! The commander at Iron Gate sent word of me!"

The second man he'd wounded moaned, lying in the muddy street.

The one still on his feet spoke rapidly, through shock and fear. "This is known! Your presence is required! It was judged you might decline to come. We were sent to ensure it happened." He bowed, jerkily.

Tai heard a rustling sound. He looked up quickly, saw someone hurtling down from a rooftop, behind the four other soldiers who had rushed up from the far end of the lane. He made as urgent a decision as he had in a long time.

"Song, no! Wait! *Leave them!*"

Wei Song landed, rolled, and stood up. She hadn't been going to a courtesan house: issues of courtesy had not applied. She drew both her swords from the scabbards behind her and extended them.

"Why?" was all she said.

Tai drew a steadying breath.

"Because there are twenty more soldiers here, not all of them incompetent, some with bows, and you are in a city I control."

The voice was assured, and amused. It came from the square behind Tai. He turned, slowly.

There were half a dozen torches by a curtained sedan chair. The small square was otherwise empty, kept that way by soldiers at the edges, blocking each street. At least twenty men. The curtains of the litter were drawn back on this side, so that the man within might see what was happening—and be seen in the cast torchlight.

Tai still felt anger within himself, a hot stone. He was dealing with the sick sensation that could follow violence. The two men on the ground were silent now. He didn't know if he'd killed them. The first one, probably, he thought. He walked slowly over to the sedan chair and the torches.

"Why have you done this?" he asked, his voice demanding, too arrogant. He was aware of the tone. He didn't care. He was fairly sure who this was.

"You look like your father," said the thin, very tall man in the litter, stepping out to stand gazing at Tai. He used a stick, a heavy one, to support himself.

And that made it certain. *A city I control.*

Tai bowed. It was necessary, whatever anger he felt. He cleared his throat. "Sir, I told your officers outside the walls that I would be honoured to call upon you in the morning."

"And I have no doubt you would have done so. But I am an impatient man, and disinclined to follow the prefect in a matter such as this. You would have had to attend upon him first."

A matter such as this.

It would always be the horses now, Tai thought.

Governor Xu Bihai, commanding both the Second and the Third Military Districts, smiled at him. It was a cold smile.

Tai sheathed his sword.

"The Kanlin," the governor said, in a paper-thin voice. "She is retained by you?"

No time wasted. Tai nodded. "She is, my lord."

"And was assigned to guard you tonight?"

"Assigned to do so always." He knew what this was about. He was afraid again, suddenly.

"She was not walking with you."

"Kanlin are conspicuous, sir. I chose to remain otherwise. She was not far away. As you see."

The cold smile again. The military governor had to be sixty years old, his long chin-beard and hair were white, but his posture and manner were commanding, notwithstanding the stick he held.

"In that case, she will be permitted to live. You do not object if she is beaten? Twenty strokes?"

"I do object. I would take it as an insult and an injury to me."

A raised eyebrow. The torches flickered in a flare of wind. "She drew weapons on soldiers in my city, Master Shen."

"She drew blades on men in darkness who appeared to be attacking me, Governor Xu. I say this with respect. I would have had cause to dismiss her, or worse, had she not done so."

A silence.

"I will indulge you in this," Xu Bihai said finally. "In memory of your father, whom I knew. I served under him in the west."

"I know that. He spoke of you often," Tai said. Not quite a lie. He did know how the governor's leg had been injured. "Thank you," he added. He bowed again.

It was entirely the governor's right, even a duty, to have Song executed or beaten to crippled incapacity. This was a market town, thronged with drunken foreigners and transients. Hard men from the long roads. The soldiers were charged with keeping order. Certain rules followed upon that.

"Wei Song, sheathe weapons, please," Tai called. He didn't look back. He heard, with relief, the doubled *snick* as she obeyed.

"Thank you," he said again, to her this time. She was Kanlin. They weren't servants, to be ordered about as such.

Neither was he. He said, "I am honoured, of course, beyond my worth, that the governor has taken himself abroad in the night to hold converse with me. I had been greatly looking forward to your counsel and tidings in the morning. I still am. What hour would be convenient?"

"This one," said Xu Bihai. "You weren't listening. I said I was disinclined to see you after the prefect."

"I was listening, sir. I do not decree the protocols of our glorious Ninth Dynasty, governor. And I am disinclined to have my appointments for a day—or a night—decided by others, however greatly I honour them."

The white-bearded governor appeared to be considering this. Distant sounds drifted, music and laughter, one voice briefly lifted in anger, but they were alone in this square with the soldiers and Wei Song.

"I don't see that you have a choice," Xu Bihai said, at length, "though I note your disinclination. I will not apologize for protecting the interests of this military district, but I can offer you mare's teat grape wine at my residence and an escort to the entertainment district afterwards."

Tai drew a breath. He needed to decide, swiftly, how far he would take this—and how far the governor would.

He was still angry. His father had liked this man. Elements to be balanced. Inwardly, he shrugged. A princess in Rygyal had changed his life. A moment such as this was part of that change. It was unlikely to be the last.

"I have not tasted mare's teat wine in more than two years," he said. "I should be honoured to be your guest. Shall we invite the prefect to join us?"

For a moment, the governor's lean face betrayed astonishment, then he threw back his head and laughed. Tai allowed himself to smile.

"I think not," said Xu Bihai.

IN THE EVENT, Tai came to understand, the governor wished to say only one thing to him, but he wanted quite urgently to say it. And to do so before anyone else spoke to the young man who now controlled enough Sardian horses to play a role in the balance of power towards the end of a long reign.

The wine was luxuriously good. It was spiced with saffron. Tai honestly couldn't remember the last time he'd tasted that.

The two young women who served them were Xu's daughters, unmarried. Each wore flawless silk, one in pale green, the other in blue, low-cut in a fashion that had evidently emerged, so to speak, since Tai had left Xinan.

Their perfume was intoxicating, each different from the other's. They both had painted moth-eyebrows, tinted blue-green, and a side-falling hairstyle with extravagant hairpins. They wore jewelled, closed-toe slippers, gold rings and jade earrings, and had amused, confident eyes.

It was, he thought, unfair.

The governor, cross-legged on a platform couch opposite, clad in doubled black robes, with a black hat and a red belt, seemed oblivious to the effect his daughters were having on his guest, but Tai was entirely certain that the wine and lamplit room, and the two exquisite, scented women had been carefully orchestrated.

Wei Song was in the courtyard with the soldiers. The two men Tai had wounded were expected to live. He'd asked, on arrival here. This was good, of course, but reminded him that his skills were not what they'd once been: he had been trying to kill.

They ate five-spice dried river-fish in three sauces, and early fruits served in ivory bowls by the daughters, not servants. They drank the saffron wine, cups steadily refilled. Talked of spring crops outside the city walls and along the river, of thunderstorms and a tail-star apparently seen in the east earlier that month, what it might presage. The two women brought water and hand cloths for them to wash and dry their fingers as they ate. Curving towards Tai, offering a lacquered bowl of scented water, the one in green allowed her hair (in strategic disarray to one side) to brush his hands. This was the "waterfall" hairstyle made popular by the Precious Consort, Wen Jian herself, in Xinan.

It *was* unfair.

Xu's daughter smiled very slightly as she straightened, as if sensing, and enjoying, his response. Her father said, briskly, "Commander Lin writes that he proposed to you a position of high rank in the cavalry of the Second Army, a number of the Sardian horses to remain as yours, and your selection of officers to serve under you."

So much for polite discussion of stars, or millet and its ripening time and best-suited soil.

Tai set down his cup. "Fortress Commander Lin was generous beyond my merits, and behaved with impeccable courtesy to his guest, on behalf of his military district."

"He's ambitious, and clever enough. He would," said Xu Bihai.

"I imagine he will serve the district well if promoted." Tai thought he owed the commander that much.

"Perhaps," said Xu indifferently. "He isn't well liked and he isn't feared. Makes it harder for him to rise. Your father would have agreed."

"Indeed," said Tai noncommittally.

He received a glance from the other couch. The two daughters had withdrawn to the door, either side of it, decorative beyond words. He very much liked the one in green. Her eyes, that knowing half-smile.

"Perhaps further persuasion from me will be of use in causing you to reconsider his offer?"

"I am honoured you would even consider me worthy of persuading," murmured Tai. "But I told Commander Lin—a man I liked, incidentally—that it would be folly for me to contemplate a course of action before I consult with those at court."

"First Minister Wen Zhou?"

"Indeed," Tai repeated.

"Your elder brother, advising him?"

Tai nodded, uneasy suddenly.

"Two men I understand you have reason to dislike."

"I should regret if you continued in such an understanding," Tai said carefully. His pulse had quickened. "My duty to the Son of Heaven, may he rule a thousand years, surely requires that I take counsel in Xinan with his advisers."

There was a silence. It was not a statement that could be challenged, and both men knew it. Governor Xu lifted his cup, sipped thoughtfully. He put it down. Looking at Tai, his expression changed. "I can almost pity you," he said.

"I should regret that, as well," Tai said.

"You do know what I mean?"

Tai met his gaze. "I might have chosen a simpler life, had it been my own decision, but if we accept the teachings of the Sacred Path, then we also accept—"

"Do you? Do you follow those teachings?"

The discussion had become uncomfortably intimate. Tai said, "I try. The balancing. Male and female, hot and cold, awareness of all five directions. Stillness and motion, polarities. The flow between such things suits my nature more than the Cho Master's certainties, however wise he was."

"You learned this on Stone Drum Mountain?"

It was curious how many people seemed to know of his time there. He remembered Rain telling him that—and what else she'd said. How it might be useful. Shaping a mystery about him ...

He shook his head. "From before. My own readings. It was a reason I went there." He saw no reason not to be honest, to a point. It *had* been one reason.

Xu Bihai nodded, as if a thought had been confirmed.

He stared at Tai another long moment, then, as if speaking only of cultivated fields again, or early-summer rainfall, said quietly, "I understand you must consult at the palace before acting, but I would sooner kill you tonight and lose all the horses for the empire and be exiled to the pestilent south, or ordered to commit suicide, than have you give them to Roshan. This, Master Shen Tai, you need to know."

THE PROMISED ESCORT took him in the governor's sedan chair to the entertainment district. He hadn't been in one of those for a long time. The cushions were soft, there was a scent of aloeswood. He was slightly drunk, he realized.

The bearers stopped. Tai opened the curtains to reveal the quite handsome entrance of the White Phoenix Pleasure Pavilion, which had a new roof, a covered portico, lanterns hanging by the entrance, wide steps going up, and doors open to the mild night.

The leader of Tai's escort went up and spoke to an older woman at the entrance. Tai knew—and there was nothing he could, in courtesy, do about it—that he was not going to be permitted to pay for anything here tonight.

The soldiers indicated that they would wait for him. He wanted to dismiss them, but that wasn't possible if they had orders from the governor, and he knew they did. They would take him back to the inn eventually. If he spent the night here they'd remain outside until morning with the sedan chair. This was the way things were going to be now. Men were investing in him. He could try to find it amusing, but it was difficult.

I would sooner kill you tonight. This, you need to know.

Murder as an alternative to investment, he thought wryly. And given consequences so sure and so severe, even for a governor—since word had gone ahead to Xinan and they would know about the horses very soon—Governor Xu's statement carried its own uncompromising message.

Roshan was not to be allowed to claim these.

Roshan was a nickname, given by soldiers long ago, adopted by the court. The man's real name was An Li. He was a one-time barbarian cavalryman, then an officer, a general, now a military governor himself commanding the Seventh, the Eighth, and most recently also the Ninth District armies. A man everyone watched. And feared.

Tai had been away too long. There were elements—balances—he needed to learn, and he didn't have a great deal of time.

I can almost pity you was the other thing Xu Bihai had said. And at Kuala Nor among the ghosts a blue-tattooed Taguran had said nearly the same thing.

He had seen Roshan only once, in Long Lake Park, watching princes and aristocrats at a polo game. The general, visiting from his base in the northeast, in Xinan to receive yet another honour (and the gift of a city palace), had sat with the imperial party. He had been unmistakable in his colossal bulk, clad in brilliant, overwhelming red, his laughter ringing across the meadow.

He hadn't always been so fat, but one needed to be older than Tai to remember An Li's fighting days. He would destroy a horse under him today.

It was said that he laughed all the time, even when killing people, that he had never learned to read, that he was advised by a steppe demon, and had given the emperor certain potions for the delights of darkness in that time when Taizu first turned his aging eyes—and heart—to the youthful glory of Wen Jian.

It was also said that the only man Roshan had ever feared—and he had very greatly feared him, as everyone did—was the infinitely subtle, calculating, now-deceased first minister, Chin Hai.

With Chin gone, there was a new prime minister, and though Wen Zhou might be a favoured cousin of the Precious Consort, and owe his appointment to that as much as anything else, Roshan was also beloved of the emperor and had long been said to be equally close to the exquisite Jian—and perhaps more than merely *close*, depending on which rumour you heard and believed.

In the night street before a courtesan house in Chenyao's pleasure district, remembering a summer day in the park, Tai recalled looking across at the corpulent figure of the military governor from a distance and flinching inwardly at the image of such a figure embracing, crushing, the most beautiful woman of the age.

Jian was already named by then in poems, and had been painted, as one of the Four Great Beauties of Kitai, going back to the First Dynasty and the Empress Jade Pearl, among the immortals now.

To Xu Bihai tonight, Tai had simply said that he would seek counsel from as many people as he could before deciding what he would do, and expressed a willingness to come back west and meet the governor here, drink and dine again—perhaps in the presence of his charming daughters.

One of them had giggled at that from by the door, not the one in green. That one had simply looked across at Tai, her expression suddenly difficult to read.

Thoughts of the two of them drew his mind back to the house in front of him. He wasn't in the best condition, after so much saffron wine, to deal with matters of court and rival governors. Such issues could surely be deferred for a night? His first in a city after two years?

The doors of the house were wide open. He saw lights within. The attendant woman smiled from under two red lanterns. Of course she'd smile a welcome. It was her assignment here, and she would have just been informed that anything—anything—the young man wanted was to be offered to him, and charged to the governor.

The young man wanted more wine to start with, he decided. *The sage in the cup*, the poets said. The rest could follow as the spring night deepened and the late moon rose.

He heard a voice inside, speaking poetry.

He went up the wide, handsome steps, between lanterns, and entered the White Phoenix, giving a coin to the woman at the door.

CHAPTER VIII

The ridiculous Kitan adoration—and that feels like the right word!—of poetry and of declaiming, drunken poets is an endless mystery to Amber, and deeply annoying. Amber is from Sardia, has honey-gold hair, therefore her name. Not particularly inventive, but courtesan names never are.

She is beautiful (green eyes!). She's long-legged, has perfect skin, is very young. Beauty has been enough to ensure her a stream of clients since arriving here, even infatuated ones, though she can't sing or play one of their instruments, and poetry puts her to sleep.

Not every silk merchant or off-duty officer in need of a woman for a wintry afternoon or summer night wants the girl to discourse upon philosophy, or pluck "The Bandits of the Gorge" on a *pipa* before he takes her upstairs and throws her across a bed.

Amber makes a point of giggling when they do this to her. Men tend to be excited by that. She may not be educated, but she understands certain things.

In bed (or on the floor beside it) she knows exactly what she's doing, has a talent, especially if the man is young and not offensive in manner or appearance.

A few of the women who have been here longer are constantly urging her to listen more carefully to the poetry, even memorize some of it, to practise harder at her music. They are always pointing out that the men with real money, the ones who leave additional sums for the girl (they are allowed to keep half of this), will usually be those with some worldliness. That's just the way of things here in Kitai, even in a western market town.

Bright Amber (she *likes* the name they gave her, as it happens) doesn't entirely disagree, but she also knows that a merchant just off the long road will be generous to a pretty girl with smooth legs and an easy laugh and green eyes, and that many of those men will be indifferent to (or *bored* by, as she is) obsessive distinctions between eight-line regulated verse and any other of the hopelessly contrived forms poetry takes here.

Poetry! In the name of the bull-god! You even need to be a poet to rise in the civil service here. Can there be a clearer sign of a culture that has lost its way? Amber doesn't think there is, when she thinks about it at all, though she does concede the point Jade Flower makes: if Kitai has lost its way, why does it control so much of the world?

Maybe it would be different in a pleasure house in Xinan or Yenling, where the aristocrats are. Maybe she'd accept that it was worth her while to work on other skills. But Amber is happy in Chenyao, has thoughts already about one or two merchants and one extremely handsome officer of the Second District cavalry.

She's perfectly content to spend a year or two in the White Phoenix and then cajole or induce the right man to buy her as his concubine. It is as good a life plan as any for a girl.

She is from a hard world, after all. Orphaned in a plague summer, sold at twelve by her oldest sister to a brothel-keeper, noticed there by a merchant heading east, bought by him to sell. Her good fortune, that, no doubting it. She is distinctive in Kitai, and the White Phoenix is the best house in Chenyao. She has food and a bed of her own, firesides in winter, two days a month to herself, and half the festival holidays. Life has not dealt badly with her.

Chenyao is as far into Kitai as Amber feels any desire to go. They recite more poetry in pleasure houses east, among other things. She's been told that often enough. You need to pretend to listen and admire and *understand* it, strum accompaniment on your *pipa*, or else the men in fine silks of their own will laugh the wrong way, or ignore you entirely. A waste of a pretty girl, as far as Amber is concerned.

Let the older women, who need to spend time each day painting away lines, struggle to find ways to keep the attention of clients: clapping and smiling at drunken, mumbled verses, placing a *pipa* strategically in front of fallen breasts. Amber tends to find that standing a certain way, then just looking across the room at a man is enough.

At this particular moment of an almost-summer night, however, in the large, subtly lit reception room of the White Phoenix, crowded with a variety of men and a number of perfumed women, circumstances are otherwise.

No one is looking at Amber, though she's positioned herself by her favourite lamp near an archway and knows her hair is beautiful tonight.

Even one of her regular clients, the cavalry officer she has thoughts about, is among those crowding the central platform. On that platform, a soft-bellied, badly groomed, considerably intoxicated man well past his middle years is reciting a verse about—as best Amber can tell—a wife and her absent husband.

It is, she feels strongly, insulting.

The poet is proceeding slowly—in part, because he stops to take a drink every few lines. This poem is not (alas!) one of their brief, formal things. This one, he declared (his voice is not deep but it carries), is a ballad, whatever that is.

Well, Amber knows one cursed thing it is: *long*.

She makes herself smile with that. No one notices. One of the other girls, looking as if she was on the cresting edge of extreme desire, had breathed the word *immortal* when the poet came in some little time ago.

The Banished Immortal.

It is laughable. Amber *wants* to laugh but knows she'd be in trouble if she did. Where she comes from, an immortal, exiled from heaven for whatever reason, would have to look a great deal more as if he knew how to use the sword that lies beside the poet now, and would surely have the dignity to not be so obviously unable to stop himself from drinking cup after cup of their best grape wine.

It hasn't happened yet, but she expects his voice to start slurring soon—if he even manages to remain upright. This one isn't going to be much use to himself or the girl he takes upstairs, Amber thinks. Sometimes, if the man is too drunk to use you properly he leaves a larger sum, to have a girl keep quiet about his embarrassment.

She doesn't think this one, this *immortal* in his dusty, wine-stained clothing, is likely to care.

He is still reciting to an unnaturally silent room, and still drinking another cup every few lines. He's impressive in that, at least, Amber concedes. Two of the girls, hovering by the platform, visibly excited, hasten to refill his cup, taking turns. Amber wonders if their nipples are hard. She is tempted to have a coughing fit or cause a lamp to topple, so annoyed is she by this spectacle. No one is looking at her, no one is talking or even whispering to anyone else, no one is taking *any* of the women to another room, and the owner doesn't look as if she cares in the least.

Incredulously, Amber realizes that some of the girls—and many of the men—have tears in their eyes. *Tears!* Bright Amber is from a land famed for horses and women, and for men who fight bare-chested with knives, priding themselves on their scars.

She is seventeen and a half years old, has been in the White Phoenix for a little more than two years now. But honestly, she thinks, she could live among these Kitan till she was dried up like an end-of-autumn grape, bent like an ox-cart wheel, and she'd never understand them, or how the Celestial Empire dominates the world they know.

She is thinking this, outraged and aggrieved, when another man steps quietly into the room, following Lotus through the open doorway. Lotus just watches at the entrance now, greets arrivals, too old to ever be asked to go to a room with a man any more. Her hands are twisted, painful in rain and wind, she can't even play the *pipa* properly. Apparently she was the best of all of them, once.

Amber sees Lotus bow to this man, as low as she can, twice, as she backs out to the portico. That—of course—is the usual sign to all of them: this one is important, has money.

No one but Amber is even looking.

She runs a quick hand to her bright hair, checking the pins that hold it in place. Prepares her smile for when his gaze finds her beside the lamp.

It doesn't. He stops where he stands. His mouth opens. He stares—it is *too* upsetting—at the poet on his raised platform. The new arrival's expression is awed, disbelieving.

He has money to spend, Lotus has signalled it. He's young, presentable. You might even call this one handsome (unusual, deep-set eyes). Amber wants him to look at *her* with that dazzled expression, as she unbinds her golden hair and slowly, teasingly, discards silken clothing in a private room and kneels gracefully to attend to him.

She swears, not quietly enough. Two of the older women turn back to glare at her. Amber offers the response that makes the most sense at this particular moment: she sticks out her tongue.

∾

In the teachings of the Path, beliefs to which he'd tried, erratically, to adhere, Tai knew that coincidence, the fortuitous encounter, was to be accepted with composure.

If grim and unpleasant, such moments were properly understood as tasks, lessons one was meant to master. If benevolent, they were gifts to be humbly received.

Sometimes there was no obvious tilt towards one side or other of that balancing, there was simply a moment, an event, that startled in its unexpectedness.

Regarding these, there was a dispute among teachers. Some said the wayfarer's task was to interpret the meaning of the moment as best he could, and respond appropriately. Others taught that there *were* moments in a life that did not admit of understanding until long after. At such times, they counselled, one was merely to experience, and strive towards comprehension in the fullness of time.

That Sima Zian, the Banished Immortal, most beloved poet of the empire, should be in the reception hall of the White Phoenix Pleasure House of Chenyao, declaiming one of the poems Tai loved most in the world, felt—immediately—to be one of those moments that could not possibly be grasped.

There was no point even trying. *Be in the room*, Tai told himself. *Be aware of all of this. Gather it.*

Before anything else, however, it made sense to close his mouth, which was hanging open like that of a child watching fireworks at the Chrysanthemum Festival.

He took a few cautious steps forward. The women, their silks in many colours, like butterflies or flowers, were exquisitely trained in an expensive house. Perfumed deliciously, they made way for him, lingering close in subtle and less-subtle ways to read how he responded, what he liked.

Girls like these, and the wine they offered, and their flute and *pipa* music, had been what he'd dreamed about for two years. They almost didn't matter now.

He moved forward a little more, among other men around the platform. Merchants and soldiers, provincial bureaucrats in their belted gowns. No students, not in a border town, or a house this expensive.

Up close, there was resistance as Tai tried to get nearer to the poet. He saw a willowy girl bend, her hair swept up stylishly, the curves of her perfect breasts showing, to pour for Sima Zian as he paused between verses. He waited for her, smiled, drank off the entire cup. He hesitated, resumed:

I remember my careless maiden time.
I did not understand the world and its ways
Until I wed you, a man of the Great River.
Now on river sands I wait for the wind to change.

And when, as summer begins, the winds are fair
I think: husband, you will soon be here.
Autumn comes, the west wind whistles,
I know you cannot come to me.

Sima Zian paused again, lifted his cup. It was refilled from his other side, another girl, lissome as the first, her dark hair pleasingly disordered, brushing the great man's shoulder.

He smiled at her and Tai saw—for the first time, so near—the poet's notorious tiger-eyes, wide-set.

Dangerous, you might even say. Eyes that would know you, and the world. On the other hand …

The poet hiccupped, and then giggled. "Oh, dear," he said. "I have friends in Xinan … I *do* still have friends in Xinan … who would be disappointed in me, that this small sampling of a good wine should cause me to lose the thread of my own verse. Will someone …?"

He looked around, optimistically.

Tai heard himself, before he was aware that he was speaking:

But whether you go or come, it is always sorrow,
For when we meet you will be off again too soon.
You'll make the river ford in how many days?
I dreamt last night I crossed the waves in wind

And joined you and we rode on grey horses
East to where the orchids are on the Immortals' Isle.
We saw a drake and duck together in green reeds
As if they were painted on a silk-thread screen.

The crowd by the raised platform parted, turning to look at him. Tai moved forward, aware that he wasn't entirely sober himself, light-headed with what he was doing, overwhelmed to be among this many people after so long alone, all these women. His gaze was met—and held—by tiger-eyes.

He stopped. Had reached the last verse.

Sima Zian smiled. No danger in it at all, only good-natured, inebriated delight.

"That was it!" he exclaimed. "Thank you, friend. And have you left the ending for me?"

Tai bowed, hand in fist; he didn't trust himself to speak. He had loved the words of this man, and the legend of him, since he'd left childhood behind.

When he straightened, a tall girl in crimson silk attached herself to his side, hip against his, a long arm lightly around his waist, head tilted to rest on his shoulder. He breathed the scent of her, felt a surge of desire, over and above and through all else.

Sima Zian, the Banished Immortal, who had never held a single post in the imperial civil service, never even sat an examination, who had been banished from Xinan (as well as heaven!) three times that Tai knew about, who was reliably reported to have not been entirely sober in decades, who could nonetheless extemporize a poem, write it on the spot with immaculate brushwork, and break your heart, said softly, into the hush:

Take pity upon me now. When I was fifteen years old
My face and body were ripe as a summer peach.
Why did I wed a merchant who travels the Great River?
Water is my grief ... my grief is the wind.

There was a further silence. Surely there would always be, Tai thought, a silence after this, everywhere. The hand around his waist lingered. There was musk in her perfume, and ambergris. Both were expensive. This really was, he thought, the best house in Chenyao, if the girls wore such scents.

"Thank you, master," he said.

Someone had to say it, he thought. Sima Zian didn't turn his head at first. He lifted a hand, holding the empty cup. The first girl moved beside him and refilled it. The poet drank it off, held it up again. The second woman, refusing to yield her rights, came forward this time.

The poet's eyes, pale and brilliant in the lamplight, finally turned to look at Tai.

"Join me," Sima Zian said, "if your mourning time is over. It must be, since you are among us. We can drink together."

Tai opened his mouth, realized he had no idea what to say.

The girl beside him pressed her head briefly against his shoulder, a reminder of her presence, a promise, and withdrew. Tai stepped up to the platform, bowed, and slipped off his own sheathed sword, laying it near the poet's. He sat opposite the other man, cross-legged. A cup was handed to him, wine was poured. He lifted the cup in salute. He decided to be careful how much he drank.

He had no idea how Sima Zian knew who he was.

The poet, seen close, was a bigger man than Tai had imagined. His long hair was mostly grey, tied at the back with a nondescript blue strip of cloth, no hairpins. His robe was stained. His face was remarkably unlined, round, flushed, and benign. The bright eyes were unsettling, however. His hands were steady, large, the fingers long.

He said, "I knew of your father, of course. His death was a loss. It has always seemed to me that the best military leaders are gentle in their souls, aware of what war means. I thought this might be true of Shen Gao."

He lifted his cup and drank. Tai did the same, cautiously.

Tai cleared his throat. It was necessary to speak, or be thought simple-minded. The two girls had withdrawn down the two steps, leaving them a space of privacy on this platform. The evening activities of the chamber had resumed. He heard *pipa* music begin, then a flute, and laughter; saw men and women retiring through curtained doorways.

Tai wished he were sober. He said, "Our family is honoured, of course, that you even know who he was. Or ... who I am."

The pale eyes were briefly sharp, then amusement returned. "You *have* been long away," said the poet. "I know your brother, as well. Shen Liu is too close to the first minister not to be known ... and judged."

Tai said, "Judged, but not admired?"

Sima Zian grinned again. A smile seemed to be his natural expression. "Not by all. The same is true, of course, of the first minister himself. We live in challenging times. Assessments are going to be made."

Tai looked quickly around. Only the two girls with their wine were in possible range of hearing this.

The poet laughed. "You are concerned for me? What would Wen Zhou do? Exile me from Xinan again? He would like to, I suspect. So would others. It was decided by friends who care for me that this might be a good summer to absent myself from the capital. That's why I'm drinking in a pleasure house in the west. In part."

A deliberate pause, an obvious invitation. Taking it, Tai murmured, "In part?"

That laughter again, uninhibited, infectious—though Tai was not in a state to share amusement. "The prefect was kind enough to tell me of your arrival, over dinner this evening. He mentioned that you'd inquired about where the best courtesan house in town might be. A sensible query. I wanted to meet you."

"I am ... I am humbled ..." Tai heard himself stammering.

"No," said Sima Zian. "Not after that lake beyond borders. What you did there." His wide gaze was suddenly direct.

Tai nodded, a single awkward bob of the head. He felt flushed. Wine and the room's warmth, the intensity of the eyes holding his.

The poet murmured:

Alone among the pines,
He is a servant of no man.
How could I dream

Of ascending such a mountain?
From below that starlight
I bow my head.

The lines were well known. Zian had written them himself for a friend, years ago. Another poet, older, now gone.

Tai lowered his eyes. "You do me too much honour."

Sima Zian shook his head. "No," he said again. "I do not." Then, quietly, "Do you see ghosts here tonight?"

It was a real question. Tai was startled, looked at the other man and then away. Zian held up his cup and one of the women came forward. She gestured at Tai's and he shook his head. The poet made a face.

Tai tried to ignore that. He said, "I never *saw* them. At Kuala Nor."

"Heard?"

Tai nodded, more slowly. "Every night. Once ... once only, by day." Last afternoon, sun going down. A wind that was not wind.

"Are they angry?"

The girl had stepped back down again, with the wine.

This was difficult. "Some of them. Others are lost. Or in pain."

The poet looked away this time. At length, he shook his head. "Did you ever write about it?"

"How did you know that I ...?"

The smile again, more gently. "You were studying for the examinations, I understand, when your father died. All of you write poetry, son of Shen Gao."

"Or we try," Tai amended. "I had paper and ink. Wrote little I judged worth keeping. I am not equal to their story."

"Perhaps none of us are."

Tai drew a breath. "What else did the prefect tell you?"

He wanted, he badly wanted, a man he could trust. He wanted it to be this man.

Sima Zian hesitated for the first time. Then, "He did inform me about your Sardians, the Heavenly Horses. The princess's gift."

"I see," said Tai.

It was too large a tale to keep, he thought. Every man who heard it would tell.

"They will probably know in Xinan soon," the poet added.

"I hope so. I sent word ahead."

The eyes were thoughtful. "Because?"

"The horses are being held for me at the border. The gift is revoked if I do not claim them myself."

"Clever," the other man said, after a moment. "It might save your life." He didn't smile now.

"A Taguran captain thought of it."

Tai wasn't sure why he'd said that.

"A friend, clearly."

"I think so. While we're at peace."

"Ah. You believe we might not be?"

Tai shook his head, suddenly uneasy. "I've been away two years. I have no information. What should I know?"

Abruptly, he lifted his cup. It seemed he did want another drink. The poet waited until a girl had come with wine and withdrawn, slender and young, in wine-coloured silk that rustled as she moved.

Sima Zian's gaze drifted across the crowded, lamplit room, came back to Tai. "As to saving your life," he murmured, under the music, "don't look away from me, but is there a chance uncivilized men would be here with ill intent towards you?"

His voice was relaxed, almost lazy, as if they were discussing poetry or world affairs.

"It is possible," Tai said carefully. He felt his heart beginning to hammer. Kept his gaze on the poet's.

"Even with that message you sent ahead? The loss of the horses should you die? Of course, they might be here for *me*."

"Truly?"

The poet shrugged. He was deceptively broad-shouldered; the softness hid it. "Unlikely. I offended the prime minister and the chief eunuch in the same room, which is difficult, but I don't believe it was a deadly insult for either. Remind me to tell you the story later."

"I will," said Tai. *Later.* That meant something, didn't it?

He cleared his throat. It took some effort not to look around. He made a decision. He would acknowledge, after, that some of it had to do with the sense of the person that came through in the poetry, and that this might not be a sound basis for judging a man. Nonetheless: "There was an assassin sent west for me, before the gift of the horses was known."

Sima Zian's expression changed again. Watching him, Tai saw curiosity and then—unexpectedly—a hint of pleasure.

"You killed him?"

It was widely reported that the poet had been an itinerant warrior in his youth, two horses, two swords and a bow, sleeping in caves or under stars, defending peasants against landlords and tax collectors like one of the hero-bandits of folk tales. There were stories— legends, really—about his deeds along the Great River in the wild country by the gorges.

"It was a woman," Tai said. "But, no, I didn't. She was killed by the Tagurans and … and the ghosts."

You had to trust *some* people in life.

The poet considered this, then: "Look now! Near the door. Do you know them?"

Tai turned. There were two men to the left of the entranceway. They were in profile, engaged by three girls. Neither man was dressed for an evening in the pleasure district, let alone the best house there. Their boots and clothing were dusty and stained. They carried two swords each. One of them glanced over his shoulder just then— directly at Tai. Their gazes met, the man flicked his eyes away. It was enough, however. They *were* here for him.

He looked back at the poet. "I don't know them."

Sima Zian said, "They know you." The poet gestured to the girl whose turn it was with their wine. "Sweet joy, are those two often here?" he asked, indicating with his chin. "Are they ever here?"

She was a composed young woman. Would have stature among the girls, to have been chosen to serve the poet. Her glance towards the door was brief, appraising. She poured the wine and murmured,

"I have never seen them." She made a disapproving face. "They are not dressed suitably."

"Not at all," Zian agreed cheerfully. He looked at Tai, a brightness in those eyes now. He stretched, like a big cat. "I wouldn't mind a fight. Shall we kill them together?"

"I could ask the mistress to have them escorted out," said the girl, quickly, "if they distress you, my lord."

The proper thing to say. Fights were bad for a pleasure house. Killing was, obviously, worse. The poet made a face, but nodded reluctantly, was in the process of agreeing, when Tai spoke.

He heard the anger in his own voice, sharp, like the spikes of an assault ram breaking through a gate. He was *tired* of being acted upon: threatened, attacked, treated as an object of malice—or even apparent benevolence—with no resources of his own. No chance to shape his own course. He did have resources in Chenyao tonight, and not just his sword.

"No," he said. "Be so good as to go out to the governor's sedan chair in front. Advise the soldiers there that two men are inside with ill intent towards me, and that this threatens the Second Military District, the governor's authority, and the security of the empire. I would like them detained and questioned. I wish to know who sent them. I will await the governor's answer later tonight at my inn. Can you do that?"

The girl smiled. It was a slightly cruel smile. She set down the wine flask on a low table. "Of course I can, my lord," she murmured. She bowed to him, withdrawing. "Please excuse a brief absence."

She walked down the two steps and crossed to the entrance. They watched her go. Her movements were graceful, unhurried.

"I believe," said Sima Zian thoughtfully, "that one would make a memorable companion."

Tai found himself nodding.

"Do you know the military governor yet? Xu Bihai will not be gentle with them," said the poet.

"I met him tonight," Tai said. "Not by my own choice. And so I believe you. I need to know these things, however." He hesitated.

"The assassin who came to the lake? She killed the friend of mine she guided west under the pretext of serving him. I buried him at Kuala Nor."

"A soldier?" asked Sima Zian.

Anger still, sorrow returning.

"Nothing like. A scholar taking the examinations with me. A man without harm in him."

The poet shook his head. "I am sorry to learn of it. We live in troubled times."

Tai said, "He was coming to tell me something. Came all that way to do it. She killed him before he could."

A clattering from near the doorway. They turned. Six soldiers entered the White Phoenix.

There was a stir, but not an unduly disruptive one. The room was crowded and large. Men came in and went out all the time. The girl, who had come back with the soldiers, pointed to the two men Zian had noted.

They were approached. A brief, intense conversation ensued. One of the two went—foolishly—for his sword.

He was carried out a moment later, unconscious. The other man was hustled through the doorway between soldiers. It had only taken a moment. The music and laughter from the other side of the room hadn't even paused. Two girls were dancing, a flute was being played.

This, Tai thought grimly, was the way of life in cities. An assault could occur in a public place and not even be noticed. He needed to remember this, relearn it. Xinan would be more of the same, and infinitely worse. The dust of the world.

Sima Zian had turned back to look at him.

"I'd have enjoyed a fight," the poet said.

"I believe you." Tai forced a smile.

"It is unlikely those two can tell them anything. You do know that?"

"Because?"

"If this is from Xinan, from power, there will be many people between the order and those sent to execute it."

Tai shook his head. He was still angry. Too much wine, too much helplessness, and the memory, the image, of Chou Yan.

"Perhaps," he said. "Perhaps not so many people, if this is being kept quiet for whatever reason."

Zian grinned happily. "For someone without any rank and two years away from the world, you know more about such things than you should."

Tai shrugged. "My father. And my older brother advises the prime minister, as you noted."

"He does do that, doesn't he?" said the poet thoughtfully. "An honour for your family."

"A great honour."

He knew his voice didn't match the words, and that the other man would hear it.

Sima Zian said, softly, "If these two are in Chenyao looking for you, they'll have been given their orders some time ago. To watch for you coming back east. Probably in the event the assassin by the lake should have failed."

The voice of his own thought.

He stared at the other man. "I still don't know why anyone would have wanted me dead. Before the horses."

The poet did not smile. "I do," he said.

In the dense, canopied forests along the Great River, gibbons swung and shrieked at the boats bobbing and spinning east with the current or being pulled upstream along the gorges. Birds wheeled, crying, above the water and the crags. Tigers lived among the trees and killed men in the dark, should they be foolish enough to be abroad at night.

It was easy to see a tiger in the wide eyes holding his, Tai thought. For all the wit and worldliness of the poet, there was also something feral, a link to the wilderness that lay outside the walled and guarded cities. Sima Zian had been a bandit, on rivers and roads, never entirely a part of court or courtesan district.

You could see it.

The poet smiled again, compassion in his face now. But tigers weren't like that, Tai thought. They never looked kind. *You are going to have to do better with your images*, he told himself. There was too much complexity here for a jungle cat.

The other man said, gently, "You came here for a woman, I must imagine. It has to have been a long time, and that is not good for any man, let alone one with hard decisions to make. Go upstairs, Shen Tai. I will do the same. Make use of tonight, because you can. Let us meet here a little later. We will both be the better for it, then we can decide what we will do with what I have to tell you."

What we will do.

Tai cleared his throat. "I ... whatever this is, it is surely not your trouble, or task."

The smile deepened. "Call it wisdom in the cup, if you like, which is not always wisdom, as we know. But I have lived my days making decisions this way and I am too old to change. Poetry, friendship, wine. The essence of a man's life. And then there is ..."

The poet rose, smoothly enough, but he swayed a little when upright.

He looked down at Tai. Spread his feet a little. Rumpled, food-stained, greying hair inadequately tied. The wide eyes afire, though. He said, "You will know the passage: *There is another world / That is not the world of men.*"

He looked around unsteadily for the girl they'd sent to carry the message. She was beside him already. She bent, took his sword, handed it to him. She said, with a slow smile of her own, "Though it is your other sword I want now, my lord, in all truth."

Sima Zian laughed aloud, and went with her down the two steps and then from the room through the nearest of the curtained doorways.

Tai sat a moment longer, then stood, uncertainly, claiming his own sheathed sword as he rose.

A scent was beside him in that same moment, musk, ambergris. A slender hand at his waist again. He looked at her. Crimson silk.

Her hair was gathered with pins of ivory and jade, some of it artfully allowed to fall.

"I have been patient," she murmured. "Not without distress."

He gazed at her. She was as beautiful to him just then as moonlight on a high meadow, as the Weaver Maid herself, as everything he remembered about the grace and mystery of women, and she did not have golden hair.

"I may not be as patient," he said, hearing the change in his voice.

Her expression altered, a darker note in the dark eyes. "That will please me, too," she said. His pulse responded. "Please honour my need and come upstairs, my lord."

Pipa music, quiet singing, flutes. Laughter and talk in a carefully lit room fading behind him, behind them, as she led him up the stairs to a room with a very wide bed and lamps already burning, lit by servants, flickering light waiting for them (for whoever it was who came), incense on a brazier, a window open to catch the late-spring breeze. There was a *pipa* on a table.

"Shall I play for you, my lord?"

"After," Tai said.

And took her in his arms with hunger and need, with fear beneath those, and an urgency that came from all of these and found its centre in the rich red of her mouth tasting his and the slipping down of silk as she let it fall and stood before him, jewelled at ears and throat, wrists and fingers and ankles, the lamplight playing with and over the beauty of her body.

He had a sense, even as she began to disrobe him and then drew him to her upon the bed, that after this, after he went back downstairs, his life would change yet again, as much as it had when the horses were given to him. And therein lay his fear.

She was skilled and clever, unhurried, intricately versed in what it was that women were to do here, and to know about men and their needs (hidden or otherwise), in a house this well appointed. She made him laugh, more than once, and catch his breath in quick surprise, and draw breath sharply (he saw her smile then), and cry aloud, both times she took him to, and through, the long-deferred crescendo of desire.

She washed him after, using water from a basin on the table. She murmured the words of a very old folk verse as she did, and her movements were languid, replete, slow as aftermath should be. And then she did play for him, quietly, upon the *pipa* left in the room, bringing him back with all of these, movement by movement, mouth, fingers, fingernails, with whispers in his ear of shocking things and subtle things and, finally, with music—back from Kuala Nor to the world.

At length, Tai made himself get up. He clothed himself again as she watched, still naked on the bed, posed artfully to let him see her to best effect in the muted light, breasts, belly, the dark, inviting place between her thighs. She would attend to herself, come downstairs after him, that was the way it was done properly.

He finished dressing, found his sword, bowed to her, which was something Chou Yan had initiated among their circle: a tribute to the woman, even when one didn't know her name and might never see her again, if she had given of herself beyond expectation and reached to needs held deep within. He saw that she was surprised.

He went out of the room and down the stairs towards the next change of his life.

The poet was on the platform, same place, likely the same cup in his hand. The two girls were there again. He wondered idly if they'd both been with him upstairs. Probably, he thought.

The room was quiet now. It was late, and though the pleasure districts never really stopped in any city, the mood would change as night deepened. The best houses let some of the lanterns go out in their reception rooms, the ambience grow gentler, the music softer and sometimes even melancholy, for men could take a kind of pleasure in sadness, remembrance of loves long ago or the days of their youth. Someone was singing "The Windmill Above My Village," which was only played late and made some listeners cry.

He placed his sword where it had been before, and sat opposite the poet again. The taller of the two girls came forward with a cup for him, poured wine, withdrew. Tai drank. He looked at the other man, waiting.

"It is about your sister," said Sima Zian.

PART TWO

CHAPTER IX

Li-Mei has her own yurt, assembled every evening for her when their travels finish for the day, taken down in the morning when they rise to go on.

The sun is west now, near the end of their fourth day outside of Kitai. She has never been this far. She has never wanted to be this far. There are two ladies attendant on her from the court. She doesn't know them, doesn't like either of them. They cry all the time. She is aware that they resent serving her instead of the real princess.

She's a princess now. Or, they call her one. They made her royal before this journey north started from Xinan. There was a ceremony in the Ta-Ming Palace. Li-Mei, in red-and-gold silk with a too-heavy headdress decorated with white jade, and tortoiseshells and pearls from the south, had paid little attention. She'd been too angry. Her brother had been standing behind the prime minister. She'd stared at him the whole time, never looking away. Making certain that he knew exactly how she felt, as if that would mean anything to Liu at all.

She is still more angry than anything else, though she is aware that this could be a way to hide fear from herself, and from others. It is anger that stops her from being gentler with the two women who

are hers now. They are afraid. Of course they are. She could be
gentler. None of this is their fault.

There's no shame to their grief, she thinks. Or their terror, which
has grown worse, predictably, since they left Shuquian behind—the
last major city north of Xinan—and then reached the Golden River's
great bend and the Wall.

Shuquian had been many days back. They'd passed through the
Wall and entered wilderness four days ago. Soldiers saluted from
above as their party went through.

Li-Mei is counting, keeping track of time as best she can. A habit
of mind. Her father used to say he liked it in her. Her father is dead,
or this would not be happening.

The leader of their imperial escort had bowed three times to the
princesses, and then he and the Flying Dragon Army from Xinan
had turned back at the heavy gates in the Long Wall—back towards
the civilized world. Li-Mei had left her sedan chair to stand in a
yellow-dragon wind to watch them go. She saw the gates of the world
swing shut.

The nomads, the barbarians, had taken custody of two Kitan
brides, negotiated—traded—for furs and camels and amber, but
mainly for horses and military support.

This is the first time the Bogü have aimed so high, or been given
so much.

The actual princess, thirty-first daughter of the Glorious
Emperor Taizu (may he live and reign forever, under heaven), will
become the newest wife, in whatever ceremony they use on the grasslands, of Hurok, the ruling kaghan, lord of the steppes, or this part
of them, loyal (for the most part) ally of Kitai.

It has been duly judged, by the clacking, black-garbed crows who
serve the Imperial Throne as advisers, that with a momentarily
overextended military, and issues as to both army costs and the
supply of horses, it is a sage and prudent time to allow the *kumiss*-
drinking steppe-barbarians this otherwise unthinkable honour.

Li-Mei should not be here, does not want—the gods know it!—
to be a princess. Had her father not died, putting a two-year halt to

all family ceremonies and celebrations, she'd surely have been married by now, and safe. Her mother and Second Mother had been working on that marriage, through the proper channels.

She is not remotely a true member of royalty, only an attendant to the aging, exiled-to-the-countryside empress. But Li-Mei is also the sister of an ambitious, brilliantly positioned brother, and because of that she is about to become, soon now, the whatever-the-number wife of Hurok Kaghan's second son, Tarduk, currently his heir.

Not that there is anything certain about remaining an heir on these steppes, if you've listened to the stories. Li-Mei is someone who does listen to what is said around her, always has been, from childhood—and her second brother, Tai, had come home from the north with a tale, years ago.

There are—as with everything done in the Ta-Ming Palace—precedents for elevating lesser women to royalty for this purpose. It is a kind of sly trick played on the barbarians. All the subject peoples want, ever, is the ability to *claim* a link to Kitan royalty. If a woman is called a princess that is more than enough for the second or third member of a wedding party. For the foreign ruler (this has happened a handful of times, though never with the Bogü) a true princess is … made available.

There are more than enough daughters, with this particular emperor, after forty years on the throne and ten thousand concubines from all over the known world.

Li-Mei has thought about the lives of these women, at times. Locked behind walls and gates and silk-paper windows in their wing of the palace, at the top of eunuch-guarded stairways. Most of them have grown old, or will, never having even been in a room with the emperor. Or any other man.

The true princess, the emperor's daughter, has not stopped having one of her attendant women (she has six of them) sing and play "Married to a Far Horizon" for her since they left Shuquian. They are weeping, day and night, Princess Xue and her women. Endless lamentation.

It is driving Li-Mei to distraction.

She wants a deeper calm around her in this wilderness, this wind, to nurture the fury within, ward off terror, think about her brother.

Both her brothers. The youngest, Chao, still at home by the stream, doesn't really count yet. Thinking of home—cascading images of it—is a bad thing to do right now, Li-Mei realizes.

She concentrates her mind, as best she can, on the brother she wants to kill, and on the one who ought, somehow, to have saved her from this.

Although, in fairness, there would have been nothing Tai could have done once Liu had—brilliantly, for his own purposes—proposed his sister as the second princess for the Bogü alliance and had that accepted. But why be fair? Why be *accepting* in this place of wolves and grass, when she is leaving everything she's ever known for empty spaces and primitive yurts, yellow-dust wind off the western desert, and a life among barbarians who will not even speak her language?

This would never have happened if her father were alive.

Eldest Son Liu has always been eloquent and persuasive, and daughters are tools. Many fathers would have acquiesced, seen the same family glory Liu did, but Li-Mei, only girl-child of her family, is almost certain that the general, even in retirement, would have stopped his first son from using a sister this way. Liu would have never dared propose it. Ambition for self and family was proper in a balanced man, but there were limits, which were part of balance.

She wants to think this, but has been with the court long enough—arriving the year before the empress's exile—to picture it otherwise. She can almost hear Liu's polished, reasonable voice: "What is so different from offering her as an attendant to the empress, in my proposing her elevation to a princess? Are they not both exaltations for our family? Has she any other duty, or role in life?"

It is difficult, even in the imagination, to shape a sufficiently crushing reply.

Tai might have done so, equally clever, in a different fashion. But her second brother is impossibly far away right now, west, among the ghosts. It is an absolute certainty that Liu took *that* absence into account, as well, when he shaped his plans. Nor could Li-Mei's sad, sweet empress, exiled from the palace, lost to endless prayers and a dwindling memory, do anything to shield her when the summons to the Hall of Brilliance came.

Li-Mei, being carried north, is beyond all borders herself now. The difference is, Tai—if he is alive—will be going home soon. She never will.

It is a hard thing to live with. She needs her anger.

"Married to a Far Horizon" starts up again, the worst *pipa* player of the six this time. They appear to be taking turns. Li-Mei allows herself to curse, in a very un-royal fashion. She *hates* the song by now. Lets that feeling help drive and shape the fury she requires.

She peeks out of her litter (they will not let her ride, of course). One of the Bogü is just then passing, riding towards the front. He is bare-chested, his hair loose, almost all the way down his back. He sits his horse in a way that no Kitan ever has. They all do, she's come to realize. The nomads *live* on their horses. He looks at her as he goes by. Their eyes meet for an instant before Li-Mei lets the curtain fall.

It takes her a few moments, but she decides that the expression in the rider's face was not conquest or triumph or even a man's lust, but pride.

She isn't sure what she wants to make of that.

After a time, she peers out again. No rider now, he's moved ahead. The landscape is hazy. The evening wind blows dust, as usual. It has done that for several days now. It stings her eyes. The sun is low, blurred above the endless grass. They have seen vast herds of gazelles the last two days. Heard wolves at night since leaving the Wall behind. The Kitan have a terror of wolves, part of the fear and strangeness these northern grasslands evoke. Those stationed in the garrisons past the Wall must hate it like death, she thinks.

Squinting towards the orange sunset, Li-Mei finds herself devising ways in which she might have killed her brother Liu before any of this happened, sent him over to the night.

The visions are briefly satisfying.

She's angry at Tai, as well, she's decided. She doesn't have to be fair to anyone in this wind. He had no business leaving them for two years, not with a father and husband buried. He was *needed*, if only as a counterweight to Liu. He ought to have known that, foreseen it.

She lets the curtain drop, leans back against pillows, thinking about the two of them, sliding towards memory.

Not necessarily a good thing. It means remembering about home again, but is she really going to be able to keep from doing that? It is, if nothing else, a way of *not* dwelling upon what is waiting for her when this journey from the bright world ends, wherever it does, in this emptiness.

SECOND MOTHER, their father's only concubine, was childless. A tragedy for her, cause of nighttime sorrows and sleeplessness, but—in the difficult way of truth sometimes—an advantage for the four Shen children, because she diverted all of her considerable affection to them, and the general's two women did not have competing children as a source of conflict.

Li-Mei was six years old, which means Liu was nineteen, preparing for the first round of examinations in their prefecture. Tai was two years younger than him, training in military arts, already bigger than his older brother. Chao, the baby, was toddling about the yard, falling happily into piled leaves that autumn. She remembers that.

Their father was home, end of a campaign season (another reason she knew it was autumn, that and the paulownia leaves). Li-Mei, who had been diligently studying dance all summer with a teacher arranged by her mothers, was to offer a performance for the family one bright, windy festival-day morning with everyone home.

She remembers the wind. To this day, she believes it was the wind that caused her problem. Were her life not shattered and lost right now she could manage to be amused that she still clings to this explanation for falling.

She *had* fallen. The only time she'd done that after at least a dozen rehearsals in the days before, for her teacher and her mother. But with both mothers, and father, and her older brothers watching, and the drummer hired to accompany her, she had spun too far halfway through her first dance, lost her balance, tried to regain it, wobbled the other way, and tumbled—ignominiously—into leaves at the edge of the courtyard, as if she were no older than the baby playing in them.

No one laughed. She remembers that.

Liu might have done so in a certain mood, but he didn't. Li-Mei sat up, covered in leaves, shocked, white-faced, and saw her father's immediate, gentle concern, and then his almost-masked amusement at his short-legged little girl-child.

And *that* made her scramble to her feet and run from the courtyard, weeping uncontrollably. She had wanted to show him—show them all—how she was growing up, that she wasn't an infant any more. And what she'd done was entirely the opposite. The humiliation welling within her was beyond enduring.

Liu found her first, in the orchard under her favourite peach tree at the farthest end of a row, by the stone wall. She was sprawled on the ground, ruining her dance costume, her face buried in her arms. She had cried herself out by then, but refused to look up when she heard him coming.

She'd expected Second Mother, or perhaps (less likely) her own mother. Hearing Eldest Brother's crisp voice speaking her name had startled her. Looking back, she has long since realized that Liu would have told the two women to leave her to him. By then they'd have listened to his instructions.

"Sit up!" he said. She heard him grunt, crouching beside her. He was already plump, it wasn't an effortless position for him.

It was simply not done, to ignore a direct instruction from a first brother. You could be whipped or starved in some other families for that.

Li-Mei sat up, faced him, remembered to bow her head respectfully, hands together, though she did not stand up to do it.

He let that pass. Perhaps her mud-stained face, the tracks of her tears caused him to be indulgent. You could never tell with Liu, even back then.

He said, "Here is what you will learn from this." His voice was controlled, precise—not the tone with which one addressed a child. She remembered that, after. He was quiet, but he made her pay attention.

He said, "We train to avoid mistakes, and we do not go before others unless we believe we have trained enough. That is the first thing. Do you understand?"

Li-Mei nodded, eyes wide on her oldest brother's round face. He had the beginnings of a moustache and beard that year.

He said, "Nonetheless, because we are not gods, or of the imperial family, we cannot ever be certain of being flawless. It is not given to ordinary men, and especially not women. Therefore, this is the second thing you will remember: if we are in public and we err, if we fall in the leaves, or stumble in a speech, or bow too many times or too few ... *we continue as if we had not done so.* Do you understand?"

She nodded again, her head bobbing.

Liu said, "If we stop, if we apologize, show dismay, run from a courtyard or a chamber, we force our audience to register our error and see that it has shamed us. If we carry on, we treat it as something that falls to the lot of men and women, and show that it has not mastered us. That it does not *signify.* And, sister, you will always remember that you represent this family, not only yourself, in everything you do. Do you understand?"

And a third time Li-Mei nodded her head.

"Say it," her brother commanded.

"I understand," she said, as clearly as she could manage. Six years old, mud and overripe fallen fruit on her face and hands and clothing. Representing her family in all she did.

He stared at her a moment, then rose with another grunt and walked from the orchard down the long row. He wore black, she remembers now. Unusual for a nineteen-year-old, bordering on presumption (no red belt, mind you), but Shen Liu was *always* going to pass the exams, all three levels, and become a mandarin in the palace in Xinan. Always.

Tai came into the orchard a little later.

It was a certainty that he'd waited for Liu to come and go, as a second brother should. The images of that day are piercingly sharp, a wound: she is equally certain, thinking back, that Tai knew pretty much exactly what Liu had said to her.

She was sitting up still, so this time she saw her brother's approach. He smiled when he drew near, she'd known he would smile at her. What she hadn't expected was that he'd be carrying a basin of water and a towel. He'd guessed she'd have been lying on muddy ground.

He sat down next to her, cross-legged, careless of his own clothing and slippers, and placed the bowl between them, draping the towel elaborately over a forearm, like a servant. She thought he'd make a funny face to try to make her laugh, and she was determined not to laugh (she almost always did), but he didn't do that, he just waited. After a moment, Li-Mei dipped her cupped hands and washed her face and hands and arms. There was nothing she could do about her specially made dance costume.

Tai handed her the towel and she dried herself. He took the towel back and set it aside, tossing the water from the basin and putting that beside him, as well.

"Better," he said, looking at her.

"Thank you," she said.

She remembers a small silence, but an easy one. Tai was easy to be with. She'd worshipped both her older brothers, she recalls, but Tai she'd loved.

"I fell," she said.

He didn't smile. "I know. It must have felt awful. You would have looked forward so much to dancing."

She nodded, not trusting her voice.

He said, "It was very good, Li-Mei, until the wind picked up. I started worrying when I felt it."

She looked at him.

"Perhaps ... perhaps next time, maybe even tonight ... you might do it inside? I believe that is a reason dancers dislike performing out-of-doors. Any breeze affects how their clothing flows, and ... they can fall."

"I didn't know ... do they prefer inside?"

"I know it for certain," her brother said. "You were very brave to do it in the courtyard on an autumn morning."

She'd permitted herself to briefly claim the notion she'd been brave. Then shook her head resolutely.

"No, I just did it where mother and the drum man decided. I wasn't brave."

He smiled. "Li-Mei, just saying that makes you honest and brave. And that would be true, it *will* be true, when you are twenty-six, not six. I am proud of you. And father was. I saw it as he watched. Will you dance again for us. Inside? Tonight?"

Her lip quivered. "He was ... father was almost laughing."

Tai grew thoughtful. "Do you know a truth about people? When someone falls, if they don't hurt themselves, it *is* funny, little sister. I'm not sure why. Do you have an idea?"

She'd shaken her head. She didn't know why it was funny, but she remembered giggling when Chao toddled and toppled into leaves.

Tai added, "And father didn't laugh. He was afraid for you at first, then afraid he would hurt your pride if he smiled, so he didn't."

"I saw. He was holding it back. He covered his mouth with his hand."

"Good for you, seeing that. Yes. Because he'd been very proud. He said he hopes you'll try again."

Her lip wasn't quivering any more. "Did he? Truly, Tai?"

And Tai had nodded. "Truly."

She still doesn't know, to this day, if that last *was* the truth, but they'd walked out of the orchard together, Tai carrying the basin and the towel, and she'd danced for them again that night (the dancing costume hurriedly cleaned), among carefully spaced lanterns in the largest reception room, and she hadn't fallen. Her father had smiled throughout, watching her, and patted her cheek when she came over to him after, and then he had stood up and bowed formally, without laughing at all, and given her a string of copper coins, the way one paid a real dancer, and then a sweet from one of his pockets, because she was six years old.

IF SHE WERE TO ADDRESS within herself—or explain to someone who might ask and have any claim to an answer—a few of the very great differences between her older brothers, Li-Mei thinks, those long-ago conversations in the autumn orchard would do well enough.

Liu had told her—that day, and endlessly after, in person and in letters from Xinan—that she represented the family in all she did. She accepted it as true: for her, for any woman or man. That was the way of things in Kitai. You were nothing in the empire without a family behind you.

But she is beyond the empire now. The nomads, with their strings of long-maned horses and huge wolfhounds and their primitive yurts and harsh-sounding language … don't *know* her family. Her father. Don't care at all about that. They don't even know—the thought comes hard to her—that she's part of the Shen lineage. She's been named as one of the imperial dynasty. That is how the Bogü see her, that's why they look so proud, glancing at her as they ride by.

The honour of it eludes her, just now. She is the embodiment of a smug deception and of her brother's cold ambition. And no one at home by their small stream will ever see her again.

She wonders, controlling emotion, if a letter will even reach her mother and Second Mother, if she sends one, or a dozen, with Bogü riders to the trading place by the river's loop in spring.

Tai had called her brave, had repeated over and again how clever she was, growing up, how both these things would help her in life. She isn't so sure any more. He wouldn't have been lying, but he might have been wrong.

Bravery might mean only that she doesn't weep at night, or insist on hearing the same interminable lament as they travel, and Li-Mei has no idea at all how *cleverness* might play out for the second or fifth wife of the kaghan's heir.

She doesn't even know what number she'll be.

She knows nothing of the man she's travelling to wed—whose bed she'll share, if he even chooses. In her carried litter, Li-Mei draws a deep breath.

She can kill herself. That has been done by women married in this fashion. It is considered a disgrace, of course. She isn't sure she cares. She can decide to cry and mourn all the way north, and after they arrive.

Or, she can represent her father's bright, tall memory, and the version of herself Tai has held up like a bronze mirror all her life. The version of Shen Li-Mei that an aged empress had loved and trusted in her own exile after the Precious Consort came and bewitched with music and wit and beauty, changing the world.

A woman *could* change the world.

And Li-Mei is not the first woman to be exiled from her life and home, through marriage, through the ending of marriage, through someone's death, through birth, through the inability to bear a child ... in one hard way or another.

She hears shouted orders. She recognizes some words by now, having paid attention. They are finally stopping for the night. The approach of summer on the steppe means very long days.

The routine has been established: the two princesses remain in their litters while their yurts are prepared. They step out when summoned and proceed directly into the yurts where a meal is brought to them. After, they are readied for bed by their women, and they sleep. They rise so early that, even nearing summer, there is sometimes frost on the grass, or a mist rising.

In the litter, as it is set down, Li-Mei makes a face. It is somewhat childlike, in fact, although she wouldn't like to be told that. She pushes bare feet into slippers.

She draws back her curtain herself—all the way this time—and she steps outside into evening light and the dusty wind of the wide steppe.

The grass around her, the world, is green as emeralds. Her heart is beating fast. She hopes no one can tell that.

One of her litter-bearers cries out, startled. A rider turns at the sound, sees her standing there and comes galloping back through the tall grass: the same one who glanced at her before. He swings off his horse before it has even stopped, hits the ground smoothly, running then slowing, an action done half a thousand times, Li-Mei thinks.

He comes up, anger and urgency in his face. He speaks fiercely, gesturing at the litter for her to re-enter, no ambiguity in the message though she doesn't understand the words.

She does not move. He says it again, same words, more loudly, same harsh, pointing gesture. Others have turned now, are looking at them. Two more riders are coming quickly from the front of the column, their expressions grim. It would be wisest, Li-Mei thinks, to go back into her litter.

She slaps the man in front of her, hard, across the face.

The impact stings her hand. She cannot remember the last time she struck someone. She cannot remember ever doing so, in fact.

She says, enunciating clearly—he will not understand, but it doesn't matter: "I am the daughter of a Kitan general, and a member of the imperial family of the Celestial Emperor Taizu, Lord of the Five Directions, and I am bride-to-be of the kaghan's heir. Whatever rank you hold, any of you, you will listen to me now. I am *done* with staying in a litter or a yurt all day and night. Bring me someone who understands a civilized tongue and I will say it again!"

It is possible he might kill her.

She may be standing at the edge of night here, of crossing over. His shame will be very great, struck by a woman.

But she sees indecision in his eyes and relief floods through her. She is not going to die in this evening wind, they have too much vested in her coming north to this marriage.

He had looked so proud moments before, riding past, gazing at her. With nothing but instinct as her guide, Li-Mei steps back, places her feet together, and bows, hands formally clasping each other inside the wide sleeves of her robe.

Straightening, she then smiles, briefly, royalty condescending to ease a hard moment.

Let them be confused, she thinks. Let them be uncertain of her. Showing anger and independence, then courtesy and even grace. She sees that the curtain of the other princess's litter (the real princess) has been pulled slightly back. Good. Let her watch. At least the idiotic song has stopped.

Li-Mei hears birds; they are passing overhead, in great numbers. There is a lake nearby. That will be why they've chosen this place to stop for the night.

She points to the water. "What lake is that? What is it called in your tongue?"

She looks at the man in front of her. The other two have reined up by now, have remained on their horses, visibly uncertain as to how to proceed. She says, "If I am to live among the Bogü, I must learn these things. Bring me someone who can answer!"

The man in front of her clears his throat and says, amazingly, "We name it Marmot Lake. There are many of them here. Marmots, their burrows on the hills, other side."

He speaks Kitan. She raises her eyebrows and favours him— again, keeping it brief—with a smile.

"Why did you not tell me you spoke our language?"

He looks away, manages a shrug that is meant to be disdainful, but fails.

"You learned it trading by the river's loop?"

He looks quickly back at her, startled (but it wasn't a difficult surmise).

"Yes," he says.

"In that case," she says, coldly now, "if you have anything to say to me, including requests I may or may not agree to, you will say it from now on in the language I know. And you will tell the others what I said to you just now. Do you understand me?"

And, gloriously, after a short pause, he nods.

"Tell them," she says, and she turns her back on them to look east towards the lake and the birds. The wind is tugging at her hair, trying to pulls strands of it free of the long pins.

There is a poem about that, the wind as an impatient lover.

She hears him clear his throat again, then begin to speak in his own tongue to the riders who have gathered.

She waits for him to finish before she turns back, and now she gives him something, gives it to all of them. "I will be trying to learn your language now. I will have questions. You must show me the riders who know Kitan. Do you understand?"

He nods again. But, more importantly, one of those on horseback lifts a hand, as if asking permission to speak (which is proper!) and says, "I speak also your tongue, princess. Better than this one." He grins, crooked-toothed. An edge of competition here. He is a bigger man.

And Li-Mei sees, with pleasure, that the one standing before her looks angrily at the new claimant. She smiles at the one on the horse this time. "I hear you," she says, "though I will form my own conclusions as to whose speech is best among those here. I will let you all know, after I've had time to judge."

They must be played, she thinks, kept in balance, the men here. Any woman from the Ta-Ming knows something of how to do that. Meanwhile, this is useful, the first good thing in who knows how long. All her life she has been known for asking questions, and now she might find some answers here.

She needs to learn as much as she can about the man she's marrying and the life of women on this steppe. If existence is to become a dark horror, she *will* end it herself. But if days and nights can be shaped in any way here beyond the Wall and the known world, she has decided to try. She is trying now.

She looks at the one standing before her. "Your name?" She keeps her tone and bearing imperious.

"Sibir," he says. Then adds, "Princess." And inclines his head.

"Come with me," she says, bestowing this upon him as a gift for the others to see and envy, "while they put together the yurts. Tell me where we are, how far we have yet to travel. Teach me the names of things."

She walks away without waiting for him, going towards the water, out of this jumbled column of riders and litters and disassembled yurts. The long sun throws her shadow ahead of her. *Be imperial*, she reminds herself, head high. The sky, she thinks, is enormous, and the horizon (the horizon she is married to) is astonishingly far. Sibir bestirs himself, follows quickly.

It pleases her that he does not fall into stride beside her, remaining half a step behind. This is good. It is also good that her heartbeat has slowed. Her right hand stings from when she slapped him. She cannot believe she did that.

The ground is uneven; there are rabbit holes, and those of other animals. Marmots. The grass is astonishingly high, almost to her waist as she nears the lake. Grasshoppers jump as she walks through. She will need better shoes, she realizes. She is unsure what clothing they packed for her at the palace. She deliberately ignored all that at the time, lost in anger. She will have one of her women open the trunks and boxes they are bringing north, and look.

"I intend to do this each morning before we start and every evening when we make camp," she says, looking around. "Also at midday when we stop to eat, unless you tell me there is danger. I want you to attend upon me. Do you understand?"

Do you understand? She is sounding like her brother Liu. And yes, there is irony in that.

The one named Sibir does not answer, unexpectedly. She looks over her shoulder, uneasily. She is not as confident as she sounds. How could she be? He has stopped walking, and so does she.

His gaze is not on her.

He says something in his own tongue. An oath, a prayer, an invocation? Behind them, in the column of riders, the others have also fallen silent. No one is moving. The stillness is unnatural. They are all looking in the same direction—towards the lake, but beyond it, above, to the hills where the marmot burrows are supposed to be.

Li-Mei turns to see.

There is another stirring of wind. She brings up both hands and crosses them on her breast protectively, aware again, powerfully, of how alone she is, how far away.

"Oh, father," she whispers, surprising herself. Why did you leave me to this?"

Of all creatures living, the Kitan most fear wolves. A farming people—rice and cereal grains, irrigation and patiently cultivated fields—they always have. The wolves of the northern steppe are said to be the largest in the world.

On a hill slope beyond the lake there are a dozen of them, in the open, motionless against the sky, lit by the late-day sun, looking down upon them, upon her.

Sibir speaks, finally, his voice thick with tension. "Princess, we go back. Quickly! This is not natural. They let themselves be seen! Wolves never do. And—"

His voice stops, as if the capacity for words, in any language, has been ripped away from him.

She is still looking east. She sees what all of them see.

A man has appeared on the hilltop, among the wolves.

The beasts make room for him. They actually do that.

And Shen Li-Mei knows with sudden, appalling certainty that her life's journey is about to change again. Because paths can and do fork, in ways no man or woman can ever truly grasp, for that is the way the world has been made.

CHAPTER X

That same evening, in the Ta-Ming Palace, bordering the northern wall of Xinan, with the vast, enclosed Deer Park visible through open balcony doors, a woman is playing a stringed instrument in an upper-level audience chamber, making music for the emperor and a select company of his courtiers. His heir, Shinzu, is also present. The prince is cradling a steadily replenished cup of wine.

The Emperor Taizu, Serene Lord of the Five Directions, ruling with the mandate of heaven, never takes his eyes from the woman making music. That observation applies to most of the people in the chamber. (One mandarin is also watching, out of the corner of his eye, a prodigiously large man near the emperor, trying—and failing—to see into his heart.)

Wen Jian, the Precious Consort, is accustomed to being the object of all gazes. It is the way things are, the way she is. This is so whether she is making music, as now, or simply entering a room, or riding through one of the city or palace parks alongside water or wood. It is acknowledged as her due. She is already named among the legendary beauties of Kitai.

She is twenty-one years old.

She takes the breath away, alters the rhythm of the heart. First time seen, every time after: as if memory is erased, then renewed. One thinks of impossible ripeness, then of porcelain or ivory, and tries to reconcile these images, and fails, seeing Wen Jian.

This evening, her instrument is western in origin, a variant of the *pipa*, played with the fingers, not a plectrum. She was singing earlier but is not doing so now; only rippling notes fill the room, which has columns of alternating jade and alabaster, some of the latter so finely wrought that lanterns placed within them cast a light.

A blind man sits with a flute on a woven mat beside the woman. At a moment of her choosing, she strokes a final note and he knows this for his cue and begins to play. She rises, and it can be seen she is barefoot, crossing the pink marble floor to stand before the throne that has been carried to this room.

The Son of Heaven smiles behind the narrow, grey-white length of his beard. He is robed in white. His belt is yellow, the imperial colour. He wears a soft black hat pinned upon his head, black silk slippers stitched with gold, and three rings upon each hand. One of the rings is a green jade dragon. Only the emperor can wear this. Forty years ago, a little more, he killed his aunt and two of his brothers, and sixty thousand men died in the weeks and months following, as he claimed and secured the Phoenix Throne after his father's passing.

Bold and capable on the battlefield, learned, imaginative (much more than the brothers who died), a hardened leader, Taizu had secured the Ninth Dynasty and shaped the known world, using war to bring expansion and peace, and then that peace—enduring, for the most part—to begin the flow of almost unimaginable wealth to Kitai, to this city, this palace, which he'd built beside the smaller one that had been his father's.

He is no longer young. He is easily wearied now by affairs of state and governance after so many decades of diligent care. He is building his tomb northwest of Xinan, beside his father's and grandfather's, dwarfing them—but he wants to live forever.

With her. With Jian, and her music and youth, the beauty of her. This improbable discovery, treasure beyond jade, of his white-haired latter days.

She moves before them now in a high room, beginning to dance as the blind man lightly plays. There is a sound among those watching, a collective intake of breath, as from mortals glimpsing the ninth heaven from a distance, a hint given of what existence might be like among the gods.

The emperor is silent, watching her. Jian's eyes are on his. They are almost always on his when he is in a room. Flute music, that soft breath of anticipation as her dance begins, and then one voice cries out, shockingly, an assault: "Oh, very good! You will dance for us now! Good!"

He laughs happily. A voice oddly high-pitched in a stupefyingly massive body. A man so large his buttocks and thighs overspill the mat set out for him next to the throne. He has been permitted to sit, leaning upon cushions, an acknowledgement of necessity and a sign of honour. No one else is seated other than the emperor and the blind musician, not even Taizu's heir. Shinzu stands near his father, drinking wine, carefully silent.

It is usually wise for a prince in Kitai to be cautious.

The very large man, not careful at all, had been born a barbarian in the northwest. He was arrested, young, for stealing sheep, but permitted to join the Kitan army instead of being executed.

He is now so powerful it terrifies most of those in this room. He is the military governor of three districts in the northeast, an enormous territory. A very large army.

This has never happened before, one governor for three districts, it has never been permitted to happen.

The man's thick legs are thrust straight out before him; there is no possible way he could cross them. His eyes are almost-hidden slits in the creases of a smooth-shaven face. His hair, under a black hat, is thinning; there isn't enough left to tie into a knot. When he comes to Xinan, or when he leaves the imperial city, returning to his northern districts, twelve men bear his sedan chair. Gone are the days when a horse could carry him, into battle or anywhere else.

His name is An Li, but he has been known for a long time as Roshan.

He is hated by a great many, but there are those who adore him, as passionately, as intensely.

The emperor is one who loves him, and Jian, the Precious Consort, has even adopted him as her son—though he is past twice her age—in a child's game, a mockery of ceremony, seen by some as an abomination.

Earlier this spring the women of her entourage, thirty or forty of them, giggling amid clouds of incense and the scent of mingled perfume, had stripped him of his garments as he lay upon the floor in the women's quarters, and then they had powdered and swaddled and pinned him like a newborn in vast cloths. Jian, entering, laughing and clapping with delight, had fed him milk, pretending—with exposed breasts some said—it was her own.

The emperor, it was whispered, had come into the room that day in the women's quarters, where the gross man who had been—and in many ways still was—the most formidable general in the empire was wailing and crying like a newborn babe, lying on his back, fisting small eyes with his hands, while sleek, scented women of the Ta-Ming Palace laughed themselves into raptures of amusement to see Jian and Roshan so merrily at play at the centre of the world.

Everyone in Xinan knew that story. Other tales were whispered about the two of them which were unspeakably dangerous to say aloud in the wrong company. In any company, really.

To speak out, as Roshan does this evening, just as Wen Jian's dance begins, is a violent breach of protocol. For those who understand such things it is also a ferociously aggressive display of confidence.

He is uncouth and illiterate—proudly declares it himself—born into a tribe bordering desert dunes, among a people who had learned to survive raising sheep and horses, and then robbing merchants on the Silk Roads.

His father had served in the Kitan army on the frontier, one of many barbarian horsemen filling that role as the imperial army evolved. They had stopped the raiding, made the long roads safe for commerce and the growth of Xinan and the empire. The father had risen to middling rank—preparing the way for a son who had not always been so vast.

An Li, in turn, had been a soldier and an officer, then a senior one, whose soldiers left mounds of enemy skulls on his battlefields for the wolves and carrion birds, subduing swaths of territory for Kitai. Following upon these conquests he'd been made a general and then, not long after, a military governor in the northeast, with honours beyond any of the other governors.

He assumes a licence, accordingly, to behave in ways no other man would dare, not even the heir. Perhaps especially the heir. He *amuses* Taizu. In the view of some in this room, he acts this way deliberately, interrupts crudely, to show others that he can. That only he can.

Among those with this opinion is the first minister, the new one: Wen Zhou, the Precious Consort's favoured cousin, holding office because of her intercession.

The *last* prime minister, the gaunt, unsleeping one who died in the autumn—to the relief of many and the fear and grief of others—was the only man alive Roshan had visibly feared.

Chin Hai, who had steadily promoted the gross barbarian, and kept him in check, has gone to his ancestors, and the Ta-Ming Palace is a different place, which means the empire is.

Eunuchs and mandarins, princes and military leaders, aristocrats, disciples of both the Sacred Path and the Cho Master—all of them watch the first minister and the strongest of the military governors, and no one moves too quickly, or calls attention to himself. It is not always a good thing to be noticed.

Among those observing Jian's first slow, sensuous motions—her cream-and-gold silk skirt sweeping the floor, then beginning to rise and float as her movements grow swifter, wider—the most suspicious view of Roshan is shared by the prime minister's principal adviser.

This figure stands behind Zhou in the black robes (red belt, gold key hanging from the belt) of a mandarin of the highest, ninth degree.

His name is Shen Liu, and his sister, his only sister, is a great distance north by now, beyond the Long Wall, serving his needs extremely well.

He has a cultured appreciation for dancing such as this, for poetry, good wine and food, painting and calligraphy, gems and brocaded *liao* silk, even architecture and the subtle orientation of city gardens. More, in all these cases, than the first minister does.

There is also a sensual side to his nature, carefully masked. But watching this particular woman, Liu struggles to resist private imaginings. He frightens himself. The very fact that he cannot help but picture her in a room alone with him, those slender hands upraised, wide sleeves falling back to show long, smooth arms as she unpins night-black hair, makes him tremble, as if an enemy might somehow peer into the recesses of his thought and expose him on a precipice of danger.

Impassive, outwardly composed, Liu stands behind First Minister Wen, beside the chief of the palace eunuchs, watching a woman dance. A casual observer might think him bored.

He is not. He is hiding desire, and frightened by Roshan, perplexed as to what the man's precise ambitions might be. Liu hates being unsure of anything, always has.

The first minister is also afraid, and they believe they have reason to fear. They have discussed a number of actions, including provoking Roshan into doing something reckless, then arresting him for treason—but the man controls three armies, has the emperor's love, and Jian, who matters in this, is ambivalently positioned.

One of Roshan's sons is here in the palace, a courtier, but also a hostage of sorts, if it comes to that. Liu is privately of the opinion that Roshan will not let that deter him from anything he decides to do. Two of the governor's advisers were arrested in the city three weeks ago at the first minister's instigation: charged with consulting astrologers after dark, a serious crime. They have denied the accusations. They remain incarcerated. Roshan has appeared serenely indifferent to the matter.

The discussions will continue.

There is a rustling sound. A lean cleric of the Path, an alchemist, appears beside the throne bearing a jade and jewelled cup upon a round golden tray. The emperor, his eyes never leaving the dancer, whose eyes never leave his, drinks the elixir prescribed him for this hour. She will take hers later.

He might never need his tomb. He might live with her forever, eating golden peaches in pavilions of sandalwood, surrounded by tended lacquer trees and bamboo groves, gardens of chrysanthemums beside ponds with lilies and lotus flowers floating in them, drifting amid lanterns and fireflies like memories of mortality.

☙❧

Tai looked across the raised platform at the poet, and then away towards a lamp and its shadow on the wall. His eyes were open, but seeing nothing more than shapes.

Sima Zian had finished the tale, what he knew. What was, he'd said, beginning to be known among people with links to court or civil service.

It was a story that could easily have reached the scholars-in-waiting, come to the ears of Tai's friends: two princesses to be sent as wives to the Bogü in exchange for urgently needed horses for stock breeding and the cavalry, and increased numbers of the nomads to serve for pay in the Kitan army. One of the princesses a true daughter of the imperial family, the other, in the old, sly trick . . .

It is about your sister, the poet had said.

A great deal had become clear in this softly lit reception chamber of a courtesan house, late at night in a provincial town far from the centre of power. From where Tai's older brother, trusted confidant and principal adviser to First Minister Wen Zhou, had achieved . . . what people would regard as something brilliant, spectacular, a gift to their entire family, not just himself.

Tai, looking towards shadow, had a sudden image of a little girl sitting on his shoulders, reaching up to pick apricots in the—

No. He pushed that away. He could not let himself be so cheaply sentimental. Such maudlin thoughts were for slack poets improvising at a rural prefect's banquet, for students struggling with an assigned verse on an examination.

He would conjure, instead, mornings when General Shen Gao had been home from campaigning, images of the wilful girl who had listened at a doorway—letting herself be seen or heard, so they could dismiss her if they chose—when Tai spoke of the world with their father.

Or, later, after the general had retired to his estate, to fishing in the stream, and sorrow, when Tai had been the one coming home: from the far north, from Stone Drum Mountain, or visiting at festivals from studying in Xinan.

Li-Mei was not some earnest, round-faced little girl. She had been away from home, serving the empress at court for three years, had been readying herself to be married before their father died.

Another image: northern lake, cabin aflame, fires burning. Smell of charred flesh, men doing unspeakable things to the dead, and to those not yet dead.

Memories he would have liked to have left behind by now.

He became aware that he was clenching his fists. He forced himself to stop. He hated being obvious, transparent, it rendered a man vulnerable. It was, in fact, Eldest Brother Liu who had taught him that.

He saw Sima Zian looking at him, at his hands, compassion in the other man's face.

"I want to kill someone," Tai said.

A pause to consider this. "I am familiar with the desire. It is sometimes effective. Not invariably."

"My brother, *her* brother, did this," Tai said.

The women had withdrawn, they were alone on the platform.

The poet nodded. "This seems obvious. Will he expect you to praise him for it?"

Tai stared. "No," he said.

"Really? He might have done so. Considering what this does for your family."

"No," Tai said again. He looked away. "He will have done this through the first minister. He'll have had to."

Sima Zian nodded. "Of course." He poured himself more wine, gestured towards Tai's cup.

Tai shook his head. He said, the words rushing out, "I have also learned that First Minister Wen has claimed for himself the woman I ... my own favoured courtesan in the North District."

The other man smiled. "As tightly spun as a regulated verse! He'd be another man you'll want to kill?"

Tai flushed, aware of how banal this must seem to someone as worldly as the poet. Fighting over a courtesan now. A student and a high government official! To the death! They performed this sort of shallow tale with puppets for gaping farmers in market squares.

He was too angry, and he knew it.

He reached over and poured another cup after all. He looked around the room again. Only a dozen or so people still awake. It was very late. He'd been riding since daybreak this morning.

His sister was gone. Yan was dead by the lake. His father was dead. His brother ... his brother ...

"There are," said Sima Zian gravely, "a number of people in Xinan, and elsewhere, who might wish the prime minister ... to be no longer among the living. He will be taking precautions. The imperial city is murderously dangerous right now, Shen Tai."

"I'll fit in well then, won't I?"

The poet didn't smile. "I don't think so. I think you'll disturb people, shift balances. Someone doesn't want you arriving, obviously."

Obviously.

It was difficult, despite everything, to picture his brother selecting an assassin. It was painful as a blow. It was a crack, a crevasse, in the world.

Tai shook his head slowly.

"It might not have been your brother," said the poet, as if reading his thoughts. The Kanlin woman, Wei Song, had done the same thing a few nights ago. Tai didn't like it.

"Of course it was him!" he said harshly. There was a dark place beneath the words. "He would know how I'd feel about what he did to Li-Mei."

"Would he expect you to kill him for it?"

Tai slowed the black drumming of his thoughts. The poet held his gaze with those wide-set eyes.

At length, Tai shrugged his shoulders. "No. He wouldn't."

Sima Zian smiled. "So I thought. Incidentally, there's someone on the portico, keeps crossing back and forth, looking in at us. Small person. Wearing black. It may be another Kanlin sent after you ..."

Tai didn't bother to look. "No. That one is mine. Kanlin, yes. I hired a guard at Iron Gate. A Warrior who'd been sent by someone in Xinan to stop the assassin."

"You trust him?"

He thought of Wei Song in the laneway tonight, when the governor's men had come for him. He did trust her, he realized.

Once it would have irritated him, to have someone post herself so visibly on guard: the loss of privacy, the assumption that he couldn't take care of himself. Now, with what he'd learned, it was different. He was going to need to think that through, as well.

Not tonight. He was too tired, and he couldn't stop his thoughts from going to Li-Mei. And then to Liu. First Son, elder brother. They had shared a room for years.

He pushed that away, too. More sentimentality. They were not children any more.

"It is a woman," he said. "The Kanlin. She'll have seen the governor's soldiers leave with their prisoners, decided someone needed to be on watch. She can be difficult."

"They all can. Women, Kanlin Warriors. Put them in one ..." The poet laughed. Then asked, as Tai had half expected, "Who is the *someone in Xinan* who sent her?"

He had decided to trust this man, too, hadn't he?

"The courtesan I mentioned. Wen Zhou's concubine."

This time the poet blinked. After a moment, he said, "She risked that? For someone who's been away two years? Shen Tai, you are …" He left the thought unfinished. "But if it is the first minister who wants you dead, even costing the empire your horses might not change his mind."

Tai shook his head. "Killing me *now*, after word of the horses has arrived, Zhou or my brother runs the risk of someone—you, Xu Bihai, even the commander at Iron Gate—linking it to him. The loss of so many Sardian horses would make my death important. His enemies could bring him down with that."

The poet considered it. "Then what is this about? There was nothing you could do for your sister from Kuala Nor, was there? You were much too far, it was already too late, but an assassin was sent. Was this about eliminating a new enemy before he returned?" He hesitated. "Perhaps a rival?"

There was that.

Her hair by lamplight.

And if someone should take me from here when you are gone?

He said, "It might be."

"You are going on to Xinan?"

Tai smiled, first time since coming back down the stairs. Mirthlessly, he said, "I must, surely? I have sent word. I will be anxiously awaited!"

No answering smile, not this time. "Awaited on the road, it might also be. Shen Tai, you will accept an unworthy friend and companion?"

Tai swallowed. He hadn't expected this. "Why? It would be foolishly dangerous for you to put yourself …"

"You helped me remember a poem," said the one called the Banished Immortal.

"That's no reason to—"

"And you buried the dead at Kuala Nor for two years."

Another silence. This man was, Tai thought, all about pauses, the spaces between words as much as the words themselves.

Across the room someone had begun plucking quietly at a *pipa*, the notes drifting through lamplight and shadow, leaves on a moonlit stream.

"Xinan is changed. You will need someone who knows the city as it has become since you left. Knows it better than some Kanlin pacing back and forth." Sima Zian grinned, and then he laughed, amusing himself with a thought he elected not to share.

The poet's hand, Tai saw, reached out to touch his sword.

Friend was the word he had used.

ⓧ

A journey does not end when it ends.

The well-worn thought comes to her in the chill of night as she waits in her yurt alone. Li-Mei is not asleep, nor under the sheepskin blankets they lay out for her at night. It can grow cold on the steppe under stars. It is black as a tomb inside, with the flap closed. She cannot even see her hands. She is sitting on the pallet, fully clothed, holding a small knife.

She is trembling, and unhappy about that, even though no one is here to see her weakness.

The doctrines of the Sacred Path use the phrase about journeys and destinations to teach, in part, that death does not end one's travelling through time and the worlds.

She does not know, there is no way she could know, but Bogü belief lies near to the same thought. The soul returns to the Sky Father, the body goes to earth and continues in another form, and then another, and another, until the wheel is broken.

Li-Mei understands something else tonight. She *knows* something else. And this was so in the moment she saw the wolves on the slope and the man with them, and watched the nomads behind her hurled into chaos and panic—these hard, fierce men of the steppe whose very being demands they show no fear to anyone, or to themselves.

Something is about to happen. A journey, one sort of journey, *will* end, possibly right here.

She is awake and clothed, waiting. With a knife.

So when the first wolf howls she is unsurprised. Even with that, she is unable to keep from jerking spasmodically at the lost, wild sound of it, or stop her hands from beginning to shake even more. You can be brave, and be afraid. She fears she'll cut herself with the blade and she puts it aside on the pallet.

A lead wolf by itself at first, then others with it, filling the wide night with their sound. But the nomads' dogs—the great wolfhounds—are silent, as they have been since the first wolf sighting towards sundown.

That, as much as anything else, is why she is so certain something strange is happening. The dogs should have gone wild at the sight of the wolves before, and hearing them now.

Nothing. Nothing at all from them.

She does hear movements outside, the riders mounting up. They will be happier on horseback, she has come to realize that. But there are no shouts, commands, no warlike cries, and no dogs. It is unnatural.

The wolves again, nearer. The worst sound in the world, someone called their howling, in a long-ago poem. The Kitan fear wolves more than tigers. In legend, in life. They are coming down now. She closes her eyes in the dark.

Li-Mei wants to lie on her small pallet and draw the sheepskins over her head and wish this all away, into not-being-so.

There was a storyteller in the town nearest their estate who used to offer a marketplace tale, a fable, of a girl who could do this. She remembers extending to him a copper coin the first time, then realizing he was blind.

She wants so much to be there, to be *home*, in her own bedchamber, going back and forth on the garden swing, on a ladder in the orchard picking early-summer fruit, looking up to find the Weaver Maid in the known evening sky …

She realizes there are tears on her face.

Impatiently, with a gesture at least one of her brothers would have recognized, she presses her lips together and wipes at her cheeks with the backs of both hands. In her own way, though she might wish to deny it, showing distress disturbs her as much as it would the nomads outside on their horses.

She forces herself to stand, makes certain she's steady on her feet. She's wearing riding boots. She'd made her two women find them in the baggage when she came back from that walk at sundown. She hesitates, then takes the knife again, drops it into an inside pocket of her tunic.

She might need it to end her life.

She draws a breath, lifts back the heavy flap of her yurt, and ducks outside. You have to be afraid for it to count as bravery. Her father had taught her that, a long time ago.

A wind is blowing. It is cold. She is aware of the hard brilliance of the stars, the band of the Sky River arcing across heaven, eternal symbol of one thing divided from another: the Weaver Maid from her mortal love, the living from the dead, the exile from home.

The man is standing before her yurt. She'd had a thought about him before, what he might be, but it turns out she is wrong. It is difficult to tell his age, especially in the night, but she can see that he's dressed as any other Bogü rider might be.

No bells, no mirrors, no drum.

He isn't a shaman. She had thought this might be why the horsemen were so afraid. She knew about these men because her brother had told her, years ago. Though, if truth was being demanded, Tai had told their father—and Li-Mei had listened nearby as father and Second Son talked.

Did it matter? Now? She knew some things. And they could have sent her away from the stream, or closed the door, if they'd wanted to. She hadn't worked very hard at remaining hidden.

The man in front of her yurt is the one from the lakeside slope. She has expected him to come. In fact, she knows more than that: she knows *she* is the reason he's here and that he is the cause of the dogs' silence—though wolves are with him in the camp now, half a dozen of them. She decides she will not look at them.

The Bogü riders are rigid, an almost formal stillness. They sit their horses at intervals around her yurt, but no one is moving, no one reacts to the intruder among them, or his wolves. They *are* his wolves, what else can they be? She sees no nocked arrows, no swords unsheathed. These men are here to escort the Kitan princesses to their kaghan, to defend them with their lives. This is not happening.

Stars, a waning moon, campfires burning between yurts, sparks snapping there, but no other movement. It is as if they have all been turned to moonlit statues, the man and his wolves, the horsemen and their horses and the dogs, as in some legend of dragon kings and sorcerers of long ago, or fox-women working magic in bamboo woods by the Great River gorges.

The Bogü look, Li-Mei thinks, as if they *could* not move.

Perhaps that is true. An actual truth, not a fable told. Perhaps they are frozen in place by something more than fear or awe.

It isn't so, she decides, looking around her in the firelit dark. One man twitches his reins. Another draws a nervous hand down his horse's mane. A dog stands up then sits quickly again.

Folk tales and legends are what we move away from when the adult world claims our life, she thinks.

For a brief, unstable moment, it crosses her mind to walk up to the man with the wolves and slap him across the face. She does not. This isn't the same as before. She doesn't understand enough. She doesn't understand any of it. Until she does, she can't act, can't put her stamp (however feeble) on events. She can only follow where the night leads, try to hold down terror, be prepared to die.

The knife is in a pocket of her robe.

The man has not spoken, nor does he now. Instead, looking straight at her, he lifts a hand and gestures, stiffly, to the east— towards the lake and the hills beyond it, invisible now in the dark. She decides she will treat it as an invitation, not a command.

Not that it makes a difference.

The wolves—six of them—immediately get up and begin loping that way. One passes close to her. She doesn't look at it. The man does not turn to watch them. He continues to face Li-Mei, waiting.

The riders do not move. They are not going to save her.

She takes a hesitant step, testing her steadiness. As she does, she hears a sigh from those on horseback: a sound like wind in a summer grove. She realizes, belatedly, that everyone has been waiting for her. That is what this stillness has been about.

It makes sense, as much as anything does in this wide night in an alien land.

He has come for her, after all.

CHAPTER XI

He was tired. It had been a very long day and his body was telling him as much. Tai was hardened and fit after two years' digging graves by Kuala Nor, but other factors could enter into making someone weary at day's end.

It would also be dishonest to deny that a measure of his languor could be traced to an encounter upstairs in the White Phoenix, just now.

He was aware that the woman's scent was still with him, and that he didn't know her name. That last wasn't unusual. And whatever name he'd learned wouldn't have been her real one. He didn't even know Rain's real name.

That suddenly became a sadness, joining others.

Stepping outside with the most celebrated poet in the empire, his new companion—the reality of *that* was going to take time to settle in—Tai saw someone waiting, and decided he'd be happier if his recently hired Kanlin guard hadn't looked so smugly amused. Registering her expression, he wished he were sober.

Wei Song approached. She bowed. "Your servant trusts you are feeling better, my lord." She spoke with impeccable courtesy—and unmistakable irony.

Tai ignored her for the moment. A useful tactic, when your thoughts offered no good reply. He looked around the night square. Saw the governor's sedan chair behind her. Other soldiers had replaced those who'd taken the would-be assassins. Caution— another new thing—made him hesitate.

"You saw these men arrive?" he asked, gesturing.

Song nodded. "I spoke with the leader. You may safely ride with them." Her tone was proper, her expression barely so. He really wished she hadn't said what she'd said back at Iron Gate, about women waiting for him in Chenyao.

Tai became aware of an extreme delight showing in the face of the rumpled poet beside him. Sima Zian was eyeing Tai's bodyguard with appreciation by the light of the lanterns on the porch.

"This is Wei Song, my Kanlin," he said, briefly. "I mentioned her inside."

"You did," agreed the poet, smiling.

Song smiled back at him, and bowed. "I am honoured, illustrious sir." She hadn't needed an introduction.

Tai looked from one of them to the other. "Let's walk," he said abruptly. "Have the soldiers follow. Song, is there word from the governor? About the men they took?"

"A report will be sent to us as soon as they have something to tell."

Us. He considered commenting and decided he was too tired for a confrontation, and not sober enough. He didn't want to argue. He was thinking about his sister. And his brother.

"We're leaving at sunrise," he said. "And we'll be riding faster now. Please advise our soldiers from Iron Gate."

"Sunrise?" protested Sima Zian.

Tai looked at him.

The poet grinned wryly. "I'll manage," he said. "Send this one to wake me?"

Wei Song laughed. She actually laughed, flashing white teeth. "I'll do that happily, my lord," she said.

Unable to think of anything to say to that, either, Tai began walking. Sima Zian caught up with him. He showed no evidence of fatigue or the wine he'd drunk. It was unfair. Song walked behind them. Tai heard one of the governor's men snap a command as they lifted the empty sedan chair and hurried to follow.

Something occurred to him.

Without breaking stride or looking back, he said, "Song, how did those two men get inside?"

She said, "I had the same thought, my lord. I was guarding the back. There is an entrance there. I believed that soldiers of Governor Xu could stop anyone at the front. I have spoken with them about this failure. They know I will mention it to their commander."

It was difficult to catch her out, Tai thought. As it should be. She was a Kanlin, after all.

"They will not feel kindly towards you," the poet said. Zian glanced back at Song as they walked.

"I'm certain that is so," she said. Then, after a pause, she murmured, "I saw the fox-woman again, Master Shen. Near the laneway when you fought the soldiers."

"A fox-spirit? Inside the city?" The poet looked at her again. His tone had changed.

"Yes," she said.

"*No,*" Tai snapped in the same moment. "She saw a fox."

There was silence from the other two. Only their footsteps and distant noises from other streets. The city, Tai thought. He was in a city again, at night. By the waters of Kuala Nor the ghosts would be crying, with none to hear their voices.

"Ah. Well. Yes. A fox. I wonder," the Banished Immortal said thoughtfully, "if it will be possible to find an acceptable wine at this inn. I hope it isn't far."

THERE WAS NO MESSAGE from the governor when they reached the inn. Nor was there a room available for the poet. Song spoke to the attendant in the reception pavilion, and Zian was assigned her chamber.

She would sleep outside Tai's room again. The staff of the inn were embarrassed by the awkwardness, eager to provide a pallet on the covered portico. It wasn't unusual for guards to sleep outside doorways.

There was little Tai could do about it. The poet invited Song to share his room. She declined, more sweetly than Tai would have expected.

He stared at her as the attendant hurried off to give orders. "This is because of those two men?" he asked.

She hesitated. "Yes, of course. And your friend needs a chamber. It is only proper to—"

"It's the fox, isn't it?"

He couldn't say why that upset him so much. Anger was too easily his portion. He'd gone to Stone Drum Mountain, in part, because of that. He'd left for the same reason, in part.

She met his gaze, eyes defiant. They were still in the reception pavilion, no one else nearby.

"Yes," she said. "It is also that."

Kanlins, he recalled, were enjoined not to lie.

What was he going to say? It was unexpected on her part, given how controlled she was, otherwise. An embracing of folk legends, ancient tales, but she certainly wasn't alone in doing that.

The poet had wandered off through the first courtyard into the nearest pavilion, where music was still playing. As Tai glanced that way, Zian reappeared, grinning, carrying a flask of wine and two cups. He came back up the steps.

"Salmon River wine, if you can believe it! I am very happy."

Tai lifted a warding hand. "You will undo me. No more tonight."

The poet's smile grew wider. He quoted, *"At the very bottom of the last cup, at the end of night, joy is found."*

Tai shook his head. "Perhaps, but sunrise will also be found soon."

Sima Zian laughed. "I thought the same, so why go to bed at all?" He turned to Wei Song. "Keep the room, little Kanlin. I'll be with the musicians. I'm sure someone there will offer a pillow if I need one."

Song smiled at him again. "The chamber is yours, sir. Maybe the pillow—or the someone—will prove unsatisfactory. I have my place tonight."

The poet glanced at Tai. He nodded his head. He didn't look nearly intoxicated enough.

"I will instruct that any message from the governor tonight be brought to me." Song had the grace to bow to Tai. "If that is acceptable."

It probably shouldn't have been, but he was weary. Too much of too many things. *It is about your sister.*

He nodded. "Thank you, yes. You will wake me if you judge it proper."

"Of course."

Two servants carrying a rolled-up pallet appeared, moving briskly, managing to bow sideways as they passed. They hurried out to the courtyard, past lanterns, towards a building on the left. Zian went out after them, but turned right again, towards *pipa* music and flutes and a ripple of late-night laughter. There was, Tai saw, an eagerness to his stride.

Tai and Song followed the pallet the other way. It was set down on the covered portico of the first building, outside the closed door of his own chamber. The servants bowed again and hurried away, leaving them alone.

There were torches burning at intervals along the portico. Faintly, from the far side of the courtyard, they could hear the music. Tai looked at the stars. He thought about the last time Song had spent a night outside his room. He wondered if there was a bolt on the door.

He remembered that he'd meant to check on Dynlal before retiring. He could ask Song to do it, and she would, but it didn't feel right. She'd been awake as long as he had. It was unlikely to be necessary: one of the Iron Gate soldiers, that first one who'd seen Tai approaching, from up on the wall, hardly ever left the horse. Odds were good he was sleeping in the stables.

He didn't know where the other soldiers were ... sharing one of the larger rooms, most likely. They'd be long asleep by now.

Night clouds, thin moon, stars,
But a promise of the sun
Remaking the world,
Bringing mountains back.

In a way, Sima Zian had the right idea. Tai had spent entire nights drinking before, many times. With Spring Rain, with Yan and the other students and their women. He wasn't up to that tonight.

"You'll wake the men?" he asked Wei Song.

"I'll wake all of you before dawn."

"Just knock, for me," he said. He managed a smile.

She made no reply, just looked at him a moment, hesitating. When she stood so near, he realized how small she was.

"I'll go tell the stable hands to have the horses fed and watered before sunrise. We'll need a horse for Master Sima. And I'll look in on Dynlal." She bowed briefly, walked quickly down the three steps to the courtyard. He watched her crossing it.

She didn't look tired either, he thought.

He went into the room, closed the door. Then he stood, just inside, keeping extremely still.

After a moment he opened the door again. "Wait here," he said to the empty portico. "Come if I call you." He left the door ajar, turned back into the chamber.

It was her perfume that had registered.

That, and the amber glow in the room: three lamps were lit, which was extravagant, so late. The servants of the inn would not have done that.

There was another entrance, from the covered porch on the opposite side, a private space from which to look at flowers or the moon. The sliding, slatted doors had been pushed back, the room was open to the night. The gardens of the inn went all the way down to the river. Tai saw a star in the opening, quite bright, flickering.

She had changed her gown. She was wearing red now, gold threads in it, not the green of before. He wished it hadn't been red.

"Good evening," he said quietly to the daughter of Xu Bihai.

It was the older one, the one he'd liked: sideways-falling fashion of her hair, clever look in her eyes, an awareness of the effect she'd had, bending to pour wine. Her jewellery was unchanged, rings on many fingers.

The governor's daughter was sitting on the edge of his canopied bed, alone in the room. She wore gold, open-toed sandals. Her toenails were painted red, Tai saw. She smiled, stood up, moved towards him, exquisite.

It was still unfair, in almost every possible way.

"My Kanlin guard ... she's just outside the door," he lied.

"Then shouldn't we close it?" she asked. Her voice was low, amused. "Would you like me to do that? Is she dangerous?"

"No. No! Your father ... would be very unhappy if his daughter was in a closed bedchamber with a man."

"My father," she murmured, "sent me here."

Tai swallowed.

It was just possible. How urgently, how desperately, did the military leader of two western districts want to keep Tai—and his horses—from rivals? From Roshan, as an example. As the best example. What would he do to achieve that?

He'd given an answer, hadn't he, earlier tonight? *I would sooner kill you*, Xu Bihai had said, over saffron wine.

Was this—a lissome daughter sent to bind him—an alternative short of murder? It would preserve the horses for the empire. And for the Second and Third Military Districts. If Tai was killed the horses were lost. And Governor Xu, if known to have caused that to happen, was likely to be exiled, or ordered to end his life, for all his power and accomplishment.

But a man could be seduced by an elegant daughter with the worldly skills of well-bred women in Ninth Dynasty Kitai. Or he could be compromised, perhaps, forced to behave with honour after a night ... lacking honour, defined by skills. There was that possibility.

And daughters—*like sisters*—could be used as instruments.

He was not, he realized, tired any more.

The governor's daughter, tall, slender, came slowly up to him. Her perfume was delicious, expensive, disturbing, and the red gown was cut as low as the green one had been earlier tonight. A green dragon amulet still hung between her breasts on a golden chain.

Silk brushing against him, she glided past, to close the half-open door.

"Leave it! Please!" Tai said.

She smiled again. She turned towards him, very close. Large eyes, looking up, claimed his. Her painted eyebrows were shaped like moth wings. Her skin was flawless, cheeks tinted with vermilion. She said, softly, "She might become envious or aroused, your Kanlin woman, if we leave the door ajar. Would you like that? Would that add to your pleasure, sir? To imagine her looking in upon us from the dark?"

If, Tai thought, a little desperately, she was doing this on the instructions of her father, she was a very dutiful daughter.

"I ... I have already been to the White Phoenix Pleasure House tonight," he stammered.

Not the most poised or courteous thing to say. Her fingernails were also red, and they had golden extensions, a fashion he remembered from two years ago in Xinan. The fashion had reached this far west. That was ... that was interesting, Tai thought.

It wasn't, really. He wasn't thinking very clearly.

Her breath was sweet, scented with cloves. She said, "I know where you were. They are said to be well trained, the girls there. Worth the cost to any man." She cast her eyes down, as if shyly. "But it is not the same, you know it, my lord, as when you are with a well-born woman you have not bought. A woman who has risked a great deal to come to you, and waits to be taught what you know."

Her right hand moved, and one of those golden fingernails stroked the back of his hand, and then, as if carelessly, moved slowly up the inside of his forearm. Tai shivered. He didn't believe there was a great deal this one needed to be taught. Not by him, not by anyone.

He closed his eyes. Took a steadying breath and said, "I know this is foolish, but are you … could a *daiji* be within you?"

"That took longer than it should have!"

A third voice—from the small porch leading to the garden and the river.

Tai and the governor's daughter turned, very quickly.

Wei Song stood framed in the space between the sliding doors. One sword was drawn, levelled at the girl.

"I can be a little dangerous," he heard his Kanlin Warrior say calmly. She wasn't smiling.

The other woman lifted shaped eyebrows, then turned, very deliberately, away from Song, as if from someone inconsequential.

"My name," she said to Tai, "is Xu Liang. You know it. My father introduced us tonight. I am flattered you think me fair enough to be a *daiji* spirit, but it is an error. It would be another error if your woman-servant harmed me."

It was said with the utmost composure. There really was something, Tai thought, about being well-born. You could call Kanlin Warriors woman-servants, for one thing.

It is an error. He glanced towards the porch. Song was biting her lower lip; he doubted she was aware of it. He was trying to remember if he had ever seen her look this uncertain before. It might have been diverting at any other time. She kept her sword levelled, but without force or conviction now, he saw.

He was still trying to define a proper target for his own rising outrage. Was there *no* privacy in a man's life when he travelled with a guard? Or, for that matter, when some military leader encountered on the road decided to bind him with a daughter? Everyone could just wander into his room as they pleased, when they pleased, day or night, eliciting embarrassing fears of shape-changing spirits?

The daughter in question murmured, still not bothering to look at Song, "Did you not see my guards, Kanlin, in the garden? They rowed me here, to the water gate of the inn. I am surprised, and a little unhappy, that neither of them has killed you yet."

"It would be difficult for them, my lady. They are unconscious, by the trees."

"You *attacked* them?"

She turned to glare at Song. Her anger was pretty clearly unfeigned, Tai decided. Her hands were rigid at her sides.

"I found them that way," Wei Song said, after a hesitation.

Lady Xu Liang's mouth opened.

"They are not dead," Song added. "No blows that I could see, no cups or flasks for poison, and they are breathing. If you have not been claimed by a fox-spirit, governor's daughter, and used for her purposes, it may be ... because something kept the *daiji* away."

Tai had no idea what to make of this. Shape-shifting fox-women were the subject of erotic legends going back to the earliest dynasties. Their beauty impossibly alluring, their physical needs extreme. Men could be destroyed by them, but in such a manner, spun of world-changing desire, that the tales aroused fear *and* inchoate longings.

Further, not every man made the nighttime recipient of a *daiji's* fierce hunger was destroyed. Some of the tales suggested otherwise, memorably.

Wei Song hadn't yet lowered her blade. Tai said, first of half a dozen questions jostling in his head, "How did you know to come back?"

She shrugged. "You couldn't smell that much perfume through the door?" A cool glance at the governor's daughter. "And I was quite certain you hadn't asked for another courtesan. You did say you were tired. Remember, my lord?"

He knew that tone.

Xu Liang folded her arms across her low-cut gown. She looked younger suddenly. Tai made his decision. This was not a girl possessed by a fox-spirit that had chosen to make use of her body— and his—for what was left of tonight. He didn't even *believe* in fox-women.

That did mean, if you were functioning well enough to consider the matter, that the governor's older daughter was remarkably seductive and alarmingly poised. He'd address that issue later.

Or, perhaps better, he wouldn't.

He concentrated on his black-clad guard, not much older than Xu's daughter. "So you went …?"

Song rattled it off impatiently. "I came back around on the garden side. I saw the two guards in the grass." She looked at Liang. "I never touched them."

The governor's daughter looked uneasy for the first time. "Then what? How were they …?"

A footfall on the porch, behind Wei Song.

"I'd have to agree it was probably a *daiji*," said Sima Zian.

The poet came up the steps into the room. "I just had a look at the two of them."

Tai blinked, then shook his head in indignation.

"Shall we," he asked caustically, "wake our soldiers and invite them in? Oh, and perhaps the governor's men out front might want to join us?"

"Why not?" grinned Zian.

"*No!*" said Xu Liang. "Not my father's guards!"

"Why? You said his soldiers brought you here. It won't be a secret," Song said dryly. These two, Tai realized, had decided not to like each other.

"You are wrong, again, Kanlin. It *is* secret, my being here. Of course it is! The two in the garden are men I can trust," Liang said. "My own guards all my life. If they have been slain …"

"They are not dead," the poet said. He looked around. Probably hoping for wine, Tai thought. "If I were to shape a conjecture, and I confess I enjoy doing that, I would say that Master Shen was the target of a *daiji*, that our clever Kanlin is correct." He smiled at Song, and then at the governor's daughter. "Your arrival, gracious lady, was exquisitely timed for the fox-spirit—or was guided by her." He paused, to let that thought linger. "But something here, perhaps within our friend, kept the spirit away—from him, and from you. If I am correct, you have cause to be grateful."

"And what would *something* be?" asked Xu Liang. Her painted eyebrows were arched again. They really were exquisite.

"This is ... this is nothing but conjecture!" Tai snapped.

"I did say that," Sima Zian agreed calmly. "But I also asked if you saw ghosts at the White Phoenix tonight, when first we spoke."

"You are saying that you did?"

"No. I have only a limited access to the spirit world, my friend. But enough to sense something about you."

"You mean from Kuala Nor? The ghosts?"

It was Wei Song this time, her brow furrowed. She was biting her lower lip again.

"Perhaps," said the Banished Immortal. "I would not know." He was looking at Tai, waiting.

Another lake, far to the north. A cabin there. A dead shaman in the garden, mirrors and drum. Fires, and then a man, or what had once been a man ...

Tai shook his head. He was not about to speak of this.

When pressed, ask a question. "What could my being at Kuala Nor possibly mean to a *daiji*?"

The poet shrugged, accepted the deflection. "You might draw one as you passed by. She could become aware of your presence, conscious of those protecting you, hovering."

"There are spirits attending upon Master Shen?"

Xu Liang didn't sound fearful. You could say, if you wanted, that she appeared to find the notion intriguing, engaging. She'd uncrossed her arms again, was looking at Tai. Another appraising glance, not dissimilar to ones she'd given him from by the door in her father's reception room.

He really had been away from women too long.

"There are spirits near *all* of us," Song said from the porch, a little too emphatically. "Whether we see them or not. The Way of the Sacred Path teaches as much."

"And the *Dialogues* of Master Cho assert that this is not so," murmured the woman in the red gown. "Only our ancestors are near us, and *only* if they were improperly consecrated to the next world when they died. Which is the reason for our rituals."

Sima Zian glanced happily from one woman to the other. He clapped his hands. "You are both splendid beyond description! This is a wonderful night. We must find wine!" he cried. "Let us continue this across the way, there is music."

"I am *not* entering a courtesan pavilion!" said Xu Bihai's daughter with immediate, impressive propriety.

The fact that she was standing, scented and bejewelled, in a man's bedchamber and had been on the verge of closing the door (lest someone be made envious by what was apparently to transpire) seemed entirely beside the point, Tai thought, admiringly.

"Of course! Of course you aren't," the poet murmured. "Forgive me, gracious lady. We'll bring a *pipa* player here. And perhaps just one girl, with cups and wine?"

"I think not," said Tai. "I believe that Wei Song will now escort the Lady Xu Liang back to her father's mansion. Is the boat waiting for you?"

"Of course it is," Liang said. "But my guards ..."

Tai cleared his throat. "It appears, if Sima Zian is correct, and my Kanlin, that they may have encountered a spirit-world creature. I have no better explanation. We are told they are alive."

"I will return and watch over them myself," Song said, "and tell them when they wake that their lady is home and well."

"They won't believe you if I'm not here," Xu Liang said.

"I'm a Kanlin," said Song simply. "We do not lie. They will know that, if others, less experienced, do not."

The poet, Tai thought, looked ridiculously pleased by all of this.

Liang, he realized, was looking at him again, ignoring the other woman. Tai didn't entirely mind that. He was briefly tempted by the notion of agreeing with Zian, summoning music and wine.

But not really. His sister was a long way north, beyond the Wall by now. And tonight, here in Chenyao, men had—

"I did say earlier," Xu Liang murmured, eyes demurely downcast, "that my father had sent me. You have not asked why."

Indeed. Well, he'd had what seemed a good notion why.

"My apologies." He bowed. "Is it permitted for your servant to ask now?"

She nodded. "It is. My father wished to advise you privately that those two men, when encouraged to discuss their adventurism tonight, suggested only one name of possible significance before they each succumbed, sadly, to the exacting nature of the conversation."

She looked meaningfully at the poet, and then at Song on the porch. Tai understood. "One is my guard," he said. "The other my companion."

Liang inclined her head. She said, "The assassins were bandits from the woods south of here. The man they named lives in Chenyao. He, in turn, when invited for a conversation, was kind enough to offer another name—from Xinan—before lamentably expiring."

Tai was listening very closely. "I see. And that other name is?"

She was crisp, efficient. She said, "Xin Lun—a civil servant at court, we understand—was the name given. My honoured father offers his deepest regret that he was unable to be of greater assistance, but dares to hope this will be of some use to Master Shen."

Xin Lun. Again. Yan had spoken that name before he died. He'd been killed as he said it.

Lun. Drinking companion, fellow student, convivial and clever. Not a student any more, it seemed. If he was in the palace he'd passed the examinations while Tai was away. A card and dice player once, ballad singer at night, a lover of—as it happened—Salmon River wine. Wearing the robes of a mandarin now.

Because of Yan, it wasn't a revelation, not devastating news of betrayal. More a confirmation, an echo. He'd been waiting for a different name, perhaps two, behind these assassins ... and had been deeply afraid to hear one of them spoken aloud.

He showed none of this in his face, he hoped.

He bowed to the governor's daughter. "My thanks to your father. And to you, gracious lady, bearing these tidings so late at night. I do understand why Governor Xu would not trust them to anyone else."

"Of course he wouldn't," she murmured.

She looked directly at him as she said it, then let that slow smile shape her lips, as if the guard and the poet weren't in the room. As if she and Tai were continuing a conversation interrupted earlier, and *so* unpleasantly, by another girl with a blade.

THE OTHER GIRL escorted her out the sliding doors and through the garden. Sima Zian walked them down to the river. Standing on the porch, Tai watched the three of them go towards the trees and the water beyond. He lost them in the dark, then saw the one man come back a short time later and head across towards the music again, head lifted, steps quickening, hearing it.

Tai waited in silence for a time, listening to the night. He caught the scent of flowers, citrus. There were peonies. A slight breeze from the north, towards the river. The stars that ended the night this time of year were rising.

"Daiji?" he called, greatly, recklessly daring.

He couldn't say why, but it felt as if there might be an answer to something, to *part* of this story, out in the garden.

Nothing stirred in the dark but fireflies. *Flashing go the night-travellers.* The old song about them. He thought of the tale of the poor scholar who could not afford oil for lanterns, gathering fireflies in a bag each evening, studying by their light. They used to joke about that story, in Xinan, the students. Chou Yan, Xin Lun, Shen Tai, the others.

There were other night-travellers tonight. He wondered where his sister was, where in a too-wide world. A hard pull upon the heart. His father was dead. This would not have happened, otherwise.

Deaths, even quiet ones, had consequences.

Three men had died in Chenyao tonight under questioning. For attempting to have him killed.

No movement in the garden, no approach to his call, his foolishness. He didn't believe there had been a fox-creature following him, though it was interesting that Wei Song seemed to fear them. He hadn't noticed her biting her lower lip that way before. He had thoughts about how those two guards had ended up unconscious.

Wind in leaves. Distant music. The bright, low star he'd seen before was still there. It felt as if a great deal of time had passed since he'd come into this room, but it wasn't so.

Tai didn't call again. He turned and went back inside. He washed and dried himself using the filled water basin and towel. He undressed, put out the three lights burning in the room, drew the sliding doors and hooked them shut. Some air came in through the slats, which was good. He closed the main door, which was still ajar.

He went to bed.

A little later, drifting towards sleep as to the shore of another country, he suddenly sat up in the nearly black room and swore aloud. He half expected to hear Song from the portico asking what was wrong, but she wouldn't be back from the governor's mansion yet.

They couldn't leave at sunrise. He'd just realized it.

It was not possible. Not in the empire of the Ninth Dynasty.

He had to visit the prefect tomorrow morning. *Had* to. They were to take a morning meal together. It had been arranged. If he didn't attend, if he simply rode off, it would bring lasting shame upon himself, and upon his father's memory.

Neither the poet nor the Kanlin would say a word to refute this. They wouldn't even think to try. It was a truth of their world, for good or ill. As much a part of it—this ritualized, unyielding, defining formality—as poetry was, or silk, or sculpted jade, palace intrigues, students and courtesans, Heavenly Horses, *pipa* music, or unburied tens of thousands upon a battlefield.

CHAPTER XII

They are walking east in the night, around the shore of the small lake, then ascending the slopes of the hills that frame it on the far side. No one has followed them. The wind is from the north.

Li-Mei looks back. The campfires glow. They seem fragile, precarious, in the vastness stretching in all directions. The firelit presence of men—some women are down there, but not her, not her any more—surrounded by all of night and the world.

It is cold in the wind. Swiftly moving clouds, then stars. Deerskin riding boots are better than jewelled slippers, but are not adequate to this steady walking. The wolves keep pace on either side. She is still trying not to look at them.

The man has not said a word since they walked out of the camp. She hasn't seen him clearly yet. She needs more light. His strides are long, ground-covering, though somehow awkward, stiff. She wonders if it is because he's accustomed to riding. Most of the Bogü are. He walks in front, not bothering to see if she is keeping pace or has tried to run away. He doesn't need to do that. He has the wolves.

She has no idea where they are going or why he is doing this. Why he has come for her, and not the real princess. It is possible that this is a mistake on his part, one that their guards permitted, encouraged, to protect the bride of the kaghan.

Loyalty, Li-Mei thinks, requires that she continue the deception, let the princess get as far away as possible. She doesn't think he intends to kill her. He could have done so by now if that was why he was here. Nor does this feel like someone seeing a chance of wealth, kidnapping Kitan royalty. That had been her thought, waiting in the yurt, holding a knife in the blackness. Kidnapping isn't uncommon back home, in the wild country along the Great River gorges, certainly. But she doesn't think this is a man looking for money.

He may ... he may want her body. Difficult to shield that thought. The allure of a Kitan woman, the exciting mystery of strangeness. This might be that sort of abduction. But again, she doesn't think it is. He has hardly even looked at her.

No, this is different: because of the wolves and the silence of the wolfhounds when he came for her. There is something else happening here. Li-Mei has prided herself all her life (had been praised by her father for it, if ruefully) on being more curious and thoughtful than most women. More than most men, he'd added once. She has remembered that moment: where they were, how he looked at her, saying it.

She is skilled at grasping new situations and changing ones, the nuances of men and women in veiled, elusive exchanges. She'd even developed a sense of the court, of manoeuvrings for power in her time with the empress, before they were exiled and it stopped mattering.

Her father hadn't been this way. She has the trait, very likely, from whatever source her oldest brother does. Though she doesn't want to think about Liu, acknowledge any kinship, any sharing, with him.

She wants him dead.

What she also wants, what she needs, is a rest just now, and to be warmer. The wind, since they have climbed higher—skirting the steepest of the hills, but still ascending—is numbing her. She is not dressed for a night walk on the steppe and she has carried nothing with her at all, except a small knife in her sleeve.

She makes a decision. Inwardly, she shrugs. There are many ways to die. As many, the teachings tell, as there are ways to live. She'd never thought about being torn apart by wolves, or ripped open in some Bogü sacrifice on the plain, but ...

"Stop!" she says, not loudly, but very clearly.

It does sound too much like a command, in the huge silence of the night. It is mostly fear, infusing her voice.

He ignores her, keeps moving. So, after a few steps to consider that, Li-Mei stops walking.

Being ignored is not something she's ever been inclined to accept, from girlhood. They are on a ridge. The lake lies to their left and below, the moon shows it to her. There is beauty here for a landscape painter. Not for her, not now.

The nearest wolf also stops.

He pads towards her. He looks directly at Li-Mei, the eyes glowing the way they do in tales. One of the things that is true, she thinks. His jaws open, teeth showing. He takes two more silent steps nearer. Too near. This is a *wolf*. She is alone.

She does not weep. The wind is making her eyes tear, but that is an entirely different thing. She will not cry unless driven to a deeper abyss than this.

She resumes walking, moving past the animal. She does close her eyes in that moment. The wolf could shred her flesh with a twist of his head. The man has slowed, she sees, to let her and the animal catch up again. He still has not looked back. He seems to know what has happened, however.

She doesn't know anything, and it can be called intolerable.

Li-Mei takes a deep breath. She stops again. So, beside her, does the wolf. She will not look at it. She calls out, "If you intend to kill me, do it now."

No reply. But he stops this time. He does do that. Does this mean he understands her? She says, "I am very cold, and I have no idea where you intend to walk like this, how far. I will not willingly go farther unless you tell me what this is. Am I being abducted for money?"

He turns around.

She has achieved that much, she thinks.

For a long moment they stand like that in the night, ten paces apart. She still cannot make out his features, the moon is not enough. *Does it matter?* she thinks. He is a big man for a Bogü, long arms. He is bare-chested, even in this wind, his loose hair whipped around his face by it. He will not be sympathetic, Li-Mei thinks, to a claim of being cold. He is gazing at her. She cannot see his eyes.

"*Shandai,*" he says. She is shocked. The fact of speech. "You follow. Shelter. Horse." He says this in Kitan. Awkwardly, but in her tongue.

He has already turned away again, as if this terse handful of words is all he feels capable of saying, or inclined to say. A man unused to speech, explaining himself. Well, he would be, she thinks, glancing at the wolves.

"Shandai?" she repeats. "That is ... where we are going?" She had not looked at any maps before they set out. Regrets it now.

He stops again. Turns, slowly. She can see the stiffness in his posture. He shakes his head impatiently. "*Shandai!*" he says again, more forcefully. "Why this. Why you. Come! Bogü will follow. Shaman."

She knows what a shaman is. She'd thought he might be one.

He starts walking again, and she does the same. She is working on it, puzzling it out. She doesn't feel as cold now, or even tired, with a thought to pursue. He doesn't want to be caught by a shaman. That seems reasonably clear. Her guards had had none, and feared him. A shaman ... will not?

Some time later, directly ahead, she sees the first grey begin to soften the sky, then there is a pale band, and pink. Morning. She looks around. Mist, rising. A rolling away of grass in all directions, between them and every horizon.

Married to a distant horizon.

Perhaps not. Perhaps a different tale?

Just before the sun rose in front of them, making bright the tall grass and the world, under heaven, she understood the word he'd spoken to her.

॰∞॰

The imperial way, running utterly straight for eighteen *li* through the exact centre of Xinan, from the main gate of the Ta-Ming Palace to the southern walls, was four hundred and ninety paces wide.

There was no thoroughfare so broad and magnificent in the empire or the world. It had been designed to overawe and intimidate, proclaim majesty and power on a scale worthy of the emperors ruling here in glory with the mandate of the gods, and as a reasonably effective firebreak.

It was also difficult for anyone to cross, after curfew, without being seen by one of the Gold Bird Guards stationed at every intersection.

You had to run a *long* way, without any hint of concealment.

Thirty of the guards were at all important crossroads (there were fourteen major east-west roads), five guards at the smaller ones. You faced thirty lashes with the medium rod if found on a major roadway after the drumbeats sounded to lock the ninety-one wards. The night guards were authorized to kill, if one ignored a command to halt.

Order in the capital was a priority of the court. With two million inhabitants, and vivid memories of famine and violent unrest, this was only sensible. Within the wards—each one enclosed by its own rammed-earth walls—one could be abroad after dark, of course, else taverns and pleasure houses and the local dining places, peddlers and snack wagons, men selling firewood and lamp oil and cooking oil, would have had no trade. They did their best business after the two huge city markets closed. You couldn't slam a city shut at night, but you could control it. And defend it.

The massive outer walls were four times the height of a man. A hundred of the Gold Bird Guards manned the towers above every major gate, day and night, with twenty at the lesser ones. There were three very large gateways through the walls to east and south and west, and half a dozen to the north, four of them opening into the palace courtyards, the administrative offices attached, and the emperor's vast Deer Park.

Four canals flowed into the city, diverted from the river to provide drinking and washing water, irrigate the city-gardens of the aristocracy (and create lakes for the larger gardens). One canal was assigned to floating in logs for the endless construction and repair and to carrying flat barges with coal and firewood. At the point where each canal came through the walls there were another hundred guards.

Being found in a canal was punished with sixty lashes if it happened after dark. If found in the water by daylight, without an acknowledged labour (such as shifting the logs if they piled up), the punishment was thirty. It was also recognized that men, drunk at sunrise after a long night, could fall into the water without ill intent. The Emperor Taizu, Lord of the Five Directions, was a merciful ruler, ever mindful of his subjects.

Less than thirty lashes with the rod seldom killed, or caused permanent incapacity.

Of course few of these rules and restrictions applied to aristocrats, to imperial couriers, or to the black-clad civil service mandarins from the Purple Myrtle Court—the crows—with their keys and seals of office. Ward gates would be opened or closed for them on command if they were abroad on horseback or in carried litters during the dark hours.

The North District, home to the best pleasure houses, was accustomed to late arrivals from the Ta-Ming and its administrative palaces: hard-working civil servants from the Censorate or the Ministry of Revenue, finally free of their memoranda and calligraphy, or elegantly attired noblemen exiting city mansions (or the palace itself), more than slightly drunk, seeing no compelling reason not to prolong an evening with music and silken girls.

Sometimes it might be a woman travelling one of the wide streets in a discreet sedan chair, curtains drawn, an anonymously clad officer of her household alongside to deal with the Gold Bird Guards and shield her assignation.

In Xinan, after darkfall, it was fair to say that someone on a main thoroughfare was—if not an officer of the guard—either at risk, or part of the court.

Prime Minister Wen Zhou normally took pleasure in riding his favourite grey horse down the very centre of the imperial way at night. It made him feel as if he *owned* Xinan, to be so conspicuously at ease, a powerful, handsome, richly dressed aristocrat proceeding south from the palace to his city mansion under moon or stars. He had guards with him, of course, but if they kept behind and to either side he could imagine himself alone in the imperial city.

The distant outer edges of the road had been planted with juniper and pagoda trees by the present emperor's father, to hide the drainage ditches. There were beds of peonies—king of flowers—running between the lamplit guard stations, offering their scent to the night in springtime. There was beauty and a vast grandeur to the imperial way under the stars.

But this particular night, First Minister Wen found no pleasure in his night ride.

He'd been afflicted with such anxiety (he would *not* call it fear) this evening—after his cousin's dance in that upper chamber of the Ta-Ming—that he'd felt an urgent need to remove himself from the palace lest one of the appallingly astute figures of court or civil service note apprehension in his features. That would not be acceptable. Not in a first minister (and president of seven ministries) in his first year of office.

He could have asked Shen Liu to come home with him, and Liu would have done that, but tonight he didn't want even his principal adviser beside him. He didn't want to look at that smooth, unforthcoming face, not when he felt his own features to be revealing depths of indecision.

He trusted Liu: the man owed everything to Wen Zhou, his own fate by now completely tied to the first minister's. But that wasn't always the point. Sometimes you didn't want your counsellors to see too clearly into you, and Liu had a habit of appearing able to do that, while revealing next to nothing of himself.

The first minister had other advisers, of course, a vast bureaucratic army at his disposal. He had done his own investigations, had learned a good deal about Liu—and his family—some of it complex, some of it unexpected.

Liu's subtlety made him enormously useful, because he could read others in the palace with acuity, but it also meant there were times when you were just as happy to arrange for morning attendance from the man, and spend the night with others.

Zhou had to decide if he wanted Spring Rain alone tonight or to pair her with one of his other women. He was angry and uneasy, that might affect what he needed. He reminded himself, again, not to use—even in his mind—her name from the North District. He was the one who had changed it, after all.

He looked around. Not far now from his ward gates.

His home in Xinan, provided by the emperor, was in the fifty-seventh ward, east of the imperial way, halfway down. There lay many of the most luxurious properties in the city.

Including, as of this same night's proclamation by the emperor, the newest mansion of the military governor of the Seventh, Eighth, and Ninth Districts: An Li, widely known as Roshan.

Whom Wen Zhou hated and feared and wished dead—in all his bloated grossness—and consumed by eyeless, crawling creatures without names.

His hands tightened on the reins, and the high-strung horse reacted, pacing sideways restively. Zhou handled it easily. He was a superb rider, a polo player, enjoyed speed, and the most challenging horses. Enjoyed them more than, say, calligraphy displays or landscape painting or poetry improvised in a palace room. Dancing, he'd concede, was pleasant enough if the dancer was even nearly as skilled—or as stunningly desirable—as his cousin.

His cousin, who had changed the empire. Jian, to whom he owed everything he was now and everything he had. But who refused, capriciously, to be unequivocal in supporting him against a monstrous general's obvious ambition. She'd even adopted Roshan as her child some months ago! What game—what *possible* woman's game—was she playing at?

The obese barbarian had to be thirty years older than her. His odious *sons* were older than her! The adoption had been a frivolity, Zhou had to assume, meant to divert the court—and the emperor.

The first minister was among those who had not found it diverting. From the moment Chin Hai had died and Zhou had manoeuvred swiftly from his position as president of the Ministries of Revenue and Punishment to succeed him, he had been aware that An Li was his greatest danger—among many.

Roshan, with Chin Hai gone, was like a beast of the jungle uncaged. And why, *why* did the emperor and his exquisite concubine not see that, beneath the clownish act Roshan offered them?

Zhou forced himself to be calmer, if only for the horse. He looked up at stars, the waning moon, racing clouds. He was saluted by the next set of guards as he approached their station. He nodded vaguely to them, a straight-backed, broad-shouldered, impressive man.

It occurred to him, undermining any movement towards tranquility, that if he was—and he *was*—contemplating having his enemy ruined or killed, it was possible that Roshan was shaping similar thoughts about him.

These night rides from the palace might become less prudent, going forward. It was a consideration to be weighed. In fact ... he gestured his guards in closer. Motioned one to ride ahead. They were nearly at their gate: someone would need to signal for admittance.

Even in the presence of the emperor, Roshan seemed to know no fear, inhibition, no idea of restraint—his very bulk suggested as much. He had been mortally afraid of Chin Hai, however, would break out in a sweat if Prime Minister Chin spoke to him, if they were even in the same room. Zhou had seen it, more than once.

No great surprise, that terror; everyone had feared Chin Hai.

Whatever any man might accuse Zhou of doing since accepting office—in the way of choosing persons for exile or elimination, with formal design, randomly, or for a personal reason—no one could honestly suggest that he was *introducing* this as a feature of government. Not after what Chin Hai had done for most of the emperor's reign.

It was Shen Liu, his so-clever adviser, who had pointed this out, not long after Zhou had been appointed to succeed the one called (privately) the Spider. Some men simply had to be dealt with, Liu had said, if one were to properly discharge the duties of office and establish the proper tone as first minister.

If one were new, and relatively young—and Wen Zhou was both—weakness might be anticipated, and probed, by some within the court, the wider empire, or abroad. Any such misconception on their part needed to be swiftly addressed.

A measure of effectively employed terror, Liu had suggested, was almost always useful.

One might argue, he'd added, that it was imperative in challenging times. Kitai might be wealthy beyond description, but that could make it more vulnerable to destructive ambition, more in need of loyal men to have narrow eyes and suspicious hearts. To be cold and vigilant while others played at polo games, wrote poems, danced to foreign music, ate golden peaches brought from far corners of the world, built lakes in private gardens, or used extravagantly expensive sandalwood for the panels of pavilions.

Polo was Wen Zhou's favoured sport. Sandalwood, he happened to believe, was entirely proper for a display of wealth. He had it in the walls of his bedchamber. And the man-made lake behind his mansion had jade and ivory rocks on the island built within it. When he had guests for a party, courtesans hired from the best houses would play music from that isle, dressed like creatures from legend. Once they'd worn kingfisher feathers, rarer, more expensive than jade.

But the new first minister had taken Liu's central point: a firm hand was needed for the Ta-Ming Palace and the civil service and the army. Perhaps especially the army. Chin Hai, fearing the aristocrats in his own early days, had gradually placed barbarian generals in many of the military governorships. It had made him safer (what could an illiterate foreigner, who owed him everything, aspire to be, or do?), but there were consequences. All the more so since the celestial emperor (may he live a thousand years!) was older now, distracted, less firmly attentive to imperial matters, month by month, day over day.

Night after night.

It was widely known that Roshan had sent the emperor an alchemist's potion shortly after Taizu had summoned his very young Precious Consort to the palace and installed her there. Shortly *before* the illustrious empress was gently persuaded to take up her new residence at a Temple of the Path outside Xinan.

Wen Zhou wished—he so dearly wished—he'd thought of sending that potion himself. Firmness. You could make a joke about firmness.

He didn't feel amused or amusing. Not tonight. The city palace just given as a gift this evening (another gift!) to the pustulent barbarian toad was Chin Hai's own mansion, conspicuously uninhabited in the nine months since he'd died.

What did it *mean* that it had now gone, in its unrivalled splendour and notoriety (tales of interrogation chambers underground, walls made proof against screaming), to the military governor of three districts and their hard, trained armies in the northeast? A man who was scarcely ever in Xinan to even make use of the mansion? Did the emperor, did Zhou's empty-headed cousin, did no one realize what sort of message this sent?

Or, rather more frightening, did they realize it?

The ward guards recognized them, of course. There was a shout and a signal from atop the wall. Men began hastily unbarring the gates as the first minister and his men approached, angling across the imperial way. Not the best ward security, perhaps, but mildly gratifying, the alacrity—and fear—with which they responded to his presence.

He should be used to it by now, perhaps, but why did becoming accustomed to something have to render its pleasures stale? Could one of the philosophers answer him that? He still enjoyed saffron wine, and being serviced by women, did he not?

Passing through, he asked casually, addressing the night, not deigning to look anywhere near an actual person, who else had come through after curfew. He always asked them that.

Someone answered. Two names. Neither one, for different reasons, brought Zhou any of the pleasure he'd just been thinking about. He rode on, heard orders behind him, the gates creaking closed, the heavy bar sliding.

Even here, within the ward, the main east-west street running between the gates at each end was sixty-five paces wide. Long expanses of wall on either side, lanterns at intervals, shade trees planted by mansion owners. The walls were interrupted on the north side of the street by the massive doors of homes that were better described as palaces. To his right there were only occasional servant-doorways: back-garden exits from someone's property. All front doors faced south, of course.

He saw the second of the men who had come through earlier, waiting in a sedan chair with the curtains back so he could be seen and known under the lanterns hanging by the doors of Zhou's own home.

He hadn't intended, or desired, to see this man tonight, and his principal adviser would have known that. Which meant that if Liu was here, something had happened. Something even more than the disturbing news they'd heard this evening, of the gift given to Roshan.

Roshan himself was the other man who'd passed through after nightfall. Come, undoubtedly, to boastfully luxuriate in his newest extravagant possession: a city palace larger, and more potently symbol-laden, than any other in Xinan.

Perhaps, Zhou thought, he could ride over there himself, suggest a drink by way of celebration, poison the wine.

Roshan drank very little. He had the sugar sickness. Zhou wished it would kill him already. He suddenly wondered who the governor's personal physician was. It was a thought ...

Chin Hai's former mansion was only a short distance on horse-back, two streets over and one north from here. The property was gigantic, even by the standards of an aristocratic neighbourhood: it stretched all the way to the northern wall of the ward—the southern border of the fifty-third. There were rumours that a tunnel went beneath the wall into the fifty-third.

The mansion's servants had been kept on, he knew, paid by the court, even with no one living there. The pavilions and rooms and furnishings, the courtyards, gardens, banquet halls, women's quarters, all would have been impeccably maintained, awaiting whoever might be honoured—exalted!—at the whim of the emperor with the dead prime minister's home.

Well, now they knew.

Zhou swung down from his horse, tossed the reins to one of the servants who hurried up, bowing. The doors were open, wide enough for a carriage and horses. The first courtyard was brightly lit, welcoming. His own was an entirely magnificent home. It just wasn't …

Seeing the first minister dismount, Liu stepped out of his sedan chair. There was mud in the roadway from rain the night before. His adviser placed his feet carefully, a fastidious man. Zhou found it amusing. The prime minister, booted, accustomed to polo and hunting, utterly unfazed by dirt and mud, strode over to him.

"He came through the gates just before you," he said. There was no need to say the name.

Shen Liu nodded. "I know. I asked."

"I thought of riding over to welcome him to his new home. Bring poisoned wine."

Liu's face took on a pained expression, as if his stomach were ailing him, one of the few ways he revealed himself. His adviser carefully restrained himself from glancing around to see who among the guards or servants might have heard. Zhou didn't care. Let the gross barbarian know what the first minister of Kitai thought of him and his too-obvious designs.

As if Roshan didn't know already.

"What are you doing here?" he asked. "I said you were to come in the morning."

"I received tidings," Liu murmured. "Or, I was advised of tidings that have come to the palace."

"And I needed to know this tonight?"

Liu shrugged. *Obviously*, was the import of the gesture.

He was an irritating man, and disturbingly close to indispensable. Wen Zhou turned and strode through his open doors into the courtyard, splashing through a puddle. He crossed and entered the first reception hall and then the private room beside it. Servants sprang to action. An interval passed in which boots became slippers, court garb turned into a silk robe for a night at home, and cypress-leaf wine was warmed on a brazier. Liu waited in the adjacent chamber.

There was music from a pavilion across another small courtyard, a more intimate reception room with a bedchamber attached. Spring Rain was playing her *pipa* for him, having awaited his arrival as she always did. She would be adorned with jewellery, he knew, her hair exquisitely pinned, her face painted. Waiting for him. His.

Her name was Lin Chang now, a change made on his own order once he'd brought her here. It was far more suited to her status as a concubine of the first minister of Kitai. He hadn't been able to stop thinking of her by the North District name yet. Not that it mattered.

She belonged to him, and would wait. It was her role. Although, looked at another way, *he* was going to have to wait until whatever Liu had on his mind tonight was shared.

The prime minister decided that he was likely to remain in a troubled mood. He walked back into the reception chamber, was handed the wine. He sipped. Threw the cup down. It bounced and rolled against a wall.

The servant, cringing and bowing, almost to the floor, mumbling desperate apologies, scurried to the brazier and added coal to the flame below. He crawled over and picked up the discarded cup. His hands were shaking. There were stains on the carpeting.

The first minister had made extremely clear by now his preference as to the temperature of his wine at night (which was not the same as in the morning or at midday). Servants were required to know these things or accept consequences. Consequences, in at least one case, had left a man crippled and dismissed. He begged in the street now, behind the mansion. Someone had told Zhou that.

The *pipa* music continued from across the small courtyard. The sliding doors were open, window shutters were folded back on a mild night. The silk-paper windows did little to keep out sound. He thought about silencing the instrument, but the music was beautiful—and promised a mood very different from this one, once he'd dealt with Liu.

He gestured, Shen Liu took one side of the platform. Zhou sat opposite, cross-legged. A breeze, music, late night. The two men waited. The servant, bowing three full times, eyes never leaving the floor, brought the wine again and extended it with both hands. Wen Zhou tasted.

He didn't nod, he didn't need to. Keeping the cup was sufficient. The servant poured for Liu, backed up, bowing all the way to the edge of the room. He was expecting to be beaten later. The wine had been too cool. Zhou looked at his adviser, and nodded permission to speak.

"What do you think happens," Liu asked, his round face placid, as usual, "when we make jests about killing him?"

He hadn't expected that as a start. "*We* don't," Wen Zhou said coldly. "I do. Unless you have become a humorist when I am not present?"

Liu shook his head.

"I thought not. What happens," the prime minister went on, his mood congealing further, "is that I amuse myself."

"Of course, my lord," said Liu.

He said nothing more. He'd made his accursed point: sometimes you weren't allowed to amuse yourself.

Zhou was inclined to disagree. If he wanted a woman or a horse, they were his until he grew tired of them. If he wanted a man dead he could have him killed. Why else *be* what he was? This came with his power, defined it.

"Why are you here?" he growled. He gestured, the servant scurried forward with more wine. Liu declined a second drink. The first minister had long intended to see his adviser drunk; it hadn't happened yet.

From across the courtyard the *pipa* music had stopped.

She'd have been told that her lord was engaged with his principal adviser. Rain—Lin Chang—was impeccably trained, and intelligent. She'd not wish to distract them, he knew.

His adviser waited until the servant had withdrawn to the far wall again. He said, "Word came tonight, a military courier from the west. From Iron Gate Fortress."

"Well, that *is* west," said the prime minister, amusing himself slightly.

Liu did not smile. He said, "You know that my ... my brother has been at Kuala Nor? You asked about my family last year and I told you?"

He did remember asking. It was before he'd taken office. He remembered this piece of information very well. And the man. He hadn't liked Master Shen Tai. Hadn't known him at all, but that didn't matter.

The first minister nodded, more carefully. His mood had changed, he didn't want it noticed.

"Burying bones," he said indifferently. A flick of one hand. "A foolish thing, with all respect to your father. What of it?"

"He's left the lake. He is coming back to Xinan. They made him a member of the Second Military District army to shorten his mourning time, permit him to return."

The two men in this room had done the same thing not long after Shen Gao had died, to allow Liu to come back to the palace—to assist the ambitious cousin of the woman the emperor favoured above all others.

The first minister considered this a moment. Still carefully, he said, "I wonder why? We know this from Iron Gate?"

Liu nodded. "He passed through for one night. He sent a message ahead to the Ta-Ming, along with the fortress commander's formal report."

One night meant he wasn't lingering as he travelled. Wen Zhou affected a yawn. "And why would the movements of your brother—diverting as the topic might be for you, personally—be of interest to me, or of importance to the empire?" He thought he'd said that well enough.

Liu looked discomfited. An extreme rarity. He shifted position. A rider could look like that after too long in the saddle. It was interesting. The prime minister kept his gaze on him.

"Well?" he added.

Liu drew a breath. "He … my brother reports first that an assassin was slain at Kuala Nor, having been sent there to kill him."

"I see," said Zhou, keeping his voice level. "That is first. Of little importance to us, as far as I can see. What else?"

His adviser cleared his throat. "It seems … it seems that the White Jade Princess, in Rygyal … Cheng-wan, our, our own princess …"

"I know who she is, Liu."

Another throat clearing. Liu was unsettled. That, in itself, was disturbing. "She's given him a gift," Liu said. "To honour what he was doing by the lake. With the dead."

"How pleasant for your brother," Wen Zhou murmured. "But I fail to see—"

"Two hundred and fifty Sardian horses."

Like that. A hammer.

Zhou felt his mouth go dry. He swallowed, with difficulty. "He is … your brother is riding from the border with two hundred and fifty Heavenly Horses?"

It was impossible, he thought.

In a way, it was. "No," said Liu. "He has arranged to have them held by the Tagurans. He must go back and claim them himself, only he can do it, after it is decided what is to be done with them. He writes that he is coming to Xinan to inform the celestial emperor. And others."

And others.

Now he understood why this was information he needed to know.

He also understood something else, abruptly. He struggled to keep this from showing in his face. Liu's unpleasant younger brother had told the soldiers at Iron Gate Fort, and written a letter, about an assassin sent after him. He was a figure of significance now, with those horses. There would almost certainly be an inquiry, where there might never have been one before.

Which meant ...

It meant that someone in Xinan had to be dealt with. Tonight, in fact, before word of Shen Tai's journey and his gift—likely racing through the palace and the Purple Myrtle Court even now—spread too widely, and reached the man in question.

It was unfortunate. The person he was now thinking about had his uses. But he also knew too much, given these sudden tidings, for the first minister's comfort.

It was still possible, for certain reasons, that the extremely irritating Shen Tai might not reach Xinan, but everything was changed with this information.

"What does that mean, he has to claim the horses himself? Did you read the letters?"

"I did." The prime minister didn't ask how Liu had achieved that. "If he does not go back for them himself the gift is revoked. It is a gift from the princess to *him*. There was ... there is a third letter, from a Taguran officer, making this clear."

Inwardly, with great intensity, the prime minister of Kitai began shaping the foulest oaths he could imagine. He felt a droplet of sweat slide down his side.

It was worse than he'd imagined. Because now if Shen Tai died on the road—if he'd already died—his death cost the empire those horses.

Two hundred and fifty was an absurd, a *stupefying* number. The man was coming back as a hero, with immediate access to the court. It was about as bad as it could get.

And someone needed to be killed, quickly.

The silence continued. No *pipa* music across the way. Liu was very still, waiting for him, clearly shaken himself. You might have thought it a good thing for him, for his family, but not if you knew these brothers—and something else that had been done.

Zhou said it aloud, with the thought. "Your sister is beyond the Long Wall, Liu. He can't do anything about her."

Liu's eyes wouldn't meet his gaze. This was rare, told him he'd hit upon the concern—or one of them—in his adviser's mind. "You are," he added tartly, "the eldest son, aren't you? Head of the family. This was within your rights, and I approved it and proposed it at court. It brings you honour, all of you."

It had also put Liu even more in his debt.

His adviser nodded, though with something less than his customary crispness.

"What else do I need to know?" the prime minister asked. Relations within the Shen family were not his most compelling problem. He needed to dismiss his adviser. He had someone else to summon tonight. "Who will know of this?"

Liu lifted his eyes. "Who will know? Everyone," he said. "Tonight, or by mid-morning. It was a military dispatch, two copies, one to the Grand Secretariat, one to the Ministry of War, and nothing in the Ta-Ming stays secret."

He knew that last. *Nothing in the Ta-Ming stays secret.*

A man was coming, a troubling man, with control of an impossible number of Sardian horses and a profoundly exalted stature, for so-very-virtuous actions in the past two years.

He *would* be received by the Son of Heaven.

There was no way to prevent it. And depending on what Shen Tai wanted, he could become an immediate, unpredictable factor in a game already too complex for words.

Although, possibly, he'd be killed, or had already been killed, on the road from Iron Gate. But that had different implications now, given the horses. The court would investigate, undoubtedly. And First Minister Wen knew altogether too much about those chances of death on the road.

It had been such a small, private matter when set in motion. An impulse as much as anything, a casual flexing of power. But now . . .

if it emerged that the empire had lost two hundred and fifty Sardian horses because of someone's recklessness, pursuing entirely personal interests ...

It could happen, if someone talked.

There was a man who absolutely needed to die before he arrived at the same conclusion regarding his own risks—and tried to protect himself. By speaking to someone in the palace, for example. Tonight. Possibly even right now.

Or—the prime minister felt himself growing pale at the thought—perhaps by attending upon a certain military governor with what he had to say, asking for guidance and protection.

A scenario too terrifying to even contemplate.

He sent his adviser home.

Too abruptly, perhaps, given a shrewd man, but there wasn't time to be subtle here and he was not about to share *this* story with Liu. He'd have to rely on the fact that Liu was distracted and uneasy. Because of what he'd done with the sister, of course, and the brother's return.

This was all because of the same man, Zhou thought bitterly. The one coming back along the imperial road from beyond the border. He might have the power—and the desire—to ruin them both.

When he was alone, except for the still-cowering servant who did not matter, Zhou began to swear aloud. The person he cursed—without speaking the name, he was hardly so great a fool—was the seventeenth daughter of the celestial emperor, the serene and beautiful, the White Jade Princess, Cheng-wan.

Who, from far-off Rygyal on its mountain-ringed plateau, had capriciously, irresponsibly, altered so much. The way a woman could.

He heard the *pipa* music begin again.

She'd have been told of Liu's departure. Would assume Zhou was free now, the toils of the day falling away. He wasn't. They weren't. He could not go to her. He couldn't slake or assuage or channel fear or anger yet. He needed to deal with something immediately, and that meant trusting another man. And hoping it was not already too late.

He knew the man he needed, gave orders for him to be brought. As to trust, he could always have this one killed as well, after. These matters rippled outwards, the prime minister thought, like the waters of a still pond after a single stone fell.

There. Think of that image! He was an accursed poet, after all.

He lifted his cup, the servant hastened to bring him wine. He tried not to picture someone riding, or being carried from the Purple Myrtle Court in a litter, even now, across the night city. Arriving before the doors of the new mansion of Roshan. Being admitted. Telling him …

The guard he'd summoned was announced. Zhou bade him enter. A big man. A scar on his right cheek. His name was Feng. He bowed in the doorway.

Wen Zhou dismissed his servant, then said what had to be said. He did so with precision, his voice calm. Feng accepted the orders with another bow, no flicker of response in his face.

Which was all as it should be. You simply could *not* guide and govern an empire this vast, with so many challenges from within and without, while being the sort of gentle-souled person who might be deemed worthy of admission to holy orders.

And any fair-minded man evaluating the times would agree that this was even more the case if one's emperor was no longer young, no longer the driven, brilliant leader he had been when he seized the throne himself (killing brothers, it needed to be remembered) and began shaping a reign of glory.

If the late Prime Minister Chin Hai, at the emperor's side for decades, had taught the court anything it was that sometimes the darker, disturbing deeds of government needed to be shouldered by the first minister. Why else were there said to have been those soundless rooms underground, or the secret tunnels in and out of the city palace, that now belonged, as of tonight, to the most dangerous man in Kitai?

And if a beleaguered, overburdened first minister, directly responsible for no fewer than nine ministries, forswearing his own best-loved pleasures and diversions in the tireless service of his emperor, should have invoked the power of his office in the trivial matter of a chosen woman and an irritating man she'd known too well … well, were there to be *no* benefits attached to dealing with so many tasks? To the sleepless hours, for example, that lay ahead of him tonight while he waited for the return of the man he'd just sent out?

In their nine heavens, Wen Zhou decided, the gods would understand.

SHE HAS NEVER ACCEPTED the name he chose for her when he bought her from the Pavilion of Moonlight Pleasure House and had her brought here.

Lin Chang means nothing to her, it has no weight at all. Neither had Spring Rain at first, but she has at least grown accustomed to her courtesan name, and was even offered choices when they proposed it, asked if it felt right.

Zhou hadn't done that. He hadn't needed to, of course, but neither had the women at the Pavilion of Moonlight when she'd arrived there. He hadn't even told her the source of her new name, what it meant to him, if anything. It certainly wasn't Sardian. No acknowledgement of her origins. He'd wanted something more dignified than a North District pleasure girl's name, and there it was.

And it isn't worth hating. It really isn't. That is the change in her. You did need to decide what mattered, and concentrate on that. Otherwise your life force would be scattered to the five directions, and wasted.

A woman needs to accept some truths in the world.

Wen Zhou is immensely powerful. He is not cruel to his servants or his women, certainly not by the standards of Xinan. Or those of Sardia, as it happens.

He is young, not unpleasant to be with in most humours. And his needs with women, though he likes to think they are decadent (men are often that way), are hardly so, for a girl from the pleasure district.

No, if she hates him now—and she does—it is for a different reason. The intensity she brings to bear upon this anger is extreme.

He had not needed to order a rival killed.

Tai wasn't even a rival, in any way that signified. He had gone away for his mourning years, leaving her where she was, and what man—what student, having not yet even taken the examinations—could set himself against the first minister of the empire, the Precious Consort's kinsman?

You could, if you wished, draw upon your knowledge of how fragile men were, even the most powerful. How much they could be shaped, or guided, by women and the needs they aroused. Was not the august emperor himself the clearest illustration?

You could understand how even a man of the stature of Wen Zhou might dislike remembering nights in the Pavilion of Moonlight when he'd arrived unexpectedly and discovered her already with another, and perhaps too obviously enjoying that.

But you could also draw a line in your own mind, straight as string, as to what you'd accept in the way of actions following upon that—and killing was on the far side of such a line.

It had not been difficult to shape a space for herself when she'd arrived here in the compound. She had been able to render two of the servants infatuated with her. Had she been unable to do that she'd hardly be worth desiring, would she? She'd begun working on the task of gathering information as soon as she'd come, without any purpose in mind. It was just … what you did.

She'd made it clear (let them appear to deduce it, which worked with most men, high or low) that her reasons for wanting to learn the current mood, conversations, comings and goings of their lord had to do with her sustaining desire to please him, to know his needs at any hour.

She behaved—behaves still—impeccably, in the compound, or when she leaves it in a litter, guarded, to shop at one of the markets, or accompanies Zhou to banquets or polo games.

No one here has cause to hate her, unless it is the other concubines, and she has been careful with them. She still calls herself Spring Rain among the others, to avoid seeming to put on airs.

Her real name, from home, is hers to keep, and hasn't been spoken by anyone in a long time. She put it aside when she crossed the border at Jade Gate years ago. It is possible that there is no one in all of Kitai who knows it. An unsettling thought.

Zhou's wife is of little consequence, a woman of extreme breeding—selected for that—and even more extreme piety, which means she and her husband lead widely divergent lives. One of the concubines has offered the view that she might have been less virtuous if more attractive. An ungenerous thought, though not necessarily an untrue one.

The first minister's wife is often away at one sanctuary or another. Her generosity to holy men and women is well known. Her husband encourages it. She also frequents astrologers, but is careful about it. The School of Unrestricted Night has an ambiguous place in the court of the Emperor Taizu.

Tonight, Rain knew that Adviser Shen had come to their doors before Zhou was even home, and that he'd been nervous about something. Normally, Shen Liu would be admitted to wait inside, but he had declined that invitation, staying in the street under the lanterns, watching for Zhou. The nervousness—reported by Hwan, her primary source of information—was unusual.

Shen Liu does not know of her connection to his brother, Rain is almost sure of that. She is less confident of some other things about him. She will need a certain Kanlin Warrior to return and report before she knows—if any sure conclusion is possible. Shen Liu is a cautious man.

It is unlikely to be obvious if he's been part of a plan to kill his brother.

Rain has been waiting in Number Two Pavilion, elegantly attired. She wears no perfume, as usual. That makes it easier for her to cross dark courtyards, linger on porticos. Perfume is an announcement, after all.

Only when she knows Zhou is coming to her will she use her scent. It has become a gesture she's known for here, a signature, like a calligrapher's brush stroke. Another way his newest concubine honours her master.

These devices are not difficult for a woman who can think, and with men who don't realize she can.

She'd heard the two men come in to the chamber across the small courtyard. Had begun playing her *pipa* then, to let Zhou know she was here. She stops when she hears—too faintly to make out words—that they have begun to talk. They will, she knows, think it a courtesy of hers.

She crosses the wet courtyard, barefoot, to save her slippers, carrying her *pipa*. That is her excuse: if anyone sees her, she is on the portico, out of sight, to offer music to her lord and his adviser if a request for it arises. Music is her domain here.

The sliding doors are open on a spring night and silk-paper windows block little sound. She hears, quite clearly, what they are saying.

Her heart begins pounding. Excitement, and there is fear, but she has made her peace with that, and her own decisions, some time ago. Betrayal, it can fairly be called. It will be called that, if what she's done emerges from night into bright day.

But he'd sent a trained assassin, a false Kanlin, and arranged for two more, in an excess of casual, murderous inclination, and Rain would have called it a betrayal of herself to do nothing about that.

Tai wasn't at his father's home, it seemed, even in their mourning period. Wen Zhou, evidently, knew where he was. Rain did not. It was maddening. She was too isolated here—the city, the empire, the world beyond these stone walls were all wrapped in a cloud of not-knowing.

She had done what she could. Hwan, usefully in love with her by then, had arranged for a Kanlin, a real one this time, to come to her from their sanctuary at Ma-wai. The woman—she'd asked for a woman—had come over the wall at the back of the compound for a night meeting in the garden.

Rain had told Hwan it had to do with a threat she needed to quietly guard against—and that much had been true. She had paid the Kanlin, and sent her to Tai's family, which was the only place to begin. Surely there they would know where he was, and why he was away?

Tonight, listening from the portico, Rain finally knows where Tai had gone. It is a wonder.

Walking back to the Number Two Pavilion, having a maidservant wash her feet, beginning to play her instrument again for the man now waiting for someone else to return tonight, Rain tries to decide if she wants the guard—his name is Feng—to succeed in killing Xin Lun.

She remembers Lun: quick, irreverent company in the Pavilion of Moonlight. A good singing voice, a loud, high laugh, generous with money. None of that matters. What concerns her is if it will be better if Tai is able to find the man alive when he returns. If he survives, himself.

She tries to make her heart be calm. There is no place here for desire, or dreams, though dreams are difficult to control. Whatever else might be true, she cannot be his now.

He should not have gone away without her. She had told him what might follow. Men didn't listen enough. A truth of the world.

But ... what he had done at Kuala Nor. What he had *done*.

And now two hundred and fifty horses from her own land. It is beyond words, it reaches past music, and it can change so much—though not for her.

It is extremely late when Zhou comes to her. She has been certain he will, though not what his mood will be. Hwan and her maidservants had been asleep when Feng returned to the compound.

Zhou seems almost cheerful when he crosses the courtyard to her. She believes she has an idea what that means.

He takes her with some urgency. From behind first, against the wall, and then more slowly, face to face on the wide bed while she touches him in the ways he likes. He does not awaken any of the other women to play with them, or to watch.

After he is done, she washes his body while he sips wine her maidservant has readied. She is careful about his wine.

She is thinking hard, hiding it, as ever.

Xin Lun is dead. Zhou will have protected himself, ended that risk of exposure. She will need to consider this, she thinks, her hands moving over the body of the man, lightly, then strongly, then lightly again.

She will be wrong in some of her guesses and conclusions. There are limits to what a woman in her position can know, however intelligent and committed she might be. There are too many constraints on someone confined to the women's quarters of a compound or a curtained sedan chair, relying for information on infatuated servants.

There have always been such limits. It is the way of things, and not all men are foolish, though it might seem otherwise at times.

Tonight, she wonders—caressing him, smiling a little as she does so, as if in private pleasure (he likes this)—if he will order the guard slain now.

He'll probably send Feng away first, she decides. South, to where his family and power base are. Raised in rank, to disguise the purpose, make it appear a reward, then accidentally dead in a faraway prefecture.

Alternatively, he might decide he needs a man like Feng in Xinan, with events unfolding as they seem to be.

Either is possible, Rain thinks, singing for him now, a song of the moon reflected in the Great River, autumn leaves falling in the water, floating past the silver, moored fishing boats, drifting towards the sea. An early verse of Sima Zian, the Banished Immortal, set to music, a song that everyone knows, only ever sung late at night, bringing peace with it, carrying memories.

CHAPTER XIII

It was possible, Tai knew, to be asleep, and dreaming, and somehow be *aware* you were dreaming, entangled, unable to wake up.

After the night he'd had: intense in the White Phoenix, violent earlier, and with unsettling tidings given him, he found himself alone in a bedchamber in Chenyao, dreaming himself lying on his back, bed linens scattered around him, while he was mounted and ridden by a woman whose face he could not see.

In the dream he could hear her breathing become more rapid, and could feel his own excitement. He was aware of his hands on her driving hips as she rose and fell upon him, but try as he might, in the darkness of dream (heavier than any in the waking world), he couldn't *see* her, didn't know who this was arousing in him such a fever of desire.

He thought of the fox-spirit, of *course* he thought of that, even in dream. Perhaps especially because this was a dream.

He tried to say the word again: *daiji*. But words, even the one word, would not come to him, just as clear sight was not given. Only movement, touch, the scent of her (not perfume), her quickened breathing—small gasps now—and his own.

He wanted to reach up and touch her face like a blind man, find her hair, but his dream-hands would not leave her hips, the smooth skin there, the muscles driving.

He felt wrapped and gathered, cocooned like a silkworm in this enclosed, indeterminate space of not-waking-yet. He feared it, was aroused and wildly excited by it, wanted never to leave, wanted *her* never to leave him.

Some time later he heard a different sound, and woke.

He was alone in the room, in the bed. Of course he was.

A hint of light through the slatted doors to the garden. The bed linens were in disarray. He might have tossed them off in restless sleep. He was confused, tired, not sure why he was awake.

Then he heard again the sound that had reached him: metal on metal, from the portico past the door.

Something heavy fell, hitting the wall outside.

Tai leaped from bed, scrambled into his trousers, didn't bother knotting them, or with a shirt or boots or tying his hair.

He did take his swords. He jerked open the door, noting that he hadn't barred it the night before, though he remembered intending to.

There was a man on the threshold. He was dead. Sword wound, right side.

Tai heard fighting to his left, the garden. He stepped over the dead body, ran towards the sound of swords, barefoot down the portico, his hair swinging free, sleep gone, the dream gone, in this first light of morning. He reached the end, leaped over the railing without breaking stride.

Wei Song was in the courtyard, spinning Kanlin-style—fighting five men.

It had been six, at least, with the one behind Tai. She was battling in a deadly, whirling silence. Tai swore savagely under his breath: she *could* have shouted for help! He had an idea why she hadn't. He didn't like it.

Sprinting towards them, he screamed: a release of pent-up rage, as much as anything else, directed at anyone and everyone and everything just then. At all of these people acting upon him, and for him, and even *through* him—from the moment Bytsan sri Nespo had given him a rolled-up parchment at Kuala Nor with a gift of too many horses.

It had gone far enough, this passiveness, this acceptance, absorbing the designs of others—benign, or otherwise. It was not what he was, or would allow himself to be, under the nine heavens. Perhaps he could declare that, with two swords in his hands.

One of the men facing Song half turned towards Tai's sudden cry. That turning closed the scroll of his life.

Song's left-hand sword took him on the side he'd exposed. The blade was withdrawn, as cleanly as it had entered, drawing life away with it.

She dropped and rolled through a flower bed, peonies crushed under her. They sprang back up as she did. A sword stroke from the nearest man, meant to decapitate, whistled through air.

Tai was among them by then.

The essence of Kanlin training, as he saw it (others might differ), was the continuous, patient, formal repetition of the movements of combat. Without swords, with one blade, with both, over again, every day of one's life, ideally, the movements becoming so instinctive that the need for thought, awareness, planning in a fight disappeared. The body knew what it needed to do, and how to do it.

So it was without anything resembling deliberation, without a thought given to how long it had been since he'd done this, that Tai planted his right-hand sword in the earth, left it quivering there, and hurled himself into a twisting dive. A movement which—when properly executed—let the left-hand sword slide under one's own flying body and sweep like a scythe, parallel to the ground, at someone facing him, or turning to do that.

His blade caught the nearest man, biting deep, just above the knee, sending blood spurting like some primitive sacrifice to the rising sun.

Tai landed (a dangerous moment, with a blade in one hand) and, from his knees, killed the wounded, falling man with a straight thrust to the chest.

Three left. All three turned to him.

"Get away!" Wei Song screamed.

Not likely, thought Tai, anger-ridden.

You each chose a man on either side when there were three lined up straight against two—if they made that mistake.

He switched his single blade to his right hand. Took the man farthest from Song: that was routine. He parried a slash from the bandit, and rolled again through the air to his left, a different move, one he hadn't realized he remembered. You needed to be careful not to cut yourself with your own sword doing this one, too—*that* awareness came back in mid-air—but as he completed the movement, before he landed, he slashed at the bandit, and felt the sword bite.

The man screamed, went down. Tai landed in flowers, was up (almost) smoothly, and dispatched this one, too, on the ground. He looked quickly over, dropping down in anticipation of an attack, then stepping back.

No immediate danger. The middle figure was also down.

Song had adapted to what they had given her. She'd used both her swords, slicing as the man turned towards Tai. You could call it elegant, though there was a great deal of blood.

The last of the bandits turned, not surprisingly, to flee.

Unfortunately for him, his way was blocked by a rumpled, irritated-looking poet with grey hair untied and askew.

Sima Zian looked for all the world like one of the grotesque guardian statues placed by the doorway of a house or the entrance to a tomb, to frighten away demons.

"You took me from my first cup of wine," he said grimly. "Let fall your weapon. Doing so offers you a small chance of living. Otherwise there is none."

The bandit hesitated, then—evidently—decided that the "small chance" wasn't real. He shouted what sounded like a name and hurtled full tilt towards the poet, blade swinging. Tai caught his breath.

He needn't have bothered. He knew the tales, after all. Sima Zian had been an outlaw himself for years in the wild country of the gorges, and his sword—the single one he carried—was famed.

He sidestepped the wild charge, dropped, leaning away, and thrust out a leg. The running man tripped and fell. Before the bandit could recover from where he sprawled by the portico, Master Sima was upon him, dagger to throat.

The sun appeared over a pavilion to the east.

A servant walked into the courtyard from that side, carrying a water basin. He stopped. His mouth gaped.

"Summon the governor's men!" Song shouted. "They are in front!" She looked at Tai. "And are about as useful as they were at the White Phoenix." She walked over and handed him his second sword. She had already sheathed her own pair.

"These came in through the water gate?"

She nodded.

The poet had the bandit's left arm twisted high behind his back. It would crack, Tai saw, with only a little pressure. The dagger remained at the man's throat.

"Why are you here?" Sima Zian said quietly. "You know the governor's questioners will be merciless. Answer me, I'll do what I can."

"Who are you," the man rasped, face to the earth, "to offer anything in Chenyao?"

"You'll have to believe I can. They will be here soon. You heard her send for them. Speak!"

"You will kill me, if I do? Before they …"

Tai winced, closed his eyes for a moment.

"I swear it," said the poet calmly. "Why are you here?"

"It was my brother they tortured last night. After the two men named him."

"Your brother hired men to kill Shen Tai?"

"He was told a man of that name might come from the west. To watch for him. Good money if he came to Chenyao and did not leave."

"Your brother was the one directed in this way?"

"Yes. A letter. I never saw it. He only told me."

"Who wrote the letter?"

"I do not know."

"Then why are you here? If it was his task?"

There came a sound from the man on the ground. "Why? They carried him back to his wife last night. Dropped his body in the street. His servant summoned me. He was naked in the mud. He had been castrated, his organ stuffed in his mouth. His eyes had been carved out and they had cut off his hands. This was my brother. Do you hear it? I was here to kill the one who caused this."

Tai felt himself swaying where he stood, in the spreading light of day.

"The ones who caused this are not here," said Sima Zian, gravely. It was as if he'd expected these words, Tai thought. "You must know that. They work for Governor Xu, who sought only to stop violence and murder in his city, as he must do for the Son of Heaven we all serve in Kitai. It is ... it is not easy to amend a broken world."

That last was from a poem, not his own.

They heard a jingling sound. Soldiers, half a dozen of them, entered the courtyard at a run. One of them shouted an order.

Sima Zian murmured something Tai didn't hear.

The poet's knife moved. The bandit, face down among earth and flowers, died instantly, before the guards arrived to claim his living body for more of what had been done to his brother in the night.

"How dare you kill him!" the lead guard rasped in fury.

Tai saw the poet about to reply. He stepped forward, lifting a quick hand. Zian, courteously, was silent, but he remained coiled now, like a snake who might still strike.

"How dare *you* let assassins into this inn yard!" Tai snapped. "Into a garden you were here to guard! I want your names given to my Kanlin, right now. I will wait for Governor Xu to advise me how he intends to make redress for this."

The soldier looked, Tai decided, very like a fish extracted from his element, suddenly lacking easy access to breathing.

Xu Bihai was, it was already clear, not a man given to half measures. He'd regard this second failure by his guards as a stain upon his honour. These soldiers might well be executed, Tai thought. He wasn't sure, at this particular moment, if that distressed him.

He took a breath. "I'm sorry your morning was disturbed," he said to Zian.

The poet flexed his shoulders and neck, as if to loosen them. "Hardly your fault. And it isn't as if I was asleep."

"No?"

"Well, perhaps I'd dozed a little. But I was having my first cup. Will you join me now?"

Tai shook his head. "You must excuse me. I have to change for breakfast with the prefect. I forgot about it last night."

"Ah!" said the poet. "We'd have been late for a dawn departure, even without this diversion."

"We would have been."

Tai turned to Song. She looked pale. She had cause. "You are all right?"

"They barely touched me." It wasn't true, he saw, there was a line of blood on her left side, showing through her slashed tunic. Her expression changed. "That was a foolish leap for someone who has not fought in two years! It was folly to even come out. What were you thinking?"

Tai stared at her, small and resolute, wounded, glaring up in fury. It was a *maddening* question. "What was *I* thinking? Who fights six men without calling for help?"

She looked away, then shrugged. "You know the Kanlin answer to that, my lord. Your servant offers apologies if you believe I erred." She bowed.

He started another sharp retort, then stopped. He looked more closely. "Your hand is also hurt."

She glanced at it indifferently. "I rolled over some rocks. I will get these soldiers' names and have them taken to the governor. Is there a message?" She paused meaningfully. "For anyone else?"

Tai ignored that. "What happened to the two men in the garden last night?"

"They revived. I spoke with them. They took the river path home."

"You were awake?"

She nodded. Hesitated. "It is why I saw when these others came up the garden."

He thought about that. "Song, how would they know my chamber?"

"I think we will discover that someone here told them—under duress, or not. We can leave that, unless you wish otherwise, to Governor Xu's inquiries."

"Yes," said Tai. "We are leaving as soon as I return from the prefect."

"As soon as *we* return," she said. She met his gaze. Her mouth was firm, her eyes resolute, indomitable.

He looked back at her. She had just fought six assassins, in silence, to keep him from coming out and possibly being killed in a fight.

He would need to ask her, though not just now, if she truly thought he was best served by being left to lie in bed to be attacked—unarmed and defenceless—in the event they killed her as she fought them alone.

"Your servant will escort you, and wait," Song murmured. "If that is acceptable, my lord."

She lowered her eyes, presenting a small, neat, lethal image, all deference and duty, in a black Kanlin robe.

"Yes," he sighed. "It is acceptable."

What was the point of saying anything else?

ꙮ

"*Shandai* is my brother!"

Li-Mei's voice is louder than she's intended it to be. They are alone, after all, only the wolves around them in a vast expanse, the sun just risen. But her heart is racing. "That is what you are trying to say? His name? Shen Tai?"

He turns to look at her. There is light, pale and benevolent, warming the land, mist is rising, dispersing. She can see him clearly for the first time, and she knows who this man has to be.

Tai had told them what happened. Well, he'd told their father, with Li-Mei among the willow trees near the stream.

This man with the stiff, ground-covering gait and the lightless eyes will surely be the one assailed by shaman-magic all those years ago, who had almost died. Or half-died. Or had been made into some ... thing suspended between living and dead.

Tai hadn't been able to tell their father which, so Li-Mei didn't know. Couldn't know, even looking now. But what fit was the identity, the remembered name—Meshag, son of Hurok—like the puzzle pieces of wooden toys her mother or Second Mother would sometimes bring home for her on market days long ago.

She should be terrified, Li-Mei thinks. He could be a monstrous spirit, a predator like his wolves, malignant, devouring.

He isn't, though, and so she isn't. He hasn't touched her. The wolves haven't. *He is ... he is rescuing me*, the thought comes. And he is rescuing her, not the true princess, the emperor's daughter, because—

"You are taking me away because of what Tai did?"

He has been staring at her, accepting her gaze in the growing light. After another long moment, his untied hair moving in the breeze, straying across his face, he nods his head once, down and back up.

"Yes," he says. "Shan ... Shendai."

Li-Mei feels herself beginning to tremble, is suddenly much too close to tears. She hates that, but it is one thing to be fairly sure of a guess, it is another to be standing here with a spirit-figure and wolves, and be told it is true.

"How did you know I was with them? How did you know to come?"

She has always been able to think of questions to ask. Her voice is smaller. She is afraid of this answer, for the same reasons, most likely, that the Bogü riders were afraid of him last night.

Magic, whether the foretellings of the School of Unrestricted Night in Xinan, the potions and incantations of the alchemists, or darker, bloodier doings up here with mirrors and drums ... this is not easy ground.

And the story her brother told, all those years ago, is still the worst she's ever heard in her life.

Perhaps the man senses that? Or perhaps for an entirely different reason, he only shakes his heavy head and does not answer. Instead, he takes the leather flask from his hip and extends it to her, his arm straight out.

She doesn't repeat her question. She takes the water, drinks. She pours some into one hand and washes her face with it, a little pointlessly. She wonders if he'll be angry at the waste, but he says nothing.

His eyes are deeply disturbing. If she thinks about how they became so black and flat she will be afraid. *He isn't dead,* she tells herself. Repeats it, within, as if for emphasis. She may need to keep telling herself this, she realizes.

He says, awkwardly, but in her tongue, "Cave not far. You rest. I find horses."

She looks around at the grassland stretching, all directions. The lake is gone now, behind them. There is only grass, very tall, lit by the risen sun. The mist has burned away.

"A cave?" she says. "In *this?*"

For a moment she thinks he is amused. His mouth twitches, one side only. Nothing in the eyes. Light is swallowed there; it dies.

She hands him back the flask. He seals it, shoulders it, turns to walk on. She follows.

Shandai.

The world, Li-Mei decides, is a stranger place than any sage's teachings can encompass. You have to wonder why the gods in their nine heavens have made it this way.

They reach the cave quite soon.

She'd missed the depression in the landscape ahead of them. From the edge, she sees this is a shallow valley, with another small lake within it. There are wildflowers on the banks. On the far side, the slope back up is steeper.

They descend and start across. It is full morning now, the air is warmer. At the lake Meshag fills his flask. Li-Mei washes her face properly, shakes out and reties her hair. He watches her, expressionless. *He is not dead,* she tells herself.

The lead wolf takes them to the cave at the eastern end. Its entrance is entirely hidden by tall grass. She'd never have seen it. No one who didn't know this was here would see it.

This is not the first time, Li-Mei realizes, that the man and these animals have been here. He gestures. She finds herself crawling, elbows and knees, holding down fear, into a wolf lair.

The tunnel is narrow, a birth chamber, the smell of wolf all around, and small bones. She feels these, with her hands, under her knees. Panic begins to rise in the blackness, but then the cave opens up. She is in a space with rough stone walls and a ceiling she can't even make out. She stands. It is still dark but not completely so. Light filters in farther up, openings high on the cliff face. She can see.

The strangeness of the world.

Meshag comes through the tunnel. The wolves have not followed them. On guard outside? She doesn't know. How could she know? She is in a wolf cave in the Bogü grasslands beyond the borders of the world. Her life ... her life has carried her here. *The strangeness ...*

He hands her a satchel and the flask. "Here is food. Not leave. Wait. My brother will come after us, very soon."

My brother. His brother is the kaghan's heir. The man she is supposed to marry. She is a Kitan princess, a treaty-bride.

She looks at the man beside her. His speech, she decides, is already clearer. Can the dead *learn* things?

He isn't dead, she reminds herself.

"Where are you going?" she asks, trying to keep apprehension from her voice. Alone, a cave in wilderness, wolves.

He looks impatient. It is almost a relief to see such a normal expression—if you don't look at the eyes.

"Horses. I told before."

He had. She nods. Tries, again, to assemble facts she can work with. She can't say why it matters, but it does. "Your brother. You are opposing him? For me? For ... for Shen Tai? For *my* brother?"

There is enough light for her to see that his eyes remain flat. There is nothing to find in them. It makes her consider how much of what she's known—or thought she knew—of any person has come from their eyes.

"Yes," he says, finally.

But he's taken so long she decides it isn't entirely true, this reply. That might be an error she's making. He might have simply been trying to decide *whether* to tell her. But she still feels ...

"What would he do to you? Your brother?"

Again, he stares. Again, a hesitation.

He says, "He wants me destroyed. He has never found me. Now he will think he can."

Destroyed. Not killed. But it might be just language again, words. She is working hard.

"He thinks he can find you by following me?"

He nods, that single down and up. "All of us. The wolves. I have allowed myself to be seen."

"Oh. And you haven't done that? Before?"

"Not so near him. Or his shamans. Not difficult. Grasslands are large."

You might imagine you saw a smile there, almost.

She lowers her head, thinking.

She looks up again. She says, "I am grateful. You took ... you are taking a great risk. For me." She bows. Twice, right fist in left hand. She has not done so yet to him, and it is proper. They may call her a princess but she isn't, and it doesn't matter, anyhow.

Meshag (she needs to start using the name, she thinks) only looks at her. She sees that he is not discomfited by her gesture. *He was the kaghan's heir,* she thinks.

She is nowhere near her home.

He says, quietly, "I wish him destroyed, also."

Li-Mei blinks. He looks at her, dead-eyed, bare-chested, hair to his waist, utterly strange, in this cave where they stand, faint light filtering from above.

He says, "He did this to me. My brother."

And it begins, piece by puzzle piece, to come clearer.

HE HAS NOT YET RETURNED. It is now, she judges, well into the afternoon, though it is difficult to measure time inside a cave. There is more light filtering down now, the sun is higher. She has eaten, has even dozed fitfully, lying on earth and pebbles, her head pillowed awkwardly on the satchel. She is obviously not a princess if she can do that.

Awakened by what was probably an imagined sound, she's untied and then retied her hair, used a little of the water to wash her hands again.

She is not to go outside. She can ignore this—she's ignored so many instructions through her life—but she isn't inclined to do so. Nor does it occur to her to run away.

For one thing, she has no idea where to go. For another, the man she's been sent to marry is looking for her. She has no doubt of that, and she doesn't want to be found. She doesn't want to live her life on these steppes. She may end up with no choice (short of death), but for the moment, at least, there appears to be a glimmering of one, like glow-worms in a night dell, or a cave.

She has no idea what Meshag intends to do, but he is helping her away, and that is a start, isn't it? It might get her killed, or he might decide to claim her body as a prize in a war with his brother, take her right here on earth and stone. But what control does she have, in any of this?

What she'd *prefer* (it feels an absurd word) is to be with the empress still, serving her, even exiled from the Ta-Ming. Or, even better, to be home right now at this beginning of summer. She can picture it too well. Not a helpful channel of thought or memory.

She is sitting, hands around drawn-up knees. She permits herself to cry (no one can see), and then she stops.

She looks around for what must be the fiftieth time: the low, narrow tunnel leading out, the curved cave walls rising towards light spilling softly down from the openings on the one side. Stones and pebbles, bones scattered. The wolves will have needed to eat, feed their cubs. She shivers. There is one other tunnel, larger than the entranceway, leading farther in. She'd seen it on first entry here.

She can't say why she decides to explore it now. Anxiety, a desire to *do* something, make a decision, however trivial. Patience is not a skill she has. Her mother used to talk to her about it.

She finds she can stand in the second tunnel if she bends over. The air seems all right as she goes. She isn't sure how she'll know when it isn't. She keeps her hands on the rough walls to either side and strains her eyes, for the light begins to fade.

It is a short distance, actually. Another birthing passage, she thinks, though she can't say why that thought has come to her, twice now.

She straightens in a second chamber, not as large, or as high. It is colder. She can hear, faintly, the sound of water dripping.

Something else is different. There is no wolf smell here. She doesn't know why. Wouldn't they extend their lair as far from outside as they could? Protect the cubs? What is it that has kept them away? And does that mean she shouldn't be here either? She doesn't know. The answers are too remote from any life she's lived.

Then, as her eyes adjust to fainter light, Li-Mei sees what lies in this chamber.

Both hands go to her mouth, as if to lock in sound. As if a gasp or cry would be sacrilege. Her next thought is that she might know, after all, why the animals have not come here. For this must be— surely it must be—a place of power.

On the wall in front of her, dim in the darkness, but clearly conjured forth, Li-Mei sees horses.

Innumerable, jumbled chaotically, piled on each other all the way up into shadow. Full-bodied, half-forms, some with only heads and necks and manes, in a racing, tumbling, spilling tumult. A herd, all facing the same way, *moving* the same way, deeper in, as if thundering across the curved cave walls. And she knows, she *knows*, in the moment of seeing, the moment they emerge from darkness on the wall, that these painted, surging figures are unimaginably old.

She turns, in the centre of a cascade. On the opposite wall is another herd, galloping the same direction, the horses superimposed upon each other in wild, profligate intensity, so vital, so vivid, even in barely sufficient light, that she can imagine sounds, the drumming of hooves on hard ground. The horses of the Bogü steppes.

But before the Bogü tribes were here, she thinks. There are no men on these walls and the horses are untamed, free, flowing like a river in spate towards the eastern end of the cave, deeper in—where there is a third tunnel, she now sees.

Something rises within her, primitive and absolute, imperative, to tell her she will *not* go in there. It is not for her. She does not belong, and she knows it.

High above that slit of an entranceway, the largest by far of all the painted horses looms: a stallion, deep-chested, red-brown, almost crimson, its sex clearly shown. And on its body, all over it—and on this one, only—Li-Mei sees the imprint of human hands laid on in a pale-coloured paint, as if branding or tattooing the horse.

She doesn't understand.

She does not ever, in her life, expect to understand.

But she feels an appallingly ancient force here, and senses within herself, a yearning to claim or possess it. She is certain that those who placed their handprints on this wall, on the painted body of this king-horse, whether they did so ages ago or have come recently through these tunnels, were paying tribute, homage, to this herd.

And perhaps to those who put these horses here, leading the way deeper in.

She will not follow them there. She is not such a person, and is too far from home. There is a barrier in her mind where that third tunnel begins. It is not an opening she can take. She has not led a life guided by magic, infused or entwined with it. She doesn't like that world, did not, even at court—alchemists hovering, stroking narrow beards, astrologers mumbling over charts.

Still, she looks at these horses, unable to stop turning and turning, aware that she's becoming dizzied, overwhelmed, consumed by the profusion, the *richness* here. There is so much power on these walls, humbling, evoking awe, enough to make someone weep.

She has a sense of time stretching, back and back so far it cannot be grasped. Not by her, at any rate. Not by Shen Li-Mei, only daughter of the Kitan general Shen Gao. She wonders, suddenly, what her father would have said had he been with her in this hidden place. A hard thought, because if he were alive she wouldn't *be* here.

And in that moment she hears a sound that makes her halt her spinning. She stands motionless suddenly, silent. She listens. The drip of water. Not that. She is almost certain she heard a horse. Fear comes with that.

Then another sound: someone coming into this inner cave from the first one. Instead of frightening her, this reassures. Meshag went to get horses. He knows where she is. The sound she's heard—faintly—is from outside. A real horse, not the supernatural neighing of a spirit stallion on these walls.

She sees him come through. He straightens. She is about to speak when he holds up a hand, three fingers to his lips. Fear returns. Why silence? Who is out there?

He gestures for her to follow, turns to lead her through the short tunnel to the wider, brighter cave, the first one. She takes a last look at the horses all around, at the king-horse with the human hands upon him, and then she makes her way out.

In the larger cave, with the high openings lending light, Meshag turns again, once more with fingers to his lips urging silence. He is wearing a long, dark tunic now, a leather vest over it. She wonders what clothing he has found for her. She opens her mouth to whisper a question (surely they can whisper?) but his gesture, seeing that, is imperative. His eyes gleam, flashing angrily in the thin light from above.

She registers this, says nothing. She draws a slow breath.

He gestures again for her to follow, turns to take them back towards daylight.

She approaches closely, behind him. And at the edge of the tunnel that will lead them out, in the moment when he bends low to enter it, Li-Mei stabs him in the throat from one side with the knife she's carried in her sleeve all this way.

She drives the blade in then rips it towards her with all her strength, knowing she'll have only this one chance, *not* knowing how to kill a man, where the knife must go. She tears it out and stabs him again, and a third time, sobbing. He grunts only once, a queer chest sound.

He falls with a clattering noise, right at the entrance to the tunnel.

Still weeping (and she is *not* a woman who weeps), Li-Mei strikes again with the knife, into his back. It hits metal, twists in her hand. She is frantic, terrified, but he lies where he's fallen, and now she sees how much blood there is.

She scrabbles away, clutching the marred blade. She backs up against the cave wall, eyes never leaving him. If he gets up, if he even *moves*, she knows she will begin to scream and not be able to stop.

Nothing, no movement. Her rapid, ragged breathing is loud in her ears. The light in this chamber falls as before. It is the light that saved her, that told her. *If* she is right in this. Her hands are still shaking, spasms she cannot stop. She puts the knife down beside her. She has killed a man. She is quite certain she has killed a man.

It is not Meshag. It is not him. She says that last aloud, shocking herself with the sound, the harshness of her voice. It cannot be him, must not be.

She needs to know. Can only do that if she looks. That means going back to where he lies, face down, before the tunnel. It requires courage. She has more, in fact, than she knows.

Holding hard to inner control, she does crawl back, bent knife in hand. There are stones on the cave floor, they hurt her knees. Her wrist hurts, from when the knife twisted. Why did it twist? She thinks she might know. Needs to touch him to be sure.

She does that, too. Drags him by his legs from the tunnel's entrance. More light where he lies now. With an effort, grunting, she pushes him onto his back. Into her mind there flashes a horrifying image of this man rising up as she does so. Rising to ...

He is dead. He will not rise. And he is not Meshag.

An older man, lean face, thin grey hair. He looks nothing at all like Meshag, son of Hurok. Now. But he *had* before. Had looked exactly like him, in all but one respect. Which tells her what this man is. What he was, she corrects herself. He is dead. She killed him.

She rips through his tunic, chest to belly, with her reddened, twisted blade. Tears it open with both hands. Metallic mirrors appear, strapped around his body, glinting in the pale light from above.

∞

It is a truth about the nature of human beings that we seek—even demand—order and pattern in our lives, in the flow and flux of history and our own times.

Philosophers have noted this and mused upon it. Those advising princes, emperors, kings have sometimes proposed that this desire, this need, be *used,* exploited, shaped. That a narrative, a story, *the* story of a time, a war, a dynasty be devised to steer the understanding of a people to where the prince desires it to go.

Without pattern, absent that sense of order, a feeling of randomness, of being lost in a world without purpose or direction can undermine even the strongest man or woman.

Given this, it would certainly have been noted as significant by any such philosopher or adviser that the second son and the only daughter of General Shen Gao, honoured in his day as Left Side Commander of the Pacified West, each killed a man on the same morning, a long way from each other.

The son had done this before. The daughter had not, had never expected to.

As to the meaning to be attached to such a conjunction, a pattern discovered embedded in the tale ...

Who can number, under nine heavens, the jewel-bright observations to be extracted from moments such as these? Who will dare say he knows with certainty which single gem is to be held up to whatever light there is for us, in our journeying, and proclaimed as true?

༄

Eventually Li-Mei begins to think about the horse sound she'd heard: she fears an animal will give her away, reveal the cave, if it is still out there.

It might not be. The wolves might have driven it away. Or killed it. It leaves her feeling oddly passive, after the hideous spasm of action before: someone is lying not far away, blood thickening on stone. It is as if she's exhausted her reserves of force, her ability to play any further role, help herself, can only wait to see what will follow. It is an unexpectedly peaceful state.

You sat, leaning against a wall, legs extended, in the midst of stones and animal bones and the smell of wolf and the sometimes flutter of a bat or bird overhead, and you waited to see who—or what—would come for you. You didn't have to do anything, there didn't seem to be anything left to do.

There is no point going outside to be seen. Where will she walk from here, or even ride, alone? She has no adequate clothing, no food, and the wolves are out there.

So there is a curious measure of tranquility in her when she hears the sound of someone else coming into the cave through the tunnel. She looks over, but she doesn't stand up, or try to hide. She holds her bent knife in her hand.

Meshag enters and straightens and looks around.

She can see him absorb what has happened. She looks at him closely, of course, though she is very sure the deception isn't happening again.

He kneels beside the fallen man. She sees that he avoids the blood on the cave floor. He stands and comes towards her. She looks at his eyes.

"He was a shaman?" she asks, though she knows the answer.

He gives his short nod.

"He made himself look exactly, almost exactly like you. He never spoke. He was taking me outside when I …" She doesn't finish.

"What was not me?"

She stands before answering. Brushes at her leggings and tunic to remove some of the rock dust. There is blood, too, she sees. That isn't going to disappear so easily.

"His eyes," she says. "His … yours couldn't have been so bright." She wonders if this will be wounding, for what it implies.

But it looks as if he smiles. She is almost sure she sees it before the expression goes away. He says, "I know. I have seen my eyes in water. In … pools? That word?"

"Yes, pools. This is since what happened to you?"

A stupid question but he only nods again. "Yes, since. My eyes are dead."

"No, they aren't!" she says with sudden force. He looks surprised. She *feels* surprised. "Your eyes are black, but they aren't … you aren't dead!"

No smile this time. "No. But too nearly something else," he says. "Before Shan … before Shendai came. That day."

That day. "And it was your brother who …?"

"Yes."

"You *know* this?"

"I know this."

"And this one?" She gestures at the body. "He was sent by him?"

Unexpectedly, he shakes his head. She had thought she was beginning to understand. "No. Too soon. I think he sees me when I leave to find horse. Or before, as we came here."

"He just saw a chance to take me?"

"For himself, or for reward, might be. He sees me to know me. Who I am. Watching the wolves might have told him. Then it takes time to make a spell to shape-change."

Li-Mei is thinking hard.

"He could have just come in and seized me when you left? No?"

He considers that. "Yes. So must have meant to take you to them. Maybe afraid you kill yourself, so he changed."

She clears her throat. Her hand is hurting.

"Must go now," he says.

"What about him?"

He looks surprised. He gestures at the bones around them. "Leave to wolves. It is what we do." He pauses, looks a little awkward. Then he says, "Was good, killing this one. Was very bravery? Is the word?"

She sighs. "Brave. I suppose it is the word."

Again he hesitates. He motions with a stiff hand. "You see what is next cave?"

"The horses? I saw. I didn't go farther. I felt … not brave."

"No," he shakes his head. "Was right. Not to go. For priests, spirit-walkers. Very old. But you see last horse? Above?"

"I saw it."

He looks at her, seems to make a decision. "Come. One thing we do, then go."

She has exhausted her reserves for resisting. She lets him lead her back into the dimness of the horse-cave with those animals on the wall, laid upon each other long ago. And she watches as he does go into the last cave, the one she would not enter. *Very old.*

He comes out with a shallow earthen bowl, and mixes into it water from a second flask he's carrying, and he stirs with a wooden stick, his motions stiff as they always are. There is no grace to him, how he moves. She is surprisingly certain there was, once.

He signals her nearer. She goes. He takes her right hand—the first time he's ever touched her—and lays it flat in the bowl. There is a paint of sorts, white, or very nearly.

At that point she realizes what is happening.

He leads her over by the wrist and he lays her hand on the flank of the king-horse above the tunnel leading to the third cave, so that a fresh imprint is made there among all the others, which means that her existence, her presence, her *life* having been here has now been recorded, registered. And perhaps (she will never know) that does play a role in what follows.

It is so hard to see the patterns, to be sure that they are there.

They leave that cave and then the other one, go back out into sunlight. She blinks in the day's brightness.

He has found one horse only, but the dead shaman's is still tethered here, unmenaced by the wolves, though lathered with fear—and so they have two mounts, after all, along with the food and the clothing Meshag has taken from who knows where.

He helps her on the smaller horse, and then he mounts and gentles the shaman's, and they ride a path out of that valley and go east with the sun overhead and the wolves beside them.

Li-Mei has no notion, no least idea where he is taking her, but she is alive, and not going placidly into the fate devised for her against her will and desire, and, for now, for this moment under heaven, that is enough.

CHAPTER XIV

Wujen Ning, of the Second District cavalry, had been the first to see Master Shen Tai and his horse appear like ghosts out of a grey dawn west of Iron Gate Fortress.

Now, not many days after, he was dimly aware that his life might be changed—or might have already been changed—by them.

It was not normal for peasant labourers or soldiers without rank to undergo such alterations in the flowing of their lives. You worked your fields, dealt with flood or famine, married, had children born, had them die (and wives). Events far away rolled on, vaguely apprehended, perhaps heard about over rice wine in a tavern, if you went to taverns.

Or you joined the army, were posted where they posted you— usually far from home these days. You dug ditches and latrines, built and rebuilt garrison walls and buildings, patrolled for bandits or wild animals, caught fevers, lived or died, marched, *did* go to taverns and brothels on leave in market towns. Sometimes you fought, some of you died in battle, some lost an eye or an arm and wished they'd died. The sweep of distant events among the great might come more often to your ears in the way of army talk, but it tended to have just as little impact, short of a major campaign, or perhaps a rebellion.

Change wasn't a part of life as Wujen Ning had understood or experienced it. This truth was currently ... undergoing change.

For one thing, he was shockingly close to Xinan, to seeing the capital for the first time in his life. Only a night or two away now, they told him.

The countryside had been altering as they'd ridden east from Chenyao. Wheat and barley fields, the occasional mulberry grove (silk farms set back behind them, away from the noise of the road) had given way to village after village, and larger towns, so frequent now you could say they were continuous. People and more people. Temple bells ringing not in haunting isolation but barely audible amid loud populations. Small farms—potatoes, broad beans—were tucked in between the villages, squeezed.

There was an endless line of market carts or wood-cutters' wagons going both ways along the imperial road, clogging it, slowing them. This was the outermost sprawl of Xinan, he was told. They were getting close now.

It was not something Ning had ever thought about, or wanted. The capital had been as remote to his grasp of the world as the sea. It terrified him, to be honest: so *many* people. Already. He tried not to let that show, and since no one in their company was really looking at him and he talked little, he thought he'd kept his secret. He did catch himself whistling nervously sometimes.

He wondered, as they travelled, how the other soldiers felt about coming to the capital. There were thirty riders now, not just the five that had set out from Iron Gate to escort Master Shen. Governor Xu had insisted that Shen Tai, as an honorary officer of the Second District army, carrying tidings (and riding a horse) of greatest importance, be accompanied—and protected.

There was some anger and some amusement among the Iron Gate soldiers (Ning didn't see the humour, but he wasn't good at that, he knew) arising from the belief that it was carelessness among the governor's guards that had come near to having Master Shen killed in Chenyao.

One of Ning's fellows from Iron Gate, a man with no shortage of opinions or wine-soaked breath to voice them with, said he didn't think any of those soldiers who had been on guard outside their inn that night were still alive.

Governor Xu might no longer be in the prime of youth, he said, but he wasn't showing any inclination to retire to fruit orchards and trout ponds. He was wealthy, aristocratic, known to have rivalries with other military governors. One big one in particular, he'd said with a knowing look, as if everyone at their table would realize the one he meant. Ning didn't. It didn't bother him.

Had Shen Tai been killed (or the horse, Wujen Ning thought, with genuine horror) it would, apparently, have reflected very badly on the governor. Ning didn't understand or think much about this either, but from the time they'd left Chenyao he had made it his task to stay as close as he could to Master Shen and Dynlal. He honoured Shen Tai; he loved the horse. How could anyone, Wujen Ning thought, not love the horse?

The Kanlin woman, who frightened all of them a little (and elicited some crude talk at night), appeared to have decided Ning was all right. After an amused expression or two, she had accepted him as having a place close to them while they rode, or when they settled for the night.

(Ning didn't understand her glances. He didn't know what anyone could find amusing in any of this, but he had learned to accept that what made others smile could be a source of perplexity for him.)

They were stopping at large inns now at sundown, imperial posting stations. Good meals, a change of horses. They had documents, signed by the governor.

Ning was always entrusted with Dynlal at the end of a day's ride. He tried not to let his pride show, but it probably did. He talked to the horse at night, waking and walking out from whatever space he shared with the other soldiers, bringing apples to the stable. Sometimes he'd sleep there.

Master Shen didn't look at him much as they rode, or at any of them. He spoke occasionally with his Kanlin guard, more often with the poet who had joined them (another mystery). His preoccupation was with speed. None of the soldiers knew why, not even the one who acted as if he knew everything.

If Wei Song and the poet knew the reason, they weren't telling. The poet's name was Master Sima. The others said he was famous. Immortal, one of them declared. Ning knew nothing about that but he didn't think anyone was immortal. Maybe the emperor.

What he did know was that Shen Tai was in a great hurry to get to Xinan.

Ning wasn't, at all, but his own wishes and desires were as those of the silkworm that spins in subdued light amid a hush, and lives only to do that.

ON THE FIFTH DAY out of Chenyao, just before crossing an arched river bridge Tai had always loved, they'd come to a road branching south, running alongside the stream.

He had known it was coming, of course.

He'd been careful not to look down that road as they reached the junction, or to speed up his horse in feigned indifference as they went across the bridge above bright water. There were plum blossoms in the stream, he saw.

It was difficult. He knew that southern road as surely as he knew his own face in a bronze mirror. Every turn, every fall and rise. Knew the towns and hamlets you would pass, the fields and mulberry groves and silk farms. The one genuinely good wine shop, and the places to find a woman and a bed between the imperial road they were on and the home where he'd grown up, where his mothers and youngest brother were, and his father's grave.

Not him. Not Liu. Not Li-Mei.

The three of them were in the world, entangled in it. In the dust and noise, jade-and-gold. After two years by the lake he didn't know how he felt about that, he'd been moving east so fast he hadn't had time to think about it. That was, he decided, a component of the dust and noise: never enough time.

For Li-Mei it would be worse. Tai remembered the dust storms of the north. Real ones, stinging, blinding, dangerous, not a poet's imagery. There was so much anger when he thought of her.

He'd felt a tug within, a feeling nearly physical, as they passed the cut-off south. Two years and more since he'd been there, seen the gates in the stone wall, the worn-smooth statues beside it (to frighten demons away), the always-swept path, the goldfish ponds, the porch, garden, stream.

His father's grave-marker would be raised by now, he thought. The allotted time had passed. His mother would have done things properly, she always did. But Tai hadn't seen the headstone, hadn't bowed before it, didn't know what was inscribed, what verse had been chosen, what memorial words, who had been selected to do the calligraphy.

He'd been at Kuala Nor. And was going elsewhere now, riding past the road that would bring him home. There could be peace there at night, he thought, after two years of hearing the dead.

He knew that this speed was almost meaningless. It crossed into some showy gesture, a display of love for his sister, driving riders and horses hard towards Xinan, and to no point.

She'd already been gone when Sima Zian left the capital. He'd said so. The decision had been made before poor Yan had set out for Tai's family estate, thinking to find him there, to tell him what was being done to her. There might have been enough time if he'd been home.

Too late now. So why was he pushing on so fiercely, all of them awake before sunrise, riding till nightfall? The days were longer now, too, approaching the summer festival.

No one complained, not by word or glance. The soldiers would not (would never!), but neither did Wei Song, who had given considerable evidence of a willingness to advise him as to correct conduct. And Sima Zian, older and presumably suffering most from their pace, did not seem to be suffering at all. The poet never spoke to Tai about their speed, the folly of it, the absence of proportion.

Perhaps, with a lifetime of observing men, he'd understood from the beginning what Tai only gradually came to grasp: he wasn't thundering down this road on his glorious horse in a wild attempt to rescue his sister.

He was going to his brother.

Accepting that truth, acknowledging it, didn't bring anything like the calm that resolving uncertainty was supposed to do. For one thing, there was too much anger in him. It seemed to find new channels with every *li* they rode, every watch of the nights when he lay awake, even in the fatigued aftermath of the day's riding.

He didn't talk about any of this with the poet, and certainly not with Song, though he had a sense they both knew something of what was troubling him. He didn't enjoy the feeling of being understood so well, even by a new, dazzling friend, and certainly not by a Kanlin woman who was only here to guard him, and only because he'd made an impulsive decision at Iron Gate. He could have dismissed her by now. He had thirty soldiers.

He didn't dismiss her. He remembered, instead, how she'd fought at sunrise, in a garden in Chenyao.

IT WAS LATE in the day. Tai felt it in his legs and back. The sun was behind them, a mild summer's day, slight breeze. The imperial road was thronged with traffic. It was too crowded, too noisy, for any attempt to appreciate the beauty of late afternoon, the twilight to come.

They were three days past the cut-off to his home now, which meant less than two days from Xinan. They might even be there tomorrow, right around curfew. He knew this part of the road very well, had gone back and forth often enough through the years.

Even with the crowds they were going quickly. They used the middle of the three lanes, reserved for soldiers and imperial riders. A pair of imperial couriers, galloping even faster than they were, shouted for them to make room and they did, jostling some farm carts and laden peasants right off the road towards the drainage ditch. The couriers carried full saddlebags, obviously packed with more than message scrolls.

"Lychees for Wen Jian!" one of them shouted over his shoulder as the poet threw out a query.

Sima Zian laughed, then stopped laughing.

Tai thought about helping the farmers right their carts and goods, but there was too much urgency in him. They would help each other, he thought, and looking back saw that it was so. It was the way of life for country folk: they'd probably have been fearful and confused if soldiers had stopped to aid them.

He looked over at the poet. Zian's horse was beside his. Dynlal could have outrun all the others easily; a foolish thing to do. It might not be as foolish in a day or so. Tai had been thinking about that, of making his way ahead, entering Xinan quietly, before the gates closed at dusk. He had someone to see, and it might be more possible after dark.

The other man's expression was grave, as they watched the couriers disappear into dust ahead of them, carrying a delicacy for the Precious Consort. Lychees. The military post, wearing out horses with them.

"That is wrong. It is not …" Sima Zian began. He stopped.

Recklessly, Tai said, "Not proportionate?"

Zian looked around to ensure that no one else was near them. He nodded. "One word for it. I fear chaos, in the heavens, here on earth."

Words that could have you beaten and exiled. Even killed. Tai flinched, sorry he'd spoken. The poet saw it and smiled. "My apologies. Shall we discuss the verses of Chan Du? Let us do that. It always brings me pleasure. I wonder if he's in Xinan … I believe he is the best poet alive."

Tai cleared his throat, followed the lead. "I believe I am riding with the best poet alive."

Sima Zian laughed again, waved a hand dismissively. "We are very different men, Chan Du and I. Though he does enjoy his wine,

I am happy to say." A brief silence. "He wrote about Kuala Nor when he was younger. After your father's campaign. Do you know them, those verses?"

Tai nodded his head. "Of course I do." He had studied those poems.

Zian's eyes were tiger-bright. "Did they send you there? To the lake?"

Tai thought about it. "No. My father's sadness sent me there. One poem ... may have given me a task."

The other man considered that, then said:

Why sir, it is true: on the shores of Kuala Nor
White bones have lain for many years.
No one has gathered them. The new ghosts
Are bitter and angry, the old ghosts weep.
Under the rain and within the circle of mountains
The air is full of their cries.

"You thought it was a poet's imagery? About the ghosts?"

Tai nodded. "I imagine everyone does. If they haven't been there."

A short silence, and then the poet asked, "Son of Shen Gao, what is it you need to do when we arrive? How may I help you?"

Tai rode a little. Then said, very simply, "I do not know. I am eager to be counselled. What *should* I do?"

But Sima Zian only repeated back to him, "I do not know."

They rode on, the light very rich now, nearing day's end, the wind behind them. Tai felt it stir his hair. He reached forward and patted the mane of his horse. He loved the horse already, he thought. Sometimes it took no time at all.

The poet said, "You told me you wanted to kill someone."

Tai remembered. Late night in the White Phoenix Pleasure House. "I did say that. I am still angry, but trying not to be unwise. What would you do, in my place?"

A quick answer this time. "Take care to stay alive, first. You are a danger to many people. And they know you are coming."

Of course they did. He'd sent messages, the commander of Iron Gate had, Governor Xu would have sent letters, using all-night riders.

But Tai took the point, or what might have been part of a subtle man's point: it truly would not be wise to ride alone through the walls, to do whatever it was he wanted to do, if he decided what he wanted to do.

He realized that Zian was reining up beside him. Slowing Dynlal, Tai looked ahead, towards the side of the road, at a grassy space across the ditch. He realized, doing so, that it had become more than just foolish, any notion of slipping quietly into the city as darkness fell.

He stopped his horse. Lifted a hand so the others would do the same. Wei Song came up beside them and so, a little behind her, did the gap-toothed soldier whose name he could never remember. The one who always took care of Dynlal.

"Who is it?" Song asked quietly.

"Isn't it obvious?" asked the poet.

"Not to me!" she snapped.

"Look at the carriage," said Zian. There was an edge to his voice. The sun from behind them lit the road, the grass, and the carriage he was eyeing. "There are kingfisher feathers on it."

"That *isn't* the emperor!" Song said. "Stop being obscure. I need to know, to decide what—"

"Kanlin, look at the soldiers!" said Sima Zian. "Their uniforms."

A silence.

"Oh," said Song. And then she said it again.

The poet was looking at Tai. "Are you prepared for this?" A real question, the large eyes grave. "You may not have any more time to decide what you wish. He cannot be ignored, my friend."

Tai managed a thin smile. "I wouldn't dream of doing that," he said.

He urged Dynlal forward, towards a tight cluster of forty or fifty soldiers surrounding an enormous, sumptuously extravagant carriage. A carriage so big he wondered how they'd got it across the small bridge that carried the roadside ditch. Maybe, he thought, one of the bridges was larger, farther east? At a crossroads?

It didn't matter. The mind, he decided, could be peculiar at times like this with what it chose to dwell upon or ponder.

He heard hoofbeats. Looked back. He wasn't alone, after all: rumpled poet, small, fierce, black-clad Kanlin.

He reined up, looked across the ditch at the carriage. Kingfisher feathers decorating it, as the poet had pointed out. In the strict code of such things, these were reserved for the imperial household, but some, near enough to the throne, in high favour, might display that favour by using them.

He reminded himself that those in the palace—in all the different factions—would be wanting to enlist him to their cause if they could, not end his life.

He moved Dynlal across the roadway to the grass beside the ditch.

The door of the carriage was opened from the inside. A voice, unexpectedly light, slightly foreign, used to commanding, said bluntly, "Master Shen Tai? We will talk in here. Come now."

Tai drew another breath. Let it out. He bowed.

He said, "I will be honoured to converse with you, illustrious lord. Shall we speak at the posting station east of us? Your servant must attend to the needs of his soldiers and friends. They have been riding all day."

"No," said the man in the carriage.

Flat, absolute. Tai still couldn't see the speaker, not from where he was beside the road astride Dynlal. The voice added, "I wish not to be seen and known."

Tai cleared his throat. "My lord," he said, "there can be no one on this road who matters who does not know who is in this carriage. I will meet you at the posting inn. Perhaps we can dine together. It would be a great honour for me."

A face appeared in the window of the carriage. Enormous, round as a moon, under a black hat.

"No," repeated An Li, usually called Roshan, governor of three districts, adopted son of the Precious Consort. "Get in or I will have your soldiers killed and your friend decapitated and have you brought in here anyway."

It was surprising, given how crowded the road had been, but a space seemed to have somehow been shaped where they were, in both directions, east and west. Tai looked ahead, then over his shoulder, saw that other travellers were holding back. It was quiet, suddenly.

It matters, he told himself. *It matters what I do now.*

So he said, speaking very clearly, "Sima Zian, it is a grief to me, as it will surely be to the empire, that our friendship may end your illustrious life, but I must trust you to understand why this is so."

"Of course I do," said the poet. "What is friendship if it comes only when the wine cups are readily filled?"

Tai nodded. He turned to the Kanlin. "Wei Song, be good enough to ride back and advise Governor Xu's escort that they must prepare to be attacked by cavalry of the—" he glanced over at the horsemen by the carriage—"is it your Eighth or Ninth Army, honourable governor?"

From within the carriage there came no reply.

The man would be thinking hard. Tai had just said something, perhaps two things, that would register. He was pleased to note that his voice had remained level, as if he did this sort of thing every day.

"I believe it is the Ninth," said the poet.

"I obey, my lord," said Song, in the same moment.

He heard her galloping back to their cavalry. He didn't turn to watch. He looked at the carriage, at the round, silent moon-face within, just visible.

He said, quietly, "My lord, I am—honorary though the commission may be—an officer of the Second Military District, commanding cavalry, some of them assigned to me by Governor Xu himself. Regulations must shape my actions more than inclination. I carry important information for the court. I believe you know this. I believe that is why you have done me the honour of being here. I am not in a position to follow my desires and accept the privilege of hidden converse with you. There is too much embodied by that, with so many watching a carriage that bears kingfisher feathers. I am certain you will agree."

He was certain, in fact, of the opposite, but if he had any hope of remaining free in his own alignment, his decisions, surely he needed to—

From within, coldly, An Li said, "This is truly that drunken poet beside you? The one they call Immortal?"

Tai inclined his head. "The Banished Immortal, yes. I have the honour of his companionship and counsel."

Sima Zian, on his horse next to Tai's, sketched his bow. He was smiling, Tai saw, amazed. *That drunken poet.*

From within the carriage, a moment later, came a string of oaths startling in their crudeness, even to someone who had been a soldier.

In the silence that followed, the poet's smile deepened. "Are those formal requests of me, my lord? I admit I would find some of them difficult, at my age."

Roshan stared out at them both. The general's eyes were nearly lost in the creased folds of his face. It was hard to see them to get any reading of his thoughts. He was, Tai realized, even more frightening because of that.

It was said that once, fighting in the northeast, he had defeated an army of Shuoki tribesmen beyond the Wall, part of a border insurgency. He had ordered his soldiers and their Bogü allies to cut off one foot from each man captured, then he and his army had ridden off, taking the enemy horses, leaving the Shuoki to die in the grass, or survive, somehow, maimed.

There were other stories.

Now, in that oddly high, accented voice he said, "Don't be clever, poet. I have little patience for cleverness."

"My apologies," said Sima Zian, and Tai had a sense he might mean it.

"Your being here limits my actions."

"For that," said the poet, calmly, "I must decline to apologize, my lord, if your actions were to be as you suggested."

Roshan leaned back in his seat. They couldn't see him any more. Tai looked to his right. The sun was setting, he had to squint. Wei Song was arranging their men in a defensive alignment. They had not yet drawn their weapons. Traffic had come to a halt. The tale of this encounter, he knew, would race ahead of them now. It would be in Xinan before him.

That was the reason he was acting as he was. But there was a risk of dying here, of others dying for him. If a celebrated poet had not been with them …

From within the carriage he heard, "Son of Shen Gao, accept my sympathy for the passing of your honourable father. I knew of him, of course. I have journeyed two days from my own route to speak with you. I will not, for my own reasons, go back to that posting inn. They are not reasons you require to know. But if you enter my carriage, if you … honour me by doing so … I will begin by telling you what happened to a man you will be looking for, and show you a letter."

Tai registered the changed tone. He said, carefully, "That man would be?"

"His name is Xin Lun."

Tai felt his heart thump.

"Lun?" he repeated.

"Yes. He arranged for the assassins sent to kill you."

Tai swallowed hard. His mouth was dry. "How do you know this?"

"He told me himself."

"When did he … what did happen to him?"

A mistake, perhaps, asking this. It created an obligation of courtesy if the other man answered.

The other man answered. "He was killed some nights ago."

"Oh," said Tai.

"The same night word came that you were on your way to Xinan, and the news of the White Jade Princess's gift. The horses. Your own is magnificent, by the way. I assume you will not sell him?"

"The same night?" Tai said, a little stupidly.

The vast, incongruous face reappeared in the carriage window like the moon from behind clouds. "I said that. He sent me an urgent request for sanctuary, explaining why. I offered it. He was murdered on his way from the Ta-Ming to my house." A fat finger appeared, pointed at Tai. "Master Shen, you know your trouble isn't with me. It is with the first minister. Your life depends on realizing that. It is Wen Zhou who is trying to kill you. You need friends."

Tai was badly shaken. Lun was dead. Drinking companion, fellow student—a man he'd intended to kill himself, in Yan's name. Discharging an obligation to another ghost.

One less obligation now? Was that good? Did it free him?

It didn't feel that way. There was a letter. It might tell him the other thing he needed to know—and feared to learn.

"Get in," said Roshan. Impatience in the voice, but not anger.

He swung open the carriage door again.

Tai took a breath. Sometimes you just went with the way the wind was blowing. He dismounted. He handed Dynlal's reins up to the poet, who said nothing. Tai jumped down into the ditch, and accepted the hand of an officer of the Ninth District to climb to the other side.

He entered the carriage, closed the door himself.

IT WAS A RESPONSE to the realities of the main imperial roads that in most of the posting inns along them the stables were larger than the accommodations available for travellers.

Civil service messengers and military couriers, the most regular users of the staging inns, were constantly wearing out and changing horses, often not lingering for the night. A meal, back in the saddle. The whole point was to ride through the darkness down the middle of the road, not to seek out a feathered bed, let alone wine and a girl. Time mattered in a far-flung empire.

There were merchants and army officers on the roads, aristocrats going to and from country estates, moving with rather less urgency, and there were civil servants travelling to or returning from postings to various prefectures, or on tours of inspection there. For these, of course, rooms and adequate food were required.

The inns nearest to Xinan tended to be different. Their wine was generally excellent, and so were the girls and music. High-ranking mandarins making short journeys from the capital didn't need their carriage horses changed but did demand a better quality of chamber and meal if, for example, they wished to time a return to the city for the hours before curfew fell.

The Mulberry Grove Rest House, not far from Xinan, qualified as one of the more elaborately appointed places to spend a night on the main east-west road.

Mulberry trees were long gone from the environs of the inn, as were the silk farms associated with them. The inn's name evoked quieter days many hundred years ago, before Xinan had grown into what it now was. There was a plaque in the main courtyard, inscribed in the Fifth Dynasty: a verse extolling the serenity of the inn and its countryside.

It made for some irony. By the time Tai and his company rode into the inn yard, well after darkfall, it was as noisy and crowded as the road had been. Two riders had been sent ahead to arrange their stay, or finding rooms would have been doubtful.

Torches were lit in the inn yard. The night had been starry as they approached, the Sky River showing, a sliver of moon. These were lost in the smoky, clattering chaos of the main courtyard.

Tai's horsemen were bunched around him. On guard, aggressively alert. He imagined Song had given the orders. Issues of rank in their company had been worked out; his Kanlin Warrior could speak for him. The soldiers might hate her for it, but that would have always been the case with a woman. In any event, Song didn't seem inclined to worry about being well liked by soldiers.

Tai was too preoccupied as they rode in to be unhappy about how protective they were. In fact, with some ruefulness, he realized that he didn't even mind it any more. He'd been frightened in that carriage by the road, and was still disturbed.

The two advance riders they'd sent reported to Song and their captain. Their company had three rooms, seven or eight to a room. There was a chamber for Tai and Sima Zian to share. The other soldiers would sleep in the stable. There were to be guards posted tonight, Tai learned, listening without much concentration to orders being given in his name. He ought to be paying closer attention, probably. He found it difficult.

He had no problem sharing a room with the poet. For one thing, Zian hadn't made it to their chamber from the pleasure pavilions in the other inns where this had happened. This was a man who had earned legendary status in diverse ways. Tai could never have sustained the hours and the drinking the poet managed—and Sima Zian had to be twenty years older than Tai was.

They dismounted in a clatter of weapons and armour and the stamp and snort of tired, hungry horses. Servants ran in every direction through the courtyard. It would not, Tai thought, be difficult to kill him here. One suborned servant, one assassin with a knife or on a rooftop with a bow. He looked up. Smoke from torches. He was very tired.

He forced himself to stop thinking about it. Held to the core truth underlying all of this: killing him now, with word of the Sardian horses already in Xinan, represented a reckless, possibly suicidal act for anyone.

Even an enormous, and enormously powerful, military governor of three districts. Even the first minister of Kitai.

He looked around, trying to bring himself into the present, not let his thoughts run too far ahead, or linger behind. Song was at his elbow. So, until a moment ago when Tai dismounted, had been the gap-toothed soldier from Iron Gate.

He shook his head, suddenly irritated. "What is the name of that one who always takes Dynlal?" He spotted the man, leading the horse towards the stables. "I should know it by now."

Song tilted her head a little, as if surprised. "A border soldier? Not really. But he's called Wujen. Wujen Ning." He saw her teeth flash. "You'll forget it again."

"I will not!" Tai said, and swore under his breath. He took immediate steps to fix the name in memory. An association: Ning was the metalsmith in the village near their estate.

He looked at the woman in the flickering light. Torches were above them, over the portico. Other lights moved through the yard. Insects were out now after dark. Tai slapped at one on his arm. "We are less than a day from your sanctuary," he murmured. "Do you wish to go home, Kanlin?"

He'd caught her by surprise, he saw. Wasn't sure why, it was an obvious question.

"Do you wish to dismiss your servant, my lord?"

He cleared his throat. "I don't think so. I have no cause to question your competence."

"I am honoured by your trust," she said formally.

Zian strode over from—predictably—the direction of the music, to the right of this first courtyard.

"I have arranged a table," he said cheerfully, "and I have requested that their best saffron wine be heated, seeing as we have had a long, difficult day." He grinned at Song. "I trust you will approve the expense?"

"I only carry the money," she murmured. "I don't approve the spending of it, except for the soldiers."

"Make sure they have wine," Tai said.

The poet gestured with one hand, and Tai went with him through the crowd. Song stayed beside them, her expression alert. It made him weary, this need for vigilance. It was not a life he'd ever wanted.

How many men were allowed the life they wanted?

Maybe this one, he thought, looking at the poet moving eagerly ahead of him towards where they could just hear a *pipa* being played, in a room beyond the courtyard noise. *This one, or maybe my brother.*

"YOUR BROTHER," Roshan had said without preamble, as Tai closed the carriage door and sat opposite him, "is not named in the letter. It was read to me several times. I do not," he'd added, "read, myself."

It was widely known. A source of derision among the aristocrats and the examination-trained mandarins. It was regarded as a principal reason why the endlessly subtle Chin Hai, once first minister, once feared everywhere, now gone to his ancestors, had allowed Roshan and other barbarian generals to acquire so much power on the borders. An illiterate had no chance of threatening him at the centre of his webs in the Ta-Ming, the way an aristocrat with an army could.

Such, at any rate, had been the view of the students taking the examinations, or preparing to. And, of course, whatever they agreed upon had to be true, did it not?

Settling into the carriage, Tai had immediately felt out of his depth. Which was, he was certain, the point of Roshan's remark.

"Why would you imagine I'd consider that possible? That my brother could be accused of anything regarding me?"

He was delaying, trying to get his bearings. The governor leaned back against a profusion of cushions, eyeing him. An Li was, from this close, even more awesomely vast. A size that seemed mythic, a figure of legend.

He had, when not yet promoted to the rank of general, led three companies of Seventh District cavalry through five brutal days and nights of riding to turn the tide of battle against an incursion from the Koreini Peninsula. The Koreini of the far east, ambitious under their own emperor, had elected that spring to test the Kitan emperor's commitment to the building of garrison forts beyond the Wall.

They had been given an answer, to their very great cost—but only because of Roshan. That was twenty years ago. Tai's father had told him about that ride.

He had told Liu, as well, Tai remembered.

An Li shifted on his cushions again. "Your brother is principal counsellor to the first minister. Shen Liu has made his choice of paths. The letter—you may read it—indicates that Prime Minister Wen had his reasons for wishing you no longer among us, or in a dear woman's thoughts. Or perhaps able to disrupt your brother's plans for your sister. He does, after all, depend on Shen Liu for a great deal. It was the first minister who formally proposed your sister's elevation to exalted status. You did know that?"

Tai shook his head. He hadn't, but it made sense.

The governor sighed, fluttered a hand. His fingers were unexpectedly long. He wore a sweet, floral scent, it filled the carriage. He said, "Spring Rain? Is that the charming creature's name? It will puzzle me until I draw my last breath how men can be so undone by women." He paused, then added, thoughtfully, "Not even the highest among us are immune to the folly of that."

Nothing he says is unplanned, Tai told himself. And that last remark was treason, since *the highest among us* could only mean the emperor.

Tai said, possibly making a mistake, "I might risk such a course myself for a woman."

"Indeed? I had thought you might be different. This Lin Chang—that is her name now?—is she so *very* appealing? I confess I grow curious."

"I never knew that name. We called her Rain. But I am not speaking of her, my lord. You have mentioned two women."

Roshan's eyes were slits. Tai wondered how well the man could even see. The governor waited. He shifted in his seat again.

Tai said, "If you can bring my sister back from the Bogü lands before she is married there, I will claim and then assign all of my Sardian horses to the armies of the Seventh, Eighth, and Ninth Districts."

He hadn't known he was going to say that.

An Li made a small, involuntary movement of one hand. Tai realized he'd startled the other man. The general said as much: "You are more direct than your brother, aren't you?"

"We have little in common," Tai said.

"A sister?" the other man murmured.

"And a father of distinction, as you were gracious enough to mention. But we see different paths to extending the family honour. I have made you a formal proposal, Governor An."

"You would do this, you would give them to me, *all* of them, for a girl?"

"For my sister."

From outside Tai heard sounds again: traffic on the roadway had resumed, creaking cartwheels, laughter, shouts. Life moving, on a spring day. He kept his gaze on the man opposite.

At length, Roshan shook his head. "I would do it. For two hundred and fifty Sardian horses? Of course I would. I am thinking now, right here, of how to do it. But it is impossible. I believe you know that. I might even accuse you of toying with me."

"It would be untrue," Tai said quietly.

The man across from him shifted yet again, stretching a massive leg to one side, with a grunt. He said, "Five horses would have been generous as a gift. Princess Cheng-wan has shaken your life, hasn't she?"

Tai said nothing.

"She has," the governor went on. "Like a storm shakes a tree, or even uproots it. You have to choose what to do now. You might be killed to *stop* you from choosing. I could do it here."

"Only if it did not get back to the Ta-Ming, to the first minister, whose action cost the empire those horses."

An Li stared at him with those slitted eyes.

"You all want them too much," Tai said.

"Not if they go to an enemy, Shen Tai."

Tai noted the word. He said, "I just offered them to you."

"I heard you. But I cannot do it, since it cannot be done. Your sister is gone, son of Shen Gao. She is north of the Wall by now. She is with the Bogü."

He grinned suddenly. A malicious smile. No sense of any genial, amusing figure of the court, the one who'd allowed himself to be swaddled like a baby by all the women. "She may be with child to the kaghan's son as we speak. At the least she will know his inclinations. I have heard stories. I wonder if your brother knew them, before he proposed her as wife to the kaghan's heir."

The sweetness of the perfume was almost sickening suddenly. "Why be uncivilized?" Tai said before he could stop himself.

He was fighting anger. Reminded himself again that the other man was not saying these things—was not saying *anything*—without purpose.

Roshan seemed amused. "Why uncivilized? Because I am! I am a soldier all my life. And my father's tribe warred with the Bogü. Shen Tai, you are not the only one to be direct by inclination."

"Let me see the letter," Tai said. Being direct.

It was handed across without a word. He read, quickly. It was a copy, the calligraphy was too regular. No mention of Liu, as Roshan had indicated. But ...

Tai said, "He is clear, Xin Lun. Says he expects to be killed that night. Begs you to guard him. Why did you not send men to bring him to you?"

The expression on the other man's face made him feel, again, out of his depth. Childlike.

An Li shrugged, turned his neck one way and then the other, stretching it. "I suppose I could have. He did ask for protection, didn't he? Perhaps you are right."

"Perhaps?" Tai was struggling, heard it in his voice.

The general betrayed impatience. "Shen Tai, it is important in any battle to know your own strengths and weaknesses and to understand your enemy's. Your father *must* have taught you this."

"What does that have to do—?"

"Wen Zhou would have learned of your horses and your survival as soon as word reached the palace. As soon as anyone learned it that night. That is why Xin Lun knew he was in danger. The first minister could not let him live, knowing what he knew, and with what he'd done. Zhou is a fool, but dangerous."

"So why not send your soldiers for Lun?"

The general shook his massive head, as if sorrowing for the ignorance of the world. "Where was this happening, Shen Tai? Where were we all?"

"Xinan. But I don't—"

"Think! *I don't have an army there.* It is not permitted to me, to anyone. I am on my enemy's ground without my forces. If I shelter Lun in the capital, I am declaring war on the first minister that very night, where he has the weapons he needs and I do not!"

"You ... you are the favourite of the emperor, of the Precious Consort."

"No. We are *both* favoured. It was a policy. But our so-glorious emperor is unpredictable now, too distracted, and Jian is young, and a woman, which *means* unpredictable. They are not, son of Shen Gao, reliable. I could not bring Lun into my home and be halfway certain of leaving Xinan alive."

Tai looked down at the letter in his hand. Read it again, mostly to give himself time. He was beginning to see.

"So ... you let Lun believe you would. You offered him sanctuary. That led him to start down through the city."

"Good," said An Li. "You are not a fool. Are you as dangerous as your brother?"

Tai blinked. "I may be dangerous to him."

The general smiled, shifted again. "A good answer. It amuses me. But come, work it through. What did I do that night?"

Tai said, slowly, "You did send men, didn't you? But not to escort Xin Lun. Only to observe."

"Good, again. And why?"

Tai swallowed. "To see when he was killed."

An Li smiled. "When, and by whom."

"The killer was seen?"

"Of course he was. And by the Gold Bird Guards, as well. My men made certain of it. The Guard were persuaded not to do anything yet, but have recorded what they saw that night."

Tai looked at him, the small eyes, florid face. "One of Wen Zhou's retainers killed Lun?"

"Of course."

As simple as that.

"But if Lun is dead …?"

"The honourable Xin Lun is as useful to me murdered as alive. Especially if the city guards know who did it. The letter is what I needed, along with the observed killing of the letter-writer by a known person. The first minister has generously obliged me. Xin Lun in my home might have had me arrested. Xinan was the wrong place for me to begin a battle."

Tai let that last sink into awareness, stone in a pond.

"Are you beginning a battle?"

There was a silence. He wasn't entirely sure he wanted an answer. Sounds from outside again. The customary back and forth of the road. An irritated outcry, an oath, more laughter. A day moving towards a usual end, sunset and the stars.

"Tell me," the man opposite said, "were you really burying dead soldiers at Kuala Nor for two years?"

"Yes," Tai said.

"Were there ghosts?"

"Yes."

"That was bravely done, then. As a soldier I honour it. I could kill you here, if I decided your horses would somehow determine the course of events."

"You don't think they will?"

"They might. I have decided to act as if it is not so, and to spare you." He shifted position yet again.

"You'd have lost—"

"Rank, title, all granted lands. Possibly my life. And so, Shen Tai, what does that tell you, by way of answering the question you asked?"

Are you beginning a battle? he'd asked.

Tai cleared his throat, managed a half-smile. "It tells me I need to be grateful you've decided the horses might not matter as much as some others seem to think."

A moment of stillness, then the carriage rocked to Roshan's laughter. It lasted a long time.

When he finally subsided, coughing, the governor said, "You can't see it, can you? You have been too long away. I am being pushed towards my destruction or to resisting it. Wen Zhou is rolling dice. That is his nature. But I cannot, I *will* not linger in Xinan to see what the emperor does, whether Jian chooses her cousin or ... her adopted child."

Tai had never seen a smile so lacking in mirth.

He shivered. The governor saw it, of course. The narrow eyes in the folds of flesh. Roshan said, "You may keep that copy, it might be of use to you. And perhaps to me, if you choose to remember who gave it to you, eventually." He shifted his outstretched leg one more time.

Eventually. Everything he said had layers of meaning.

And so, Tai abruptly realized, with a sudden hard shock of understanding, did his movements. They had nothing to do with restlessness. The man was in pain. Once you saw it, it was obvious.

Tai looked away, an instinct to hide what he'd realized. He wasn't at all sure how he'd intuited this, but he was certain he was right. And that An Li would not be pleased to have it noted.

"I ... I am not part of this," he said, thinking hard. He wondered now about the scent, that too-sweet perfume. Was it covering something else?

"I'm afraid that is not true. Everyone will be part, if this happens. That includes you, unless you go back to Kuala Nor, and the dead. And maybe even there. I told you, the princess in Rygyal has seized hold of your life." He gestured, his hands outspread. "I would be very cautious with those horses. You may find yourself between cliffs and tigers, as we say in the northeast." He dropped one hand in his lap, motioned with the other. "You may go, son of Shen Gao. I have my own road to take now. Remain guarded in Xinan."

"You are not going back?"

The other man shook his head. "It was a mistake to go to court this spring. My oldest son said as much, tried to stop me. I sent him back north four days ago. To our own ground." That cold smile. "He knows how to read, my son. Even writes poetry. I don't understand it."

Another piece seemed to be trying to slide into place, like one of the puzzle toys his sister used to love. Tai tried to remember what he knew about the sons.

"But you came this way yourself to—"

"To meet you, and decide if you might give your horses to Wen Zhou. I have satisfied myself you will not."

Tai felt a calmness descend. "And if you had satisfied yourself otherwise?"

"There would have been a fight here. A small, first battle. Your cavalry would have been killed, and probably the poet. But certainly you, first of all. I would have had no choice."

"Why?"

A reckless question but he never received an answer to it. Not in words. Only another mirthless smile.

It was then, looking at that expression, that a feeling overtook Tai unlike any he'd ever known.

He said, before an instinct for caution could stop the words, "Governor An, honoured general, you do not have to shape your son's legacy. You have your own to devise yet, my lord. We who follow great fathers, we must make our own paths and choices. This empire has been defended by you all these years. Surely you can allow yourself some rest now? Some easing of ... of painful burdens?"

Too close, too much said. The look he received was as bleak and frightening as anything he'd ever experienced. He thought of wolves, of teeth and claws in his own flesh. Coming directly after the earlier, inward sensation, an impulse sharp as a thorn, it almost made him ill. An Li did not speak again. Tai said nothing more.

The carriage door was opened for him by the governor, leaning over to do so. A gesture of courtesy from someone of such rank. Tai bowed where he sat, then stepped out and down into the late-day light and what looked, surprisingly, to be the ordinary world.

HE WAS IRRITABLY AWARE that Wei Song was watching them from the far side of the room, near the doorway to the courtyard. He was in a recessed alcove with the poet, drinking good wine too quickly. Quiet music was playing.

There was food. He wasn't hungry. He'd felt a need to become drunk, wasn't there yet. He didn't want to be dealing with the thoughts he was carrying. *A river too deep*, as a friend had written once.

Not a very good line, in truth, though it lodged in the mind.

It didn't matter how deep a river was, what mattered was how swiftly the water flowed, how cold it was, if there were dangerous creatures in it, if it had rapids or falls.

Tai drained another cup of saffron wine. Looked around the room, saw his Kanlin watching him, some distance away.

He didn't like the set of her too-wide mouth, or that intense, alert scrutiny. The mixture of concern and disapproval in it.

So, I'm drinking, he wanted to say. *There a reason I shouldn't be?* It wasn't as if she'd ever cast that sort of glance at Sima Zian, though the man spent every single night and most of the days doing exactly this.

It occurred to him, gazing across the crowded room, that he'd never seen her in anything but the black tunic and leggings or robe of a Kanlin, and he never would. Her hair had been unbound, that first sunrise, at Iron Gate. He'd thought she was another assassin. She wasn't. Rain had sent her. Rain was sleeping now a little more than a day's ride from here. In Wen Zhou's home. In his bed, perhaps. Or maybe she was in his bed and not asleep.

She had tried to tell him this might happen.

It came to him to be irritated again by the too obviously professional appraisal his Kanlin was still giving him. His Kanlin. That was why the poet never got this look. Zian hadn't hired her. He just ... enjoyed her presence.

The poet was an easy companion. He could talk if that was your mood, or sit as quietly as you needed. Tai shook his head. Found himself returning, against his will, to the end of the encounter in Roshan's carriage.

The reason he was drinking.

The *pipa* subsided, a flute took up the melody. Across the small platform the poet was, as best Tai could tell, a few drinks behind him for the first time ever. No judgment in those eyes. No amusement either. You could say that was a judgment of sorts.

Tai didn't feel like saying it, or thinking it, or having his mind working on anything at all tonight. He gestured vaguely and a sleek figure in pale-blue silk was beside them, filling his cup. He was vaguely aware of perfume, the cut of her gown. Xinan fashion for this season, he imagined. They were almost there. He'd been away two years. They were almost there.

"A woman is generally better than wine for pushing thoughts away. And almost always better for your head." Zian smiled gently.

Tai stared at the other man.

The poet added, quietly, *"In the depths of the wood I hear only birds. You need not say anything, but I am listening."*

Tai shrugged. "I'm here. We're all alive. My brother's name wasn't in that letter. I'd say it was a *good* encounter. Respectful. Illuminating."

"Would you?"

It was, more than the words, the calm, forest-deep gaze that brought him up short in his striving for irony.

In the depths of the wood ... His reply had been unworthy: of this man, of what had just happened, of what Tai was dealing with. The *pipa* resumed, joining the flute. The players were very good.

"I'm sorry," he said. He lowered his head. Looked up. "You told me earlier today that it felt as if something was approaching. You called it chaos."

"I did."

"I think you are right. I think it is almost certain."

"And you want to do something? That is what troubles you? Shen Tai, we need to remember what we are, our limitations."

And so Tai did end up saying, after all, what he'd been thinking (or trying not to think). "I could have killed him. In the carriage. He is not young. He is in great pain, all the time. I had my knife. Do you understand? I was *there*, and I listened to him speak and I thought: this is what I must do! For the empire. For all of us." He looked away. "I have never had such a feeling in my life."

"Well, you spoke of killing someone, while we rode."

He had. He'd meant Xin Lun. "That was about Yan's death. A response. This was different. It felt as if I *owed* Roshan's death, and my own, to ... to everyone else. That it was required of me. Before it is too late."

He saw that he'd disturbed the other man, finally.

"What does he intend?"

"He's left Xinan, going back northeast. His son has already gone. He feared remaining in the city. Says Wen Zhou was forcing him. He has Xin Lun's letter. It shows the first minister tried to kill me."

"Will anyone believe it?"

"I think so. Roshan has people, including the Gold Bird Guards, who saw that Zhou had Lun killed. Because he knew too much."

He had never seen the poet look like this. "He went northeast to do what?"

Tai just looked at him.

"You'd have been killed immediately," Zian said, finally. "Surely, you know it."

"Of course I do! Sometimes you have to accept that, don't you? Isn't that what courage is? In a soldier? I think I was a coward, today."

Tai drained his cup again.

The poet shook his head. "No. Ending a life, two lives that way? And other people on that road. You weren't ready to pretend to be a god."

"Perhaps. Or I wasn't ready to accept my own death. Offer it. It might have been that."

The poet stared at him. Then said:

Full moon is falling through the sky.
Cranes fly through clouds.
Wolves howl. I cannot find rest
Because I am powerless
To amend a broken world.

Sima Zian added, "I love the man who wrote that, I told you before, but there is so much *burden* in Chan Du. Duty, assuming all tasks, can betray arrogance. The idea we can know what must be done, and do it properly. We cannot know the future, my friend. It claims so much to imagine we can. And the world is not broken any more than it always, always is."

Tai looked at him and then away, across the room.

Wei Song had gone. He didn't know where. The music continued. It was very beautiful.

PART THREE

CHAPTER XV

He woke from another dream that escaped him, slipping away like a salmon from his childhood grasp in a cold river. Awareness of morning came.

It was not a dream of a fox-woman, not this time. No desire, no sense of desire spent. Instead, wistfulness, loss, as if something, someone, was leaving, was already gone, like the dream itself. A path in life, a person, a shape to the world? All of these?

I am powerless to amend a broken world.

It occurred to him, still half asleep, that the way Chan Du had phrased that celebrated grief, it suggested other worlds than this. Others that might need mending—or amending. The two words were not the same, Tai thought, though they glided into each other, in the way the best poetry did.

Then that thought, too, fled from him as a rapping came at his door, and Tai understood that he had heard it already, asleep, that it was the knocking that had awakened him, sending the dream away down the river of night with the moon.

He glanced over. The second bed was empty, had not been occupied—as usual, although the poet's manner had been sombre when Tai had left him after their talk last night.

Wei Song and two of the soldiers had been in the courtyard when he'd crossed it to go to bed. They'd walked him to the door of his room. It was clear they were going to stay outside. Three guards now. Roshan had warned him to be cautious. Tai hadn't told that to Song but she'd made changes anyhow. He'd said nothing, not even a good night.

Another knocking. Not imperative or demanding. But it was also—he knew this from the courtesy of that sound—not his Kanlin summoning him.

From outside came a voice, carefully pitched, exquisitely cultured: "Honourable Shen Tai, be so gracious as to acknowledge a humble servant's presence and request."

Tai sat up in bed. "You haven't made any request, and I don't know whose presence I am acknowledging."

"I bow twice in shame. Forgive me, noble sir. My name is too unworthy to be offered. But I am entrusted with the office of second steward in the household of the Shining and Exalted Companion. You are invited to present your honourable self."

"She is here?"

The steward said, with the faintest hint of asperity, "No, no, she is at Ma-wai. We are sent to bring you there, with all courtesy."

Tai began dressing very quickly.

It was beginning. You could say it had begun by Kuala Nor, when Bytsan sri Nespo had brought him a letter. Or at Chenyao, when the governor of the Second and Third Military Districts had sought to claim him and his horses, had even sent a daughter to him at night. A sign, in silk, of what might come.

You could say there never was a clear beginning to anything in life, unless it was the moment you drew your first breath in the world.

Or you could say it was beginning now.

Because the Shining and Exalted Companion was also called Precious Consort and Beloved Companion, and her name was Wen Jian. The court hadn't waited for him to get to Xinan. It had come for him.

He splashed water on his face at the basin. Tied his hair hastily and then did it again to marginally better effect. Rubbed his teeth with a finger. Used the chamber pot. Put his swords on, his boots.

He went to the door. Just before opening it, a thought occurred.

"Wei Song, please report."

Silence. Tai drew a breath. He truly didn't want a confrontation here, but ...

"Steward, where is my Kanlin guard?"

On the other side of the door, the steward cleared his throat. His voice was as smooth as before, however. "The Shining and Exalted Companion is not always enamoured of Kanlin Warriors, my lord."

"Not everyone is. What does that have to do with the present circumstance?"

"Your guard was assertive in trying to prevent us from knocking at your door."

"As was her duty, since I was asleep. Once more: where is she?"

A hesitation. "She is here, of course."

"Then why is she not answering me?"

"I ... do not know, my lord."

Tai knew. "Steward, unless Wei Song is released by those holding her, and until she speaks to me, I am not opening my door to you. I have no doubt you can break it down, but you did speak of respect, and of courtesy. I expect both."

This was not the mildest way to begin a day. He heard quick, low speech outside. He waited.

"Master Shen," he heard her say, finally. "I am shamed. I could not prevent them from disturbing your rest." They would have been holding her. She would have refused to speak until she was free.

He opened the door.

He took in the scene before him. The steward was bowing. There were a dozen soldiers in the courtyard's morning light. Two of them had wounds: one was on the ground, being attended to, another was upright but holding a hand to a bleeding side. Both, he saw with relief, looked as if they would be all right. Song stood among them with her own swords removed from her. They lay beside her. Her head was lowered.

She had, evidently, fought imperial soldiers for him. He saw his other two guards of the night. They were kneeling to one side, unharmed.

Tai's soldiers, far outnumbering these new arrivals, were standing in the middle of the courtyard. But the difference in numbers was meaningless. This steward was leading men of the imperial guard of the Emperor Taizu, might he rule a thousand years in joy upon the Phoenix Throne. These were elite soldiers of the Ta-Ming Palace. You didn't fight them, or deny them anything, unless you were keen to have your head on a spear at the city gates.

Tai saw the poet among his own soldiers. Zian didn't seem amused or curious this morning. He looked concerned and alert, though rumpled as ever: hair untied, belt askew.

There was a crowd in the courtyard beyond all of these. Gathered, early of a morning to see what was happening, why a company from the court was here. Who it was they had come to seize, or summon, or honour.

The second son of General Shen Gao, once Left Side Commander of the Pacified West, said, carefully, "Steward, you do me too much honour."

The man straightened from his bow, a practised movement. He was older than Tai, had little hair, just fringes at the sides. He affected a thin moustache, likely a fashion. No sword. The black robe of a civil servant, red belt of rank, key of office dangling at his waist.

The steward bowed again, fist in palm this time, in response to Tai's words. They were doing this very formally, Tai thought. It made him nervous.

He had a sudden image in his mind, vivid as a master-painting, of the mountains ringing Kuala Nor in springtime, rising up, and up. No men to be seen, just birds, mountain goats and sheep on the slopes, and the lake below.

He shook his head. He looked to his left, and saw a sedan chair waiting for him. He blinked. It was dazzling. It gleamed in the sunlight. It made Roshan's carriage yesterday look like a farmer's market cart.

There was gold adorning the four pillars. The rods the bearers would hold were banded in ivory and onyx, and he was fairly certain, even from here, that the wood was sandalwood. The curtains were heavy, worked silk, with the phoenix symbol, and they were yellow, which only the emperor's household could use. Kingfisher feathers were everywhere, iridescent, shimmering. Too many of them; an opulence that was almost an assault if you knew how rare they were, brought from how far, what they would have cost.

He saw jade decorations at the cross pieces, top and bottom, of the curtained cabin on the rods. White jade and pale-green and dark-green. The rods were long enough for eight bearers, not four, or six, and there were eight men standing by, expressionless, to carry him to Ma-wai.

He had tried, vainly in the event, to keep some control, some distance yesterday when An Li had summoned him beside the road. He tried again.

"Wei Song, reclaim your weapons and make arrangements for Dynlal to be saddled." He glanced at the steward. "I prefer to ride. I will be grateful for your escort, however."

The steward looked utterly composed, his expression formally regretful. "I fear your Kanlin cannot be permitted arms. She drew upon the imperial household guard. She must, of course, be punished."

Tai shook his head. "That is not acceptable. She was under orders that my night not be disturbed. There have been—I imagine your mistress knows this—attempts upon my life. If I die, the empire suffers a great loss. And I am *not* referring to my own unworthy life."

The slightest hint of unease in the man's smooth face, adjustments being made. "Even so, my lord, it remains that she—"

"She did exactly what she was ordered to do in the interests of Kitai and her current master. I am curious, second steward, did your soldiers explain their purpose? Did they invite her to knock at the door and address me?"

A silence. He turned to Song.

"Wei Song, report: were these things done?"

Her head was high now. "I regret it was not so, my lord. They came up on the portico, ignored requests to stop. Ignored requests for an explanation. This one, the steward, went straight to your door."

"Surely you saw their imperial livery?"

"My lord, livery can be a disguise. It is a known device. Men have been slain through that artifice. And the sedan chair did not arrive until after I had engaged the soldiers. I am shamed and sorry to have caused you distress. I will, of course, accept any punishment due to me."

"None is due," Tai said flatly. "Steward, I will make answer to your mistress for my servant, but I will not accompany you willingly if she is in any way harmed, or impeded from guarding me."

"Soldiers have been injured," the steward repeated.

"So was she," Tai said.

It was true. He saw blood on Song's shoulder, a rip in her tunic. She would be, he thought, more distressed at being defeated (by a dozen of the best-trained soldiers in the Ta-Ming) than anything else. He let his voice grow cold. "If there is anyone who can confirm the report she has offered, I daresay the fault—and the punishment—does not lie with my guard, and I will say as much at Ma-wai." He lifted his voice. "Sima Zian, will you be good enough to assist?"

It was useful sometimes to have a celebrated name to bring into a conversation, and see what ensued. In a different time and place, he might have been amused.

The steward wheeled, stumbling, as if caught in a swirl of wind. He spied the poet, who had obligingly stepped forward to be spied. The steward achieved two bows with speed, but his composure was clearly shaken.

Zian smiled genially. "I do not believe, to my great distress, that the Lady Wen Jian is fond of me this spring. I would be honoured and grateful to have the chance to express my respect for her, should the opportunity arise."

He'd hinted to this effect, Tai remembered, in their first conversation. A reason he'd left Xinan.

"Master Sima," the steward spluttered. "This is unexpected! To find you in the … in the company of Master Shen Gao, er, Shen Tai."

"Poets turn up in strange places. I was here this morning to see your soldiers refuse a request to explain themselves at Master Shen's doorway. I believe a Kanlin must respond to that refusal, by the code of their order. Han Chung of the Seventh Dynasty has a verse on the subject, praising their dedication. The poem was a favourite of the glorious emperor's illustrious father, now with the gods and his ancestors. Perhaps he is even listening to Han Chung recite in one of the nine heavens." Zian lifted a hand piously. "We can only hope, amid the dust and noise of the world, that it might be so."

Tai felt an impulse to laugh, so befuddled did the steward look.

He schooled his features. He said, as gravely as he could, "Steward, I am accompanied by the illustrious Master Sima, by a Kanlin guard, and by a company of soldiers personally assigned to my command by Governor Xu Bihai. I will ride among them. I am humbled by your mistress's invitation to attend upon her and will make my way to Ma-wai immediately. Would you do me the honour of riding with us?"

He said it loudly, he wanted people to hear.

From this point forward, he thought, a great deal of what happened would be for display—positions, and posturing. He knew that much about the court.

The steward of Wen Jian knew more, of course. But the man seemed acutely uncomfortable now. He cleared his throat again, shifted his feet. An awkward silence descended. He seemed to be waiting. For what, Tai didn't know.

"Ride with me," Tai repeated. "There has been a minor embarrassment here, nothing of consequence. I will happily tell your mistress that you were properly zealous in her cause."

"Master Shen, your entirely unworthy servant begs forgiveness. It was not considered that you might decline the sedan chair. It is known that you are attached to your horse and we wished to ensure it came safely with us. Some of our soldiers took it already this morning, from the stables here. They are to meet us at Ma-wai. Of course no harm will come to—"

"*You took my horse?*"

Tai felt a hard pulsing at his temples. He was aware that Wei Song had reclaimed her weapons, just below him in the courtyard. The imperial soldiers made no movement to stop her. Zian stepped forward to stand beside her. The poet's face was cold now, the wide eyes watchful.

Tai said, to Song, "Dynlal was guarded?"

"As always, my lord," she replied.

The steward cleared his throat again. This morning's encounter had not, quite evidently, unfolded as he had expected it to. "Two of the three men by the horse, I understand, were prompt to stand aside, as was proper, given who we are."

"And the third?" said Tai.

"The third, I greatly regret, also elected to draw blade upon officers of the imperial palace guard."

"Defending my Sardian horse—a gift from the Princess Cheng-wan! As he'd been instructed to do. Steward, *where is he?*"

Another silence.

"I am informed that he unfortunately succumbed to wounds incurred, my lord. May I offer my regrets? And the hope that the passing of a nameless soldier will not—"

Tai threw up both hands, fingers spread, palms outward, compelling silence. It was a gesture of force, arrogance, a superior stilling an underling—in public. Even as he did it he was trying to sort through if he *did* carry rank against this man. Tai was a middle-level, purely symbolic military officer, but also an honoured general's son and—importantly—younger brother to the prime minister's principal adviser.

But this steward, in the red-belted black robe of a mandarin of the eighth degree, high in the household of the Beloved Companion, outranked him by any and all possible—

No. He didn't. And *that* was why the man bowed yet again, instead of snarling in outrage at Tai's gesture. The steward knew.

Tai was, over and above all other possible truths and alignments and ranks, brother to royalty now. To Li-Mei. *Princess* Li-Mei, elevated into the imperial family before being sent north in marriage.

In Kitai, in the Ninth Dynasty of the Emperor Taizu, that relationship mattered. It mattered so much. It was *why* Liu had done what he'd done, sacrificing a sister to his ambition.

And it was why Tai could stand here, hands thrust forward to silence another man, and see a Ta-Ming Palace mandarin stand abashed before him.

Through clenched teeth, fighting anger (rage could undo him here, he needed to *think*), Tai said, "He is not nameless. His name was Wujen Ning. A soldier of the Second District army posted to Iron Gate Fortress, assigned by his commander to guard me and my horse, serving the emperor by obeying the orders of his officers, including myself."

He was trying, even as he spoke, to remember the man, his features, words. But Wujen Ning had never said anything Tai could recall. He'd simply been *there*, always near Dynlal. A worried-looking, gap-toothed expression came to mind, thinning hair exposing a high forehead. Sloped shoulders, or maybe not ... Tai was relieved he'd remembered the name. Had been able to offer it to this courtyard assembly, to the gods.

He said, "Steward, I await the formal response of office to the killing of a soldier and the theft of my horse."

Theft was a strong word. He was too angry. He saw Zian glance at him, lips pursed together, as if urging caution.

Then—a small motion in a crowded courtyard—he saw something else. Discreet as the movement was, it seemed as if every man and woman (girls from the music pavilion had come out by now) in that open space in morning light saw the same thing, and responded to it as if a dancing master had trained them all.

A hand appeared through the silk curtain of the sedan chair.

It gestured to the steward, two slowly curled fingers.

There were rings on those fingers, Tai saw, and the fingernails were painted red. Then he was on his knees, head to the ground. So was everyone in the courtyard except her guards, and the steward.

Tai allowed himself to glance cautiously up and look, heart pounding, mind askew. The steward bowed three times then walked slowly across to the curtained chair as if towards his own beheading.

Tai watched the man listen to whatever was being said to him from within. The steward stepped aside, bowed again, expressionless. The hand reappeared through yellow silk and beckoned a second time, exactly the same way, two fingers, but this time to Tai.

Everything had changed. She was here herself, after all.

Tai stood. Offered the same triple bow the steward had. He said, quietly, to Song and Zian, "Stay with me if you possibly can. We won't be going quickly in that. I'll do my best to ensure your safety, and the soldiers'."

"We aren't in danger," Sima Zian said, still kneeling. "We'll be at Ma-wai, one way or another."

"Master Shen," he heard his Kanlin say. Her expression was odd, looking up at him. "Be careful. She is more dangerous than a fox-woman."

He knew she was. Tai took the steps down from the portico, crossed the dusty courtyard through a crowd of kneeling people, and found himself beside the curtained sedan chair.

He said loudly, looking at the steward, and at the captain of the imperial escort beside him, "I give my companions into your protection. If my horse is missing or harmed I lay that upon you both." The officer nodded, standing straight as a banner pole. The steward was pale.

Tai looked at the closed curtain. His mouth was dry. The captain gestured at Tai's swords and boots. He removed them. The steward pulled the curtain back, just enough. Tai entered. The curtain of the sedan chair fell closed with a rustling sound. He found himself enveloped by scent in a softened, silk-filtered light that seemed to not be entirely of the world he'd just left.

It wasn't, of course. It wasn't the same world in here.

He looked at her. At Wen Jian.

He had known lovely women in his life, some of them very recently. The false Kanlin who'd come to kill him by the lake had been icily beautiful, cold as Kuala Nor. The daughters of Xu Bihai were exquisite, the older one even more than that. Spring Rain was golden and glorious, celebrated for it. The preferred courtesans in the best houses in the North District were lovely as flowers: the students wrote poems for them, listened to their singing, watched them dance, followed them up jade stairs.

None of these women, none of them, were what this one was in the brightness of what she offered. And she wasn't even dancing now. She sat opposite, leaning upon cushions, gazing at Tai appraisingly, enormous eyes beneath shaped eyebrows.

He had seen her from a distance, in Long Lake Park, at festival ceremonies with the emperor and court in their elevated place on a Ta-Ming balcony, removed from ordinary men and women, above them, nearer heaven.

She wasn't removed from him here, she was annihilatingly close, and they were alone. And one small, bare, high-arched foot seemed to be touching the outside of his thigh very lightly, as if it had drifted there, all unawares.

Tai swallowed hard. Jian smiled, took her time assessing him, utterly at ease.

An entire courtyard of people at an imperial posting station had seen him enter this sedan chair. A man could be killed for being alone with the emperor's beloved. Unless that man was a eunuch, or—an abrupt thought—was made into one as an alternative to having his throat cut. Tai tried to find a safe place to rest his gaze. Light came gently through silk.

She said, "I am pleased. You are handsome enough. It is better when men are pleasant to look upon, don't you agree?"

He said nothing. What did you say to this? He lowered his head. Her foot moved against his thigh, as if idly, a restlessness. She curled her toes. He felt it. Desire was within him. He worked fiercely to suppress it. Head down, avoiding those eyes, he saw that her toenails were painted a deep red, almost purple. There was nowhere safe to look. And with every breath he caught the scent she wore.

He made himself look up. Her mouth was full and wide, her face heart-shaped, skin flawless, and the silk of her thin blue summer gown, patterned in a soft yellow like the curtains, was cut low. He saw an ivory pendant in the shape of a tiger between the rich curves of her breasts.

She was twenty-one years old, from a well-known family in the south. Had come to Xinan to be married at sixteen to a prince of the imperial family, the eighteenth son.

Then the ever-glorious Emperor Taizu, her husband's father, had seen her dance one night in the palace to the music of a flute (the story was very well known) and the course of her life and the empire's course had been altered forever by the time the music and the dancing stopped.

The pious had declared (quietly) that what followed was a profanation of marriage and family. The eighteenth son accepted a larger mansion, another wife, and exquisite concubines. Time passed at court, pleasantly. There was music in the palace and at Ma-wai and a woman danced for the emperor. Poets began to write of four great beauties.

The empress was invited to follow her own clear inclination towards devotion and withdraw to a retreat outside Xinan and the palace, to enfold her life in prayer.

Tai's sister had gone with her. He used that quick image of Li-Mei—brave and bright—to bring him back from what felt, truly, like intoxication. There was, he thought, no wine in the world like the presence of this woman. There might be a poem in that, it occurred to him.

Someone had probably written it.

He said, as the chair was lifted and they began to move, "My lady, your servant is too greatly honoured by this."

She laughed. "Of course you are. You won't be killed for being here, if you are thinking about that. I told the emperor last night I intended to come and bring you myself. Will you take a lychee? I can peel it for you, Master Shen Tai. We could even share it. Do you know the most enjoyable way to share lychee fruit?"

She leaned forward, as if inclined to show him right then. He said nothing. He had no words, no idea what to say.

She laughed at him again, the eyebrows arched. She regarded him another moment. Nodded her head, as if a thought was confirmed. "You reminded me of your brother when you held your hands up to my steward just now. Power hidden behind courtesy."

Tai looked at her. "We are not very like, my lady. You believe he shows power?"

"Liu? Of course he does. But carefully," said Wen Jian. She smiled. "You say you are greatly honoured. But you are also angry. Why are you angry with me, my lord?" She didn't have to call him that. The foot moved again, unmistakably.

She would use her beauty, any man's desire for her, as an agency, a weapon, he told himself. Her long neck was set off by golden earrings to her shoulders, set with pearls, the weight of the gold making her seem even more delicate. Her hair was coiled, but falling to one side, famously. Her own invented style, the "waterfall," copied throughout the empire now. The hairpins were jewelled, variously, and he didn't even know the names of all the gems he saw.

She laid a hand, as if carelessly, upon his calf. He caught his breath. She smiled again. She was measuring his responses, he realized.

"Why so angry?" she asked again in a voice suddenly like a child's, grieving at being punished.

He said, carefully, "One of my soldiers was killed this morning, illustrious lady. I believe you heard. A soldier of the emperor. My Kanlin guard was wounded, and two of your own men. And my Sardian horse—"

"I know it. It was uncivilized. There was violence in my presence, which is never permitted." She lifted her hand from his leg. "I have instructed my under-steward to kill himself when we reach Ma-wai."

Tai blinked, wasn't sure he'd heard correctly.

"You ... he ...?"

"This morning," said the Beloved Companion, "did not proceed as I wished it to. It made me unhappy." Her mouth turned downwards.

You could drown in this woman, Tai thought, and never be found again. The emperor was pursuing immortality in the palace, men said, using alchemists and the School of Unrestricted Night, where they studied the stars and asterisms in the sky for secrets of the world. Tai suddenly had a better understanding of that desire.

"Your brother," she said, "doesn't look like you."

"No," said Tai.

She was going to do this, he realized: change topics, make him keep up with her, test him that way.

"He advises my cousin," she said.

"I know this, illustrious lady."

"I don't like him," she said.

Tai was silent.

"Do you?" she asked.

"He is my brother," Tai said.

"He has measuring eyes and he never smiles," said Wen Jian. "Am I going to like you? Do you laugh?"

He took a breath, then answered more seriously than he'd thought he would. "Less often since my father died. Since going to Kuala Nor. But yes, your servant used to laugh, illustrious lady."

"In the North District? I have been told as much. You and my cousin appear to have admired the same woman there."

Treacherous ground, Tai thought. And she was doing it deliberately.

"Yes," he said.

"He has her now."

"Yes."

"Do you know how much he paid for her?"

"No, illustrious lady." How would he have known?

"A very great sum. More than he needed to. He was making a declaration, about himself."

"I see."

"I have seen her since. She is ... very lovely."

He considered that pause.

He said, "There is no wine in Kitai or the world as intoxicating as the Lady Wen Jian."

The smile that brought him was a gift. He could almost believe she was flattered, a girl reacting to a well-turned compliment.

Almost. She said, "You never answered about your brother, did you? Clever man. You might survive at court. They tried to kill you?"

They. Such a dangerous word.

He nodded, not trusting himself to speak.

"Twice?"

He nodded again. The palace would have known this several nights ago. Xu Bihai had written, the commander at Iron Gate had sent word. She would know what the Ta-Ming knew.

"Twice, that I know about," he said.

"Was it Roshan?"

Terrifyingly direct. This was no girl-woman seduced by a turn of phrase. But he could sense apprehension, as she waited for his reply. There was, he thought, a *reason* she'd come to speak with him alone. This might be it.

"No," said Tai. "I am certain it wasn't."

"He persuaded you of that yesterday?"

This had become a precise interrogation—amid silk and scent, with a bare foot against his thigh.

He had been certain that a report of yesterday's encounter in the carriage by the road would reach the court, but the *speed* of it made him realize something, belatedly: she'd have had to travel half the night from Ma-wai to be here now. He calculated distances quickly. She'd have left almost as soon as word came of his meeting with An Li.

He didn't know what to make of that. He had never been part of the court, never even near it. He was coming from two years of solitude beyond Iron Gate.

"He did persuade me, illustrious lady."

"You believe what he told you was true?"

"I do."

She sighed. He couldn't interpret that. It might have been relief.

What he didn't say, yet, was that he *knew* that what Roshan had told him was true because he'd already known who had tried to kill him in the west—Spring Rain had risked her life so he could know this.

He was going to need to see her.

Jian said, "Because An Li can order men killed without a thought."

"I have no reason to doubt it, illustrious lady." He chose his words carefully.

She smiled slightly, lips together, noting his caution. "But he still made you believe him."

Tai nodded again. "Yes, my lady."

He didn't know if she wanted him to say more. It crossed his mind to consider that this questioning was being done here and in this way by a woman, the emperor's dancer-love, his late-in-life dream of eternity.

It came to Tai that this was a part of why the Ninth Dynasty might be as precarious as it was dazzling. Why Sima Zian had said what he'd said yesterday: *I feel chaos coming.*

This matchless creature across from him, lovely as a legend, was the cousin of the first minister *and* the supporter (the adopting mother!) of the man who was his rival, and she had the trust and passion of an emperor who wanted to live forever because of her.

The balance of Kitai—of the known world—might be reclining across from him. It was, Tai thought, a great burden to lay upon slender shoulders.

He sat there, the sedan chair moving steadily along the road, breathing perfume in an enclosed, intimate place removed from the ten thousand noises of the world, and he waited for the next question. The one that could plunge him—all of them—into the chaos Zian feared.

It wasn't Roshan? Who was it, then? she was going to ask him.

She never did. Either she knew already, or she was afraid to know, or to have it said aloud. Be brought into the world, compelling a response. Her hand lifted from his calf where it had been resting again. She selected a lychee from a bowl beside her, peeled it expertly.

She extended it towards him.

"Please," said Wen Jian.

Tai took the ripe, slippery fruit from her fingers. It tasted like the south, and summer, like memories of sweetness lost.

That last, he realized, was what he was feeling. Something slipping away, almost gone. Yesterday's encounter by the road and now this one. Both of them coming to meet him on the way. Entirely different encounters but also the same at their core. Power approaching, to know what he was going to do. Needing to know, because power always needed that—knowledge was how power preserved itself, or tried.

He had set out from a mountain bowl, the battleground his father had never left behind, determined to reach Xinan to do … to do what, precisely?

He had never decided, he'd been moving too fast.

Kill a man, he'd told the poet yesterday, as an answer for Yan's death. But Xin Lun was dead already. No fault of Tai's, no achievement of his, no credit to his name with Yan's ghost by the lake. And Lun had only been an instrument.

What else? What else had he been racing here to do, straight down the imperial road past the cut-off south that could have taken him home? Deal with the horses, somehow, that life-claiming gift.

Life-claiming. The thought reverberated strangely in his mind. Tai hadn't lived a life where enemies, on a murderous scale, had played any kind of role. But the first minister wanted him dead. On a whim, most likely. Because he *could*. Wen Zhou, who was this woman's kin, holding office because of her.

He looked at Jian, across from him. She had peeled her own lychee and, as he gazed, placed it delicately between her front teeth and bit down. Tai shook his head, then smiled. He had to smile, she was so obviously playing with her own desirability.

"Oh, good!" she said. She licked her lips, glistening with the fruit. "This will be a tedious journey if you are serious all the time."

The back and forth of it, he thought. Hard questions, ripe fruit bitten, a slow tongue tracing wet lips, a foot or fingers touching him, conjuring desire. Then the questions would come again.

In that moment, Tai arrived at a decision. It seemed obvious enough, and it had the virtue of simplicity. He'd only needed to finally grasp something: that he could never be subtle enough to match those waiting for him. He didn't have time to know enough, or gain an awareness of relationships, at a level that would let him move with these men and women to their music. He wouldn't even *hear* the notes they heard.

He wasn't able to probe for what they knew or wanted, play the game of words spoken and unspoken with the court and the higher civil servants and even some of the governors, in and around the Ta-Ming Palace and the emperor.

He would be among them today. And he couldn't learn that rhythm, not in the time he had. So he wouldn't even try. He'd go another way, like a holy wanderer of the Sacred Path choosing at a fork in the road, following his own truth, a hermit laughing in the mountains.

Tai drew a breath. He said, "I offered the horses to Governor An yesterday."

She stared, sat up straighter. Carefully put down an unpeeled lychee she'd just picked from the bowl.

"All of them?"

He nodded. "But I had a condition, and he declined."

"An Li rejected two hundred and fifty Sardian horses?"

"I said they were his if he brought my sister back from the Bogü. He said he could not do it. The horses are yours, illustrious lady, if you can do this."

"*All* of them?"

He nodded again. She was clearly shaken. Roshan had been, as well.

"I don't ... Is she your lover, your sister?"

He could not allow himself to be offended. This was the court. Such thoughts would occur to people. He shook his head. "Nothing like that. This is to honour my father as much as anything. He would never have let my brother do this. In our mourning period, it was an act of disrespect."

She was staring as if dazed. And the woman in this sedan chair was no simple concubine or dancer, however exquisite. This was someone who *defined* the life of the Ta-Ming now, who shaped and balanced it, in a dangerous time.

He was beginning to understand how dangerous, since yesterday and the thought he'd had: of the knife he carried, and committing murder in that carriage by the road.

"You are not suggesting it was wrong to give your sister to this marriage and send her north?"

He needed to be careful. "The Son of Heaven cannot be wrong."

"No, he cannot." Her voice was emphatic.

"This is a personal request, my lady, only that."

"You do understand," she said, her voice controlled now, "how much you can expect at court as the last hero of Kuala Nor and brother to a new princess? Have you considered that the emperor cannot be less generous than the Lion of Tagur or he is shamed? He must give you gifts that exceed those horses from Sangrama."

He hadn't thought about that. At all. Including, before this morning, the connection to Li-Mei, how much her elevation meant for him. He said as much.

Jian shook her head impatiently. Her earrings made a jingling sound. "Son of Shen Gao, you are angry with your brother for what he did. You are a rival to my cousin for a woman. Very well. Do you think *their* ranks and honours are set in jade, reserved to them forever? Do you think they might be just a little fearful of your coming?"

Tai's turn to be unsettled. "I don't know enough to judge such matters. I have little experience, or guidance. Sima Zian's, perhaps."

The woman made a face. "Not the surest counsellor, Master Shen. He has never held office, and he owes me a sweeter poem than the last he offered."

"Perhaps later today?" Tai said. "If he is permitted to—"

"I have other intentions today. Some people have been summoned to Ma-wai. This is too important to go any longer unad-dressed."

"What is?"

"You are, son of Shen Gao! *You* are too important. Why do you think I am here?"

"Because ... because of the horses?"

A slow smile, honey poured to sweeten a drink. A hand, shining with rings, touched his unshod foot where he had kept it carefully against the side of the sedan chair. "You are permitted to think it is only them. But consider what I have said. I will be disappointed if you prove unintelligent. Or lack decisiveness."

Fingernails moved. He said, a little desperately, "Illustrious lady, you do not want the horses?"

"Ten of them," she said promptly. "If you wish to give me a gift in exchange for company on this road and lychees peeled for you. I want to train them to dance, I have been told it can be done. But what would I do with more than that? Lead them to war?"

"Then ... then surely the emperor? I will give the Sardians directly to the Son of Heaven."

"You *are* anxious to be rid of them, aren't you? No. Think, Shen Tai. Our exalted emperor is not permitted to be indebted to any of his subjects. His is the duty of supreme generosity. He'd have to return more than you gave him or be shamed in the eyes of the world. You control more of these horses than Kitai has received at any one time, ever. The Son of Heaven must honour you as soon as you arrive. And if you also give him the horses ...?"

Tai suddenly wished he'd taken that turnoff south, that he were riding home along a road he knew. Not all men, surely, needed to be part of the ten thousand noises, the swirling dust, the palace strug-gles, the guiding of the world?

He closed his eyes. Not the wisest thing to do. Her foot moved immediately, as if she'd been waiting for that. The toes flexed against his thigh. If she chose to move just a little more ... Tai opened his eyes, quickly.

"Have you ever made love in a sedan chair?" Wen Jian asked, guilelessly. Those enormous eyes met his from under perfect, painted eyebrows. "It can be done." She moved her foot.

Tai made a small, involuntary sound.

Directness. He had decided upon that.

He said, "My lady, you are making my heart pound. My mouth is dry with desire. I know you are toying with me, like a cat, and I wish only to honour you and the emperor."

That smile again. "You know I am doing this … this toying, do you?"

He nodded his head, too rapidly.

"And that is my only purpose, you have decided?"

He stared at her. Couldn't speak.

"Poor man. Would a lychee help at all? That dryness …?"

Tai laughed. He couldn't help it. Her expression was mischief incarnate. A moment ago she'd been crisply explaining affairs of the empire and the world, now she was enjoying her beauty and the power it gave her. She took and peeled another fruit without waiting for his answer. She extended it. Her fingers touched his.

She said, quietly, "I told you, the emperor, may he live eternally and in joy, knows I am here, knows you are with me. He will ask me at Ma-wai if you were respectful and I will tell him you were, because indeed, you are. Does this make you feel easier?"

He was doing a lot of nodding or shaking of his head. He nodded again.

She said, "I have arranged that compensation will be paid to the family of your soldier. My under-steward has been instructed to do this before he attends to his own affairs and ends his life."

He'd forgotten about that. Tai cleared his throat. "May I ask, gracious lady, that the steward be permitted to live? Wujen Ning, my soldier, and my Kanlin will both have been aggressive in defence of me, and of the horse."

The eyebrows arched again. "You may ask. I am disinclined, however. This morning was incorrectly undertaken. It reflects badly upon me, and the throne." She selected another lychee. "In a short while we will reach a waiting carriage and your horse and companions. You will ride to Ma-wai, escorting me. I like this chair, but not for longer journeys. Do you like it?"

Again, he nodded. Then said, "Illustrious lady, I think I would like being anywhere you are."

That unhurried smile: genuine pleasure it seemed (though he truly couldn't be sure). "A smooth-enough tongue, Shen Tai. As I said, you might survive in the palace."

"Will you help me?" he asked.

He hadn't known he was going to say that.

Her expression changed. She looked at him. "I don't know," said Wen Jian.

A SHORT TIME LATER they halted at a place where—when the yellow silk curtain was pulled back—he saw that a carriage was indeed waiting. This one, too, had kingfisher feathers.

Beside it on the road (not the imperial road now, they had turned off, northeast) Tai saw Zian and Song and his soldiers on their horses, and the restless, magnificent figure of Dynlal.

He gave his horse a lychee by way of apology, and mounted up.

No great speed now, they were escorting a carriage. A west wind blew. There was birdsong as the sun climbed. They saw green hills ahead of them. They rode that way. These were the forested slopes where the most extravagant country estates of Xinan's aristocracy were to be found. The Five Tombs District it was called, near the burial place of the last emperor and his ancestors, and the vastly larger tomb the Emperor Taizu (might he live another thousand years) was building for himself.

Just before they reached the first foothills they passed a large postal station inn on this northeast-southwest road, then they came to a small lake surrounded by trees, a place celebrated for hot springs and healing waters. On the western side of the lake were a silk farm and a Kanlin retreat, on the other shore lay Ma-wai.

CHAPTER XVI

Li-Mei has lost track of how long they've been riding. Five nights? The landscape is unvarying, remorseless. The approach of summer has made the grass very tall and there are few paths or tracks. Time blurs. She doesn't like it. She has lived her life anticipating possibilities, knowing what is happening, where she is going. *Shaping* where she is going, to whatever degree she can.

She is much like her oldest brother in this, but would not happily acknowledge that.

She knows how to ride, was taught as a child because her father thought it important, even for a girl, but this much time on a horse, day after day, is hard for her, and Meshag is not inclined to rest very often.

She is in pain at the end of each day and then weary through the next morning's riding because nights sleeping under stars are cold and not restful. She'd hoped this discomfort would pass.

She says nothing about it, but is aware that he knows. She has a sense they are travelling more slowly than he wants to, because of her. She's tried to shorten their rest times herself, being the first to stand up, but Meshag has simply ignored her when she does this. He will only move when he is ready to move, or decides that she is, more likely.

But he'd said, back in the cave (another world, where she killed a man), that his brother would follow them, with shamans, and it is clear to her that whatever Meshag, son of Hurok, has become, whatever dark link he might have to wolves and the wild and spirits, he doesn't want the shamans catching them. Surely for her sake, possibly for his own.

He's avoided his people, hasn't he? Stayed clear of his brother all these years since *her* brother saved his life (maybe saved his life). But now, for her—for Shen Li-Mei, a woman from Kitai—he's approached the Bogü again, stolen her away, and they are being pursued. So he has told her. Li-Mei has no way of knowing the truth. It leaves her uneasy, even angry. She asked him, some time ago, why they hadn't already been caught, since they weren't travelling at great speed.

"They have to find us," he said. "Have other princess to carry north. They do not know which way we travel. He had to wait for a shaman."

A long answer, for him.

She has only the barest idea of where they are. They have been riding east. These are Shuoki lands, but if she remembers rightly they move north as the weather warms. The Shuoki are enemies of the Bogü. There are Kitan garrison forts somewhere in this direction, northern outposts. The Long Wall is south of them, of course. She doesn't know how far, but it will be rising and falling with the land like some serpent heading to meet the sea. Ahead of them will be nothing but grassland if the Shuoki are indeed north. The Bogü do not graze their herds this far east, and they are nowhere near the Koreini Peninsula.

He is taking her into emptiness.

It has been two days since any sign of human life—morning smoke by a distant lake. Meshag had decided not to go that way for water, though they'd been rationing theirs by that point. He'd found a small pool towards evening. They camped there, the wolves on guard.

So she does have some notion of time, after all, she tells herself. A pool of water two nights ago, a slight rise in the land last night in the open. No real shelter since the cave with the horses on the walls.

They have made no fires of their own at night. He hasn't touched her, except to help her on her horse. She has thought about that. Has thought about it a great deal.

She'd expected to have been taken physically by now, has been preparing for it from the time she waited in the yurt, in darkness. She is a woman alone with a man in an expanse of empty land—certain events usually follow upon that.

Meshag is too different, however, in visible, unsettling ways. She doesn't know what to think any more.

She has never made love to a man, has only played with the other girls at court, giggling or whispering explorations to little import. Some of the others have done more—with each other, with courtiers (or one of the princes) in the Ta-Ming—but Li-Mei has not. The empress, even when they were still in the palace, was devout and demanding: *her* women were expected to observe rules of well-bred conduct, which were clear on this matter.

Once, the emperor's named heir, Prince Shinzu (a special case, of course), had come to stand behind Li-Mei during a musical performance in the Min-Tan, the Hall of Light.

As the musicians played and the dancers began, she had felt sweetened breath on her neck, then a hand brushing her lower back, through silk, gliding down, back up, down again. Shinzu was regarded as vividly irresponsible, charming, rarely sober. There were endless rumours as to how long he'd remain heir, or even why he was Taizu's chosen successor among so many sons.

She remembers that day extremely well, remembers standing, eyes forward, towards the dancers, not moving at all, breathing carefully, suspended between outrage and excitement and helplessness as he touched her from behind, unseen.

He hadn't done anything more. Hadn't even spoken with Li-Mei afterwards, then or at any other time before she went away from the palace with the empress into exile.

With a murmured phrase (she hadn't even heard the words clearly) he'd moved on when the music ended. She'd seen him talking to another lady of the court, after, laughing, another wine cup in his hand. The woman was laughing, too. Li-Mei could recall ambivalent feelings, seeing that.

She has never considered herself the sort of beauty to drive a man to excesses of desire or recklessness. Nor, even, was she the kind of woman who normally elicited even transitory attention on an autumn afternoon in the Hall of Light.

Had her father been alive she'd be married by now, undoubtedly, and would know much more about this aspect of the world. Men and women. She's been ready to learn for a while. Were Shen Gao still living, his daughter would not now be alone with a barbarian rider and wolves among the grasslands of the north.

Meshag sleeps a little apart from her. The wolves take stations like sentinels in a wide circle around them. The stars have been more dazzling each night as the moon wanes. She sees the Weaver Maid set each evening, then the Sky River appear overhead as darkness deepens, and then the lost mortal lover rising east, on the far side of the River.

She is never easy about the wolves, still tries not to look at them, but they aren't going to harm her, she knows now, because of Meshag. Every day he has ridden away before sunrise, mist rising from the grass. He's made her keep riding alone, heading into the sun as soon as it is up and the mist has burned away. The wolves guide her, guard her.

She still hates them. You couldn't change a lifetime's thinking and feeling and fear in a few days, could you?

Each time, Meshag has caught up with them before midday, with food. He is hunting, in the hunter's time before dawn. He even brings firewood, kindling on his back. He tramples grass, shapes a space, builds low, careful daytime fires.

They eat rabbits, or marmots most recently—today—skinned and cooked, a whittled stick through them. He gives her some kind of fruit to peel. She doesn't know the name of it. It is bitter but she eats it. Drinks water. Washes her face and hands, always, more symbol than anything else. She is Kitan, and her father's daughter. Stands and stretches, does it before Meshag does.

They ride on, the sun overhead, clouds, no clouds, the days mild, evenings chilly, the nights cold. The plain stretches, all directions, unlike anything she's ever known, the grass so high, nearly hiding them, even on horseback, as they go. It does conceal the wolves, she can just about forget that they are there.

She can almost imagine they will ride like this forever, in silence, through tall grass, with wolves.

NOTHING IS FOREVER, not since the world changed after the war in heaven.

Late that same day, the sun behind them. Li-Mei is weary, trying to hide it, glad Meshag rides in front and seldom looks back. He leaves it to the lead wolf to be sure she is keeping up. She has been reciting poetry, not with any theme or coherence, only to distract herself, keep herself riding until he calls a halt.

Then he does halt, too sharply. She hasn't been paying attention, almost bumps his mount with hers. She pulls up quickly, twitches her reins, comes around beside him.

He is looking at the sky.

A few clouds ahead of them, some to the north, pink and yellow in the light of the low, long sun. No sign of rain, any kind of storm. The wind is easy. It isn't anything like that.

She sees a swan. Sees that this is what he is watching. His face has become very still. *It is just a bird,* she wants to say. But she has been among strangeness long enough now to know that he would not be looking up like this, looking like this, if it were simply a bird flying by.

She sees him draw the short, thick Bogü bow from his saddle.

He hadn't had a bow when he'd come for her. He'd taken this one when he stole the horse. Li-Mei moves her own mount away, to give him room. The swan is flying south, towards them.

It is springtime. Even she knows a swan should not be flying south in spring. It is alone. Perhaps lost, having wandered in the high roads of the sky? She doesn't really think that. Not when she looks at the man beside her, arrow now to bowstring, the bow lifted. It is a very long shot, she has time to think.

She hears the arrow's release. *Red song of war arrows, red sun.* There are so many poems about bow-songs and war in Kitai, back a thousand years to the first shaping of the empire.

Meshag has not looked awkward or rigid, she realizes. Not claiming his bow, fitting the arrow, letting it fly.

The swan falls out of the sky. So white against the colours of the clouds and the blue. It disappears into the grass.

She sees two wolves go after it, swift, avid. There is silence.

"Why?" she asks, finally.

He is looking back west. Sky and grass. He puts the bow away.

"He has found me," he says. "Ill chance."

She hesitates. "Your brother?"

He nods. The wind moves his hair.

"The ... a *swan* was searching?"

He nods his head again, absently this time. It is clear that he is thinking. Devising.

He says, "Now when shamans will call it there is no answer. They know direction each bird was sent. Will know I killed it."

She is afraid again. It is the strangeness of all things that frightens her most. You killed a bird in the sky, just as you killed rabbits or marmots in morning mist, and that meant ...

"Couldn't it have been hunted for food? By someone else?"

He looks at her. The black eyes. "Bogü never kill swans."

"Oh," she says.

He continues to gaze at her, a longer look than any she can remember. His eyes take in light and swallow it.

He says, "My brother would hurt you."

She has not expected this. "*Hurt* me?"

"He is ... like that."

She thinks a moment. "Some men are, too, in Kitai."

He seems to be working with a thought. He says, "When I was ... I was not like him."

When I was. When he was a man? She doesn't want to go towards that, it is dark in that direction.

She says, to fill silence, not really needing an answer, "Why would he hurt me? A Kitan princess, bringing him glory?"

He moves a shoulder, the awkward shrug. "Far too many questions. You are always asking. Not proper for women."

She looks away. Then back. "Then I need to thank you again, and be grateful I am not going to him, don't I? Will they catch us now? Where are we riding? What have you decided to do?"

They are a test of sorts, these swift, immediate inquiries. She is the way she is.

She sees the expression she has decided to call a smile.

There are ways of beating back fear, strangeness, the sense of being profoundly lost in the world.

THEY HAVE RIDDEN until darkness has almost gathered the land, eating cold meat in the saddle and the remains of the fruit. The waning moon has set. Li-Mei, in real discomfort, has continued to remain silent about it. They will be pursued now. He is trying to save her. This is no springtime ride in the Deer Park to see animals feeding or drinking at twilight.

He brings her to water again. She isn't certain how, this far from Bogü lands. It is the wolves, she decides.

He tells her they can rest only a short while, that she is to sleep right away. They will ride in darkness now, will do this every night. But then, after staring towards her in the almost-lost gloaming, his features difficult to see, he orders her to lie face down on the short grass by the pond.

She obeys. *Now it begins*, she thinks, her heart beginning to race against her will. (How does one control a heartbeat?)

But she is wrong, again. He comes to her, yes, but not in need, or hunger. He kneels beside her and begins to work the muscles of her back, his fingers mingling pain with the easing of pain. When she tenses, wincing, he slaps her lightly, the way you might slap a restive horse. She tries to decide if she's offended. Then makes herself settle into his hands. She is going to be riding again soon, this is no time or place to carry pride. What can *offended* mean here? His movements remain stiff, but very strong. She cries out once, apologizes. He says nothing.

She wonders abruptly—perhaps an illumination?—if his physical restraint, this indifference to her being a woman, is caused by what happened to him those years ago. Could it be he has been rendered incapable of desire, or the accomplishment of it?

She knows so little about this, but it is possible, surely. And it would explain ...

Then, at one point, as his hands slow, and then slow again, and linger near her hips, she becomes aware that his breathing has changed. She cannot see anything by then, is face down in the grass, can only be aware of him as a presence, touching her.

And though Shen Li-Mei, only daughter of an honourable house, has never shared a bed or couch with any man, or explored very far along even the first pathways of lovemaking, she knows—with instinctive certainty—that this man is not indifferent to her as a woman in the dark with him, and alone. Which means, if he is holding himself back it is not because he cannot feel—

And in that moment she understands another part of what is happening. Now, and since he came for her between the campfires, back west. She closes her eyes. Draws her own slow breath.

His is, in truth, a gesture, from a largeness of spirit she's not been prepared for. These are barbarians. Everyone living outside the borders of Kitai is a barbarian. You didn't expect ... grace from them. You couldn't, could you?

She listens to his breathing, feels his touch through her clothing. They are alone in the world. The Weaver Maid, alone as well, is shining in the west. Li-Mei realizes that her heartbeat has steadied after all, though she is aware of something new within herself.

She thinks she understands more now. It calms her, it always has. It makes such a difference. And *Shandai* was, after all, the first word he'd spoken to her. The name.

She says, softly, "Thank you. I think I will sleep now. You will wake me when it is time to ride?"

She shifts position, onto her side, and then up on her knees. He stands. She looks up at him against the stars. She cannot see his eyes. The wolves are invisible. She knows they are not far.

Still on her knees, she bows to him, her hands touching the earth.

She says, "I thank you for many things, son of Hurok. For my unworthy self, in my father's name, and in the name of my brother Shen Tai whom you are honouring by ... in the way you guard me." She does not say more. Some things cannot be made explicit, even in the dark.

Night breeze. He says nothing, but she sees him nod his head once. He walks off, not far but far enough, nearer the horses. Li-Mei lies down again, closes her eyes. She feels the wind, hears animal sounds in the grass and from the waters of the pond. She becomes aware, with surprise, that she is crying, for the first time since the cave. Eventually, she sleeps.

☯

Spring Rain has not thought of herself by the name her mother gave her since she left Sardia years ago.

She had come to Kitai as part of a small company of musicians and dancers sent as tribute to Taizu, the Son of Heaven. The Sardians were a careful people, offering annual gifts to Kitai and Tagur, and even to the emerging powers west of them. When your small homeland lay in a fertile valley between mountains, that was what you needed to do. Sometimes (not always) it sufficed.

She wasn't enslaved, and she wasn't abducted, but she hadn't had a great deal of *choice* in the matter. You woke up one morning and were told by the leader of your troupe that you were leaving your home forever. She'd been fifteen years old, singled out for her appearance already, and for skill in singing and on the *pipa*, all twenty-eight tunings of it in the Kitan fashion, which may have been why she was chosen.

She remained with that troupe for two years in Xinan, all twelve of them coming to terms with the fact that the great and glorious emperor had twenty thousand musicians. They all lived in a vast ward east of the palace—it was like a city in itself, larger than any in Sardia.

In two years they had been summoned to play three times, twice for minor court weddings, once at a banquet to welcome southern emissaries. On neither occasion was the Son of Heaven present.

You might be green-eyed and yellow-haired, lovely and lithe and genuinely skilled in music, and still see your life disappearing down the years. You could be invisible and unheard among the Ta-Ming Palace entertainers.

To the court, perhaps, but not to those on watch for a particular sort of woman. Rain had been noticed at that second wedding, apparently. She'd been seventeen by then. It was time to begin achieving something, she'd thought. A life, if nothing else.

She accepted an invitation to enter the pleasure district and be trained in one of the best houses there—trained in many things, and on terms that were (she knew by then, having paid attention) better than most girls received. Green eyes and yellow hair made a difference, after all. Her ability to leave the musicians' district was a matter of bribing the eunuchs who controlled the Ta-Ming entertainers. It happened all the time.

She was to become a courtesan, and was under no illusions about what that meant. She was taught to be a mistress of the table, the highest rank among the pleasure district women. They were the ones hired to perform at banquets by aristocrats or high mandarins. To perform, also, more privately and in other ways after the feasting had ended.

And when there were no wealthy courtiers on a given evening or afternoon in the Pavilion of Moonlight, there were always the students studying for the examinations—or not actually studying (not if they were in the North District) but aspiring to the rank that would come with passing the exams.

Spring Rain tended to like the students more than the courtiers, which wasn't the cleverest way for a girl to be. But their enthusiasms, their dreaming, spoke to something in her that the extravagance and hauteur of Ta-Ming aristocrats didn't touch—and they made her laugh sometimes.

The palace guests gave better gifts.

It was a life—while a woman was young, at any rate. A better life, most likely—though no one could ever say this for certain—than she'd have had back home. Xinan, under Emperor Taizu, was the centre of the world. She did sometimes wonder if the centre of the world was always the best place to be.

She can remember the moment, years before, as they'd passed through Jade Gate Fortress into Kitai, when she'd made the decision to leave her name behind.

The girl born to that name was gone, she'd decided. She was almost certainly never coming back—to home, family, the view of the mountains north of them, range upon range, to heaven. The girl travelling east would leave her name with her memories.

At fifteen, it had felt like a way to go forward, to survive.

But if her birth name is long since gone, that does not mean she must accept, in her mind, the one Wen Zhou has chosen for her, as if selecting among fabrics or polo horses.

She answers in the compound to Lin Chang because she must, and does so smiling, effortlessly gracious, but that is as far as she will go. The surface of a lake.

He cannot see what she is thinking or feeling. She has a talent for deceiving men by now. She's had time to learn. It is a skill like any other a woman can teach herself: music, conversation, lovemaking, simulating yearning and the tumult of desire.

She ought to be more grateful, she tells herself many times a day, or lying at night, alone or beside him. Hers is a destiny, thanks to Zhou, that marks, like a banner, the highest summit of the dreams of every courtesan in the North District.

He is the second most powerful man in the empire—which means in the world, really. She lives in a vast compound with servants at her whim and call. She entertains his guests with music or witty talk, watches him play polo in the Deer Park, shares his pillow many nights. She knows his moods, some of his fears. She wears silks of the finest weaving, and jewellery that sets off her eyes or dazzles by lamplight at her ears, in her golden hair.

He can dismiss her at any moment, of course. Cast her out, with or without any resources to survive—that, too, happens all the time to concubines when they age. When skilful use of masicot, onycha, indigo sticks for beauty marks, sweet basil, plucked eyebrows and painted ones, powder and perfume and exquisitely adorned hair are no longer enough to sustain necessary beauty.

It is her task to ensure that he has no cause to send her from his presence, now, or when that day comes when the mirror of men's eyes tells a darker tale.

In which case, she has not been acting prudently at all. Kanlin Warriors hired secretly. Listening on porticoes.

She has been distracted and disturbed the last few days, is afraid that it might show. There are other eyes besides his in this compound. His wife is famously inattentive to the women, her gaze turned towards the heavens and alchemical mysteries, but the other concubines are not her friends, and each of the important ones has servants devoted to her.

A household like this can be a battleground. There are poets who have seen this, lived it, written of it.

Events seem to be moving faster now. Late this morning a messenger came from Ma-wai. Wen Zhou and his wife left the compound by carriage not long after. Zhou was swearing, flushed and angry, through the flurry of preparations.

His cousin had evidently requested their presence for the afternoon and evening. Short of the absolute dictates of warfare or crisis, this is not an invitation that may be declined, even by the prime minister.

He holds office because of her, after all.

A case could be made, and she knows Zhou wishes he could do it, that they *are* in a time of crisis, but the growing tensions with Roshan are not the sort of matter he can use as an excuse to offer his regrets to Jian. Not until he's ready to reveal this, raise it with the emperor, and Rain knows he isn't. Not yet.

There are too many dangers, and they need working through.

He has already sent word to his principal adviser. Liu will follow to Ma-wai in his own carriage. Zhou always wants him nearby when there is any likelihood they might see the emperor, and in Ma-wai there is a good chance.

The first minister is increasingly dependent on Liu. Everyone in the compound knows it.

What Rain does *not* yet know, though she has done her best to find out, is whether Liu was privy to, or even the agent of, certain instructions given with respect to a man coming back now (it seems) from the far west, having escaped attempts upon his life.

Escaped them, possibly, because of her.

That, of course, is how she's been most reckless. Zhou would kill her and she knows it. At least one man in Xinan has already died in this affair in the past few days: Xin Lun, after word of Tai's journeying had come.

Lun was killed to preserve a secret. If Tai chooses to reveal it, the prime minister will be exposed. She's made her peace with that. Any loyalty to the man who brought her here stops short of this attempted assassination. A woman, as much as a man, is surely allowed her own sense of right conduct in the world.

No, her real fear right now is of herself.

Word has come by courier from Chenyao. That was days ago. Travelling at any normal speed, a horseman from that city could be here tomorrow, or even tonight. And Tai is riding, if the tale is to be believed, a Sardian steed. A Heavenly Horse, from her home.

Rain is too self-possessed, too controlled (always has been), to attach meaning or weight to that last. Nor is she a poet, as some of the courtesans are. She sings the songs others have written. But still ... Sardian horses?

And he is alive, very nearly here. After two years.

The morning passes, a midday meal, a rest in her rooms, a walk in the gardens by the bamboo grove. Time crawls at a pace that kills.

It occurs to her, sitting on a stone bench by the artificial lake, shaded from the sun by sandalwood leaves, that if Zhou has been summoned to Ma-wai for this afternoon, and a banquet after, he will not be home tonight.

It is just about then that the second messenger arrives. The household steward stalks into the garden to find Mistress Lin. She doesn't think he likes her, but he doesn't like anyone so it isn't significant.

It seems there is another message from Ma-wai, this one sent to her. That has never happened before. She wonders if she's being summoned to play for them ... but no, it would be too late by now. And there is hardly a deficiency of performers at Ma-wai.

The courier is escorted through the sequence of public rooms and courtyards back through the garden, preceded by the steward and a warning to her that someone is coming—so that she can be properly seated and composed on one of the benches. She is, or presents herself as such.

The courier bows. She is, after all, the newly favoured concubine of First Minister Wen. There can be power in that for women. He hands her a scroll. She opens it, breaking the seal.

This message is also from Wen Jian, the Precious Consort. It is very short. *Do not retire early tonight, unless you are excessively fatigued. Not all windows above jade stairs need be seen through tears.*

The second line is derived from a celebrated poem about a woman left alone too long. Jian has changed three words. You can imagine her smiling as she wrote or dictated that.

Actually, that isn't quite true: it is difficult to imagine that woman. She eludes too easily, and frightens because of that.

You can begin to feel your own heartbeat going too fast, however, as you consider those words on the scroll, dismiss the courier with a grave expression, give instructions that he be offered food and drink before starting back to Ma-wai.

For one thing, how does Wen Jian even know of her existence? For another, why would she be disposed to assist Rain in anything, if indeed she is doing that? If this is not some trap, or test?

Rain feels like a child, overwhelmed by complexities.

The steward leads the courier past pagoda trees. Her maidservant lingers, ready if called. Rain sits alone, looks across the water at the island he'd had made in the lake he'd had made. The light breeze ruffles leaves overhead, touches her skin and hair.

She'd liked amber and apricots and music, very young. Horses a little later, but only to look at them. They'd frightened her. Her eyes had drawn attention, very young. Her mother had named her *Saira* when she was born. A sweet name left behind, many years ago.

CHAPTER XVII

"I should like," said Wen Jian, "to be entertained. Cousin, will you offer a poem for me?"

Her cousin, the first minister, smiled. He was as Tai remembered him in the North District, or glimpsed in Long Lake Park … a big man, handsome and aware of it. He wore blue silk with dragons in silver. There was a lapis lazuli ring on his left hand.

A breeze entered through unshuttered windows, rippling pennons outside. It was late afternoon. They were in Ma-wai, where the hot springs had eased imperial weariness for centuries, and where the decadent games of various courts had been notorious for as long. Just north of here, not far away, were the tombs of the Ninth Dynasty.

Poets had written of this conjunction of symbols, though doing so carried risks and one needed to use care.

Tai wasn't feeling careful just now, which was unwise and he knew it. He was tense as a drawn bowstring. Wen Zhou was here and Tai's brother was here.

They didn't know he was in the room.

Jian, amusing herself (or perhaps not so), had arranged for Tai to enter before her guests, and to seat himself on an ivory bench behind one of two painted room screens (cranes flying, a wide river, mountains rising, the tiny figure of a fisherman in his boat).

He hadn't wanted to do this. It felt too passive, acquiescent. But he didn't know, on the other hand, what he did want here. He had arrived. This was the court. He had decisions to make, alignments to choose or reject. It would also be useful, he thought wryly, to remain alive. One person here had been trying to kill him.

At least one person.

For the moment he would accede to what the Beloved Companion wished of him. He could start that way, at least. Jian's women had bathed him when their party arrived, and washed his hair (gravely, with propriety, no hint of rumoured immorality). After, in a chamber overlooking the lake, they had laid out silks more fine than any he'd ever worn in his life. *Liao* silk: compared to ordinary weaving once, in a poem, as what a glistening waterfall was to a muddy stream dried out in summer heat.

He remembered that image as he dressed. His robe was a shimmering, textured flicker of greens, the colours of a bamboo grove in changing light. His slippers and belt and soft hat were black, with pale-yellow dragons on them. His hatpin had an emerald.

Two women had led him, silently, hands in full sleeves, eyes downcast, along corridors of marble and jade, then across a courtyard and down more corridors to the chamber where Wen Jian evidently purposed to receive certain guests.

Tai had not seen her since they'd arrived. She had told him in the sedan chair that she had a plan for this afternoon. He had no notion of what this might be, or of his own role in it.

At Kuala Nor each night, watching the stars set and rise, or the moon, he'd known his task at every moment. What he was there to do. Here, he was one of many dancers, and he didn't know the dance.

He wished Zian were with him. Wei Song he'd released for the afternoon, to report to her own Kanlin sanctuary farther along the shore. It had crossed his mind that now that they'd arrived, her duties, her employment, could be considered over. He'd felt oddly exposed when she'd bowed and gone away.

The poet was somewhere in Ma-wai. He'd been a guest here before. They hadn't had a chance to speak before being led in different directions. Zian was almost certainly sampling some celebrated wine. Tai wondered if the women were as proper with the Banished Immortal as they had been with him.

His two escorts had led him into this audience chamber, showed him the room screens (the paintings were by Wang Shao) and the low seat behind one of them. They'd invited him, prettily, to sit. He could have refused. But he didn't know what he'd achieve by doing so. It seemed wisest, for the moment, to see what Jian was doing. What she was playing at—if it was a game.

He discovered he could see quite well through tiny holes in the screen. He hadn't noticed them from the painted side. He was entirely certain the viewing holes, his ability to observe the room unseen, were not accidental. The ceiling, he saw, looking up in wonder, was of beaten gold. There were lotus flowers and cranes worked upon it. The walls were sandalwood, the floor was marble.

Jian smiled at his screen when she walked in with her steward—a different man from the one this morning. (The one this morning was probably dead by now.) It was not, Tai thought, the smile she'd offered when they were alone on the road.

He'd asked, just before getting out to ride Dynlal the rest of the way, if she'd help him here at court.

I don't know, she had said.

This wasn't about helping him, he decided. He might be wrong, but it didn't feel that way. He felt cowardly sitting here. He wanted to confront Wen Zhou and his brother. He had a quick, clean image of drawing swords with them. Liu was hopeless with a blade. Zhou was likely a match for Tai, or more than that. It was an idle thought: no weapons were allowed here. He'd been made to surrender his when they arrived.

Seen through the screen, Jian looked very different: cooler, more serene, with a gravity that had not existed (could not exist) while she reclined in a perfumed sedan chair, peeling lychees, curving a bare foot against his thigh.

She was in green as well, with imperial phoenixes in the same pale yellow as his own dragons. He wondered if that meant something. Her hair was as before: the widely imitated, side-slipping style. It could do things to a man, looking at her.

There was a small, discreet door behind him. He could get up right now and walk out—if the door wasn't barred. He wondered if it was. He wondered if there was a door behind the other painted screen, set diagonally to this one against the same wall, the two of them framing a space for Wen Jian and her friends, at Ma-wai, in springtime.

He stopped wondering about such things when Jian seated herself on a platform in the centre of the chamber, accepted a cup from the steward, and gestured for her guests to be admitted.

Tall doors opened. A number of men came in, no women. Jian was the only woman in the room. Even the servants, pouring wine into jade cups, were men. There were no musicians.

Among the arrivals was Sima Zian. A surprise. The poet was properly dressed and groomed, with a dark hat and his hair neatly pinned. His expression was alert, amused, as ever. Tai registered this, but didn't look at him for long. His attention was pulled away. Not to the first minister, though Wen Zhou had also entered the room.

Hidden, silent, afraid, and fighting anger, Tai looked at his older brother for the first time in two years.

Liu had gained weight, it showed in his face, but he was otherwise unchanged. Smaller than Tai, softer. In a mandarin's rich, sober black silk, with the dark-red belt of highest rank and symbolic key at his waist, he entered discreetly, bowed formally, took a place behind Wen Zhou, a little to one side.

Tai was staring at him. He couldn't stop. Fear, and fury.

He recognized another of those who entered: the imperial heir. Another surprise, if Jian intended anything serious today. Prince

Shinzu was notorious for sensuous luxury, though seldom seen in the city, and never in the North District.

Women were brought to him. He didn't go to them. He was an even bigger man than the first minister, affecting a short beard, but wider than the mandarin fashion. He already carried a cup of wine, Tai saw. Scanning the room, from a position he took near an open window, the prince smiled at Zian, who bowed, and smiled cheerfully back.

Jian waited until her guests had wine, then spoke her first words to her cousin: inviting a poem, entertainment.

From behind his screen, Tai saw Zhou offer his confident, lazy smile. "We retain people to offer poetry, cousin. You ask the one man here whose effort would surely not amuse you."

"But surely he will make an effort? If only to please me?" Tai could hear the sly smile in her words.

"I love you too much for that," said Zhou. One man laughed appreciatively. Tai couldn't see who it was. Wen Zhou added, "And we seem to have, for some reason or other, a poet among us. Let *him* divert you, cousin. Is he here for any other purpose?"

A fair question: the poet had left the city under one of his usual clouds and it had to do with Jian and a poem. The Banished Immortal, as in heaven so on earth. That was the way the stories ran.

Jian only smiled. She had, Tai was realizing, more than a dozen ways of smiling. This one was closer to the cat with a mouse he'd sensed in the sedan chair. It occurred to him that she wasn't really pursuing amusement here. He wondered if Zhou knew that yet.

He shivered suddenly. Wasn't sure why. In the tales his nursemaid used to tell, you shivered that way when someone was walking across the ground where your grave would one day lie. If you never shivered so, she used to say, you were doomed to die in water, or lie unburied.

His brother knew those same stories from the same source. Liu knew the same orchard fruits, the same tree-swing in the farthest garden, stream for fishing or swimming, paulownia leaves on the path all at once in autumn, the same teachers, sunsets, birds returning at winter's end, the same lightning-riven summer storms of child-hood in a room they'd shared, listening for thunder.

"I am afraid to have Master Sima offer any lines after the last ones he gave us in the Ta-Ming," said the Precious Consort. "A poem about an ancient emperor and his beloved." She looked at the poet, and did not smile.

"It is a grief to my soul, and will last all my days, if anything your servant has ever written brings you or the Son of Heaven other than pleasure," Sima Zian said earnestly.

"Well," said the prime minister, grinning, "a number of them have failed to bring *me* pleasure, I can tell you that." Another laugh from someone, probably the same person.

Zian looked at him. He bowed again. "Some griefs," he murmured, "we learn to expect in life."

It was Jian who laughed this time. She clapped her hands. "Cousin, cousin," she cried, "never play at words with a poet! Don't you know that?"

Wen Zhou flushed. Tai was fighting an impulse to grin.

"I'd have thought a disgraced poet without rank or office would be the one who needed to be careful," the first minister said coldly.

Tai looked instinctively to his brother. He had spent a good deal of his childhood looking at Liu, trying to read what he might be thinking. Liu's face was impassive but his watchful eyes went from the woman to the poet, then quickly to the man who—unexpect-edly—broke the ensuing silence.

"There are many ways of measuring rank, as the Cho Master has taught," said Prince Shinzu quietly. "On the matter of taking care, as it happens, I have a question of my own for the first minister. Though I fear to interrupt our dear Jian's pleasures."

"You, of all men, need never fear doing so," said Wen Jian, prettily.

Tai had no idea how to interpret that. Or the manner of the prince, leaning against the wall by a window, a cup held so casually it almost spilled its wine. Shinzu's voice was more crisp than Tai had expected. He'd never actually heard the heir speak. He only knew the tales.

"I am, of course, at your service, illustrious lord." Wen Zhou bowed.

He had to, of course. Tai didn't think it pleased him. Already, from his place of concealment, he was exhausted trying to trace the lines of connection and tension here, read surface meaning, let alone what lay beneath.

"I am grateful," said the prince.

He sipped his wine. Gestured to a servant, waited for the cup to be refilled. The room waited with him. When the servant had withdrawn, Shinzu leaned back again, at ease. He looked at Wen Zhou.

"What have you been doing with An Li?" he asked.

Behind his screen, Tai found himself breathing carefully.

"My lord, you invite a discussion of state policy here?" Zhou looked pointedly at the poet and then at two or three other men in the room.

"I do," said Shinzu calmly. "Among other things, I would like to know what state policy *is* in this matter."

There was another silence. Did the emperor's heir have the right to demand this of a prime minister? Tai had no idea.

"Cousin …" began Zhou, turning to the woman in the room. "Surely a pleasant springtime gathering is not—"

"In truth," Jian interrupted, gently enough, "I admit I should like to know, as well. About An Li. After all," she favoured the room with an exquisite smile, "he *is* my adopted child! A mother always has concerns, you know. Everlastingly."

The silence this time was almost painful. Zhou looked back over his shoulder at Liu. Tai's brother stepped forward a little (only a little). He bowed to Jian, then to the prince.

"My lord prince, illustrious lady, it is our understanding that Governor An has left the capital." Which was true, and Tai happened to know it, but wasn't an answer to anything.

"He did," said Shinzu promptly. "Three days ago, in the evening."

"And his eldest son left before that," added Jian. She wasn't smiling now. "An Rong rode northeast with a small company on good horses."

"Roshan went west, however," said Liu. His brother was shifting them away from whatever questions the prince had, Tai realized.

Not successfully.

"We know that," said the prince. "He met with your brother on the road to Chenyao."

Tai stopped breathing.

"With *my* brother?" said Liu.

He looked shaken, and this would not be an act. Liu was skilled at hiding feelings, not simulating them.

"With Shen Tai!" said the first minister in the same moment. "Why did he do that?"

"I'd imagine it was regarding the Sardian horses," said Shinzu carelessly. "But that isn't what I wish to discuss."

"It should be!" snapped the prime minister. "Roshan is obviously—"

"He is obviously interested in their disposition. He is commander of the Imperial Stables, among other offices. It is his duty to be interested, is it not?" The prince shifted himself off the wall. "No, my question is for you, first minister—and your adviser, of course, since he seems well informed. Why, pray tell me, have you been engaged in actions designed to drive him from the city, or worse?"

Tai swallowed hard, made himself breathe again, carefully.

"The Son of Heaven did invite him here, cousin. We all know that." Jian shook her head. "I even asked for him myself, he amuses me so whenever he comes to court."

It was only in that moment that Tai realized that she and the prince were working together, and it was not spontaneous at all.

"Drive him from the city?" Wen Zhou repeated. "How could I do that?"

The prince sipped his wine. "By planting stories in the Ta-Ming and the mandarin courtyards as to his intentions. And doing so while he was *in* Xinan, away from his soldiers, and feeling vulnerable because of it."

There was nothing idle about the room now.

Tai saw two or three of those present begin to back away, as if removing themselves from a combat. Sima Zian's wide-set eyes went from one speaker to another, avidly, absorbing it all, like light.

"Sometimes," said Tai's brother softly, "my lord prince, sometimes the stories being told can be true."

Shinzu looked at him. "They can. But there are *ways* of dealing with a man as powerful as An Li. These do not include making him feel as if his back is to a stone wall, or that he faces ruin at the hands of a first minister."

"Ruin? Not from me," said Zhou, regaining his composure. "I am no more than a servant of the empire. It would be our glorious emperor, may he live forever, who decreed anything at all!"

"In that case," said the prince in a voice delicate as silk, "might it not have been wisest to advise the glorious emperor, and others perhaps, as to your intentions? This is," he added, "a game so deeply perilous, Minister Wen, it beggars description."

"Hardly a game, my lord!" said Wen Zhou.

"I believe I will disagree with you," said the prince.

There was nothing remotely indolent or drunken about him, Tai thought. What *was* this moment? What was happening here?

He saw the prince set down his wine on a lacquered table. Shinzu added, "This feels, I am sorry to say, to be about two men and power, not the empire, or the emperor, may he rule another thousand years."

"I am distressed to hear you say so," Zhou murmured.

"I'm certain you are," agreed the prince. "My father was, as well." He said it quietly.

"You ... you spoke of this with the emperor?" Zhou had flushed again.

"Yesterday morning. In the Pagoda Tree Garden here."

"My lord prince, if I may?" It was Tai's brother. "We are confused. Please enlighten us all. You say there are ways of dealing with

Roshan. That suggests you agree he needs to be dealt with, if your servant may be so bold. The first minister and all of us who labour, unworthily, to assist him in his heavy tasks will be grateful for guidance. How *does* one address the danger General An represents for Kitai and this dynasty?"

There was nothing, *nothing*, Tai thought, of the amusing here now.

The prince, Taizu's heir, said, speaking as quietly as Liu, "By giving him honour and power. By summoning him here to be given *more* honours and *more* power—which is what the Precious Consort and my exalted father have been doing. Offering him banquet after banquet in the Ta-Ming or here at Ma-wai—and then watching him die of the sugar sickness, which he is doing in any case."

Wen Zhou opened his mouth.

Shinzu held up a hand. "And, after the great and glorious An Li has lamentably gone to join his ancestors, by giving him the most sumptuous funeral any barbarian military leader has ever had in the long history of Kitai."

He paused. The room was riveted. "And then, by bringing his eldest son into the palace, to whatever forms and variations of luxury appeal to him most. Making that son a supreme officer of the Palace Army, or leader of the Hundred Horsemen, or both! And doing the same thing for the younger sons. Keeping them *all* here for life. Giving them every woman in Xinan their fancy might turn towards. Every horse they wish to ride. Giving mansions and jade and country homes, endless wine and finer clothing than they have ever worn— while three new governors take control of the armies and districts in the northeast."

He looked at Zhou. "*That* is what you do, First Minister Wen, if you are thinking about the empire and not a private war between two men who hate and fear each other. Private wars, Wen Zhou, can become more than that."

A silence. No man rushed to fill it.

"*Every* woman?" said Jian, a hand to her breast. "Oh, dear!"

Prince Shinzu laughed aloud.

Tai realized he'd been forgetting to breathe again. He resumed, as silently as he could.

"It is not, my lord prince, so simple as that!" said Wen Zhou strongly. "Not when the man in question, ill as he might or might not be, remains ambitious beyond words."

"Nothing at court is simple," said Jian, before the prince could speak. "You are tasked, cousin, with guiding an empire. An Li is one of those charged with expanding and defending it. If you spend your days and nights circling each other like fighting cocks with metal claws, what happens to Kitai? Do we just watch and place wagers?"

From his place of hiding, Tai could not help but ask in the silence of his mind: *And where is the emperor in all of this? Is it not his task to resolve such matters, for his people, under heaven?*

Then something occurred to him and he caught his breath, again.

"Fighting cocks?" Wen Zhou repeated, head high.

Shinzu nodded. "A good description. Who shall be lord of the battle ring, vanquish the other, whatever the cost. Minister Wen, with the burdens that lie upon you, great privileges also come. This was true of Chin Hai before you. He was—we all know it—a potent, fearsome man. Roshan has chosen to test you in your first year. Can anyone be surprised? Military leaders exploring the strength and will of the Ta-Ming Palace? How do you think you have responded, first minister of my father?"

Wen Zhou's voice was firm. "I have warned the exalted emperor repeatedly. I warned the Censorate, the Treasury, and the ministers, including those supervising the army. I warned my lovely cousin. Had you expressed the least interest in these affairs before today, my lord prince, I would have warned you! You are, my lord, being unjust. Cousin, I have spoken to *all* of you about Roshan."

"But he," said Jian, smiling gently, "also warned us about you. Where does that leave the Son of Heaven, cousin?"

"He … An Li has spoken to you about *me*?"

"You think him a fool, cousin?"

"Of course not. He'd not be a danger if he was."

"That is not always so," said the prince. "Folly can be dangerous."

Tai was being forced, moment by moment, word by word, to change everything he'd ever thought he knew about Shinzu.

"Cousin," said Jian, "until lately, the danger has seemed to be from each of you to the other, not to the empire. But if Kitai is placed in peril because two men hate each other ..."

She left the thought unfinished.

"You arrested two of his advisers this spring. For consulting astrologers." The prince's eyebrows were level.

Tai's brother said quickly, "The inquiry established it was true, my lord prince."

"Did the inquiry also establish it mattered very much?" the prince said, just as swiftly. "Or was this simply provocation? Do tell me, adviser to the first minister."

Zhou lifted a hand, a small enough gesture, to forestall Liu's reply.

Wen Zhou bowed then, to the prince, to Jian. With dignity he said, "It is possible I have erred. No servant of the emperor should regard himself as infallible. I desire only to serve Kitai and the throne to the best of my abilities. I am prepared to be counselled."

"Good," said Jian.

"Indeed, good," said Shinzu. "And surely no more need be said about this on a lovely afternoon in Ma-wai. But before we turn to our diversions, will you tell me, first minister, where I may find one of your guards? Feng is his name, I am told."

"What?" said Zhou. "The honourable ... the prince is asking after one of my household?"

"I am," said the prince affably. He had reclaimed his wine cup. He held it out to be refilled. "I sent some of my own men to your compound to bring him to the Ta-Ming. He appears to have left Xinan. Where might the fellow be?"

Tai looked at his brother. Instinct, again. Liu's face showed perplexity. Whatever this was about, Liu didn't know it.

Wen Zhou said, "My guardsman? You want to speak with one of my guards?"

"I did say that," the prince murmured. "I also said he seems to have disappeared."

"Not at all," said Zhou. "He's been sent to my family. My parents are at greater risk with all these instabilities, and I thought they should have an experienced guard supervising their household retainers."

"Instabilities," the prince repeated. "So he'll be there now?"

"Still on his way, he departed only a few days ago."

"Actually, no, he's here in Ma-wai," said Jian.

Her voice was gentle. The room turned to her. "Perhaps I ought to have informed you both, cousin, my lord prince. I had the man followed and brought back, after receiving certain information."

"You knew he'd left?" The prince's expression was admiring.

"It seemed a reasonable expectation he would do that."

"You stopped my man on his journey?" Zhou's voice was odd.

"Greatly esteemed lady, please, what ... information?" It was Liu.

Tai didn't know whether to be amused by his brother's confusion, or to pity it. Liu hated, even more than Tai did, not understanding what was unfolding, anywhere, any time.

"We received a suggestion," said Jian, still gently, "that the man might have committed a murder before leaving. Dear cousin, this will all be new to you, of course."

It *wouldn't* be, of course. Tai reminded himself: he was among the dancers, and he didn't know the music.

"Of course it is new!" the first minister exclaimed. "Murder? Who alleges such a thing?"

"The Gold Bird Guards have submitted an account of something they say happened a few nights past. They were alerted that an act of violence might take place and some of them were there when it did. They made no arrest, seeking counsel from the palace first. You will appreciate why they did this: the murderer was your guardsman."

"I am shocked! Who alerted them to this terrible thing?"

The prime minister did not, Tai noted, ask who had been killed.

Zhou's demeanour, under the circumstances, was remarkable. Aristocratic breeding did make a difference, Tai thought. The Wen families of the south were not among the very wealthiest in this dynasty, but they had a lineage that went back a long way.

That was, of course, how Jian had become a lesser prince's wife, before rising beyond that.

"Who alerted us? Roshan did, as it happens," said Prince Shinzu.

Liu asked the question: "What man is he alleged to have slain?"

"A minor civil servant," said the prince. "I am told he was a drinking companion of your own brother. His name was Xin. Xin Lun, I am told."

"And … you say An Li told the Gold Bird Guards that this might be *about* to happen …?" Liu was struggling.

"Well," said Jian, sounding regretful, "the fellow, Master Xin, seems to have feared he might be in danger after certain tidings reached the Ta-Ming from the west. He wrote Roshan asking for protection."

Tai was watching the first minister. Zhou was impressive in that moment, showing nothing of what would have to be extreme agitation.

"And Governor An …?" Liu asked.

"… alerted the Gold Bird Guards, quite properly. They arrived too late, it seems, to prevent a death. It is," said Jian, "an unfortunate business."

"Most unfortunate," the first minister murmured.

"I can imagine how it distresses you, cousin, to have been sending such a violent man to guard your dear parents. My own uncle and aunt. The spirits shield them!" said Jian. "We will, of course, learn more when this Feng is questioned."

"This … has not yet happened?" Wen Zhou's voice was a little strained. Tai was suddenly enjoying himself.

That didn't last long.

"We were waiting for Master Shen Tai," said Jian, matter-of-factly. "To learn what he might add to the story. I spoke with him earlier, myself."

"With … you spoke with my brother?" said Liu.

"I did, since this seems to have to do with him." Jian looked at her cousin, and she wasn't smiling. "I think I like him. I decided he should have a chance to listen before speaking himself."

It was Liu who figured it out.

He looked at the two screens, from one to the other. His face was unreadable. Almost. If you knew him well, there were clues. Jian glanced over, as if casually, to where Tai was hidden.

And that was, Tai thought, as clear a signal to join the dance as he was ever going to get.

He stood up, straightened his clothes. Then he stepped around the screen, brushing the rich sandalwood of the wall, and came out to be seen. There was a degree of astonishment that—he supposed—the Precious Consort might find enjoyable. He didn't.

He had no idea what he was expected to do. He bowed to the heir, to Jian. Not to the first minister or his older brother. Both would have been proper, of course. He managed a brief smile for Sima Zian. The poet was grinning, clearly delighted by this theatre.

Tai cleared his throat. A roomful of high-ranking figures was staring at him. "Thank you, exalted lady," he said. "I admit I was unhappy about concealing myself, but your servant defers to your greater wisdom."

She laughed. "Oh, dear. You make me sound ancient! Greater wisdom? I just wanted to see their faces when you came out!"

Which wasn't the truth, and he knew it. All of them knew it. But this was a part of how Jian danced at this court, Tai was realizing. How she made others dance. This lay beneath the silk and scent. You didn't have to be with her long to see it.

Now that he was among them, the fact that he and she were wearing similar colours was unmistakable. Tai had wondered if it was deliberate. Of course it was.

He'd made a decision before, he reminded himself. If he could not weave subtle intentions towards a known design, he would have to do things differently. There wasn't really a choice, was there? Either he was a puppet, or a piece of wood in a river in spate, or he had *some* control over what was happening.

And he could do that here only one way.

He turned to Wen Zhou. "How did you know I was at Kuala Nor?"

He ought to have phrased it with courtesy, prefaced by bows and a deferential greeting. He ought not to have asked it at all.

Zhou stared bleakly at him. Said nothing.

"Second Brother," said Liu, a little too loudly. "Be welcome back among us! You have brought great honour to our family." Liu bowed, and not just the minimal salute of courtesy.

There was no way forward here, Tai thought, but straight.

"And you have shamed our father's memory, Eldest Brother. Did you never think how *he* would have felt about Li-Mei being sent north to barbarians?"

"But of *course*!" cried Prince Shinzu. "I had forgotten that our newest princess was of this family! How interesting!"

Tai doubted he'd forgotten it at all. Liu did not answer him. That could come later.

He turned back to Zhou. "You haven't responded, first minister." He could only be direct here. Or accept being a wood chip in rapids.

"I am unaware," said Wen Zhou coldly, "of any protocol in any dynasty that would require a prime minister to respond to a question phrased that way. A beating with the rod is possibly in order."

Tai saw Zian signalling with his eyes, urging caution. He declined. He was here. Li-Mei was gone. Yan was dead by a cold lake. And his father was dead, lying under a stone Tai hadn't even seen.

He said, "I see. Roshan suggested you might avoid the question."

Zhou blinked. "You spoke with him?"

Tai's turn to ignore a question. "A beating with the rod, you said? How many? People die under the rod, first minister. That could cost the empire two hundred and fifty Sardian horses."

If he was doing this, Tai thought, he was going to *do* it. There was exhilaration in having the chance, to be out from concealment, standing before this man and saying this. "Protocol might be amended, don't you think, when murder is involved? I ask again, how did you know I was at Kuala Nor?"

"Murder? You seem healthy enough. Are you a ghost yourself, then, Shen Tai?"

It was upon them, Tai thought. The poet had stopped trying to get his attention. The prince moved forward from the wall again. Only Jian seemed composed, sitting (the only person sitting) on her platform in the midst of all of them.

Tai said, "No, first minister. I am not dead yet. But the scholar Chou Yan is, at the hands of the assassin sent after me. Admissions have been made. By that false Kanlin who killed my friend. By two other assassins who confessed their purpose to Governor Xu in Chenyao." He paused, to let that name register. "Those two were also seen by my friend Sima Zian, and the governor's own daughter brought us the name the killers offered up. So there are others who can speak to this. And then, first minister, Roshan presented me with a copy of the letter sent him by Xin Lun, saying he feared he would be killed, since he knew too much."

"A copy of a letter? From *Roshan*? He cannot even read!" Zhou actually managed a laugh. "After all we've heard this afternoon— some of us skulking behind a screen—about his designs? You don't think that would be an obvious forgery meant to damage me? The only one openly resisting him? Surely you are not so entirely—"

"It is not a forgery," Tai said. "Lun died that night. Exactly as he feared he would. And the Gold Bird Guards saw who did it."

He turned to his brother, as if ignoring Zhou. As if there was nothing left to say to him at all. He looked at Liu. His heart was pounding.

"Someone tried to kill you at Kuala Nor?" Liu asked. He said it quietly. Assembling information—or that was how it sounded.

"And at Chenyao."

"I see. Well. I did know where you were," said Liu.

"You did."

It was strange, speaking to his brother again, looking at him, trying to read his thoughts. Tai reminded himself that Liu was easily skilled enough to dissemble here.

"I tried to persuade you not to go, remember?"

"You did," said Tai again. "Did you tell the first minister where I was?"

The question he'd been waiting to ask since leaving the lake and the mountains.

Liu nodded his head. "I think I did, in conversation." As simple as that, no hesitation. Someone else could be direct, or appear to be. "I would have to check my records. I have records of everything."

"Everything?" Tai asked.

"Yes," his brother said.

It was probably true.

Liu's face, carefully schooled from childhood, gave nothing away, and the room was much too public for what Tai really wanted to say again, face to face this time, a hand bunching Liu's robe tightly at the collar: that his brother had shamed their father's memory with what he'd done to Li-Mei.

This wasn't the time or place. He wondered if there would ever be a time or place. And he also realized that, for reasons that went far beyond his own story, this encounter could not turn into anything decisive about murder attempts. There were issues too much larger.

His thought was mirrored, anticipated. There was a dancer here. "Perhaps we should wait for my cousin's guardsman to answer some questions," said Jian. "Perhaps we can talk of other matters? I don't find this as amusing as I thought I might."

An order to desist, if ever there was one.

Tai looked at her. She was icily imperious. He drew a breath. "Forgive me, illustrious lady. A dear friend was killed in a place beyond borders. He died trying to tell me about my sister. My sorrow has made me behave unpardonably. Your servant begs indulgence."

"And you have it!" she said promptly. "You must know you will have it—from everyone in the Ta-Ming—for the honour you have done us."

"And for the horses!" said Shinzu cheerfully. He lifted a cup towards Tai. "Whatever questions or troubles any of us might have, surely our task now is to amuse our hostess. What sort of civilized men could we call ourselves, otherwise?"

A servant appeared at Tai's elbow, with wine. He took the cup. He drank. It was pepper wine, exquisite. Of course it was.

"I *asked* for a poem," Jian said plaintively. "Half a lifetime ago! My cousin declined, our wandering poet declined. Is there no man who can please a woman here?"

Sima Zian stepped forward. "Gracious and exalted lady," he murmured, "beauty of our bright age, might your servant make a suggestion?"

"Of course," said Jian. "It might even earn you forgiveness, if it is a good one."

"I live only in that hope," said Zian. "I propose that someone present a twinned pair of subjects and our two brothers, the sons of Shen Gao, each offer you a poem."

Tai winced. Jian clapped her hands in delight. "How *very* clever of you! Of course that is what we will do! And who better to offer the subjects than our Banished Immortal? I insist upon it! You choose, General Shen's sons improvise for us. I am happy again! Does everyone have wine?"

His brother, Tai knew, had passed the imperial examinations in the top three of his year. He had been preparing for them all his life. His poetry was immaculate, precise, accomplished. It always had been.

Tai had spent two years at Kuala Nor trying to make himself a poet in a solitary cabin at night, with little success, in his own estimation.

He told himself that this was just an entertainment, an afternoon's diversion at Ma-wai where they liked to play, not a competition that signified anything. He felt like cursing the poet. What was Zian doing to him?

He saw Liu bow to Jian, grave, unsmiling. *He never smiles,* she'd said in the sedan chair. Tai also bowed, and managed a wry smile. It probably looked apprehensive, he thought.

Sima Zian said, "Xinan, and this night's moon. Any verse format you choose."

The prince chuckled. "Master Sima, did we even have to wonder? Do you always choose the moon?"

Zian grinned, in great good humour. "Often enough, my lord. I have followed it all my days. I expect to die by moonlight."

"Many years from now, we hope," said the prince, graciously.

Tai was wondering, amid all else, how everyone had been so wrong about this man. He did have an answer, or part of one: it had been fatally dangerous through the years for an imperial heir to show signs of ambition, and those signs might all too easily be thought to include competence, intelligence, perception. It was safer to drink a great deal, and enjoy the company of women.

Which did raise a different question: what was Shinzu doing now?

Zian murmured, "Do you know ... well, no, you can't possibly know, since I have never *told* anyone ... but I have sometimes dreamed of a second moon to write about. Wouldn't that be a gift?"

"I'd like a gift like that," said the Beloved Companion, quietly. She was, Tai remembered (it needed remembering sometimes), very young. She was younger than his sister.

Jian turned to look at him, and then at Liu. "The First Son must surely go first, whatever other protocols we are abandoning."

Wen Zhou had stepped back as this new game began. He smiled thinly at this, however. Tai felt as if his senses had become unnaturally sharp, as if he was seeing and hearing more than he ever had. Was this what life at court was like? What the dance involved?

Liu folded his hands carefully in his full black sleeves. He had been doing this all his life, Tai knew, preparing for such moments as this. Xinan, and tonight's moon, he reminded himself. It was customary in such contests to pair two images.

Liu said, looking at no one, measuring stresses:

No one ever rests in Xinan.
Under a full moon, or the hook moon of tonight
As springtime turns a pale face to summer.
A place for winning renown, if deserved,
And gems and trappings of great worth.
The city is alive all night and even more

From the drumming-open of the great gates
As the white sun rises dispelling mist.
Here the Son of Heaven
Shines forth his Jade Countenance
Upon his beloved people, and so
Here the world is all the world may be.

There was a kind of pain in Tai's chest, shaped by and entangled with memory. This was his brother, they were at the heart of the court, the heart of empire, and Liu could do this, effortlessly. *All the world may be.*

But what else had he done, what else could he do, as easily?

Everyone in the room seemed to be looking at Tai. There had been no response at all to Liu's exquisite offering: that, too, was proper. When two or more people had been set a verse challenge you waited until the last one was done. They did these in the North District, often very drunk, often very late.

Tai sipped his wine. He was impossibly sober. He thought of Yan, of his sister. He looked across at Liu.

"If deserved," he murmured. "I like that."

His brother's mouth tightened. Tai hadn't expected a reaction. Nor had he expected to have to compose a poem in this setting. This was the court, not a pleasure house among fellow students. He took another drink. He had only one thing to bring to this room, he realized, that these elegant dancers would not have.

He looked at Zian. The poet's face was attentive. It would be, Tai thought, when poetry was concerned. This was his life, air and water.

Tai thought of a first phrase, and then—quite suddenly—of a conclusion, a contrast to his brother's, and he began, speaking slowly, picking his way, as through a moonlit wood. And as the words came, so, too, did images he'd lived with:

South of us Xinan lies under a sickle moon.
Lanterns will soon be bright in the spring night.
Laughter and music and rich wine poured.

Far to the west where all roads end
Cold stars shine on white bones
Beside the stone shores of a lake.
Thousands of li *stretch empty from there*
To east and west and mountains rise.
Birds wheel when the sun goes down
And grieving ghosts are heard in the dark.
How may we live a proper life?
Where is the balance the soul must find?

He looked at Liu first, in the silence that came when he was done, a stillness coming into the room like the breeze from outside. He'd spent so much of his childhood looking to his brother for approval. Liu turned away, reflexively, and then—it must have been difficult, Tai thought—back to his younger brother.

"A bright loom," he said. Old phrase. Poetry and silk.

"It is more than that," said Sima Zian, softly.

Laughter was heard. "Well. That didn't take long, did it?" said Wen Zhou, caustically. "Only a few moments out from hiding, and Shen Tai hastens to remind us of his so-heroic time in the west."

Tai looked across at him. And he realized two things in that moment. That he *could* do this, could dance to at least some of the music here if he chose—and that someone else in the room had even more anger than he did.

He stared at the handsome figure of the prime minister. This was the man who had taken Rain. Had killed Yan.

Tai took his time. They would wait for him, he realized. He said, "There were past a hundred thousand unburied there. Half of them were ours. I wouldn't have thought you'd need reminding, first minister of Kitai."

He saw his brother wince, which meant he knew how deeply Tai had thrust—and couldn't hide it.

"You will spoil my pleasure if you quarrel," said Jian. She let her voice sound petulant. Tai looked at her: the exaggerated downward curve of that lovely, painted mouth. She was toying with them again, he thought—but with a purpose.

He bowed. "My apologies again, illustrious lady. If I am to spend time at this court, I shall need to show restraint, even when others do not."

He saw her suppress a smile. "We have little intention of letting you leave us, Shen Tai. I imagine the emperor will wish to receive you formally very soon. Where are you staying in Xinan?"

He hadn't given it a thought. You could find that amusing. "I have no residence there any more, gracious lady. I will take rooms somewhere and I will—"

She seemed genuinely astonished. *"Take rooms?"*

Prince Shinzu stepped forward. "The Precious Consort is right, as ever. It would be a shocking lapse on the part of the court if you were allowed to do that. Will you accept one of my homes in Xinan for the present? Until my father and his advisers have had time to consider the proper ways to honour you."

"I have … I have no need for honours, my lord prince. I did what I did at Kuala Nor only—"

"—only out of respect for your father. I understand. The world is permitted to honour this, is it not?" The prince grinned. He drained his cup. "And there *are* those horses. One of my men will call upon you this evening, to make arrangements."

There were, indeed, those horses, Tai thought. He wondered—yet again—if Princess Cheng-wan in Rygyal on its far plateau had had any idea what she was doing to him when she decreed that gift.

The other woman who seemed to be entering and shaping his life now, the one who seemed to know precisely what she was doing, declared an end to her gathering.

Guests bowed to her and began filing out the doors. Shinzu remained in the room. Tai looked at the screen he'd hidden behind. The viewing holes were invisible.

He looked at the other screen.

He went out, last to leave. The steward closed the door. Tai's exquisitely delicate escorts were there, hands demurely in sleeves. He saw Zhou and Liu striding away together. He'd wondered if his brother would linger to speak. He wasn't certain if he was ready for that.

Sima Zian had waited.

"Can you spend a few moments with me?" Tai asked.

"I would be honoured," the poet said gravely, no hint of irony.

They started down the first long hallway together with the two women. Sunlight came from the west through tinted, silk-paper windows, casting a mild afternoon light at intervals. They walked through it as they went. Light and shade, then light and shade.

CHAPTER XVIII

The sun is low, reddened, there is a murky tint to the air. It has been cooler today, windy. Li-Mei wears a Bogü shirt over her tunic and a camel hair vest over that. She has no idea where Meshag found these for her in this emptiness. She has seen no signs of human life, not even smoke on the wind.

In the luxurious hot springs retreat of Ma-wai to the south and west across grasslands, the Wall, the wide, dangerous river, her older brothers are reciting poems for members of the Kitan court in a room of sandalwood and gold. Their listeners drink spiced pepper wine, and a sweet breeze softens the spring air.

Li-Mei keeps looking over her shoulder. She's been doing that, nervously, from the time the sun rose, offering light enough to see. They'd begun riding under stars, the thin moon down, the wolves invisible. Night noises. Some small animal had died in the dark, she'd heard a short scream.

Meshag never looks back. He allowed only two brief halts in a very long day. He told her during the first rest that they would not be caught that day, or the next. "They will have had to wait, to learn which way we go. They know now, but there is a dust storm. It will cost them some of a day."

"And us?"

He shook his head. "The storm? Not this far. Only wind."

Only wind, and endless grass, and a sky so much farther away than any she's known. It is difficult to feel that your life means anything under this sky. Are the heavens more removed from humankind here?

Do prayers and souls have a greater distance to travel?

Meshag signals another halt towards sunset. She's anticipated this one. Sunset is the other time he hunts. She dismounts. He nods curtly, his awkward motion, and rides off, east this time, along the way they've been going.

She has no idea how he chooses his direction. If she understood him yesterday, these are lands where his people rarely travel. The Shuoki here are enemies, and have also been restive, unsettled in their submission to Kitan authority. She doesn't know much about the Shuoki. Remembers a story about General An Li suppressing a rebellion, a heroic ride, something of the sort.

They haven't seen anyone. She has a sense it would be bad if they did, if they were found here. The grasslands are vast, however, beyond belief. That may be what saves them, she thinks.

No water this time, where he's decreed their evening rest. She was hoping for a pond. She badly wants to be clean again. It is a part of how she understands herself. This begrimed, lank-haired creature on a Bogü horse in Bogü clothes (the shirt is much too large and smells of animal fat) is not who, or what, Li-Mei considers herself to be.

She's aware that this is more and more inadequate as a way of thinking with every day that passes, every *li* she travels. The person she was has already been altered, destroyed, by the decision to name her a princess and send her north.

If she were really strong-minded, she thinks, she'd declare the girl who'd been raised by a stream near the Wai River, the woman who'd served the empress at court and in exile, to be dead.

She'd leave her behind with memories, like a ghost.

It is hard to do. Harder than she expected. Perhaps it ought not to surprise her. Who can so easily lay down habits and images of a life, ways of thinking, an understanding of the world?

But it is more than that, Li-Mei decides, stretching out her aching back. She is living—and riding—in a fragile but undeniable condition of hope, and that changes things.

Meshag, son of Hurok, is strange beyond words, barely human at times, but he is helping her, because of Tai. And his dead eyes do not undermine or refute steadiness and experience. He killed a swan with a single arrow. And he has the wolves.

He returns to her before night has completely fallen.

She is sitting in the tall grass, looking west. The wind has died. The hook moon has set. She sees the star of the Weaver Maid. There is a song about how the moon swings past her, then under the world through the night, and comes back up carrying a message to her love on the far side of the sky.

Meshag has water in the flasks and a saddlebag full of red and yellow berries. Nothing else. She takes the water, uses some to wash her face and hands. She wants to ask about rabbits, other meat. Does not.

He crouches beside her, places the leather bag between them. He takes a fistful of berries. He says, as if she's spoken aloud, "Would you eat marmot not cooked?"

Li-Mei stares at him. "Not ... not yet. Why ...?"

"No fires. Shuoki. More swans, maybe at night."

Searching for them. He has said she asks too many questions. She is not ready to let this part of her be dead or lost. She takes some of the berries. The yellow ones are bitter. She says, "Is it ... am I allowed to ask where we are going?"

His mouth twitches. "You *did* ask," he says.

She wants to laugh, but it is too difficult. She runs a hand through her limp, tied-back hair. Her father used to do that when he was trying to think. So do both her older brothers. She can't remember (a sorrow) if her little brother does.

She says, "I am afraid. I don't like feeling that way."

"Sometimes fear is proper. It is what we do that matters."

She'd not have expected a Bogü rider to admit the idea. She says, "It helps me when I know what is to come."

"Who can know this?"

Li-Mei makes a face. It occurs to her that they are having an actual conversation. "I only mean our intention. Where we are riding."

He is already harder to see. It has grown dark quickly. She hears the lead wolf in the grass, not far from them. She looks at the sky. She is looking for a swan.

Meshag says, "There is Kitan garrison not far. We sleep now, ride tonight. See it in morning."

She had forgotten about the garrison. The soldiers posted beyond the borders—here in the north, in the southwest, or west along the Silk Roads beyond Jade Gate—these seldom enter the thoughts of the Kitan. And many of them are recruited barbarians, she knows, moved from their own homelands to serve the emperor in a far place.

But that is not what she is thinking about now.

A hand goes to her hair again. She says, "But I cannot go to them! When they learn who I am they will take me back to your brother. You must understand." She hears her voice rising, tries to control it. "The emperor is dishonoured if they don't. I was ... I was *given* as a bride. The garrison commander will be terrified if I arrive! He will ... he will hold me and send for instructions and they will tell him to escort me back! This is not—"

She stops, because he has held up a hand in the darkness. When she falls silent, the night is very still around them, the only sound the wind in grass.

Meshag shakes his head. "Do Kitan women all speak so much, not listen?"

She bites her lip. Resolutely says nothing.

He says, quietly, "I said we see garrison. Not go there. I know they take you back west. I know they must do this. We see walls and turn south. Kitan fortress is protection for us from Shuoki, they not go near it."

"Oh," Li-Mei says.

"I take you …" He pauses, shakes his head. "Difficult tongue. I *am* taking you to Long Wall, is only three days if we ride quickly."

But the Wall, she thinks, the Wall's soldiers will do exactly the same thing, whichever watchtower they come to. She remains silent, waiting.

He says, "Soldiers there also send you back. I know. We go through Long Wall into Kitai."

"But how?" She cannot help herself.

She sees him shrug with one shoulder. "Not difficult for two people. You then see. No. You … *will* see."

She is heroically silent. Then she hears a strange sound, and realizes he is laughing.

He says, "You are try so hard not to ask more."

"I am!" Li-Mei says. "You shouldn't laugh at me."

He stops. Then says, "I take you through your Wall, sister of Shendai. Near to it is flat mountain. Drum Mountain, you call it? We go … we are going there."

Her eyes widen. "Stone Drum Mountain," she whispers.

He is taking her to the Kanlin Warriors.

ços

The two women bowed at the tall doorway to Tai's chamber. One of them opened the door. Tai let Sima Zian enter first. The women waited in the corridor. They didn't lower their eyes now. It was clear that they would come in if he invited them. It was equally clear that there was little he or the poet might think to request that would not be granted. Zian smiled at the smaller, prettier one. Tai cleared his throat.

"I thank you both. I must speak now with my friend. How may I summon you if needed?"

They looked perplexed. It was Zian who said, "They'll be right here, Shen Tai. They are yours until you leave Ma-wai."

"Oh," said Tai. He managed a smile. Both women smiled back. He closed the door, gently. The two large windows were open, screens rolled up. It was still light outside. He didn't imagine any real privacy existed here, but he didn't *think* anyone would be spying on him.

There was wine warming over a brazier on a small, lacquered table. He saw that the cups set beside it were gold. He felt overwhelmed. Zian crossed to the table, poured two cups. He handed one to Tai. He lifted his own in salute and drained it, then poured himself another.

"What just happened?" Tai asked.

He set his own wine down. He was afraid to drink any more. The intensity of the gathering they'd just left was washing over him. This happened in wartime, too, he knew.

This afternoon had been a battle. He'd been placed as an ambush, had engaged in single combat. Not necessarily with his true enemy. *Enemy.* That word again.

Zian raised his eyebrows. "What happened? You created a very fine poem, so did your brother. I will make copies of both."

"No, I mean ..."

"I know what you mean. I can judge the poems. I can't answer the other question."

Zian crossed to the window, looking out. From where he stood Tai could see that the gardens were glorious. This was Ma-wai. They would be. A little way north of here were the Ninth Dynasty tombs.

Tai said, "I think the emperor was behind the other screen."

"*What?*" Zian turned quickly. "Why? How do you ...?"

"I don't know for certain. I think. Two painted screens, and what Lady Jian and the prince did together in there ... it felt like it was meant for an audience, and it wouldn't be me."

"It might have been."

"I don't think so. I've never heard of Prince Shinzu behaving in such a ... talking so ..."

They were both fumbling for words.

"So strongly?"

"Yes."

"Neither have I," said Sima Zian, almost reluctantly.

"He was challenging Zhou. And he couldn't have done it without knowing—surely!—that his father would learn of it. So it seems to me ..."

"That he might have been doing it *for* the emperor?"

"Yes."

Zian's last word hung in the room, with all its obvious implications, and all those they could not see. The breeze at the window was mild, scented with flowers.

"Could you see us? From where you were?"

Tai nodded. "She'd arranged for that. So what happened there? I need help."

The poet sighed. He refilled his cup again. He gestured, and Tai reluctantly drained his own. Zian crossed the room and poured for him. He said, "I have spent my life between cities and mountains, rivers and roads. You know it. I have never had a place at court. Never sat the examinations. Shen Tai, I am not the man to tell you what is unfolding."

"But you listen. You watch. What did you hear in that room?"

Zian's eyes were bright. The afternoon light streamed in. The room was large, gracious, inviting. A place to be easy, to seek tranquility. That was what Ma-wai had always been about. The poet said, "I think First Minister Wen was given a warning. I do not think it will cost him his position."

"Even if he was plotting murder?"

Sima Zian shook his head. "No. Not even if he had *achieved* your killing. What, they will say, is the meaning of so much power if you can't use it to rid yourself of someone you dislike?"

Tai looked at him, said nothing.

Zian went on, "They'd have cheerfully allowed him to have you killed—before the horses. It would have been a matter of no consequence. Whether he did it because of a woman, or to prevent you from threatening his adviser, your brother. No one here would have blinked if you'd died at Kuala Nor or on the road. The horses have changed that. But I think today was about Roshan. Your presence was that warning to Zhou. He's at risk. They were telling him that." He poured another cup. He smiled again. "I very much liked 'cold stars shine on white bones.'"

"Thank you," said Tai.

There were two pre-eminent writers among thousands in Ninth Dynasty Kitai. This man was one of them. You could go happily to your ancestors carrying praise from Sima Zian for lines you'd written.

Tai said, "You just gave me guidance, after all."

"Treat it with caution," said the poet. "I claim no wisdom."

"Those who claim are those who lack," said Tai. It was a quote, the poet would know it.

Zian hesitated. "Shen Tai, I am not a humble man. I am only being honest. I keep returning to this jade-and-gold, it draws me. Sandalwood and ivory, the murmur and scent of women. But to visit, to taste. It is no home. I need to be here, and when I come, I need to be gone. A man must see it as his home to understand the court."

Tai opened his mouth to reply, but realized he didn't know what he wanted to say.

Zian said, "There is more beauty in the Ta-Ming, or here at Ma-wai, than anywhere else where men have built palaces and gardens. It may be that there is more beauty here, right now, than there has *ever* been. Who would deny the wonder and glory of that? Or resist seeing it?"

"Or fear that it might end?" Tai asked.

"That is ... one fear, yes. Sometimes I am happy I am no longer young." Zian put his cup down. "I am awaited, friend. There are two women who promised me flute music and saffron wine when the sun went down."

Tai smiled. "No man should keep another from that."

"Truly. Will you come?"

Tai shook his head. "I need to think. I imagine there will be a banquet tonight? I have no idea how to conduct myself."

"Because of Wen Zhou?"

"Yes. No. Because of my brother."

The poet looked at him. "He should not have done what he did."

Tai shrugged. "He is head of our family. He will say Li-Mei brings us honour, stature in the world."

The poet looked at him. "He is correct in that." His eyes were bright again, a trick of the light. "Still, I could understand if you killed him for it. But I am not a clever man in these ways."

Tai said, "I'm not certain I am, either."

Zian smiled, a wintry look. You were made to remember that he'd been a warrior in his time. "Perhaps. But you must be clever now, Tai. For a little while, or for longer than that. You have importance now."

"*The world can bring us gifts, or poison in a jewelled cup,*" Tai quoted.

The poet's expression changed. "I don't know that. Who wrote it?"

"My brother," said Tai quietly.

"Ah," said Sima Zian. "I see."

Tai was thinking of summer thunderstorms watched from a shared-bedroom window.

He was walking towards the door to open it for the poet when the knocking came. It didn't come from the hallway outside.

Both men froze where they were. A moment later the tapping came again. Tai turned to look at the wall beyond the handsome bed.

As he watched, a door-shaped panel swung away into shadow, and then a second panel did. Double doors, hidden in the wall. No one appeared. From where Tai stood he couldn't see within the recess. A corridor? An adjacent room?

The two men looked at each other. "This is not a time for me to be here," said Zian quietly. The poet's expression was grave. Close to Tai's ear, he murmured, "Be clever, friend. Be slow to act. This will not play out in a day and night."

He opened the door to the hallway himself. Tai's escorts were still there, one against the windows, the other across from her. The corridor was now lit by lanterns all the way down, in anticipation of sunset.

They smiled at the two men. Zian went out. Tai closed the door behind him, turned back into the room.

Six soldiers came in quickly, almost running.

They took positions, paired, by the two windows and the door, moving past Tai, ignoring him, their expressions impassive. They had swords and helmets and leather armour. The four at the windows looked out, carefully, but did not close them. The light coming in was beautiful, this time of day.

One of the soldiers knelt and looked under the bed. He stood up and nodded towards the recessed passage.

Wen Jian entered the room.

She didn't look at Tai, either. She walked across to the window opposite, then turned back to face the double doors, her expression sober. She was still wearing the green silk with pale-yellow phoenixes decorating it.

Tai's heart was pounding. He was afraid now.

Through the doors in the wall came six more soldiers carrying a curtained palace chair on poles. The curtains hid the figure they were carrying. You knew, however. You knew who this was.

The chair was set down in the middle of the room.

Tai dropped to his knees, forehead to the floor, hands stretched before him. He didn't look up. He closed his eyes for a moment, trying not to tremble. He remained that way, prostrate.

That was what you *did* when the Serene and Exalted Emperor of Kitai, ruling in glory through the mandate of heaven, entered a room. Any room, let alone your own bedchamber, having come to you in secrecy through a passage in the walls.

"You have permission to stand, son of Shen Gao." It was Jian who spoke.

Tai scrambled to his feet. He bowed, three times, towards the curtained chair. And then twice to the woman by the window. She inclined her head but did not smile. The soldiers who'd carried in the chair took positions along the walls, heads high, eyes staring directly ahead.

The curtains enclosing the chair were red, decorated with yellow suns. There were nine on this side, Tai saw, and there would be nine on the opposite, for the legend. Too much brightness for mortal men. That was the meaning here.

He had seen the Emperor Taizu three times in his life, from a distance.

The emperor had stood on a high balcony of the Ta-Ming overlooking a throng in the square before the palace on three festival days. The imperial party had been so far away and so far above that one of the students had said they might easily have been people hired to pose in imperial colours, under banners, while the real court were hunting or at ease in the Deer Park beyond.

"The august shepherd of our people wishes you to answer a question," Jian murmured.

Tai bowed to the curtains again. He was sweating. "Your servant is honoured beyond deserving," he stammered.

From behind the red curtain a voice came, stronger than Tai had expected. "Did you truly hear the voices of the dead at Kuala Nor?"

Tai dropped to his knees again, forehead to floor.

"You have permission to stand," said Jian a second time.

Tai stood. He had no idea what to do with his hands. He clasped them in front of his waist, then let them fall to his sides. His palms were damp.

"Your servant did, gracious and exalted lord," he said.

"Did they speak to you?" There was vivid interest in the voice. You couldn't miss hearing it.

Tai refrained, with an effort, from kneeling again. He was still trembling, trying to control that. He said, "Gracious lord, they did not. Your servant only heard them crying in the night, from the time the sun went down until it rose again."

"Crying. In anger, or in sorrow, son of Shen Gao?"

Tai looked at the floor. "Both, exalted lord. When … when … when bones were laid to rest, that ghost would cease to cry."

There was a silence. He glanced at Jian out of the corner of his eye. She stood by a window, late sunlight in her hair.

"We are well pleased," said the emperor of Kitai. "You have done us honour, and your father. It is noted."

Tai knelt again. "Great lord, your servant is not worthy of such words."

There came a chuckle from behind the curtain. "Do you mean that I am wrong in what I have said?"

Tai pressed his forehead to the floor, speechless. He heard Jian's laughter. She murmured, "Dearest love, that is unkind. You terrify the man."

Dearest love.

The Emperor Taizu, unseen, but also laughing, said, "A man who lived two years among the dead? I hope it is not so."

Tai didn't move, didn't speak.

"You have permission to stand," Wen Jian said again, and this time there was exasperation in her voice.

Tai stood.

He heard a rustling of the curtain—but it was on the other side, away from him. A moment passed, then the rustling again.

The emperor said, "We will formally receive you when such matters have been arranged. We wished to express our approval, privately. We always have need of brave men in the Ta-Ming Palace. It is good that you are here."

"Your servant thanks you, great lord," Tai murmured. He was perspiring now.

The emperor, in a quieter voice, said, "Honour falls into three parts, son of Shen Gao. One part restraint. One part right-thinking. One part honouring ancestors. We will leave you."

He didn't care what the woman had told him three times now: Tai fell to his knees again and put his head to the floor. He heard the soldiers moving, a creak as the chair was lifted, then the floorboards as they carried it back through the hidden doors.

He was thinking of those last words, trying without success to remember if he'd ever heard or studied them. Then, wrongly, *entirely* wrongly, the thought came to him that the unseen man who'd spoken them had taken his young son's young bride for his own concubine, was pursuing forbidden immortality with hidden alchemies, and was also building himself a tomb that dwarfed his father's and all those of his line.

One's own thoughts could be terrifying.

He heard the tread of the other soldiers, again almost running across the room. After a moment, he looked up.

Jian was by the double doors, alone, smiling at him.

"That was well enough done," she said. "I will confess, for my own part, that I find restraint to be over-praised. Do you not agree, Shen Tai?"

It was too much. Too many different directions for a man to be pulled in one day. Tai simply stared at her. He had no idea what to say.

She could see it in his face, obviously. She laughed, not unkindly.

"You are excused from my banquet tonight," she said.

He flushed. "I have offended you, illustrious lady?"

She shook her head. "Not so. There are gifts from the Phoenix Throne on the bed. These are the emperor's, not mine. My gift is your freedom tonight. The little Kanlin, so fierce in your service, is waiting outside this room with nine other Warriors. You will need guards when you go to Xinan tonight."

"I am going to Xinan?"

"And had best leave soon. Darkness will find you on the road."

"I … what am I …?"

"My cousin," said Jian, with a smile that could undo a man's control over his limbs, "is here with me tonight, and with others tomorrow morning, in discussions about Roshan."

"I see," said Tai, although he didn't.

"She has been told you are coming," said Wen Jian.

Tai swallowed. Found that he could say nothing at all.

"This is my gift. Your Kanlin knows where your horse is stabled. And you have a steward now, for the city home the emperor has just presented you. You will need a steward."

"A steward?" Tai repeated, stupidly.

"He was mine this morning. I have reconsidered a decision taken. He owes you his life. I expect he will serve you well."

The smile deepened. There was no woman on earth, Tai thought, who looked the way this one did.

But there *was* another woman, in Xinan, with golden hair. Who had put her life at risk for him, who had warned him, more than once, of what might happen if he went away.

She had also told him, Tai remembered, that he was going to need to be much more subtle, if he had the smallest hope of surviving in the world of the court.

"They will send word when you are summoned," said Wen Jian. "There will be an audience, and then, of course, you will need to go back west to bring your horses."

"Of course, gracious lady," said Tai.

"You have promised me ten of them," she reminded him.

"I have," he said. "For dancing?"

"For dancing," she agreed. "One more gift." She turned and laid something down on the bed and then went out through the doors in the wall. Someone closed them. The room was as it had been. It was still light outside.

On the bed lay a heavy key. Beside it was a ring, set with an emerald larger than any Tai had ever seen in his life.

There was a third object as well, he saw.

A lychee, not yet peeled.

He took the fruit, he took the key—it would be for the house in Xinan. He placed them in a pocket of his robe. He took the ring and put it on the ring finger of his left hand. He looked at it there for a moment, thinking of his father and mother. Then he took it off and placed it in his pocket, as well.

He drew a strained breath, let it out. For no good reason he removed his hat.

He crossed to the door and opened it.

"I am happy to see you," he said to Wei Song. She stood there, straight, small, unsmiling, fierce as a grassland wolf.

She made a face. Said nothing. Did incline her head, mind you. Behind her were, as promised, other Kanlins, black-clad.

Beside Song, kneeling, was the steward from this morning at the inn. The man who'd been ordered by Jian to kill himself when they reached Ma-wai. *I have reconsidered a decision.*

"Please stand," said Tai. The steward stood up. There were, embarrassingly, tears on his cheeks. Tai pretended not to see them. He took out the key. "I will assume you have been told which gateway, which house in Xinan, this will unlock?"

"I have, gracious lord," said the steward. "It is in the fifty-seventh ward, the very best. A handsome property. It is even close to the mansion of the first minister!" He looked proud, saying this.

Tai blinked. He could almost hear Jian's laughter.

He said, "I wish you to take horse or carriage, whichever is easier for you, and prepare this house for me tonight. There will be servants there?"

"Of course! This was a home belonging to the emperor, may he live a thousand years. They will be waiting for you, my lord. And they will be honoured and grateful, as ... as I am, to serve you."

Tai scowled. "Good," he said. "I will see you in Xinan."

The steward took the extended key, bowed, turned, went hurrying down the hallway. A man with a clear, shining purpose again, in a life he'd thought was over.

"His name is Ye Lao," said Song. "You neglected to ask."

He looked at her. The neat, calm figure in black. Her intense features. She had killed for Tai, had been wounded again this morning.

"Ye Lao. Thank you. Would you prefer him dead?"

She hadn't expected that. She shook her head.

"No." She hesitated. "This is a different world," she said. She wasn't as calm as she seemed, he realized.

He nodded. "It is. It will be."

She looked up at him. He saw her smile, the wide mouth. "And you will have your thighs torn raw, my lord, if you try to ride to Xinan on a Sardian horse while wearing *liao* silk. Have you riding clothes?"

He looked to the window and then the wall. His two women were still there, looking fearful and proud.

"Have I riding clothes?" he asked.

They hurried (gracefully) past him into the room. He heard them opening a chest, heard rustling sounds, giggling.

He went in a moment later. He did, it seemed, have riding clothes, exactly fitted, and his own boots had been cleaned. He changed. Neither woman looked away, he noted.

He kept the ring and, for no very good reason, the lychee fruit. He went back out, joined Song and the other Kanlins assigned to him. They led him to the stables, to Dynlal and horses for all of them, and they rode out from Ma-wai near the end of the day, towards the city of dust and noise, of two million souls, where lights would be shining by the time they arrived, and would shine all through the night.

No one ever rests in Xinan, his brother Liu had just said, in a poem.

And Rain had been told he was coming.

CHAPTER XIX

There is a rosewood gazebo near the back wall of the compound. It is set among fruit trees and flower beds, a long way beyond the artificial lake and the island set within it, past the grassy space for entertaining guests, and the bamboo grove with its laid-out paths, and the open area where Wen Zhou's guards practise swordsmanship and archery.

For Rain, the gazebo is a favourite place. She has many reasons. Rosewood is named not for its colour, but for its scent, which she loves. The wood itself is dark, with lines running through it as if trying to reach the surface, to break through. You can see that, imagine that, in daylight. Rosewood comes to Xinan from forests in the far south. It is imported overland and then along rivers and up the Great Canal, at a cost that does not bear thinking about.

There are nightingales here sometimes, this far back from the rooms and pavilions of the compound. (The street beyond the wall is quiet at night in a sedate, very wealthy ward.) They can be heard most often in summer; it is early in the year to expect one tonight.

She has meandered back this way, carrying her *pipa*, plucking it as she walked through the twilight. She has noticed that when she carries the instrument people don't look at her as closely, as if she's part of the setting, not a woman to be observed. Or carefully watched.

It is dark now. She'd had Hwan, the servant who loves her a little too much, light one of the gazebo's lanterns for her, and then she'd dismissed him. She doesn't want it to appear as if she's hiding: see, there is a light. Although you'd need to come a long way back and look through trees to see it. Earlier, in the afternoon, Hwan had run a different errand for her outside the compound. She has done what she can do, and is here.

Rain plays a few notes of an old song about the moon as messenger between parted lovers. Then she decides that's the wrong music to be thinking about tonight.

She is alone here. She's confident of that. Her maidservants have been dismissed for the night. One will remain in the suite of rooms against her mistress's return, but Rain has stayed out late in the garden with her *pipa* before. A mild eccentricity, usefully established.

And Wen Zhou doesn't spy on his women. His mind doesn't run that way. He can't actually conceive, Rain believes, that they would not be devoted and compliant. Where, and how, could they have a better life? No, his fears are cast, like a shadow, outside these walls.

He and his wife have been gone all day. Summoned to Ma-wai, no warning. He wasn't happy about the suddenness. On the other hand, there was never a great deal anyone could prudently do in the way of resisting when Jian wanted them. Rain sees fireflies among the trees, watches them for a time. Moths flutter around the lantern.

The compound has been quiet since the master left this morning, or at least since the arrival of the second message from Ma-wai. The one sent to her. *Not all windows above jade stairs need be seen through tears.*

No jade stairs here. Neither real jade nor a poet's symbol-shaped imagining. She sits on a bench with her instrument in a rosewood gazebo, roofed, but open to the night on all sides.

The scent of the wood, scent of the air. Nearly summer now. No jade, and no tears, Rain decides, although she knows it would be

possible to make herself weep. She isn't going to do that. She is thinking too hard.

Mostly about Wen Jian.

NO ONE KNOWS this mountain where I dwell.

Tai found it ironic, in an over-elaborate way, that when the nearness of Xinan first announced itself—a wide, diffused glow on the
southern horizon—the phrase that came to him was from a poem
about solitude.

Yan would have had a remark about that, he thought.

So would Xin Lun, actually. The one man gentle, amused, the
other wittily astringent. Both were dead. And the memories he was
conjuring were more than two years old.

So was the memory, rich as the emerald he carried (but didn't
wear), of the woman he was riding through the night to see.

He wasn't sure why he hadn't put on the ring. He wasn't ready yet,
he decided, for people to look at him the way one looked at a man
with so much wealth on display. He didn't want Rain seeing him like
that, though he couldn't say why. It wasn't as if she would be unused
to opulence in the first minister's house.

Even in the Pavilion of Moonlight, she had moved through a
world that included extravagantly wealthy men. It had never seemed
to touch her. She'd been as happy—or had made them think she
was—among the students, singing for them, teasing, listening to
late-night philosophy and verse and plans to remake the world.

That was what a skilled courtesan did, of course: induce every
man to think he was the one she'd choose, had she only the freedom
to pursue that innermost desire.

But he knew, Tai *knew*, that to think that way about her was to
deny a deeper truth about the golden-haired woman behind the walls
(so many of them). Xinan's walls loomed now in the middle distance
beyond the bridge they were clattering across. The bridge had bright
lanterns, and soldiers guarding it.

Two years ago, Rain had told him—had *warned* him—that the stylish southern aristocrat Wen Zhou, cousin to the emperor's beloved, might be minded to take her away from the North District.

Both of them had seen it happen many times. Mostly, it was a dream for a courtesan that this might occur. A doorway opening on a better life.

Tai, immersed in his studies and friendships, trying to decide what his own idea of a properly lived life should be, had been painfully aware that what she said might be true, but there was nothing a student preparing for the examinations, the second son of a retired general, could do if an aristocrat with wealth and connections wanted a North District woman for his own.

And then his father had died.

He was thinking of her, green eyes and yellow hair and the voice late at night, as they came to the city walls. Tai looked up at the enormous, many-storeyed tower above the gates. There were lights now, hiding the stars. The gates were locked, of course. It was after darkfall.

That didn't seem to matter: Jian had sent word ahead of them.

The leader of his Kanlin escort (not Wei Song, there was a more senior figure now) handed a scroll through a small sliding window, and a moment later the Gold Bird Guards manning this entrance through the northern wall opened for them, with a shout.

Then, as he and his Kanlins rode through, the city guards—those on the ground and those in the tower and on the nearby walls—all bowed twice, to Tai.

He truly wasn't prepared for this. He looked at Song, who had stayed close through the hours of this ride. She didn't meet his glance, was staring straight ahead, hood up, watchful and alert. She'd been wounded this morning. Seemed to show no signs of it.

The gates swung closed behind them. He turned in the saddle and watched, patting Dynlal absently. Tai wondered why he wasn't exhausted. They had been travelling most of the day, except for an interlude at Ma-wai that was likely to change his life.

He was in Xinan again. Heart of the world.

He still didn't know why Jian was doing this. His best guess was that it was a small part of the endless balancing act she performed in the palace: Wen Zhou and Roshan, ambitious mandarins, the heir, other governors, the eunuchs, other princes (and their mothers) …

And now one more man, arrived from the west. The brother of an influential adviser and of a newly named princess. A man with an absurd number of Sardian horses in his control.

To a woman in Jian's position, it would only make sense to assert a claim to such a man. And so, when it had emerged, through routine inquiry, that he'd had a relationship with a singing girl in the North District, a girl who might even be the reason Jian's cousin had sought to have him killed …

Well, you might undertake certain things in such a circumstance, set them in motion, if you were a clever woman dealing with a fiendishly difficult court. And with an aging emperor, tired of protocols and conflicts and finance and barbarians, obsessed with you, and with living forever, while shaping the most opulent tomb ever built, should that second dream not come to pass because the gods did not wish it so.

Gates had been opened for Tai, not just symbolically, as in a verse, but real ones, massive and intimidating, looming by torch and lantern light.

He had never done this: enter the city after dark.

If you approached Xinan towards day's end you found an inn, or a farmhouse with a barn (if you were a student, watching your money), and listened from outside the walls to the long ceremony of drums that closed the gates. Then you entered with the market crowd in the morning amid the chaos of another day among two million souls.

Not now. Now, the gates had just swung wide. Four of the Gold Bird Guards even came with them, to preclude the necessity of showing their scroll all the way through the city.

The streets were eerily quiet. Within the lanes and alleys of some of the wards there would be raucous, violent life even now, Tai knew, but not along the main roads. They turned east immediately inside the gate, passing in front of the vast palace complex until they turned south down the central avenue. The widest street in the world, running from the Ta-Ming to the southern gate, straight as a dream of virtue.

She had pressed her fingers to his mouth, their last night, to stop him from being clever, he recalled. He had once been a man who prided himself on being clever. He remembered her scent, her palm against his face. He remembered kissing her hand.

He looked around him. He had never done this either, ride a horse right down the central avenue, after dark. He didn't like being in the middle of the wide street. It felt too much as if he were laying claim to something. He wasn't. He'd have liked to claim a cup of wine in the Pavilion of Moonlight, if she had still been there.

"Over more, please," he said quietly to Song. "Too much of a procession, where we are."

She looked quickly at him. They were near a guard station, with lanterns. He saw concern in her eyes, then they moved from the light and he couldn't see her face any more. Song twitched her horse's reins, moved ahead, and spoke to the man leading them. They began angling southeast across the vast, open space, to continue along the roadway, nearer one side now.

There were only a handful of people abroad on the street, and no group so large as theirs. Those on the far side, west, were so distant as to be almost invisible. There were guard stations at intervals, large ones at the major intersections, all the way down the centre of the road. He saw a sedan chair being carried north. The bearers stopped as their company passed by. A hand pulled a curtain back, to see who they were. Tai glimpsed a woman's face.

They carried on, ten Kanlin Warriors, four of the Gold Bird Guards, and the second son of General Shen Gao, down the principal avenue of Xinan, under stars.

All journeys come to an end, one way or another. They reached the gate of the fifty-seventh ward.

HE HAD BEEN BORN in the south, beyond the Great River, in lands that knew tigers and the shrieking of gibbons. His family were farm labourers for generations, going back further than any of them could have counted. He, himself—his name was Pei Qin—had been the youngest of seven, a small child, clever.

When he was six years old his father had brought him to the under-steward of one of the Wen estates. There were three branches of the Wen family, controlling most of the land (and the rice and salt) around. There was always a need for capable servants to be trained. Qin had been accepted by the steward to be raised and educated. That had been thirty-seven years ago.

He had become a trusted, unobtrusive household servant. When the eldest son of the family decided to make his way to Xinan and the courtly world not quite four years ago (observing the useful, astonishing rise of his young cousin), Qin was one of the servants he'd taken north to help select and teach those they would hire in the capital.

Qin had done that, capably and quietly. He'd been a quiet child, was unchanged as a man. Never married. He had been one of the three servants entrusted with laying out clothing for the master, with preparing his rooms, with warming his wine or tea. Had he been asked at any time, he'd have said that his was a privileged life, since he knew the conditions in which his siblings lived, among the rice and salt.

One evening—the wrong evening, for reasons heaven decreed—he had been distracted by the inadequately supervised presence in the compound of a dozen girls from the pleasure district. They were being fitted with costumes for a pageant Zhou was hosting on his lake. (The lake was new then.)

Hearing their uninhibited laughter, worrying about who was watching them, Qin had overheated the master's evening wine.

The wine had, evidently, burned Wen Zhou's tongue.

Thirty-five years with the family had been as nothing, Qin would think, after. Decades of service had been less than nothing.

He was beaten. In itself, not unusual. The life of a servant included such things, and a senior retainer could be required to perform the beating of a lesser one. Qin had done that. The world was not a gentle place. No one who'd seen a brother mauled by a tiger would ever think that. And a short time in Xinan could make a man realize there were tigers here, too, even if they might not have stripes or pad through forests and fields after dark.

The thing was, Wen Zhou had ordered sixty strokes with the heavy rod for Qin. His tongue must have been *quite* badly burned, one of the other servants said bitterly, afterwards.

Or something else had greatly distressed the master that night. It didn't matter. Sixty strokes of the rod could kill a man.

Two and a half years ago, that was, in the days just before the Cold Food Festival. Qin did not die, but it was a near thing.

The household steward (not a bad man, for a steward) arranged for two doctors to attend upon him, taking turns, day and night, in the small room where they'd brought him after the public beating in the Third Courtyard. (It was important for all the servants to see the consequences of carelessness.)

He survived, but never walked properly again. He couldn't lift his right arm. That side of his torso was twisted, like some trees above the Great River gorges that grow low to the slanting ground to stay out of the wind and suck moisture from sparse soil.

He was dismissed, of course. An aristocrat's compound was not a place for the unemployable. The other servants undertook to look after him. It was not something he'd expected, not something normally done. Usually a man as deformed as Qin would be taken to one of the markets and do what he could to survive by begging there.

It might have helped if he could have sung, or told tales, or even served as a scribe ... but he had no singing voice, was a small, shy man, and his writing hand (he'd been taught by Wen Zhou's father's steward how to write) was the one that was twisted and useless after the beating.

He'd have been better off dying, Qin thought for a long time. He shaped such thoughts in the street behind Wen's compound, where the other servants had placed him after he was dismissed. It was not a busy thoroughfare, not a good place for a beggar, but the others had said they'd look after him, and they had done so.

Qin would limp on his crutch to the shady side of the street in summer and then cross as the sun moved, or huddle in an alcove in rain or winter winds. Begging brought little, but from the compound each morning and many evenings food and rice wine came out for him. If his garments grew threadbare, he would find that one day the person bringing his meal would be carrying new clothes. In winter they gave him a hooded cloak, and he even had boots. He became skilful with the crutch at beating off dogs or rats eyeing his provisions.

Last autumn his life had even changed for the better, which was not something Pei Qin had thought was possible any more.

One cold, clear morning, four of the household servants, walking the long distance around from the south-facing front doors, had come along the street towards where Qin kept his station against the compound wall. They carried wood and nails and tools, and set about building a discreet shelter for him, set in a space between an oak tree and the stone wall, not easily seen from the street, not likely to offend.

He asked, and they told him that the new concubine, Lin Chang, had heard Qin's story from one of Zhou's other women—apparently meant as a cautionary tale. She had made inquiries and learned where he was.

She had given instructions that he be provided with a shelter, and his food rations became more substantial after that. It appeared that she had assumed responsibility for him, freeing the servants from the need to feed him out of their own allocation.

He never saw her. They told him she was beautiful, and on five occasions (he remembered them perfectly) he heard her play the *pipa* towards the back of the garden. He knew it was her, even before they confirmed for him that it was Mistress Lin, of all the women, who played and sang best, and who liked to come alone to the gazebo.

Qin had decided she was playing for him.

He would have killed, or died for her, by then. Hwan, the servant who most often brought his food or clothing, clearly felt the same way. It was Hwan who told him she'd been bought from the North District, and that her name there had been Spring Rain. He also told Qin what the master had paid for her (it was a source of pride). Qin thought it an unimaginable sum, and also not enough.

It was Hwan who had told him, at the beginning of spring, that a Kanlin Warrior would be coming to meet privately with Mistress Lin.

Hwan—speaking for the lady, he made clear—asked Qin to show this Kanlin how to get over the wall using his own shelter-tree, and to give her directions to the gazebo from there (it was a distance back west in the compound).

It brought intense joy to Qin's battered body and beating heart to be trusted with such a service for her. He told Hwan as much, begged him to say so to Mistress Lin, and to bow three times in Qin's name.

The Kanlin came that night (a woman, which he hadn't expected, but it made no difference). She looked for Qin in the darkness, carrying no torch. She'd have had trouble seeing him, had he not been watching for her. He called to her, showed her the way over the wall, told her where the gazebo was. It was a cold night, he remembered. The woman climbed with an ease Qin would never have matched even when he had his legs and a straight back. But Kanlin were chosen for their aptitude in these things, and trained.

Qin had been chosen for intelligence, but had overheated wine one night.

You might call the world an unjust place, or make of life what you could. He was grateful to the servants, in love with a woman he would never see, and he intended to live long enough to celebrate the death of Wen Zhou.

He watched the Kanlin woman disappear over the wall and saw her come back some time later. She gave him a coin—silver, which was generous. He was saving it for an extravagance. Lychees would be in season now in the south, where he'd been born. The court might have them already, the Xinan marketplaces would see them soon. Qin intended to ask someone to buy him a basket, as a way of remembering childhood.

He'd actually gone once to the nearer, eastern market the summer before, just to see it again. It had been a reckless, misguided thing to do. Getting there had taken him most of a day, limping and in pain, mocked by children. He'd fallen several times, and been stepped on, and had then been at real risk, at day's end, of not getting back inside the ward when the drums began.

You were beaten by the gate guards for that.

He would ask someone to buy him lychees. There were several of the servants he trusted, and he would share his bounty. They had saved his life, after all. And surely there was value in any life, even one such as his?

Earlier today, Hwan had come out again, taking the long walk around to tell him someone else would be coming along Qin's street tonight, and would need to be shown the tree and how to climb, and where the gazebo might be found.

"It is for her?" was all Qin asked.

"Of course it is," Hwan said.

"Please bow three times. Tell her that her most humble servant in the world under heaven will ensure that it is done."

That night a man did come walking, with five Kanlins. One of these, Qin saw, was the woman who'd come before. He knew because he didn't need to call out to them, she came straight over to his tree. Since it was the woman who'd been here they didn't need instructions. The man looked down at Qin in the darkness (they carried no torches). He saw the small shelter built for him.

He gave Qin two coins, even before going over the wall. Three of the Kanlin went with him, two remained in the street, on guard.

Qin wanted to tell them that he would have served as a guard, but he wasn't a foolish man. These were Kanlin, they had swords across their backs. They wore black, as ever, and melted into the night. After a time he had no idea where they were, but he knew that they were there.

HER *PIPA* RESTS on the wide, smooth, waist-high railing. She is standing by one of the gazebo's rosewood pillars, leaning against it. It is chilly now but she has a short jacket, green as leaves, with gold thread, to cover her bodice, which is gold. Her green, ankle-length skirt has stripes running down it, also gold. The silk is unexceptional. It would have been noted had she worn finer silk, with the master away.

She wears no perfume, same reason.

She is on her feet because she has heard someone coming—from the eastern side of the garden, where the oak tree can be climbed.

The one lantern casts an amber glow. The gazebo will seem like a cabin in a dark forest, she imagines, a refuge, sanctuary for a lost traveller. It isn't, she thinks. There is no sanctuary here.

Footsteps ascend the two steps and he is here.

He kneels immediately, head lowered, before she can even see his face, register his presence properly. She has not expected him to do this. She's had no real idea what to expect. *No jade stairs*, she reminds herself. *No tears at window ledges.*

He looks up. The remembered face. She observes little change, but it is not light enough to see closely here, and two years need not alter a man so much.

She murmurs, "I am not deserving of this, my lord."

He says, "I am not deserving of what you did for me, Rain."

The voice she also remembers, too vividly. Why, and how, does one voice, one person, come to conjure vibrations in the soul, like an instrument tuned? Why a given man, and not another, or a third? She hasn't nearly enough wisdom to answer that. She isn't sure if anyone does.

"Master Shen," she says formally. "Please stand. Your servant is honoured that you have come."

He does stand up. When he looks at her, his face, beneath the lantern, shows the intensity she recalls. She pushes memories away. She needs to do that. She says, "Are you alone, my lord?"

He shakes his head. "Three Kanlin are with me, to keep watch. Two more in the street. I'm not allowed to be alone any more, Rain."

She thinks she understands that. She says, "Is the one I sent to you ...?"

"Wei Song is here, yes. She is very capable."

Rain allows herself a smile. She sees him register that. "I thought she might be. But did she ... how did you survive?"

He hesitates. He *has* changed, she decides. Is weighing his words. "You know where I was?"

She nods. She is glad of the pillar behind her, for support. "I didn't know, before. I had to have her find your home, start there. I didn't even know where your father's home was."

"I am sorry," he says, simply.

She ignores that. Says, "I know that Wen Zhou had Lun hire a woman to kill you."

"Sent with Yan."

"Yes. Is he all right?"

"He's dead, Rain. She killed him. I was saved only by ... by the ghosts. And Tagurans who came to help, when they saw riders."

By the ghosts. She isn't ready to ask about that, to know about it. Yan is dead. A hard thing to learn. A sweet man.

"I'm sorry," she says.

He is silent, looking at her. She is accustomed to men looking at her, but this is different. He is different.

Eventually he says, "He was dead the moment she became his guard, I think."

She wishes there was wine. She ought to have brought some. "So I did nothing at all?" she says.

He shakes his head. "There was a second attempt. At Chenyao. Wei Song fought a number of men alone, outside my room."

"A *very* capable woman, then." She isn't sure why she's said it that way.

Tai only nods. "As I said." He hesitates again. He isn't being awkward, she decides, he is choosing what to say. It is a difference from before. "Rain, you would have been killed if this had been discovered." It is a statement, not a question.

"It was unlikely it would be," she says. He hasn't moved from under the lantern, neither has she, from her place by the pillar. She sees fireflies behind him. Hears crickets in the garden. No sign of the Kanlins he mentioned, or anyone else. There is a silence.

"I *had* to go away," he says, finally.

This will become difficult now, she thinks.

"I know," she says. "Your father died."

"When did ... when did he bring you here?"

She smiles at him, her smile has always been an instrument she could use. "Not long after his appointment."

"As you tried to tell me."

"As I did tell you, Tai."

She hadn't meant to say that so quickly. Or use his name. She sees him smile this time. He steps closer. She wants to close her eyes, but does not.

He says, "No perfume? I have remembered it for two years."

"Have you really, my lord?" she says, the way she might have in the Pavilion of Moonlight.

He looks down at her, where the light touches her features, catches yellow hair. She has not posed herself, it was simply a place against a column where she could lean back for support. And be on her feet when he came.

He says, "I understand. You wear scent now only for him, and he's away."

She keeps her tone light. "I am not sure how I feel about you becoming this perceptive."

He smiles only a little. Says nothing.

"I can also move more easily undetected without it," she says. But she is disconcerted that he has so swiftly understood.

"Is that important?" He is asking something else now, she knows.

She lifts her shoulders again, lets them fall.

"Has he been cruel?" he asks. She hears strain in his voice. She knows men well, this one very well.

"No. Never," she says.

A silence. He is quite close.

"May I kiss you?" he asks.

There it is. She makes herself meet his eyes.

"No. Never," she says.

And sees sorrow. Not anger, not balked desire. Sorrow, which is—perhaps—why and how another's voice or soul can resonate within you, she thinks.

"Never?" he asks.

He does not move nearer. There are men who would, she knows. She knows many of those.

No jade stairs, she tells herself.

"Are you asking my views on eternity and the choices of life?" she says brightly. "Are we back to discoursing upon the Sacred Path?"

He waits. The man she remembers would have been eager to cap her own half-witticism with a quip of his own. That, or take the exchange deeper, despite her teasing.

She says, to delay: "You have changed in two years."

"Where I was," he says.

Only that. He has not touched her.

She lifts a hand to his cheek. She had not meant to do that. She knows exactly what she'd meant to do among the fireflies tonight. It was not this.

He takes her hand in his, and kisses her palm. He inhales, as if trying to bring her back within himself after so long.

She closes her eyes.

SHE HAS NOT CHANGED, Tai thought, and he realized that it had been childish for him to imagine that she'd appear to him like some fragile princess abducted into sad captivity.

What had happened to Rain was not, he finally understood, his sister's fate. It was a difficult truth. Had he merged the two of them in his mind, journeying east?

What, truly, was better about a singing girl's life in the Pavilion of Moonlight? Serving any man who had money and desire? Compare that with existence in this compound with one powerful man she knew—*clearly* she knew—how to entrance and lure? As for when she grew older: also clear as moonlight on snow, her chances of a protected life were better here. This destiny was what the North District girls all longed to find.

He felt a wave of self-reproach, and sadness.

Then she touched his cheek, and then she closed her eyes.

He bent and kissed her on the lips. He did it gently, trying to acknowledge what had happened, the reality of it, and that he'd been away two years. Her mouth was soft, her lips parted. His own eyes closed.

He made himself draw back. He said, "Rain, there has never been a woman who reaches into me as you do."

Her eyes opened. The gazebo was lit by only one lantern, so it was hard to see how green her eyes were, but he knew, he remembered. He wondered—a shockingly hard thought—if he'd ever see those eyes again.

For that was where this night was travelling, he realized.

She said, "I am sorry for it, my lord. And pleased. Am I permitted to be both?"

"Of course," he said.

She had slipped, effortlessly, into the mixture of formality and intimacy that had characterized her manner in the Pavilion of Moonlight. He tried to match it. Could not.

He said, "Why did you come tonight?"

She shook her head, suddenly impatient with him. He remembered that, too. "Wrong question, Tai. Would you have me shame myself with an answer?"

He looked at her. "I'm sorry."

She was angry now, he could see it. "I came because the Beloved Companion sent a note advising me not to sleep tonight, and she quoted the jade stairs poem."

"I see." He thought about it. "She told me you were alerted I might come. She kept Wen Zhou at Ma-wai. Gave me guards and a pass into the city after dark."

"So we are both serving *her* needs?" He heard amusement under the bitterness. "How compliant of us."

He smiled. "Rain, I would say the feel of your mouth, the taste of you, serves my needs very well."

She looked up at him for a long time. Then away into the dark, and then she said, with finality, "I cannot be your lover, Tai. There is no proper way for it to happen. I did not send a Kanlin to you for that."

"I know," he said.

Sorrow in the quiet dark. The astonishing truth of this woman: proud and seductive, more subtle than he was. *Needing* to be more subtle, he thought, in the life she'd lived.

"I could accuse Zhou of trying to kill me," he said. "It was almost said at Ma-wai today, not by me. He did have Yan murdered, and Lun. It might change your—"

"You would accuse the first minister of Kitai, governing this empire, of killing students or minor civil servants? And this would accomplish what, Tai? Who would care? How would you prove it?"

"Others would do that. Wen Jian has the man who killed Lun."

"What? Feng?"

He saw that she was startled by this. "He was heading south to Wen Zhou's family. She told us all that she had the man. There were important people in the room, including Prince Shinzu."

He didn't mention the emperor. It was not the sort of thing you spoke about. He said, "I think ... we think ... that she is giving her cousin a warning. He's in difficulty, Rain, mainly because of Roshan."

She crossed to the bench, sat down, looking up thoughtfully at him now. Moths darted around the one light. The air was cool. He remembered this about her, the way her mind could be so suddenly engaged.

"Who is *we*?" she asked. Not the question he'd expected.

"I was befriended on the road. Sima Zian has been with me since Chenyao."

She stared. Then inclined her neck, as if in submission. "The Banished Immortal? Oh, my. How may a singing girl from the North District, a simple girl, ever hope to keep the interest of a man with such illustrious connections?"

Tai laughed softly. "For one thing, she isn't simple at all. For another, she isn't in the North District. And her own connections are more potent than his." He grinned. "How else may I assist you?"

He saw her return his smile this time. "If I said, *You could kiss me again*, that would be wrong, wouldn't it?"

He took the one step necessary, and did so. Her mouth came up to meet his. It was Rain who pulled back this time. She looked away. "That *was* wrong," she said. "Forgive me."

He sat on the bench beside her. He was aware that she'd left room for him to do so. "Rain, your life has changed. I have been foolish in my dreaming."

"Most of us are foolish in our dreams," she said, still looking the other away. "The trouble comes when we bring folly out of dream."

"Rain, listen to me. If I am right, if Jian is sending a warning to her cousin and it has to do with me … does that endanger you?"

She thought about it. "I don't think so. There is a servant who could destroy me, but he won't. If you were seen here I would be killed." She said it matter-of-factly. "But Wen Zhou is worrying about Roshan right now, not you. An Li left the city a few days ago, and so did his oldest son."

"I know," said Tai. "I spoke with him on the roadside, coming here."

He saw that he'd shaken her again. He was young enough to feel a flicker of pride in that, and old enough to know it was unworthy.

She said, "Tai, what is all this? You are in a swift river."

"Yes," he said. "Because of the horses. Only that."

"And the ghosts," she said. "What you did."

"The horses come from what I did. It is the same."

She was silent, considering that, then said, "Sardian horses."

"Second thing from that country to change my life."

She smiled. "I haven't changed your life."

"You might," he said. "Rain, we can't know what the next days will bring us. Sima Zian thinks something grave is happening."

He could see her thinking about it.

He said, "I have a house in the city now, in this ward. If you need to get word to me, can someone do that?"

"If I need to? Or if I wish to?" She turned to look at him.

His turn to smile. With every word they spoke some of the old manner was coming back, like the steps of another dance. It was unsettling.

He said, "You were always better at judging. You will know if there is danger for you, or something I need to be told."

She took his hand. Looked at the interlacing of their fingers. "I think I am not so much better than you any more, Tai. If I ever was."

"You were. You are. And you risked your life. What is it I can do? Please ask."

He was wondering how many men had said *I love you* to this woman, late at night. He wondered what Zhou said to her.

Her head remained lowered, as if she were fascinated by their twined fingers on her lap. She wore no perfume. He'd understood why immediately, but there was a scent to *her*, to her nearness after so long, and it conjured desire, drew it forth.

She said, "I will have someone learn where your house is. If I need to send word, I can. The man by the wall may be trusted with messages. They will get to me. The servant here to approach is named Hwan. No one else." She fell silent, still gripping his hand. When she spoke again her voice had changed. "I think ... Tai, you need to leave, or I will relinquish my pride. This is more difficult than I thought it would be."

He drew a breath. "And for me. I am sorry. But ... Rain, I am also pleased. Am I permitted to be both?"

She squeezed his hand hard for that. It was painful, because a ring of hers bit into his skin. She *meant* to hurt him, he knew, for so neatly echoing her phrase from before.

"How clever," she said. "You students are all alike."

She released his hand. Clasped hers together in her lap. Her gaze remained lowered, as if submissively. He *knew* she wasn't submissive at all. He didn't want to leave, he realized.

There came a rustling sound from the trees, then a voice beyond the spill of light. "Gracious lady, Master Shen. Someone is walking past the lake. We can kill him, but it would not be wise."

It was the Kanlin leader. "Where is Wei Song?" Tai asked quickly.

"Farther along the garden, awaiting instruction."

"Kanlin, is the man carrying wine?" Rain asked.

"He is, gracious lady."

She stood up. "That's Hwan. Do not harm him. Tai, I mean it … you must go."

He hesitated, then did something she couldn't see, or the Kanlin. He stood up, looked at her in lantern light.

She clasped her hands before her, bowed formally. "My lord, it was too kind of you to visit your servant."

"I will see you again?" He found it difficult to speak.

"I would like that, but it is hard to know the winding of paths. As you said, my lord. Tonight's … was not the greeting I would have most wanted to give you."

She still knew exactly what to say to set his heart beating.

"Nor mine for you," he said.

"It pleases me to hear that," said Spring Rain, eyes demurely lowered.

"Come, my lord!" said the Kanlin.

Tai turned, and went from her.

SHE WATCHES HIM go down the steps and away into darkness. She hadn't even seen the Kanlin, only heard a voice in the night. She looks to her *pipa* on the railing, sees the moths still fluttering.

Then she sees what he has left behind him on the bench where they've been sitting. She picks it up. Looks at it under the light. Her hand begins to tremble.

She swears aloud, in a voice that would shock many of the men who once valued her for serene grace in the Pavilion of Moonlight.

She looks up. The guard had said …

She calls out, "Wei Song? Are you still there?"

A moment, no sound, no woman appearing from the blackness. Then, "I am, my lady. How may your servant be of use to you?"

"Come here."

Out of the night garden the woman comes. The one she'd met here earlier this year, had hired and sent west. The Kanlin woman bows.

"The servant will be here very soon," she says.

"I know. He has seen you before."

"I remember."

Rain looks at her. A small woman, hooded. She extends the ring Tai has left for her.

"Take this. Give it back to Master Shen. Tell him I could never sell it, or wear it, or even have it cut down to sell, without being at risk. There is writing on the band! This is from the emperor, isn't it?"

"I have never seen it," says the other woman. "He didn't wear it, riding." Her voice is odd, but Rain has no time to work that through. "I believe the emperor might have been with …"

"Indeed. This ring suggests he was, or sent someone. Tell Tai he must have this, and be seen to have it. He has to wear it. It will *protect* him. He needs to learn these things. He can't go around making gifts of something like this. Take it."

The ring is stunningly beautiful, even in this light. It would match her eyes. She believes—in fact she is certain—that Tai will have thought of that. Not his *reason* for doing this, but a part of his wanting to.

The Kanlin hesitates, then bows again, takes the ring. "I am sorry I failed you," she says. "I did not reach Kuala Nor, and I—"

"Master Shen told me," Rain says briskly. "He also said you fought attackers for him. And he is alive. No one failed. Do I need to pay you more, to continue guarding him?"

The Kanlin, who is smaller than Rain remembered, draws herself up straight. "No," she says. "You do not."

"Why not?" says Rain.

"We have been retained by Lady Wen Jian. Ten of us. He is defended."

"She did that? I see. It is out of my hands, then," says Rain. She isn't sure why she says it that way. She looks at the woman more closely, but the light isn't strong, and the Kanlin is hooded.

The other woman seems about to say something. She doesn't. She goes down the stairs and east through the garden, the way the others have gone.

Rain is alone. Not for long, and she knows it. She picks up her *pipa*, is tuning it when she hears Hwan calling to let her know—quite properly—that he is approaching.

He comes into the gazebo bearing a round tray with a small brazier heating wine, and a cup for her.

"Why are you here?" she asks coldly.

He stops, shaken by her tone. He bows, handling the tray carefully. "My lady. It is cold now. I thought you might want—"

"I left instructions, did I not, Hwan?"

She *knows* why he is here. There is a balance to be achieved in this, as in all else. She needs his devotion, but he must not be allowed to assume, or presume. There are lines to be drawn, not to be crossed.

"My lady," he says, abjectly. "Forgive me. Your servant thought only that you might—"

"That I might want wine. Very well. Leave it and go. You will not be punished, but you are aware that the master has instructed that servants are to be beaten for failing to follow instructions. He said it is our task to ensure this."

It is not, she knows, the response he expected. That is all right, she thinks. He bows again, the tray wobbles slightly.

"Put it down and go," Rain says again. She allows her voice to soften. "It was a kind thought, Hwan. Tell my woman that I will be back shortly. I will want a fire, to take the edge off the night."

"Of course, my lady," he says, and backs away. "Do you ... do you wish an escort back through the garden?"

"No," she says. "I just gave you your instructions, Hwan."

"Yes ... yes, my lady."

She smiles, makes certain he sees it. She is in the light. "No one will be told of this. You are a loyal servant and I value you for it."

"My lady," he says again, and leaves her, bowing twice.

Dealing with men of all stations and all ranks, learning their needs and anxieties ... is this not what a girl from the North District, especially from one of the best houses, is supposed to be able to do?

She actually does want the wine he's brought. She removes the top of the warmed flask and pours for herself. Trained girls know how to pour, another skill they are taught.

She seems to be crying, after all.

She sips the spiced wine and puts down her cup. She takes the *pipa* and begins to play, for herself, but she knows someone will be listening, and she owes him this.

An emerald ring, she is thinking. From the emperor. Perhaps from his own hand. Tai hadn't said. A delicacy in that. The world is a place of surpassing strangeness, she thinks. And then she is thinking, without knowing why, of her lost home in the west.

QIN SAW THE MAN and his guards come back over the wall. It was harder to get up and out. You needed to be boosted over, and the last one had to be exceptionally skilled at climbing. The last Kanlin was the woman, Qin saw, and she seemed to do it easily.

The man seemed distracted, not even certain which way to walk. The Kanlins led him away, including the two who'd been waiting here in the street. The fellow—clearly an aristocrat of some kind, though he wasn't dressed like one—did pause long enough to offer Qin two *more* silver coins. That made four, in all, which was more money than anyone had ever given him out here.

He saw the last Kanlin catch up with the man and draw him aside. He saw them speaking, saw her hand over something small. They walked on, farther into the ward, and were lost to sight down the street.

Qin had managed to push himself to his feet, and offer what passed for a bow with him, when he was given the money, but he wasn't sure the fellow noticed. He sat down again, looking at the four coins. Silver! A breeze came up, stirring the dust. He was thinking about lychees, and when they'd reach the markets. Then he stopped thinking about that.

From within the garden, *pipa* music began. The sound came faintly to him, for she was some distance away from where he sat against the wall, in the small hut she'd had made to shelter him.

She was playing for him. Qin *knew* she was. A music more precious than any coins anyone could give. He heard sadness, sweet and slow, in the plucked strings, and thought about how a beautiful woman, from within her sheltered, easeful life of luxury and power, was offering sorrow to the spring night, for what had been done to him.

Qin listened, claimed unconditionally by love. He imagined that even the stars were still and listening, above the haze and lights of Xinan. Eventually the music stopped and the night street was quiet. A dog barked, far away.

CHAPTER XX

As he had promised her, they see the Kitan fortress before sunrise. Even in the night and far away, it is imposing.

It is another unsettling moment for Li-Mei, among so many: looking under stars at something her own people have built here, this heavy, squared-off structure on the grass. Something set solidly, walls rising. An assertion about permanence in a world where the presence of mankind was transitory, lying lightly on the earth. Everything carried with you where you went.

What did it mean, wanting to proclaim this permanence? Was it better, or wiser—a new thought for her—to be a people who knew there was no such thing?

It is as if, she thinks, looking at the fortress her people have erected, some giant, heavenly civil servant had taken his scroll-stamp—the seal he used to signify he'd read a document—and dropped it on the grass, and left it there.

There is something so unnatural, so foreign, about the walled fort being here that she misses the important thing.

Meshag does not. He mutters something beside her, under his breath in his own tongue, and then, more clearly, he says, "It is empty."

She looks quickly over at him. "How do you know?"

"No torches. No one on the walls. The pastures, there should be night guards for the horses. Something has happened." He stares ahead. They are on a rise of land, the fortress lies in a shallow valley.

Meshag makes a sound to his horse. "Come," he says to her. "I must see." Fearfully, hating her fear, she follows him down.

The fortress is even larger than she'd realized, which means it is farther away. There is a hint of grey in the sky as they finally come up to it. Li-Mei looks to left and right, and now she can see their wolves.

This close, she can see the strangeness of the fort, the thing he understood right away. There is no one here at all. Not on the wall walks, not above the gates, in the squared corner towers. This is a hollow structure, lifeless. She shivers.

Meshag dismounts. He walks to a fenced pasture ahead of them. Goes to the gate, which hangs open, unlatched. It creaks in the wind, banging at intervals against the post. A thin sound. She sees him kneel, then walk a distance south and kneel again. He stands and looks that way.

He turns and walks towards the main gate of the fort. It is far enough that she loses sight of him against the looming walls, in the dark beyond the pasture. She sits her horse, beside wolves, and feels fear blow through her like a wind.

At length, she sees him walking back, the loping, rigid stride. He mounts up. His face is never easy to read, but she thinks she sees concern in it, for the first time.

"When did they leave?" she asks. She knows that is what he's been trying to determine.

"Only two days," he says. "Towards the Wall. I do not know why. We must ride quickly now."

They ride quickly. They are galloping the horses up out of the valley along the southern ridge, the sun about to rise, when they are attacked.

It is called the raider's hour on the steppe, though that is not something Li-Mei has any way of knowing. Attacks in darkness can become confused, chaotic, random. Daylight undermines surprise. Twilight and dawn are—for hunters of any kind—the best times.

Li-Mei is able to piece events together only fitfully, and only afterwards. She experiences the attack in flashes, images, cries cut off, the screaming of horses.

She is sprawled on the ground before she even understands they are being attacked. He must have pushed her down, she realizes. She looks up, a hand to her mouth, from deep grass. Three, no, four now, of the attackers fall before they even come close.

Meshag's movements are as smooth as they were when he shot the swan. He is shooting men now, and it is the same. Sighting, release, another arrow nocked and fired. He keeps his horse moving, wheeling. The raiders have bows, too, she sees—that is why he pushed her down. There are a dozen of them, at least, or there were. One more falls, even as she watches. The others move nearer, screaming, but there is something strange about their horses, they rear and wheel, hard to control.

She is in the grass. They can see her horse, but not her. She doesn't know who these are. Shuoki? Or the pursuing Bogü, come upon them? This is a battle, she has time to think. This was her father's world all his life. Men die in battle. And women, if they find themselves in the wrong place.

Two riders come thundering towards her, whipping their mounts into control, tracking her by her own horse. She can feel the earth vibrate. They are close. She is going to scream. These are not Bogü. Their hair is short, shaved on both sides, long in the middle, there is yellow paint on their faces. They are near enough for her to see this, and understand that these painted features may be her last sight, under nine heavens.

Then the wolves rise up.

They rise from the grasslands that were theirs to rule before men came with their families and herds, whether treading lightly or trying—hopelessly?—to set wooden structures down to endure as a stamp upon the land.

And when the wolves appear from hiding, she realizes how many more of them there are than she's been aware of in these days of journeying. She's seen only the nearest of them—the lead wolf, a handful of others. But there are fifty or more, rising like grey death in the dawn. They have been hidden by the tall grass, are not any more.

They go straight for the Shuoki horses, panicking them wildly into screams and rigid, bucking halts. The horses thrash, kicking out, but to no avail, for there are fewer than ten riders left now, and five times as many wolves, and there is a man (if he is a man) shooting steadily, lethally at them, again and again. And the wolves are his.

Li-Mei sees a yellow-painted Shuoki fall very close to her. She hears something crack as he hits the ground. He screams in pain, in throat-raw terror. Four wolves are on him. She looks away, burying her face in the earth. She hears the man stop screaming, she doesn't watch it happen. Snuffling sounds, snarling. Then another sound she never forgets: flesh being torn, ripped away.

Nothing frightens her more than wolves.

She would be dead or taken if they were not here.

The world is not something to be understood. It is vanity, illusion to even try.

Her body is shaking where she lies. She can't control it. And then, as suddenly as the first cries came, and the terrifying vision of those riders, there is stillness again. The light of morning. Dawn wind. Li-Mei hears birdsong, amazingly.

She makes herself sit up, then wishes she had not.

Beside her, much too near, the dead Shuoki is being devoured. He is blood and meat. The wolves snap and grunt, biting down, snarling at each other.

She is afraid she is going to be sick and, with the thought, she is, on her knees in the grass, emptied out in spasms.

A shadow falls. She looks up quickly.

Meshag extends one of the water flasks. She sits up. Takes it and unstoppers it. She drinks and spits, does so again, heedless of dignity or grace or any such concepts from another world. She drinks again, swallows this time. Then she pours water into her hand and wipes her face. Does that again, too, almost defiantly. Not everything is lost, she tells herself. Not unless you let it be.

"Come," Meshag says to her. "We take four horses. We can change, ride more fast."

"Will ... will there be more of these?"

"Shuoki? Might be. Soldiers have gone. Shuoki come to see why."

"Do we know why?"

He shakes his head.

"Come," he says again. He reaches a hand. She gives him back the stoppered flask, but though he takes it and shoulders it, he puts his hand out again, and she understands that he is helping her get up.

HE CHOOSES two more horses for each of them. The Shuoki horses have scattered, but are well trained and have not gone far. She waits by her own mount, and watches him. He reclaims his arrows, first, approaches one Shuoki horse, examines and leaves it, takes another. She has no idea how he's making these choices.

Around her, hideously, the wolves are feeding on the dead.

She remembers from another life Tai telling their father (she is in the trees, listening) how the Bogü take their dead out on the grass, away from the tribe, to be devoured under the sky, souls sent back that way.

The sky is very blue, the wind milder today.

He has left her a flask. She drinks again, but only a little, to take the bad taste from her mouth.

She watches him ride back. He has four horses looped to each other, tied to his own. He doesn't appear to say anything at all, but suddenly wolves spring up and lope away, to be lost in the grass.

Li-Mei takes her reins and does the leap (not graceful) she's taught herself to get up on a horse without his aid. When you lose your access to pride in almost all things, perhaps you find it somewhere else? She says, "Shouldn't two of them be tied behind mine, to make it easier?"

"Not easier. We must go."

"Wait. Please!"

He does wait. The sun is washing the land in morning light. His eyes are dark, nothing comes back from them.

"Forgive me," she says. "I told you, when I don't understand, it makes me fearful. I am better when I know things."

He says nothing.

She says, "Can you, do you control wolves? Do they follow you?"

He looks away, north, the way they've come. Says nothing for so long she thinks he's chosen not to answer, but he hasn't moved yet. She hears birds singing. Looks up, almost involuntarily, for a swan.

He says, "Not all. One pack. This one."

The lead wolf is near them again; he is always close to Li-Mei. She looks at him. Fights a new horror and an old fear.

She turns back to Meshag, the black eyes. The wolf's are so much brighter. The man is waiting. She says only, "Thank you."

He twitches his reins and she follows him south, leaving the dead behind under birds and the sky.

UNDER STARS, that same night. They have ridden all day, two brief halts. No cooking fires, berries only, but they've stopped by a pond this time. Li-Mei takes off her clothes and bathes in the dark: a need to wash away the memory of flesh being shredded, the sound it made.

After dressing again, she asks him, "What you said before? About the wolves? This is because of what was done to you?"

It is easier to ask in the night.

He has been crouching in the grass, after watering the horses. She sees him look away. She says, "I'm sorry. You don't have to—"

He says, "Shaman in north was making me a wolf-soul. Bound to him. His command? Hard magic, bad. Not ... not done. Wolf his totem creature. He summoned a wolf to come. Your brother killed him as he was doing this. I was ... I am caught between."

"Between?"

There are frogs in the pond. She hears them croaking in the night. He says, "Man and wolf. This body and the other."

The other. She looks over, against her will. The lead wolf is in the grass, the grey shape. She'd seen him tearing flesh at sunrise, blood dripping from those jaws.

The animal looks back at her, steadily. She can barely make it out but these eyes, unlike Meshag's, seem to shine. A fearful sensation comes over Li-Mei, and the realization that it would be wrong, *wrong* for her to push him more, to ask for more.

She lowers her head. Her hair is wet, she feels it dripping down her back, but the night is mild. She says, "I am sorry. Perhaps it would have been better if Tai had not—"

"No!" he says strongly. She looks up quickly, startled. He stands, a shape against horizon and stars. "Better this than what I would have been. I am ... I have choices. If that shaman bind me, I am only his, and then die. Shandai gave me this."

She looks up at him.

He says, "I *choose* to come for you. To honour Shan ... Shendai."

"And after? After this?" She had just decided not to ask more questions.

He makes his one-shoulder shrug.

She looks over at the wolf again, a shadow more than something you can see. There is a question she cannot ask.

"Ride now?"

He actually puts it as a question.

"Thank you," she says.

Li-Mei gets up and walks over and mounts one of her horses, by herself. They are changing mounts every time they stop. Just before sunrise he shoots a second swan, but a third one, following behind, wheels away west, very high.

Someone had a wolf for a totem, she thinks. Someone has a swan.

YOU CAN FALL ASLEEP on a horse, but not when it is galloping. Li-Mei collapses into an aching, fitful slumber whenever he allows a halt.

She knows why he's pushing so hard, since shooting the second swan, but body and mind have their demands.

She lies on her back in shorter grass now. Consciousness reasserts, recedes. She has been dreaming of swinging—the swing in the garden at home—arcing higher and higher among spring blossoms, back and forth. She doesn't know who is pushing her, she never looks to see, but she is not afraid.

The pushing is Meshag, shaking her shoulder.

She opens her eyes. Pale light. Morning. He hands her the water flask, gestures towards the saddlebag beside her. More berries. If there are further days of nothing but this, Li-Mei thinks, a rabbit eaten raw might begin to seem appealing. Then she remembers the wolves and the Shuoki, and that thought slides away.

She drinks, splashes water on her hands and face. Takes a fistful of the berries, and then does it again. She has learned to avoid the unripe ones, picks them out. She *is* a Kitai princess, isn't she?

She's too weary to be amused by her own irony.

She gets to her feet. Her legs hurt, and her back. Meshag is already mounted. He is scanning the sky as it brightens. She does the same. Nothing to be seen. Another fresh day, high clouds. She goes to the horse he's freed from the line for her. She flexes stiff limbs and gets herself into the saddle. She's become better at this, she thinks.

She looks at him.

"It will change now," he says.

"What do you mean?"

"The land. You will see. We are leaving the steppe. Your Wall is not far."

Even fatigued as she is, this makes her heart beat faster. Just the words. The Wall means Kitai, and an exile's return, if they can get through it to the other side. He'd said they could.

We are leaving the steppe.

She looks back, turning in the saddle. As far as she can see under the risen sun and the high sky the grass stretches, yellow-green, darker green, tall, moving in the breeze. There is a sound to its swaying, and that sound has been a part of her existence since the

Bogü claimed her. Even in the sedan chair she'd heard it, incessantly. The murmur of the steppe.

Gazing north, her eyes filled with this vista, imagining how far it goes, she thinks, *If there was a morning in the world, this is the way it looked.* And that is not a thought natural to her people.

They start south. Li-Mei looks to left and then right, and sees the lead wolf beside them. The others are out there, she knows. But this one is always near.

BY MIDDAY the land begins rising, the grass is shorter, differently textured, darker, and there are clumps of green and silver-green shrubbery, and then bare rock in places. When she sees a stand of poplar trees it is almost shocking. She realizes she isn't fatigued any more.

They cross a shallow river. On the other bank Meshag halts to let the horses drink. He refills the water flasks. Li-Mei dismounts as well, to stretch her aching legs. She keeps looking at the sky. More wind today, the clouds moving east. Sometimes they pass before the sun and a shadow slides along the land and then away.

She says, "Do you know how close they are, behind us?"

He stoppers the flasks. He takes the line that holds the four horses behind his and makes the changes needed to give each of them new mounts. He swings himself up and Li-Mei does the same.

He says, "Most of a day. I think we are enough ahead."

She is afraid to ask him how he knows this. But she also thinks she knows the answer: not all the wolves are with them here.

"Thank you," she says.

They begin to ride again, south, under the high sky and the coming and going of light and shadow across the changing land. One more stop, mid-afternoon. He switches their horses again.

They see a swan, late in the day, flying too high for an arrow. A little after that they crest the long, steady rise of land they have been climbing. There is a downward slope in front of them.

Beyond it, stretching to the ends of sight, west and east, lit by the long, late sun, is the Wall.

He has brought her home.

෨෨

Tazek Karad had never made any real distinction between the nomads of the grasslands, however much they might have hated each other. He looked out over Shuoki lands now, having been abruptly shifted two hundred *li* east of his normal gatehouse on the Wall.

Both the Shuoki and the Bogü were domesticated, nose-wiping sheep-herders to him. Their women dominated them in their yurts, by day *and* by night. That, his fellow Kislik joked, was why so many of the steppe-men slept with their sheep.

They might boast of their thick-maned horses, of battling grass-land wolves, hunting gazelle, but what did these things mean to a Kislik? His were a people of the desert, where men murdered for half a cup of water, and sometimes drank the blood of the victim, too. Where you'd have to drag your camel down to the ground and shelter against it, wrapping your face completely, to *try* to survive a sandstorm.

The deserts killed; these steppes nurtured life. You could make a guess, couldn't you, as to which land produced harder, more worthy men?

Tazek would have denied it if someone had called him bitter. Still, when it came to talking about *worthy* you could make a case that command of only fifty men in the Kitan Sixth Army after twelve years along or north of the Wall was not even close to showing proper respect. A *dui* was nothing. He ought to have had two hundred or more, by now.

True, Kitai and its empire had fed and clothed him since he was fifteen, and had made women and wine (or *kumiss*, more often) available for soldiers posted along the Wall. True, he had not died in desert sand as his father and two brothers had.

Serving the Kitan emperor was a way of life, and not the worst. But surely anyone worth being named a man wanted to *rise*, to move nearer the centre. What sort of person would come this close, and look, and say, "It is enough, what I have. I don't need more."

Not the person Tazek Karad was, at any rate.

Add the fact—it was on his record—that he'd accepted, uncomplainingly, doubled six-month shifts at outpost forts in the grasslands three times, and you had to concede that the officers either had it in for him, for some reason, or they were just too incompetent in the Sixth District to recognize a man ready for promotion.

Not that he was bitter.

Part of the problem was that the flaccid sheep-lovers of the steppe were too quiet these days. The Bogü had become a subject people of the emperor, selling him horses at the spring gathering by the river's loop, requesting Kitan intervention in their own squabbles, but not fighting nearly enough in those to let good soldiers engage in the sort of actions that got you promoted.

The Shuoki were more contentious, and the forts in their lands— Near Fort and Far Fort, the soldiers called them—saw some combat. The nomads here had even tried to break through weak places in the Wall on raids. A mistake, and they'd suffered for it. But the two outpost forts and the Wall below them had been manned by soldiers of Roshan's Seventh Army, so the glory (and citations) from that fighting didn't get anywhere near Tazek Karad or his fellows in the Sixth.

In the Sixth Army they supervised horse trading, heard whining complaints about sheep raids levelled by one rancid-smelling tribe against another, and let long-haired Bogü riders through with furs and amber, destined for markets in Xinan or Yenling.

It was predictable, safe, unspeakably dull.

Until four days ago, when *dui* commander Tazek Karad had received urgent orders to lead his fifty men east to take up a position at the gatehouse and towers directly south of Near Fort.

Other officers and men went with them, some halting sooner, some going farther east, thinning the numbers at their own guard posts. Along the way, changing orders overtook a number of them, causing confusion. There was an apparent need to move quickly.

The emerging report was that the soldiers of the Seventh along the Wall had been withdrawn. All of them. They were gone. The gates and the watchtowers between gates were undefended. It was almost inconceivable.

No one told them why. No ranking officer (in the Sixth Army, anyhow) would bother telling a lowly commander of fifty men anything.

Nor did anyone explain why, just two days ago, the garrison soldiers of the Seventh and Eighth, posted in Near Fort and Far Fort, had come marching and riding back, both armies together, thousands upon thousands of them funnelling through the Wall section Tazek now controlled. They disappeared south through a curtain of dust that took most of the morning to settle, leaving an eerie, empty silence behind.

Soldiers had asked soldiers what was happening as the garrisons passed through. Soldiers didn't know. They never did.

And although army life was almost always lived in a state of ignorance and one grew accustomed to that, there were times when sudden and shifting orders could unsettle the most dour and steady of minor officers, even one with the western desert in his blood.

The sight of the Seventh and Eighth garrisons approaching his gate and passing through and disappearing south had done that for Tazek Karad.

He felt exposed, looking north. He was commanding an important, unfamiliar gate, he was undermanned, and he was above Shuoki lands now. A man might want the chance to fight the barbarians, earn a reputation, but if the nomads raided right now in any numbers he and his men could be in serious difficulty.

And with both forts emptied out, there was a good chance the Shuoki *would* come down to, at the very least, see what was happening here. Tazek didn't even want to think about what they would do to the two forts. Not his problem, until someone made it so.

He stood in the wooden gatehouse at sundown and looked east and west along the rise and fall and rise of the Long Wall of Kitai, to where it vanished in each direction. They'd used rammed earth to build it here above the grasslands, pressed between wooden frames, mixed with lime and gravel carted north. They'd used stones, he'd been told, where the Wall climbed towards mountains over rocks.

It was a staggering achievement, difficult to think about. They said it stretched for six thousand *li*. They said four hundred thousand men had died in building and rebuilding it over the centuries. Tazek believed that last part.

He hated the Wall. He'd lived twelve years of his life defending it.

One of his men said something. He was pointing north. Tazek sighted along the man's extended finger.

Two traders approaching, still far off, a string of horses behind them. Here in Shuoki lands this was uncommon. It was the Bogü who went back and forth, who had the spring meeting by the Golden River's bend where thousands of horses were brought and bought and led away south for the Kitan army's endless need.

The Shuoki traded more sporadically. Often the goods were stolen horses—often from the Bogü. It wouldn't surprise Tazek if that were so now. As the pair drew nearer he saw four horses in addition to the two being ridden. In theory, he could arrest the would-be traders, hold them for tribal justice (which was never pretty), and keep the horses as the price of inconveniencing Kitan soldiers.

In reality, they tended to let traders through. Standard army policy these days: horses mattered too much, you wanted the nomads to keep bringing them, they would stop if it meant being captured. The usual practice was for the gate commander to accept discreet compensation for looking the other way while stolen goods went into Kitai.

He waited for the thieving Shuoki to get closer. He had questions to ask. He needed information more than the horse or the handful of coins they'd likely offer. Their mounts were tired, he saw, even the ones being led on a rope. They'd been ridden hard, probably confirmation they were stolen. Tired horses sold for less.

Tazek stared stonily down at the approaching riders. He wasn't a happy man.

The two men came up to his gate and halted below.

They weren't Shuoki. First sign of the unexpected.

"Request to pass through with horses to sell," the larger one said. He was a Bogü, you could see it in the hair. He spoke Kitan like the barbarian he was. The smaller one was hooded. Sometimes they did that, out of fear in the presence of Kitan soldiers.

Well, fear was *proper*, wasn't it.

This was a father and son, Tazek decided, stealing together. But it was a surprise to find Bogü this far east, especially just a pair of them. Not his problem. His problems were different.

"What have you seen to the north, thieving Bogü?" he demanded.

"What do you mean?" No reaction to the insult, Tazek noted.

"The garrison!"

"Fortress empty," agreed the big man. He was bare-chested, kept his eyes cast down. This, too, was normal—and appropriate. These were barbarians talking to an officer in the Sixth Army of Kitai.

The man said, "Tracks of horses and men go this way. They not come here?"

That was none of his business, was it?

"What about the other fort?"

"Not go so far. But many soldiers go this way. More than one fort. Two days, maybe?"

He didn't look up, but he had it right. The nomads knew how to read their grass.

"Anything happen up there?"

"Happen?"

"You see any Shuoki?"

"No," said the big one.

"I need a better answer!" snarled Tazek.

"No, honourable sir," the man said, which would have been funny, some other time.

"Any of those shit-eaters coming this way? You see them?"

"No Shuoki. There are Bogü behind us."

"Why?"

"We are … we are exiled from tribe, honourable sir."

And *that* put an answer in place as to why these two were so far east. Interesting that they were being pursued, but not interesting enough. The tribes had their laws. If they stayed north of the Wall and didn't bother the garrisons, it had nothing to do with Kitai. Or with Tazek Karad of the Sixth.

It could, however, get complicated if the Bogü showed up, and he was *seen* letting these two through. There were horses. Horses mattered. Tazek looked north. Emptiness.

He nodded to the man beside him. "Open them up."

He looked down at the two riders. "Where you taking these?"

"These horses requested by Kanlins," the bigger man said.

A surprise. "You aim to go all the way to Stone Drum Mountain with these?"

"Requested by them. Three smaller horses. Some Kanlin are women."

Well, the gods send a sandstorm to blind fools! As if Tazek didn't *know* some of the black-robed ones were women? And that the women could kill you as easily as the men?

"In that case, we have a problem, my shirtless friend. Stone Drum is what, six days? I am not letting Bogü horse-thieves ride alone that far through Kitai."

"It is only four days, *dui* officer. You are properly cautious, but it is all right, we are here to escort them."

The voice was behind him. Speaking impeccable Kitan.

Tazek turned quickly—and saw three Kanlin Warriors, astride their horses, just inside his gates.

It had happened to him before: they could be right up on you, in among you, before you were aware they'd even been approaching. Two men, one woman, he saw. They had hoods down in the evening light, carried swords across their backs, bows in saddles.

Tazek stared down. If he'd been unhappy before it was as nothing now.

"How did you know they were coming?" he demanded.

The first Kanlin smiled. He seemed amused. "It had been arranged," he said. "It is not hard to watch for riders from places along the Wall."

Well, fuck your by-the-hour mother, Tazek wanted to say. "You learn anything about the garrison soldiers? The ones who came through?"

"Seventh and Eighth Armies," the Kanlin said, promptly. "They are all moving south. Do you have enough people to deal with this stretch of the Wall?"

"Course I do!" snapped Tazek. As if he was going to admit anything to a black-robe.

"Good," the man said equably. "Be generous enough to let our horses through? And please accept, for you and your soldiers, some rice wine we have brought as a humble offering to those who defend us here. It might be better than what you have."

Might be better? It couldn't *help* but be better, because the accursed soldiers of the Seventh, the ones posted here before, the ones who'd gone away south, had taken all the wine and most of the food stores with them.

He had sent word about the stores as soon as they'd arrived. He was expecting provisions from the west, as soon as tomorrow, with luck. On the other hand, the sun was going down and a dry night stretched ahead.

He nodded to the three in the black robes, and then to the soldier beside him. The man barked the orders.

The gate bars were pulled back. The heavy gates swung inward, slowly. The Bogü father and son waited, then rode through with their horses. Three of the horses were, Tazek saw, smaller ones.

He still didn't know how the Kanlin had gotten a message, a request for horses, through the Wall to Bogü exiles. That part didn't make sense. He was trying to decide if it mattered.

He decided it didn't. Not his problem.

He looked down and saw that the three Kanlins had dismounted and were shifting flasks from their pack horse into the extremely eager hands of his own soldiers.

"Hold off opening those till I get down!" he shouted.

He'd need to count and estimate, figure out how to do this. But rice wine meant that at least one good thing had happened today. Pretty much the only good thing.

He was turning to go down the steps when, out of the corner of his eye, he saw a grey shape streak through the gate.

"The fuck was that?" he roared.

"A wolf, I think," the Kanlin leader said, looking up.

"It just went through my Wall!" Tazek shouted.

The Kanlin shrugged. "They do go back and forth. We'll shoot it for you if we see it. Is there a bounty this spring?"

There sometimes was, it depended how many there were. Tazek had just arrived here. He was short of men, of food, of water and wine, and he had no idea what had happened with the Seventh and Eighth.

"No," he said sourly. There might well have been a bounty for all he knew, but he felt like saying no to someone. "Shoot it anyhow."

The Kanlin nodded, and turned. The five of them rode off, the extra horses trailing after the big, bare-chested Bogü.

Tazek watched them for a while, discontented. Something was still bothering him, a thought teasing at the edge of his mind. Then he remembered the wine and went quickly down the stairs. He never did chase down that stray thought.

When a party of Bogü riders appeared the next morning he ordered his men to begin shooting as soon as the riders were in arrow range. He was undermanned; he did *not* want the nomads to get close enough to realize it.

They were chasing the horse-thieves, obviously. Well, he'd made his decision to let those two pass through. An officer in the Kitan army didn't show uncertainty or doubt to barbarians, or his men. You didn't get promoted that way, and your soldiers would lose faith in you. They were allowed to hate you, they just couldn't worry about your competence.

He watched the Bogü withdraw out of range and linger there, arguing amongst each other. They had wolfhounds with them, he saw. He had no idea what the quarrel was about. He didn't care. He watched—with the quiet satisfaction of a man who had done his assigned task well—until they turned and rode off.

Two swans appeared, flying towards the Wall. Tazek let his men amuse themselves shooting at them. They brought one down.

The other wheeled away, higher, and went back towards the steppes.

ৎ৹

She is in Kitai again. The Kanlins, silent, courteous, bring them to an inn as darkness falls. Li-Mei sees torchlight and lanterns, hears music. She is shown by bowing servants to a room with walls and a bed, and she bathes in a brazier-heated bath chamber, with hot water, and servants to attend her, and she weeps as they wash her hair.

Her hands are shaking. The girls make pitying sounds when they see her nails and fingers, and one of them spends a long time with brush and file, doing the best she can with them. Li-Mei weeps through this, as well.

They tease her gently, trying to make her smile. They tell her they cannot paint her eyebrows or cheeks if she will insist on crying. She shakes her head, and they leave her face unpainted for this first night. She hears the wind outside, and the knowledge that it will *be* outside tonight, that she will sleep sheltered, sinks into her like a promise, like warm wine.

She goes downstairs, unadorned, but in clean robes and sandals, and sits with the Kanlin Warriors in the dining pavilion. They speak politely and gracefully. One addresses her by name.

They know who she is.

Fear, for a swift, shattering moment, until she understands that if they were going to expose her, reveal her identity, they'd have done so at the Wall.

"You are taking me to Stone Drum Mountain?" she asks.

The leader, an older man, nods his head. "Both of you," he says. "My lady."

"How do you know who I am?"

The briefest hesitation. "We were told," he says.

"Do you know who is with me? Who he is?"

A nod. "They wish to see him at Stone Drum, as well."

Li-Mei realizes that there is wine in front of her. She sips, carefully. It has been a long time since she drank rice wine.

"Why?" she asks.

The Kanlins exchange glances. The woman is very pretty, Li-Mei thinks. She has silver hairpins, for the evening.

The older man says, "You will be told when you are there. Questions will be answered. But you do know your brother was among us, once."

So it is Tai, she thinks. It is Tai again, even so far away. One brother had exiled her, another is drawing her home.

"He told us that when he left Stone Drum, some of you … some were not …"

"Some were not happy, no," the Kanlin leader says. He smiles.

"Not everyone who comes to the Mountain becomes a Warrior," the woman says. She sips her wine. Fills three cups. She gestures with the flask to Li-Mei, who shakes her head.

"Where is Meshag?" she asks.

He's outside, of course. Wooden walls, a wooden roof, a room full of people, Kitan people. He'll be out in the night he knows, although the land is no longer known. A thought occurs to her.

"You mustn't kill the wolf," she says.

"We know that," says the Kanlin leader. "The wolves are why they want to speak with him at the Mountain."

She looks at him, a thought forms. "It was a wolf that brought you word of our coming, wasn't it? You weren't looking out from the Wall for us."

It sounds impossible, even as she says it. But he nods his head.

"You are very like your brother," he says.

She begins to cry again. "You knew him?"

"I taught Shen Tai for a time. I sorrowed when he left us. I asked to be one of those sent to bring his sister."

She is *not* a woman who cries. They wait, patient, even amused. She wipes her eyes with her sleeve.

She says, looking at the leader, "What has happened? The armies have all left the garrisons, the Wall. Why?"

Again they look at each other. The older one says, "I think it is better if you are told this at the Mountain."

"There is something to tell?"

He nods his head.

She asks no more questions. She eats with them, and there is a singer (not very skilled, but they are in a remote place), and then Li-Mei goes to her chamber and sleeps in a bed and dreams of wolves.

There are three more nights' travelling. Meshag stays with them. She wasn't certain he would do that. He keeps to himself, sleeps outside each night. She never sees the wolf, though she'd watched him burst through the gate at the Wall.

On the second day she sees Stone Drum Mountain for the first time, rising from tableland, magnificently alone, green slopes like jade in the sun, one of the Five Holy Mountains.

On the fourth afternoon they reach it. The Kanlins lead them up a slow switchback path along the forested slope, until finally they come to the flat summit that gives the Mountain its name, where the sanctuary is, and she is welcomed there with courtesy, because of her brother. And that evening she is told, as promised, what has happened—by the Wall, and elsewhere—and what it means for the empire and the times into which they have been born.

ᘒᘔ

At least three historians of a later dynasty, working within the Hall of Records (after it had been rebuilt), expressed the view that tens of millions of people might have been spared famine, war, displacement, and death if someone had stopped the kingfisher-feathered carriage of Governor An Li as it sped northeast that spring, returning to his own territories. And his armies.

The soldiers of the command posts that carriage passed had no reason to do so, the historians agreed. They were not attaching censure to the officers and men who watched it go by, rolling heavily through mild days and nights along the roads of Kitai.

They were only observing a truth, the historians wrote.

Others, from the same period and later, dissented. These writers suggested that *truth* when examining events and records of the past was always precarious, uncertain. No man could say for certain how the river of time would have flowed, cresting or receding, bringing floods or gently watering fields, had a single event, or even many, unfolded differently.

It is in the nature of existence under heaven, the dissenting scholars wrote, that we cannot know these things with clarity. We cannot live twice, or watch as moments of the past unfurl, like a courtesan's silk fan. The river flows, the dancers finish their dance. If the music starts again it is starting anew, not repeating itself.

Having noted this, having made the countervailing argument as carefully (and in one case as lyrically) as possible, these historians, without exception, appeared to join in accepting the number of forty million lives as a reasonable figure for the consequences of the An Li Rebellion.

CHAPTER XXI

An Tsao, second son of General An Li, resided in the Ta-Ming Palace and had done so for three years, enjoying the many pleasures of courtly life and the honours appropriate to a son of a distinguished father.

He had formal rank as a commander of one thousand in the Flying Dragon Palace Guard, but—along with most other officers in a largely symbolic army—his days were spent hunting in the Deer Park or farther afield, playing polo, or riding abroad in pursuit of diversion, with sons of aristocrats, mandarins, and senior officers of the army.

His nights were given over to pleasure, in various houses of the North District, or among sleek, lithe women invited to city mansions or the palace itself to entertain the wealthy and empowered with their music and their bodies.

On the same day word reached the Ta-Ming of his father's rebellion in the northeast, Roshan proclaiming himself emperor of Kitai and founder of the Tenth Dynasty, An Tsao was decapitated in a garden of the palace.

The engraved sword that did this was wielded by the first

minister, Wen Zhou, himself. A big man, skilled with a blade, somewhat impulsive.

This action was widely considered among senior mandarins to have been a mistake, even at the time. The son had been useful alive, as a hostage or an earnest of good faith in negotiating peace. Dead, he was worthless, and possibly worse than that, if the father proved vengeful.

Wen Zhou was also, of course, the proclaimed reason for General An's treacherous rising: the need to free the empire from the reckless, incompetent stewardship of a corrupt first minister, whose presence in power proved that the aged emperor had lost his way—and the mandate of heaven.

That was the declaration sent in a letter to the Ta-Ming carried by a Kanlin courier. The Kanlins were important in times of conflict: they could be hired and trusted by either side.

Given this stated cause of revolt, the fact that Wen Zhou had killed the son himself was seen by many, with wringing of hands and shaking of heads, as worrisome.

It was noted by some, however, that judgments and reactions among the civil service in those first days of the rebellion could not be called calm or poised—or sound.

There was, in truth, panic in the palace and abroad.

An attempt to suppress news of the rebellion proved predictably unsuccessful. Xinan was not a place where tidings could readily be contained. And once word spread through the capital, it began running everywhere.

Someone said that a red fireball had been seen in the northern sky the week before. That this had been reported to the astrologers in the School of Unrestricted Night.

True or not, there *was* an army, a large one, in the north, and it appeared to be moving down towards the second city of the empire, the obvious initial target. Yenling was east of Xinan, nearer the Great Canal, on the far side of Teng Pass. Roshan's advance put nearly a million of the emperor's loving subjects in extreme peril behind those city walls.

They were likely to surrender.

A number of cities north of the Golden River had already done so, it appeared. Word came that Roshan was treating prefecture officials with courtesy, that many were crossing over to him. It was difficult to judge the truth of this.

Distances were great, communication became uncertain.

There were obvious truths: the armies to resist Roshan were south and west and northwest and could not possibly reach Yenling in time to defend it. The best they could do—and it became the immediate military plan—was to defend Teng Pass.

In making these decisions, it was agreed, First Minister Wen showed decisiveness and confidence. Amid military leaders and mandarins in various stages of terror and uncertainty, he expressed the steady view than An Li would falter soon, that turmoil behind him would stop his progress.

Kitai, he declared, would never accept or support an illiterate barbarian as emperor. As soon as people started to think this through events would take their course.

The Sixth Army was pulled back from the river's bend and stations along the Wall and sent east to disrupt Roshan's supply lines, put the northeast in play, force some of his rebel soldiers back that way.

The Second and Third and Fifth Armies were commanded to proceed as fast as they could to seize and hold Teng Pass. Five thousand of the Flying Dragon Palace Guard were sent there immediately from Xinan. These were hardly distinguished soldiers, but the Pass was narrow, famously so, and could be held for a time by even a small number if they had any courage at all and adequate commanders. It had happened this way many times in the history of Kitai.

Yenling was sent instructions to hold out as best it could. Delaying the rebels mattered.

The First and Fourth Armies were kept where they were, along the northwestern and western borders. Calamity would result if Kitai lost control of the Silk Road fortresses and the corridors there, and it was considered unwise to withdraw from the Tagurans at any time.

From the south would come three other armies, but messengers had a long way to go just to summon them and those forces would be some time in coming.

Wen Zhou predicted a short campaign.

Others were less certain. Roshan had command of the Seventh, Eighth, and Ninth, and had merged them. These soldiers were the most battle-hardened in Kitai, and since General An had *not* been shifted from district to district—once the rule for military governors—their loyalty to him was absolute. If the Golden River was crossed and Yenling besieged, they would have made their own commitment.

Roshan had also been the Imperial Stable-master for years, and had assigned to his own cavalry the best of the horses obtained from the Bogü at the river's loop each spring.

In hindsight, not the wisest power to have given him, either.

Beyond all of this (as if this were not enough to make a civil servant panic), appeasing the northeast had always been a delicate matter for this dynasty. That region was the home of powerful families with intermarrying lineages that they claimed (truthfully or not) went back a thousand years, to the First Dynasty itself. There were many in the northeast who saw the Ninth Dynasty as ill-bred interlopers. Xinan's measures to reform taxation and land ownership to the benefit of the farmers had not been well received in the northeast. The aristocracy there called themselves the Five Families, and their response to rebellion could not be known with certainty.

It was entirely possible that they might see a gross, illiterate general in precarious health as an improvement for their own purposes, because he would surely be transitory, and easily manipulated. Once change was set in motion, clever men could very well shape where it went.

And, as it happened, both Chin Hai, the first minister who had instituted the loathed reforms, and Wen Zhou, now, were from southern families, and therefore rivals.

It could matter, something like that.

Another element might also be important, someone pointed out in the Ta-Ming (it was the imperial heir who said this). Given the size of the empire, the vast distances that had to be dealt with for communication, and the always critical importance of cavalry, two hundred and fifty Sardian horses were suddenly even more important than before.

The second son of General Shen Gao was summoned to the palace.

ලා

The message from the court came at the end of two weeks of intense frustration, even before news of rebellion began to run through Xinan.

Tai had heard stories of how slowly the wheels of the Ta-Ming turned in matters such as audiences granted and decisions made within the multitude of layers in the civil service. There were one hundred and forty thousand mandarins in Xinan, through the nine degrees. Speed was not a strength.

He'd never had anything near the importance that would have caused him to experience this directly. Had never been someone who might expect a summons to court, in anticipation or apprehension.

That had changed. He wore the emperor's ring. He hadn't wanted to, hadn't even wanted to keep it, thinking it more important for Rain to have. A secret access to funds for her in the event of ...

Of what? And had he entirely lost his bearings in the world, to think she couldn't find jewellery to sell if she needed to? In that compound? Concubine to the first minister? How else, he thought ruefully, had she managed to hire a Kanlin Warrior in the first place?

He'd asked Wei Song about that. Predictably, she'd given him a scornful glance. As if, as *if* a Kanlin would answer such a question.

She wasn't the one who'd made him wear the ring, though she'd brought it back to him in the street the night they climbed the wall, two weeks ago. He hadn't seen Rain since then. Hadn't seen many people at all. And the summons to the palace had not come.

His Kanlins had told him he could not go to the North District. Too dangerous, they'd said, the lanes and alleys after dark. He knew those alleys extremely well.

"No one can attack me now!" Tai had snapped angrily. "The horses are my protection, remember?"

"Only from a known assassin," the Kanlin leader had replied calmly. His name was Lu Chen. "Not if it is unknown who attacks you, if they escape."

"How do you plan to stop me from going?" Tai had demanded.

Song had been present that evening, behind her leader, head lowered, hair neatly pinned, hands in the sleeves of her robe. He'd suddenly remembered the first time he'd seen her, coming across the courtyard at Iron Gate Fortress, just risen from sleep, her hair unbound. It wasn't so long ago, he thought. He knew her well enough by now to read her posture. For a Kanlin, she didn't hide her feelings well. She was angry. He could see it.

"We can't stop you, Master Shen," Lu Chen said quietly. "But our assigned task, from the Precious Consort and the Imperial Heir, is to guard you, and Xinan is an uncertain place. You understand that if harm comes to you, all of us forfeit our lives."

Song looked up then. He could see fury in her eyes.

"That's ... that's not fair," Tai said.

Lu Chen blinked, as if this was an observation that had no immediately obvious meaning.

Tai didn't go to the North District. He didn't try to see his brother, either, though the thought crossed his mind several times a day that he might as well just go to Liu's house and confront him.

He knew Liu spent many nights at the Ta-Ming in the Purple Myrtle Court of the mandarins, but it was easy enough to have a servant track his movements. He had servants now, and a steward who seemed effective, and alarmingly dedicated. He had a city mansion. He could ride out, or even be carried out in a sedan chair, and confront Liu.

Such a false-sounding word. Confront, to say what? That what Liu had done to their sister was a disgrace to their father's name?

He'd already said that at Ma-wai. Liu would simply disagree again, smoothly. And the bitter truth was that most men—and women— at higher levels of the court would agree with Adviser Liu, the first minister's trusted counsellor, and not with his inexperienced younger brother.

How could it possibly be wrong to have a sister elevated to the imperial family? How could that *not* be a glorious thing for the Shen line? Did it not border upon an insult to the Phoenix Throne to even hint at less than rapture?

The offence, the nature of the wrong, was unique to their family: to their father, and how he'd seen the world. And perhaps, in truth, only to General Shen as he'd become later in life. After Kuala Nor.

On the other hand, Tai could accuse his brother of trying to have him killed. He could do that. The conversation there was even more predictable. And he wasn't sure, in any case, about this. If he ever *was* certain, his proper task might be to kill his brother. He wasn't ready to do that.

Late one night, struggling with a poem, he looked out the window at the stars and an almost-full moon shining, and realized it was likely he never would be ready to do that. Someone might call it a weakness.

Wen Zhou he avoided. Easy enough. One didn't encounter the prime minister in the marketplace or riding outside the walls.

Sima Zian visited often, sharing wine and talk and not-quite-sober good humour. He urged patience or careless indifference in the waiting period, depending on his own mood.

Tai made sure the poet had chambers in his new mansion, ink and good paper, spiced wine kept warm, and whatever else he might want. Zian came and went. Spent some nights with Tai, others abroad.

He wasn't forbidden the North District.

Tai rode Dynlal in Long Lake Park. The vast green space in the southwest of the city was open to all, and much loved. He took the track around the lake, under plum blossom trees.

There were memories here, as if in ambush. Gatherings with friends three years ago, less than that. Rain and other girls—allowed out from the Pavilion of Moonlight three days each month, and at festivals. Tai even had images of Xin Lun from that time when they were all students together, dreaming of what might be. Lun, who was playful and brilliant, in the general view likeliest of them all to pass the examinations with honours, rise to rank and distinction in the Purple Myrtle Court.

The general view hadn't been especially reliable, Tai found himself thinking as he rode.

Wei Song was with him on those rides, with four of the other Kanlins. All of them poised, alert, even before word of Roshan's rising came, and panic began.

Heads would turn to watch as they rode past. Who *was* this unsmiling man on a magnificent Sardian horse, guarded by the black-robed ones?

Who, indeed?

HE HAD NEVER BEEN inside the palace. Never nearer than standing in crowds at festivals to receive the emperor's elevated blessing. Xin Lun made the same joke every time: how did they know it was Glorious Emperor Taizu up there, so far away, in white and gold?

Three hundred thousand bodies could be in the square at festivals, a crushing, dangerous press in the vast space before the Ta-Ming's inner wall. People did die: trampled, a lack of air, sometimes knifed in a quarrel, then kept upright by the dense mass of people even after they were dead, while the murderer squeezed himself away. Nimble-fingered thieves could retire on what they stole at such times. Lun had said that, too, often.

There was no crowd this morning as Tai rode up with his Kanlins. The Gold Bird Guards were present in numbers, keeping traffic moving briskly through the square and along the streets. No one was being permitted to linger and look up at the palace. Not with a rebellion under way. Order and flow were the mandate, Tai realized, or at

the very least a simulation of such things, the illusion of calm.
Appearances mattered.

His own appearance was formal. His steward had been unyielding. The man showed indications of being a tyrant. Tai wore blue *liao*
silk, two layers, two shades, a wide black belt, black shoes, a soft felt
hat, also black. The pins holding it, placed carefully by the steward
himself, were gold, with ivory elephants for decoration. Tai had no
notion how he'd come to own gold hatpins with elephants.

He wore the emperor's ring.

The emerald was noted, he saw, by all those in the chamber into
which he was finally ushered. He had proceeded, under escort,
through five enormous courtyards and then, after dismounting and
leaving Dynlal with his Kanlins (who were not allowed any farther),
up a prodigiously wide flight of fifty stairs, through two large chambers into this one, the ceiling supported by massive pillars of pink-
and-yellow marble.

Twelve men were seated cross-legged on couch platforms, advisers standing behind them, servants in the distant corners of the
room.

At the head of the gathering was Wen Zhou.

Tai made a point of meeting his gaze, and so tracked the prime
minister's glance as he approached. Approaching took time, the
room was ridiculously oversized. He had to cross an arched marble
bridge over a pool. There were pearls embedded in the railings of the
bridge.

Because he was watching, refusing to look away, he saw when
the first minister's expression shifted from frigid to uneasy—in the
moment Wen Zhou's gaze registered the emerald ring.

Sima Zian had predicted this would happen.

It was very simple, he'd said the night before, drinking the
season's first lychee-flavoured wine. Tai had not yet been formally
received. Newcomers to the court were *not* seen by the emperor
without precise observance of protocol and priority. No one knew of
the emperor's visit through the walls at Ma-wai two weeks ago.

The ring was a signature, it was known to be Taizu's. And tomorrow a new arrival, a man who hadn't even taken the examinations, let alone passed them, who had no military rank that mattered, no claim by birth to favour, was going to walk into the Ta-Ming wearing the emperor's ring.

The poet had expressed a wish that he could be there to see it.

Tai looked away from the first minister, beyond him to his brother behind Wen Zhou. For the first time in his life—and it was unsettling—he saw extreme anxiety in Liu's face, staring back at him.

Tai stopped with his palace escort beside the platform couch opposite the first minister's, the one evidently left for him. He bowed, turning slightly each time, to include all those here.

He saw the heir, Shinzu, halfway along one side. The prince had a cup of wine, the only one there who did. He smiled at Tai. If he noticed the ring, if it surprised him, there was no sign of it.

Tai had briefly wondered if Jian would be here, but it had been an idle thought. Women did what they did *behind* such scenes as this—not among a council tasked with running an empire facing an armed rebellion.

He'd known, not being a complete innocent, that the emperor would not be present. Once, he might have been. Not any more. Kitai's glorious emperor would receive a report—or more than one—in due course. Although …

Tai looked around, trying to do so casually. There were tall room screens behind Zhou, between him and the doors at the back. If someone wanted to listen and observe, unseen, it would not be difficult. The servants would see him, or her, but servants didn't matter.

"Be seated, Second Son of Shen Gao." Zhou's voice was almost casual. "We have been discussing the movements of the Sixth Army. This does not concern you. Your presence has been solicited on a small matter, by the imperial heir."

Tai nodded, and bowed again to the prince. He gathered his robes and sat down opposite the first minister. There was something almost too direct about that. Shinzu was between them, on Tai's right side.

Wen Zhou went on, "We saw no reason—as ever—not to accede to the illustrious prince's wish to summon you."

We, Tai thought. He wasn't sure what that meant.

He inclined his head again. "I am anxious to be of any possible assistance, among such august company."

"Well," said Zhou airily, "I believe I have a sense of what his excellency has been thinking. In truth, the matter is already in hand."

"Indeed? How so, first minister?"

It was Shinzu. And though he still held his wine cup at a lazy, indifferent angle, his voice wasn't lazy at all. Instinctively, Tai glanced at his brother again: Liu's expression was transparently unhappy.

Suddenly uneasy himself, Tai looked back at the prime minister. Zhou said, with an easy gesture, "It is the western horses, of course, my lord prince. How else could this fellow be of significance? Accordingly, I dispatched twenty men yesterday to fetch them from the Tagurans. I trust your lordship is pleased." He smiled.

Tai stood up.

It was almost certainly barbaric, he thought, to do so at such a gathering. It might even be an offence. There were precise rules for how one spoke to power in the Ta-Ming, especially if one had no proper standing. He didn't care.

What was astonishing was how calm he'd suddenly become. It was when you *cared*, he thought, that you felt at risk. He said, without any salutation, "Did you ask your adviser, my brother, before you did that? Did Liu really let you do something so foolish?"

There was a shocked silence. Wen Zhou stiffened.

"Have a care, Master Shen! You are in this room only—"

"He is in this chamber at my invitation, first minister. As you noted. What were you about to say, Master Shen, while wearing my revered father's ring as a sign of very great honour?"

So he had noticed. The prince put down his wine.

Tai couldn't help himself: he looked again at the room screens behind Zhou. It was impossible to tell if anyone might be behind them.

He bowed again, before answering. "I only asked a question, august lord. Perhaps my brother might be allowed to answer, if the first minister remains disinclined?"

"My advisers do not speak for me!" Wen Zhou snapped.

Shinzu nodded briskly. "A sound policy. It would undermine confidence in the first minister even further if they did. So tell us, was this done after consultation with your advisers?"

Even further. No possible way to miss that.

"The proceedings of the first ministry are hardly a matter for this council. Decisions are taken in widely varied ways. Anyone with experience of governance knows that."

A return arrow shot at a dissolute prince.

"Perhaps," said Shinzu. "But I must tell you, I would dismiss any adviser who had urged me to send those men."

"Ah! The prince wishes now to discuss the staff of the first ministry?"

"Too boring in every possible way." Shinzu smiled thinly.

Wen Zhou did not smile back. "My lord prince, this man has not yet been received by the emperor. He is placed in the list for attendance. Until he appears before the Phoenix Throne he cannot leave the city. The horses matter, as you have said yourself. Therefore I sent for them. What, my lord, do you wish to tell me is improper about that?"

It sounded impeccably reasonable. It wasn't. Tai opened his mouth, but the prince was before him.

"I wish to tell you that those men were stopped on the imperial road last night, at the first posting station."

This time Zhou stood up.

Protocol was taking a fearful beating here, Tai thought. His heart was racing.

"No one would dare such a thing!" Wen Zhou snapped.

"A few of us might have thought it necessary, but only one would dare. You are almost correct, first minister. Your riders were halted by soldiers of the Second Military District, who happened to still be at Ma-wai after escorting Master Shen Tai from the west."

"What is this? How can we defend ourselves against Roshan if we—?"

"If we ignore very clear information as to the conditions under which those horses will be released! Master Shen is *required* by the Tagurans to collect them himself. They are his!"

Zhou shook his head. He was taut with fury. "The Sardian horses are a gift to Kitai from the exalted emperor's own beloved daughter. The Tagurans would not embarrass themselves by denying a gift merely because a small aspect of the transfer—"

"Please!" said Tai. Zhou stopped. They all looked at him. "My lord first minister, allow your adviser to speak. For himself, not for you. Brother, did you urge this course upon him?"

Liu cleared his throat as all eyes turned to him. He was an accomplished speaker, with a real skill at pitching volume and tone to circumstances. He had worked at this all his life, from before he could grow a beard.

He was visibly uneasy now. He looked from Wen Zhou to the prince. He said, "His gracious lordship, the prince, was surely correct when he suggested we require those horses more than ever, with the need to communicate over great distances."

"Which is why I invited your brother to join us," said Shinzu. "The horses are an honour given to one man. If twenty soldiers simply ride up to the border and demand them we'll be insulting Tagur by ignoring their conditions. We'd shame ourselves with our actions!"

"Who stopped my men?" Wen Zhou said, ignoring what the prince had said. There was a hard edge to his voice. A wolf cornered, Tai thought—or thinking he might be.

Tai knew by now. Zhou had to know, as well.

"Your cousin gave the orders," said Shinzu quietly. "The Lady Wen Jian told me I might say as much, if asked."

It would have had to be her, Tai thought. And it meant so much, that she would do this, that she was watching her cousin so closely. The empire was facing open rebellion and the two men she'd favoured, had tried to keep in balance, were at the centre of that. One in this room, one with his armies moving even now.

The prince paused, then added, even more softly, "Also, I was to tell you that she has now spoken with that man of yours, the one stopped some weeks ago, riding south."

The one who had killed Xin Lun.

"A conversation I should enjoy learning about," said Zhou, with genuinely impressive calm. "But this is a far more important matter!"

"My lord first minister," Tai said, and he said it formally this time. "The august prince is surely right. We risk losing two hundred and fifty Sardian horses. The terms of a supremely generous gift, one far beyond my deserving, were conveyed. I wrote myself, so did the Tagurans, so did the commander of Iron Gate Fortress."

"How vulgar and vainglorious to see yourself as so important, second son of Shen Gao. And do note: *supremely generous* gifts are in the giving of the emperor of Kitai, not tributary, subordinate nations who beg imperial daughters from us as a sign of heavenly favour."

Tai knew what he had to do next. It was not in his nature, and he was realizing that more and more with each passing moment. This was not where he wanted to be, not now, and perhaps not ever. But he *could* dance a little here.

He held up his hand, with the ring. "I know all too well how supremely generous to his least-deserving servant our beloved emperor can be, may he live and rule a thousand years."

There was a short silence.

"May it be the will of heaven," said that emperor's son and heir. Zhou said nothing.

Tai turned to Shinzu. "My lord prince, do you wish me to take men and go west for the horses? I am at the service of the court. They are being held across the border from Hsien."

"So we understand."

"I am prepared to leave immediately."

The prince shook his head. Zhou was still on his feet, Tai saw. He faced the first minister, down the length of the council space in a vast and echoing chamber. If Zhou had somehow obtained the horses, Tai thought, there would have been nothing to stop him from having a certain second son killed. Nothing at all.

The prince said, "As it happens, the prime minister is correct in one respect. You cannot leave Xinan while awaiting an audience. Your name has been put forward."

Tai stared at him. "I would rather serve the emperor, as best I can, than seek an appearance at court."

Shinzu smiled. He had an effortless charm. It might have been, Tai thought, one of the things that had kept him alive all this time. That, and a reputation—disappearing moment by moment—for indifference to imperial affairs.

The prince shook his head again. "Events must flow as they are decreed under nine heavens, Master Shen. The palace and the empire will spin into disarray if they do not. When the periphery is unstable, as the Cho Master taught, the centre must be firm. My father will receive you. You will be given honours that—because they *must*—will exceed those given by Sangrama in Rygyal. This is the way the world unfolds. And then, if it should be the desire of the Phoenix Throne, you may be asked to ride for your horses."

"My lord, time might matter."

"Which is why I sent for them!" interjected Wen Zhou.

"Is it?" asked Prince Shinzu. The prince looked at Tai. "Time always matters. But order, right conduct, right thinking have always mattered more. It is our way."

Tai lowered his head. He felt self-conscious now, standing so conspicuously. "I do understand, my lord. But if that is so, why am I here? You said you asked for me ..."

A flicker of amusement in Shinzu's eyes. This was, Tai suddenly thought, the son of a man renowned for intelligence and command. If the emperor had grown old and weary (thoughts not to be spoken), it did not take away from the lineage.

The prince said, "I asked for your attendance as soon as we learned of those riders sent for the horses. Those men would have been rejected at the border. We all know it, or should have known it. *Your* presence will be required there, and then the horses will be required by the empire, if you are good enough, of course, to make them available. Accordingly, I have asked you here, in the presence of the first minister, because we have need of his great power."

Tai blinked. He looked at Zhou.

And only now did Shinzu turn that way. "First minister, I would dedicate myself and my own limited abilities to protecting this man, for the sake of Kitai and my father, but the times are dangerous and my own resources are meagre. I ask you, in the presence of this council, to pledge your office and life to guarding him for us. Only someone with your wisdom and power can ensure his safety in troubled times, and we *know* Roshan is aware of those horses."

The expression on Zhou's face was genuinely interesting. Defeat was there, unmistakably, but behind it Tai thought he saw an amused, aristocratic flicker of irony: acknowledgement of a game well played, as if this had been a match on a polo field, and the ball had just been elegantly struck into his goal.

He agreed, of course.

THERE WAS NO WAY, Sima Zian said, over Salmon River wine that evening, that he could have failed to agree.

The moon, past full, was overhead. They were on a curved stone bench under lanterns in the garden of Tai's home. The garden was nowhere near the size or intricacy of Wen Zhou's, but it had a small pond, a bamboo grove, winding paths, an orchard. The scent of flowers was around them.

"The prince," said Tai. "He's changed."

Zian thought about it. "He is letting people see now what he has always been."

"He was hiding it?"

Zian nodded.

"Why now?"

"Perhaps it is time."

Tai's turn to think about it. "Is he in danger because he's doing this?"

"Shinzu?"

"Yes."

The poet drank his wine. A servant filled his cup, and withdrew. "Perhaps. But no more than any of us. There are a quarter of a million soldiers moving on Yenling."

He looked at Tai, and then away, and murmured:

Bitter wind blows battle smoke.
Wild geese and cranes fly.
Later, moon's disk in the water.
Plum blossoms mirrored in the river,
Until they fall.

He'd written that himself, during the last Taguran war. Tai's father's war.

Tai was silent a while, then said, "The first minister seems to think it will be over quickly. That the northeast will not accept Roshan's ambitions, will rise up behind him, and the Sixth Army will cut his supply lines."

Sima Zian's enormous tiger-eyes met Tai's. "We must hope," he murmured, "that the first minister is correct."

TAI DREAMED THAT NIGHT that he was back in the north. By that cabin beyond the steppe, watching men burned and devoured beside a jewel-bright blue lake. It wasn't a dream that came often any more, but the memory was never entirely absent, either.

Smoke was drifting, and through it leering faces surged, bare-chested Bogü looming close, waving severed limbs of human beings in his face, offering them as if they were gifts, then drifting away. Blood dripped from arms and from hacked-off slices of thigh. The cabin burned with a roaring sound. Tai felt terror, and an overwhelming grief. He had a sense that he was crying aloud, in the dream, and in Xinan.

He became aware, as if in fog and mist, half asleep, of a voice soothing him. He was trying to see. He looked for yellow hair. A hand brushed his forehead, or so it seemed to him. Someone beside his curtained, canopied bed in the dead black of night. He felt himself struggling to wake, then surrendered and slipped back into sleep—an easier sleep, without the horrifying images of memory.

In the morning, waking at sunrise, he said nothing about his night, and no one else did, either.

NINE DAYS AFTER THIS, the Second Son of General Shen Gao was summoned to the Ta-Ming Palace and received in the Hall of Brilliance by the Emperor Taizu in the presence of the most illustrious members of his court, including the Precious Consort.

Tai, clad by his steward in white for the occasion, approached the Phoenix Throne, making the triple obeisance three times, as instructed. He stopped the stipulated distance from the imperial presence, his eyes cast down, also as required.

He was then presented, by an admiring and grateful empire, with an estate in the Mingzhen Hills, the aristocracy's hunting and riding playground north of Xinan. He received another estate and considerable land in the south, near the Great River, once the property of a minister convicted of stealing from the Treasury.

The corrupt minister had been executed, his property confiscated. It now went to the brave man who had lived among the ghosts of Kuala Nor, laying them to rest.

He was further presented with a staggeringly large sum of money, ceremonial artifacts, jade, coral, pearls, ivory, and precious gems, and two ceremonial swords that had belonged to an emperor of the Fifth Dynasty.

Not speaking (speech was forbidden), Tai rose at a tall eunuch's discreet hand signal and bowed again, nine times, as he backed slowly away from the throne.

Outside, light-headed, but breathing in a sunlit courtyard, he fully expected that orders would now come for him to set out immediately to claim his horses. It did not happen that way. Events intervened.

Word came that same afternoon that Yenling, second city of the empire, east of them on the far side of Teng Pass, had surrendered to Roshan. He had declared it the capital of his Tenth Dynasty.

His soldiers had, it was reported, left the general population substantially unharmed, but they were butchering every civil servant and soldier who had not managed to flee when the rebels appeared before the walls.

More ghosts, Tai thought. More to come.

CHAPTER XXII

 It is not one of the things she's ever thought about, but Li-Mei has never been on a mountain. She never even climbed the hills east of their home. Women didn't do that. She remembers dreaming about seeing the sea. A different sort of thought.

In her first days here, with no tasks, no need to rise in darkness and ride anywhere, clutching the unimaginable luxury of time to herself, she walks the broad, flat top of the mountain and the green terraces below. There isn't even anyone escorting her. Not here, there is no need.

Stone Drum, one of the Five Holy Mountains, stands out vividly because of where it is, above mostly level land in all directions. The top looks as if some god had taken a sword and sliced, creating the level summit. She can see a long way, whichever direction she looks. Sometimes she imagines she can even see the Wall, but she knows that is an illusion.

She has no restrictions, can wander anywhere. She wears the grey robes of a Kanlin acolyte, though she isn't one. She watches them training in combat, or with the bow, or practising movements that seem nearer to dance than fighting. She watches men and women run up walls, spring back across open space, and down a different wall, and then do it again.

She hears the bells that summon the Kanlins to prayer and she drifts that way, among grey and black figures on a green mountain.

She loves the sound of bells in this high place. She stands at the back of a temple, watching the rites, tall candles burning, hearing the chants rise and fall, feeling more peace than she can remember.

It is the same at twilight, when she finds a quiet place on one of the terraces and watches the sky grow dark and the stars appear.

She has to deal with some guilt. Slipping into peace at this moment is surely selfish, even shameful. They know by now why the Long Wall and the garrisons beyond have been emptied out. They know where the armies of Roshan have gone, are going.

Even so—or perhaps, more honestly, because of this—by the evening of her third day on Stone Drum, Li-Mei has decided she wishes to remain on the Mountain all her life, training to be a Kanlin, or simply serving them.

Early the following morning, summoned before the trio of elders who govern the sanctuary, she learns that she will not be allowed to do this. She is to leave almost immediately, in fact.

They do not look like men inclined to alter any decision made, she thinks, standing before them. Their faces are austere. Two are very tall, the third has only one hand. They wear the unadorned black of all the Kanlins she has ever seen. They sit on cushions on platform couches in a pavilion open to light and wind. The sun is rising.

She has questions.

She sinks to her knees. Isn't sure if that is the proper thing to do, but it feels correct. She says, looking from one to the other, "Am I so unsuited to becoming a Kanlin?"

Unexpectedly, the elder in the centre, the one with a single hand, laughs aloud, a high-pitched, merry sound. He isn't so remote, after all, she thinks. Neither are the others: they are smiling.

"Unsuited? Hopelessly so!" says the laughing one, rocking back and forth in mirth. "Just as your brother was!"

She stares. "You knew my brother?"

"I taught him! We tried. He tried." He calms himself, wipes his eyes with his sleeve. He looks more thoughtfully at her. "His was not a spirit meant to grow within a larger group, a shared belief. Neither is yours, daughter of Shen Gao." His voice is actually kind. "This is not to be seen as a failure."

"It feels that way," she says.

"But it is not so. Your brother had too strong a feeling of what he was, within. So do you. It is a nature, not a flaw."

"I don't want to leave." She is afraid of sounding like a child.

"You love the Mountain because you have come through peril and it is peaceful here. Of course you want to linger."

"I cannot? Even as a servant?"

One of the tall ones stirs. He is still amused, she sees. He murmurs, "You are a princess of Kitai, my lady. Circumstances have now changed in the world, and it is nearly certain you will not go back north. You cannot be a servant. It shames the Ta-Ming Palace, and us, too many people will know who you are."

"I didn't ask to be made a princess."

This time all three of them laugh, although it is gentle enough.

"Who chooses their fate?" It is the third one, the tallest. "Who asks to be born into the times that are theirs?"

"Well, who accepts the world only as it comes to them?" she says, too quickly.

They grow quiet. "I do not know that passage," the one in the centre says. "Is it from a disciple of the Cho Master?"

She says, not fighting a ripple of pride, "It is not. It is from General Shen Gao. My father said that to all his children." She remembers him saying it directly to her, his daughter, more than once. It was not something she'd only overheard.

The three men exchange glances. The tallest inclines his head. "It is a challenging thought, and places burdens on those who heed it. But, forgive me, it only makes more clear why you are not meant to be a Kanlin. We are of many minds, and natures, but our way is to find fulfilment and harmony in the larger identity. You know this."

She wants to fight, but finds it difficult. "My brother could not do that?"

"No more than he could find harmony in the ranks of the army," says the one on the right. "It seems your father succeeded in shaping independence in his children."

"Kanlins cannot be independent?"

"Of course they can!" It was the small one again, in the centre. "But only in some measure and only after acceptance of the self as gathered into our robes and the duties they bring."

She feels foolish, young. These are things they might have expected her to know. She says, "Why are you helping me, then?"

They look surprised. The one in the centre—he appears to be the leader—gestures with his one hand. "For your brother, of course."

"Because he was here?"

Three smiles. The tall one on the left says, "Not that. No. Certainly not that. It is because of Kuala Nor, my lady."

And so she asks, having never learned what it was that Tai had done after he left home and went west in the mourning period.

They tell her, on a far-off mountain. They explain about the horses, and the attempts upon his life, one by a woman disguising herself as a Kanlin—trained here, in fact, before leaving the order, though still wearing the black robes, deceiving people. Something they deeply regret, the tallest one says. A burden they feel.

It is a great deal to absorb.

Li-Mei has the sensation that the world she left behind when she departed from Xinan in a litter, travelling north to the Bogü, is coming back in a rush of words and thoughts.

"Why would anyone have wanted to kill him?" The first question that comes.

They shake their heads. Do not answer. Choose not to answer.

"Is he all right?" she asks.

"He is in Xinan, we are told. And guarded. By Kanlins, which is as it should be. The horses will be even more important now, and they are his. It is a good assurance," the tallest says. They are not smiling now, she sees.

A good assurance. She shakes her head.

It is all so strange, enough to change the way you understand everything. But it seems as if her second brother has done something astonishing, and that, even so far away, he has been with her, has protected her, after all. Here on Stone Drum, and before that, on the grasslands, because of—

"What about Meshag?" she asks suddenly. "The one who brought me. Will he be allowed to stay? Can you do anything for him? Do you understand what has happened to him?"

The one on her left answers this time. "Our teachings and our understanding do not go so far into the north."

She stares at him. They have been nothing but kind to her. Still, she dislikes being told something untrue. They are right, of course: hers is not a Kanlin nature. These are elders, wise and revered.

She says, "Forgive me, but that is not correct, is it? Someone here understood a wolf messenger. Isn't that how three of you came to meet us by the Wall?"

She has had several days to think about it.

"Kitan do not like wolves," the one in the centre says. The one who had been Tai's teacher here. It is not an answer.

She says, "He's *bound* to the lead wolf, isn't he? Meshag. That is what happened to him? His life ends when the wolf dies?" She's had time to think about this, too.

"Perhaps," says the elder on her right. "But it would be a presumption for us, for anyone, to believe we understand this."

For anyone. That means her. And here, again, she knows what he says is true. How could what happened by that far northern lake be grasped?

"You won't let him stay." She doesn't ask it as a question.

"He has no wish to stay," the one in the middle corrects her, gently.

She hasn't seen Meshag—or the wolf—since the evening they arrived. Surely, she thinks, he would say farewell before going back. It isn't necessarily a well-founded belief. She has no ... good assurances.

She tells herself it must not be allowed to matter. The world came to you, and you tried to make of it what you wanted it to be. If you broke upon rocks, as the seas did in room screen paintings she'd seen at court, you broke with your pride.

But no one *was* allowed to choose the times into which they were born. Her father was right, and the elders were. There was no true contradiction in the teachings.

She stands up, and bows. "Where will you send me, my lords?"

The small one has a kind face, she decides. It is a kindness hidden by scars, his bald head, the black severity of the Kanlin robes. But it is a gentle face, nonetheless, and so is his voice.

He explains, speaking for the three of them, what is to happen to her. She feels a flicker of fear, listening, like the first tongue of flame as a fire is started, but she pushes it down.

She is, after all, a princess of Kitai, and her father's daughter, and she sees now, with clarity, that it would have been pursuing a false simplicity to live out her days upon this mountain, pretending otherwise.

SHE GOES LOOKING for Meshag and his wolf when she leaves the pavilion and the elders.

She doesn't expect to find them unless he wishes it, but she is still certain he will not have gone away, not without speaking with her.

As she winds her way down green terraces late in the day, away from others, among pine trees, the scent of them, she is remembering the cave where she placed her handprints on the body of the king-horse on the wall—before the entrance to the last cave, where she'd been afraid to go.

He'd gone in there, Meshag.

She watches the sun go down.

Late at night, she lies in the narrow bed they have given her, in a simple room with a fireplace, one small table for a washbasin, a chest for belongings, and nothing else, and he comes to her.

A tapping at the door, once and then again. Soft, you could think you had imagined it.

"Wait," she says. She has not been asleep.

She rises and dons her grey robe and goes to the door and opens it. Moonlight in a cold, clear night. She is barefoot. Goes out nonetheless to where he stands a little distance from her threshold.

She sees, without surprise, the grey wolf not far away, the yellow-gold of its eyes. It is achingly quiet upon the Mountain's summit. No one stirs. No bells in the dark hours. The moon dims all but the brighter stars. A wind blows.

"Thank you," she says.

He is lit by moonlight but she cannot see his eyes, which is always the case at night. He is wearing the leggings and boots he wore on their journey.

The wolf sits. It is alert but calm, she thinks. She doesn't understand wolves, however. She might easily be wrong.

He says, "You were looking for me, before?"

His Kitan has improved, she thinks. Several days of talking with the Kanlins. The open space and the buildings here are silver in the moonlight, otherworldly.

"I was afraid you had gone."

"Afraid? But you are safe now."

She had thought he might say that. It pleases her to be right, if only in small things. It is a way of not being lost.

"There is a rebellion. I wonder if anyone is safe."

"They will not send you back. They have told me this."

"They won't. Someone else might. I don't know."

She hears the wind. The wolf rises, moves a little, settles.

Meshag, standing very still, says, "I do not think so. Too much will change now, Kitan and Bogü, and others. But if … if they do this, I will know it. And I will come for you again."

And with that, she begins to cry.

She sees the wolf stand up again as she does so, though she is silent, only the tears sliding down her face. Meshag does not move. And because she hates to cry—she tells herself later—because of that, she steps forward and reaches up and takes his head in both her hands and kisses him. First time she has ever done such a thing, outside of dream.

It feels like a dream here, on the Mountain, in silver light. She holds her eyes open, as long as she can, and so she sees when his dark eyes shut, and only then does she close hers, knowing he is not, after all, entirely gone from the world and needs of men.

His mouth is unexpectedly soft, but his arms do not come around her, and when she steps back, light-headed, a little unsteady on her feet, her heart pounding much too fast, he says, gravely, "I did not take you from my brother to claim you for myself."

"I know!" she says, too loudly. "Of course I know that."

The small movement of his mouth she has learned to call a smile. "You are so certain?"

She feels herself flush. Finds she has nothing to say.

He murmurs, "I lose what there is in this, if I take you now."

"I understand."

A silence, wind. She is suddenly aware that the wolf has gone. At length, he says, softly, "In different lives …"

He leaves the thought unfinished. He doesn't have to finish it.

"I understand," she says again.

Eventually, she adds, "You are leaving now?"

"Yes."

She's expected that. She feels the tears on her cheeks in the night. She manages a smile. "I have questions," she says.

She hears the sound that is his laughter. "Always."

Another sound, to her right. The wolf is back, and has growled, though softly. Meshag says something to it in his own tongue. He looks back at her. That stiff nod, last time. He lifts one hand—it is not at all a graceful lover's motion—and touches the side of her face.

Then he goes, running after the running wolf.

His horse will be waiting somewhere, she knows. Probably two or three horses, for the Bogü seldom ride just one when they have a long way to travel.

She thinks of walking out to where she can overlook the slopes and the plain below them to the north; she might see them go. It is cold, though, and there really is no reason to go look.

She stands in the moonlight, alone on the mountain. She wipes at her cheeks with the sleeve of her robe. The world, she thinks, is impossible to measure.

TWO MORNINGS LATER she leaves as well, with a good-sized party of Kanlins, heading south. She is dressed in black, with a hood, as if she is one of them.

They are riding to Teng Pass.

The elders, considering and communing, have decided that this is where Kanlins will be needed. This has happened at that pass, it seems, years ago, and before that, and before.

 space

In warfare there are times of frenzied urgency and violence that saturate the churned earth with blood, and there are periods when everything seems to slow, or even come to a halt.

The rebel armies had taken Yenling with alarming ease and some savagery. An Li's well-horsed cavalry thundered down from the north, forded the Golden River, and appeared before Yenling's walls before any opposing force could arrive to defend the second city of the empire.

This had been anticipated within the Ta-Ming Palace. It was accepted by the emperor's senior mandarins in the Purple Myrtle Court that this would be so.

There would be casualties in the east, lamentably. How not? This was an armed rebellion, and no one was unaware of how ruthless An Li could be.

Teng Pass, which protected Xinan itself, was manned and guarded. Not with the very best soldiers at first. Roshan might possibly have been able to fight through, had he moved immediately from Yenling, but the pass was notoriously narrow, easy to defend. And going south of it through the hills, or crossing and recrossing the river north, were appallingly treacherous (especially with horsemen). Attempting such manoeuvres had destroyed armies over the centuries. Teng Pass was a central square on the Kitan gameboard.

Put another way, warfare could also be a dance, and often the steps and music were well known by both sides.

The vanguard of the rebels—now calling themselves the Tenth Dynasty of Kitai—consolidated their hold on Yenling, killed anyone they decided to kill, seized control of the Grand Canal ports nearby, and waited for their foot soldiers to subdue the north and join them.

Subduing the north proved a difficult matter, however, made more so by the arrival of imperial forces from the Sixth Army to attack supply lines. Rebel troops were forced to remain northeast in order to prevent cities from being retaken—or even throwing open their gates to the emperor's troops.

Roshan and his generals had nourished hopes that the Five Families, long displeased with certain measures taken regarding taxation and land rights, might join the rebellion, or at least not oppose it. In the event, though there was some discussion among the northern aristocracy, this did not happen.

Instead, almost from the start, there were insurrections north of the river, in the supposed heartland of the newly proclaimed Tenth Dynasty.

One might dislike the current imperial family, find them presumptuous, of modest lineage, and far too inclined to consolidate power in Xinan ... but compared to a barbarian and his vulgar sons and generals? Well, there was really nothing to choose between, was there? And no one in the northeast, having lived with Roshan as governor for years, was inclined to be seduced by the notion that he would be easily manipulated once in power.

In addition to which, the proud leaders of the Five Families knew their history and geography as well as anyone.

Roshan had probably missed a chance, they agreed, exchanging elegantly scripted missives on silk paper, or meeting at one estate or another over summer fruit and wine. He had erred: by waiting in

Yenling to have himself crowned, then setting up the trappings of a court, by not moving swiftly enough with the advantage of the first army in the field.

It was understandable that he might try to assume the mantle of legitimacy, of a new emperor. A hero of the suffering Kitan people, bent on destroying a corrupt first minister, and replacing an aged, hapless, love-snared emperor.

This was the tale as Roshan needed it told. But keeping his army in the field, away from barracks and families, as summer heated up and autumn's harvest came—and was not gathered—was going to be a challenge.

With Teng Pass secured and Xinan safe, the emperor's forces could slowly gather from all directions, assemble ranks and regiments, and eventually squeeze the rebels, north and south, as a man might squeeze a grape between his fingers.

This was, in fact, the almost universally accepted opinion among historians of what should have happened.

∾

For all his disclaimers that he'd never held a position at court, never wanted one, and would not pretend to understand manoeuvres there, it was Sima Zian who continued to anticipate the events that began the change of the world.

Zian did not write the "Song of Everlasting Sorrow." That was a younger poet, years after. But the Banished Immortal did, over lychee wine in Tai's city garden on a summer evening, indicate what he thought was about to happen. The Second Army, under Governor Xu Bihai himself, was in Teng Pass by then, blocking the rebels.

There were skirmishes, no major engagements. Armies of both rebels and empire were moving all over Kitai. *Locusts crossing ruined fields*, a poet had written during another war long ago.

A second blazing star had been reported, falling in the east.

It had to do with apprehension, Zian said that night, amid fire-flies. "Great events often begin in fear. And the Ta-Ming is a fright-ened place. Mistakes can be made."

Tai remembered looking around, even in his own garden, to see who might be placed to overhear. They were alone except for two of his Kanlins, at some remove. They were always with him now. He'd stopped permitting himself to be unhappy about it.

Zian, not even nearly sober, had expounded on what he expected in the not-too-distant future. He quoted two poems and a passage from the Cho Master.

Tai had listened, and looked at him under two lanterns burning, and had said, when the poet was done, "My brother would not permit that. It will not happen."

Zian, he remembered, had laughed: that uninhibited amusement that was so near to the surface in him. An ability to find joy in the world.

"Not permit?" the poet said once he'd subsided. "Have you considered that your brother's influence is not what it might once have been?"

"It isn't?" said Tai. He put his wine cup down. "Why not?"

"Because you came back to Xinan! Liu reminds the first minister of you. Think about it!"

"What am I thinking about?"

"Those twenty riders he sent for your horses. You think your brother approved those?"

Tai knew the answer to that. He'd seen Liu's face that day.

"No," he said. "He knew it was wildly foolish."

"*Wildly foolish.* That is good! But Wen Zhou still went ahead, didn't he? Do you think Liu was even told it was happening?"

"I doubt it."

"You see? I speak for the sage in the cup! Pour me more of your good wine, friend." He waited for his cup to be filled, then added, softly, "We will pick our way through the shards of broken objects that folly leaves behind. And some of what breaks will be very beautiful."

Tai would remember that, too.

෨෨

She has always been able to tell when he is uneasy. It is a part of her training—and her nature. The ability to read a man's mood is critical in the North District. It is one of a singing girl's essential skills.

When it comes to Wen Zhou it is not—unlike some other men— an important signal when he shows no inclination to make love. He can absently take her on a bed or against the wall when he is disturbed, his attention entirely elsewhere. Or he can linger at ease, let her make music for him, on an evening when his thoughts and mood are perfectly tranquil.

With Zhou, gauging his mind often has to do with how he answers when she speaks to him. Or does not answer. Rain can almost feel the whirling of his thoughts some nights, and knows that though he is with her, though he might even be inside her, he is scarcely present—and is even (though he'd be angered if she were ever so foolish as to say this) afraid.

But he is. For several nights now, when he arrives home late from the Ta-Ming and comes to her, she has sensed his disquiet, and tonight it is even stronger.

Although she has no understanding of what has happened, she is aware that Shen Liu, his most trusted adviser, has not appeared at the compound for days.

They must be meeting at the palace, she decides.

She very much misses one aspect of the North District: all kinds of tidings arrived there in a steady, endless flow, like a river. You needed to be skilled in extracting what was true (or might be true) from what was only the idleness of streets and markets, but you *heard* things in a house like the Pavilion of Moonlight, you felt connected to the world.

Here, ironically, in the home of the most important man in Kitai, according to some, Rain is cut off from events and their report. The other women are useless in this regard, and the servants alternate between stolidly uncurious and wildly credulous.

She knows that the rebels have taken Yenling and that the emperor's forces are holding Teng Pass. It is summer now, fighting season, but when autumn comes, with winter to follow, the rebels in the field should be in serious difficulty. The imperial forces might be in trouble, as well, mind you, since Grand Canal supplies will be interrupted, but the west is theirs, and Roshan is bottled up in the northeast and in his proclaimed capital of Yenling.

On the other hand, Zhou is clearly uneasy, so there must be something she doesn't know. She puts aside her *pipa* and says, a slight risk, "You are quiet, my lord."

He does not answer.

After a moment she takes up the instrument again, and begins to play. They are in her chamber, it is very late. The sliding doors are open to the summer.

Gazing out, he says quietly, as if he'd not even heard her words, "Rain, have I ever been cruel to you?"

She is genuinely startled, hides it as best she can. "My lord, your servant knows—all your servants know—how good you are to us!"

His expression is odd. "But have I been cruel? To you?"

Rain shapes a smile. "Never, my lord. Not ever."

He stares at her a long time. He stands up and finishes his wine, sets the cup down. "Thank you," he says, and walks out.

She hears him speaking commands. He wants his horse, and guards. He is going back to the palace. At this hour?

And ... *Rain*. He'd called her by her North District name. He never does that. And expressing gratitude? It is disturbing.

The next day she dismisses her servants mid-afternoon, claiming a need to rest after a tiring night with the master, and she sets about filling a discreet cloth bag with some of her most valuable jewellery.

Later, walking alone, as is her carefully established custom, towards the far end of the garden—not far from the rosewood gazebo—she buries those jewels at the base of a cherry tree.

The flowers on the tree have come and gone by then: beautiful for a little time, then falling.

☙

In the Ta-Ming Palace, and in Ma-wai when she wishes to be there, a woman dances for the emperor of Kitai.

PART FOUR

CHAPTER XXIII

There have been rebellions before in Kitai, civil wars from the time the earliest dynasties of the empire were forged, and shattered, and reforged.

In one of these conflicts, notoriously, a Sixth Dynasty army was treacherously undone by a false order sent to its generals, purporting to be from the palace. Since that time, measures have been undertaken to offer commanders on a battlefield assurance that communications from court are truly their orders.

A certain number of imperial seals are made, fired in a small and guarded kiln on the grounds of whatever palace the emperor is using. On these seals dragons are variously depicted. On the backs of the seals are numbers, in a recorded sequence.

In the presence of military leaders and mandarins from the Purple Myrtle Court, these seals are ceremonially broken in half. It is considered an honour to be the man entrusted with doing this.

Before taking his army to the field, a commander is given a certain number of these seals—or half-seals, to be precise. Orders relayed to him from court are accompanied by the matching half-seal. The messengers carrying these have been Kanlin Warriors, for several hundred years. They are trusted by all parties to any conflict, and in that trust lies their sanctity.

The military commander must ensure that the piece they bring to him fits, in shape and number, one he carries.

If it does match, he must accept those orders, or death and shame (and ruinous dispossession) will invariably follow, as wolves follow sheep through summer grass.

ତ୨ର

Of the two men who met on a summer morning at the eastern end of Teng Pass, one arrived on horseback, as a general in the field always should, in his own view. He needed help dismounting, however, and used a walking stick to make his way forward, swinging a stiff leg.

The other man approached the shadows of the pass from the open ground east, carried in an enormous sedan chair by eight large men. The number is a concession to the circumstances; normally there are twelve.

Behind this, two other soldiers could be seen bearing a western-style chair, very wide, cushioned and backed in yellow cloth. It was, when viewed closely, a throne, or meant to be seen as one. The colour indicated as much.

They placed this on level ground, not far inside the pass. The sedan chair was also set down. The curtains were drawn back. With assistance, a fabulously large figure emerged and made his way to the throne-chair and subsided into it.

The other man waited, leaning upon his stick. He wore a battle sword (not a decorative one). He smiled thinly throughout all of this, watching with interest. Birds circled in the updrafts overhead. It was windless below. A hot day, though cooler in the shade of Teng Pass.

Each of the two men had five others accompanying him (aside from those allowed by agreement to carry the sedan and the throne, and to handle the general's horse). None but the general was armed.

His sword was, in truth, a transgression, as symbolic in its way as the throne and the kingfisher feathers on the sedan chair.

There were, in addition, fifty Kanlin Warriors in the pass, supervising this parley—as Kanlins had done during such encounters for hundreds of years.

Five of these were sitting cross-legged before writing tables with brushes and paper and black ink. They had arrived before anyone else. These would record, with precision, to be checked against each other, everything said this morning.

One scroll would be presented to each party attending, after the gathering was over. Three would be kept and archived by the Kanlins, as evidence of any agreement emerging here.

There was no great expectation on anyone's part that an agreement would emerge from Teng Pass today.

The other black-robed ones were spread out around the canyon, and these men and women bristled with weapons. Two dozen of them held bows where they were posted some distance up the slopes on either side of the pass. They were here to monitor—or to preserve—the peace of this meeting and the safety of all who came to it.

The Kanlins, even the ones preparing to write, were hooded. Their identities meant nothing here. They were emblematic of their order and its history. No more than that, but certainly no less.

General Xu Bihai, commanding the imperial armies of Kitai in Teng Pass, waited until the other man had settled himself in the large chair. It took some time. Xu Bihai's thin smile never wavered, but one would have been deceived in thinking there was anything but ice in his eyes.

It was, in most instances of this sort, customary for one of the figures behind the principals to speak first, addressing the Kanlins, formally requesting them to begin transcribing. This did not happen.

Instead, General Xu said, "I have a personal proposal for you, An Li." No title. Of course, no title.

"I await it with eagerness!" said the other man.

His voice was unexpectedly high if you were hearing it for the first time. A slight accent, even after so many years.

"Why don't you and I settle this conflict with a single combat right here, after the fashion of ancient days?" said Xu Bihai.

All those gathered, where sunlight did not penetrate, seemed to grow still, to breathe more shallowly. Roshan stared at the other man. His creased eyes widened, and then he began to shake—his prodigious belly, his shoulders, the folds of face and chin. High-pitched laughter, wheezy and urgent, echoed in the narrow pass. A startled bird flew up and away.

Xu Bihai, eyes still hard, allowed his own smile to grow wider. One is always pleased when a jest, however barbed, encounters an enthusiastic response.

Gasping, quivering, Roshan lifted an unsteady hand, as if pleading for mercy. Eventually he regained control of himself. He wiped at his small, streaming eyes with a sleeve of his *liao* silk robe. He coughed. He wiped his face again. He said, "A fight for poets that would be! You'd kick me to death with one leg or I'd sit on you! Crush the life out of you!"

"Right out of me," agreed the other man. His thinness, the lean, austere appearance, seemed shaped by a mocking deity to provide as vivid a contrast as possible to An Li. His smile faded. "I could fight your son?" The son, bulky and fit, stood beside his father's chair.

The man in the chair was no longer laughing. His eyes, nearly lost in the folds of his moon-face, became as cold as Xu Bihai's.

"He would kill you," he said. "You know it. The Ta-Ming would not allow it, or honour it. We are not children. These are not the ancient days. You asked for a meeting. The black-robes are writing. Say what you have come to say and then leave my presence."

Blunt, heavy, harsh. All of these things, and deliberately so.

The standing man's turn to be amused, or pretend to be. "Ah, well. You would have to leave *my* presence, wouldn't you? Since it is my army that holds this pass. Why don't you attack, Roshan? Or do you like camping on the hot plain out there? Is it soothing for your afflictions?"

"I hold the Grand Canal," An Li said, grimly.

"You hold the northern ports of it. But have you not heard? The weather has been glorious in the southwest. We have great hopes for that harvest. And have you not also heard? The Twelfth Army is on its way here even as we enjoy a morning together. And the Five Families are restless behind you, or so our tidings tell."

Roshan smiled. "Ah. The Five Families. Do your tidings also tell of the fate of Cao Chin and his family ... behind me, as you say? Or has that news not yet reached the Ta-Ming? Be the first to know! His castle has been burned down. His wives and daughters taken by my soldiers. Granddaughters too, I believe. The men did need some diversion, after all. Cao Chin hangs naked, castrated, meat for carrion birds, from a hook on a pillar outside the ruins of his home."

When it grew quiet, as it did now, you became more aware there was no wind. It was clear to anyone watching that Xu Bihai had not known this, and equally clear that he believed what he was being told.

"That was a great name," he said softly. "It brings even more shame upon you."

Roshan shrugged vast shoulders. "He was a traitor to the Tenth Dynasty. The Families needed to learn there are consequences to the elegant exchanges of missives, and musings over wine discussing which way to turn, when an army is among them. I doubt the north-east is as restless now as you might think."

Xu Bihai stared. "Time and the winter will tell, whether you can feed the army that keeps them quiet. You are trapped here and you know it. Perhaps you would prefer to withdraw to Yenling? I enjoy siege warfare, myself. When autumn comes without an eastern harvest, you are done, Roshan."

Birds calling. No breeze in the pass.

"May I tell you something?" the man in the chair said. "I don't like you. I never have. I will enjoy killing you. I will begin by hacking off your crippled leg and showing it to you, then dripping your own blood in your open mouth."

It was, even for such a setting as this, savage enough to elicit another silence.

"I tremble," said Xu Bihai finally. "Before I commence to babble like a terrified child, hear the words of the emperor of Kitai. You are declared accursed of men and the gods. Your life is forfeit, and your sons'—"

"He killed my son," said An Li.

"One of them. A hostage to your own conduct. He was executed when that conduct became treacherous. Wherein lies your grievance? Tell me!"

There was something magnificent about the lean, thin-bearded man standing there with his heavy stick.

"He was no hostage! Do not shape lies that are being written down. He was an officer in the Flying Dragon Army, and a member of the court. He was killed by a fool in an act of fear. Will you pretend you approved?"

"I was in Chenyao," said Xu Bihai.

It was an admission of sorts.

"Nothing near to an answer! But I *know* your answer. However much you hate me, Governor Xu, I will wager the lives of my remaining sons against your daughters' that you despise Wen Zhou as much!"

There was no reply.

Roshan went on, his voice a hammer now, "You were afraid to challenge him, all this time! You stayed west and let a vain polo player, whose only claim to rank was a cousin in the emperor's bed, turn Kitai into his own fiefdom, while Taizu drank potions to straighten his male member and drank others to live forever!"

He glared at the other man. "Was yours, Governor Xu, the conduct of someone mindful of his duty to the state? Do you *accept* the fool whose cause you are serving here? I require Wen Zhou at my feet, blinded, and begging for death."

"Why? Are you the first man to lose a battle for power?"

"He is worth nothing!"

"Then neither are you the first to lose to a lesser man! Will you kill so many, destroy an empire, for it?"

"Why not?" said An Li.

The words, unadorned, hung in the air.

"Because you cannot blame Wen Zhou for this. *You* rose against the throne, your son died for it. You had to know it could happen. And sons die every day in the world."

"So," said Roshan, "do daughters."

Xu Bihai shook his head. Gravely now, he said, "Ministers of the empire come and are gone, leaving memories, or only tracks in sand. The Phoenix Throne is more than the man who sits it, or those who serve him, well or badly. I have my views on the first minister. I have no inclination to share them with a foul and accursed rebel."

"I am neither, if I win," said Roshan.

"You are both, now and until you die, and the words will cling to your name forever, wherever your body lies." Xu Bihai stopped, then he said, "Hear my offer."

"I am listening," said An Li.

"You and your eldest son have forfeited your lives. You will be graciously permitted to commit suicide and be buried, though not with monuments. I have the names of five of your commanders who must also accept their deaths. All others in your army, here or in the northeast or in Yenling, are offered pardon in the name of the Glorious Emperor Taizu, an offer to be recorded now by the Kanlins, and with my own name and honour behind it."

His voice grew quiet. "You are dying. You know it. All men who look at you know it. With your life, already ending, and six others, you can save all those who follow you, and Kitai, from this."

He ended. Five Kanlin scribes, their hands dipping brushes, shaped words. Otherwise, there was a stillness in the pass.

"Why would I do that?" Roshan said.

He sounded genuinely puzzled. He scratched at the back of one hand. "He drove me to this. Wen Zhou was stripping me of choices, poisoning the emperor against me, erasing anything I might offer my sons. What should a man with any pride in what he leaves behind do in the face of that?"

"Is that it?" said Xu Bihai. "Legacy?"

"It is different for you," said Roshan, dismissively. "You have only daughters." He shifted in his chair. "If this is all you came to say, we have wasted a morning. Unless it is of importance to you to understand that I do know of your daughters, and I will find them, to their very great regret. You may trust me in this."

The thin man appeared undisturbed. "I thank you," he said. "You turn the duty of destroying you into a pleasure, rare and delicate."

That last word, *delicate*, lifted into the air and was recorded, strange as it sounded in that place, on pale silk paper by five brushes moving swiftly, dipping and stroking—delicately, in fact.

The yellow-backed throne was carried out of Teng Pass. Roshan waited in the kingfisher-feathered sedan chair, curtains drawn, respecting—perhaps surprisingly—formalities. It may have been the case that, having named himself an emperor, these mattered more to him than they might once have done.

Eventually, three hooded Kanlins walked over, two escorting the one carrying a scroll that preserved the record of what had been said. The Kanlin extended the scroll. A hand reached through the curtain and took it.

The sedan chair was lifted and carried away into sunlight.

LI-MEI IS DEEPLY DISTURBED, not even close to working through all the reasons for this. One of them, however, is surely the savage intensity of what has just happened in Teng Pass, the words spoken, violence embedded—and with more to come. Surely, now, to come?

Another reason, on an infinitely smaller scale, shameful, almost unworthy of acknowledging, is that she's still recovering from the effect of the heavy, too-sweet smell that had come from An Li's sedan chair when she'd accompanied the Kanlin carrying the scroll to him. She'd been next in line when he was given the completed record. They'd motioned for her, and one other, to go forward.

A sweetness of perfume overlaying, thickly, an odour much darker, something corrupt. She feels ill in the aftermath of it, and the air in Teng Pass is too still, too dense, when she tries to breathe deeply. It will be very hot outside the pass, where the rebels are camped in the sun.

She remains shaken by a thought that came to her, walking towards Roshan, standing by, watching the scroll being extended to him.

She isn't remotely capable with a sword or knife, but there was surely a chance that, armed as she was—as a Kanlin for today—she could have stabbed him, ending this.

Ending all safety and tradition and respect for the Kanlin Warriors, too, mind you.

Hundreds of years of being judged worthy of trust, destroyed in a moment by Shen Li-Mei, only daughter of General Shen Gao— after they'd welcomed her on Stone Drum Mountain, given her shelter and guidance and even a way to make her way home through civil war.

Not to be thought of. Or, if thoughts cannot be barred, not to be permitted to be more than that.

Roshan is dying, in any case. That was the odour she smelled. The thin-bearded man who'd faced him down (she knew who he was, remembered her father speaking of him) had said it in blunt words. Words she'd watched being recorded in swift calligraphy by the scribes.

Killing him, she thinks, wouldn't have ended anything, necessarily. The sons—the one standing here, and there are two others alive (she believes)—and, probably, the five men whose names are carried on a second scroll, the ones whose deaths are required: these would carry on, even if An Li died.

Rebellion might not always be tied to one man's will and life. Perhaps it took on its own force, after a given point was reached and passed. You could turn back, and turn back, and then you couldn't.

Has that happened here?

She'd like to ask someone, but can't. She is disguised as a Kanlin, no one is to know who she is, and a Warrior would not be asking questions like that, of anyone.

They'd made her carry twin swords on her back during the ride south so she wouldn't look awkward and inept, moving with them when the time came. They'd been heavy at first, the swords, painful against her spine in their back-scabbards. She's more accustomed to them now.

A person—a woman—can adapt to more than she might have thought she could. What she's unsure about is when that stops being a virtue and turns to something else, leaving you too much changed, undefined, unanchored, like a fisherman's empty boat drifting on a river, with no way to be returned to where it belongs.

Thinking so, ashamed to be dealing with thoughts of her own life at such a time, Li-Mei sees three riders racing towards them up the pass from the western end.

The leading one carries a banner, the imperial insignia. These are couriers, she'd seen them often enough in her days with the empress. The second rider is a Kanlin. He is the one who dismounts from his lathered horse before the stallion has even entirely halted. He approaches General Xu, bows. He is perspiring from the heat. The black robes are soaked with sweat. He extends a small object. It is a seal, broken in half. Li-Mei knows what this signifies, though she's never actually seen one. The courier also extends a scroll to the general.

Xu Bihai accepts both. He hands the half-seal to one of his officers. This man reaches into a leather satchel he carries and extracts a similar object, rejects it, pulls out another. No one speaks. The man holds this second piece to the one the courier has brought. He looks at the fit, examines the back, nods his head.

Only then does Xu Bihai untie the scroll and read.

Li-Mei sees him grow older before her eyes. He leans on his stick for a moment. Then he straightens. "When was this given to you?" he asks the couriers. His voice is thin. Li-Mei is suddenly frightened, hearing it.

The courier bows before speaking. He is clearly exhausted. "Three nights ago, my lord. We left in the middle of the night."

"And it came from?"

"From the first minister himself, my lord general. His hand to my own, the scroll and the half-seal."

Rage appears in Xu Bihai's features; it is impossible to miss. He breathes in and out, slowly.

He says, very clearly, "He is afraid. He has decided that the longer we are here holding them back, the more likely it is that someone might decide this can be ended by delivering him to An Li."

No one says a word in Teng Pass. Li-Mei is remembering someone else this morning: *I need Wen Zhou at my feet, blinded, and begging for death.*

After a moment, General Xu says, quietly this time, as if to the stillness of the air, not to anyone beside him, "If I were a different man, and Roshan were, I might even have done it."

What Li-Mei feels, hearing this, standing so near, is fear. It chases away, as wind chases fallen leaves, all thoughts of her own destiny. There is too much more here now.

NOT LONG AFTER THAT, eight Kanlins ride west out of the pass, through the assembled armies of the Second and Third Districts. The armies are stirring. Orders have been given.

The eight riders go swiftly once beyond the canyon, with the wide river on their right and hills to the left—the features that make Teng Pass what it is, vital for so long in Kitai.

Two of these riders are bound for the Kanlin sanctuary at Ma-wai with three of the records of the morning. From there, two scrolls will be sent on to other sanctuaries, for greater security.

Two of the other riders will go only as far as Xinan, with the scroll for the Ta-Ming Palace, along with newer ones: the just-dictated words of General Xu Bihai, sent to the imperial heir and the Beloved Companion, but not to the first minister.

Three of the riders are escorting the last one farther west, and south, because of a promise made at Stone Drum Mountain. These four will branch off halfway to Xinan.

That last one, wrapped in fear and doubt as they ride, is the daughter of General Shen Gao.

 ∾

There have been many chronicles of warfare in Kitai, from the First Dynasty onwards.

Disagreements as to strategy and tactics, not surprisingly, are everywhere in the texts, and a component of the civil service examinations is for students to analyze two or three such writings and express a preference for one of them, defending that choice.

Victory or defeat in battle can be attributed to many different elements. Some writers stressed the (somewhat obvious) point that numerical superiority, all else being relatively equal, could usually determine a combat, that a prudent general would wait for such superiority, decline to engage without it.

Others noted that all else was rarely equal.

Weaponry, for example, made a great difference. An often-cited example was the fate of an army in the northeast some time ago, an incursion into the Koreini Peninsula: undone before the crucial battle by a sudden rainstorm that soaked their bowstrings, eliminating the archers from playing any role, leading to a terrible defeat.

This incident was also cited in the context of preparation. The fact that the leaders of the expedition had failed to anticipate the rain was judged significant. All of the surviving generals were later executed, or ordered to kill themselves.

Other writers placed emphasis on terrain, positioning. The army with higher ground or territory protected by natural features would have a significant advantage. The capable commander sought such terrain.

Supply lines played a role. Food, clothing. Horses. Even boots for a marching army. So could the ratio of infantry to cavalry, and the quality of horsemanship. Experience, in general. Battle-hardened soldiers were worth much more than new recruits.

Surprise, whether by way of an unexpected assault (at night, in difficult weather, sooner than anticipated) or a battle conducted using new tactics, could make a difference. There were examples. Those taking the examinations were expected to know them.

Morale and passion were seen as important, and were linked to leadership.

There was a very old tale of a commander who committed his army to battle with a river in spate behind them, having refused to move forward from the edge of the water to better ground, waiting for the enemy there.

His soldiers had no possible retreat.

They did not retreat. They won a famous victory that day against significantly greater numbers. When men have nowhere to escape, the lesson went, they will fight more bravely, and often prevail.

So, too, will soldiers who are aware that defeat for them is decisive, and likely to mean death.

On the other hand, an army that knows there need not be (for them) finality to a given field, that flight is possible, is less likely to engage the enemy with the same ferocity.

This last distinction, it was subsequently agreed with a degree of consensus, was the best explanation for the victory of the An Li rebels against the forces of the Second and Third Armies in the battle joined east of Teng Pass.

The imperial army had an advantage in numbers, and they did surprise the rebels—who'd had no thought that General Xu Bihai would lead his forces out of an impregnable pass and onto a sun-broiled battlefield.

The initial appearance of the emperor's troops caused extreme consternation in the rebel ranks. General Xu had increased this likelihood by moving most of his men into position outside of the pass during the night, so the rebels woke to see their enemies gathered, and then had to face a charge.

This surprise changed, swiftly, to something else. Something that could be described as hope, or even joy. Short of an attack such as this (a mistake such as this) they had been almost certainly fated to withdraw from here and face the uncertainty of autumn and winter with too little ground gained, a large army to feed and house through the cold months, and unrest in their own base. All the while learning of the steady mustering of even greater numbers of imperial forces, readying themselves for the resumption of fighting in spring.

The attack out of the pass, once the initial shock was over, presented itself to An Li and his forces as what it was: a gift, an opportunity unlooked for.

It was a gift they did not fail to grasp.

There were a great many casualties on both sides that day. There were more in the imperial army. When the dead and wounded reached a certain number (there is always such a number for any army), the soldiers of General Xu Bihai broke and fled.

They raced back up Teng Pass, pushing through the rearguard left to hold the pass, running over them, pursued with triumphant ferocity by the rebel cavalry, into the pass, and along it through shadows, and out the other end into light again.

At the end of that day, more than half of the Second and Third Armies lay dead east of the pass or within it, or overtaken in flight to the west.

Most of the others were scattered in their frenzy to get away—to let others take on the burden of resisting these rebels while serving a court that issued commands that made no sense, forcing them out of a secure position into unnecessary battle.

General Xu was one of those who escaped the wreckage of that battlefield and headed west, riding at speed with his guards towards Xinan, which lay open now, undefended before Roshan.

Xu Bihai was seen to be weeping as he rode, though whether the tears were of rage or grief no man felt able to say.

It was a catastrophe for Kitai, that battle, leading to chaos that would last a long time. The ensuing nightmare ended eventually (all things end), but not before the changing of the empire and the world.

Beauty was not easily sustained in that time, nor music, nor anything that might be linked to grace or serenity. Not easily sustained at the best of times, those things. Sorrow lasts longer.

WORD OF THE DISASTER reached the Ta-Ming in the dead of night three days later.

The glorious emperor was awakened from sleep and informed as to what had happened. At all costs, Taizu, beloved of heaven, had to be saved. Xinan had fallen before. It could be lost and retaken. But not if the dynasty fell.

With little time for decision-making, with Roshan's army of hardened soldiers approaching and Xinan wide open to them—and with panic certain in the morning when these tidings became widespread—a small imperial party, escorted by some of the Second Army who had been left with them, proceeded in secrecy out a northern gate of the palace into the darkness of the Deer Park, and then through another gate in the walls of the park, on the road towards Ma-wai, under stars, with the wind rising.

CHAPTER XXIV

Wei Song woke him in the dark of night.

The Kanlins had never let Tai bolt his chamber door in Xinan. There were entrances to his bedroom through sliding doors from porticoes on two sides; these were guarded, but they needed to be able to enter, at need, or so they'd told him. He'd thought about making a jest about *needs* in a bedchamber but never had.

He'd been deeply asleep, not dreaming. It took him time to fully rouse to her voice and her touch on his shoulder. She stood by the bed, holding a candle. Her hair was unbound. She'd been sleeping, too, he realized.

"What is it?"

"You are summoned. To the palace. An escort is waiting."

"Right now?"

She nodded.

"What has happened?" He was naked under the bedcovers.

"Trouble east, we think."

East meant the rebellion. There should not be any trouble there now, not with two armies blocking Roshan in Teng Pass.

"Who sent for me?"

"I do not know."

She handed him the scroll she carried. She ought to have done that first, he thought. She never did things properly.

He took it. Sat up. "Do you know what this says?"

She nodded. "A Kanlin brought it. That's why we're allowing you to go."

Allowing. He ought to correct her, but there was no point. If any harm came to him his Kanlins would die.

He untied the scroll, read it by the candle's light. It clarified nothing: was simply a command to come immediately, with a permit to pass through the ward gate and up to the Ta-Ming. The permit was signed by a senior mandarin, not a name he knew.

"Get Dynlal for me."

"It is being done."

He looked at her. Sometimes, not often, you were reminded of how small she was, for someone so fierce. "Then go put up your hair and let me dress."

She looked embarrassed. It occurred to him that Song might be as uneasy about a middle-of-the-night summons as he was. With armies in the field, the times were deeply troubling. She put the candle on the table that held his washbasin and went to the door.

On impulse, he added, "Is Master Sima here?"

He never knew whether the poet had come in late or lingered wherever else he'd spent the night.

She turned in the doorway and nodded.

"Please wake him, Song. Say that I would like him with me." The *please* and her name were an apology.

In the courtyard, another thought came. He hesitated. He might be making a large thing out of a small one, but *trouble east*, and a summons under stars carried weight, didn't they?

He saw the poet, rumpled as ever, but moving quickly, alert, walk into the courtyard. Zian had his sword across his back. Tai felt a measure of relief, seeing him.

He beckoned Lu Chen, the leader of his guards, and arranged for two of the Kanlins to carry a message. He called for paper and ink and wrote that message, quickly, by torchlight, on a small table brought on the run into the courtyard. Then he sent the two Kanlins to deliver it to Spring Rain, by way of the crippled beggar who lived in the street behind Wen Zhou's mansion.

The two guards had been there before, the night he'd met her in the garden, they would remember how to find the man. He instructed them to be respectful, request his aid, then stay until there was a reply. If they saw the Lady Lin Chang (that was her name now) they were to guard her life as surely as they'd been ordered to defend his.

He could give that order. He could assign them as he chose. There was no time to shape a better plan. *Possible danger*, he'd written, in hurried, ungraceful script. *Be very alert. Two Kanlins in street behind garden awaiting word from you.*

He didn't sign it, to protect her, but the reference to Kanlins probably undid that measure, if anyone saw this. There wasn't time for clearer thought. He didn't have a clearer thought.

He rode out of the gate on Dynlal, taken again—always, in the moments when he mounted up—by the sensation of being on such a horse, his bay-coloured Sardian.

They went down the night street of the ward, and through the ward gate, then north towards the Ta-Ming along the starlit main avenue of Xinan. Tai saw Gold Bird Guards at their stations, patrolling. Then a handful of people on the far side of the wide street, increasing the sense of emptiness. Their horses' hooves were the only sound.

The Kanlin who'd brought the summons was with them. At the city-side gates of the Ta-Ming another was waiting. The gates were opened at a signal, then closed behind as they rode through. Tai heard the heavy bar slide shut.

They continued north through the vast palace complex with its hundred buildings and courtyards. No paths were straight here, so that demons (who could travel in a straight line only) might be forestalled in any evil designs against heaven's beloved emperor within his palace.

The emperor, Tai learned, was not in the Ta-Ming any more. He was on the road, heading northwest.

He exchanged a glance with the poet.

They reached the northern wall of the palace complex, and passed through another gate into the Deer Park, and rode through that. Continuing north, they'd have eventually reached a stone wall by the riverside. They turned west instead, led by their Kanlin escort. Song was at his side, Tai realized, hair precisely pinned, swords on her back.

They passed a bamboo grove on their right, an open space, an orchard, then they came to a western gate in the park wall and went out. They began riding quickly now, in open country.

Not long after, they saw the imperial party ahead of them on the road. Torches under moonlight.

Fear and strangeness were in Tai as they caught up with the others. He saw Prince Shinzu near the back of the small procession. It was shockingly small, in fact: two carriages, some riders from the court. Twenty or thirty cavalry of the Second Army guarding them. No more than that.

Normally, the emperor would journey to Ma-wai accompanied by two or three dozen carriages, preceded by an army of servants and five hundred soldiers, and escorted by five hundred more.

The prince looked back, hearing them approach. He slowed when he saw the Kanlins. He greeted Tai, who bowed in the saddle. Briskly, with nothing in the way of warning or preamble, Shinzu told them of the disaster that had happened east.

Or the first disaster.

With Teng Pass fallen, there was much more now to come.

Tai felt his mouth go dry. He swallowed hard. Had the world, their world, come to this? The emperor, they were told, was in the carriage just ahead—no kingfisher feathers. Jian was with him. The prime minister was riding at the front of the party.

"It is good that you are here," said the prince. He was riding a handsome stallion, though it was almost a full head smaller than Dynlal.

"I don't understand," said Tai. "What can I do?" He felt lost. This night ride felt dreamlike, as if through some star-world not their own.

"We need your horses, Shen Tai. More than ever. As cavalry mounts, or for couriers. We are going to be spread very widely. Distances will need to be covered swiftly. When we reach the posting station ahead I am going to propose we head north to Shuquian. The Fifth Army is still mostly there, and we will summon the First Army from the west now. I think we can hold Roshan in Xinan while other forces come up from the south. We ... we have to do that, don't we?"

Don't we? Why was a prince asking him? Was he waiting for a considered answer? A disagreement? What was Tai expected to know?

It was obvious the prince was shaken. How could he not be? It was the middle of the night. They were fleeing the capital, the palace, with twenty or thirty men, and an army of rebels was behind them, would be approaching Xinan unopposed. Was the mandate of heaven being withdrawn right here? Could the shape of the world change in a night?

"I am to go to Shuquian with you?"

He was confused, himself. The prince shook his head.

"You will take riders southwest to the border. You must claim your horses, Shen Tai, then bring them as speedily as possible to wherever we are."

Tai drew a breath. Precise instructions were good, they freed him from the need to think. "My lord, there are a great many of the Sardians."

"I know how many there are!" said the prince sharply. There was a half-moon shining but it was hard to see his eyes.

Another voice: "My lords, let the Kanlins do this. Take fifty of us, Master Shen, from our sanctuary ahead." It was Wei Song, still beside him (she was always beside him through that night, he would later remember). It made sense, what she said.

"Are there enough of you? At the sanctuary? Will they release so many?" Tai was calculating quickly. "If they are good with horses, we can do this with sixty, five horses behind each rider, ten to guard us."

"There are enough," she said. "And they will be good with horses."

The prince nodded. "Attend to it, Kanlin."

"This is why you sent for me, my lord?" Tai was still wrapped in strangeness, struggling to believe what had happened.

"I didn't send for you," the prince said.

It took a moment. They looked ahead, at the nearest carriage.

It wouldn't have been the emperor. Once, perhaps, in his burnished, brilliant youth, new to the throne or ready to claim it, but not now. Not any more.

It was Jian who had summoned him, Tai realized. Awakened in the middle of the night herself, amid panic, preparing to fly from all they knew, she had thought of this.

A question came. It ought to have been, he thought, his first. "My lord, forgive me, but I don't understand. How was there a battle? General Xu *held* the pass. He would never have—"

"He was ordered out," said Shinzu flatly.

And then, very deliberately, he looked ahead, towards where a handsome, moonlit horseman rode at the front of their small procession.

"In the name of all nine heavens!" exclaimed Sima Zian. "That cannot be. He would not have done that!"

"But he did do that," said the prince. He smiled, mirthlessly. "Look where we are, poet."

It seemed as if he would say more, but he did not. The prince flicked his reins and moved up beside his father's racing coach, then they saw him go past it to ride with the soldiers guarding them.

Just as the sun rose on a summer morning they reached the posting station by the lake at Ma-wai.

TAI HAD BEEN WARNED that the soldiers were beginning to murmur amongst each other as the night drew to an end.

Lu Chen, a shrewd, experienced man, had moved up for a time among the cavalry escort. Then the Kanlin drifted back towards Tai, where he and Zian and Song had kept to the rear of the party.

Chen had spoken to Song first, then brought his quick Bogü horse over beside Dynlal. "My lord," he said, "I am not certain how it is, but the soldiers know what they should not."

"What do you mean?"

"Someone has spoken to them about Teng Pass. Word is spreading as we ride. The Second Army was in the pass, my lord. These men will be grieving, and angry."

Zian moved up. Song shifted her mount to let him. The road was wide; they rode four abreast in the night.

"They know who gave Xu Bihai that order?" the poet asked.

"I believe that is so, my lord." Lu Chen was invariably courteous to the poet.

"Do you think it was intentional? That they know this?" Zian's voice was grim. Tai looked quickly over at him.

"I do not know, my lord. But I believe it would be wise to be cautious at the posting station." He glanced at Tai. "My lord, I have determined that your honourable brother is in the other carriage. I thought you might wish to know."

Never much of a horseman, Tai's honourable brother, to their father's regret. Even less so now, undoubtedly. Clever in the extreme, however, hard-working, ambitious, precise, with foresight and discipline.

He would never have let Wen Zhou send that order to Teng Pass.

Tai knew it with certainty. As surely as he understood how Liu could send their sister to the barbarians, he knew he would not have ordered Xu Bihai out of that pass into battle.

His Kanlins were gathered tightly around him now. Someone had obviously given instructions. He looked ahead at the carriage nearest to them. The emperor of Kitai was in there, rolling through the night, *fleeing* in the night. Could the world really come to encompass such a thing?

Tai knew it could, that it had before. He'd studied a thousand years of history, hadn't he, preparing for the examinations? He knew the legacy of his people, the dark and the brightly shimmering. He knew of civil wars, palace assassinations, slaughter on battlefields, cities sacked and burned. He had not thought to live through any of these.

It suddenly occurred to him, belatedly, how almost all of the court and imperial family—children, grandchildren, advisers, concubines—had been left behind tonight, to get away as best they could, or face Roshan when he came.

And there were two million people in Xinan, undefended.

His heart twisted. *Be very alert,* he'd written to Rain. So helpful, that. What would she do? What was possible? Would she even get his message, from that twisted figure in the street? He'd left two Kanlins behind for her—at least he'd done that.

His mouth was dry again. He spat into the dust beside the road. Zian handed over a wine flask. Wordlessly, Tai drank. Only a little. He needed to be clear-headed, surely, above all else.

He glanced ahead. Wen Zhou was still among those up front. Lit by torches, he was easy to see, on a splendid black horse, a riding posture to be envied. Born to ride, they said about him.

The light grew as they went on. All but a handful of the brightest stars disappeared, then these, too, were gone. Individual trees took shape on their right, and fields on the other side of the road, ripe with summer grain. Torches were extinguished and discarded.

End of night. Morning, soft and clear. Tai looked back. Thin clouds east, underlit, pale pink, pale yellow. He caught a flash of blue, bright between trees, then he saw it again: the lake, ahead and to the right.

They came to the branching road that would lead around its shore to the extravagant luxury of the hot springs at Ma-wai. Jade and gold there, alabaster and ivory from the Silk Roads, porcelain, flawless silk, marble floors and columns, sandalwood walls, room screens painted with mastery, rare dishes from far lands, exquisitely prepared. Music.

Not today. They carried on along the road straight past that lakeside cut-off so often taken by this court, and not long after they came to the postal station inn and yard and stables, instead.

Riders had galloped ahead. They were awaited. The officers and attendants of the station were assembled in the courtyard, some bowing three times, some already prostrate in the dust, all visibly terrified to have their emperor suddenly among them like this.

There was a clatter of coach wheels and horses and orders shouted, then an odd, intense near-silence as they came to a halt. Birds were singing, Tai would remember. It was a summer morning.

The imperial carriage stopped directly in front of the station's doors. It was a handsome posting inn, Ma-wai's, so near Xinan, so very near the hot springs and aristocrats' country estates, and the tombs of the imperial family.

The carriage door was opened and they saw the emperor step down.

The Exalted and Glorious Emperor Taizu wore white, unadorned, with a black belt and hat. Alighting behind him, in a vivid blue travelling robe, with small gold flowers for decoration, came Jian.

The two of them went up the three steps to the station's porch. It was deeply disturbing to see the emperor walking. He was carried, always. His feet seldom touched the ground—not in the palace, and certainly not here in the dust of an inn yard. Tai looked around, and saw that he wasn't the only one unsettled by the sight. Wei Song was biting her lip.

Too much had changed too swiftly in a night. The world was a different place, he thought, than it had been when they went to bed.

On the porch, the emperor turned—Tai hadn't thought he would—and looked gravely out at those in the courtyard. He lifted a hand, briefly, then turned and went inside. He held himself very straight, Tai saw, leaning on no one. He didn't *look* like a fleeing man who'd lost the guidance of heaven.

Jian went in behind him. The prime minister and the prince followed, handing their horses to servants, going quickly up the steps. They didn't look at each other. The other carriage door was opened by a servant. Tai saw his brother step down and walk into the station as well. Three other mandarins alighted and followed.

The posting station doors were closed.

There followed an interlude of disquiet in the courtyard.

No one seemed to have any idea what to do. Tai gave Dynlal's reins to a stable boy, with orders to feed and water the horse and rub it down. Uncertainly, he went up on the covered porch, standing to one side. Zian came with him, and then Song and five of the Kanlins, staying close. Song was carrying her bow, had her arrow-quiver at one hip. So did the other five.

On the western side of the yard Tai saw a company of soldiers, fifty of them, a *dui*, such as he had commanded once. They appeared to have just arrived.

Their banners and colours marked them as also being of the Second Army. A mixed unit: forty archers, ten cavalry escorting them. Their presence was not unusual. When the main east-west road was congested troops would routinely be diverted this way. The posting stations were used by soldiers in transit throughout the empire, to change horses, eat and rest, receive new orders. These men would be coming from the west, assigned to the capital very likely, or they might even have been heading all the way to Teng Pass, to join their fellows there.

Not any more, Tai thought.

Some of the soldiers who had escorted their party here could be seen making their way across the inn yard to talk to the others. They were all of the Second Army. And there were tidings to share.

"This is not good," said Sima Zian quietly.

The two companies of soldiers were intermingled now, talking with increasing intensity in small clusters. Tai looked for their officers, wondering if they'd assert control. That didn't seem to be happening.

"The *dui* commander just drew his sword," said Song.

Tai had seen it, too. He looked at her.

"I have sent two of our people for sixty riders from the sanctuary," Lu Chen said. "They cannot be here before end of day." He said it as if apologizing.

"Of course not," said Tai.

"They will not be in time to help," said Chen. He had stepped in front of Tai and the poet, holding his bow. They were towards one end of the porch, away from the doors.

"We are not the target of their anger," said Tai.

"It doesn't matter," Sima Zian murmured. "This mood finds targets as it goes."

And with that, Tai thought of a cabin in the north, long ago, when anger had turned into flames, and worse. He shook his head, as if to shake off memory.

He said, "Keep together. No aggression. There are more than seventy of them. This cannot become violent. The emperor is here."

The emperor is here. He'd actually said that, he would recall later. Invoked the imperial presence like a talisman, a ward, something magical. Perhaps once it would have been, but too much had changed by the time that day's sun had risen.

An arrow flew in morning light.

It struck one of the doors of the posting station straight on, burying itself, vibrating there. Tai winced as if he'd been hit himself, so shocking was the sight, and the sound it made hitting the wood.

Three more arrows, and then ten, rapidly. The archers of the Second Army were widely known for their skill, and they were shooting only at doors, and not from far away. This was solidarity, the *dui* acting together. None of them would leave any others to face consequences alone. Tai looked for the *dui* commander again, hoping he could stop this.

A vain hope, entirely awry. The commander, not a young man, grey in his short beard, cold anger in his eyes, strode to the foot of the steps leading up to the porch and shouted, "Where is the first minister? We demand to speak with Wen Zhou!"

Demand to speak. *Demand.*

Knowing this might end his own days, aware of what men in such a state as this could do (they would be thinking about their fellows at Teng Pass), Tai stepped forward.

"Do not!" he heard Song say, a low, strained voice.

He didn't feel as if he had a choice.

"*Dui* commander," he said, as calmly as he could. "This is unseemly. Please hear me. My name is Shen Tai, I am the son of General Shen Gao, a name of honour among soldiers, and you might know it."

"I know who you are," said the man. Only that. But he did sketch a bow. "I was in Chenyao when the governor assigned you an escort and gave you rank in the Second Army."

"We share that army, then," said Tai.

"In that case," said the commander, "you should be standing with us. Have you not heard what happened?"

"I have," said Tai. "Why else are we here? Our glorious emperor is consulting even now with his advisers and the prince. We must stand ready to serve Kitai when they emerge with orders for us!"

"No," said the officer below him. "Not so. Not until Wen Zhou comes out to us. Stand aside, son of Shen Gao, if you will not come down. We have no quarrel with the man who went to Kuala Nor, but you must not be in our way."

Had this been a younger man, Tai would later think, what followed might have been different. But the officer, however low-ranking, had clearly been a soldier for a long time. He'd have had companions, friends, at Teng Pass, and he would have, just this moment, learned what happened there.

The *dui* commander gestured towards the door.

More arrows struck, all together, loudly. They had to sound like a hammer blow inside, Tai thought. A hammering from the changed world. He thought of Jian, more than any of the others in there, even the emperor. He wasn't sure why.

"Come out to us, or we will come for you," the officer shouted. "First Minister Wen, commander of the armies of Kitai, your soldiers are waiting! We have questions that must be answered."

Must be. From an officer of fifty men to the first minister of Kitai. Tai wondered how the sun was climbing in the sky, how birdsong sounded as it always did.

The door to the posting station opened.

Wen Zhou, whom he hated, came out.

LONG YEARS AFTER, when that rebellion was another part of the past—a devastating part, but over with, and receding—the historians charged with examining records (such as remained from a disjointed time) and shaping the story of those days were almost unanimous in their savage writings as they vied to recount the corrupt character (from earliest childhood!) and the foul treachery of accursed An Li, more commonly known as Roshan.

Virtually without exception, for hundreds of years, Roshan was painted in text after text as the grossest possible figure, pustulent, oozing with depraved appetite and ambition.

In these records, it was generally the view that only the heroic and wise first minister, Wen Zhou, had seen through the vile barbarian's dark designs—almost from the first—and done all he could to forestall them.

There were variations in the writings, complicated by certain aspects of the records, and by the need (until later dynasties) not to be at all critical of the Great and Glorious Emperor Taizu himself.

Accordingly, the most common explanation of the events at the outset of the An Li Rebellion involved incompetence and fear among the generals and officers assigned with defending Teng Pass—and Xinan, behind it. A certain General Xu Bihai, an otherwise inconsequential figure, was routinely described with contempt as physically infirm and a coward.

This solution to the problem of explaining what happened was obvious, given that official historians are civil servants and serve at the court of any dynasty—and can readily be dismissed, or worse.

It would have been deeply unwise to imply, let alone assert, any error or failing on the part of heaven's emperor, or his duly appointed ministers. Easier, and safer, to turn one's gaze and calligraphy to the soldiers.

The handsome, aristocratic, preternaturally wise first minister was also, of course, part of a legendary tragedy, one embraced by both the common people and the artists of Kitai—and this, too, surely played a role in the shaping of official records.

When the desire of the court and the tales of the people meld with the vision of great artists, how should any prudent chronicler of the past set himself to resist?

THE FIRST MINISTER, showing no sign of unease, stopped at the front of the porch, above the three steps leading to the yard.

It left him, Tai thought, looking disdainfully down on the *dui* commander and the soldiers. Wen Zhou had had no real choice but to come out, but this encounter needed care, and part of that, surely, was to make clear the gulf, wider than the Great River in flood, between himself and those below.

Tall and magnificent, Zhou looked out into the sunlight of the yard. He was dressed for riding: no court silk, but perfectly fitted cloth and leather. Boots. No hat. He often disdained a hat, Tai remembered, from days in Long Lake Park, seeing him at a distance.

A much greater distance than this.

Zhou extended an arm and swept it, one finger extended, in a slow, wide arc across the inn yard. He said, his voice imperious, "Each man here has forfeited his life for what has just been done. The officers must be executed first."

"No," murmured Sima Zian, under his breath. "Not that way."

Wen Zhou went on, "But our infinitely merciful emperor, mindful that these are difficult times for ordinary men to understand, has elected to let this moment pass, as if it were the troublesome behaviour of small children. Put away your weapons, form ranks. No punishment will be visited upon any of you. Await orders when we come out. You will be needed in defending Kitai."

And he turned, amazingly, to go back inside without waiting to see what they did, as if it were inconceivable that anything other than immediate compliance could take place.

"No," said the *dui* commander.

Tai could see that it cost him a great deal to say that single word. The man was perspiring in the sunlight, though the morning was mild.

Wen Zhou turned. "What did you say?" he asked. His voice and manner, Tai thought, could freeze a soul.

"I think you heard me," the officer said. Two others came to stand with him. An archer and one of his officers of ten.

"I heard treason," said Wen Zhou.

"No," said one of the archers. "We have learned of treason just now!"

"Why was the army ordered out of Teng Pass?" cried the grey-bearded commander, and Tai heard pain in his voice.

"*What?*" snapped Zhou. "Will the heavens crack above us? The sun fall? Are common soldiers asking questions of the Ta-Ming now?"

"They didn't have to fight!" cried the *dui* commander. "Everyone knows it!"

"And you are fleeing from Xinan, leaving it to Roshan!" shouted the archer, a small, fierce figure. "Why was *any* of this done?"

"They say you gave those orders directly!" the officer of ten said.

First hesitation in Wen Zhou, Tai saw. His mouth was dry again. He didn't move. He couldn't move.

Zhou drew himself up. "Who says such a thing?"

"Those who rode with you have told us!" cried the archer. "Your own guards heard it on the ride!"

Tai turned to Sima Zian. The poet's face was stricken. Tai wondered how he looked himself. He heard Wen Zhou again. "This encounter is over. Soldiers! Take custody of these three men. Your *dui* commander is relieved of his post. Bind them and hold them for execution when we come out. Kitai will *fall* if such chaos is permitted! Soldiers of the Second Army, do as you are ordered."

No man moved in the inn yard.

A flurry of wind stirring the dust. Birdsong again, and always.

"No. You must answer us," said the archer. His voice had altered. Tai heard Song draw a breath behind him. He saw Wen Zhou look down into the inn yard with the withering, lifelong contempt a man such as he would have for those below. He turned, to go back inside.

And so the arrow that killed him struck from behind.

Sima Zian, the Banished Immortal, master poet of the age, who was there that day at the Ma-wai posting inn, never wrote a word about that morning.

A thousand other poets, over centuries, did take those events as a subject, beginning with the death of Wen Zhou. Poets, like historians, have many reasons for varying or amending what might have taken place. Often they simply do not know the truth.

Before the prime minister fell, there were five arrows in him.

The bowmen of the Second Army would not let one of their number carry the burden of this deed alone.

By the time the poems of lament were in full spate, like a river, some versifiers had twenty-five arrows (with night-black feathers) protruding from the first minister's back as he lay in his red blood upon the porch: poets straining for pathos and power, oblivious to the excesses of their images.

Tai stepped forward. His swords remained sheathed. His hands were shaking.

"No, my lord!" cried Song. "Shen Tai, please. Hold!"

And, *"Hold!"* echoed the *dui* commander below, eyeing him narrowly, visibly afraid. Frightened men were dangerous.

Tai saw that the man's hands were also trembling. The commander stood alone now, exposed in the dusty inn yard. The archer was no longer beside him, nor his officer. They had withdrawn, blending back in with their fellows. Tai was quite sure he could recognize the archer, the man who'd fired first.

The bowmen in the yard all had arrows to string. So, he saw, glancing back, did Song and the other Kanlins. They stepped forward to surround him. They would be killed before he was.

"This must stop!" he cried, a little desperately.

He pushed forward, past Song. He looked down at the *dui* commander. "You know, surely you know it must stop."

"You know what he did," said the commander. His voice was harsh with strain. "He sent all those men—an army!—to their deaths, left Xinan open to ruin, and only because he feared for himself if the officers in the pass decided he'd caused this rebellion."

"We can't know that!" cried Tai. He felt weary and sick. And afraid. There was a dead man beside him, and the emperor was inside.

"There was no reason for our army to leave the pass! That one there sent the order in the middle of the night, with the half-seal. He gave it himself! Ask those who escorted you here."

"How do you *know* this?" cried Tai. "How would they know?"

And the officer in the inn yard below, not a young man, said then, quietly, "Ask the prince you came here with."

Tai closed his eyes, hearing that. He felt suddenly as if he might fall. Because it fit. It made a terrible, bitter kind of sense. The prince would be readying himself to take command now, with a full-fledged war upon them and his father so frail. And if the prime minister was the one who had created this sudden nightmare ...

They had seen Shinzu ride ahead in the darkness on the road, to join the escort from the Second Army, speak with them.

A man's actions could have unexpected consequences, sometimes; they could come back to haunt you, even if you were a prime minister of Kitai. Also, perhaps, if you were a prince of Kitai.

Tai opened his eyes, found himself unable to speak just then. And so, instead, he heard, in that bright, clear morning light near Ma-wai and its blue lake, another man do so, from among the gathered soldiers, lifting his voice. "One more must die now, or we will all be killed."

Tai didn't understand, not at first. His immediate thought was, *You are all going to die, in any case.*

He didn't say it. He was too shaken to speak. Very near him, blood slowly spreading on the wooden porch, lay Wen Zhou.

"Oh, please, no," said Sima Zian, barely a breath. "Not this."

Tai remembered that, too. That it was the poet who realized first what was happening.

He turned quickly to look at the other man, then wheeled back to the courtyard.

And with a sorrow that never left him, that lay in memory, in his days forever after, as powerful, in its way, as the terrible images of the

Bogü by the northern lake, Tai saw the soldiers step forward, together, well trained, and he heard the one who had just spoken speak again, and this man—whose face Tai never properly saw, among seventy or so of them—said, very clearly, "He was prime minister for only one reason. All Kitai knows it! We will be slain in vengeance—by her. She destroyed the emperor's will with her dark power and has brought us all to this, through her cousin. She must come out to us, or this cannot end."

Dancer to the music. Bright as morning light. Lovely as green leaves after rain, or green jade, or the Weaver Maid's star in the sky when the sun goes down.

CHAPTER XXV

"This will not happen!" said Tai.

He said it as forcefully as he could, feeling a frantic need to push back against where the morning had now gone.

A trickle of perspiration slid down his side. Fear was in him, a twisting thing. He said, "She was working to control her cousin. Wen Zhou had even tried to kill me, at Kuala Nor. She was gathering information on that. Against him!"

He felt ashamed, telling soldiers this, but the moment was surely beyond shame, or privacy.

Hidden among the others, the archer (he would remember the voice) shouted, "This family has destroyed Kitai, driven us to civil war! As long as she lives they will poison us!"

That was clever, a part of Tai was thinking. A moment ago it had been about their own safety, those who had killed Wen Zhou—now it was something else.

"Bring her out," said the *dui* commander.

Tai felt like cursing him. He held back. This was not a time to let anger overwhelm. He said, as calmly as he could, "I am not going to allow another death. Commander, control your men."

The man shook his head. "I will. But after the Wen family poison is purged from among us. Our companions were sent out from Teng Pass. Will you measure two against so many? You have been a soldier. You know how many men are dead there. Does not the Ta-Ming invoke execution when someone in power has erred so greatly?"

"She is only a woman. A dancer." He was dissembling now, but desperate.

"And women have never shaped power in Kitai?"

Tai opened his mouth and closed it. He stared at the man below.

A twist of the officer's mouth. "I sat the examinations twice," he said. "Studied eight years before accepting that I would never pass them. I know some things about the court, my lord."

Tai would wonder about this later, too. If the world as it went forward from that day might have been otherwise had another leader and his fifty men been shifted to the northern route from the congested highway to Xinan.

There are always branches along paths.

"I will not permit this," Tai said again, as coldly as he could.

The commander gazed up at him. He didn't look triumphant or vengeful, Tai thought. The man said, almost regretfully, "There are … eight of you? We have better than seventy men. Why would you wish to kill your Kanlins, or yourself? Do you not have tasks in the war upon us now?"

Tai shook his head, aware again of anger. He fought it. The man was telling only truth. Tai could kill a great many people with the wrong thing said or done here. Even so: "I have no task greater than stopping this. If you wish to move into that posting station, you will have to kill me and my guards, and deprive Kitai of two hundred and fifty Sardian horses."

He was willing to play that card, too.

There was a short silence.

"If we must," said the *dui* commander. "Eight more deaths will not change what is to come, along with however many of us fall, including myself. I don't matter. I know enough to know that. And the horses are your duty, not ours. Stand aside, my lord. I am asking you."

"Tai," said Sima Zian softly, at his elbow, "they are not going to stop for you."

"Nor I for them," said Tai. "There comes a point when life is not worth enduring if one steps back."

"I agree, Master Shen."

A woman's voice, from the open doorway to the posting station. She had come out.

Tai turned and he looked at her. Their eyes met. He knelt, near the blood of her cousin where it was spreading on the porch. And, with a shiver, he saw that not only did his Kanlins also kneel, and the poet, but every soldier in the inn yard did the same.

The moment passed. The soldiers stood up. And Tai saw that the archers still held their bows, arrows to strings. It was only then that he accepted that this was going to happen and he could not stop it.

In part, because he saw in her eyes that she willed it to be so.

"Poet," she said, looking at Zian with the mocking smile Tai remembered, "I still grieve that you chose to be ironic with your last verse about me."

"Not more than I do, illustrious lady," said Sima Zian, and Tai saw that he had not risen from his knees, and there were tears on his face. "You brought a shining to our time."

Her smile deepened. She looked pleased, and young.

Tai stood up. He said, "Will the emperor not come? He can stop this, surely."

She looked at him for what seemed a long time. Those in the courtyard were waiting, motionless. The posting station of Ma-wai felt to Tai as if it were the centre of the empire, of the world. All else, everyone else, suspended around it, unknowing.

"This is my choice," she said. "I told him he must not." She hesitated, holding Tai's gaze. "He is no longer emperor, in any case. He gave the ring to Shinzu. It is … the right thing to do. There will be a hard war, and my beloved is no longer young."

"You are," said Tai. "It is too soon, my lady. Do not take this brightness away."

"Others are taking it. Some will remember the brightness." She gestured, a dancer. "Shen Tai, I remember sharing lychees with you on this road. I thank you for it. And for ... standing here now."

She wore blue, with small golden peonies (royalty of flowers) embroidered on the silk. Her hairpins were decorated with lapis lazuli and two of her rings were also of lapis, he saw. She wore no earrings that morning. Her slippers were silk, and golden, with pearls. He was near enough to tell that she had not left the Ta-Ming in the middle of the night without the scent she always wore.

Nor had she left without considering the Sardian horses at the border, and sending a messenger through the night city for the only man who could claim them for Kitai.

"You must let me go," Jian said softly. "All of you."

He let her go. He dreamed of it, and saw it in his mind's eye waking, all the rest of his days.

He watched her turn, poised, unhurried, stepping lightly past her fallen cousin who had brought them all to this. She went down the steps alone—lifting her robe so it might not catch—and into the yard, and she went forward there, in morning sunlight now, to stand before the soldiers who had called her out to kill her. It was a dusty inn yard, filled with fighting men, not a place for silk.

They knelt. They knelt down again before her.

She is too young, Tai thought. In the room she had left, an old emperor and a new one remained out of sight. Tai wondered if they were watching. If they could see.

With mild surprise, he saw tears on Song's face, too. She was wiping at them, angrily. He didn't think she'd ever trusted or liked Jian.

Perhaps liking was without importance sometimes, with some people. The dancers, like summer stars. You didn't say you *liked* a star in the sky.

He moved to the top of the steps leading down. He had no idea what he was doing, he was living inside sorrow.

Jian said, clear as a temple bell sounding across fields, "I have a request, *dui* commander."

The officer was still kneeling. He looked up for an instant, then lowered his head again. "My lady?" he said.

"I would not like to die as my cousin did, to have arrows disfigure my body, or perhaps my face. Is there a man here kind enough to kill me without marring me? With ... with a knife, perhaps?"

That faltering, her first since coming out.

The commander looked up again, but not directly at her. "My lady, such a man would be too clearly marked for death. It is not proper for me to name anyone in my company to that."

Jian seemed to consider it. "No," she said. "I understand. I am sorry to have troubled you with such a request. It was ... childish of me. Do as you must, *dui* commander."

Childish. Tai heard a footfall behind him. Then a voice by his side.

"I will do it," said the voice. "I am marked in any case."

The tone was precise. Not beautiful as a temple bell, but firm, no uncertainty.

Tai looked at his brother.

Liu was gazing at the commander in the yard, his posture and expression defining authority, a man accustomed to being heard without raising his voice. He wore his mandarin's robe and a soft hat, and the belt and key of his rank, as always. The man he had served was lying in blood at his feet.

That was it, of course. Add Wen Zhou's death to the emperor's abdication, a new emperor for Kitai. Consider Liu's position as the first minister's principal adviser, and ...

And you had this, Tai thought. Added to the other moments unfolding here one by one, a morning tale.

The *dui* commander nodded his head jerkily. He seemed, for the first time, overawed by what they'd set in motion. Not so as to falter (his soldiers would not allow it by now), but by the weight, the resonance of this.

Liu lifted a hand in a practised gesture. "One moment, then, *dui* commander, and I will be with you." Jian had turned, was looking up at the two brothers. "My lady," said Liu, and bowed to her.

Then he turned to Tai. "This needs to happen," he said crisply, quietly. "I was the prime minister's man. There is a price to be paid for a failure such as this."

"Did you have anything to do with that order? Teng Pass?"

Liu looked contemptuous. Tai knew that look. "Am I such a fool in your eyes?"

"He never spoke of it?"

"He stopped seeking my counsel on some things from the time you returned to Xinan, Second Brother." Liu's thin, superior smile. "You might say your return caused all this."

"You mean my failure to die at Kuala Nor?"

"Or Chenyao, if I understand it rightly."

Tai blinked. Stared. Anger slipped away.

Liu's smile also faded. They looked at each other, the sons of Shen Gao. "You didn't truly think I had anything to do with that?"

The sensation was so strange. Relief like a wave, and then another wave, of sorrow.

"I wondered," Tai said. "We knew it came from Wen Zhou."

Liu shook his head. "It would have made no sense. I knew how far away you were, if you were still alive. You could do nothing about Li-Mei even if you were foolish enough to want to. Why would I need you dead?"

"Why would he?" Tai looked down at the dead man beside them.

"He didn't. Which is one reason he never told me about it. It was nothing but arrogance. He did it because of the woman, and because he could."

"And Teng Pass?"

"He was afraid of Xu Bihai. Afraid the general would decide the rebellion *was* Zhou's fault and come to an arrangement with the rebels. I think he feared all soldiers." A slight smile. "Makes this morning amusing, doesn't it?"

Tai said, "That wouldn't be my word for it."

Liu flicked his fingers dismissively. "You have," he said, "no sense of irony. Listen now, and carefully." He waited for Tai to nod, an instructor confirming a student's attention.

Liu said, "The horses will save your life. Let it be said abroad— by the Kanlins, if you can do it—that I *did* try to have you killed. They won't lie, you must make them think you believe it."

"Why? Why do I need to—?"

The familiar, impatient look. "Because Shinzu is more clever than any of us suspected, and if he thinks you are linked to me ..."

"I *am* linked to you, First Brother!"

Liu's expression was impatient again. "Think. In this imperial family, brotherhood can mean hatred and murder as easily as anything else. Shinzu will know that. Tai, there is a clear path to power for you, for our family. He honours you already. He will have need of advisers, his own men, over and above your bringing the horses."

Tai said nothing. Liu didn't wait for him to speak.

"Also, the lands given you, by the Great River. A very good property, but not safe for the next while. I have no idea which way Roshan will go, but he might move south. After they take Xinan and finish killing there."

"He will allow killing in the city?"

A small headshake, as if it pained Liu that someone might not see these things. "Of course he will. Wen Zhou slew his son, and the rebel soldiers are hard men, more than half of them barbarians. Almost all of the imperial family are still in the city. They are dead when he finds them. Xinan will be a bad place for the rest of this summer at least. People will be leaving in panic. As soon as today." His voice was brisk, low, no one else could hear. The soldiers were waiting. Jian, Tai thought, was waiting.

Liu seemed to come to the same awareness. "I cannot linger to teach you," he said. "Our own estate will likely be safe for our mothers, but have an eye to them, wherever you are. Keep Shinzu content, stay as close to him as you can. If this rebellion lasts a long time, and I think it will now, there is a man in Hangdu, near our property. His name is Pang, he has only one leg, you cannot miss finding him at the market. He has been buying and storing grain for me, for our family, in a hidden barn I had built some time ago. He needs to be paid three thousand a month, the middle of every month. You are wealthy now, but there will be shortages of food. Try to keep buying. These things are yours now to look after. Do you understand, Second Brother?"

Tai swallowed. "I understand," he said. "Pang, in Hangdu."

Liu looked at him. No affection, no fear, not much of anything to be read in the soft, smooth face.

Tai said, "I am sorry for this, brother. I am … pleased to know you did not send the assassins."

Liu shrugged. "I might have, if I had thought it prudent for any reason."

"I don't think so, Liu."

A superior smile, well remembered. "You did until now."

"I know. My error. I request forgiveness."

His brother glanced away, then shrugged again. "I forgive you. What I did for our family, Li-Mei made a princess, I would do again. Tai, it was a master stroke."

Tai said nothing. His brother looked at him, then away towards the courtyard.

"So was Kuala Nor," Liu added softly.

It was suddenly difficult to speak.

"I didn't think of it that way."

"I know you didn't," said Liu. "If you can, have me buried beside father in the orchard." Another thin smile as he glanced back. "You are skilled at quieting ghosts, are you not?"

And with that, he went down the steps to the sunlit yard, drawing a jewelled court blade from the sleeve of his robe.

Tai saw him approach Jian and bow to her. The *dui* commander was the only one near them, and now he withdrew, backing away a dozen steps, as if to, belatedly, distance himself from this.

Tai saw his brother say something to Jian, too softly for anyone to hear. But he saw her smile, as if surprised, and pleased, by what she heard. She murmured something to Liu, and he bowed again.

He spoke one more time, and after a motionless instant she nodded her head. She made a dancer's spinning movement, a last one, the sort that ends a performance and releases the audience's approval and applause.

She ended it with her back to Liu, to the posting station. She faced south (her people had come from the south), towards the cypress trees lining the road and the summer fields beyond them, bright in morning light, and Tai's brother placed his left hand around her waist, to steady the both of them, and he thrust his knife cleanly into her, between ribs, into the heart, from behind.

Liu held her, gently, carefully, as she died. And then he held her a little longer, and then he laid her down on her back in the dust of that yard, because there was nothing else he could do.

He knelt beside her a moment, arranging her clothing. One of her hairpins had come loose. Tai watched his brother fix it in place again. Then Liu set down his jewelled blade and stood up and he moved a distance away from her, towards the archers of the Second Army. He stopped.

"Do it," he said. Making it his command. And was standing very straight as they sent half a dozen arrows into him.

Tai had no way of knowing if his brother's eyes were open or closed before he died. He did become aware, after a time, that Sima Zian was beside him, saying nothing, but present.

He looked out into the yard. At Liu, face down, and at Jian on her back, the blue robe spread about her, and it seemed to him that sunlight was wrong for what the moment was, what it would always be now, even as it receded. This morning brightness, the birds rising and darting, their singing.

He said that, to the poet. "Should there be birdsong?"

Zian said, "No, and yes. We do what we do, and the world continues. Somewhere, a child is being born and the parents are tasting a joy they never imagined."

"I know that," said Tai. "But *here*? Should there be so much light here?"

"No," said Sima Zian, after a moment. "Not here."

"My lords?" It was Song. Tai turned to her. He had never seen her looking as she did now. "My lords, we request your permission," she said. "We wish to kill two of them later. The commander and the first archer, the small one. Only two. But it must be done." She wiped at her cheeks.

"You have mine," said Zian, eyes gazing out upon the courtyard.

"You have mine," said Tai.

The star-cloud of her hair,
Flower-petal of her cheek,
Gold-and-jade of her jewels
When she danced …

A different poet, younger, would write that. Part of a very long verse, one that would be remembered, among all the (deservedly) forgotten ones about that morning at Ma-wai.

ON THE POSTING STATION PORCH, shaded from sunlight, two men came out a little later to stand before the soldiers.

The older one, his hands trembling, holding himself not nearly as upright as before, formally presented the younger one, his son, with the phoenix ring, in public this time, making him emperor of Kitai.

The soldiers, all of them, the posting inn servants, the Kanlins on the porch, Shen Tai, the older of the surviving sons of Shen Gao, and the poet Sima Zian, all knelt, faces to inn yard dust or wooden porch, and so became the first to pay homage to the Glorious and Exalted Emperor Shinzu of the Ninth Dynasty of Kitai, in the first year of the An Li Rebellion, just before Xinan fell.

THE NEW EMPEROR'S COMMANDS were exact, measured, appropriate. There were three dead people here. The Kanlins were asked to attend to them, with assistance from their sanctuary.

Jian would be carried to the imperial family tombs, close by. The oldest son of General Shen Gao was, after a consultation with his brother, also given to the Kanlins, with the request that his body be preserved and taken to his family's estate for burial. Word would go ahead to the family.

The body of the former first minister, Wen Zhou, was to be burned by the Kanlins on a pyre at their sanctuary, duly shrouded and with rites, but not with courtly honours. The ashes would be scattered, not preserved. The absence of ceremony was obviously— and cleverly—designed to allay the fears of the soldiers who had killed him.

The father-emperor, Taizu, who had awakened in the middle of this night as ruler of Kitai, frail-seeming, grieving and bewildered in the bright day, was to be escorted to safety in the far southwest, beyond the Great River.

In due course, it was hoped, he would recover his strength and purpose, and be brought back, with dignity, to his son's renewed court in Xinan.

The Emperor Shinzu himself would go north. He would make Shuquian, in the loop of the Golden River, his base. It had served that purpose before in Kitai. Xinan could not be held, but it could be retaken.

There was no hint of concession to the rebels in the new emperor, no flicker of doubt or surrender. An error had been made by a minister. The man (and his adviser) were dead, as required, here this morning.

The woman lying in the dust might be considered a source of regret, now and afterwards, but no one judging the matter with clarity of mind could deny that her family was at the root of this disaster. Just as women in Kitai could reap the benefit of the deeds of the men they knew, they could not be immune when those men fell.

One small incident, noted by only a handful of people in that inn yard, occurred just before Taizu re-entered his coach to be escorted from Ma-wai. An alchemist, a lean cleric of the Sacred Path, emerged cautiously from the second coach, where he had evidently remained through the violent events of the morning. He approached Taizu, bearing what was—evidently—the morning's elixir, designed to help pursue immortality.

The emperor, the former emperor, waved this man away.

Shortly afterwards, Master Shen Tai, a person of some importance now, was summoned by the new emperor into the posting station. He knelt there and was presented with another ring, pale jade—the first gift offered by Shinzu as emperor of Kitai.

Shen Tai was instructed to leave with the retired emperor for the posting station on the imperial road to Chenyao. From there, as soon as his sixty Kanlin Warriors arrived from their sanctuary, he was to proceed swiftly to Hsien, on the border with Tagur, to claim his horses and bring them safely back to Shuquian. The emperor formally requested that the Sardians be made available to the empire. Shen Tai formally acceded to this, expressing great happiness at being able to be of use to Kitai.

XINAN WAS ABOUT TO BE one of the most terrible places on earth. Tai had realized it at some point on the night ride to Ma-wai, and then his brother Liu had said the same thing to him, and his brother Liu was someone who was—who had been—brilliantly clever about courts and armies and the world.

And if this was so, if a red violence was approaching from the east, dust rising even now beneath an army's marching tread and their horses' hooves, there was a woman to be taken from the city.

Especially since that woman had been the concubine of the man who would surely be the most hated in Xinan, even before the rebels came. Vengeance could give birth to horrors not to be spoken aloud. So could fear.

One woman who had given all of them music (and more) was dead this morning, in her youth and grace. Tai wasn't ready to lose another now because of Wen Zhou.

He had always known that actions could have unintended consequences, any man's actions, of whatever rank. But sometimes events could also be shaped. Words had been spoken to soldiers by the imperial heir, on their ride from the palace. Consequences had followed.

Wen Zhou. Jian. Tai's brother. And the emperor yielding the throne that same morning to his son. Tai had knelt before the Serene and Exalted Emperor Shinzu, ruling now with the mandate of heaven, and realized he didn't know how much had been foreseen, or intended, by this man.

He didn't ever expect to know for certain.

He would do his duty. Kitai was an empire at war now, beset from within. But the Kanlins from the sanctuary could not be at the imperial highway inn before nightfall, at best. So he had a little time, though he'd have to move at speed, and probably through the night again, depending upon what he found in Xinan.

As ordered, he started from the inn yard with his own Kanlins, Taizu's carriage, and the soldiers who'd escorted their party from the palace in the night.

The other fifty men of the Second Army were going north with the new emperor. It was a great honour. Their *dui* commander had them standing in rigid, disciplined order in the courtyard, awaiting the command to set out.

Tai had watched Wei Song observing this. He thought about the idea that these men were being honoured. He said nothing. Sometimes it was better not to know the details of what might come. And he had his own task to attend to now.

A short distance from Ma-wai he reined Dynlal to a halt and in the middle of the roadway told Song and Zian and Lu Chen his intention. He didn't present it as a matter for discussion.

They all came with him. His other Kanlins stayed with Taizu and the soldiers. They'd wait at the inn for the sixty riders from the sanctuary.

Tai and three companions set out across the fields, cutting south to intersect the imperial highway. They rode through a late-summer morning and then an afternoon that ought to have registered as beautiful. High white clouds and a breeze from the west.

He was thinking of death. Behind them and at Teng Pass, and increasingly, as they rode, with a cold awareness of more to come in the days ahead.

The road system near Xinan was exceptionally good. It was rare that riders had to cross farmland or skirt the edges of what small bamboo forests remained. They found a track leading east, then another running off it south towards the highway, passing through village after village, a blurred progression.

People came out to watch them gallop through, or stopped in whatever they were doing. Riders moving so fast was unusual. Something to talk about on a quiet day. Dynlal was a glory, running easily. The other three had changed mounts at the station. Even so, he could have outstripped them had he chosen to. He almost did make that choice, but he knew he'd need them when he entered the city.

He never entered the city. He never came close to doing so.

They heard the noise, like a heavy storm or a waterfall, before they saw anything: a roar of sound as they raced up a rise in their small roadway near the highway. Then they crested that rise and saw what was happening below.

The city was emptying out, in panic. His heart aching, Tai saw the imperial road thronged with the people of Xinan, pushing west in a tumultuous mass that spilled into the drainage ditches and across them into the clogged going of the summer fields beside the road.

People were struggling with their belongings on their backs, or pulling carts with children and the elderly and their goods. The noise was punishing. At times a scream or cry would rise above it, as someone was pushed into the ditch, or fell and was trampled. If you fell you were likely to die. Progress was agonizingly slow, Tai saw, and the mass of people stretched back east as far as he could see.

He couldn't even see the city gates, they were too far away. But he could imagine them. All the gates. Word of disaster had arrived. Xinan's inhabitants were not inclined, it seemed, to wait for Roshan to come to them.

"They will starve out here," said Sima Zian softly. "And these are just this morning's vanguard. Only the beginning."

"Some will stay," said Lu Chen. "Some always stay, for their homes, their families. They will keep their heads down and hope that bloodshed passes."

"Eventually, it probably will," said Tai. "He wants to rule, doesn't he?"

"Eventually," agreed Lu Chen. "But that can seem like forever."

"Is it going to be forever, this war?"

Tai looked at Song, who had asked that, gazing down on the crawling-forward multitude on the road. She was biting her lower lip.

"No," he said. "But much will change."

"Everything?" she asked, looking at him.

"Much," he said again. "Not everything."

"Tai, we can't get into the city." It was Zian. "We must hope she received your warning and responded. But there's no way to swim against this current."

Tai looked at him, a bleakness in his heart. Then he shook his head. "Yes, we can. Swim is a good idea. We'll get in through the canals."

It *was* a good idea, but it didn't matter. Sometimes that happens.

They spent the rest of the afternoon cutting overland across fields and along small roads again, forcing their way east. Even the back roads and rutted cart tracks had crowds by late in the day, all fleeing west. It became difficult to make any headway. People cursed the four of them on their horses. If it hadn't been for the Kanlins, the respect and apprehension they engendered, they might even have been attacked. Tai fought anger and panic, aware that time was running against them.

When they finally reached a vantage point, forcing tiring horses up a ridge from which they could see Xinan's walls, he heard a voice cursing, and realized it was his own.

In the evening light, Xinan, capital of the empire, glory of the world, was spread below them. The city looked like a hive with all the insects in flight from it, pouring out of every gate, along all roads. And within the walls, they could see smoke rising.

Roshan was days away, and already Xinan was burning.

"Look at the Ta-Ming," Sima Zian said.

The palace was on fire.

"They'll be looting it," said Tai.

"Where are the guards?" Song cried.

"Looting it," Tai said wearily.

Zian murmured, "They know the emperor has fled. What could the city understand from that, other than that he's abandoned it? Abandoned them."

"He left to regroup! To gather armies. The dynasty will fight!" Song's tone revealed a great strain.

"We know that," the poet answered, gently. "But how does that help those down there, with An Li coming for them?"

Tai was looking at the canals, where they flowed lazily into the city under arches in the walls, bearing firewood and lumber, marble and other stone and heavy goods and foodstuffs on any normal day. There were substantial punishments for being found in a canal; they were known to be a weakness in the city's defences.

There were thousands of people, he saw, who had chosen to take the risk of a beating today. So many bodies were in the water, pushing, fighting their way through, bearing goods on their heads, children on their backs, or carrying nothing at all but terror and the need to get away.

People will drown, he thought.

Lu Chen lifted a hand and pointed. Tai saw a new tongue of flame within the Ta-Ming Palace.

The others sat their horses beside him on the ridge. They said nothing. They were honouring his sorrow, Tai knew, by letting him be the one to say it. To surrender the day's hopeless quest. They had come with him, and stayed by him.

He sat astride Dynlal gazing at a nightmare, or the beginnings of a nightmare. The sun was setting, its long light falling upon Xinan, making the walls seem gold. He was thinking of Rain, of green eyes and yellow hair, and a mind shrewder than his own, even in the days when he'd been immersed in his studies, trying to understand ancient courts and long-dead sages and the forms and rhythms of poetry.

He was thinking of her singing for him, of her hands in his hair, the two of them on a bed in a lamplit room.

There were so many poems over so many hundreds of years about courtesans, young or not young any more, at upper windows above jade or marble stairs, at twilight time or by moonlight, waiting for lovers to return. *The night comes, and the stars, the streets are lit by lanterns on stone walls. The nightingale cries in the garden. Still no sound of horse's hooves beneath my open window ...*

"We can't do this," he said. "We have to go back. I am sorry."

He was, for so many things, as a long summer day finally went down to the dark. They turned west again, leaving the fires behind.

IT TOOK MOST OF THE NIGHT to reach the inn on the Imperial road. The same one where he'd awakened on a morning in spring to find Song wounded and held by soldiers, and Wen Jian waiting to take him to Ma-wai.

Because they were riding, even on tired horses and off the main roads, eventually they outpaced the struggling, exhausted vanguard of refugees from Xinan. They'd made their way down to the highway. It lay open before them under moonlight, serene and beautiful.

The Kanlins from the sanctuary, sixty of them, as promised, were waiting when they reached the inn. Taizu was asleep, they reported.

Tai had Dynlal led away to be watered and rubbed down and fed. They all needed to rest, he knew it, but he was unable to sleep. He was bone-weary and heartsick.

Song and Lu Chen went off with the other Kanlins. He thought of inviting her to stay with him, he'd seen how distressed she was. He didn't feel able to offer comfort. She'd be better off with the Warriors, he thought.

Or perhaps not. He didn't know. He didn't have that much clarity in him tonight. Ma-wai, what had happened there. And Xinan on fire, with Spring Rain inside the walls. Or perhaps trapped among tens of thousands on one road or another.

He didn't know. He walked through the reception chamber of the inn. Saw frightened men standing there, unsure of what to say or think. They bowed to him. He went through into the courtyard, the garden.

A little later Zian came out and found him. Tai was sitting on a bench under a mulberry tree. The poet carried wine, and two cups. He sat down and poured and Tai drained a cup, then held it out again. Zian filled it a second time and Tai drank that, too.

The poet was a quiet, comforting presence. It felt illicit, somehow, to take comfort in anything tonight. Friendship, starlight. The night breeze.

Zian said, "You will need to rest."

"I know."

"You will leave in the morning?"

"Before sunrise. We should stay ahead of those fleeing the city." Tai looked at the other man, a shadow beside him. The leaves above blocked the moonlight. "You are coming with us?"

A short silence. Then Zian shook his head. "It may be arrogant of me, a delusion, but I believe I can do more good with the emperor. The ... father-emperor."

"Taizu can't keep up with us."

"Of course not. But he will be grieving, and he has only that fool of an alchemist with him, and soldiers. He has a long way to go and the roads are hard. Heaven's way is bent like a bow now. Perhaps an old poet can help."

"You aren't old."

"Tonight I am."

There was a silence in the garden, and then Tai heard the poet speak again, offering him a gift:

Together our spirits soared to nine heavens
But soon we will scatter like stars before rain.
I follow a fading dragon over hills and rivers.

You must journey to far borders.
Perhaps one day you will go home, my friend,
Crossing a last bridge over the River Wai.

Tai said nothing for a time. He was moved, and very tired. The wine, the words, the stillness. "I will see you again?"

"If heaven allows. I will hope so. We'll drink good wine in another garden, listening to *pipa* music."

Tai drew a breath. "I will hope so. Where ... where will you be?"

"I don't know. Where will you be, Shen Tai?"

"I don't know."

CHAPTER XXVI

Ye Lao, once under-steward to the Beloved Companion Wen Jian, was now principal household steward to the honourable and distinguished Master Shen Tai (son of the famous general). This meant, of course, that he was burdened with formal responsibility for Master Shen's quite substantial compound in Xinan in extremely uncertain times. Household stewards, without exception, preferred certainty.

Ye Lao had never endured a major rebellion or the arrival of angry soldiers in any city or palace he'd known. You heard tales about such times, you didn't live through them—if the gods in the nine heavens were kind.

They weren't always kind, of course.

Being quite good at his job, and priding himself on it, Lao refused to allow himself to be unduly frightened or flustered (and, most definitely, did not permit the household servants to see a hint of such feelings in him) until the army of An Li was actually sighted at the eastern gates of the city, seven days after the emperor and a handful of the court had fled.

At that point, as rebel soldiers began pouring into Xinan, and reports of shocking conduct reached Master Shen's compound,

Ye Lao found himself becoming slightly perturbed. *The jackals were in the city,* someone quoted, *the dragons were in the wild.*

Xinan was left open for Roshan, of course: only fools would close city gates when there were no soldiers to defend them. But this courtesy had not induced any immediate limiting of violence.

One expected, in the usual way of soldiers arriving in a civilized place, a certain amount of intoxication, destruction, looting, even killing, unnecessary though it was.

It was undoubtedly wisest to keep women out of sight, and hope the poor girls in the pleasure districts proved equal to the task of assuaging a drunken army.

About half a million citizens of Xinan had, if widespread reports were accurate, chosen to flee ahead of the rebels. They'd streamed out in all directions, trampling each other in their haste. Some had even gone east, right into the approaching storm, probably towards country homes and family, hoping to scurry north and south around the advancing army and get back to their farmland roots.

Most of those escaping went west or south. A certain number were reported to be making their way north, once word arrived that the new emperor, Shinzu (it was a difficult idea, a new emperor), was rallying the Ninth Dynasty there.

In Ye Lao's view, most of the people in flight were making a mistake.

Unless they had family in the country with room for them, an actual place to go, starvation outside Xinan was a real possibility. In fact, with so many on the move it was hard to imagine how they could all be sheltered and fed, even with family waiting.

It was assumed by those who stayed that An Li and his sons intended to establish themselves in the Ta-Ming Palace, and would therefore act in a manner befitting a self-proclaimed new dynasty.

There would be some measure of undisciplined behaviour, but that would surely be brought under control, and life in the capital would resume in acceptable fashion.

With this underlying thought in Xinan, one that he shared, it was profoundly shocking for Ye Lao to learn of wanton slaughter in the palace from the first hours, and continuing.

There were public executions in the square before the Ta-Ming's walls. It was reported that the hearts of dead members of the imperial family were being ripped out and offered as a sacrifice to the ghost of An Li's slain son. It was said that some were executed by having the tops of their heads ripped off with iron claws.

Bodies were piled in the square and it was forbidden to claim them for burial. Huge bonfires were built and men and women were burned with black, choking smoke rising, and an appalling stench. It was barbarous, in Ye Lao's view.

All mandarins found, even newly graduated lowly officials, were killed within the Purple Myrtle Court, if they hadn't had the foresight to discard their robes and belts and hide themselves in the city, or flee.

The women of the palace were, report had it, being fearfully abused. Many of Taizu's concubines and musicians were being shipped in wagons, as slaves, back towards Yenling and the rebel soldiers left behind there. Roshan knew what needed doing, to keep an army happy.

There was a widespread smashing-in of private gates, almost at random, as inebriated soldiers crashed through, spilling destruction and death. Not all of Xinan's wives and daughters—or younger boys—were successfully hidden.

There were fires everywhere in those first days.

You risked your life walking the streets in search of food. The markets were closed. Bodies lay among refuse and wild animals, smoke and yellow dust, and the smell of burning.

Word was conveyed by military heralds moving through the city that anyone offering to the new dynasty's illustrious leaders the whereabouts of children or grandchildren of Taizu—once emperor, now unmasked as a coward and having lost the mandate of heaven—any such information would be met with a reward and formal assurances of household safety.

What followed was ugly, as the hiding places of Taizu's many offspring and their children (often very young) were promptly reported, their disguises revealed. These helpless, hapless princes and princesses were, every one of them, brought to the bonfires before the Ta-Ming walls and beheaded.

Steward Ye Lao's distaste for such conduct was beyond his capacity to express. This man, An Li, had proclaimed himself an emperor? Successor to nine dynasties of glory in Kitai? Men, Lao thought grimly, were no better than beasts, they were wolves or tigers.

He kept his head up and his ears open, gathered what information he could, and ensured that the household of Master Shen remained as orderly as possible, under trying conditions. Some of the staff had fled in the first days but most had nowhere to go and had stayed, fearfully.

There was a private well in the second right-side courtyard of the compound, a pleasing indication of its importance. Lao arranged for every bucket and pail on the property to be filled and kept in readiness, should the fires one could see everywhere now reach them. He had linens soaked in water every morning.

Food was a difficult matter, but not yet impossible. After ten days Roshan allowed the markets to reopen, for those brave enough to venture forth, either to sell or to buy.

Some farmers began hesitantly coming in after that, with milk and eggs, vegetables and poultry, millet and barley, picking their way past dead bodies, and crying, abandoned children, and smouldering ruins.

Prices were high. You could call them outrageous, except that you really couldn't, under the circumstances. Ye Lao expected them to go higher.

He took thought one morning and an idea came to him, a recollection: hadn't Master Shen had an encounter with Roshan himself, on his way back to Xinan from the west? If memory served, it had been the day before Ye Lao himself (and his former mistress) had encountered Shen Tai at the posting inn on the imperial road.

He didn't know any details, and no one in the compound knew more (he asked), but on impulse—a steward's instinct based on his master's nature—Ye Lao composed a brief, careful note and had it conveyed by a terrified under-servant (one he judged expendable) to the Ta-Ming, once Roshan had ordered the killing there to stop. He was occupying the palace himself, and had probably realized he needed some people to run it.

(An experienced steward could have told him that, from the outset.)

Word was that the Phoenix Throne itself had been smashed to fragments, and the gemstones embedded in it removed, by some members of the imperial family before they'd fled. This to prevent a barbarian usurper from placing his gross body on that throne.

Ye Lao approved, quietly.

He never did learn if his note was received. There was no reply. In it he'd simply advised the palace, all who might be there serving the Revered and August Emperor An Li of the Tenth Dynasty, who owned this particular property.

He did note in the days and weeks that followed, allowing himself a small measure of satisfaction, that no soldiers came to their gates, no one smashed them open, to do what they were doing elsewhere.

It was disturbing to learn, as they did learn, what had been done to the household of the late first minister within his city compound, not far away at all, in this same ward.

As if those poor men and women had had any role in the crimes attributed to Wen Zhou. The first minister was dead, a ghost, denied honourable burial. Why would anyone feel a need to take brutal, blood-drenched vengeance on household servants, concubines, stewards?

Ye Lao was angry, a disturbing feeling for a man who prided himself on a trained steward's composure.

He continued to manage the compound as best he could through the late summer (which was hot that year, and dry, increasing the risk of fires). As the days passed, the city was slowly brought under control. Bodies were removed from the streets; a subdued, hesitant rhythm returned to the capital. The sunrise drums, the evening drums. Most of the rebel soldiers left for battlefields north and south. Shinzu appeared to be rallying the Ninth Dynasty forces against them.

In Xinan, the killings and looting diminished, if they never entirely stopped. Some of it by now was pure thievery, Lao knew, criminals using chaos for their own purposes. Every so often another member of Taizu's family would be discovered in hiding, and killed.

Ye Lao awaited instructions of any kind, though without any real confidence that they'd come. He had no idea if Master Shen was even alive. He knew he'd left the city—he'd watched him go, in the middle of a night. He did think, perhaps too trustingly, that they'd have heard if he were dead, even with the empire fractured by war. They'd learned of other deaths, for example—including that of the first minister and the Lady Wen Jian.

That news had come right at the outset, after the emperor fled, well before Roshan's arrival. To Ye Lao, the tidings had, for many reasons, brought great sadness.

Over time he heard that there were poems being written about her passing. A brightness fallen from the world, a star returning to the heavens, words to such effect.

Ye Lao had no ear for poetry. On the other hand, later in what turned out to be a very long life, he would tell stories about her, warming himself on winter nights with the glow in people's eyes when they understood that he'd served Wen Jian, that he'd knelt before her, been spoken to, kissed the hem of her robe.

She had passed into legend by then.

Back in that summer when the rebels came, his task, as he came to understand it, was straightforward: to preserve order in one small place, one household, in a world that had lost all sense of order or claim to being civilized.

He didn't give it a great deal of thought, caught up in his day-to-day tasks, but one morning, in autumn, it suddenly came to him that the men and women here in Master Shen Tai's compound trusted him completely, relied upon him, were doing whatever he ordered, for reasons that went beyond rank or deference.

He was keeping them alive.

കൈ

Most nights now Rain awakens afraid, disturbed by sounds that turn out to be nothing at all, whether they are in some small inn on the road or a larger one in a city, as now.

She doesn't like being so fearful, it isn't how she thinks of herself, but the times are very dangerous, and she knows she isn't the only one feeling this way.

She is alive to feel anything at all—and she's acutely aware of this—only because of a note sent in the middle of the night, and because two men turned out to be loyal beyond anything she might have expected.

And because of the Kanlins, of course.

Perhaps, also, her own decisiveness, but when she looks back at that night it doesn't seem to her that she'd felt decisive. She had been panicked as much as anything, acted on impulse, instinct. Fear.

Small things, a difference in her own mood that night, a message not sent, or lost, or not delivered until morning (by which time it would have been impossible to get away). Smallest differences: living or dying. Such thoughts could keep you awake at night.

They now know, here in Chenyao to the west, a little of what happened in Xinan after they left. The two Kanlins, still with her, have ways of discovering information even in wartime. A time when letters go astray, when posting inn horses are all claimed by the army, when news of any kind is worth a fortune.

In particular, they have learned what took place in the city compound of the recently deceased first minister, Wen Zhou, when the rebel army arrived in the capital.

Is it so surprising, really, if she startles awake at alarming sounds in the dark, or never even falls asleep?

It is the narrowness of survival, of her being here and alive, that unsettles as much as anything. That, and the awareness of how many are dead, and how savagely. She knows names, remembers faces. It is impossible not to think about what would have been done to her, as favoured concubine. There are sickening stories, worse than anything ever heard about the barbarians beyond Kitai's borders.

She is *from* beyond those borders. Sardia is a beleaguered little kingdom that has always known warfare and contended with invasion. Even so, Rain has never heard tales such as those that come to them from Xinan.

Xinan, which lies behind her only because Tai sent a note in the middle of the night. He'd been summoned to the palace—she understands that from the Kanlins. Wen Zhou had been sent for as well.

That was what had put her on edge that night. He'd been with her when the message came. Sitting up in bed, watching him read it by the light of a quickly lit lamp, Rain had understood that this wasn't any routine summons to the Ta-Ming. Those didn't come at this hour, and they didn't shake him so profoundly.

He'd dressed in haste and left immediately with guards, saying nothing—nothing—to her, to anyone. Also disturbing. He'd burned the note, or she'd have retrieved it and read it as soon as she was alone.

Some time later—the passage of time that night is blurred—Hwan had come with another message, this one addressed to her.

He might so easily have waited until morning. That would have made all the difference. Or the note might not have reached her at all.

It had been carried by Qin, the crippled beggar in the street.

She understood, and it humbled her even now, that he had entrusted it to no one. Had paid coins to a drunken tradesman (and why had *he* been in the street, passing by, so late?) to carry him—*carry* him—all the long way around to the front gates of the compound. And he'd stayed there, painfully on his feet, banging at the gates and shouting, until someone had sleepily, angrily come.

And then he'd demanded, loudly, fiercely, without backing down, that Hwan be brought to him, and no one else but Hwan.

And, improbably (another source of fear in her imagining those moments), they hadn't beaten him and turned him away. Hwan, awake since the master had ridden out, had come to see what the disturbance was.

The disturbance.

He had accepted the note, hand passing it to hand, and brought it to her. Immediately, not waiting for morning. Perhaps he'd known she'd be awake. Perhaps he'd been frightened. She's never asked, though he's been with her all the way here, to Chenyao.

So has Qin.

She can't say with certainty why she kept them with her, but it had seemed proper, it had seemed ... needful. As she'd read Tai's note, Rain felt some inner imperative overtaking her.

Possible danger. Be very alert, he'd written.

Alert meant remembering Zhou's face as he read the summons from the palace, as he burned it, as he went away. No good night, or goodbye.

You could describe the first minister in many ways, but he had never been a coward—and he'd looked afraid that night. And Rain had already had enough of a feeling of danger to have hidden jewels in the garden.

It had been enough—she remembers now, in Chenyao, middle of another night, late summer. All these things together, and a sense (her mother had also had it) of when something decisive needed to be done.

Decisive. There'd been only one action she could take. Like a gambler throwing dice in a late-night game in the pleasure district, staking everything he owned.

She'd been a little unkind to Hwan then, trading upon his love for her, the love she'd nurtured for her own reasons. On the other hand, she'd almost certainly saved his life.

Her instructions had been precise, much more assured than she'd felt. Inside, she'd been terrified. He was ordered to go out the gates alone. He was to find a sedan chair in the streets of the ward—there were always one or two of them, even late at night, bearers ready to carry someone to an assignation, or home from one.

He was to get the beggar, Qin, into that sedan chair, and lead it around to the back of the property.

Hwan's eyes had widened, she remembers.

He was to do this immediately, she'd said coldly, or never find favour in her sight again. If he did do this, she'd said, looking straight at him by the light of the lantern, wearing her night robe, he would find very great favour.

He'd left to do as she'd said.

She rose and dressed by herself, moving quickly now that a decision had been made, as if speed could overmaster second thoughts. The gods alone knew what was to come, but if she was wrong about this she was unlikely to live through the day.

She took more gems from the chest in the room. There was no point leaving them. She walked back alone through the vast and silent garden, past the lake and isle and the small, moored boats and the bamboo grove and the grassy space where Wen Zhou had played at games with others of the court. The path wound through night flowers. She breathed their scent.

She came to the gazebo, found the tree where she'd hidden that small bag. She claimed it (dirtying her hands) and then she climbed the wall herself, using the elm tree at the eastern end.

She'd learned how to climb as a girl in Sardia, had been good at it, better than most boys, treating a skinned knee or elbow as a mark of honour. She still has a scar on her left knee. There'd been little call for climbing in the North District, or here at the compound, but some things the body remembered.

The two Kanlins appeared out of shadow as she dropped down into the street. She hadn't doubted for a moment that they'd be there.

"I am leaving now," she said. "Because of the message you brought. Will you stay with me?"

They had stayed with her.

They'd done more than that, through the flight west. For one thing, it was the Kanlins who had gotten them out of the ward in the night. No gate official was going to deny them. It brought bad luck, at the very least. The understanding was, if the black-clad ones were abroad they had reason to be, and so did those they were escorting. That was the way of things.

Because of this, they'd made it all the way across Xinan and to the western gate, were right there before curfew's end opened the city. While they waited for sunrise and the drums Rain had Hwan arrange a carriage, and two good horses for the Kanlins.

With the coming of morning they were out of Xinan, moving along the western road against the flow of traffic coming in with goods for the markets. They bought food as they went, wine, millet cakes, dried meat, peaches. Hwan had brought cash. She didn't ask where he'd gotten it. Her jewels weren't going to help until they reached a market town. You didn't buy boiled eggs or barley cakes with amber earrings set in gold.

She was to understand later that they had been able to leave the city only because they'd moved so quickly, were out and going west before word spread of the disaster at Teng Pass. And with it, tidings of the emperor's flight.

Later that day the capital learned of these events, and Ma-wai, and panic erupted in the city, choking every gate and every road with terrified people in flight.

Rain and her party had left the imperial road by then. She'd decided there were too many people who might know her at the well-known posting inn on the road. It was used by the court, which meant by people who might have visited the Pavilion of Moonlight Pleasure House.

They branched off, found another east-west road, kept going all day along that. Stopped the first night at a small inn near a silk farm.

Rain never knew it, no one can ever know such things, but had they stayed on the imperial highway, stopped at the posting inn that first night, her own life, and the lives of many others might have been different, going forward.

This is a reason why we sometimes feel as though existence is fragile, precarious, that a random wind can blow, changing everything. They might have gone to the inn on the imperial road—it was an impulsive thought to leave the road. She might not have been able to sleep, could easily have risen to walk in the garden late, and seen two men in conversation on a bench under a mulberry tree ...

THE KANLINS KEPT THEM moving quickly, staying on secondary roads. They changed horses each day until horses became hard to come by. One evening a discussion was started, courteously, by the older of the two. His name was Ssu Tan. They wished to know whether she intended to continue west, or planned to go south, or even north. A perfectly good question.

But it meant she needed to have an idea where she was going.

She'd chosen Chenyao, told them so that night, as much to name a destination as anything else. It was close, by then, large enough to let them melt into the city, sell some jewels. It had roads leading in all directions, was accustomed to travellers coming through, often from far away.

People had stories in Chenyao, and they didn't have to tell them.

When they arrived, Hwan negotiated the lease of a good-sized house, with a staff to run it. He was apparently skilled at such bargaining, but it had also helped, Rain knows, that both Kanlins went with him and were standing by. No one was inclined to offend the black-clad ones in any possible way, and someone who had two of them serving her was not to be troubled.

An uncharacteristic lack of energy or will had settled on Rain from the time they took the city house. She knew it, knows it tonight, weeks later, lying awake.

She has no clear (or even vague) idea what to do next. Along with everyone else—Chenyao is crowded with refugees from Xinan and elsewhere now—they watch the movements of soldiers from the west and northwest, passing through, riding or marching, grim-faced. Some of the faces seem very young to Rain.

Armies are moving all through Kitai this summer.

They seize on news, or the rumour of news. Qin spends mornings in the market begging for coins, though it is hardly necessary. But he finds that people talk to a crippled beggar and he learns almost as much as the Kanlins do through their own channels.

Rain has never asked what these channels are. She's too grateful for their presence, unwilling to intrude. At night they gather and share what they know.

They know that the Ta-Ming Palace had seen wholesale slaughter, as did much of Xinan. That it is quieter in the capital now, but strange, tense, a city under occupation. Crouched against another blow, someone said.

They know that the Emperor Taizu is now the father-emperor, reportedly heading southwest, beyond the Great River. Shinzu rules them now, although Xinan and Yenling are held by the rebels, which makes it a fair question if anyone can be said to rule Kitai.

There was a battle in the northwest, not far from the Long Wall. Depending on who tells the tale, it was a victory against the rebels, or a victory for them.

They have known from near the outset of their journey that Zhou is dead, and Jian.

Awake at night again because some animal has screamed in the street, Rain thinks about war, the boys' faces seen in the army ranks, about Kitai, this land that she came to years ago with her *pipa*, her yellow hair and green eyes, and so young.

In summer darkness, stars in her south-facing window, she makes—or accepts—a decision in her heart. There is fear again with it, and sorrow, but also a kind of easing of disquiet and distress, which is what acceptance is said to bring, is it not?

With that, it seems her clarity returns, the sense that she can sort matters through, make plans, a choice and then the next one. For one thing, none of the four men with her is to be burdened with this. It is her decision, and is to be hers alone, she thinks.

She falls asleep.

IN THE MORNING, when the men are out and about, in the market, buying goods for the household, pursuing information, she has one of the servants call a sedan chair and she makes her way to a merchant's place of business, alone.

It is almost certain that he cheats her on the price he offers for a jade necklace and a golden brooch in the shape of a dragon, but she doesn't think he's been outrageously dishonest, perhaps intimidated by her manner and a casually dropped reference to Kanlins awaiting her at home.

She makes one other stop, conducts another negotiation, and is back at the house before the others.

That evening, in her chamber, she calls for brush and ink and paper and, some time later, by lantern light, writes a single message addressed to the four of them.

Chenyao, she suggests, is a good place for Hwan to remain for now. He and Qin will have money (the point of this morning's first transaction) to keep the house, to buy food, to live ... if the war does not last forever.

The Kanlins, she knows, will not accept money from her. They were hired and paid by Wen Jian. It is another strangeness for Rain, that these two—who have meant so much to her this summer, who have saved her life—she owes not just to Tai (whom she is leaving now) but to the Precious Consort, who is dead.

She thanks them by name: Ssu Tan, and the younger one, Zhong Ma. She asks them to accept her gratitude and to convey it to the leaders at their sanctuary. And also, if they will be so very kind, to convey that same gratitude, and farewell, to Master Shen Tai, who sent them to her, should they encounter him again.

There is sadness, and she doesn't write this part quickly, or easily. But what woman has ever been promised a life, has ever lived a life, without sadness? And at least she is not sitting above jade stairs in moonlight, waiting, waiting while life recedes.

He had asked her not to do that when he went home after his father died. He had ended up at Kuala Nor among the ghosts. She had ended up with Wen Zhou.

Or, no, she thinks. She has ended up here.

She finishes writing and puts the brush aside, blows on the letter until the ink dries. She leaves it on the writing table and she rises and takes the money she's received today and places most of it on the table.

They will be all right, she thinks. If the war does not last too long.

She looks out her window. Sees summer stars. It is time. She has not changed into her night robe. She is not going to sleep. She'll need to be quiet, leaving, but the sedan chair she hired ought to be outside the door by now, and the household is accustomed to her restlessness. It ought to be all right.

She takes the part of the cash she's kept back for herself, and the small bag with the jewellery she will need for a journey. A long journey. A hard one. She's hired two guards, paid them a third of the negotiated fee, and she's arranged to join a good-sized group leaving at sunrise. The two guards are her contribution to their safety. That is how these things are done.

There are always parties of one sort or another leaving Chenyao. The leaders of this one seemed to know what they were about, talking with her this morning, which is good. It is not truly safe, of course, especially not now, and for a woman, but the world never is. She wishes she had her *pipa*, a distracted thought.

Perhaps she'll find one on the way. It is time to go. She crosses the floor silently and opens her door to the dark hallway. She will need to step over the third step on the stairway down, she remembers. It creaks. She'd tested for that earlier today.

As it happens, it doesn't matter.

All four of them are in the corridor. Hwan, Qin, both Kanlins. They are dressed to travel.

"Ah, good," says Ssu Tan. "We had just decided to wake you. The chair has been outside for some time. We have to go, if we are to join the caravan before it leaves."

Her mouth is open. Hwan is holding, shielding with his hand, a single candle. She can see their faces. Amazingly, all of them are smiling.

Rain says, "You can't … this isn't a journey I can ask any of you to take!"

"You didn't ask," says Qin. When he has a wall to lean against, he can stand for a time. "We have chosen."

"You can't!" she says again. "Do you even know where I'm going?"

"Of course we do," says Ssu Tan. "We thought you'd decide this some time ago. We talked about it."

"You … you talked about what I'd decide?" She would like to be angry.

Hwan says, quietly, "We talked about what *we'd* do, my lady, once you made your decision."

The younger Kanlin, Zhong Ma, has said nothing. His eyes have never left her, and he's still smiling.

"But I'm going to Sardia!" she cries.

"You are going home," says Ssu Tan.

"But it isn't *your* home."

"It isn't," he agrees. "But Zhong Ma and I had you entrusted to our care, and it would shame us both to let you slip away."

"You have no duty once I leave Kitai!" she says. She's begun to cry, however, which makes it difficult to fight well.

"Not so," says Zhong Ma, quietly.

Tan smiles. "You may argue as to Kanlin duties once we're on the road. We will have much time, I believe."

"It is the Tarkan Desert," Rain says, despairingly. "People die there!"

"The more reason for us to be with you," says Hwan. And then, "We bought you a *pipa* in the market this morning. For the journey."

IT TAKES HALF A YEAR, a little more, the Silk Road journey through the deserts and then up the narrow, climbing mountain passes to Sardia. They do not die. She almost certainly would have, without them. Qin, it emerges, can ride a camel.

They are attacked twice, the attackers are beaten off. There are sandstorms. The second of these costs Ssu Tan his right eye, but there is a physician with them (the party leader is experienced) and he applies an ointment and gauze bandages and Tan survives. He wears a patch over the eye after that. Rain tells him it makes him look like a bandit from ancient days.

He and Zhong Ma no longer wear their black robes by then. They had removed them after they passed through the third and last of the garrisons in the Kanshu Corridor. At that point, really, they had left the empire behind.

Around that same time she'd made another decision.

"My name is Saira," she told them.

There is a taste in her mouth like spring cherries, saying it. All of them use it, or refer to her that way, surprisingly easily, from then on.

At the end of the very long road, burnt and weary, they arrive past the end of sand and rock to high, green pastureland surrounded by mountains. When she sees the horses for the first time, the Heavenly Horses (they still frighten her a little), she knows she is home.

It has been nine years. Her mother and father are alive. All but one of her brothers and sisters. There is little of glitter and jade, but less dust and noise, entirely. Merchants go both ways, east and often west now (new powers rising there). Over time she is able to sell, piece by piece, her jewels. Kitan work is highly valued west of here, she learns. The sky is blue and the mountain air is entirely unlike what she'd learned to live with in Xinan, with the yellow wind blowing and two million souls.

There are young children in her own family, amazingly. There is music. She teaches herself not to be afraid of horses, and eventually she rides one, a moment never to be lost. There is sadness, there are memories.

Qin stays, is made welcome in her father's home at first, and then in hers. Hwan stays. She is wealthy enough to need a steward to run a household.

Zhong Ma goes home. He is young, proud of his journey, and of being a Kanlin. She gives him a letter to carry back. It takes her time to write this one. Sadness, memory.

Ssu Tan stays. She marries him. One of their children, a green-eyed girl, though with darker hair than her mother, is gifted beyond words at learning music. She masters all twenty-eight tunings of the *pipa* before she is twelve years old.

The world, Saira thinks, through her days, can bring you surprising gifts.

CHAPTER XXVII

He had not been happy in that small fort above Kuala Nor, but Bytsan sri Nespo could not truthfully say that his self-described "flanking manoeuvre" to get away from there had improved his life yet.

His idea for dealing with the horses given to the Kitan had been approved. He'd been promoted and was now understood to have had direct communication with the palace in Rygyal, which was useful, obviously. He was in a far larger fortress now.

On the other hand, he had no clear role in the chain of command here, which was awkward and made him disliked. He outranked longer-serving officers, but he was here only to await one specific person, or message, from across the border.

He also knew, each morning and through each day and into each long summer evening, what his father thought of all this.

Principally, because his father was the commander of Dosmad Fortress. Dosmad, where Bytsan was posted to await the possible arrival of a Kitan gifted with an absurd number of Sardian horses.

Bytsan hadn't known who had just been made fortress commander here when he'd offered his clever suggestion about the

Sardians. One of the (many) unfortunate aspects of having been in such an isolated fort.

It was an unhappy surprise.

His father entirely and unreservedly disapproved of the royal gift. He thought it was an act of decadent folly. But since it was impossible in Tagur, even for a high-ranking officer, to say anything like that, Fortress Commander Nespo discharged his ire on his own worthless son, who happened to be serving under him now, and who had evidently proposed amendments to the gift, making it more likely to happen.

The horses were here at Dosmad, in large pens outside the walls. They needed to be fed and watered, ridden regularly, monitored for health. To send defective horses east would reflect badly upon Tagur, Commander Nespo had been caused to understand, and this, in turn, might have implications for him, nearing retirement.

A small army of men had arrived with the horses to discharge these duties, adding to the burdens of a fortress commander. He'd placed his son in charge of them. It was beneath Bytsan's new rank, but the Sardians were the only reason for his son's promotion, so he could make sure their hooves and diet were tended to and the shit and mud brushed off them when they rolled in it. He could do it himself, for all Nespo cared. In fact, he'd have preferred it that way. He'd said that to Bytsan.

It was easy to blame his son for all of this: Bytsan had been the one to propose to the court that they hold the horses here.

As far as Nespo sri Mgar was concerned, it was a foolish idea added to a foolish gift. The thing to do, if you *had* to go through with this, would have been to dump all two hundred and fifty of them on the Kitan at Kuala Nor and let him do what he could to get them back to wherever he wanted them. If the horses were stolen or scattered, grew sick, or died on the way, so much the better for Tagur, in Nespo's view.

You didn't give Sardian cavalry horses to a once enemy who might be a future enemy. You didn't *do* that. And he wasn't going to listen to anyone, especially his hopeless son, going on about the treaty signed after Kuala Nor, or honouring the wishes of the so-lovely princess they'd been so kindly granted by the eternally untrustworthy Kitans.

In fact, Nespo had declared to his son one evening earlier in the summer, this whole business of the princess and the horses might be part of Kitai's intricate plotting.

Bytsan, who was far too modern in his thinking and too inclined to disagree if his father said the sun was shining at noon on a blue-sky day, had said, "After twenty years? Long time to hatch a plot. I think you're too much afraid of them."

Nespo had thrown him out of his chambers for that.

He did that often, throwing Bytsan out. He'd call him back the next night, or the one after if he'd been really angered, because ... well, because this was his son, wasn't it? And because not every last thing he said was foolish.

It was possible, just, for an old army officer in Tagur to accept that the world was changing. He didn't have to like it, mind you.

And he wasn't sure how he felt when messengers came from across the border in late summer, two riders under a banner of peace, to say that the Kitan from Kuala Nor had come for his horses—which meant his clever son had been proven right.

THEY MET, with half a dozen attendants each, on open ground near a stand of elm trees. The hilly country between Dosmad Fortress and the prefecture town of Hsien was one of the places of relatively open land between Kitai and the Taguran Plateau.

Shen Tai, he saw, riding up to where the other man was already waiting, had Kanlin Warriors as his escort. It surprised Bytsan a little, how pleased he was to see the other man.

Nespo had wanted his son to wear armour—he was enormously proud of Taguran linked-mail, better than anything in Kitai—but Bytsan had declined. It was a hot, humid day, they weren't going into battle, and he'd be embarrassed if the Kitan decided he was wearing the armour for show.

Shen Tai dismounted first, from Dynlal. It affected Bytsan to see his own horse again, looking well cared for.

The Kitan walked forward. He stopped and bowed, hand over fist. Bytsan remembered this about him. He swung down from the saddle and did the same thing, not caring what his own soldiers thought. Shen Tai had done it first, hadn't he? And the two of them had shared a night in a cabin among the dead.

He said, in Kitan, "You haven't had your fill of Kanlins?" He grinned.

The other man smiled a little. "That one was false, these aren't. I am pleased to see you again."

"I am pleased you survived."

"Thank you."

They walked together, a little apart from their escorts. It was a heavy day, a chance of rain, which was needed.

Shen Tai said, "Dynlal is beyond magnificent. Would you like him back?"

They could do that to you, the Kitan—or some of them could. Bytsan shook his head. "He was a gift. I am honoured that he pleases you."

"You have chosen three horses from the herd?"

Bytsan had done so, of course. Hadn't been shy, either.

He said, "I'm afraid I took three of the best."

Shen Tai smiled again, though there was an odd feeling that smiling came hard for him. Bytsan looked more closely, and wondered.

The other man registered the gaze.

He made a jest, too deliberately. "Ah, well, how would a Taguran know a good horse?"

Bytsan allowed himself to smile back. But now that he'd noticed it, it was obvious that even with the Kitan skill at hiding their thoughts, Shen Tai had changed since he'd left the lake.

Well, why shouldn't he have?

"Did you find out who tried to kill you?" he asked.

He saw the other man stiffen, hesitate.

"You were there," said Shen Tai, too lightly. "The false Kanlin did."

It was a rebuff. Bytsan felt himself flushing, humiliated. He turned away, to hide it.

TAI REGRETTED HIS WORDS as soon as he spoke them. He hesitated again, this was difficult. The other man was Taguran, and Kitai was in the midst of a rebellion.

He took a breath. He had decided to trust this man, back by the lake. He said, "Forgive me. That was a shameful answer. But I have not talked of this with anyone."

"Don't force yourself to—"

"It was Wen Zhou, the first minister, who sent that assassin. And there were others on the road. As you thought there might be."

He saw the Taguran, broad-shouldered, tanned by the summer sun, turn to look at him. There was no one nearby, which was good. Tai heard a distant roll of thunder. There would be rain.

"The first minister of Kitai hates you that much?"

"He hated me that much," Tai said.

"He doesn't, any more?"

"He's dead."

And if that told the Tagurans something they hadn't yet learned, so be it. They were going to learn it, and it might as well be this man, his ... well, his friend, who relayed the news.

Bytsan was staring. "This may be known in Rygyal, but I'm not certain it is."

"There was an uprising in the northeast," Tai said. "First Minister Wen Zhou accepted the blame for allowing it."

That was enough for now, he thought.

"And he was killed?"

Tai nodded.

"So ... you aren't in danger?"

"No more than any man in difficult days."

"But did ... were you honoured by the emperor? As you deserved to be?"

"I was. I thank you for making it possible."

It was true, of course. Tai had wealth, a great deal of property, and access to power if he wanted it. Though the emperor who had given him these things was travelling somewhere south of here, even now, towards the Great River, and he didn't rule Kitai any more.

You didn't need to tell all the truth, not with armies moving.

"And you?" he asked. "You are not in your fortress any more. This is good?"

"Mostly so. I am at Dosmad, obviously. My ... my father is the commander."

Tai looked at him. "Did you know that he ...?"

"Am I so obviously a fool? He'd just been transferred."

"This is not good?"

Bytsan sri Nespo shook his head so gloomily, Tai laughed.

"I'm sorry," he said. "Fathers and sons ..."

"I blame you," said the Taguran wryly. And suddenly they seemed to be as they'd been during a long night by the lake.

"I am your friend," said Tai with exaggerated seriousness. "One role of friends is to accept such blame unquestioningly."

He was jesting, but the other man didn't smile.

After a moment, Tai added, "I know that this has also changed your life."

The other nodded. "Thank you," he said. Bytsan looked at the clouds overhead. "I can bring the Sardians by late today, or tomorrow morning, if that suits better."

"Tomorrow suits very well. I will have sixty Kanlins with me. They will have weapons, they always have them, but they are only here to lead and guard the horses. Please tell your men not to be alarmed."

"Why would a Kitan alarm a Taguran soldier?"

Tai grinned.

Bytsan smiled back. "But I will let them know." The Taguran hesitated again. "What are you doing with the horses?"

Given the circumstances they'd shared, a fair question. Tai shrugged. "The only thing that made sense, in the end ... I've offered them to the emperor."

He didn't have to *name* the emperor, he thought. But he suddenly pictured Bytsan some weeks from now, learning the truth, realizing that Tai had …

"You do know," he said abruptly, "that Emperor Taizu has withdrawn from the Phoenix Throne in favour of his son?"

They wouldn't know. Not here, not yet.

Bytsan's mouth opened, showing his missing tooth. "Which son?" he asked quietly.

"Third Son. The heir. Shinzu of the Ninth Dynasty is emperor of Kitai now, may he rule a thousand years."

"Has … has a message gone to Rygyal?"

"I do not know. Perhaps. If you send word swiftly, it might come from you. It is all recent, I came here quickly."

Bytsan stared at him again. "This may be a gift you are giving me."

"A small one, if it is."

"Not so small, being the one with world-changing tidings."

"Perhaps," Tai said again. "If so, I am pleased for you."

Bytsan was still looking closely at him. "Are you pleased about the change?"

Near to the bone this time. "A man in my position, or yours … who are we to be happy or unhappy about what happens in palaces?" Tai suddenly wanted a cup of wine.

"But we are," said Bytsan sri Nespo. "We always have thoughts on these changes."

"Perhaps eventually," said Tai.

The other man glanced away. "So you will take the Sardians to the new emperor? You will serve him, with them?"

And it was in that moment—in a meadow by the border with Tagur, under a heavy sky with thunder to the south—even as he opened his mouth to answer, that Tai realized something.

It made his heart begin to pound, so abrupt was the awareness, so intense.

"No," he said quietly, and then repeated it. "No. I'm not."

Bytsan looked back at him, waiting.

Tai said, "I'm going home."

Then he added something else, a thought he hadn't even known he'd been carrying until he heard his voice speaking it.

The Taguran listened, holding Tai's gaze. After a moment he nodded his head, and said, also quietly, something equally unexpected.

They bowed to each other and parted—until the next morning, it was agreed, at which time the Heavenly Horses of the west, the gift of the White Jade Princess, would be brought over the border to Kitai.

LOOKING BACK, Tai would name that day as another of those that changed his life. Paths branching, decisions made. Sometimes, you did have a choice, he thought.

Riding back from the meeting with Bytsan he understood, yet again, that he'd already made a decision within, he'd only needed to acknowledge it, say it, bring it into the world. He felt a quiet within, as they rode. He hadn't felt this way, he realized, since leaving Kuala Nor.

But this awareness—that all he wanted to do now was go home to his two mothers and his younger brother and his father's grave, and Liu's by now—was not the only thing that would emerge from that day and night by the border.

The storm came that afternoon.

The heavy stillness of the air, silence of birds, had foretold it. When it broke over them, lightning lacerating the southern sky, thunder cracking like the anger of gods, they were blessedly under a roof in the trading station and inn between Hsien and the border.

In times of peace, and there had been twenty years of peace now, Tagur and Kitai did trade, and this was one of the places where it happened.

As rain drummed on the roof and thunder boomed and snarled, Tai drank cup after cup of unexceptional wine, and did the best he could to fend off a verbal assault.

Wei Song was rigid with fury, had even enlisted Lu Chen to join her attack—and the very experienced leader of Tai's Kanlins, however respectful he remained, wasn't diffident about agreeing with her.

Song was less respectful. She called him a fool. He had made what appeared to be a mistake, had told the two of them his intentions. He was going home; the Kanlins would take the horses to the emperor.

"Tai, you cannot do this! Later, yes. Of course, yes. But not until you have taken the Sardians to him yourself! He needs to see *you*!"

She'd just called him by his name, which she never did.

Another hint that she was genuinely upset. As if he needed more evidence. He pushed a cup of wine across the wooden table to her. She ignored it. Her eyes were fierce. She was very angry.

"I am touched that a Kanlin Warrior should care so much about her employer's choices," he said, trying for a lighter tone.

She swore. She never did that, either. Lu Chen looked startled.

"You aren't my employer any more!" Song snapped. "We were hired by Wen Jian, or did you forget?"

There was another roll of thunder, but it was north of them now, the storm was passing. "She's dead," he said. He was somewhat drunk, he realized. "They killed her at Ma-wai."

He looked at the two Kanlins across the table. They were alone in the dining space of the inn, on long benches at a rough table. They had eaten already. The sun would be setting, but you couldn't see it. A hard rain had been pounding down, it seemed to be lessening now. Tai felt sorry for the Kanlins who'd gone back to Hsien to bring the rest of the company. They would claim the horses in the morning and start them north.

Sixty Kanlins would. Not Tai.

He was going home. *Crossing a last bridge over the River Wai.*

He thought for a moment. "Wait. If you're paid by Jian, then you aren't being paid any more. You don't even owe me ..."

He trailed off, because Song looked extremely dangerous suddenly. Lu Chen lifted an apologetic hand.

He nodded to Chen, who said, "It is not so, my lord. The Lady Wen Jian presented our sanctuary with a sum of money to ensure you ten Kanlin guards for ten years."

"*What?* That's ... it makes no sense!" He was shaken, again.

"Since when," said Song icily, "do the women of a court have to act in ways that make sense? Is extravagance such a startling thing? I'd have thought you'd learned that lesson by now!"

She really wasn't speaking respectfully. Too upset, Tai decided. He decided he would forgive her.

"Have more wine," he said.

"I do not want wine!" she snapped. "I want you to have some sense. You aren't a member of the court yet! You *have* to be more careful!"

"I don't want to be a member of the court, that's the whole ... that's the point!"

"I know that!" she exclaimed. "But take the horses to the emperor first! Bow nine times, accept his thanks. *Then* decline a position because you feel a son's need to go home to protect his family, with a father and older brother dead. He will honour that. He has to honour that. He can make you a prefect or something and let you go."

"He doesn't have to do anything," Tai said. Which was true, and she knew it.

"But he will!"

"Why? Why will he?"

And amidst her fury, and what was also clearly fear, Tai saw a flicker of amusement in her eyes. Song shook her head. "Because you aren't very useful to him in a war, Tai, once he has your horses."

Using his name again. She sat very straight, looking at him. Lu Chen pretended to be interested in wine stains on the table wood.

Anger for a moment, then rue, then something else. Tai threw up both hands in surrender, and began to laugh. The wine, mostly, although wine could take you towards rage, too. Another crack of thunder, moving away.

Song didn't smile at his amusement. She stared angrily back at him. "Think it through," she said. "Master Shen, please think it through." At least she was back to addressing him properly.

She went on, "The emperor knows your brother was with Wen Zhou. That puts you under suspicion."

"He knows Zhou tried to kill me, too."

"Doesn't matter. It isn't Wen Zhou, it is your brother, his death. Your feeling about that. And Jian's. He knows she paid for your guards. For us."

Tai stared at her.

Song said, "He will remember that you were on the ride from Xinan, when he spoke to the soldiers about Teng Pass and caused what happened at Ma-wai."

"We don't know he did that!" Tai exclaimed.

He looked around, to be sure they were alone.

"Yes, we do," said Lu Chen softly. "And we also know it was almost certainly the right thing to do. It was necessary."

"Sima Zian thought so, too!" said Song. "If he were here he would say it, and you would listen to him! Shinzu needed Zhou dead, and could have foreseen what would happen to Wen Jian after, and even his father's reaction to her death. The empire *needed* a younger emperor to fight Roshan. Who can deny it?"

"I don't want to believe he intended all that," said Tai, gripping his wine cup.

The problem, the real problem, was that he *did* see it as possible. He had been thinking that way himself through that terrible day. And the thoughts had not left him since.

He looked at the two Kanlins. He drew a breath and said, quietly, "You are right. But that is one of the reasons I'm not going north. I accept that what you say may be true. I even accept that those are deeds men must do at court, in power, if they are to guide the empire, especially in wartime. But it is ... I do not accept it for my own life."

"I know that," said Song, in a quieter voice. "But if you are to pull away, to remain safe and not under suspicion, you need to bring him the horses first and be seen to bow, wearing the ring he gave you. The emperor has to see you are not hiding from him. Hear you petition for leave to go. Decide he trusts you."

"She is right, my lord," said Lu Chen.

"Master Sima would agree with me," Song repeated.

Tai glared at her. "Master Sima has never in his life held any position at—"

"I know," she interrupted, though gently. "But he would still agree with me. Shen Tai, take the horses north, then beg him to let you go home as your reward."

"And if he refuses?"

She bit her lip. Looked young again, suddenly.

"I don't know. But I know I'm right," she said defiantly.

HE HAD CALLED for a writing table, paper and ink, brushes, lamps for · his room.

The storm had passed. His window faced south, which meant good fortune; his was the best room, at the end of the long hallway upstairs. He'd pushed the shutters back. The air was sweet and mild, the heat broken by the rain. Tai heard the sound of water dripping from the projecting eaves. The sun was almost down when he began writing.

It was a difficult letter. He started with a full salutation, impeccably formal, summoning everything he'd learned about this while studying for the examinations. First missive to a new emperor, explaining why he was not coming back as instructed. Because his small Kanlin guard wasn't the only defiant person at this inn.

He employed every imperial title he could remember. He used his most careful calligraphy. This was a letter that could decide his life.

Because of that, he even invoked Li-Mei, thanking the imperial family, the Ninth Dynasty, for the great honour done his father's only daughter. Of course, that expression of gratitude was also a reminder that the Shen family was linked to the dynasty, and could surely be considered loyal.

He didn't mention his brother. Liu had died honourably, bravely, but it was wisest not to raise any connection to Wen Zhou.

He did hint, also obliquely, that his mother and his father's much-loved concubine were living alone with only a still-maturing young son in the household, and had been doing so for a long time.

He mentioned that he himself had not yet seen his honourable father's headstone and the inscription on that stone. Had not been able to kneel before it, or pour his ancestral libation. He'd been at Kuala Nor. Sardian horses were coming to the emperor because of that, had already arrived, if Shinzu was reading this letter.

All but ten of the Heavenly Horses (he was keeping ten, because he had people to honour and reward for their help) were humbly offered by Shen Tai to the exalted Emperor Shinzu, to use as the Son of Heaven and his advisers saw fit. It was a matter of great pride to the glorious emperor's most unworthy servant, Shen Tai, son of Shen Gao, that he could assist Kitai in this way. He used all of his father's offices and titles at that point in the letter.

He wrote of his own devotion to the Ninth Dynasty and to the emperor himself, since he who now held the Phoenix Throne (and would rise like the phoenix from the ashes of war!) had helped Tai himself, deigning to intercede one day at Ma-wai, and another time in the palace, against the murderous intrigues of a man whose disgraced name Tai would not even write.

He'd thought about that part for some time, as the night darkened outside, but it was surely right to make it clear that Wen Zhou had wanted Tai dead.

He hesitated again, sipping wine, reading over what he'd written, then he mentioned the rings the august and illustrious emperor and father-emperor, may the gods in all nine heavens defend them and grant them peace, had each given the unworthy but devoted Shen Tai, by their own hands.

He was looking at that part, and wondering about it, if it could possibly be read as a thought that the father, not the son, should be on the throne, when he heard the door to the room open.

He didn't turn around, remained on the mat before the writing table, facing the open window. There was a breeze, and stars now, but the three lamps lit the room too much for them to be clearly seen.

"If I were someone who wanted you dead, you would be by now," she said.

Tai laid down his brush. "That was one of the first things you ever said to me, at Iron Gate."

"I remember," she said. "How did you know it was me?"

He shook his head impatiently, looking out. "Who else would it be?"

"Really? Not an assassin from Tagur, perhaps? Trying at the last minute to stop their horses from crossing the border?"

"I have Kanlin guards," Tai said. "He wouldn't have gotten near this room. I recognized your footfall, Song. I do know it by now."

"Oh," she said.

"I thought I barred the door this time."

"You did. This is an old inn. The wood shifts, too much space between door and wall. A sword can be used to lift the bar."

He was still looking out the window. "Shouldn't I have heard it?"

"Probably," she said, "though someone trained can do it quietly. This is why you need guards."

He was tired, but also amused. "Really? Why would an assassin bother with me? I am apparently of no use to anyone, in wartime."

She was silent a moment. "I was angry. I didn't mean that."

"It is true, however. Once the emperor has the horses."

"I don't ... I don't think it is true, myself. I was trying to be persuasive."

Her footfall, moving into the room.

A moment later one of the lamps was blown out. The one closest to him, illuminating his writing table. And because she'd come nearer he caught the scent of perfume. She never wore perfume.

He turned.

She had already crossed to the second lamp. She bent and blew that one out as well, leaving only the one by the bed. She turned to him.

"I'm still trying to be persuasive," Wei Song said, and let her tunic slip from her shoulders to the floor.

Tai stood up quickly. He looked away a moment, then his eyes were pulled back to her. The lithe form. She had a long, shallow gash across the ribs on one side. He knew how she'd received that wound.

"Please forgive my shyness with the lights," she murmured.

"Shyness?" Tai managed to say.

The single lamp beside her lit one breast more than the other, and the left side of her face. Slowly, she lifted both her hands and began unpinning her hair.

"Song, what … this is to persuade me to go north? You do not have to—"

"It isn't," she said, hands lifted, exposing her body to his gaze. "That wasn't true, about persuading. It just sounded like a clever thing to say. A pleasure district remark? They are clever there, I know. And beautiful."

She set one long pin on the table by the bed, and then removed and set down another, moving slowly, the light falling upon her. "This is a goodbye," she said. "We may not meet again, since you will not come north."

Tai was mesmerized by her movements. She had killed for him, he had seen her do it at Chenyao, in a garden. She was barefoot now, wore only thin Kanlin trousers, nothing down to the waist.

The last hairpin slipped free and she shook out her hair.

"Goodbye?" Tai said. "You were hired for ten years! You are mine until then!" He was trying to be ironic.

"Only if we live," she said. She looked away, he saw her bite her lip. "I am willing to be yours," she said.

"What are you saying?"

She looked back at him, and did not answer. But her wide-set eyes were on his, unwavering, and he thought, yet again, of how much courage she had.

And then, for the second time that day, Tai realized that within himself something had already happened, perhaps some time ago, and that he was only, in this lamplit, after-thunder moment, coming to know it. He shook his head in wonder.

"I can leave now," she said, "and be gone before morning, to collect the horses."

"No. I have to be there, remember?" Tai said. He drew a breath. "I don't want you to leave, Song."

She looked young, small, almost unbearably exposed.

He said, a roughness in his voice, "I don't want you ever to leave."

She looked away again, suddenly. He saw her draw a breath this time, then let it out slowly. She said, "Do you mean that? It isn't because I have been so ... because I did this?"

"I have seen women unclothed before, Song."

She looked up. "I know. And I am thin, and have this new wound, which will be another scar. And one more on my leg, and I *know* I am insufficiently respectful and—"

She wasn't very far away at all. He moved forward and put a hand, gently, over her mouth. Then he took it away and kissed her, also gently, that first time. Then he did so again, differently.

He looked down at her, in the one light left burning. Eyes on his, she said, "I am not greatly experienced in these matters."

SOME TIME LATER. Her left leg across his body where they lay in the bed, her head against his shoulder, hair spread out. The lamp had been extinguished some time ago. The rain had stopped dripping from the eaves. They could see moonlight, hear a night bird singing.

Tai said, "Not greatly experienced?"

He felt more than he saw her smile. "I was told men like hearing that from a woman. That it makes them feel powerful."

"Is that what it does?"

"So I was told." One of her hands was playing at his chest, drifting down towards his belly then back up. "You were on Stone Drum Mountain, Tai. You ought to remember what happens there at night. Or did none of the women …?"

"I don't think I'm going to answer that."

"Not yet, perhaps," she murmured.

The moon laid a trail of light along the floor of the room.

"You seem to always be coming into my chamber," he said.

"Well, once I was saving you from a fox-woman, remember?"

"She wasn't a fox-woman."

"She was a trap. Extremely pretty."

"Extremely," he agreed.

She sniffed. "Even if it wasn't a *daiji*, Sima Zian and I agreed you were not in a state to resist her that night, and bedding a governor's daughter would have put you in a very difficult position."

"I see," Tai said carefully. "You and the poet agreed on this?"

"We did. They wanted you in a difficult position, of course. Xu Bihai was after the horses."

"You don't think she might simply have fallen in love with me?"

"I suppose there's that possibility," said Song. Her tone suggested otherwise.

"She was very pretty," Tai said.

Song said nothing.

"So are you," he said.

"Ah. That will surely make *me* fall in love." She laughed again. "I'd have attacked you if you'd come into my room on the road."

"I believe that."

"I wouldn't do that now," she said, mock-contrite.

His turn to laugh. "I am pleased to hear it." After a moment, he said, "Song, I wanted you on the first night at Iron Gate, when you came in."

"I know," she said. He felt her shrug. He knew that motion by now. "I didn't feel flattered. You'd been alone two years. Any woman …"

"No. It was you. I think from when you walked up in the court-yard."

"My hair was down," she said. "Men are very predictable."

"Are we? Am I?"

A silence. "Not you so much."

They listened to the bird outside.

"I'll come north," he said.

She shook her head emphatically. "No. You've made that deci-sion, Tai, bad luck to start a journey after that. Finish your letter. We will take it with us. We have decided that your sister and the fact that Zhou tried to kill you should keep you safe. With the horses."

"You have decided that?"

"Yes, Lu Chen and I."

"And what if I decide—?"

"Tai, you already did. It was an honourable choice. I was only afraid."

"And now I'll be afraid for you. There is a war, you're going a long way."

She laughed softly. "I'm a Kanlin Warrior, riding among sixty others. That is one fear you need not sensibly have."

"When is fear sensible?"

Her hand stopped moving, lay against his chest.

"And after?" he asked. "After you reach the emperor?"

She hesitated. "There is one thing I need to do."

He lay there remembering: *We wish to kill two of them later. It must be done.*

He squeezed her arm. "Song, if you kill those two yourself, and anyone links you to me—"

"I know," she murmured. "That isn't it. Those two from the Second District army are likely dead already. They shamed us, and our sanctuary will not permit that. I think the emperor knows it. I don't think he will be unhappy. That is not what I meant."

"Then what …?"

"I have to ask leave to withdraw from the Kanlins. I must do it at my own sanctuary."

He said nothing. He was deeply moved.

She misunderstood his silence. "I ask for nothing, Tai. If this is only tonight, I am—"

He placed a hand over her mouth again. "You have to come back, Song. I need you to show me another way to live."

"I have only been a Kanlin," she said, as he moved his hand away.

"Might we teach each other?"

He felt her nodding her head. "But I don't believe the world will let you stay by that stream all your days."

"It might not. But I do not want to be lost in the dust and noise. To be what Liu became. In the Ta-Ming."

"If they even reclaim the Ta-Ming."

"Yes."

"Do you ... do you think they will?"

Tai lay in darkness, thinking about it.

"Yes. It may take time, but the new emperor is wiser than Roshan, and I think Roshan will die soon. This is not the end of the Ninth Dynasty."

"There will be changes."

He ran a hand through her hair: the unimaginable gift of his being able to do so. "This is a change, Song."

"I see. You prefer me this way? Obedient and submissive?" Her hand began moving again.

"Submissive? Is that like the inexperience, before?"

"I have much to learn," she murmured. "I know it." And she lifted her head from his shoulder and slipped down towards where her hand had gone.

A little later, Tai managed, with some effort, to say, "Did they teach you that on Stone Drum Mountain?"

"No," she said, from farther down the bed. And then, in a different voice, "But I'm not a concubine, Tai."

"Hardly," he murmured.

He felt her head lift. "What does that mean? I lack the skills you are accustomed to?"

"You could possibly acquire them," he said judiciously. "With effort and time enough to—"

He made a sharp, strangled sound.

"I didn't hear that last," she murmured sweetly.

He made an effort to compose himself. "Oh, Song. Will I survive a life with you?"

"If you are more cautious about what you say," she said, sounding meditative, "I see no reason why not. But I'm not a concubine, Shen Tai."

"I said I know that," he protested. "Before you bit me."

He cleared his throat. He felt amazingly sure of himself. Sure of the world, or this small part of it.

He said, "It would be a great honour if, Mistress Wei Song, before you took my horses north, I were permitted to learn your father's name, and your mother's, and the location of their home, that my mother might correspond with them as to possibilities for the future."

She stopped moving. He had a sense she was biting her lower lip.

She said, "Your servant would be pleased if your honourable mother were willing to initiate such a correspondence."

Which formality, given where she was just then, and what she now resumed doing, was remarkable.

He reached down and drew her up (she was so small), and laid her upon her back, and shifted above her. She began, shortly thereafter, making small sounds, and then more urgent ones, and then, some time after, with the bird still singing outside, she said, halfway between a gasp and a cry, "Did you learn that in the North District?"

"Yes," he said.

"Good," she said. "I like it."

And twisting her body the way he'd seen her do springing up a wall in Chenyao or fighting assassins alone with two swords, she was above him again. Her mouth found his, and she did something with her teeth that made him realize, suddenly, that it hadn't been any fox-woman he'd been dreaming about so vividly those nights on the road from Chenyao. It had been her.

The strangeness of the world.

There was a brightness growing within him, vivid as the first spring flower against snow, and a sense that this was all deeply undeserved, that he was not worthy of such a gift.

There was also now—and Tai would not let himself turn away from it—a farewell taking place inside himself, a painful one: to green eyes and golden hair, music, and her own courage.

You were surely allowed to remember these things? It would be wrong not to remember, Tai thought.

Branching paths. The turning of days and seasons and years. Life offered you love sometimes, sorrow often. If you were very fortunate, true friendship. Sometimes war came.

You did what you could to shape your own peace, before you crossed over to the night and left the world behind, as all men did, to be forgotten or remembered, as time or love allowed.

EPILOGUE

The Second Son of General Shen Gao crossed a bridge over the Wai River and reached his home on the same day that An Li, usually named Roshan, died at the hot springs retreat of Ma-wai, not far from Xinan.

Roshan, known to be unwell, did not die of the sugar sickness. He was murdered by a servant while he rested after taking the healing waters. The servant had been instructed to do this, and provided with a weapon, by An Li's eldest son. An Rong disagreed with certain of his father's policies and was impatient by nature.

The servant was executed. A man may agree to become an instrument of violent death in pursuit of rewards. These rewards are not invariably forthcoming.

Much farther north on that same day, in the grey hour before sunrise, Tarduk, the son and heir of the Bogü kaghan, was killed by a wolf in his yurt.

No dogs had barked, none had signalled in any way that a wolf had entered the campsite where the heir and some of his followers were in the midst of a hunt. Tarduk had time to scream before his throat was torn open. The wolf was struck by at least two arrows as it fled through the rising mist.

None of the dogs went after it.

Conjunctions of this sort—events occurring at the same time, far apart—are seldom perceived by those living (or dying) through the moments and days involved. Only the patient historian with access to records is likely to discover such links, reading diligently through texts preserved from an earlier time and dynasty. He might take a scholar's pleasure, or be moved to reflection, considering them.

The conjunctions found do not always *mean* anything.

The timing of such moments doesn't necessarily change the course of history, or throw illumination backwards upon how and why men did what they did.

The prevailing view of scholars was that only if it could be shown that events emerged from the same impulses, or if a significant figure came to *know* what had happened elsewhere, and when, did it become important to record such links in the record of the past.

There were some who suggested otherwise. Theirs was a view that held the past to be a scroll wherein the wise, unrolling it, could read how time and fate and the gods showed intricate patterns unfolding, and patterns could repeat.

Still, it is likely that even those of this opinion would have agreed that Shen Tai—that son of General Shen Gao, returning home—was not important enough in those early days of the An Li Rebellion for his movements to be part of any pattern that signified.

Only a tale-spinner, not a true scholar—someone shaping a story for palace or marketplace—would note these conjunctions and judge them worth the telling, and storytellers were not important, either. On this, the historian-mandarins could agree.

Shen Tai hadn't even passed the examinations at that point! He had no formal status, in fact, though any fair-minded chronicler had to give him credit for courage at Kuala Nor, and the role his Sardian horses eventually played.

ༀ

His mother and Second Mother were in Hangdu, the prefecture town. They had taken a cart to buy supplies, Tai was informed by the household steward. The steward kept bowing and smiling as he spoke. You could say that he was beaming, Tai thought.

Yes, the steward said, Youngest Son Chao had escorted them, with several of the bigger servants carrying heavy staves.

No, trouble had not yet reached their market town in any serious way, but it was always best to be careful, Master, was it not?

It was, Tai agreed.

The steward, and the household servants piling up behind him in the soon-crowded courtyard, were clearly moved by the return of Second Son. Tai felt the same way himself. The creak of the gate was a sound that might make him weep if he wasn't careful.

The paulownias shading the walkway still had all their leaves. Autumn was not yet fully upon them. The peaches and plums had all been picked, he was informed. The family was being diligent about that this year. The Lady and Second Lady were supervising the preservation of the orchard's fruit against winter and a possible shortage of food.

Tai reminded himself that he needed to get to Hangdu as well. A man named Pang, one-legged. Owed money for supervising a hidden supply of grain. Liu had told him that.

Liu would be buried here by now.

He went through the compound and into the garden, carrying wine in an agate cup. He went past the pond where he'd spent so much time with his father, watching Shen Gao toss bread for the goldfish. The fish were large and slow. The stone bench was still here. Of course it was. Why should such things change because a man had been away? Were two years any time at all?

For human beings they were. Two years could change the world. For stones, for trees growing leaves in spring, dropping them in autumn, two years were inconsequential. A stone in a pond makes ripples, the ripples are gone, nothing remains.

When those one has loved are gone, memories remain.

Tai walked through the orchard and he came to the elevated ground where the graves were, not far from where their stream flowed south to meet the Wai and be lost.

There was a new mound for Liu. No marker above it yet, no inscription considered and incised on stone. That would come after a year had passed. No time at all for trees or stone or the circling sun, a single year. But who knew what it would bring to men and women under heaven?

Not Tai. He had no gift of sight. He was not, he thought suddenly, a shaman. He flinched, wondered why that image had come to him.

He stood before his father's grave. It was peaceful here. The ripple of the stream, some birds singing, wind in leaves. Trees shaded the place where his family lay and would lie, where he would one day rest.

He set down his cup and knelt. He bowed his head to touch the green grass by the grave. He did this three times. He stood, reclaiming the cup, and he poured the libation on the ground, for his father.

Only then did he read the words his mothers (or perhaps his brother Chao, not so young now) had put there.

It was not, it really was not so great a coincidence that they'd have selected lines by Sima Zian. The Banished Immortal was the preeminent poet of their age. Of course they'd have considered his words in choosing an inscription. But even so ...

Tai read:

When choosing a bow choose a strong one,
If you shoot an arrow shoot a long one,
To capture the enemy capture their leader,
But carry within you the knowledge
That war is brought to bring peace.

Sometimes, Tai thought, there were too many things within you at once. You couldn't even begin to sort through them, do more than feel the fullness in your heart.

"It is well chosen, isn't it?" someone behind him said.

The fullness in your heart.

He turned.

"It was Chao who decided on the inscription. I'm proud of him," said his sister.

Fullness could overflow, like a river in springtime. Seeing her, hearing the remembered voice, Tai began to weep.

Li-Mei stepped forward. "Brother, do not, or I will, too!"

She already was, he saw. Speechless, he drew her into his arms. She was clad in Kanlin robes, which he could not understand, any more than he could grasp that she was here to be enfolded.

His sister laid her head against his chest and her arms came around him, and they stood like that together by their father's grave and stone.

SHE WAS WEARING Kanlin black for safety. She had travelled that way. It was too soon to make her presence more widely known. The family knew her and the household servants, but the village understood only that some Kanlins had come from the east to the Shen estate, and then others had arrived bearing the body of Eldest Son for burial, and one of the Warriors, a woman, had remained behind as a guard.

There were three more Kanlins now, they had come with Tai from the border.

"You saved my life," Li-Mei said.

First words, when they moved to the stone bench by the stream (Shen Gao's favourite place on earth) and sat together.

She told him the tale, and the wonder of how the world was devised felt overwhelming to Tai, listening.

"He had me place my handprint on a horse painted on the wall in a cave," she said.

And, "Tai, I killed a man there."

And, "Meshag is half a wolf, but he did what he did because of you."

(As of earlier that same morning, he was no longer half a wolf.)

And then, towards the end, "I wanted to stay on Stone Drum Mountain, but they refused me, for the same reason they said they rejected you."

"I wasn't rejected, I left!"

She laughed aloud. The sound of her laughter, here at home, healed a wound in the world.

He said, "Li-Mei, I have chosen a woman. A wife."

"What? *What?* Where is she?"

"Taking my horses to the emperor."

"I don't—"

"She's a Kanlin. She's taking them north with sixty other guards."

"North? Through this? And you *let* her do that?"

Tai shook his head ruefully. "That isn't the right way to describe it. When you meet her you'll understand. Li-Mei, she is ... she may even be a match for you."

His sister sniffed dismissively, in a way he knew very well. Then she smiled. "Is she a match for you?"

"She is," he said. "Listen, I will tell you a story now."

He started at Kuala Nor. While he was talking, the sun crossed the sky, passing behind and emerging from white clouds. A servant came, unable to stop smiling, to say that his two mothers and his brother were back from Hangdu, and Tai stood up and went to them in the principal courtyard and knelt, and stood, and was welcomed home.

WATCHING, A LITTLE APART because she's already had her moments with him and her own homecoming, Li-Mei is annoyed to find herself crying again.

Tai has already told her he intends to stay here, not go to the new emperor. She understands this, of course she does: there is a long tradition in Kitai, all the way back to the Cho Master himself, of a strong man striving to balance the desire to be of service, part of the court, "in the current" ... and the opposite yearning for quiet, for rivers and mountains and contemplation, away from the chaos of the palace.

She knows this, understands her brother, realizes that some of what Tai is feeling has to do with Liu.

But she has a sense—already, that first day when he's come home—that her own needs go the other way. The empire is too much larger than this quiet estate by the stream. She has even been beyond the borders now. And she has too deep a hunger for *knowing* things, for the thrust and dazzle of the world.

In time, Li-Mei tells herself. She is not in a hurry.

There are steps and stages involved in this, traps to be avoided. But the man who is their emperor now, glorious and exalted Shinzu, had once trailed a hand down her back while watching a dance in the Ta-Ming Palace. She wonders if he remembers. If he can be caused to remember.

She looks around, sees the servants weeping and smiling, and finds herself unexpectedly remembering another dance: this is the courtyard where she'd tried once, very young, to offer a performance for her father, and had fallen into leaves because of the wind.

Tai had suggested that was why she fell. Liu had … Liu had told her never to let the performance stop, even if you made a mistake. To carry on, as if you'd never failed at all, as if you couldn't imagine failing.

She still hasn't poured a libation for her oldest brother. She isn't sure if she ever will.

Many years later she does do that—pour an offering for Shen Liu—but only after the immediate past had become the distant past. How we remember changes how we have lived.

Time runs both ways. We make stories of our lives.

ఱ

Autumn came. The paulownia leaves fell one night, were on the ground when they woke. They left them on the path for a day, a family tradition, then the leaves were swept away by all of them together the morning following.

In winter, a message came from the court of the Emperor Shinzu, from his temporary court in Shuquian.

The glorious and exalted emperor acknowledged receiving a communication from his trusted servant, Shen Tai. He confirmed the arrival at Shuquian of nearly two hundred and fifty Sardian horses, a gift to Kitai from the same loyal servant of the empire.

It was understood by the compassionate emperor that after his labours in the west, and disruptions within his family, Master Shen might wish to spend an interval with his mother, attending to affairs at his family estate. The emperor approved such devoted impulses.

It was expected that Master Shen would agree that all loyal and capable men were needed by Kitai in times so vexed as the current ones, and his presence at the court, wherever it was, would be welcomed by his emperor in due course.

In confirmation of this imperial benignity, and in recognition of services performed, the emperor saw fit to extend a grant of lands in the south and east beyond those already given by the revered father-emperor to Shen Tai. Documents were attached. The emperor was also pleased to graciously accede to Master Shen's request for seven of the Sardians. The emperor went so far as to express the personal view (this was unusual) that, under the circumstances, it was a modest number. These seven horses would be arriving, under escort, soon, if the gods willed it so.

Tai drew a series of very deep breaths, reading this and then rereading it. He had succeeded, it seemed.

The land wasn't really the emperor's to give, he thought. There was too much uncertainty in the east. Still, the documents were his, Tai held them in his hands, and fortune might one day smile upon Kitai and the Ninth Dynasty again. The important thing was that his absence from court was accepted. Or it appeared that way.

Seven horses were coming back to him. It was a number he'd chosen very simply: he'd promised ten to Jian (she'd wanted to train them to dance); he had left three with Bytsan, seven remained. Besides two for himself, he had people for whom he wanted horses.

His younger brother, his sister. A fortress commander at Iron Gate. A poet, if he ever saw him again. The woman he loved, as a wedding gift.

If he ever saw her again.

The horses did indeed come, not long after the letter, escorted by twenty soldiers of the Fifth Military District. The new soldiers stayed and were garrisoned at Hangdu. They were reassigned to the Fourteenth Army, based here, but more specifically to Tai himself. They arrived with documents making him a senior officer of the Fourteenth Cavalry, carrying responsibilities for good order in Hangdu and the surrounding countryside. He reported directly to the governor.

It was suggested he call on the governor and the prefect as soon as circumstances permitted.

He'd had his mother write Song's parents. It had caused him a day of reflection when he'd learned who her father was. In the end, perhaps to honour the man as much as anything, Tai had ended up in laughter, by the stream. It did make sense, who she was. He told Li-Mei, tried to make her see why it was amusing, but she didn't laugh, only looked thoughtful.

A reply came back, addressed to his mother, offering the formal acceptance by Wei Song's father of the Shen family's proposal of honourable marriage to his daughter.

The letter communicated personal admiration for General Shen Gao, but also noted that Kanlin women, by the code of the order, always had the right to decline such offers in order to remain among the Warriors. Her father would convey to Wei Song his own approval, but the decision would be hers.

Through the winter, which was blessedly mild in their region, given other torments unfolding, Tai dedicated himself to tasks in the prefecture.

Warfare had not yet reached the district, but fleeing people had, and there was hardship. Outlaws, whether from need or a seized opportunity, became a problem, and the soldiers of the Fourteenth were busy dealing with them.

Tai also made a decision (not a difficult one) and began doling out supplies of grain from Liu's hidden granary. He put his brother Chao in charge of that, assisted by Pang, the man in Hangdu.

Their family had assets enough. Liu's own wealth had been mostly in Xinan and was probably forfeit after his death, because of his connection to Wen Zhou. It was too soon to explore this, but Tai was wealthy now himself, and Li-Mei had been given considerable gifts when made a princess. These had made their way here, since she had been expected never to see Kitai again.

Tai gave a horse to her and another to Chao.

In the evenings when he wasn't out with his cavalry on patrol, he drank wine, wrote poetry, read.

Another letter arrived one afternoon, brought by a courier from the southwest: Sima Zian sent greetings and love to his friend and reported that he was still with the father-emperor. There were tigers and gibbons where they were. The poet had travelled to the Great River gorges and remained of the view that there was no place in the world like them. He sent three short poems he'd written.

Word came that An Li had died.

There was a flickering of hope at this, but it didn't last long. The rebellion had taken on a life, or lives, that went too far beyond that of the man who'd started it.

It rained, the roads were muddy, as always in winter.

Nothing arrived from Wei Song until spring.

In that season, when the peach and apricot trees were flowering in the orchard, with magnolias in bloom and the paulownias growing new leaves and beginning to shade the path again, a letter finally came.

Tai read it and did calculations of distance and time. It was six days to the full moon. He left the next morning, with two of the remaining Kanlins and ten of his cavalry. He rode Dynlal, and they led a second Sardian horse, the smallest one.

North along the river road they went, the one he'd travelled all his life. He knew each inn along the way, the mulberry groves and silk farms. They saw a fox once, at the side of the road.

They encountered one band of outlaws, but a party as large as theirs, heavily armed, was far too intimidating and the bandits melted back into the forest. Tai took note of where they were. He'd send soldiers up this road later. The people living here would be menaced by these men. You could grieve for what might drive men to be outlaws, but you couldn't indulge it.

On the fifth day they reached the junction with the imperial road. There was a village to the west. East of here was the place where he'd sat in a carriage decorated with kingfisher feathers and spoken with An Li, who had brought destruction upon Kitai, and was dead now, leaving ruin and war all around.

Beyond that point along the road was the posting inn where he'd met Jian. One of Tai's cavalry from Iron Gate—his name had been Wujen Ning—had died there, defending Dynlal.

Wei Song had been wounded, defending him.

They didn't have to go that far. They were where they needed to be. The full moon would rise tonight. He waited, among a company of soldiers and two Kanlin Warriors. They ate a soldiers' meal by the side of the road. He read her letter again.

I have learned from my father that he approves of my marriage. I have also received leave from the elders of my sanctuary to withdraw from the Kanlin Warriors, and have completed the rituals required for that. I will be riding south to your father's home, if that is acceptable. I have sat beside open windows through autumn and winter, and have come to understand the poems about that better than I ever did. At times I have been angry with you, for causing me to feel this way. At other times I desire only to see you, and have my dust mingled with yours when I die. It would please me greatly, husband-to-be, if you were to meet me by the bridge across your stream, where it meets the imperial road between Xinan and the west. I will be there when spring's second full moon rises. Perhaps you will escort me home from Cho-fu-Sa?

The moon rose as he looked east along the road.

And with it, exactly at moonrise, she came, riding along the imperial way with a dozen or so companions and guards. It took him a moment to recognize her: she no longer wore Kanlin black. He'd never seen her in any other clothing. She wore no elegant bridal garb. She'd been travelling, and they had a distance yet to ride. Wei Song had on brown leather riding trousers and a light-green tunic with a short, dark-green overtunic, for there was still a chill to the air. Her hair was carefully pinned, he saw.

He dismounted and walked away from his men.

He saw her speak to her escort and she, too, dismounted and came towards him, so that they met each other, alone, on the arched bridge.

"Thank you for coming, my lord," she said. She bowed.

He bowed as well. "*My heart outraced the both of us,*" he quoted. "The winter was long without you. I have brought you a Sardian horse."

Song smiled. "I will like that."

He said, "How did you know the old name for this bridge?"

"Cho-fu-Sa?" She smiled again. "I asked. The elders at Kanlin sanctuaries are very wise."

"I know that," he said.

She said, "It is pleasing to me to see you, husband-to-be."

"Do you want me to show you how pleased I am?" he asked.

She actually flushed, then shook her head. "We are not yet wed, Shen Tai, and others are watching us. I wish to make a proper appearance before your mother."

"And my sister," he said. "She is waiting as well."

Song's eyes grew wide. "What? How is …?"

"We have a few days to ride. I will tell you that tale."

She hesitated, and then she bit her lip. "I am acceptable to you, like this? I feel strange, not wearing black. As if I have lost … protection."

There was a swirl of wind. The water swirled below. Tai looked at her in the twilight. The wide-set eyes and the wide mouth. She was small, and lethal. He knew how gracefully she moved, and he knew her courage.

He said, "I have a few days of travelling to answer that, as well. To make you understand how pleasing you are in my sight."

"Truly?" she asked.

He nodded. "You make me wish to be always at your side."

She came and stood next to him on the arched bridge—at his side, in fact. She said, "Will you show me my new horse and take me home?"

They rode together under the moon, south along the river from Cho-fu-Sa.

Sometimes the one life we are allowed is enough.

∞

Tales have many strands, smaller, larger. An incidental figure in one story is living through the drama and passion of his or her own life and death.

In that time of extreme upheaval in Kitai, of violence engendered by warfare and famine, a young Kanlin Warrior was travelling back that same spring from far-off Sardia with a tale to proudly tell, and carrying a letter from a woman to a man.

He survived his return journey through the deserts but was killed for his weapons and horse and saddle in an ambush northwest of Chenyao, on his way down from Jade Gate Fortress.

His saddlebags were rifled through, anything of value seized and divided by the bandits. They fought over his swords, which were magnificent. They also fought over whether to try to sell or to kill and eat the horse. In the event, it was eaten.

The letter was discarded, tumbling in dust and wind, and disappearing.

∞

It might indeed have been thought that the death of Roshan would end the rebellion. This would have been a reasonable hope, but not an accurate one.

His son, An Rong, appeared to enjoy the idea of being an emperor. He continued to assert the will of the Tenth Dynasty in the east and northeast, with incursions south.

He had inherited his father's courage and appetites and matched him in savagery, but he had nowhere near the experience Roshan had in and around a court, nor did he know how to control his own soldiers and officers.

He couldn't have had those skills at his age, coming to power as he did. But explanations only clarify, they do not offer a remedy. An Rong proved unable to achieve any discipline or coordination among the fragmenting rebel leadership.

This could have prepared the way for their defeat and a return of peace to Kitai, except that times of chaos often breed greater chaos, and An Li's rebellion caused others to see opportunity in disruption.

A number of military governors, prefects, outlaw leaders, and certain peoples on the western and northern borders decided, independently of each other, that their own hour of glory had arrived— the moment to make more of themselves than had been possible in the decades of Kitan wealth and power under the Emperor Taizu.

Taizu was praying and mourning (it was said) in the southwest, beyond the Great River. His son was waging war in the north, summoning soldiers from border forts, negotiating for allies, and horses.

When the dragon is in the wild, wolves will emerge. When the wolves of war come out, hunger follows. The years of the rebellion— more accurately called the rebellions—led to starvation on a scale unmatched in the history of Kitai.

With all men, from beardless fourteen-year-olds to barely upright grandfathers, forcibly enlisted in one army or another across the empire there were no farmers left to sow or harvest millet, barley, corn, rice.

Disease was rampant. Almost no taxes on produce or land were able to be paid, however vicious enforcers became. Some regions, as warfare shifted back and forth across their land, found themselves facing taxation from two or even three different sets of overseers. And with armies needing to be fed—or they might rebel, themselves—what food could make its way to women and children left at home?

If there was a home left. Or children alive. In those years, children were sold for food, or sold as food. Hearts hardened, hearts broke.

One well-known lament, for the conscripted farmer-soldiers and their families, was composed by a poet-mandarin who lived through those years. He was looking back at a black period, after he'd retired from court for the third and final time to one of his country estates.

He wasn't judged to be among the very greatest Ninth Dynasty poets, but was acknowledged as skilled. He was known as a friend of Sima Zian, the Banished Immortal, and later, also, of the equally glorious Chan Du. He wrote:

Courageous women try to manage a plough
But the rows of grain never come right.
In winter officials arrive in our villages
Fiercely demanding taxes be paid.
How under heaven can that be done
In a shattered land? Never have sons!
They will only grow up to die under distant skies.

In time, the rebellion ended. The truth, as historians learn and teach, is that most things end, eventually.

Still, the fact that this is so would not have found a placid acceptance in the burned-out, abandoned shells of farms and villages throughout Kitai in those years. The dead are not assuaged, or brought back, by a philosophic view of events.

The Emperor Shinzu retook Xinan, lost it briefly, then took it a second time and did not lose it. General Xu Bihai reoccupied Teng

Pass against incursions from the east. The Ta-Ming Palace was restored, if not to what it had been before.

The emperor's father died and was buried in his tomb near Ma-wai. The Precious Consort, whose name had been Jian, was already there, awaiting him. So was his empress.

People began to return to the capital and to their villages and farms, or to new ones, for with so very many dead there was much land unclaimed.

Trade slowly resumed, although not along the Silk Roads. They were too dangerous now, with the garrisons beyond Jade Gate abandoned.

As a result, no letters came from the west, from places such as Sardia. No dancers or singers came.

No lychee fruits were brought up from the far south, either, carried early in the season by military couriers on imperial roads. Not in those years.

An Rong himself was murdered, perhaps predictably, by two of his generals. These two divided the northeast between themselves, like warlords of old, abandoning any imperial ambitions. The Tenth Dynasty ended, faded away, never was.

The number ten became regarded as bad luck in Kitai for a long time afterwards, among generations that had no idea why this was so.

One of the two rebel generals accepted an offer of amnesty from the Emperor Shinzu in Xinan and turned on the other, joining with imperial armies in a triumphant battle below the Long Wall not far from Stone Drum Mountain. In this battle, two hundred cavalry, four *duis,* mounted on Sardian horses, played a devastating role, sweeping across the battlefield from left flank to right and back, with a speed and power other riders could only dream about.

Three men, two of them extremely tall, the third with only one hand, watched that fight from the northern edge of the summit of Stone Drum Mountain.

They were expressionless for the most part, except when one or the other would raise an arm and point to the Sardians racing along the lines, a glory amid carnage. When the three old men saw this, they would smile. Sometimes they'd laugh softly, in wonder.

"I would like one of those," said the man with one hand.

"You don't even ride any more," said the tallest one.

"I'd look at it. I'd watch it run. It would bring me joy."

"Why would he give you a Sardian horse?" said the other tall one.

The one with a single hand grinned at him. "He's married my daughter, hasn't he?"

"So I understand. A clever girl. Not dutiful enough, in my view. She's better off having left us."

"Perhaps. And he might give me a horse, don't you think?"

"You could ask. It would be difficult for him to say no."

The smaller man looked at one and then the other of his companions. He shook his head regretfully. "Too hard to say no. That's why I can't ask." He looked down again at the battlefield. "This is over," he said. "It was over before it began."

"You think peace will follow now?"

"Up here perhaps. Not everywhere. We may not live to see peace in Kitai."

"You cannot know that," admonished the tallest one.

"I am pleased, at the least," said the third, "that I lived long enough to have an answer about the wolf. It was honourable of him to send us word. Unexpected."

"You thought he'd die himself when the wolf died?"

"I did. And now he is sending messages to us. It shows we can be wrong. The need for humility."

The small one looked up at him and laughed. "It shows *you* can be wrong," he said.

The others laughed as well. It is entirely possible, the teachings of the Kanlins suggest, to laugh while the heart is breaking for mankind.

They turned and walked away from the view of the battlefield.

THE REBEL GENERAL who'd accepted the offer of amnesty from Xinan might have expected treachery, might even have been resigned to it, but with the empire so desperately spent it was decided by the new advisers of the new emperor that the offered amnesty should be honoured. The general and his soldiers were allowed to live, and resume their posts defending Kitai.

Soldiers were urgently needed on the Long Wall and in the west and south, before all borders collapsed inwards under waves of barbarian incursions.

Weariness, sometimes more than anything else, can bring an end to war.

It was said to be the case that the emperor's favourite wife, regarded by some later historians as dangerously subtle and too influential, played a role in encouraging him to keep that agreement—with a view to securing Kitai's boundaries.

The first treaty negotiated and signed was with the Tagurans.

The second was with the Bogü. Their new kaghan, Hurok's successor, was a man his people called the Wolf. It wasn't clear why, then or later, but how would civilized people understand the names, let alone the rituals, of barbarians?

There *were* stories told that the same imperial princess, who was also Shinzu's second wife, understood more than she ought to have about this matter of the Bogü, but the details of this—the documents so vital to a historian—were lost.

Some even said this had been deliberate, but in truth the disruptions of those years, the burnings of cities and market towns, movements of people and armies, emergence of bandits, warlords, disease, and death, were so very great, it was hardly necessary to imagine or assume a purpose on anyone's part if records disappeared.

And it is always difficult, even with the best will in the world, to look back a long way and see anything resembling the truth.

☙❧

Seasons tumble and pass, so do human lives and ruling dynasties. Men and women live and are remembered—or falsely remembered—for so many different reasons that the recording of these would take seasons of its own.

Every single tale carries within it many others, noted in passing, hinted at, entirely overlooked. Every life has moments when it branches, importantly (even if only for one person), and every one of those branches will have offered a different story.

Even mountains alter given enough time, why should not empires? How should poets and their words not become dust? Does not the true wonder emerge when something actually survives?

At Kuala Nor the seasons turned with sun and stars, and the moon lit green grass or made silver the snow and a frozen lake. For a number of years following the events recounted here (however incompletely, as with all such tellings) two men met there each spring, sharing a cabin by the lake, and labouring together to lay to rest the dead.

Birds cried in the mornings, wheeling above the water, the ghosts cried at night. Sometimes a voice fell silent. Both men knew why that was.

Then there came a spring when only one of the two arrived by the shores of the lake. This one worked alone that season, and the next spring, and then the next, but the following springtime no one came to Kuala Nor.

The ghosts remained. They cried at night under a cold moon or stars, winter, spring, summer, fall.

Time passed, in sweeping arcs of years.

And, finally, because not even the dead can grieve forever, forgotten, there came a moonlit night when there was no lost spirit crying at Kuala Nor, and there was no one by the lake to hear the last one's final cry. It drifted into that night, within the ring of mountains, above the lake, rising there, and gone.

... peace to our children when they fall
in small war on the heels of small
war—until the end of time ...

—ROBERT LOWELL

ACKNOWLEDGEMENTS

I find writing these acknowledgements both an opportunity and a challenge. This is true for every book, but perhaps even more so this time, since I've been living with *Under Heaven* for so many years.

There are individuals who have helped in many different ways, and a number of books and essays played roles in shaping this variation upon themes of the Tang. Too many names listed becomes cumbersome and (I fear) risks seeming over-elaborate or pretentious. Leaving people out feels worse.

I'm going to begin where many of these notes end: this is a work of fiction spun out of and through history. No one named here bears the remotest responsibility for what the author has done with the time, the place, and his story. Other people have sparked my thinking and my imagination, however, and my gratitude is considerable.

On brightweavings.com I have posted essays and speeches that offer (I hope) some clarity as to why I use the prism of the fantastic to treat the matter of history. Those interested will find some answers at that site.

My gateway to Tang China was by way of the master poets of the dynasty: Du Fu, Li Bai (the "Banished Immortal"), Wang Wei, Bai

Juyi, and so many others. I read their works (and biographies) in English in many versions and the first acknowledgement I want to record here is to the poets and their translators. I am indebted to, among others: David Hawkes, Burton Watson, Arthur Waley, David Young, Red Pine, and Arthur Cooper. There are dozens of renderings of Tang poetry that I have read and profited from, but these names need to be cited.

On a much more personal level, my old friend Andy Patton—painter, poet, Tang aficionado—was profoundly important in the emergence of this book, through years of discussion and encouragement.

It is daunting to choose among the historians whose work (and in some cases personal communication) has been vital to me. I'm going to name the following: Susan Whitfield, Edward H. Schafer (his masterful *The Golden Peaches of Samarkand*, in particular), Edwin G. Pulleyblank (on the background to the An-Lushan rebellion), Howard Levy, Patricia Ebrey, Edward Shaughnessy, Jonathan Tucker (a gorgeous book on the Silk Road), Christopher Beckwith (historian of early Tibet), René Grousset (on the steppes), Howard J. Wechsler, C. P. Fitzgerald, William Hung.

The invaluable Arthur Waley wrote biographies of both Li Bai and Bai Juyi (under the then-standard anglicized names Li Po and Po Chü-i). The Cambridge multi-volume *History of China*, in the volumes treating the Tang, was enormously helpful. There's a fair bit written about courtesans and students in the Tang, which is a motif of *Under Heaven*. I'll mention here Ping Yao's "The Status of Pleasure: Courtesan and Literati Connections in T'ang China (618–907)."

The general reader looking only for a taste would do well to start with Whitfield's *Life Along the Silk Road*, or have a look at Charles Benn's *China's Golden Age: Everyday Life in the Tang Dynasty*, which is full of detail. Ebrey's illustrated one-volume history of China for Cambridge is nicely done, and so is Shaughnessy's for Oxford. The Tucker book on the Silk Road has evocative photographs.

In terms of art, the Yale University *Three Thousand Years of Chinese Painting* (multiple authors), *China: Dawn of a Golden Age*, from the Metropolitan Museum in New York, *China: At the Court of the Emperors*, from an exhibition in Florence in 2008, *The Art of the Horse in Chinese History*, from an exhibition originating in Kentucky, and Hugh Scott's *The Golden Age of Chinese Art* (focusing on the Tang) are among those I consulted with profit.

On cave art, Gregory Curtis and, especially, Jean Clottes gave me compelling ideas to work with. Colin Thubron, writing about China and the Silk Road countries today, conjures landscape and history. His books are treasures. A number of the scholars named above were generous with their time in answering e-mail queries, and so were others too numerous to name. For professional research assistance on a variety of matters I am indebted to Sarah Johnson of Eastern Illinois University.

Turning to the remarkably supportive people in my life, I must acknowledge, once again, Deborah Meghnagi Bailey of bright weavings.com, and her accomplices there now: Alec Lynch, Elizabeth Swainston, and Ilana Teitelbaum. Bright Weavings has been a source of pleasure and aid in ways I never anticipated when I gave Deborah permission to launch it in 2000, one of my more intelligent decisions.

As I type the names of my agents, I am reminded how fortunate I am to be able to draw upon the intelligence and experience of people who have also become friends over the years: Linda McKnight, Jonny Geller, Jerry Kalajian, John Silbersack, and Natasha Daneman. The same applies to my editors: Nicole Winstanley, Susan Allison, Jane Johnson—in Toronto, New York, and London, respectively. When an author writes books that challenge genre, category, convention, he requires editors willing to do that with him, and I am fortunate to have those. Martin Springett, another old friend, assumed the role of cartographer once again, with patience and flair. Catherine Marjoribanks did the copyediting, with care and good humour.

Finally, and with love, my usual suspects: Laura, Sam, Matthew, Rex—and Sybil, who does deserve to be named at beginning and end.